The Other Side of Loss

Tom Vaughan

The
Other
Side
of Loss

PENCOYD PRESS

First published in the United Kingdom in 2014 by
Pencoyd Press

ISBN 978-0-9930509-3-0

Produced by whitefox
www.wearewhitefox.com

Printed, bound and distributed by IngramSpark

DEDICATION

With grateful thanks and love I would like to dedicate this first novel to all those members of my family, extended family and friends who have been kind enough to encourage and support this endeavour. Especially my immediate family, my wife Sarah and my children, Sophia, Georgianna and Henry, who have put up with me for all these years!

Also to my muse, Sarayu.

ACKNOWLEDGEMENTS

I would like to acknowledge, with heartfelt thanks, all those who have helped and encouraged me in the writing of this novel. Too numerous to mention by name, I would nevertheless like to single out those few deserving of special thanks.

Clive Dickinson, who has so skilfully, diplomatically and cheerfully worked tirelessly with me in the editing of the manuscript to allow it to emerge in book form.

Susan Hoffman for hours and hours of patient typing, deciphering my handwriting and dealing with copious scrawled notes.

John Bond of Whitefox Publishing Services, for his professional assistance in so capably steering me through the detail and complexities of the publishing process.

Fiona Thornton for her expert copy-edit – nothing escaped her professional eye and it is a much better book for her input. I am indebted to her for her passionate involvement in the project.

Eugenie Furniss of Furniss Lawton, Charles Walker of United Agents and Broo Doherty of Wade Doherty, for their experienced, helpfully honest input and advice at various stages.

Teresa Tassell and Sarah Appleby; also Andrew Murray of Cara Networks, for their patient help with my rudimentary computer skills!

Paulo Coelho for the inspiration I drew from his seminal book *The Alchemist* and William Paul Young for his delightfully imaginative book, *The Shack*.

Emily Furniss of Emily Furniss PR for her success in generating public relations opportunities for the exposure and promotion of my book.

Becky Morrison for her artistic talent in designing the appealing front cover.

My niece, Tara Vaughan, for her invaluable help in getting to grips with the benefits of social media networking.

Paula Snow for her instinctive marketing skills, advice and creative ideas.

Robin Reed and Doug King who, unknowingly, allowed me the time for this project.

Finally, those kind enough to act as my test readers of the early first drafts; for their time, honest feedback and helpful suggestions:

Fiona Irens (especially for her tireless, enthusiastic encouragement of this project throughout)

Nick Irens

Teresa Tassell

Boo and Oliver Vaughan

Harriet Bridgeman

Bernard Heng

Chris Roberts.

1

ACROSS THE STREET, a vigorous-looking young man was surveying the run-down Church of St Mungo's from the point where Pembroke Road joins Earls Court Road. A passer-by, spotting this broad-shouldered stranger, well protected from the incessant rain in his full-length Drizabone, could have been forgiven for mistaking him for one of the itinerant residents of 'Kangaroo Valley', recently arrived in London and finding his bearings.

Such a passer-by would have been quite correct in placing Robert Melton from Australia, although he was not, in fact, a newcomer to England. They would, however, never have identified this strapping young man as the newly appointed vicar of St Mungo's.

They would have shared their surprise with the Bishop of West London, from whose comfortable drawing-room Robert had recently emerged into the surprisingly wet and dreary late summer afternoon.

'It's a challenging parish, Robert,' the bishop had told him, almost before his guest had settled himself into the armchair to which the bishop had ushered him.

This was their first meeting since Robert had been appointed and he had sensed that the bishop had been feeling less at ease than he was, as he watched the tall, stooping figure gather a thin file from the table set in the bow window overlooking the drab, rain-battered garden.

'It's a parish in immediate need of caretaking ... or rather should I say care and ... understanding,' the bishop had hurriedly corrected himself before continuing. 'Your last two predecessors found it required more than men nearing the end of their ministry could offer. But in the circumstances, what could we do?' he had added, half to himself.

Robert had smiled encouragingly. 'That's why I'm very keen to get to work there, your Grace.'

'Yes. Yes, of course. I'm sure you are.' The bishop had turned from the window and looked at him thoughtfully. 'There are so many young people in the parish these days.'

He had settled himself in the chair facing Robert, where he had fiddled with his reading glasses and opened the file, fingering through the papers inside.

'History and Theology, Peterhouse,' he had commented approvingly. 'I was up at Corpus myself, though a good few years before you, of course.'

The bishop had read on. 'Your grandparents lived near Oxford, I see.'

'Yes, in fact my grandfather's still alive, although he's in a home now.'

'Nonetheless the "dreaming spires" didn't tempt you to pursue your studies there?'

'I like to think I struck an Anglican compromise,' Robert had answered lightly, but interested to see how his reply would be received.

The bishop had smiled in acknowledgement. 'Ah, yes. Train for the world at Cambridge and for the Lord at the other place.'

'I have to thank Cuddesdon for more than my training for the Church, Bishop.'

'Quite so. I wouldn't wish it any other way. But Peterhouse is a long way from Sydney. Clearly this scholarship you were awarded carries considerable prestige in Australia, but what drew you to spend three years studying so far away from home?'

'I guess it was my history teacher at school, as much as anything,' Robert had answered. 'He had been at Cambridge too. The way he talked about it, it really fired you up, made you want to experience it yourself.'

The bishop had nodded. 'Your mother was a widow.'

'That's right, sir. My father died when I was six.'

'I'm very sorry to hear that.'

'He was killed in a construction accident.'

The bishop had looked up, encouraging Robert to say more.

'They were building a new section of underground vault for the National Bank of Australia. Dad was down there supervising the work when he saw the huge girder temporarily supporting the middle of the vault beginning to twist and sag. According to the engineer's report it should never have happened, but his men were the wrong side of the girder.

'My father was a very strong man. He put himself underneath that girder and held it. It can't have been for more than a few seconds, but it gave the others long enough to escape. It took them three days to dig his body out.'

The bishop had nodded again, but this time with a look of condolence. 'A strong man and a very brave one. It must have been hard for your mother.'

Pia Melton had been a very pretty woman but Robert's father had been the only man for her. From the day he died Robert knew he would never have a stepfather, or any half-brothers or half-sisters. Ahead of him stretched a childhood in which his mother's grief would gradually distance her from her son.

'My mother was Swedish,' Robert had answered. 'She kept her emotions in check. And she had her faith. That got her through it.'

'I'm sure it would have done,' the bishop had replied soothingly, before he turned back to Robert's file.

Robert's mother had been a deeply religious woman, who had divided her time between looking after her husband and the job she held in Sydney's newly opened Queen Elizabeth Hospital for Children. Even after Robert's birth she had managed the difficult juggling act of being a wife, mother and full-time nurse without detriment to herself or those she loved. Her secret, if secret it was, lay in her willingness to subordinate herself and her own pleasure to the absolute

3

necessity of leading a very disciplined and highly organised life. Late nights and early mornings set the pattern of her life.

In return, her one demand of the family had been that Sunday mornings saw them together at either St Andrew's Anglican Cathedral for the eleven o'clock family Communion Service or, on alternate Sundays, at St Mary's Roman Catholic Cathedral for the family Mass at ten. This ecumenical arrangement was out of deference to her husband's upbringing in the Catholic faith and a promise she had had to make at the time of her marriage that any children they might have would be brought up within the Catholic Church.

But Robert's father had long since lost any interest in religion and at first his mother's promise to raise their son as a Catholic had irked her. As she became more familiar with the Catholic faith, though, Pia Melton had realised that the differences between these two great Christian beliefs were, at the practical level, minimal. It was only academic pedants, she concluded, who wanted them kept wide apart for the sake of what they regarded as the more crucial theological differences.

'You mother was Anglican, but your father a Roman Catholic,' the bishop had commented.

'That's right, sir. And after Dad died, Mum stayed true to her word. Every other Sunday she'd take me to Mass.'

'You didn't find this confusing?'

Robert had been expecting something along these lines and he had his answer prepared. 'On the contrary. I found that it helped me cut through all the misunderstanding and misrepresentation.'

'But at some point you had to choose in which direction God was leading you. Or was that an Anglican compromise too?' the bishop asked, with a twinkle in his eye.

What Robert could not have confided was that it was biology more than anything else that had governed his decision. The powerful stirrings of teenage urges, coupled with a growing awareness of his attraction to the opposite sex and, he discovered, their not infrequent attraction to him, had persuaded him that he did not trust himself with the concept of the voluntarily enforced celibacy required of a Catholic priest.

Robert realised this was both a physical and spiritual weakness. But he knew that he had to be true to himself as well as to God.

He did not make his decision lightly. It had involved long hours of prayer and soul-searching. He liked the idea of being married first and only to the Church. Perhaps, he had wondered, what he saw in adopting a life of celibacy was a romantic similarity with the Buddhist monks and mystics of the East.

However, apart from his concern over the weakness of the flesh, he had been unable to convince himself that being celibate would, in the end, render him better equipped to serve God than he would be within the framework of marriage to a compatible partner, with whom he envisioned sharing his commitment to the work of the Church.

With the passage of time his father was, sadly but inevitably, becoming an increasingly distant figure in his memory, However, Robert had tried to consider what his wishes and advice might have been. This was complicated in Robert's mind by the fact that his father had been adopted and had lived with his adoptive parents until he had emigrated to Australia as a young man. As Roman Catholics, they had raised their adopted son as a Catholic too, but what faith, Robert wondered, had his biological grandparents practised? Had they been Anglicans or Catholics, or something else, or nothing at all? He had no idea. That unanswerable question had played on his mind as he grew older.

'My mother set me a very fine example,' Robert had told the bishop. 'I think seeing what her faith gave her helped me reach the decision that was right for me. I knew God was there. But I also knew he wanted me when I was ready. My mother was still alive when I graduated, so I returned to Sydney for a short while before I began my theological training at Cuddesdon.'

'It was your mother's death, then, that brought you back to this country?'

'Yes, I stayed with her after she had her stroke. But she was worn out and I could see what she really wanted was to be reunited with Dad. She was only in hospital for a couple of months and then her time came to go and join him. It sounds strange, almost heartless perhaps, but those weeks when I visited her every day in hospital – I wouldn't have wanted to miss them.'

The bishop had looked quizzical.

'What I mean is, Mum was so rock solid in her belief that God was guiding her, even though He had paralysed her and put her in hospital, that I saw a serenity in her that I had never seen before. She'd always been very busy – tired as well. And this was so different. It was uplifting. At least I found it uplifting. Does that seem strange?'

'Not in the least,' the bishop had answered. 'God was speaking to you, through your mother. He knew what He wanted you to do with your life. All He was waiting for was for you to understand it as well.'

'You're right about that, Bishop. Seeing my mother, so contented and at peace, I knew that was what I wanted other people to feel. Everyone: the rich and successful as well as the down-and-outs and the lonely. It's love, isn't it? When you boil it down, cut away all the trappings. It's God's pure love. My dad lost his life saving his men. My mother gave her life to helping the sick. I guess that kind of mission is in my blood.'

'Well, I hope you'll find what you're looking for in St Mungo's,' the bishop had continued. 'Looking around the parish will have shown you we have the rich and successful, the down-and-outs, the drug addicts and the lonely, as you put it, in abundance. The difficulty we face as churchmen is in bridging the void between them. And be under no illusion, Robert: that void is deep, and growing wider.'

'I know exactly what you mean,' Robert had said, leaning forward. 'I've seen so many different types of people, from all kinds of places, not just England, or Europe even. If I can harness just some of that talent, I'm convinced we can turn things round at St Mungo's. It was beginning to happen in my last parish and I wasn't even running the show.'

'Yes,' the bishop had said, turning over a page in front of him. 'The Bishop of Reading has noted your determination in that respect. You certainly displayed a talent for enterprise.'

The bishop drew another sheet of paper from the file and glanced at it before continuing. 'Appealing directly to local businesses to donate materials for church halls and even, I see, the roof of your church, was regarded as …' here he had hesitated to check the exact wording, '"being imaginative" by the Diocesan Advisory Committee and the archdeacon.'

'It may have raised a few eyebrows,' Robert acknowledged, 'but I reckoned that if the church-aided schools can do it, why can't the Church itself?'

'Why not indeed? And no one could deny the success of your venture.'

'The way I see it, your Grace, it's about utilising untapped local resources. Step out of the box. Take a chance. And with church finances as they are, what is there to lose?'

'Quite so,' the bishop had replied guardedly. At the same time, with a quiet smile of satisfaction, the bishop thought he detected a possible burgeoning financial acumen in Robert's answer. A generally unusual trait among the clergy and one that might prove useful in his young protégé's future, he thought.

Closing the file, he looked directly at Robert to say in a way that required no answer, 'After putting in so much work, I wonder that you didn't want to stay to see the results for yourself.'

'With the opportunity St Mungo's offers?'

'And, of course here, you will be your own man: "running the show" yourself.'

'That's the point, your Grace. As I told the PCC and the Diocesan Appointments Board. With God's will and your backing I know I have the drive and the vision to give St Mungo's what it needs.'

The bishop had cleared his throat again. 'Well, all we can ask of you is that you try your utmost.'

'You have my word on that, Bishop.'

'I don't doubt it,' the older man had replied, 'But if you take my advice, you'll move steadily, The people who go to St Mungo's don't respond well to unexpected change. Give yourself a few weeks to get the feel of the place. That's what I would suggest.' Then he turned his attention back to the file.

'There is one thing I wanted to ask you,' Robert had said. 'It's the church building itself, sir, St Mungo's. Looking at the parish accounts, the fabric fund looks pretty much spent out. But the church still needs a lot of work and when I spoke to the diocesan architect he seemed vague on when repairs were scheduled.'

'St Mungo's used to be one of the finest churches in west London,' the bishop had answered, getting to his feet. 'I think we could both do with a cup of coffee, don't you? My wife makes very fine biscuits, could I tempt you to one of those as well?' And after Robert had thanked him, the bishop had left the room for a moment.

'Now, where were we?' he had asked when he returned.

'The repairs to St Mungo's?' Robert had suggested.

'I know that the Church Commissioners are keeping an eye on it,' the bishop answered, hoping he sounded encouraging. 'I think you and I should leave that side of things to the people who know about it. You concentrate on your parishioners, building up the congregation again.'

'But if the church itself isn't maintained properly, there's going to come a time when there won't be anywhere for the congregation to go.'

'Oh, I think that's a little extreme, Robert. St Mungo's has weathered two centuries. I think it's good for a little while longer.'

Now it had been Robert's turn to get to his feet. 'I'm a practical man, sir. I prefer to know how things stand. I work better to a timetable, better than having things open-ended.'

'Yes, I can see that.' The bishop had taken off his glasses and had started polishing the lenses with the corner of his handkerchief. 'Well, let's see how things are looking in, say, a couple of years. Who knows, the whole economic climate might have changed by then. You concentrate on drawing people back into St Mungo's. The Church Commissioners are practical people as well. If they see the numbers increasing at services, that has to make a difference, surely. Then there's the giving of course. Keep the parish accounts in the black, pay the parish share in full and on time. That's the sort of thing they look for. And it starts with the collection plate, Robert. That's where you'll see the change – if you take my meaning,' and he had smiled at his unintended pun.

Robert would have liked to have pushed the bishop further on this point, but the drawing-room door had swung open and a slim middle-aged woman with carefully tinted hair and a winning smile had entered carrying a tray.

'Ah, coffee! Excellent,' the bishop had announced, taking the tray and setting it down on a side table.

'My dear, this is Robert Melton,' he had said.

His wife's smile had widened as she had crossed over to Robert to shake hands. 'Camilla Rogers. It's very nice to meet you and I do hope you will be very happy here in our diocese.'

Robert had thanked her, had complimented her on her biscuits, and had made polite small talk for a respectable amount of time. By the time he had finished his second cup of coffee, it was clear that his meeting with the bishop had come to an end and when he had put his cup down, he had turned to look at the rain pattering against the window before announcing, 'Well, I keep reminding myself that I didn't come to London for the weather. Perhaps, if you'll excuse me, I had better make a start. As you say, sir, there's a lot to do.'

'Of course,' the bishop had replied. 'Thank you for dropping in for this chat. Now, where's that rather fine raincoat you were wearing?' and he had opened the door to show Robert out.

9

'What a charming young man,' his wife had told him, when the bishop had returned. 'If anyone can lure people back into that damp, chilly, cavern of a church he will.'

'I wonder,' the bishop had answered, pouring himself another cup of coffee.

'Oh, come on, John. The way those blue eyes look at you. If the Reverend Melton can't fill pews at St Mungo's, I don't know who will. I think you all did just the right thing giving him the job.'

The bishop had taken a sip of coffee. 'We didn't have much choice. Robert Melton was the only candidate. He doesn't know that, of course. But it doesn't look good to the powers that be. Nor does it make it any easier for me – or for him. The good people of St Mungo's won't be in for a tranquil ride with the Reverend Melton. I've seen his kind before. He'll either make a gigantic stride towards becoming our youngest Archbishop of Canterbury, or he'll destroy himself and the parish with it.'

'Aren't you being just a little pessimistic, John?' his wife had asked.

'I wish I were, my dear. I very much fear that Robert Melton may be the last vicar of St Mungo's. I know you won't breathe a word about it, but there's talk of reorganising the whole deanery. They want to carve up Melton's parish along "socially compatible grounds". That was the loathsome phrase. It's going to save the diocese the cost of two other clergy, besides Melton's own stipend. Numbers. That's what the Church Commissioners look at, and at this present moment the numbers are not in our favour: mine or his. And we don't have time on our side.'

2

ALTHOUGH HE CHAFED against it, Robert soon recognised there was wisdom in the bishop's advice not to rush things. In fact, after only four weeks in the job, he had begun to realise that the situation in the parish was far worse and much more complex than he had feared. He was even beginning to have some understanding of, if not actual sympathy for, his two predecessors. Until now, he had been trying hard not to regard them with disdain over what he saw as their litany of failure.

Now that he had had time to familiarise himself with the physical dimensions of the parish and meet the tiny handful of regular churchgoers, Robert had come to the conclusion that the parish was not so much run down through any disadvantage of being where it was; its problems stemmed from a failure to understand the polarisation that had been quietly occurring over the years. This had now created a difficult situation in which, to succeed, he felt he would have to engage the combined powers of a skilful diplomat and a ruthless dictator.

The Church of St Mungo's itself was in fact just on the right side of one of those established, but unmarked, London boundaries between a 'good' area and a 'not so good' area, that only Londoners would know about. The parish, on the other hand, straddled both sides of this boundary. This was where a large part of the problem lay.

On the good side of the boundary the parish was, quite literally, dying. The few regular churchgoing parishioners were, by and large, genteel, elderly and infirm. They could be, and by Robert's predecessors were, forgiven for being more concerned with the next world than this one.

The remainder of those living on this side of the parish, and it was by far the largest proportion, were in youthful early middle age, with young families beginning to reach into the upper-teenage bracket. A significant number of these were hard-working executives, employed in the City.

English, American, Dutch, Swedish, French and German – this part of Kensington had, in recent years, also become an enclave for well-to-do expatriate families who were responsible for the development of a burgeoning cosmopolitan atmosphere. This was clearly manifested in the springing up of continental-style cafés, delicatessens and cheerful eateries that, on fine days, spilled onto the adjoining pavements in a very un-English way – a practice that had previously been the sole preserve of those more popular public houses of the sort that were always festooned with baskets of hanging flowers.

The international element of the area self-confidently and cheerfully co-existed with their more reserved English neighbours. It was the 'overseas crowd' who willingly got involved and took a lead in supporting community events, or neighbourhood activities, which, if left to the reclusive attitude of the English, might otherwise never have taken place, but from which all in the end benefited.

In parish terms, however, Robert had begun to realise that, regardless of nationality, this executive class was largely caught up in the self-absorbing task of wealth creation at its most personal and materialistic. In pursuit of this, they either had no time for, or inclination to acknowledge any need of, God in their well-ordered lives. Some of them who did in fact attend church from time to time, did so to conform with the standards of the peer group in which they aspired to move. So their decision to go to church was arrived at by way of the same social compass with which they selected the right schools, friends, clubs and social engagements.

However, for those in the regular churchgoing communion, to whom this approach to religion might apply, the close proximity of the well-endowed and undoubtedly magnificent St Mary Abbots was much more appealing.

St Mary Abbots had it all: beautiful monastic architecture, soaring spire, accomplished campanology, a renowned choral tradition and an illustrious congregation (that periodically included members of the royal family from nearby Kensington Palace). By comparison, impoverished, worn-out and down-at-heel St Mungo's on Earls Court Road offered little contest.

On the not-so-good side of this invisible boundary, the parish was mostly made up of the kind of itinerant backpackers from all over the world that Robert had spotted right away. They were accommodated in cheap Earls Court hostels, or more pretentious establishments in which the term 'hotel' was often incongruously coupled with the name of a god from the ancient Greek pantheon: Apollo, Dionysius and Zeus being among the favourites.

Mixed together with these was a vast array of bedsits, shoehorned into what were once substantial mansion apartment buildings. These now housed a diverse cross-section of humanity, ranging from those engaged in the oldest profession in the world, through drug-dealers to hard-working, conscientious student nurses.

The occasional exceptions to the almost uniform youthfulness of this part of the parish were the single old people. Many of them, like St Mungo's itself, had once known better days; now down on their luck, they survived in an increasingly hostile world by taking refuge in some form of harmless eccentricity or another. Usually to be found in the cheapest basement flats, in rent-controlled buildings, these were the batty old ladies who took in hundreds of stray cats and spoke to no one, except perhaps the milkman on whose kindness they relied for an affordable supply of milk.

The men in this category were fewer, but generally more outwardly sociable. They tended not to live so long and were less careful with whatever slender resources they had left, as a result of which they sometimes found themselves facing eviction by not always unkind so much as exasperated landlords, who had no wish to become an unpaid extension of the social services. In this way, the relentless downward spiral of poverty would eventually force them onto the streets. Once there, whether through ignorance or a deep-rooted shame, coupled with an antipathy towards a patronising bureaucracy, arrogantly administered by people they regarded as intellectually and educationally inferior, they regularly failed to take advantage of the economic safety net on offer to them. This left their available share of help to be exploited by less scrupulous, shameless swindlers, who had made a lifelong career out of milking the social security system for everything they could get. As Robert discovered, the parish of St Mungo's was in many respects a microcosm of the nation at large.

It did not matter from which walk of life they came – the great majority of the people living in his parish were wholly indifferent to religion, and particularly in the case of the younger people, to establishment religion. The idea of going to church had moved beyond being an inconvenience to an otherwise leisurely Sunday to become something faintly embarrassing: a complete irrelevance in their self-sufficient lives.

To the socially and financially secure middle-class element, the role of the vicar was now regarded with a patronising benevolence. His primary function was seen as a duty to mark, with due ceremony, their rights of passage in baptism, marriage and death. To the itinerant younger element the vicar was seen as an outdated, eccentric figure of fun.

Despite this, Robert's arrival had created a flurry of considerable excitement amongst the stalwart hardcore of dependable parishioners,. The older, mostly widowed, ladies of the parish were, in this respect, only teenage girls trapped in ageing bodies. They were not immune to Robert's considerable charm and striking physical presence, his robust good looks alternatively reminding them of much-loved sons and, real or imagined, secret lovers from the past. They reacted towards him with a potent mix of maternal fantasy and suppressed lust. They vied with each other surreptitiously to host a lunch or tea for the new vicar, while volunteering to undertake all kinds of small services to the church, the neglect of which had forced Robert's rather less attractive predecessor to resort to a changeless display of artificial flowers between Christmas and Lent.

Even the handful of older men in this group found they were not immune to Robert's infectious enthusiasm and they responded to his vitality and encouragement to get involved in the work of the parish in a way that made them feel both useful and younger again.

It was already clear that Robert had that rare gift of leadership. With this most unlikely, and admittedly small, volunteer army of elderly, ragtag and bobtail 'soldiers' from the genteel side of the parish, the battle to save St Mungo's had, in a sense, already begun.

Once the first couple of weeks had passed, a new, more frequent schedule of weekly services was instigated. A simple but effective church pamphlet was now being created for parish distribution: with no money to pay for it Robert had utilised the well-tried concept of local business sponsorship to good effect. In newly organised parish discussion groups, concepts previously unthought-of at St Mungo's were now being enthusiastically considered as a way to increase utilisation of the building and deliver a positive boost to raising the level of awareness of the church in the community.

With these early plans set in motion, Robert decided it was time to tackle the other side of the parish, although in contemplating this, he realised he didn't know where to begin. There was no obvious starting point. His Kensington parishioners, as he called those who lived north of Cromwell Road, had no contact with his Earls Court parishioners – those who lived, however temporarily, south of it.

From what he could ascertain, it seemed that no Earls Court parishioners had shown up at St Mungo's in years. When he announced to his Kensington parishioners that this situation was to be addressed and asked for suggestions as to how it might be tackled, his request produced blank and baffled stares from a congregation that saw no need to bring that kind of social risk into their well-ordered, complacent lives.

As he had tried to convey to the bishop, Robert felt that bringing together both sides of this parish would benefit the two quite separate communities. He pictured his elderly Kensington parishioners, drawing on their years of worldly experience, assisting the younger, impetuous and less experienced Earls Court parishioners in exchange for a vicarious share in the comradeship and youthful enthusiasm that would sustain them against the crippling loneliness of old age.

Unfortunately Robert was alone in this thinking. It was one area of muttered disagreement with their new vicar in which the Kensington side of the parish was united against him. At best, they saw this youthful idealism as naive and misguided and, at worst, as interfering and disruptive to the equanimity of the parish. There were even those who talked of 'nipping it in the bud' with a strongly worded letter to the bishop.

Robert soon realised that to succeed in this goal of parish unification he would have to overcome many preconceived notions and deeply held prejudices on both sides. He also knew he would have to find a way to do it alone.

Barely two months into his ministry, Robert had began to appreciate the Herculean task that lay ahead of him if he was to succeed in saving St Mungo's and making it matter again in the West London diocese. In that realisation he sought comfort from the Confucian saying 'A journey of a thousand miles must begin with one small step'. Not for the first time, he acknowledged, western philosophy and faith could learn much from the Orient.

It was at about this time that Robert began to recognise a pattern from a not infrequent visitor to his church; one, however, who never attended Sunday services.

Perhaps to say 'pattern' was an inaccurate description, because the visits made by this striking-looking lady of mixed race had no regularity or discernible aim, other than in a certain consistency of purpose. She seemed to visit the church fairly early in the day, maybe once or twice weekly, but never at weekends. She would come in and sit, or kneel, in a truncated pew at the very back of the church that lay directly in the shadow cast by the pillar it abutted. She was usually there for anywhere between five and twenty minutes, invariably at a time when no one else was around.

Robert had noticed her leaving the church on occasions and had watched her turn left and cross over Cromwell Road, to become engulfed in the Earls Court part of his parish.

At first he hadn't given the woman too much thought, but as the weeks passed and the difficulties within the parish became clearer, Robert started to take more interest in this mysterious visitor. If none of his other Earls Court parishioners stepped inside St Mungo's, he decided that she might be his best chance of getting to know people who lived on the other side of Cromwell Road.

He missed her next couple of visits and then came the morning when, just after nine, he saw her enter the church and go to sit in her customary place. Robert quietly positioned himself unobtrusively near the back of the church and waited for her to get up to leave. As he stood there he wondered how to approach her without making it obvious that he wanted to chat with her – something he instinctively felt might be unwelcome. Rightly or wrongly, he sensed that the hold on whatever it was she came to St Mungo's for was not strong, and that she could easily be frightened off.

When she rose to leave, Robert stepped out of the shadow to open the door and he gave her what he hoped was his most disarmingly friendly smile. 'I'm Robert Melton,' he said. 'I'm the new vicar here and I just wanted to say how pleased I am to see you coming to St Mungo's.'

Whatever response he might have expected, he could not have been more surprised by the one he got. The woman looked at him briefly, with an expression of completely blank disinterest, before stepping outside and very deliberately closing the door in his face behind her. She had not spoken a word in reply to his attempt at a friendly overture.

For a moment Robert was quite shocked. Then he opened the door and stepped quickly out into the street, still half expecting a delayed response, perhaps even an explanation or apology. He was not used to rejection, and such blunt rejection had left him temporarily speechless. But the woman was nowhere to be seen.

For the remainder of the day he found himself thinking intently about just what it was he thought he had seen, besides the studied disinterest on her face, in that brief moment of eye contact. Was it fear? Was it disdain? He could not be sure. Perhaps it was all of these and something more.

3

BRENDA HAD WALKED quickly away from St Mungo's, hoping that the young vicar didn't try to follow her.

The other one had been different. Grey-faced, with thinning hair, the lingering smell of Lifebuoy soap and a loose-fitting dog collar from which his scrawny neck poked like that of a wizened tortoise, he had always scuttled into one of his dark recesses in the church whenever he had caught sight of Brenda. She preferred it that way. Most men would make it their business to sidle up to her; the ones with hands like octopus tentacles and beer-steeped breath were the worst. But the old priest had looked intimidated rather than lecherous. Brenda realised he was more alarmed by her than she was by him and once she had felt confident that he would not disturb her, she began to find peace and a sanctuary of sorts in the sad-looking church, where even the sound of the traffic hurrying past outside seemed like an echo from a different world.

St Mungo's had provided Brenda with privacy and peace, somewhere she could spend time alone with God without the anxiety of people butting in. The old vicar was harmless enough, but it was the well-meaning churchgoers, whom Brenda knew might try too hard in their urging of her to join them at Sunday morning services, that she wanted to avoid.

Now this handsome, fair-haired young vicar had suddenly appeared. Brenda felt irritated, betrayed almost. It was as though St Mungo's itself had craftily embraced him behind her back. Brenda's private sanctuary had been discovered.

All she could hope was that her reaction had been sufficiently off-putting to make the new vicar think twice before approaching her again. A similarly blunt response from her had worked with other men in the past, why should it not work with him?

As she walked briskly down the busy pavement, though, the memory of the shocked look in the young vicar's eyes and the genuinely friendly way in which he had spoken to her began to nibble at her conscience, slowly diffusing Brenda's irritation and disappointment.

She thought of Sister Lucy regularly. Even so, Brenda was surprised that she had come to mind at this moment. Sister Lucy had read Brenda's thoughts in those early days of frustration and overwhelming sadness. But she had offered practical help too: her meagre savings, sixty dollars; the note pads and pencils; clothes; books; the imitation diver's watch. In later years, it had been the little silver cross that had come to mean most to Brenda – that, and the letter Sister Lucy had given her that she still read from time to time:

> I know nothing of your past or what may have led you to these events, but the honesty and eloquence of your eyes tell me all I need to know. You are a good person – of that I am sure.
>
> Life will be difficult for a while as you come to terms with your new circumstances. Although it will be hard, try not to dwell on your disadvantages but focus instead on your advantages …
>
> Keep the little cross in your pocket. When you are lonely, sad, frightened, or – as I know you will be again one day – happy, the touch of it between your fingers will remind you, and just you, of the journey you are on. Please know that from now on, and for the rest of my life, you will always be in my special daily prayers. One of my precious 'Starfish'. May God go with you.
>
> With great love and care for you at this Eastertide.
>
> I remain affectionately yours,
> Sister Lucy

The quiet, even the slight chill, inside St Mungo's reminded Brenda of slowly coming round years ago to the feeling of cool cotton sheets and a sense of peace through which she could hear the hushed voices of people calmly going about their business.

With gradually increasing consciousness she had become aware that her head and mouth hurt, but nothing like as much as the pain she felt in the lower abdomen and the area between her buttocks.

Through the intense ache in her head, she had tried to understand where she was and what had happened. Gradually, as she had lain with her eyes closed, full consciousness had returned and with it the memory of the nightmare of what she had endured.

Seeing a young black nun pass the foot of the bed, Brenda had tried to call out to her. A strange strangled sound she had not recognised had been all that had passed her lips. She tried to lick them. Nothing happened.

Gingerly she had put her fingers to her open mouth. Her head throbbed. The pain in her mouth and throat had been almost more than she could bear. She could not understand what was wrong. Seeing another nurse nearby, she had tried again to call out to her and had feebly attempted to wave an arm.

The young nun Brenda had first seen had come quickly to her bedside. Her face had had a look of great compassion and relief as she had gently said, 'So, you've regained consciousness. At first we weren't sure you were going to make it.'

Bewilderment had clouded Brenda's face. The nurse had placed a finger on her lips and explained, 'You were found on the roadside, four days ago. Luckily someone brought you here. But you should really rest now. You lost a great deal of blood and you're going to be very weak for a while yet.'

But Brenda could not forget how she had tried to speak again, nor how the unrecognisable sound and excruciating pain had made her grab the nun's hand and hold it tightly. Then the pain, fear and misery had given way to sobbing and tears.

'All right, now you are awake, the doctor wants to speak to you,' Sister Lucy had said, disengaging Brenda's hand and laying it gently on the bed, but not before softly stroking it. Brenda had been surprised to catch sight of the tears in the young nun's eyes.

Brenda had replayed that scene in her memory many times since. She wondered where Sister Lucy was now. More than likely still working in that same hospital in Trinidad, where she would be looking older now of course. If Brenda was still in her special daily prayers, she had often wondered what Sister Lucy would think of how she was making use of her 'special gift'. That thought would give Brenda a sick feeling in her stomach. Sister Lucy had seemed too kind to be angry with her, but would she be disappointed – ashamed, maybe? Embarrassed? How could Sister Lucy understand her situation?

This had been one of the reasons that had drawn Brenda to St Mungo's. God she felt, did understand her. But what had it been about this young vicar that had made Brenda instinctively think of Sister Lucy? Did Brenda want him to understand her as well? And why would that be important? She was not angry any more. But she was confused.

4

ROBERT TOOK HIS encounter with the enigmatic parishioner as a personal challenge. However, he had to admit it confirmed that he was now no further forward in his attempts to find a contact, or bridge, into the more volatile and fluid part of his parish. He needed a different approach, which led to his resolve to immerse himself in the cosmopolitan culture of that part of the parish in order to see if he could find a way in and make his own contacts.

He began by making a practice of crossing over Cromwell Road to have lunch in one of the area's numerous, smoke-filled pubs whenever he could. He started shopping there too. Even though it placed an increased burden on his always precarious finances, he now switched from the efficiency of Tesco's to the small individual, mostly Asian, shops that lined Earls Court Road. On the nights when he could, he would mingle with the throng at the bar of a popular pub, trendy pseudo-French brasserie, or some basement jazz club. A music lover in the broadest sense, Robert was a jazz and blues aficionado.

Work had kept him so busy that Robert had neglected his own social life and the odyssey into the colourful, multi-cultural and, above all, youthful atmosphere of this freewheeling part of the London scene held its own attraction for him. He became aware again of shapely young ladies, many of whom frequented the area's cafés, bars, clubs and restaurants. They in turn noticed him and on more than one occasion, Robert found himself being approached with a directness that he had at first found disconcerting, but later came to appreciate for its honesty.

Robert responded by being equally straightforward. He never attempted to fudge the question, always asked early on in any encounter, about what he did for a living. The initial reaction of outright disbelief would be swiftly followed by one of incredulity and thereafter, in nine out of ten cases, a complete change in manner. This involved the burial of all overt sexual interest, reducing the encounter to nothing more than an exchange of superficial pleasantries, which continued only for as long as social decency dictated was necessary. Then the girl in question would extricate herself to return to her friends or seek out another, more promising, male target.

The irony of how the honesty of the initial approach disappeared the moment he told them he was a vicar was not lost on Robert. The way in which their direct candour was immediately replaced by a thin veneer of embarrassed, insincere politeness always disappointed him. It was, however, something he had grown used to accepting. He found he felt almost sorry for having to deliver the shock he knew was coming, and he greatly resented the narrowness of opportunity for female company of his choosing that this general reaction to his calling seemed to present him with. It was as if he had somehow deceived them by infringing an unwritten law that good-looking, healthy young men could not be called by God to serve in his Church; even when that Church permitted a married priesthood.

On the other hand, Robert discovered soon after his arrival at St Mungo's that, on the Kensington side of the parish, there was to be no shortage of 'respectable' daughters and granddaughters paraded before him by openly scheming mothers and grandmothers. Here he had had time to observe another prevailing pattern. If one of these girls was pretty, fashion-conscious, glamorous, self-assured, or even just nice looking and clever with it, the prize of becoming a vicar's wife would have been strongly discouraged: the unspoken belief being that such a girl could do much better than that for herself.

It was always the less attractive, chronically shy, fat and frumpy girls that

Robert found himself being introduced to at little 'impromptu' luncheon or tea parties. Somehow it was contrived that he should sit next to the unfortunate girl in question, or find himself left alone with her on some impossibly small window seat. While he could not experience any more attraction to these poor girls than other men, the human and priestly side of his personality would never allow him to be dismissive. He hated seeing the barely disguised hope and gratitude in their eyes as he tried to focus his attention on them, reminding himself, without any conviction, that it was a person's interior disposition that mattered. Above all he strove always to treat them with kindness and respect, for which, at least, they were unashamedly grateful. It was at moments like this that he best understood, and indeed almost envied, the rule of celibacy in the Catholic Church.

Early one morning, during a foray into the Earls Court district in search of breakfast, Robert found himself seated at a window table in Café Rouge, next to the tube station. He had just started on his second cup of coffee when the door opened, heralding a blast of cool morning air and the entrance of a very attractive, mixed-race woman. She walked with an attitude of easy familiarity to a seat at the bar, where the young man serving greeted her with a cheery, 'Good morning, Brenda' and, without waiting to be asked, poured her a cup of coffee.

Until now Robert had only seen her within the shadows of the church and he was struck by two things. Firstly by how really very good looking this young woman was. She had exceptionally fine features and a manner about her that hinted at a more sophisticated past than the life she appeared to be leading at present would suggest. The other was that she didn't speak. He noted she had not replied to the barman's friendly good morning with anything other than a quick smile. The barman in turn had not appeared to expect more than this while busying himself with pouring her coffee and fetching a small jug of milk, neither of which she had asked for. Robert decided that she must be a sufficiently regular customer with habitual tastes that it made both small talk and the need to repeat an unchanging coffee order redundant. Nevertheless, he thought this silent approach exuded a coolness that bordered on the arrogant.

Robert watched her for some while, noting the shapeliness of her long legs as she sat poised, rather than perched, on the high stool. Her skirt was short, but only fashionably so. The blue silk scarf, which she wore loosely around her long neck, enhanced a face with the striking features of a model: high cheekbones, penetratingly large dark brown eyes and a refined nose set above a generous, well-defined mouth. A modestly applied hint of red lipstick provided a sensual contrast with her dark skin. Robert thought her skin was beautiful: an unblemished, burnt olive colour that had a velvet smoothness and texture more consistent with that of a teenager than a young woman who was probably in her mid-twenties.

While he was watching her, Robert noted again that, whenever another regular customer or member of staff greeted her, the young woman's only reply was a friendly smile, accompanied by a raised hand or nod of acknowledgement.

Suddenly Robert became aware that she was returning his stare with a look of mild annoyance. He was overcome with shame and embarrassment and turned hurriedly away. He wondered if he should perhaps go up and apologise for his rudeness. but he decided this might only make matters worse. Instead he finished his coffee and signalled to the waitress for the bill.

He was just putting on his coat when he realised that this silent beauty was standing beside his table. Without saying a word she handed him a small printed card and returned at once to her place at the bar, but not before Robert had caught an expression of sensitive intelligence in her dark brown eyes. Flustered, Robert put the unread card in his pocket, thanked his waitress and left.

Back at his small office attached to St Mungo's, he pulled the card from his pocket and read:

> Hello, my name is Brenda. Due to an incident when I was 16 I am no longer able to speak. This makes me comfortable with other people's physical differences.

Please understand and respect that it is only to those with physical differences that I specialise in offering my particular massage services.

Because of my lack of speech I am an excellent listener, precisely because I have the time to hear things that speaking people don't.

I charge by the hour and will quote you a rate if you wish to avail yourself of my services. Please call to make an appointment.

There followed a telephone number, with the area code of the local exchange.

The realisation of what this young woman probably did for a living struck Robert like a thunderbolt. Deep in thought, for a long time he just sat holding the card in his hand. He couldn't reconcile the image he had begun to form of this woman who regularly visited his church, with the darker picture of the sordid backstreet business he now conjured up. Added to this was the shock he felt in discovering that there was a reason why she didn't speak and the guilt at having presumed her to be both rude and arrogant.

Robert looked again at the card in his hand. It was of poor quality: the printing was both uneven and slightly crooked. Robert guessed that Brenda needed large quantities of these cards. The inside of every telephone box he passed seemed to be plastered with the same kind of notices posted by other young women offering a variety of similar services.

He looked at the telephone number and was curious to know why some-one who couldn't speak needed a phone. He thought also about the unsentimental directness of the wording on the card, wondering what could possibly have happened to render a sixteen-year-old girl mute, while showing no other outward sign of injury. But, looking again, he saw that the card quite clearly said 'incident' and not accident or illness. This seemed to imply something far more sinister.

His curiosity was getting the better of him and Robert lifted the handset from the rather old-fashioned telephone on his desk and dialled the number on the card. After a couple of business-like rings the recording of a polite female voice came on the line.

'Hello, thank you for calling,' the recording began. 'I'm speaking for Brenda, who, as you know, is mute and unable to talk. Because of this, Brenda has a special affinity for those afflicted by any kind of physical handicap or disability. If you do not qualify please ring off now.

'If you do and would like to make an appointment with Brenda, please call between six and eight on a Monday evening, when someone will be here to make appointments for the coming week.

'Brenda offers an affordable, discrete, unhurried service that is dedicated to sensitively helping and pleasing all her special customers. Your sensibilities will be treated with the utmost respect and your privacy will be assured. You will not be disappointed. Although Brenda can't talk, you will find that she speaks eloquently with her eyes and hands.

'If your message requires a response, please leave a telephone number, then please be patient. Someone will get back to you on Brenda's behalf, usually within forty-eight hours.'

There then followed a short list of rates, dependant on the amount of time allocated.

Robert was stunned by what he had just heard. He slowly replaced the receiver in its cradle, aware that any idea of the worldliness he thought he possessed had just been shaken. As he looked at the card in front of him and ran the recording through in his mind it began to dawn on him just how sheltered his own upbringing, and that of most of those he knew, had been. Yet he, as a priest, was expected to know about and embrace everyone in his parish, from whatever walk of life they came and regardless of the business they might be engaged in.

It was with wry humour that he tried to imagine the general reaction of the good people from the Kensington side of his parish if they knew the true extent of the gulf that Robert would have to bridge, if he was ever to break down their English reserve and prejudices in the reunification of his parish.

Now that he had had time to adjust to the situation into which he had stumbled, he was more determined than ever to succeed in reaching out to Brenda and those like her, whether male or female, rich or poor, or indeed from either side of his parish. He was, after all, not so unworldly as to realise that people engrossed in the single-minded pursuit of ever more material wealth were often in danger of succumbing to temptations of a far more sinister kind than mere sins of the flesh.

Robert found himself – and not for the first time – pondering the theological question of degrees of sinfulness. What circumstance might have framed the background to Brenda's current position in life? And why should she be condemned and shunned when outwardly successful, eminently respectable executives, or prominent public figures, were frequently being exposed for their involvement in large-scale corruption? Robert wondered how genuine the media indignation was that scandals like this had been allowed to carry on without regard to the serious hurt they invariably inflicted on innocent and defenceless people.

Robert was incensed that society regarded the salacious little sex scandals of some unfortunate individuals as disproportionately sinful – especially when it revelled in the personal disgrace of the individual exposed, while also taking a puerile interest in all the sordid details. When it came to the final judgement, Robert was reasonably certain that God would not necessarily take the same view.

Since Brenda had occupied a good deal of this thinking, he decided to return to the café bar where he had seen her that morning. Perhaps it was a favourite hangout where she felt comfortable and she might be there again? He realised he very much wanted to talk to her and with this in mind he thoughtfully put a ballpoint pen and pad in his pocket before setting out.

It was just after three when Robert walked in: that early afternoon period which is famously too late and at the same time too early to be a useful time for anything. The place was nearly empty. No sign of Brenda. He walked over to the centrally located bar, where he unconsciously picked the bar stool Brenda had occupied that morning.

Robert recognised the young man behind the bar, who asked him with a pleasant smile. 'What can I get you?'

Robert was momentarily thrown by this. He didn't really want anything. He'd already had a cup of coffee following lunch and it seemed early for either a cup of tea or anything stronger. However, recognising he needed a reason to be there, he quickly decided on coffee just to settle the matter. Spotting the espresso machine he asked for a cappuccino, glad of the extra time this would take as it allowed him to frame in his mind the questions he wanted to ask.

When the barman brought over his cappuccino, Robert made a comment about how quiet the place was, remarking that it had been much busier when he had been in earlier for breakfast. The young man seemed pleased to take this cue to stop what he was doing in order to chat with his customer.

'It's always quiet around this time,' he said.

'I suppose so,' agreed Robert. Then after only the slightest pause, he asked in a voice which he hoped sounded sufficiently casual, 'Who was that nice-looking coloured girl sitting here at about eight this morning? Brenda, I think I heard you calling her.'

The young man gave Robert a guarded look. After a moment's hesitation, however, he replied, 'Oh yes, that would have been Brenda, she comes in most days about the same time. One of our regulars.' Then he suddenly asked, 'You're not with the police are you?'

Robert assured him he was not, convincingly enough for the young man to continue. 'You see, Brenda's not what she seems, but if you were a friend of hers, or even if you were just someone in need, she would give her last penny to help you without any thought for herself. What she does to make a living is her business, but it's not easy in a city like this if you've no family and if you're unable to speak. She's mute you see,' he added unnecessarily.

'Brenda was one of the original regulars. Before my time of course, but whoever comes to work here gets to know Brenda. We're the closest thing she's got to any sort of extended family and we try to look out for her. It's why I asked you if you were a cop,' he added warily.

Robert wondered if he was always so trusting of the police.

'What time does she usually come in?' Robert asked.

'Why do you want to know?' replied the young man, suspicious again.

'Oh, just curious,' answered Robert lamely, adding as an afterthought in what he hoped was a conspiratorial manner when it came to the charms of the opposite sex, 'I thought she looked nice and I couldn't help noticing that she has great legs.'

The ploy worked. The younger man was flattered to be taken as a man of the world. 'Yeah, she's a beauty all right. Seems funny to think of her before the operation now though. They did a good job.'

Seeing Robert's confusion, he explained, 'I mean her sex change. Like I told you, Brenda isn't what she seems. But around here that doesn't matter. People are busy enough with their own problems to live and let live. We take each other at face value. Brenda is the kindest, most giving sort of person you could ever hope to meet. In this neighbourhood we all look out for her,' he added, in a way that Robert might have construed as a warning had he been paying attention at that point. He was not.

He was not sure how much more unreality (or was it reality?) he could take in one day. Remembering the good-looking woman the first morning he had set eyes on her at St Mungo's, he was at a loss to imagine what his reaction might have been if he had known then that Brenda had once been a man.

Robert had to face the fact that what he had at first seen as the tough, but straightforward, challenge of his parish was now being stood on its head. As part of this, he also realised that his spiritual and moral positions were in direct conflict. For the first time since taking over at St Mungo's, Robert felt an uncomfortable sensation that, had he been able to recognise it, he might have interpreted as a loss of control.

The easy option would be to ignore what he now knew. He could stick to doing only what might be reasonably expected of him in attempting to reach and embrace the potential of his unknown, marginalised parishioners, whereas probing deeper into their lives brought the risk of fully engaging with all their tumultuous spiritual, moral and emotional conflicts that lay directly in the path of honest confrontation. Did he really want to put himself through all that?

His expression must have given away some of what he was feeling, because the next thing he heard was the barman saying to him, 'You OK? You look like you've seen a ghost or something.'

'Yeah, I'm fine,' Robert replied, at the same time making a pretence of looking at his watch.

'I must be going,' he said finishing his cappuccino, which by now had grown quite cold. Wisely he remembered to leave a very good tip.

'Thanks very much,' said the barman. He hesitated a moment and then continued, 'Like I said, Brenda's one of the regulars. She often drops in for a glass of wine. Around seven, usually. It just depends on her appointments.'

As he left Robert tried not to think about this last piece of information too much. One way or another, he had quite enough on his mind as he walked back to St Mungo's.

After taking time to think things through and talk with God about what his next step should be in reuniting and re-engaging both sides of his parish, Robert decided that his original aim of enlisting Brenda's help was still the best approach in spite of what he now knew about her. He was surprised that he was still able to think of Brenda quite naturally as female, even though he now knew her to have been born a male.

It also occurred to Robert that in one respect he had an advantage over many people when it came to communicating with Brenda. When he was a youngster, his mother had encouraged him to visit long-stay patients in the children's wards. Several of them had suffered from deafness to varying degrees. They were learning to communicate in Sign and Robert had joined in their lessons, becoming as proficient as them in time. He couldn't pretend that he had practised Sign much in the intervening years, but he was pleased that it didn't take him long to pick up what was being communicated on the occasions when he switched on the live translation service on TV programmes.

Now that he had made up his mind to get in touch with Brenda, Robert retrieved the card she had given him. He dialled the number again and waited patiently for the polite and, Robert felt, genuinely encouraging, announcement to finish.

'Hello. My name is the Reverend Robert Melton. Could I ... can I make an appointment, please. With Brenda. I got this number from her business card. The card she uses to get ... so that people can make appointments to see her. But I don't want to see her like that. All I want to do is to have a talk with Brenda.'

As soon as he said it, Robert felt his armpits start to grow clammy and the skin around his collar starting to get damp. How could he have been so crass?

He rushed on, frantically hoping he had time to correct himself. 'What I mean is Brenda could write things down. Her answers. What she's thinking. Anything she wants. Or she could sign, if she knows how to sign. All I want is to ... to get to know her.'

He had managed to squeeze in that last bit just before the answerphone cut out, but when he replaced the receiver he wished that hadn't been able to.

He could hear the embarrassment in his own voice as he silently cursed the

33

machine that simply recorded what it heard in such a detached and unforgiving manner.

He debated calling back to leave a continuation message, but decided that that might be overdoing his apology. Why, he wondered, did her answering machine leave so little time for taking messages? He concluded that perhaps in Brenda's line of business, experience had taught her the need for a certain practical approach: give long enough for clients to leave necessary information, but not enough time for some crank or hatemonger to sound off.

For the next few days there was no response and Brenda did not come to St Mungo's. Robert started to worry that his clumsy persistence had, as he had always feared it might, frightened her off. It was for this reason that he did not return to the café immediately. Above all, he wanted to give her space and time to consider his request.

5

BRENDA HAD PICKED up some peculiar messages on her answering machine but the one she was listening to now was one of the more memorable. She could almost visualise the man – the priest – at the other end of the line, tripping over himself with embarrassment at making the call in the first place and then making such a mess of it.

Although he sounded confused and muddled, his voice didn't have the desperate urgency that Brenda had become used to with people who rang for the first time. A lot of her clients didn't want to talk more than was absolutely necessary and this caller's insistence that that was all he wanted to do struck her as odd. If he had been the sort of man who was used to using sex workers, Brenda would have picked up a swagger, a bravado in his message that the man who had called clearly didn't have. You didn't need Brenda's finely tuned receptors to work out quickly that this caller had never spoken to someone offering 'particular massage services' before, never mind getting to the point of arranging to visit them.

'You won't be able – or need – to give a special massage until you can read the signs,' Naomi had told Brenda, and Naomi had been right. Now Brenda could read all the signs. The man who had left the message on her answering machine certainly wasn't wanting a massage, special or otherwise. Whatever he did want with Brenda, she felt that the Reverend Robert Melton was not the kind of man who would have shied away from the likes of Naomi and herself.

Although he might have walked past the entrance to Venus and Apollo, once he'd spotted what was on offer behind its tawdry facade, he would have done so with an understanding sadness for those inside.

Brenda had needed the job. That was what she used to remind herself in the early days when memories of Sister Lucy's kindness were still as fresh as the waves of shame and self-doubt that would catch her off-guard at times when her spirits were low.

Until that terrible last day, the job washing-up in the kitchen at the Dorchester Hotel had been going well. After two years in England, Brenda had found her feet in London and was starting to rebuild her self-confidence.

It had been Sister Lucy who had first commented on her hands. 'You have such beautiful, sensitive hands,' she had said, holding Brenda's gently and turning over the palms to examine their long, sensitive fingers. 'You should think about using these in some trade, or maybe to discover a God-given talent. I don't know much about this kind of thing, but these look like they could be the hands of a musician, or a painter – maybe a sculptor.'

Brenda wondered what Sister Lucy would have thought if she could have seen those hands submerged in grimy water washing pots and pans for months on end. However, it was perhaps thanks to Sister Lucy that Brenda had paused to read the notice taped against the glass in the window of Venus and Apollo, a 'Massage Therapy Clinic', as the sign coyly announced.

'Good with your hands? Masseuse wanted. Let us train you in the ancient art of therapeutic massage. Excellent prospects,' the notice had read.

You didn't need a second glance at Naomi to see that whatever prospects she had once had, they were now as far from excellent as she could get. At a guess, Brenda would have put Naomi in her mid-forties, an age that was accentuated by her appearance.

Naomi was dressed as a teenager. Not, however, as a teenager of today, but rather as a sort of stylised fantasy teenager from a movie time warp. Her dyed blonde hair was tied in two pigtails, decorated with ribbons at the end. She was wearing a short, pleated skirt, a body-hugging jersey top, white bobby socks and white sneakers. The combined effects of age, gravity and a fondness for cheap white wine had caused her ample bust to drop and her thighs and waist to thicken. But the ravages of time had been kind to her face, which remained quite pretty and youthful under her false tan. She had a hard mouth and a weary, cynical expression in her eyes. Naomi was one of the Venus and Apollo 'stable' of girls that Brenda was about to become.

When she had first started at Venus and Apollo, Naomi had been what the proprietors had liked to call a 'Premium Girl', for whose services they could charge extra. Over the years she had gradually lost this dubious status, when the client demand for her particular services had begun to tail off. With this came a reduction in her earnings and the inevitable lowering, even further, of her own self-worth. It was a vicious circle from which she did not have enough focus or determination to escape. The arrival of Brenda at Venus and Apollo was the latest confirmation of that dismal truth. Still, it had been Naomi who had started Brenda on her way; she had to be grateful for that above everything else.

'I understand you've never had a massage yourself?' Naomi had said.

Brenda had shaken her head cautiously.

'OK then. Go and take off your clothes in Studio Number 3. I'm going to begin your training by giving you a massage. You won't be able to give a proper massage until you've had one yourself and know what it's all about.'

Brenda had not moved.

'Go on then,' Naomi said. 'Take all your clothes off and lie on the massage table face up. You can put the small modesty towel across your privates if you like. But I've seen it all in my time. You won't do anything for me. I'll be along in a minute or two,' she had said, turning to go.

Brenda had felt all the old familiar panic beginning to take hold. Unexplained delay would achieve little more than cause irritation. And explanation was impossible.

Mechanically she had undressed down to her underwear. Then with a feeling of utter dread she had lain face down on the massage table. Her mind and body were taut with apprehension as she carefully covered her buttocks with the small modesty towel, having pulled down the waist and tucked up the legs of her boys' boxer shorts as far as she could, thankful that they were of a plain white cotton that matched the white of the little towel.

Brenda had desperately hoped that perhaps Naomi would somehow understand and not insist. Of course she could always have got up and quit on the spot. But she had already known this wasn't really an option.

She had tried to control the feeling of panic by telling herself this was something she had to get through. If only she had been able to speak, she was certain she would then be able to persuade Naomi to allow her to keep her dignity.

Naomi had hardly had time to close the door behind her before she had said in a gently mocking tone, 'Oh we are being modest, aren't we? You must have been brought up in a convent. Come on now, face up like I told you. You can't expect to enjoy a Venus and Apollo "Naomi special" unless I can refresh the parts that others can't reach.' She gave a brazen wink.

Feeling trapped, Brenda had very reluctantly turned over on her back, somehow still keeping the towel in place.

'That's better,' Naomi had said. 'Now, normally I would talk with my clients at this stage to break the ice and put them at their ease. If they're regulars it's never a problem, we just pick up where we left off last time – a bit like a hairdressing salon really.

'If they're first-timers, I'm more careful. Some don't like to talk much, others never stop, and some of them are so skittish they need to be persuaded to go through with it. You get the feeling that given half a chance what they'd really like to do is get up and run all the way home, stopping only to buy a bunch of flowers for the missus to ease their guilty conscience. Pathetic isn't it? But that's life I suppose.'

Naomi had taken an exotic-looking round glass bottle of light amber oil from a shelf beside the table. She had gently warmed this in the flow of water from the hot tap in a basin against the wall as she had been talking.

'Of course you won't be able to talk to the customers, will you? But they'll be told this, so they won't be expecting it. Some will probably prefer it that way. They'll be able to cope with their own stupid guilt better in silence,' she had said.

'This is the oil we massage with,' she had explained, holding up the warmed bottle for Brenda to see. We warm it just enough to make sure it's a little above normal body temperature. That way there's no shock.'

She had poured a little into the palm of one hand and then, putting the bottle down, had rubbed her hands together to spread the oil, before placing them on Brenda's shoulders and beginning a slow, firm, kneading, her hands working in a circular motion on the shoulders, upper arms and torso.

'Of course the bottle looks wonderful and expensive, with its easy-to-read label promising all sorts of aromatherapy benefits, but whatever it used to have inside, it's been refilled, dozens of times I should imagine, with special Venus and Apollo blend; bog-standard baby oil, with a touch of corn-coloured vegetable dye and a few drops of a herbal concentrate. Anyway the punters think it's exotic so I suppose it is really.'

By this time Naomi had worked her way down each arm, gently tugging at the individual fingers of both hands. Had she not been in such a state of terror, Brenda had realised that she would have greatly enjoyed the therapeutic feeling from the contact of Naomi's smoothly oiled hands. It had been, she thought, a sensation that, under the right circumstances, could instil a great sense of calmness and physical wellbeing.

All of a sudden, Brenda had known that this was really something she wanted to do, something she could be good at. It had also been something else – something she had not felt since that ill-fated day in Trinidad.

Although the hands had been young then, untrained and inexperienced, it had been the innocent, close friendship and complete emotional trust that had given that distant contact with David an intensity that no professionally administered massage could ever hope to capture.

Brenda had become aware that Naomi's hands were now working their way down over her flat stomach. Sensing the panic rising in her, Naomi had started to speak softly in a gently reassuring voice.

'In all the years I've been doing this I don't ever remember seeing or touching such perfect skin. It's like dark velvet. The truth is, you may not be able to speak but you've got one of the best bodies I've ever seen.'

She had said this with such conviction that Brenda had not known if it had been the truth, or the sort of thing Naomi used to say to all her first-time clients to make them relax and feel good about themselves.

'Bear in mind that's a lot of bodies I'm talking about. OK, they're almost always older than you, but that doesn't take away what you've got, Brenda. You should count yourself lucky in that at least. The good Lord certainly gave you a heavenly body. I'd give anything to have a flat tummy like yours again,' Naomi had said wistfully, but also with an honest touch of envy.

Her hands had now reached Brenda's lower waist. Naomi stopped there just long enough to get some more of the massage oil. Turning back, she had deftly flicked away the modesty towel, revealing the carefully tucked up boxer shorts. If she had been surprised, her face had not shown it and she had said nothing. Instead, moving around to the bottom of the massage table, she had begun to work on Brenda's feet and legs. The sense of relief and gratitude Brenda felt at this reprieve was huge.

Skilfully and diligently working her way up through each tense calf muscle on Brenda's legs, Naomi had professionally noted again the unusual smoothness of her skin. But her thoughts had been elsewhere. What emotional nerve had she unwittingly touched? And why was Brenda so afraid to even risk being seen naked?

As her hands had gently but firmly worked up each inner thigh she had deliberately employed a technique of quick butterfly strokes into the rolled-up legs of the boxers, skilfully stopping just short of the genital area. Each time she had done this, she had seen and felt Brenda freeze.

At this moment, for Naomi, the battle between cruel envy and compassionate understanding had been lost. The recognition of her own faded looks, the self-hatred at her inability to overcome the unfairness of her hard life, with all its disappointments, and the near certain realisation that now this Brenda was about to occupy the position she had once enjoyed as the golden girl at Venus and Apollo, all came together in a rush of blind, destructive envy.

In one sudden movement, she had pulled down Brenda's boxers so quickly that she would have had no chance to react, even had she been able to overcome the state of paralysis that had taken hold of her.

Brenda had not moved. Unchecked tears had begun to run freely from behind tightly closed eyes.

Familiar as she was with the human anatomy in all its variety of shapes and sizes, what Naomi had seen nevertheless came as a complete shock. She had gasped as she recoiled from the table in horror.

'Christ,' Naomi had said hoarsely, when she had finally recovered herself enough to speak. 'Who did that to you? Listen … I'm so very sorry … I had no idea. I didn't mean to hurt you … Why didn't you tell me?'

At this Brenda had sat up, looked at Naomi, opened her mouth as wide as she could, and let out a series of soft sounds unmistakably reminiscent of a wounded, frightened animal.

For the second time Naomi had recoiled at what she saw. 'You've got no tongue,' she had blurted out. 'So that's why you can't speak. Hey, I'm really, really sorry. I feel awful about what I just did to you Brenda.'

At this point the door to Studio 3 had burst open. Standing there, Beatrice Fiske, proprietor of Venus and Apollo, had been seething.

'Sorry?' she had yelled at Naomi. 'What are you sorry for? That little black boy bitch has fooled us completely. Think about it you dim-witted tart. What use is the little mutant going to be to our punters with no dick and no tongue? The money and time I've wasted on him today buying all those clothes!'

Although she had been momentarily taken aback by Beatrice Fiske's furious outburst, Naomi's mind had already been working on another question. How had Mrs Fiske known Brenda was so mutilated?

Slipping off one of her high-heeled shoes, Naomi had turned to the little mirror on the wall and had hit the glass with all the force she could muster. The mirror had shattered into tiny fragments of glass to reveal the shocked grey face of Beatrice Fiske's husband, Gerald, peering through an open panel in the wall behind. This was at the precise point where, Naomi knew, a cheap picture of the god Apollo usually hung in the office.

With tiny shards of broken mirror glinting in his drooping grey moustache, Gerald Fiske's lugubrious features were momentarily caught blinking in embarrassed surprise before he ducked quickly out of the opening.

Naomi then turned her attention to Beatrice Fiske, looking at her coldly and said, 'If Brenda goes, I go too.'

It had been said quietly, but with such force that it had stopped Beatrice Fiske in her tracks. She had known she couldn't afford to lose Naomi, and this time she knew Naomi was making no idle threat.

Rather than risk a confrontation with Naomi that she might have come to regret, Beatrice Fiske had retreated, closing the door with a defiant slam as she left.

Naomi had picked up the bottle of 'exotic' massage oil and with an accuracy that would have done credit to a fast bowler, had hurled it straight through the opening she had revealed in the wall between Studio 3 and the Fiskes' office. She had the satisfaction of hearing the bottle explode as it shattered against the far wall spraying the cheap, imitation 'aromatic' oil in all directions.

'Now get out of the office you shrivelled old goat of a peeping Tom,' she had yelled at Gerald Fiske, 'and don't come back until Brenda and I have finished talking.'

After she had heard the office door close, Naomi had turned to Brenda, who had been getting dressed. Outwardly at least, her composure had been restored. She had looked at Naomi with a grateful but wary appreciation for her support.

'Hey, I'm really, really sorry. I feel awful about what I just did to you Brendan,' Naomi had said, using Brenda's proper name for the first time.

'You know you really do look good as Brenda. And, if you're comfortable with being Brenda, maybe you should think about making it a permanent change?' she had said kindly. 'Almost nothing in this world is what it looks like.'

6

THAT HAD BEEN the irony.

In the end, it had been Beatrice Fiske, of all people, who had been responsible for her transition. Her motives had been purely self-serving, of course: with a few clothes and a little make-up, hapless Brendan could be transformed into slinky, exotic Brenda. Beatrice Fiske knew her clientele well. They would be queuing up to enjoy the services of the latest piece of talent at Venus and Apollo.

The reception area that led off the street had been dimly lit and the impression of darkness had been accentuated by shafts of sunlight, determinedly penetrating through the grime of the only window, when Brendan had encountered the Fiskes.

A not quite stout, well-dressed woman in early middle age had looked up as Brendan had approached the ornate reception desk, decorated in a heavy baroque style that matched the intellectual pretensions of the owners whose sketchy grasp of ancient mythology had led them blithely to unite Venus, the goddess of love from the Roman pantheon, with Apollo, the sun god of music and poetry from the Greek canon.

The woman had short blonde hair, red lips and artificially pale skin that Brendan had noticed she maintained through the liberal use of face powder. A sign on the desk facing towards the front had read 'Beatrice Fiske'.

'Can I help you?' she had asked in a voice uncertain whether it should be welcoming or hostile. Brendan had handed her the job application he had written in the café round the corner, but not before first showing the card that had simply stated he was unable to speak.

Beatrice Fiske had taken the piece of paper suspiciously and had read it through slowly. Then, looking up at Brendan, she had said in a raised voice, 'The notice in the window says we're looking for a masseuse. That means a female. We don't have any masseurs here.'

Brendan had felt embarrassment rising to his cheeks. He had been so eager at the prospect of a job that he had seemed so well suited for that he had overlooked the obvious distinction between masseuse and masseur.

He had already turned to leave, feeling confused and foolish, when Beatrice Fiske had said, 'Wait a minute. Will you show me your hands?'

She had seemed to be evaluating the new arrival in a way Brendan had not yet understood. What the experienced eye of the proprietor of Venus and Apollo had seen was an exceptionally attractive, almost beautiful, young man with a dark olive skin and small, well-defined, even slightly effeminate features.

Brendan had held out his hands in silence. Beatrice Fiske had at once seen in them the same strength and yet refined sensitivity that Sister Lucy had noticed – and an idea had begun to form in her mind.

'Would you take a seat while I have a word with my partner?' she had asked, indicating a chair on the other side of the hallway.

Brendan had sat down while Mrs Fiske had disappeared through an opaque glass-panelled door beside her desk, which she had carefully closed behind her.

After a few minutes the door had opened. The woman had returned, followed closely by a tired, scrawny-looking man in his late fifties. His shoulders were visibly narrower than his waist. Bald on top of his head, he wore what remained of his hair in a long, lank fringe that was as grey as it was greasy. His cheeks were hollow and sallow. Half-hidden under a drooping grey moustache, his lips were pale and thin. His overall demeanour had not been helped by what appeared to be a naturally doleful expression suggesting a lifetime of downtrodden disillusionment.

'Brendan – I can call you Brendan, can't I?' Beatrice had said with a reassuring smile. 'Meet Mr Fiske – Gerald Fiske. I've explained your circumstances to him and he very much wanted to meet you.'

At this Gerald Fiske had put out his hand and had attempted what Brendan had assumed was meant to be his version of a smile, although more accurately it could readily have been taken for a leer. This grimace had lasted just long enough for Brendan to get a glimpse of the nicotine- and coffee-stained stumps that passed for teeth in Gerald Fiske's mouth.

'Gerald isn't only my business partner, he is also my husband,' Mrs Fiske had confided somewhat unnecessarily.

'I run what you might call the front-of-house side of Venus and Apollo. Mr Fiske prefers it that way. His talents lie in the back office, looking after the accounts, the wages and the hundred and one other things we owners of small businesses have to struggle with day in, day out.

'For reasons that will become clear later, we only ever employ females at Venus and Apollo. Most of them are girls and, as you may have gathered from the presence of the ancient Greek god, Apollo, our customers are nearly always men.

'Mr Fiske and I have been discussing a proposition that we would like to put to you. We think we might be able to find you a position on our staff, but it would have to be as a masseuse – to conform with company policy, you understand.'

She had waited to see how Brendan would respond. When the look in his eyes had shown that he understood what Mrs Fiske was getting at, but hadn't reject-ed the idea out of hand, Beatrice had continued, 'Of course, you'll have to dress as a girl, but Mr Fiske and I don't think that will present a problem, do we, Gerald?'

Mr Fiske hadn't answered, but the lascivious smile had said enough for Brendan to see that his own slim build, smooth skin and youthful features had not been lost on either proprietor of Venus and Apollo.

46

'The point is, Brendan,' Mrs Fiske had continued, 'by presenting yourself as a girl, you will be able to look after some of our more timid customers who require a … a full-participatory massage.'

As she had said this, Beatrice Fiske had given Brendan a sly wink that could have been passed off as a tick, if the young man in front of her had been sensitive about straying beyond what was legal, or worse, had revealed himself to be an undercover member of the Metropolitan Police Vice Squad.

At this point Gerald Fiske had chimed in. 'You'll find the pay very good here, and satisfied customers give very generous tips.'

Both Fiskes had then fallen silent, looking at Brendan as if they had expected him to reply.

But Brendan had already started scribbling down a number of questions, the first of which had been to ask if they had understood that he had no experience of giving, or for that matter receiving, a massage and therefore needed to take advantage of the training offered in the job advert.

Mr and Mrs Fiske had exchanged another knowing glance.

'That won't be a problem,' Beatrice Fiske had assured him with a perfectly straight face.

In answer to Brendan's question about pay, Mr Fiske had mentioned a figure that was far in excess of what he had been earning as a dishwasher. Offered regular pay like that, Brendan felt he had no choice but to take it. He had sensed that the Fiskes were glossing over some of the seamier things they were expecting him to do.

As a precaution, and to give himself time to weigh up the pros and cons, he had written down that he would like the evening to think over the proposition.

7

HAPPY AND GRATEFUL as he had been to have landed that first job at the Dorchester, Brendan had realised that he had become very tired of the loneliness of the work, in which even visual contact with other human beings had been minimal. This new job had offered the complete opposite and that had to be an improvement, even if it had its disagreeable aspects that even the sleazy Beatrice and Gerald Fiske had not been able to disguise.

Brendan had also struggled with the idea of disguising himself as a girl simply to fulfil the sexual fantasies of the kind of people who enjoyed what the Fiskes made available. However, he had also been troubled by another side to this unexpected metamorphosis: while presenting himself as a girl had made him feel apprehensive, he had not been able to deny that he had also found the idea strangely exciting.

Overriding all these thoughts, however, had been the pressure of raw fear. Fear of trying to find another job with his extreme limitations. Fear of losing his small studio flat that he had come to think of as home. Fear of starvation and street life with all its inherent dangers. Fear of being exposed as the incomplete human being he now was. And, primarily, the fear of being entirely alone – unable to speak.

Ultimately it had been the combination of these fears that had brought Brendan back to Venus and Apollo the next morning to begin the day when he would say goodbye to Brendan for ever and discover Brenda.

After reading Brendan's note of acceptance Beatrice Fiske had looked up and asked, 'When can you start?'

Brendan had quickly written 'TODAY' in large letters on his notepad.

'Well', Beatrice had said, 'I'd better tell Gerald and then maybe you and I could go shopping for the things we are going to need to transform you into a beautiful masseuse, fit to work at Venus and Apollo.'

Gerald Fiske had come out of his shadowy world behind the office door to offer his clumsy congratulations and welcome Brendan to the Venus and Apollo 'stable', which he quickly amended to 'family' after a sharp look from his wife.

Perhaps to reassure Brendan he had also advanced him twenty pounds. 'Against what you'll be bringing in,' he had added.

After this Brendan and Beatrice Fiske left to go shopping, but not before Brendan had had a chance to meet one of the other girls whom Beatrice had appointed to be in.

'Brendan, meet Naomi,' Beatrice Fiske had said. 'Naomi is one of our long-term regular massage practitioners. The customers love her. Naomi, meet Brendan, our newest masseuse. Or at least he will be, when we've turned him into a girl,' she had said with a short mirthless laugh. 'Brendan is dumb ... I mean mute – he can't speak. I'm going to want you to help me train him in the art of massage and pleasing the customers in the ways that keep them coming.'

Brendan had noticed that Naomi had not joined in the look Mr and Mrs Fiske had shared. Instead she had come over to shake Brendan's hand. 'Welcome to Venus and Apollo,' she had said in a rather bored and unconvincing way. 'You should make up into a great-looking girl. You're far too pretty to be a man,' she had added bluntly. 'What are you going to call yourself?'

Brendan had smiled and shrugged his shoulders.

'Oh, yeah, I'm sorry, I'd forgotten, you don't speak do you?' Naomi had said without a hint of embarrassment. 'I know. We'll just call you Brenda. That should be easy enough.'

It had been so casual – a throwaway remark from a jaded sex worker. But like the shifting snowflake that starts the avalanche, Brenda could look back and pinpoint this as the moment when her new life – her new existence itself – started to fall into place.

The shop assistant who had come forward to help them find the clothes Brendan needed was not much older than Brendan himself. Beatrice had decided she looked sympathetic and had taken her into their confidence to explain why they were buying girls' clothes for a teenage boy.

The sales girl had entered into the spirit of the adventure with undisguised glee. Choosing clothes to make a dishy-looking boy into an even dishier girl was far more entertaining than simply handling transactions and wrapping purchases.

Brendan had liked the look of her and had wished very much he could talk to her, which was rare these days. He had grown used to receiving other people's conversations instead of contributing to them. But his inability to speak had been compensated for by a heightened awareness of what really lay behind the things people said to each other. From the dark and complex caverns of the human heart, Brendan could accurately detect the distinction between what was said and what was meant far better than someone whose attention was focused on what they were going to say next.

For all this, it was a skill Brendan would have willingly forgone to get back his own power of speech. Particularly that day, when he had wanted to talk to this girl his own age, who had been so enthusiastically and unselfconsciously helping him buy the things he needed to be able to dress and look like her.

The sales assistant's nametag identified her as Amanda. She had been very patient and relaxed in waiting for Brendan to write down his comments or questions. She had also been completely at ease in her one-sided running conversation.

When Brendan had first shown her the card explaining he was a dumb mute, Amanda had handed it back and had said with a big smile, 'I'll bet you're not dumb, you just can't speak. Don't worry, my boyfriend always says I talk enough for two and that he never gets a word in.

'Now show me a sign for "yes" and a sign for "no" and I'll try to make all my questions or comments fit a yes or no answer from you. Then, if you like, we can use a scale of ten.'

Because Brendan was so slim and fine boned, women's clothes sizes had not presented any real difficulty. Even shoes had not been a problem. It had not taken long before all that was left was lingerie.

Resisting Beatrice Fiske's urges in favour of some very high-cut, red satin ladies' briefs that Amanda had only half-jokingly shown them, Brendan had firmly insisted on keeping on the boxer shorts he had been wearing.

Both Beatrice Fiske and Amanda had picked up on this, though Brendan's determined resistance had sent different signals to each of them. Amanda thought that perhaps she had misread the situation and the early assumption she had made that Brendan was gay might not, after all, be the case. Whereas the exciting idea came to Beatrice Fiske that perhaps Brendan was so well hung that any thought of wearing brief ladies' underwear would seem both crude and uncomfortable. Although he was slight in build, she knew that the size of the man was not necessarily any indication of the size of his equipment. Sometimes the biggest men were the most disappointing in this respect and it was the little guys who held the surprise. If this were the case with Brendan, his chance arrival might offer Venus and Apollo the opportunity to develop a new and even broader customer base, from which a further premium, above and below the counter, might be extracted.

It was getting harder to find girls prepared to work for them and Brendan's chance appearance had given Beatrice Fiske the opportunity to hit upon the idea of introducing transvestites to the business. Here was a whole new minority group from the shadows of life who could be exploited, and employing transvestites would allow the Fiskes to increase their market share by discreetly appealing to those from the gay and cross-dressing community who were looking for just this kind of titillation.

Brendan had simply felt very confused. He had realised, in spite of himself, that he had liked the idea of the red satin ladies' briefs and would have liked to have tried them on. But he had also been aware that his emotional reaction and the unambiguous physical attraction he had felt towards Amanda had been of equal surprise.

Finally, having settled on some snug-fitting and secure sports bras, that Beatrice Fiske had said she could pad out, the shopping was done.

While she had been paying the bill, Brendan had written a note saying how much he had enjoyed and appreciated Amanda's help, adding the hope that they might be able to stay in touch.

Amanda had smiled broadly as she gave Brendan the sign they'd agreed for 'yes'.

'I'd really love to see you again,' she had said, in such a way that Brendan knew she really meant it. 'Perhaps we could meet for a coffee or sandwich sometime?'

Then she had remembered something, 'You didn't give me your telephone number, though.'

Brendan had mimed the difficulties a non-speaking person would have trying to use the telephone.

After taking a moment to catch on, Amanda's eyes had opened wide and there had been an expressive little intake of breath as she had clapped one hand over her mouth again in mock-horror.

'How stupid of me, I just completely forgot. That's the second time I've put my foot in it. Will you forgive me?'

Brendan had smiled and nodded.

*

Back at Venus and Apollo, their investment having been made, Gerald and Beatrice Fiske were anxious to put their latest stable girl to work. The first stage was for her to switch sexes.

Armed with the padded bra Beatrice Fiske had provided, Brenda had changed into one of the outfits they had bought. She had emerged to be met by a look of speechless incredulity from Naomi. Not only had this been a girl emerging from Massage Studio Number 3, where she had had been sent to change, but an extraordinarily attractive girl at that.

The gasp of astonishment from Beatrice Fiske and the overtly salacious look of approval from Gerald Fiske had confirmed the complete success of the transformation.

'Well, you're definitely Brenda now,' Naomi had said. 'Christ, the clients'll love you,' she had added, unable to conceal the jealousy in her voice.

Recovering herself, Beatrice Fiske had walked all around Brenda, studying her carefully. When she had seemed satisfied nothing could be improved upon, she had become business-like in her eagerness to keep things moving.

'Right. This afternoon your training begins. You will be shown the techniques of massage and what signs to look for: that clients are enjoying the experience and how far they want you to go. Tomorrow you will work with Naomi on her clients. Two for the price of one, they'll think it's Christmas. I wonder if we could charge a premium?' she had speculated out loud with a humourless little laugh.

'Then the next day we'll allow you some clients on your own to see how you get along.' Looking at the clock on the wall, she had said, 'Now, go and get a sandwich, but be sure to be back in an hour so your training can begin.'

Brenda had turned towards the door to the studio, where she had left the clothes she had been wearing, but Beatrice Fiske had stopped her. 'No. Go out like that. You need to start getting used to looking like a real girl. And to avoid any slip-ups, I want you coming and going from work looking like that all the time. Understand?'

Brenda had felt a curious mixture of excitement, embarrassment and apprehension as she had emerged into the late midday sunshine.

She had more than half expected to hear cries of, 'Oy, why are you dressed up as a girl?' or similar taunts.

It had not happened. Instead, as she had walked up Bayswater Road towards Oxford Street, she had gradually realised how many men were checking her out and how many women were looking her up and down in a more coolly appraising manner.

Brenda had decided to forgo lunch. She was, she had realised, too excited to be hungry. She was starting to enjoy being this beautiful, sultry, young black woman, walking the pavement like a model on a catwalk. Nor could she ignore the open admiration that had greeted her from the moment she had stepped outside Venus and Apollo.

Amanda had been tidying a pile of rumpled sweaters that had been unceremoniously riffled through on a 'Sale' table. She had smiled back in the same friendly, outgoing but professionally detached fashion she had demonstrated earlier in the day.

Then, suddenly recognising the clothes she had sold to Beatrice Fiske, and looking intently at Brenda again, she had said, 'Is that you? Are you who I think you are?'

Brenda had nodded.

'Blimey! I just can't believe it. You look so good that when I saw you coming I thought you must be this supermodel or movie star or something. Wow, you look great! Hey, I'm going on my break now, do you want to come and have a cup of coffee? I know a place just behind where we could go.'

Without hesitation Brenda had made the sign for 'yes'.

'Good,' Amanda had said, 'I'll just tell my supervisor and I'll meet you at the top of the down escalator.'

In the café, Amanda had done all of the talking. She had kept Brenda in the conversation by occasionally phrasing a question that she had been able to answer with the simple 'yes' or 'no' sign.

Brenda had written that she had to get back to work. Just before it was time to leave, Amanda had said, 'Oh, by the way, I thought of how you could use a telephone after all. If you buy one with an answering machine I can come round and record a message for you. That way your friends can contact you and ask questions, or leave a message that only needs just a yes or no answer. You'd need to get one of those loud kids' clicker things. So you could give one click down the phone for "yes" and two for "no". So, if I call and say, "Would you like to meet me for a drink?" you can give one click for "yes". If, on the other hand, I call and ask you if my boyfriend has been round to see you, I'll expect to hear two clicks,' she said with mock sternness. 'See? Easy.'

As Brenda had hurried back to Venus and Apollo she had thought about Amanda's suggestion. Until that point there had been no need for a telephone. She had had no friends and no one to call her. But then, suddenly, it had been different. She had found a friend and she had realised she had to do everything to foster that friendship.

With her boost in earnings from Venus and Apollo, Brenda had installed a telephone with an answering machine before the end of the week.

8

NEARLY A WEEK had passed since Robert had left his ham-fisted message for Brenda and there had still been no reply from her. But now other concerns had pushed that toe-curling episode from his mind.

Sitting in his small office after an early breakfast, Robert re-read what was the third letter he had received from the bishop since his appointment to St Mungo's. It had arrived in the morning post: a delayed response to his request for very modest supporting funds to try and finance some of the more pressing requirements of St Mungo's and the parish, if he was going to be able to continue making the improvements he had already so successfully begun.

The fact that the bishop's letter was rejecting his request out of hand was not what was troubling him so much as what he perceived to be its underlying tone.

Robert's previous letters to the bishop had given news of how things were progressing. Following that, each of them had contained requests for small amounts of money to help him maintain his progress in revitalising St Mungo's. However, every one had drawn a negative response, distinguished only by the increasing length of time it took the bishop to answer and the brevity of its content.

The reply to his first letter had been prompt and, although rejecting his request, had done so in a way that seemed to appreciate Robert's work and encourage him to continue his efforts; this first letter from the bishop even seemed to hold out the promise of possible financial support at some unspecified time for some future project – just not this particular one.

This morning's letter had been sent in reply to one Robert had written more than two weeks earlier. It was later, shorter and blunter than the previous two – so blunt in fact that Robert could be left with no misunderstanding that he was on his own and that there would never be any money available for St Mungo's from central church funds.

Robert was at a loss to understand the vehemence of the letter's tone, or the apparent lack of interest and support. It was not as if he had asked for any outrageous sum, or that the purpose for which he had intended the money was in any way frivolous.

Since he was new to the diocese in general and to St Mungo's in particular, Robert had responded to each rejection with the assumption that the bishop, with his experience and greater wisdom, knew best and that perhaps he was testing Robert's ingenuity and ability to cope without support, either financially or, for that matter, in person. After the first few weeks it had been increasingly hard for Robert to speak with the bishop on the phone; he always seemed to be too busy. Robert had, in the end, given up trying and had taken to writing letters instead.

The PS on the bottom of the bishop's most recent missive was almost longer than the main body of the letter. It warned Robert that he had received a letter from some of his more eminent parishioners, who had taken exception to Robert's idea of squandering his slender resources in what they saw as futile attempts to encourage church participation from those on the Earls Court side of his parish. The bishop implied that 'oil and water do not mix' and more or less advised Robert to forget that part of his parish and concentrate on the more affluent and reachable Kensington side. Perhaps it would be here, the letter had suggested, that Robert should look for a solution to some of his financial problems.

Putting the letter down on the desk, Robert tried to analyse his reaction. He felt abandoned, and disappointed even. He had, he felt, begun to make a real and positive difference and would have welcomed a little encouragement.

Robert was human enough to admit to having hoped for at least some recognition and perhaps even praise for his efforts by this time. But he realised that these thoughts were leading him dangerously close to the indulgence of self-pity. He knew he must snap out of it and remind himself that all his work in all its ways, must now be in accordance with God's will. For the hundredth time since taking up the post of the vicar of St Mungo's, the image of the grain of mustard seed in relation to faith came into his mind.

He must reaffirm his decision and commitment to let God guide his life, instead of hoping to solve all his own problems in accordance with his own plans for himself. He thought too of that wonderful secular definition which describes life as being 'what happens to you while you are busy making other plans'.

Now in a more positive frame of mind, Robert rose from his desk and went into the church. Kneeling down in front of the altar he tried, as best he could, to present his whole predicament to God, humbly asking for his guidance and encouragement.

He had not been long at prayer when he heard the door at the back of the church open and close quietly. Afraid to turn around, Robert discreetly checked his watch. It was not quite nine. Whoever it was who had entered the church had elected to stay at the back. It had to be Brenda.

No longer able to concentrate on his previous prayer, Robert hastily said a prayer for Brenda instead, wondering rather clumsily in which gender to frame it and whether God minded such small confused details like this.

At the same time, Robert did not want to risk waiting too long. He turned cautiously towards the back of the church and saw Brenda kneeling with her head bowed in the shortened, shadowy pew that was her custom. Robert felt a great aura of sadness about her, as if she was carrying the weight of some huge unseen burden. Brenda also appeared to be so completely focused in prayer that she was, at first, quite genuinely oblivious to Robert's approach.

He sat down in the pew on the opposite side of the aisle and waited for her to finish. After no more than a few moments she lifted her head and turned to face him, an expression of defiance and, Robert thought, something like fear in her eyes.

Although he had planned and rehearsed in his head the many things he thought he might say when first he spoke, this preparation was all now abandoned. Without any idea of where it came from, Robert simply and silently raised one hand and, with the index finger of the other, pointed to the centre of his outstretched palm. He repeated this gesture with the other hand. Then pointing first at himself and afterwards at her, he crossed his arms, fists clenched, over his heart. He had not spoken a word, but even in the dim light he saw the change of expression on Brenda's face and, he thought, caught the glint of half-formed tears before she jumped up and fled from the church.

Robert held back from calling out in an attempt to stop her, and this time he didn't follow her out. Instead he stayed seated where he was and went over in his mind what he had just seen, and what he had learned from this brief encounter.

Brenda, he decided, had been forced to condition herself to handle hostility, rejection, even cruelty, but not acceptance or spontaneous gestures of kindness. He had also learned that she could speak Sign. He had seen the momentary look of surprised pleasure pass over her face when she realised that he too really could speak Sign. She had clearly understood his deliberate attempt to assure her that God and he, Robert, loved her.

Robert felt quite certain that he had made a breakthrough – literally. In approaching Brenda as he just had, he had breached the armour of indifference and hostility with which, he felt sure, she protected herself. Now that she could see that there was nothing hostile or threatening in Robert's approaches, he was confident that she would reciprocate the contact in her own time and in her own way.

He faced towards the big cross that hung over the altar, knelt and thanked God before returning to his office and the mundane work that lay ahead of him. The bishop's letter had certainly thrown a damper on the day, but somehow this did not seem to matter quite as much any more.

9

'BELIEVE ME, BRENDA,' Naomi had continued, 'I've seen enough in here, never mind outside these crummy doors, to know I'm right. For good or bad, almost nothing is what it seems to be. Take me for example. My name is not really Naomi. I grew up as Sharon, but inside I always wanted to be something different, something exotic, a Naomi in fact. So one day I just said "Goodbye" to Sharon and became Naomi. Did it make any difference? Did it make me exotic? Not really. But I did it for me, no one else.

'My son thinks I'm a massage therapist. He has me on this pedestal – way up there with doctors and nurses. But what am I really? A fulfiller of other sad people's even sadder fantasies at best. At worst I might as well be on the game, mightn't I? So, what I'm saying is, allowing Brendan to become Brenda is not so different in this mad world. Besides, you've got a better excuse than most transvestites.'

She had tried to sound encouraging. 'To hell with your training. Why don't we take the rest of the day off? Get the heck out of this crummy dump for a while. I could take you to this really nice patisserie I know. They've got this amazing chocolate cake,' she had entreated more than suggested. And she had said it with such genuine kindness and compassion that Brenda, unable to think clearly about what to do next, nodded gratefully.

'Good, I'll just get my things and wait for you in reception,' Naomi had said and had gone off to tell the Fiskes what she and Brenda were going to do – whether they liked it or not.

While they had been waiting for their tea, Brenda had pushed a note across the table that had simply said, 'Thank you'.

Naomi had smiled back almost bashfully.

Sadly, Brenda had realised, there wouldn't always be a Naomi to protect her in other humiliating situations. She needed to grow her own protective shell.

After they had been served and had had a chance to enjoy the first couple of mouthfuls of the truly delicious, soft, rich chocolate cake, Naomi had said, 'Look Brendan …' but she got no further as a silencing hand had been held up and another hastily scribbled note had been urgently despatched across the table reading, 'Brendan is no more. From now on, and for the rest of my life, I shall be Brenda – fully and completely.'

Naomi had continued training Brenda the following day. Once they were alone in one of the studios, Naomi had immediately reassured Brenda that she could keep her boxer shorts on this time. 'You needn't worry, love,' she had added, 'I'll stick to proper massage techniques – none of the kinky stuff, OK?'

Brenda had been very grateful, However, she had quickly written that, as long as Naomi didn't mind, she had thought she should strip completely to overcome her sense of shame and, more importantly, so that she could experience what a proper message felt like and how to give one.

'OK,' Naomi had replied, impressed at Brenda's bravery. 'Let's do this the way the real professionals do, using a small white modesty towel that can be easily moved from side to side, to keep down below covered all the time.' She had only just stopped herself from saying 'your manhood'.

Brenda had tried hard to focus on what every movement felt like and all the while Naomi had been explaining the different techniques, ranging from what was really little more than a pleasant, sensual stroking, to the deep tissue massage. This, Brenda had soon found, could feel quite painful, because the person giving the massage had to use considerable pressure to relieve tense, knotted muscle tissue, often deep under the skin.

'Of course, the real trick in getting it right,' Naomi had explained, 'is creating an atmosphere where the client feels so relaxed they sometimes even drop off for a little nap. I find this happens a lot if you're giving a head massage.'

When Naomi had finished demonstrating and explaining everything she could think of, she had said, 'Look Bren, there's a few important things you need to know about the clients. So, let's not kid ourselves, eh?

'Some of our customers are straight-up and come here for a genuine, professional massage and no more. They're often business people off long-haul flights. They usually come here with their bags, straight from Heathrow, on their way to the office or some important meeting. We let them shave and shower here as well, so it's a great stop-off for them.

'We set them up to go and conquer the universe and many have become regular clients whenever they come to London. These bookings are all scheduled by appointment only. Me and Mrs Fiske look after them. We don't mind coming in early and we've got the certificates to make it all legal and above board – should anyone start asking.

'Most of the other girls who work here are not professionally trained or certified, which brings me to what I want to make sure you understand. The majority of customers who come to Venus and Apollo don't really want or care about a "professional" massage. What they're after is a sensual body rub, which usually ends with them being tossed off … you know, masturbated,' she had added in response to Brenda's momentary look of puzzlement. 'What's known as "relief" in the business.

'They're a sad lot of losers really. Ugly as sin many of them, disgustingly fat, timid as hell, or with some other hang-up that stops them from developing normal relationships in the real world. Whatever normal relationships are,' she had added wistfully.

'What they're after is help in fulfilling some sort of fantasy relationship. Sometimes you get the time wasters. Nervous kids acting on a dare, that kind of thing. We usually send them packing, because they're more trouble than they're worth and in this game you don't want the Old Bill snooping round more than they already do.

'Then there are the nervous virgins. You'll find these are the ones who are finally getting married and who, for any number of reasons, have found themselves adults without ever getting it up. They want to talk mostly: to be told how and what to do.

'Finally you get the freaks. That's what Mrs Fiske calls the poor sods. The amputees, disabled, disfigured and deformed ones. Hunchbacks, club feet, un-repaired cleft palates, you name it, we've had them all in. Mostly Mrs Fiske won't take the last group. Says it's not fair on the girls to have to deal with all that stuff.

'She can't exactly turn them away because of their deformities, so she has a special charge card she shows them. All the prices are double and, to make sure they leave, she usually says we are fully booked all that week.

'They know they're being discriminated against, but since it's illegal to ask anyone for what they're really after, they don't give any trouble. People like that have got used to this kind of rejection anyway, or they wouldn't be coming to Venus and Apollo wanting a special massage in the first place.

'Occasionally, when business is slow, Mrs Fiske lets them in. So long as they're prepared to pay double what normal clients pay and the deformity isn't too gross. Of course, one of the girls has got to be happy to take them on too. But if they're prepared to, you should see how grateful those ones are. Sad really. But that's life. I suppose they get used to it.'

Naomi's last comment had sounded more like a platitude to ease her own disquieting prejudice than any belief that it might be true. She had also been uncomfortably aware that she had put her foot in it. This was the very group of people to which Brenda would unquestionably have belonged, if she had ever come in to Venus and Apollo in search of 'therapy'.

'Of course, I don't mean people like you, Bren,' Naomi had added clumsily. 'I mean, look, you're really beautiful and it doesn't matter you can't speak.'

For her part, Naomi always tried to handle the rejection kindly, going out of her way to come up with a face-saving excuse, usually something to do with being fully booked or short staffed. She didn't like the 'Freaks' Rates' price list Beatrice Fiske preferred to show them.

Brenda, who had been listening intently to what Naomi had been telling her, had reached for her pen and had quickly written, 'It's OK Naomi'.

'Lunch?' Brenda had added to the note.

'Sure,' Naomi had replied, with a shy smile of relief. 'And this one's on me!'

They had arrived back just as Beatrice Fiske had been saying to a potential client, 'I'm sorry, we're a bit short staffed this week, so we're only taking clients by appointment. The first opening I have would not be until late next week.'

Naomi had seen the 'Freaks' Rates' card in her hand. The man had declined with a resigned shrug of his shoulders as a strange sound had emanated from his mouth which, if carefully listened to, might have been identified as a polite 'No thanks, I'll try somewhere else'.

Brenda had only had sight of the man's back, but as he had turned to go she could immediately see he was massively disfigured from a severe cleft palate.

Whether it was the haunted, guilty look of desperation and loneliness in his eyes, his speech impediment, or her own impatience to start earning the money she badly needed, something had made Brenda gesture to this stranger to wait a moment.

Hurriedly she had scribbled a note, which she had handed to Beatrice Fiske: 'Let me take him. I've got to start somewhere.'

Mrs Fiske had glanced up at Brenda as she handed the note over to Naomi for her to see. After a moment's pause Naomi had looked at Beatrice Fiske and given a little nod.

Beatrice Fiske had turned back to the client to say, 'Well it must be your lucky day. It seems that one of our top masseuses has had a cancellation and could take you right now if you like. The rate is £60 for a half-hour massage.'

The man's eyes had widened at the steep price and there had been a moment when Brenda had thought they might lose him.

He had turned to look at her, so she had tried to give a reassuring smile that would encourage him, without giving him the idea that this price would buy him anything more than the regular massage he had supposedly come in for.

After he had nodded his agreement, Mrs Fiske had informed him that payment was in advance for all first-time customers of Venus and Apollo; a precaution she always took with the 'freak trade'.

There had been a moment of final hesitation before the man had pulled four crumpled twenty-pound notes from his pocket. He had given three to Mrs Fiske. The other he had pushed deeply back into the pocket from which it had just come. Brenda had wondered if perhaps that was all the money he had.

'Thank you, sir,' Beatrice Fiske had said, as she had taken the money. 'This is Brenda, who will be your therapist this afternoon. Brenda is one of our top masseuses, as you can see. However, Brenda ...' and here Mrs Fiske had been stuck for how to proceed.

'Brenda doesn't speak while she's working,' Naomi had chimed in.

Then she had caught the look in Brenda's eye telling her to be honest.

'In fact,' Naomi had continued, 'Brenda doesn't speak at all – because she can't.'

She had glanced at Brenda, who had smiled reassuringly.

'Exactly,' Beatrice Fiske had said, sounding relieved. 'That's what I was going on to say. Brenda understands everything you say to her, but all her communication with her clients is through her hands.'

The man had turned towards her. A look of surprised, compassionate empathy had passed briefly across his face.

The two-way mirror had already been repaired and Mrs Fiske had told Brenda to show her client into Studio 3 and to leave him there while he undressed.

As soon as the door had closed Beatrice Fiske had told Brenda, 'It's for your own safety. And also so Naomi can see what you've learned and how good we think you're going to be.'

'Don't worry, you have my word that it will only be me and Mrs Fiske checking on you,' Naomi had reassured her. 'Mr Fiske won't even be in the office.'

Through the low light, soft relaxing background music and fragrant smell of smouldering incense sticks, Brenda had seen her first client, naked and lying face up on the massage table, with a small white modesty towel correctly in place.

As she had prepared her hands with the oil in the way she had been taught, Brenda had noted that, although the disfigurement of his face made him look older, the unblemished firm skin and muscle tone of his body told of a younger man. He was almost certainly Indian, Pakistani or perhaps Sri Lankan, she thought.

Although she had given him as reassuring a smile as she could manage, she had felt very nervous as she had reached first for his hands, in order to relax him, by loosening his arms and fingers in the way Naomi had shown her. She had not been surprised to discover that he had coarse, calloused hands indicating hard manual labour of some sort.

However, Brenda's client had not been alone in experiencing something new and wonderful for the first time. As she had commenced this, the very first massage she had ever given, Brenda too had become aware of the stirrings of a sensation she had never felt before.

It had begun as a strange feeling of healing power in her hands. This had grown into an overwhelming wave of empathy as she had worked on the tense, sinewy body stretched out just below waist height on the massage table beside her. Gradually she had become aware that in some new and powerful way she was being allowed to take on all the aching loneliness and despair of this young man. In so doing, Brenda herself had been overcome by the most intense feeling of sadness she had ever known.

With no idea where it had come from, she had found the calm confidence to look directly into the upturned eyes of the young man in a way that had told him she felt no repulsion for his horrific disfigurement, because she had been able to identify with it, take it on even, and clearly to see the person behind it.

Those eyes had returned a confusion of emotions: defensiveness, fear, bewilderment, but chiefly a simple, childlike longing to be touched, to be held, to be loved. Brenda's face too must have reflected the deep compassion she felt, because she had been surprised to see tears suddenly rolling down the young man's cheeks which he had made no effort to check.

Although the massage had been meant to last only half an hour, Brenda had let the time run over closer to an hour. She hadn't wanted to break the spell between herself and the client and she had wanted to give this young man the best value for his money she could.

When she had drawn his session to a close, Brenda had left her client to get dressed while she had waited for him in the reception area. In her cursory training she had been told always to do this because it created the opportunity to insinuate the acceptability of a personal tip – and, more importantly, to solicit another appointment; always the best evidence of a satisfied punter, Mrs Fiske had stressed on more than one occasion.

The young man had emerged quite quickly, his hair still untidy and the laces on his work boots untied. Seeing her waiting there, he had come over and, taking both her hands in his, had bowed, had lightly touched the tips of her fingers to his forehead and had murmured, in what had sounded like a sort of quiet, unthreatening growl, the words 'Thank you' over and over again.

Then, quite spontaneously, he had reached into his pocket and, pulling out what Brenda was sure was his last twenty-pound note, he had tried to press it into Brenda's hand. Much to Naomi's surprise, and Beatrice Fiske's annoyance, Brenda had emphatically refused to take the crumpled note, gently gesturing that he should keep it.

This had been too much for Mrs Fiske who had bluntly blurted out from behind the reception desk, 'Well you must have enjoyed that. Would you like to make another appointment before you go?'

The young man had nodded rather sheepishly that he would.

Hardly even bothering to pretend to consult the appointments diary, Beatrice Fiske had told him, 'Well, we have an opening at the same time tomorrow ...' adding as a rather lame afterthought, 'it's just come available due to a short-notice cancellation.'

The young man had responded with a sound which was distinguishable, if barely so, as 'Friday' – in four days' time. But, having then spotted a wall calendar, he had walked over and with one hand had pointed to a date that indicated the Friday of the following week, while with the other he had pointed at Brenda.

Mrs Fiske looked momentarily irritated before making a show of opening the appointments diary. This had been followed by a frown of mock concentration coupled with a well-practised, gentle tapping of her pen on the desk.

She had waited for what she judged to be just the right amount of suspense, before looking up brightly to announce, 'Yes, fortunately it seems we do have an opening then, so shall I put you down for the same time?'

The young man had continued to point to Brenda with a look of enquiry on his face.

'Yes, your appointment will be with Brenda,' Mrs Fiske had assured him. Then, addressing herself to no one in particular, but for the benefit of all of them, she had mused out loud, 'We are going to have to charge more for Brenda's time soon, everyone seems to want to book with her.'

Beatrice Fiske had watched him go and waited until she had been sure he was out of earshot before saying tartly, 'We don't want clients thinking they can have extra treatment time they aren't paying for. Let me tell you in no uncertain terms, Mr Fiske and I have to work our fingers to the bone covering the overheads of a business like this. I'll let it go this time, because he was your first client. But I'm putting you on notice that if you ever run over time again, the money is coming out of your pay packet. I have to be fair to the other girls. That's what makes this a happy family, isn't it?' she had added, trying to sound ingratiating. 'That was quite impressive for your first massage,' she had continued, worried that she might have gone too far. 'You seem to be a natural at this.'

When they had been alone together later Naomi had told Brenda, 'You were really good in there Bren – especially for a first time. Fiskey was well impressed, I can tell you. I particularly liked the way you neatly let him have his relief without ever taking the towel away from his privates.

'How did you do that? His dick was like a ramrod. Poor chap was ready to explode by the time you got him to that point, but still it was very clever. I'd like to be able to do that, barely having to touch them or anything. No awkwardness or mess to clear up afterwards.'

Brenda had taken time to compose her answer to this question before handing it to Naomi. 'It's all in the eyes', she had written. She would have liked to tell Naomi so much more, but writing it down would have been impossible.

'When you can't speak you learn to communicate intensely with your eyes,' she would have liked to explain. 'The eyes can speak to the heart, the head and the soul in ways that words never can by themselves. The eyes can't lie and I could never have done what I did if I hadn't genuinely wanted to help him find, whether he knew it or not, what he was really looking for. Can you imagine the loneliness, the longing, the despair of the person inside that disfigured body?

'The world presumes that the maimed, the disfigured, the crippled, somehow shouldn't have the same kinds of needs other people have. For most people the idea of Mrs Fiske's freaks having any kind of a sex life is repulsive – and that goes for everyone afflicted like them.'

Later that evening Brenda had confided to her diary, 'Something happened for me today, I'm sure I now know what I must do with my life. I want to be able to help people society rejects in this very personal area of their lives, where no one else is prepared to go with them. When I was working with that young man today, I felt a powerful sensation flowing through me. It was almost like a healing force running down into my hands.

Would Sister Lucy have been shocked, Brenda had wondered? How could a nun have begun to understand a set-up like Venus and Apollo, never mind what people got up to there? Even so, Brenda had a hunch that Sister Lucy would at least have been sympathetic. If she could only have known the honesty and compassion that Brenda had felt was driving her, Sister Lucy might even have understood.

The odd thing was that whenever Brenda thought about Sister Lucy it was the only time she found it hard thinking of herself as female.

What would she make of the Brendan she had nursed back from the brink of death in hospital becoming sexy, lithe Brenda she wondered? It was always an uncomfortable thought, which had to be pushed aside.

It had not taken long following Brenda's success with her first client for her to attract a growing clientele from among those whom, recognising the irony, she now thought of as the 'untouchables'.

Beatrice Fiske, torn between her greed and her concern that this big increase in the very profitable 'freak trade' might start to have a negative impact on her 'normal' clientele, tried to get Brenda to take on more of her normal customers – the ones who, upon seeing Brenda, had demanded special services of their own and were prepared to pay extra to have them satisfied.

At the same time Brenda understood more than ever how much she needed this job that was beginning to pay her well. She knew she couldn't refuse to do what Mrs Fiske wanted her to do, but, try as she might, she couldn't make it work.

Whenever she had 'normal' clients with deviant requirements, she discovered that she was completely unable to fake the slightest interest in them, mainly because she was barely able to disguise her revulsion for them, which reduced the whole experience to a dreary mechanical process.

After massaging and sometimes having to attend to the other demands of one of these 'normal' clients, Brenda always felt dirty, cheap and used, in a way she never felt with the 'untouchables'.

Without the emotional connection, she felt fraudulent. The clients felt it too and each new appointment seemed to end in embarrassment, and an awkwardness in which the client could hardly wait to leave the premises – some of them never to return. Of those who did remain loyal to Venus and Apollo, none would ever book a second appointment with Brenda.

This was a source of mystery and frustration to Beatrice Fiske. She had made a point of watching Brenda at work in Studio 3 in an attempt to understand the difference between her skill and huge success with the 'untouchables', compared with her total failure to please the 'normals' who had paid handsomely to enjoy the heightened experience of something special with Brenda. But after observing several sessions, she was still unable to pinpoint any technical difference in her approach.

Brenda was just as puzzled by her response even to the few completely legitimate business clients, who came in for a genuine therapeutic massage. She found that she was hardly more enthusiastic working with them than she was with the deviant 'normals'.

As far as she could judge, the only difference in her response to them was that she didn't dislike or despise these innocent clients. But she still felt unable to make the same emotional connection with them that she almost always did with the 'untouchables'.

Although it was far from being the most profitable part of the business, this small regular core of corporate clients was very important to Venus and Apollo.

They provided the vital cloak of respectability and legitimacy that prevented the Fiskes and their premises from being targeted for investigation or intrusive inspection by the Kensington & Chelsea Borough Council authorities.

Beatrice Fiske knew all too well that the business could not afford to lose or jeopardise the important cover this group of clients brought to Venus and Apollo.

10

ALTHOUGH RELATIVELY YOUNG and new to the priesthood, Robert knew enough about the hierarchical workings of the Anglican Church to realise that, just as in any large corporation, there were layers of self-important middle management and overbearing personal assistants, who were little more than glorified secretaries. These individuals liked nothing more than to deal imperiously with humble enquiries or requests, sometimes without reference to their boss, having been given a broad enough mandate to just 'deal with all the day-to-day little stuff'.

Robert had been so puzzled by the extraordinary, unexplained change in attitude by the bishop, he felt sure the problem must indeed be one of communication. He knew that the bishop was a busy man and Robert concluded that in the circumstances it would be easy for someone on the bishop's staff, charged with the task of administering the smaller issues of his numerous parishes, to take any action they saw fit and thus write the 'appropriate' letter of response for the bishop to sign. At the end of another long day, the bishop might be presented with a pile of correspondence by a trusted adviser, with the soothing assurance that there was nothing of importance for him to consider and that everything had been dealt with. How easy and tempting must it have been just to sign his name and know those issues had been satisfactorily taken care of?

Although he was now frustrated at the system that made it necessary to do so, Robert felt sure that if he could speak directly to the bishop, everything would be resolved and he would get the support he so badly needed.

Robert also felt guilty at the way he had arrogantly dismissed the feeble efforts of his predecessors. From the perspective he now had, his derision had changed to sympathy and he marvelled only that they hadn't resorted to the bottle in dealing with their boredom and frustration.

Direct action was called for and Robert found himself picking up the telephone and dialling the bishop's office.

'Good morning, this is the Bishop of West London's office, how can I help you?' The voice was both polite and cordial, taking Robert a little off guard in his determination not to be fobbed off by flunkies.

'Oh, I'd like to speak to his Grace, the bishop, please.'

'I'll put you through now,' came the pleasant-sounding reply. After a moment's silence a more business-like voice came on the line.

'Bishop's office.'

'This is Robert Melton. May I speak to Bishop Rogers please?'

'I'll put you thorough to his personal assistant,' the business-like voice responded.

Another brief pause, then another voice. 'Who's calling please?'

'Robert Melton, vicar of St Mungo's in Earls Court.'

'How may I help you?'

'I'd like to speak with Bishop Rogers please.'

'Could you tell me what the nature of your call is? This is Christopher Callow, the bishop's personal assistant.'

'It's a parish matter that I'd really like to talk directly with the bishop about,' Robert persisted.

'I'm sorry, the bishop is away today, but you are talking to the right person anyway as I deal with all routine parish matters. How may I help you?'

Robert was torn between wanting to say he'd call back tomorrow and trying to ascertain if the person he was now talking to was the 'blockage' he suspected between himself and the bishop. He settled for a more assertive, 'Will you please ask Bishop Rogers to call me at St Mungo's when he has a moment? Thank you.'

But the voice at the other end, turning even more assertive in his tone than Robert had been, was not going to be outmanoeuvred by young Robert Melton.

'As you will realise, Reverend Melton, Bishop Rogers is a very busy man and as his personal assistant, entrusted completely to deal with all routine parish matters, it would at least be helpful if you told me what this was about so I can discuss it with his Grace prior to his calling you, should I be unable to help you myself.'

Short of making an implacable enemy of this man, by insisting on going above his head, Robert knew he had been checkmated.

'It's about the urgent need I have for just a small amount of financial support in my, quite modest, plans for the development and revitalisation of the parish, if I am to have even a fighting chance of saving St Mungo's from its terminal decline. The bishop and I have discussed this in depth.

'I've written to him three times outlining my plans for turning the parish around; I sent him a budget as well. So far, I have had three responses. All of them purport to be from the bishop and all flatly reject any financial assistance whatever. I simply don't understand what he expects me to be able to do and the tone of his letters has changed significantly. I feel there must be some misunderstanding somewhere – that I should talk directly to him to get it sorted out. Hence my call.'

Christopher Callow was struck by the impassioned righteousness he heard in Robert Melton's youthful voice. No longer young himself, and jaded by an earlier career in the Foreign Office, followed by a spell as a mid-level, political civil servant, he found himself almost envying this young man and his sincere belief that he could do anything and that life should be fair. But Christopher Callow had learned long ago that life is only as fair as you are allowed to make it and, until his current posting, the opportunity had always been denied him, largely because of an overriding weakness that haunted him and excited him in equal measure.

His career moves thus far had been thwarted by an inability to resist the alluring temptation that prostitutes had always held for him: to be precise, streetwalkers. He liked cheap, low-life sex and, as careful as he tried to be, at some point this invariably ended in his being apprehended by the police. In every case, the need to stifle any whiff of scandal had been satisfied through his 'voluntary' resignations.

In the Foreign Office he had survived his first such encounter with a departmental transfer, but not the second. As a civil servant he had fared better, surviving three encounters before having no alternative but to tender his resignation. He knew he was very lucky to have managed to keep his past concealed when he moved into the less exacting world of ecclesiastical administration. He also knew that if he was caught again, and the bishop should discover his record, he would get no second chance.

Still, this motivated him to be good at his job – and he was very good at it. He knew that and, more importantly, so did the Bishop of West London who came to rely increasingly on his PA's administrative skills and his undeniable ability to cope admirably with all manner of problems that crossed his desk; Christopher Callow might have been cast aside by Her Majesty's officials at home and abroad, but he reckoned he had more than proved his worth as far as the Church of England was concerned.

Whether it was the earnest sincerity he had heard in Robert's voice, or just that he could remember himself what it was like to be young and idealistic he wasn't quite sure, but, whatever it was, Christopher Callow found himself feeling uncharacteristically sympathetic. He knew, from seeing the file, that Robert Melton was young and that this was his first appointment as vicar of his own parish. He also knew Robert was Australian and, although he did not know that country well, he knew it had a reputation for being a no-nonsense sort of place where people said what they meant and meant what they said. How difficult it might be for someone from that culture to adjust to the political manoeuvrings so entrenched in the old mother country and especially so in its established Church.

'Did the bishop actually tell you that funding would be available? Or ask you to produce a budget and plan for your development ideas?' Callow asked Robert crisply.

There was an awkward silence, during which Christopher Callow knew from his long years of experience that he had all too easily won in this uneven skirmish. But this was a small victory that gave him no pleasure.

'Well … not exactly in so many words,' Robert found himself stammering in a way he had not intended, annoyed with himself for being so easily wrong-footed. 'But he certainly implied his full support when I started here at St Mungo's.'

Even as he was speaking, Robert knew this sounded pretty lame. However, he pressed on. 'I would just like to understand better, directly from the bishop, what it is he wants me to do without even a small amount of funding from the diocese,' he managed to finish more confidently.

Christopher Callow felt sorry for the younger man. 'I'll tell his Grace of your call when he gets back tomorrow.' He spoke more kindly, 'But I don't hold out much hope and, frankly, you shouldn't either.' He hoped he hadn't said too much in adding, 'The whole Anglican Church has a funding crisis at the moment and almost every parish is clamouring for some sort of financial support it is just not possible to give. I'm sure I speak for his Grace as well when I tell you how sorry I am that things aren't easier for all of us just at this time.'

'Thank you,' Robert replied before ringing off, only moments later realising that this most polished of personal assistants had smoothly managed to avoid giving any undertaking that would have actually obliged the bishop to call Robert back.

He recognised the feeling. He had felt it sometimes at Cambridge: the carefully worded jibe at his academic qualifications, the patronising note at the end of an alpha-quality essay for which he had been made to feel grateful for a grudgingly scribbled beta. Robert had had to grow up largely by himself. He hadn't been jealous of his classmates who had been supported at school events by both parents proudly backing up their sons; Robert's friends and their mums and dads had always been swift to include him in their celebrations and consolations. But riding back home alone on the bus afterwards there had always been the lingering hope that his mother might have slipped away from the hospital early to be waiting for him with the sort of tea he sometimes tucked into at friends' homes.

He acknowledged that it had been largely his own fault that he had let those early friendships fall away. But once he had set his sights on where his life was heading, Robert had not spared much time for anyone outside his tightly focused ambitions. That was why, he realised, his friendship with Andreas was so important – even if the calling they had each followed now restricted that friendship to the occasional transatlantic letter.

$$11$$

WORKING AT VENUS and Apollo may have had its down side, but the weeks ticked by, turning into months and soon the months into what had been three years. Brenda was experiencing a continuity and stability of sorts she could not remember ever having felt before.

Despite the Fiskes trying everything they could to reduce her pay, Brenda had begun earning good enough money to be able to start saving something towards a, still unspecified, future that she found too uncertain and frightening to think about very deeply beyond achieving some financial security.

She had continued to live a frugal, lonely life, cooking at home and seldom going out except occasionally when, as a treat, she would take herself to see a film at the local Odeon. The staff there had grown accustomed to her arrival, always just after the programme had started. They became used to seeing Brenda slipping into her seat in the dark, when everyone else had been focused on the screen and there was no fear that anyone would start chatting sociably with her to pass the time.

Outside work her social life, such as it was, had been centred around the two people who had befriended her: Naomi at Venus and Apollo, and Amanda. These friends, along with Amanda's boyfriend Mike, were the only people to whom Brenda had entrusted the truth of what had happened to her.

She smiled to herself as she remembered how, when Amanda and Mike had finished reading the lengthy explanation she had handed to them, she had

had to comfort and calm them both – Amanda, red-eyed and sobbing, and Mike valiantly fighting back his own tears, covering them by becoming visibly angry and loudly protesting they should all go to the Trinidadian Embassy to demand an investigation, with justice and retribution for what Brenda had suffered. But Brenda had asked them both to respect her wish to extinguish 'Brendan' completely from her past and never to reveal her true gender to anyone.

Looking at Brenda, the revelation that she had once been 'Brendan' was such a complete deception to Mike's eyes and senses that it had been hard for him to comprehend at first. Had he not been sure in his own sexuality it might have worried him.

Their friendship had developed since that time, and Amanda and Mike had become very protective of Brenda, frequently calling to see she was OK and always inviting her to join them for celebrations like Christmas, New Year and her birthday. Although she had been reluctant to become too dependent, Brenda had greatly appreciated their generosity and the complete sincerity of their friendship.

However, there had been one area of her life that Brenda chose not to share with Amanda and Mike: the precise nature of her work at Venus and Apollo.

Beatrice Fiske had been growing more and more alarmed by the ever-increasing 'freak trade' and the impact this was having on her business. At the same time she had been hopelessly torn by her greed to exploit this segment of society for all she could get. The dilemma had eventually led her to set a new, extortionately higher rate for Brenda's 'untouchables' in the hope of slowing demand, while not significantly reducing income.

When Brenda had tried to object to the unfairness, Beatrice Fiske had seen the opportunity she had been seeking to reassert her control and authority over Brenda. But this had been a move she had badly misjudged.

Unknown to her, Brenda, secretly encouraged by Naomi, had been thinking of looking around for a small studio that she could afford to rent, in order to set up in business by herself. However, the fear of letting go of the security of her job at Venus and Apollo had made this a lacklustre process. Beatrice Fiske's heavy-handed intervention had spurred Brenda on and close to the famous Earls Court Exhibition Centre Brenda had found what she had been looking for.

She had spotted the card advertising a self-contained basement flat with its own separate entrance in a newsagent's window, Described as being located in Trebovir Road, between Warwick Road and Earls Court Road, it boasted one main bedroom with a small bathroom, another small single bedroom, a compact, eat-in kitchen and a spacious living room. The cost of £175 per week had been a little more than Brenda had planned for in her back-of-the-envelope budget. But the privacy afforded by such a flat, particularly in having its own entrance, would more than make the extra worthwhile, she thought.

Not only could she avoid bumping into other tenants but also, in establishing her own massage practice, a private entrance would let her clients come and go unobtrusively.

Brenda had immediately had a good feeling about this flat and had gone at once to look at it from the outside. Her first impression had been favourable. What had pleased her especially had been the ramp leading from the basement: perfect for any wheelchair-bound 'untouchables'.

When she had called Amanda, she had given the emergency clicker code they had agreed upon if she were ever to need urgent help.

'OK, Bren,' Amanda's voice had sounded reassuringly calm. 'On a scale of ten, how urgent is this?'

Brenda had given five clear clicks.

Sounding relieved, Amanda had continued, 'So five clicks. Quite urgent, but not life threatening then? I'll tell you what, I've got my lunch break in an hour, how about you getting us something to eat and I'll come straight over to your place. We can have some lunch while you tell me what's up.'

Brenda had signalled a 'yes' to that plan.

After coming back with a Prêt-a-Manger chicken club sandwich, Amanda's favourite, and a box of sushi for herself, Brenda had used the remaining time to prepare for her friend's arrival. She had written a brief description of the Earls Court flat and her intention to use this as both a place to live and a place from which to operate her own 'private therapeutic massage service'. Although Amanda was attempting to learn Sign, her understanding was still somewhat rudimentary, so Brenda felt that with anything important, written notes were preferable to avoid any misunderstanding. But when she had come to the end of the note, she had uncomfortably realised that this was probably the moment when she was going to have to risk her friendship with Amada and Mike by telling them more truthfully the exact nature of her work and the particular clientele she had chosen to serve.

The thought had filled her with dread. Yet she knew she owed it to them to tell them honestly what she did for a living.

'Sorry, I know I shouldn't talk with my mouth full,' Amanda had apologised as she chomped her sandwich, 'but I don't have long for lunch and this is quite a thing you've sprung on me. So you want me to call this number and arrange to see this place in Earls Court with you tonight, if we can get hold of the landlord?'

Brenda had nodded with enthusiasm while gesturing her apology at the short notice.

'As it happens, tonight would be a good night for me, so long as you don't mind Mike joining us. Mike and I were only going to meet at the pub on our way home. We'd pretty much planned on a bit of telly and an early night. We're both knackered and broke after the weekend.'

Brenda had handed Amanda the telephone, pointing at the number she had written down from the ad.

'All right, all right, Bren, slow down a bit,' Amanda had said, laughing at her friend's obvious excitement. 'What time shall we try for? I get off at five-thirty tonight, my early release night as luck would have it. I'm planning to meet Mike for a drink at this pub he's heard about, the Devonshire Arms on Marloes Road.

Sounds like too posh a place for me, but he's got a meeting at some hotel just up the road, he says.'

Smiling broadly, Brenda had signed simply that she'd seen the Devonshire Arms and that it was quite close to the flat.

'My, aren't we getting smart all of a sudden,' Amanda had teased. 'Still, I'll bet there's a better class of customer wanting a massage in Kensington than you'll have been used to in Bayswater, Bren. Think of all those trim Kensington ladies who meet each other for lunch and then don't eat anything except a couple of lettuce leaves before going to the gym for the afternoon to work it off. And their equally fit husbands, who are all something big in the City and drive even bigger BMWs. Those tanned and toned bodies should be a nice change after the impoverished lumps of lard you've probably had to cater to in Bayswater.'

The look of profound sadness that had passed like a fast-moving shadow across Brenda's face had made Amanda realise she had touched some hidden nerve. Thinking it might have been her reference to the 'perfect bodies' in Kensington, Amanda had added rather lamely, 'Of course, I don't suppose they're all like that, there must be some normal, down-to-earth, real working people living in Kensington too. Anyhow, that means we could both meet Mike for a drink at his posh pub at around six. So shall I see if we can be shown the flat at about seven tonight?'

Brenda had nodded gratefully, while inwardly facing the fact that she couldn't delay much longer telling Amanda and Mike about the true extent of what she really did.

'Another foreigner in London from the sound of her,' Amanda had said as she had replaced the receiver. 'Hard to understand from her accent where she might be from. Why can't they learn to speak English properly? Anyway, your future landlady sounded foreign. No harm in that. London needs as many hard-working foreigners as we can get. She sounded OK, business-like and efficient perhaps, but not unpleasant or unwelcoming. Oops, look at the time, I'm going to have to run all the way back to Selfridges and even then it looks like I'll be late,' she had said, giving Brenda a quick kiss as she left.

'See you later then. Keep Mike out of trouble for me if he gets there before I do. Not sure I can trust him amongst all that Kensington totty! You know what men are like amongst ...' The rest of her words had been lost as a wailing siren had intruded loudly through the open door.

Although Brenda had already known what to expect on the outside, the sight of the flat as they approached had still filled her with excitement.

If anything, the description of the inside had been downplayed. Compared with where she was living in Bayswater, this flat had been light and airy.

Amanda had been right about the landlady. She turned out to be a Croatian woman who had moved from Dubrovnik to London, where she had bought the building in Trebovir Road.

Nina Sanka would not normally have rented any of the flats to someone she had not been completely sure of, but there had been something about Brenda that had appealed to her sense of compassion. Brenda had awoken a degree of protective, almost maternal, concern, and that had made Nina decide on this occasion to be guided by her heart rather than her head.

For her part, Brenda had felt an empathy with Nina. She had been delighted when she had agreed to rent her the flat for two years, with an option to renew thereafter. Brenda had also been hugely relieved that her new landlady seemed prepared to forgo some of the formalities and rigorous checks she might normally have insisted upon.

With the lease signed there and then and a deposit promised for the following morning, Brenda, Amanda and Mike had thanked Nina and gone back to the Devonshire Arms to celebrate, where Mike had ordered two glasses of champagne for Brenda and Amanda and a pint of Wadworth's best bitter for himself. With the raising of glasses, and toasting of Brenda's new flat and new life ahead, Amanda had asked Brenda about starting on her own in the massage therapy business and how she planned to go about finding customers.

This was the moment at which Brenda had known she could no longer postpone telling Mike and Amanda the truth. Dreading it as she had been, she had reached into her bag and had retrieved a neat green plastic wallet in which, some while ago, she had put the carefully folded 'confessional script' she had known she would at some point have to give them.

Brenda had removed the pages from their cover and, with her hand shaking, had slowly passed it to Amanda, but not before first scribbling quickly in her note book that she and Mike should read to the very end before saying anything or, more ominously, passing any judgement.

'Jeez, Bren, what's with the big mystery all of a sudden?' Amanda had asked apprehensively.

'Our friendship may be at stake over this,' Brenda had written back.

Amanda had never before seen such a look of fear and sadness on her friend's face.

'I don't think so,' she had said loyally and emphatically. But puzzled, and now worried herself, she had unfolded the carefully written pages. Smoothing out the creases she had laid them on the table between her and Mike so they could read together.

Brenda had prefaced the document with a plea that they should try to put themselves in her position before reacting. She had reminded them of the severely reduced options available to someone in her position who didn't want to live off welfare, who wanted to be independent, and who passionately wanted to help anyone suffering from the humiliation, aching loneliness and stigma caused by severe physical handicap or abnormality.

Thinking of her 'untouchable' clients at Venus and Apollo, Brenda had asked her friends to try to imagine what it felt like to be a multiple amputee, a hunchback, to have a badly cleft palate, club foot or something worse. And then to think about that person and the personality locked inside. These people, Brenda had explained, had grown accustomed to the empty seat next to them on the bus, the comments and abuse. For her 'untouchables' these were the constant reminders of their difference and their rejection by the rest of society.

All of that might seem bad enough, Brenda had continued, but it was as nothing to the intense longing for friendship and simple interaction with fellow human beings. Add to that the natural desire for physical contact, even of the most innocent kind: a simple touch, holding hands, an affectionate hug and, of course, ultimately sensual contact.

Brenda had book-ended this preface by adding a postscript at the end of her confession that sought to reassure her friends that what she was doing was not done exclusively for money. Nor did she get any sort of perverted, sexual thrill from it.

Amanda had been the first to finish reading, but she had kept her head bowed as if she couldn't look her friend in the face. This had not been enough, however, to prevent Brenda from having seen the tears dripping unchecked from her chin, nor the silent sobs shaking her body as she struggled to control both.

When Mike had finished, he had pushed the carefully written pages away, exhaling loudly, as if he had been holding his breath all the while.

They had both sat in silence while the hubbub of the busy pub had whirled around them. For Brenda, who had begun to fear the worst, the silence had been almost unbearable and she had already decided that being that frank, even with two such close friends, had been a serious mistake.

Finally, Mike, clearing his throat and putting a protective arm around Amanda, had spoken in a very quiet voice, close to cracking with emotion.

'I think I'm speaking for us both,' he had begun, giving a quick downward glance at Amanda, who had squeezed his hand in confirmation, 'when I say that what you've written and how you've explained it is so beautiful and so honest.

Thinking about it, I feel ashamed. Not in any way of you, Bren,' he had added hastily. 'But of myself for being so … unseeing, so unthinking, and so dismissive of this … blindingly obvious … need in others, massively less fortunate than we are – the kind of people you've described so well.

'I feel humbled by what I've just read and even a little guilty, but I wouldn't be being truthful if I didn't tell you that, if I had found out about what you did, without properly understanding your motives, I would have felt angry and betrayed – and I'm fairly sure it would have ended our friendship with you. As it is, Bren, I feel really proud and honoured to be your friend and to have your friendship.'

With that he had stood up and had said to Brenda, 'Let me give you the absolute biggest hug for being such a wonderful, caring, selfless person and our good friend – always and forever.'

Amanda, having now given in completely to her emotions, was up also and the three of them were in an embrace, the tears of relief and joy from Brenda mixing freely with the tears of compassion and understanding from Amanda.

It was Mike who brought them back to themselves when he noticed they were beginning to attract some curious glances.

'Well Bren, you are certainly full of surprises,' he had told her with a grin. 'But if you've got any more like that, please keep them to yourself for the time being. One way or another you've given us just about as much as we can handle in our friendship for a good while.'

12

THERE WAS SOMETHING about the sincerity in Robert Melton's voice that troubled Christopher Callow as he tried to return to what he had been doing before the call. Perhaps it was just the innocent sincerity itself, he thought, smiling ruefully at the realisation that this was an attribute he did not come across very often – least of all in himself. On a whim, but partly because he was now finding it difficult to concentrate, he asked the bishop's clerical secretary to bring him the file on St Mungo's together with his morning coffee.

Opening the buff-coloured folder, Christopher Callow had no need to reread the letters received from Robert Melton, nor the replies, which he himself had composed for the bishop to send back.

Behind these letters lay the one the bishop himself had written to Robert expressing his great pleasure that Robert had agreed to take on the challenge of St Mungo's and assuring him of his close interest in how he got on. Christopher Callow noted the care with which no mention had actually been made of possible financial support – something the original draft had initially done until the bishop's ever-watchful personal assistant had spotted the error and had recommended to the bishop that no such assurance be made – least of all in writing.

Behind this lay a copy of the memorandum of understanding with Barrasford Holdings. Callow read the letters again before laying them aside to sip his coffee. The bishop's signature, 'Rogers' followed by his episcopal 'X' caught Callow's eye. He put down his cup, picked up the bishop's first letter to Robert in his left hand and took the memorandum in his right. As he looked at them, a thin smile formed on his face. The date under the bishop's signature preceded his letter to Robert Melton by some weeks, as did the preparation date of the document itself. There was no doubt about it; the sale of St Mungo's was as good as completed. All that stood in its way was the almost inevitable failure of the ministry of the Reverend Robert Melton.

His decision made, he took the file to the photocopier, where he made a copy of this memorandum. Inside the file were several other documents sent over from Barrasford, held together with a paperclip and fronted by a 'With Compliments' slip. After checking that he was alone, Christopher Callow removed this and attached it to the photocopy that he had just made. Then he slipped the new document into an envelope addressed to Robert Melton together with a printed note that said only 'Strictly private. Sent from a well-wisher'.

Being the careful man he was, he had noted that Barrasford Holdings' offices were in Knightsbridge. He would post the letter from the main Knightsbridge Post Office on his way home to Paddington that night.

When, as Callow knew he would, Robert Melton accosted the bishop over this blatant betrayal, the finger of suspicion over who had sent Robert the copy of the memorandum would clearly point to someone from within Barrasford Holdings.

As further evidence of this likelihood, Christopher Callow also knew a case could be made pointing out that it was not in Barrasford's interests to have an eager young vicar suddenly turning St Mungo's around, just at the time when their planning application for its change of use was being put forward. Thus the Barrasford Holdings people would, of course, clearly be motivated to stop any sudden revival of St Mungo's in its current use as a parish church.

No – Christopher Callow wasn't worried about this little betrayal coming back to bite him. In fact he quite liked the idea of the frenzied diplomatic activity and embarrassment his little bomb would cause the bishop. It would give him another opportunity to excel in the art of damage control as he helped Bishop Rogers to bring Robert Melton around to understanding the reality of the situation facing St Mungo's. In Christopher Callow's assessment, the bishop's gratitude would help cement his Grace's reliance on his ever-dependable PA.

He smiled to himself as that evening, without any hesitation, he dropped the envelope in the letter-box outside the main post office in Knightsbridge. Walking unhurriedly back towards the tube station, he noticed that the Christmas lights adorning Harrods had already been switched on. This seemed to be happening earlier and earlier each year he thought.

Christmas was not his favourite time of year. It always reminded him of just how fundamentally lonely he was and recently, since moving from the dispassionate world of the civil service to that of the Church, how flawed he was. It was troubling to think he might be developing a conscience.

13

IT HAD ONLY taken Nina Sanka a few months to learn to speak Sign Language to the point where she could converse with Brenda at a reasonable speed. She still tended to use a combination of signing and speech, but she had little difficulty following Brenda's signing.

Well within the first few weeks of her new tenant arriving she had begun to suspect that there might be more to understanding the popularity of the massage therapy being provided to what seemed to be a growing stream of severely disabled or disfigured clients coming to the basement flat.

Nina had not been alone in this. A fellow private landlord who owned a nearby building had even come to warn her, 'People like that. They make the whole neighbourhood look like a bad place. You want to be careful, lady.'

Nina had been annoyed by his intrusion. What irritated her particularly was that this overweight, unshaven Albanian, who had presumed to lecture her in his bullying way, was himself an economic migrant. What he had expressed as his concern for Nina barely disguised his own selfish interests. And it wasn't just the value of his own uncared-for building he was concerned about. He reckoned that the kind of people he had seen going into Mrs Sanka's basement flat were just the sort that would start to attract the attention of the police and social services. He was making a tidy sum from renting out overcrowded rooms at extortionate prices to illegal immigrants and the last thing he needed was the authorities starting to snoop about.

*

In order to practise and develop her Sign Language skills, Nina had started out by inviting Brenda to join her for supper in her own flat upstairs.

Although Brenda had been grateful, she had at first been suspicious. On the first couple of occasions she had been very wary. However, as time had gone on and the fluency of Nina's signing skills had rapidly improved, the two of them had found they were becoming friends, despite the difference in their ages.

Brenda had recognised in Nina a deep sense of loss for a happier past. She had felt Nina was in some ways like herself: a misplaced person, determined to put that past behind her and equally determined to make the best of whatever lay ahead.

Equally, without realising the scale of it, Nina had also sensed some of the enormous tragedy in Brenda's past and found that, in allowing herself to get to know her, the maternal instinct, suppressed since the death of her only son, was gradually being reawakened.

To Nina it was painfully obvious that they were both lonely and craved more than superficial friendship. Apart from the necessary recital to immigration officials who had handled her asylum case, Nina had realised she had told no one the story of her present circumstances. She had suspected that the same was true of Brenda and when the tenant with whom she had by now established a close friendship invited her to supper in her own flat for the first time, Nina took this as her cue.

Dinner over, both women were sitting back enjoying their third glass of wine. 'You know, Brenda,' Nina had begun, 'if my son was still alive, I think he would be about the same age as you.'

'I didn't know you had a son,' Brenda had signed back.

Nina had nodded, taking a large sip of wine before continuing. 'Stefan was a lovely boy. Gentle, kind and so loving. We were such a happy family. You never think these things can end. But they can. They can be crushed, just like that,' and she had clicked her fingers bitterly. 'And I had to watch them die. Both of them, Stefan and his father.'

'Was that in the fighting?' Brenda had signed. 'In the Bosnian War?'

Nina had shaken her head and drunk some more wine.

'No it was in the harbour, on a beautiful summer day – the kind of day when all the tourists want to visit Dubrovnik. You've probably seen pictures. There is an ancient harbour in Dubrovnik. In the summer it is full of boats, too many boats really. And the big ferry ships, they sail in and dock by the harbour wall so the passengers and tourists can go ashore and take their pictures. It was one of those huge ships that killed them.

'My husband's father had given him the small boat. My father-in-law had built it himself and Josif, my husband, was so proud of it. Although it was small, it was a strong boat too, but no boat would have been strong enough against such a big ship. I was standing on the wall. We were going in the boat for a picnic. No one else was seeing what was happening. I was screaming at the big ship. Screaming for it to stop. But it kept coming closer and closer and no one was doing anything. Stefan was also screaming and I saw Josif trying to save him. He had his back against the wall and his two feet pressed against the side of the ship. He thought he could stop it. Push it back, you know. I hope you never have to listen to such sounds, Brenda. The side of the ship just kept on coming. In the end it was so close I was beating my fists so hard against it there was blood all over them. Of course, it did move back eventually. But it took so long and by then I knew they must both be dead. No one could have survived. Like I said, happiness can be crushed so easily.'

Brenda had watched Nina finish her wine and had fetched another bottle.

'Is that why you came to London?' she had enquired, after refilling her friend's glass.

'Dubrovnik had too many memories,' Nina had replied. 'I couldn't stay.'

Nina had let the silence settle over them for some time before she had asked in a very quiet voice, 'So, that is my story. Don't you think it's your turn to tell me yours?'

Brenda had thought back to when she had opened up to her other friends: Naomi, Amanda and Mike. But none of them had suffered what Nina had just described. It had been more than the wine. Brenda realised that Nina had trusted her with a memory so painful she had never told it to anyone else. For that alone, Brenda had decided, Nina should know – and it hadn't been as if Brenda had been unprepared.

At different times over recent years, she had revised and reflected on what she had written about her life. She had shown parts of it to friends already, but that night in her flat, she had given it all to Nina to look at, while she had told her the rest in Sign.

'My father would not have done that for me,' Brenda had begun.

Nina had looked surprised, but she hadn't interrupted.

'He used to boast to us how he had swum ashore in Trinidad with nothing but a wet T-shirt and shorts. But he was ambitious. He used to tell us all the time how hard he had to work. But he sent me and my brothers to St George's, the best school in Trinidad. My father became a powerful man on the island. He had money and people respected him. Businessmen, politicians. All kinds of other powerful people.

'I tried to make him respect me too. I played football, I was good at athletics. He sent me to boxing classes and I didn't complain. I gave up music and reading, which my mother and I enjoyed, because I thought that would please him. But nothing I did seemed right. It was my younger brother, Liam, he liked best. He used to call Liam "the real chip off the old block".

'I had one true friend. He was at school with me. His name was David Thornton. David's father was English. He worked for the government. He was ambitious like my father and David was left at home a lot of the time with the servants. That was how we started spending time together. Like friends do.

'It was the summer of my sixteenth birthday. It's hot in Trinidad in July and one evening David and I went for a walk. We came to this beautiful white sandy beach. There was no one else there, just a small bar at one end which looked all closed up.

'The cool water felt so good round our feet that we took off our clothes and ran into the sea. You must know what it's like too: swimming in water like that after a sweaty, dusty day. David and I used to swim a lot and that evening felt one of the best.

'Am I too fast for you?' Brenda had asked, taking a sip of wine and only then remembering that Nina was still comparatively new to Sign.

'It's OK,' Nina had replied. 'You give it to me like you are.'

Brenda had sighed, unsure how to continue.

'It was me,' she had signed. 'Me, not David. You know what boys are like. We had been splashing water at each other like we used to. Then David tried to trip me up – just for fun. I pulled him down and we were wrestling and laughing in the water and then the next thing I knew I had my arms round him. Our bodies were pressed together. We were naked and I was kissing David. Kissing him on the neck. And it felt so good. I felt happy, Nina. I had never felt that kind of happiness before.'

Brenda had seen Nina swallowing hard and drinking her wine.

'Did your friend feel the same?' she had asked.

'No. Not the same,' Brenda had replied. 'I thought maybe he did. But he didn't. He couldn't have. Not after …'

Then Brenda had reached for her wine glass.

'But we were both happy. We shook hands on it, like men do, you know? We promised each other we would be blood brothers for ever. And then we went back to the beach and found that all our clothes had gone.

'We started looking for them and then suddenly people grabbed us from behind and pulled bags over our heads, so we couldn't see. Then they dragged us into that bar. They had been there all the time. I don't know how many men there were, but they were all men. No women.'

Nina had reached across to take Brenda's hand. 'You don't need to say any more, if you don't want to,' she had said soothingly.

Brenda had squeezed her hand in reply. Then drawing it away from Nina's fingers, she had signed back. 'No. It's OK. I want to tell you.'

She had drained her glass, refilled it from the bottle, and then continued, 'The strange thing was everyone was silent until one man said, "I hope for your sake you weren't listening to our conversation."

'We didn't know there was anyone in there. We had been swimming, how could we have heard anything? We told them that. But I don't think it mattered what we said.

'Then another man with a rough voice said, "The dead don't speak and these two little perverts don't deserve to live anyway." But the first man knew who we were. He knew David's father was a minister in the government and he called my father "one of our principals". I didn't know what he meant – then.

'I couldn't make out what they said next, but I tried to listen carefully, because I was so scared. But we didn't have to wait long. The leader said they were going to make an example of one us; the other was going to be set free. He asked who was our leader: me or David?

'I told him we were friends who shared everything. "In that case," the leader said, "perhaps you should share what I had planned for only one of you."

'Then David ...' Brenda had stopped to take in a breath. 'David said, "I'm not his friend." His voice was so panicky. "Not a friend in that way. He started it. I've never done anything like that before. But he must have. He knew what he was doing, because he's a nancy boy. A queer." That's what David called me then. "A nancy boy".'

When Nina thought Brenda had stopped, she asked gently, 'Did you say anything, Brenda? You were not to blame.'

'I told them I was,' Brenda had continued. 'I told them everything David had told them was true.'

Nina breathed out audibly, fearful of what was coming, but riveted at the same time.

'They gave David his clothes. The leader said he would have his revenge – like they all would. But first, he said, they had a deal to celebrate. "A deal with our friends in Colombia." That's what the man called it.'

'And you?' Nina had asked.

'The leader gave the order, "Keep the pretty one naked. Tie him up." So they tied my wrists to a post and tightened the bag round my head. Then they started drinking.

'At first I thought they were going to kill me. Then as the drinking went on, I thought they had forgotten about me. But I was wrong. Wrong about both of those ideas.'

'I don't know how long the drinking lasted and I don't think it stopped when the leader gave his next order: "Untie the boy, gag him and spread him face down on the table. If it's sex with men he wants, this will be an evening for him to remember."

'And that was what they did. They tied my ankles to the legs of the table and pulled my arms across it. I couldn't move. But before they started, the leader said something else.'

Brenda breathed deeply again, and then carried on, 'He said, "The man who fathered this degenerate will stand alongside to witness his son's shame."'

'No, surely not,' Nina had gasped.

But Brenda had nodded and signed, 'My father had been there all the time. He had watched everything. He had heard everything. But he had done nothing. I think he hated me for what I was more than any of the other men.'

Nina had not been able to prevent herself asking, 'And the deal with the people in Colombia? Was he …'

'I think it was his deal,' Brenda had acknowledged. 'He was rich and powerful because of narcotics. My father was an international drugs baron.'

She let this sink in and hesitated, wondering how much Nina wanted to hear and how much could be left to her imagination.

'They made David rape me first,' Brenda had continued. 'Then the men, one after the other. I lost count of how many. The last one was the leader. I know this because he ordered them to take the bag off my head and turn me over, so I could see his face first. He was young, in his thirties, and he was white. He had a scar like a railway track all down his left cheek and he was holding an old-fashioned razor in his right hand.'

Nina had been looking down at the wine glass she had begun twisting agitatedly in her fingers. Brenda had not tried to catch her eye.

'The pain was so bad, I prayed to God to let me die. But He must have made me lose consciousness instead.

'The pain was still there when I woke up in hospital. That was how I met Sister Lucy, the nun I told you about. She said someone had found me by the side of a road. I was close to death because I had lost so much blood. But my Good Samaritan had taken me to the hospital. I never got to thank them.

'The doctor was kind, but he couldn't lie to me. He was the one who told me that my tongue had been cut out and my genitals cut off.'

Then she had fallen silent. Her heart had been pumping fast and she felt light-headed.

'Brenda, my poor, poor dear Brenda,' Nina had sobbed. 'What can I say? And your own father? He must be a monster to let such a thing happen.'

'Until then, I thought he was strong,' Brenda had replied. 'After that, I saw he was a coward. Weak and frightened – like I had been.'

'What about your friend, David?'

Brenda had shaken her head. 'David disappeared. I never saw him again.'

*

99

It had been well after midnight when, emotionally drained, the two women had bade each other goodnight with an unrestrained hug of affection, like mother and daughter. Now that she had heard her story, it no longer mattered to Nina whether she thought of Brenda as the daughter she never had, or the adored son she had lost. In a sense Brenda was both.

14

IT WAS A bitterly cold, dark grey, November morning as Robert Melton let himself in to St Mungo's by the side door on Stratford Road. Walking the short distance from Pembroke Villas, Robert's thoughts, distracted by the sudden short burst of stinging sleet targeting him as he stepped outside, turned to a nostalgic reflection of how it would now be early summer in Australia. Everyone would be in shorts and T-shirts, enjoying long hot days with the prospect of a convivial gathering of friends for a relaxing barbecue in the welcome cool of early evening.

His naturally positive nature was not given to homesickness or idle dreaming, but the combination of the bishop's response to his letters, taken together with the conversation he had had with the bishop's PA two days earlier, had knocked his self-assurance. The full realisation of just what he had got himself into was beginning to dawn. The gloom and biting cold of a drab, grey, London morning was going to do nothing to lift his flagging spirits.

Nearly frozen drops of rainwater were dripping relentlessly from the broken gutter just above the door at exactly the point where the key went into the lock. The rusting old lock itself proved more difficult and unresponsive than usual in the slow cold of the morning, with the result that by the time he had managed to get the door open, the right sleeve of his overcoat was soaking wet. For the umpteenth time he told himself he must borrow a stepladder and fix that broken gutter.

Gathering up the pile of damp mail from the stone floor inside, Robert made his way to his small office in the near darkness of the old and cold church, where extraneous lighting or heating could never be afforded. He put the mail on his desk and carefully removed his wet overcoat, hanging it on a peg behind the door, before turning on the single naked bulb that dangled awkwardly from the centre of the ceiling. It had once had a shade but this had been removed in an attempt to let more light into the room when the wattage of the bulb was lowered as a safety precaution: an electrical inspection of the church had determined that the wiring throughout the building was so old that the only sensible solution would be to carry out a rewiring of the whole place. The prospect of ever doing this was as dim as the light bulb Robert was now forced to use. However, he was fortunate to also have a small, low-wattage desk lamp with which to see to do his work.

The only heat came from a wall-mounted night storage heater that had been separately installed with new wiring about two years prior to his arrival. Due to the compactness of the room, on all but the coldest days this could provide an adequate, if less than comfortable, level of heat for most of the day, provided the door to the office was kept closed. But this was something Robert didn't like doing for two reasons. Psychologically, he just didn't like the idea that his office door was always closed. It was also important for a number of practical reasons to have some idea of who might be coming into the church and for what purpose. Churches were no longer sacrosanct places and deliberate acts of desecration, theft, or both, were on an inexorable rise.

To warm himself up before settling down to work, Robert filled an ancient Russell Hobbs electric kettle from the only tap in the small lavatory adjoining his office and plugged this into an electrical extension cord that ran under the office door, to a power source on a different circuit within the main body of the church. It was as he was spooning the Nescafé into a mug that he first noticed the white envelope protruding from close to the top of the pile on his desk. Why it had caught his attention he was not sure. Perhaps it was just because he was so used to the endless bills, in their cheap brown, window envelopes and the occasional pleading letter from some charity or another. From time to time, there were also the sad, badly handwritten letters from individuals asking for money: those down on their luck, who seemed to think that the Church's only purpose was to support them in their time of self-perceived need and asking.

Mug of coffee in hand, Robert sat down at his desk and pulled the white envelope from the pile. He was disappointed to note its printed address label as well as its style of address. Had it been handwritten, it would initially have held the intriguing possibility of a personal letter – perhaps from a friend? Equally, had the style of address not been to 'Mr R. Melton', a common enough mistake he was completely used to, it might perhaps have been from the bishop's office. He allowed himself to fantasise that it might then possibly even indicate a change of heart to his request, following the conversation he had had with the bishop's assistant. After all, the earlier letters he had received from the bishop's office had all come in similar white envelopes. But he knew they would know to use the correct form in addressing the envelope to 'The Revd Robert Melton'. Subconsciously he noted the Knightsbridge postmark before turning the envelope over to open it.

Thirty minutes later Robert Melton was still seated at his desk, his mug of coffee now cold and untouched, the remainder of the mail undisturbed from where he had dropped it down. The torn white envelope addressed to Mr R. Melton lay beside his left hand while, in his right, he held the copy of the memorandum of understanding between Barrasford Holdings, the bishop and the Church Commissioners, this together with the 'With Compliments' slip and a note proclaiming it to have been sent by a 'well-wisher'.

Robert was deep in thought. Emotionally he had moved from an initial, incredulous disbelief, in which he automatically assumed there must have been some mistake, to one of barely controlled anger when he found himself reluctantly forced to the conclusion that he had been deliberately duped by the bishop.

Robert still could not quite believe that Bishop Rogers would, or even could, have done this to him. Even now his feeling of betrayal was tempered by a nagging doubt and outright puzzlement.

Coming out of these thoughts he decided he needed to know the truth. He reached for the phone on his desk.

Christopher Callow's voice sounded surprisingly more helpful than it had on the occasions when Robert had called before.

'You're in luck today,' he said, 'the bishop's in his office. I'll put you through now' – though this did not end Christopher Callow's surreptitious involvement in that or other telephone calls of interest to him. Thanks to a very discreet earpiece, which he had been assured during his Foreign Office days did not betray his presence on the line, he listened in to every telephone call of significance to and from the Bishop of West London.

Already advised by his astute and protective assistant of Robert's earlier call, Bishop Rogers was well prepared to fend off his new young vicar's plea for funds. He was not, however, prepared for having to defend his own integrity.

'Hello Robert,' came the bishop's voice with what he hoped was just the right mixture of friendliness combined with a detached air of haste, suggestive of business. 'How are you getting on at St Mungo's? Sorry I haven't managed to make it over to see you yet, but you can imagine how busy things have been with the pending appointment of the new Archbishop of Canterbury happening at the same time as the "other lot". As you know, of course, our friendly competition down the road are also choosing a new Archbishop of Westminster. We're all hoping it won't be McGrindle. That would set the ecumenical process back twenty years. He's an old-school, straight down the line, don't rock the boat, no imagination sort of chap – just do the Pope's bidding in all things great or small, without question or thought. I'll bet the Vatican is waiting to see who we put up for Canterbury before they appoint Westminster though.'

Then, without pausing, he continued, 'Anyway, I'm sorry too that we can't afford to fund anything at St Mungo's at present. Depleted diocesan funds just won't allow for it right now. I'm afraid you'll just have to be patient and make do as best you can for the moment.'

He was about to conclude this speech with a 'Now I must be getting on', when Robert interrupted him.

'Can you give me your word that the copy of the memorandum I have been sent by Barrasford Holdings, purporting to have your agreement to the sale to them of St Mungo's, is either inaccurate or outdated? I should add that it appears to bear your signature,' Robert said, coming straight to the point.

Taken completely unawares, Bishop Rogers was at a total loss for words.

Anyone passing by the open door of the office next to the bishop's at that moment might have seen a smile of deep satisfaction and anticipation pass fleetingly across Christopher Callow's normally inscrutable features.

The bishop's silence confirmed to Robert what he already now knew to be the truth. When he finally found his voice, the bishop resumed in what he hoped was now a less perfunctory, more conciliatory and cordial tone. 'It's not like it must look to you Robert. I can explain it all. But I think it would be best if you came to see me in person. Why don't you come here and we can talk about it over a spot of lunch?' He was desperately playing for time.

In such tricky situations the bishop had found in the past that it sometimes worked wonders in getting his point of view across to extend the opulent hospitality of the Bishop's Palace as a backdrop to discussion. He made a mental note to put on all the extravagance for this particular lunch.

'Let's see. It's Thursday today, so how about a week from now?' he said, quickly studying the appointments in his diary for the following week. 'Is next Thursday at twelve-thirty good for you, Robert?'

Robert was seething, but managed to muffle his anger as he gave his curt agreement.

'Good. Well, that's arranged then. I can tell you are upset and I don't really blame you, but I've got a lot to tell you – to let you in on – and I think you'll feel quite differently when we've had a chance to speak. And anyway it will be very good to see you again. I know it's my fault, it really has been far too long,' he concluded in a tone he hoped sounded more sincere in Robert's ears than his own.

It did not.

Replacing the receiver, the bishop's face wore the worried frown of someone who is not quite sure if he has completely dodged a bullet, or merely dodged the first shot. He knew he would have to prepare well for his meeting with Robert Melton next week. Still, by proposing lunch he had gained the advantage of time to do so.

He rang for Christopher Callow to come in.

'Ah, Christopher,' he began, 'Bit of a problem has arisen. Seems those idiotic Barrasford people have sent a copy of our memorandum of understanding with them direct to Robert Melton over at St Mungo's. Why on earth they have gone and done that is beyond me, but it's really upset the applecart with young Melton, who's now bent right out of shape and mad as hell with me. I've played for time by asking him to lunch next week, but we'll have to come up with a pretty good explanation between now and then.'

Christopher Callow knew that the 'we' in that sentence really meant him. He was well prepared and now seized this faultlessly engineered opportunity to show his boss once again how completely indispensable he was: an excellent opportunity to strengthen the case for his continued employment if he was ever to be caught pursuing his little predilection again.

'Perhaps you'd better join me at the lunch with him, Christopher. You're so good in these tricky situations,' continued the bishop. 'Although it'll only be the three of us, I think we'd better use the formal dining room. So much more of a … persuasive environment,' he added, searching for the right words to describe the elegant, well-furnished grandeur of the room.

Christopher Callow had already detected from this suggestion just how rattled the bishop must be feeling. It took a lot for him to use the formal dining room when the numbers didn't warrant it.

'Don't worry, your Grace, I'll have it all taken care of and in readiness for Thursday.'

As he was speaking the words he realised his mistake. The bishop had not actually mentioned the day or date of the lunch to him. All he had said was lunch next week. Bishop Rogers, who had been about to tell his capable assistant the day the lunch was to be held, now asked instead, 'How did you know it was on Thursday, Christopher? Are you a mind reader too?'

'No, your Grace,' replied Christopher Callow smoothly. 'It's just that in thinking through your lunch appointments next week, I know Thursday was to be your lunch with Canon Cabot from St Margaret's, Westminster, and knowing of your strong friendship with the canon, I assumed you would ask him to reschedule, confident that no offence would be taken.

'Unfortunately every other day you have lunch with those who wish to pursue matters of importance – at least to them – and who therefore may not be so, shall we say, understanding?'

It had worked. With the moment of possible suspicion now dispelled, the bishop looked at his assistant with renewed admiration as he said, 'Christopher. You really carry all my diary appointments in your head? You never cease to amaze me with your efficiency! You're absolutely right, of course. I saw in my diary that Thursday was lunch with Bernard and I knew he wouldn't mind if we changed it for another day. In fact, I'd better give him a call straight away before I forget. That is if you haven't already done it for me?' he added, only half-joking.

Christopher Callow let out a silent sigh of relief. That had been close, too close, he felt. He was annoyed with himself for being so clumsy. It was unlike him, as he always prided himself in his ability to hold every tiny detail that might matter in the right order in his mind. How fortunate that he had in fact scanned the appointments for the following week while listening in to the conversation between Robert Melton and his boss.

Going back to his office he reflected that at least he had rescued himself by his quick thinking and perhaps even enhanced his own reputation in the eyes the bishop. So no harm was done – this time.

15

SITTING BACK IN his cold, cheerless little office, Robert was going over in his mind the conversation he had just had with the bishop. In his hand he was still holding the copy of the memorandum with Barrasford. He had not wanted to believe he could have been deliberately deceived by the man with whom he thought he had established such a good relationship when they had first met. However, it now seemed that it had already been decided to amalgamate the rump of his parish into St Mary Abbot's and sell off the Church of St Mungo's to property developers. It was a done deal and nothing Robert was able to do would change that.

His conversation with the bishop had done nothing to reassure him. On the contrary, the longer he contemplated the evidence he now had, the more certain he became that he had been duped. He knew that, next week, he would be offered excuses and plausible explanations in the reassuring environment of the Bishop's Palace. He might even get bought off with the offer of a more secure posting as compensation. But broke, dejected and downtrodden as it undoubtedly was, he had to admit that there was something about St Mungo's and its sorry parish that had got under his skin. He didn't want it to be broken up and the church sold off, or to see his own efforts cast aside on the altar of futility.

With the feelings of anger and hopelessness rising in him, Robert decided to do again what he had been trained to do in such crises, where no clear course would come to him. He knew he must take the problem to a higher authority.

Making his way into the main sanctuary of the church, he took a place in one of the pews on the right-hand side of the chancel, close to the main altar.

He was confident, unquestionably confident, that God already knew the full extent of his dilemma and inner turmoil. Robert felt no need to explain and so kept his prayer to one of humble submission to whatever was God's will for him, asking only for some enlightenment and understanding as to what God's plan was for the future of St Mungo's and what, if any, his role in that plan might be.

Unlike some of the other seminarians with whom he had been at theological college, Robert didn't always find prayer easy. Try as he might, his concentration could be all too easily broken by the stealthy distraction of more mundane worldly considerations. But, despite this, he had come to value his time spent in quiet prayer or, as he liked to think of it, conversations with God.

Occasionally, after a particularly difficult time of prayer, when he had found it almost impossible to concentrate, he would finish by simply saying, 'Lord, you know what I meant to say and how I meant to say it. So please just take these feeble prayers, such as they are, and validate them for me.'

Just occasionally it was different. He would become totally absorbed and focused, to the extent that he would lose complete track of time, and proper awareness of the outside world. On these occasions, when eventually his prayers were finished, he always found he had achieved an extraordinary sense of peace and well-being: an energising feeling he attributed to the unshakeable certainty of his closeness to God.

Today was one of those occasions. From the moment he had knelt down and begun his prayers, with the humble submission that this was too big a problem for him either to understand or deal with alone, and had added his final 'over to you Lord' plea for help, he had become completely absorbed.

Oblivious to the cold that had begun to seep into him, he was eventually jolted back to his surroundings by a vague awareness that he was no longer alone in the church.

When he glanced over, he did not see anyone at first in the dim light. Then a slight movement at the back of the church revealed someone sitting alone in the shadows.

Instinctively Robert knew it was Brenda. He didn't move, frightened that to do so might disturb her and make her leave. It was strange, he thought, that his passionate appeal to God for His help had been interrupted by the arrival of this most enigmatic of visitors to St Mungo's – and one whom many members of the regular congregation would look down upon as an unreformed sinner.

Robert rose cautiously from his knees and set off across the nave, as if to return directly to his office. He stole another glance in Brenda's direction. There was no one to be seen. Looking openly around now, it seemed to him the church was empty again and he was alone once more. Yet he hadn't heard the door either opening or closing, nor the sound of anyone's footsteps. How strange it was that Brenda could move so silently. He wondered if it had anything to do with the speechless world she inhabited. Had it made her hearing so acute that she could move without making any noise herself?

With his curiosity raised, Robert walked over to the back of the church to where Brenda had been sitting. Brenda had certainly gone, but on the pew Robert noticed a folded piece of paper weighted down under one corner of a prayer book.

He picked it up and was immediately struck by the clear, bold handwriting. The message, evidently meant for him, was as brief as it was unsettling. It simply read, 'Stop worrying. All shall be well.' It was signed with a capital B.

Back in his little office Robert was nonplussed. If this was the Lord working in a mysterious way in answer to his prayers, He had Robert baffled. What he did know was that the situation looked just as hopeless as it had done earlier; he was no further forward in being able to see any practical solution in his desire to save St Mungo's from what looked like its imminent closure.

However, as he had experienced in the past when facing seemingly insurmountable obstacles, he was already feeling better in himself for having consciously let go of the problem and handed it over to God to deal with – although he now began to worry that this acceptance could in fact be apathy taking hold. This was something he dreaded and knew he must guard against if his youthful drive and energy were not to get lost in a sense of hopelessness.

16

BY THE FOLLOWING Sunday the weather had turned even nastier. A bitter, raw easterly wind was blowing off the North Sea, bringing with it the sort of damp, bone-chilling, cold that Robert's Australian heritage still struggled to come to terms with.

London was dark, wet and cheerless, caught under a lid of fast-moving, leaden clouds bringing wave after wave of stinging grey sleet. It was shortly before eight o'clock and Pembroke Road, normally busy by this time, even on a Sunday morning, was eerily quiet. He saw no one in the street. Even before leaving the house, Robert knew that church attendance that day would be lower than normal. He wondered if anyone would turn up for the eight-thirty service, apart from old Bill, Michael and Pam, who would probably all make the effort as the sole supporters of the old rite in the 1662 prayer book.

On a good Sunday the eight-thirty might attract as many as eight in the congregation, usually made up of no more than six parishioners with a couple of tourists, or guests staying locally with friends or family.

There seemed little point in maintaining the eight-thirty service in its present form, but Robert knew that to abolish it would cause great distress to the handful of his most loyal parishioners, who were as generous with their time as they were with their modest resources in helping out with the day-to-day needs of St Mungo's.

He was not wrong; attendance at the eight-thirty comprised a total of four:

himself, Michael, Bill and Pam. However, by contrast, he was pleasantly surprised by the numbers at the service two hours later. There were fewer parishioners than normal, as he had anticipated, but this had been made up for by a larger than expected number of visitors, most of them tourists.

It was not unusual for visitors to give reasonably generously when the collection plate was passed round, so Robert had been disappointed to see just a few coins in the plate, and one note, hidden amongst the small Gift Aid envelopes used by the regular parishioners.

'Don't bother counting it today, Jim,' Robert said sympathetically. 'I'll do it. With that bad cold of yours, I'm sure you should be getting home. I'm sorry the church was so chilly today.' As a weary afterthought, he added, 'It's not exactly going to take me very long to count, is it?'

After his deputy church warden had gone, Robert went round switching off the lights, extinguishing those brief hours of possibility and purpose that illuminated his church once a week. A lack of money and people willing to help now restricted after-church coffee to one Sunday a month and today was not that Sunday. As far as Robert could see, St Mungo's would now remain cold and empty like this until its brief resurrection the following Sunday. And so it would continue week after week until the wrecking ball started smashing it to tiny pieces of unrecognisable masonry.

What was even more depressing was Robert's bleak realisation that it wasn't only about the money. It was as much about the complete lack of interest or support for what he was trying to do – something he had already spent months thinking about, planning and campaigning for. He couldn't remember ever feeling so tired, or fed up about anything as he did now.

As he was picking up his overcoat, scarf and keys, Robert noticed the collection plate, still uncounted on his desk. He could probably guess what the pitiful offering added up to and, feeling as he did, he was tempted just to leave it until the next morning. He knew he was supposed to count it and put it in the laughably big safe for the night. This elaborate masterpiece of Victorian security was commodious enough to have once held silver candlesticks, fine plate and gold chalices, but now mockingly attested to the better times St Mungo's had once enjoyed. The offering of the present-day faithful would sit alongside a couple of boxes of matches and a torch – with dud batteries.

Duty getting the better of him, Robert threw his coat over the back of his chair and sat down with a resigned sigh. Picking out the small envelopes first, he scanned the names on the front and knew straight away how much each contained. It never varied.

It was while he was picking up the loose coins in order of their value that Robert first noticed the piece of paper. People occasionally left handwritten notes offering everything from blessings or well-intentioned advice to outright abuse.

Robert was in no particular hurry to look at this small rectangle of flimsy paper, and it was only with the coins counted and neatly stacked in front of him that he picked it up to see what it was. Holding it to the light, he saw it was some sort of lottery ticket. Closer inspection revealed it to be an American Powerball lottery ticket, from the state of New Hampshire.

That was the last thing Robert or St Mungo's needed. Robert smiled to himself with wry bitterness as he scrunched it up and threw it into the wastepaper basket. After carefully locking up the church, he set his shoulders to the driving sleet as he made his way back the short distance to Pembroke Villas.

He didn't feel a bit like making himself anything to eat. But at least he had declined the invitation to lunch from a parishioner who was so deaf, conversation had to be kept to short statements delivered with such volume Robert knew from his own experience they could be heard in the street. However, the food was always delicious, hot and plentiful and, under other circumstances, it might have been most welcome. He felt guilty for having turned her down. He knew she was lonely and her family, such as they were, didn't seem to bother with her. He resolved he would go next Sunday if she asked him again, which he felt sure she would. Today he would just heat up a tin of soup. He couldn't be bothered with anything else. He needed time to himself and time to think.

As the day wore on, Robert found his thoughts returning again and again to the mysterious appearance of Brenda at the back of the church, just when he had been passing his insurmountable problem over to God to handle.

The little note she had left for him. What had it said again? 'Stop worrying. All shall be well?' Was there any connection and if so what did it mean? Was this a sign? If it was, what was he supposed to make of it?

It was while he was considering this that he remembered the American lottery ticket in the collection plate.

Another strange sign?

No, he reasoned. He must not think like that. He knew it would be the act of a very desperate fantasist to allow that line of thinking to develop further.

Robert passed the rest of the day with his mind in turmoil as he tried to form a logical plan to prepare himself for his lunch with the bishop on Thursday. Still, try as he might, he could not quite clear his thoughts of the series of those strange events.

Finally, through a niggling curiosity and the realisation that while he was thinking like this he would be unable to sleep, Robert decided it was an excuse to call the only person he knew in America: his close friend, Andreas Doria, a Benedictine monk at St Jerome's Abbey in Manchester, New Hampshire.

Although he had been born in New York, Andreas had studied in Cambridge at the same time as Robert. But while Robert's study of theology had directed him towards the Church of England, Andreas had always been destined to become a Roman Catholic priest, a path that had currently placed him at St Jerome's in New Hampshire.

New Hampshire! Robert sat bolt upright.

Wasn't that the name of the state on the lottery ticket he had found that morning? Another strange coincidence?

Glancing at his watch, Robert calculated that although it was quite late in London, now should be a good time to reach his friend, for whom it would be mid-afternoon. Robert fretted a little about the cost of the call, which he knew he would have to pay when his telephone bill was audited at the diocesan finance office, but he dialled the number all the same.

After just a few rings a cheerful American voice came on the line asking how she might help him.

'Andreas Doria? Yes certainly. I'll put you thorough to his room now. I know he's in. I saw him walk past less than five minutes ago.'

No way Andreas could hide, even if he wanted to, thought Robert, smiling to himself.

'Could I ask your name, please, sir?'

'Of course. It's Robert Melton. I'm telephoning from London …England.'

Moments later Andreas came on the line, sounding happy and excited.

'To what do I owe this extraordinary pleasure, when an impoverished member of the competition spends what may well be his last pennies on an expensive transatlantic telephone call to an equally impoverished monk? So how goes it, my friend? It's good to hear your voice.'

They joshed each other back and forth for a while before Robert filled Andreas in on his news and the situation at St Mungo's. Then, rather sheepishly, he asked, 'Andreas, what is a Powerball lottery in America?'

'First off, although it may seem like it to those who don't know, Powerball is not an individual state lottery,' Andreas explained. 'It's a multi-state lottery. In fact Powerball is the biggest and richest lottery in America.

'But what on earth makes you spend your last dime calling me from London at this time of the night to ask about Powerball? Unless of course you're giving sanctuary to the person who has the current winning ticket? The whole of America seems to be hunting for him, or her, right now. So what's up, my friend? Do I see the re-emergence of the theology freshman, the one whose hand I spotted more than once hovering over the *Financial Times* in the college library before dutifully gathering the *Church Times*? Hadn't you better explain?'

'I would, if you'd only shut up for a minute and give me a chance to tell you,' Robert responded, laughing; talking to his friend was doing him good.

He explained how the Powerball ticket had been left in his church collection plate that morning. But, although he would have liked to, he couldn't quite bring himself to tell Andreas about the other strange coincidences – all following on from what he now regarded as the treacherous circumstances by which he had been duped into taking on St Mungo's. Robert knew it would take far too long to explain and he didn't want to risk Andreas even thinking he might be losing it under the strain of events. Besides which, he couldn't afford this call and he knew he needed to try and keep it as short as possible – something not always easy to do when talking to Andreas.

'Did you say the ticket bore the state name of New Hampshire?' Andreas enquired after Robert had finished his explanation.

'Yes … at least I think so. I'm fairly sure that's what it said.'

'Well, I don't want to get your hopes up, but you could be on your way to fame and a truly breathtaking fortune. You've just increased the very remote chance you could be in possession of the sole winning ticket by a considerable margin. I say this because the manic search for the winner has so far revealed that the single winning ticket was indeed purchased up here in New Hampshire. Don't forget who your friends are now when you join the ranks of the world's super-rich.

'Tell me the numbers on your ticket, Robert and I'll check them. Then I'll either call you back to help you plan the biggest celebration of your life, or to condemn you to an endless continuation of impoverished ministry in your broken-down parish.'

If only Andreas knew just how accurately he had characterised these two extremes. His only error was that in all probability Robert's ministry would not be endless at St Mungo's; it would be over before he had hardly had a chance to get started.

'So come on, tell me the numbers,' Andreas's voice urged with feigned impatience. 'I'm sitting here with a pencil poised over a blank margin of today's newspaper. Problem is my hand is beginning to shake in excitement and anticipation.

'Did I mention, my friend, that I'm thinking of elevating you to being "my best friend", or even as St Mark liked to address Theophilus, "my excellent friend"? But if you don't give me the numbers soon I may no longer be able to write them down.'

'I don't actually have the ticket,' Robert began. He caught the mock gasp of horror from Andreas before continuing, 'I threw it away in disgust when I found it in the plate.'

There was a pause before Andreas replied. 'That, friend, is so typical of you. Extravagant in the extreme. To throw away the largest lottery win the world has ever known, because you're disgusted at the temptation of Mammon.

'So why are we wasting time and, more to the point, your slender resources?'

'Just stop and listen a minute will you,' Robert said, laughing again. 'I chucked it in the wastebasket beside my desk. It'll still be there tomorrow. One of the advantages of poverty is, because I can't afford a cleaner, the cleaning of the church is undertaken by volunteers and my wastebasket won't get emptied now until Tuesday. I'll retrieve the ticket tomorrow when I go to my office and I'll give you a quick call then with the numbers.'

'Good. Meanwhile I'll have looked up the winning numbers. If it turns out you do have the winning ticket, I can feel a movie script coming on. Until tomorrow then. Sleep well.'

Robert was enough of a realist to know that the chances of the lottery ticket being the winning one were still millions to one against. However, despite this and the lateness of the hour, he decided to go back to his office and retrieve the ticket. Apart from anything else, he knew he would sleep better if his imagination was not given the chance to conjure up the different ways the ticket might slip through his grasp.

17

THE BITTERLY COLD, late-night walk back to the church had been short. Robert had had no trouble in finding the scrunched-up lottery ticket. With this now smoothed out and placed safely on top of the chest of drawers in his bedroom, he had slept surprisingly well.

Monday mornings were always busy. He tried not to allow himself to be too distracted as he waited impatiently until it was eleven o'clock in London, six on the east coast of America, by which time he knew the day would have begun for Andreas.

Robert steeled himself to wait until five minutes past and then dialled Andreas's number.

The phone was promptly answered by the same friendly voice that had greeted him yesterday. 'St Jerome's, how may I help you?'

Robert asked to be put through to Andreas.

'Certainly. If you're the gentleman from England who called yesterday, I think he's waiting for your call before he goes to breakfast,' she volunteered.

'Hello my friend,' Andreas greeted him cheerfully. 'I hope you slept well on the night before you are either to be catapulted into the elite ranks of the world's super-rich, or condemned forever to be consigned to the rather larger ranks of the world's abject poor, struggling even to repay the costof this call.

'I have good news and not so good news,' continued Andreas. 'The good news is that so far the huge jackpot remains unclaimed. No winner has yet come forward or been found. So you're still in the game. The not so good news, my friend, is that the press are now in a feeding frenzy and have so far managed to locate the town and even the place of business where the ticket was bought. Not too far from here it seems, in a small town called New London. It's up in the middle of the state. More a village than a town according to the press report I read, with a year-round population of just 1,500 souls. Although apparently this quadruples during the summer months, from which one might deduce it to be a popular vacation spot.

'What I like is the possibility that the ticket to this truly huge lottery prize was bought in the tiny, no doubt picturesque, sleepy little rural town of New London and might now just be found to have turned up in the heart of vast *old* London in old England. There is poetry in there somewhere. The press would go wild over just that much, but wait until I tell them just where and how it came to be in your possession, at which point they will go absolutely nuts – off the scale!'

Robert laughed out loud. He knew his friend was playing for time, to extract the maximum fun, before he and Robert had to face the inevitable disappointment.

'It seems the ticket was bought at a place called Baynham's New England Mercantile, at 207 Main Street, New London. The press even poke fun at the address claiming it as pretentious to call it Main Street when there are no other streets. Why not call it "Only Street" one paper even asks disparagingly? All just sour grapes over their frustration at not being able to crack this story.'

But he could sense Robert's mounting tension at the other end of the line and continued, 'Right, my friend, here are the winning numbers: 3, 5, 10, 21, 28 and 35.'

The silence that followed seemed interminable. It was broken only when Robert asked in a thick voice, 'Could you give them to me again, Andreas, more slowly this time? I don't think I can have written them down properly.'

Andreas repeated them slowly.

Again there was silence, punctuated only by Robert's now audible breathing. Then in a soft, shaky voice, Robert said, 'Andreas, if those numbers you've given me are correct and I've understood how this thing works, I really, really do have the winning ticket in my hand.'

'You wouldn't be trying to put the joke over on me now, would you my friend?' rejoined Andreas in a mock Irish accent.

'No, Andreas, I'm really serious about this. I think I really might have the winning ticket. If so, what on earth do I do now?'

Andreas, now almost as stunned as Robert, knew his friend well enough to know he was not joking.

'Well, well, my excellent friend, that's a true fortune you hold in your hand, almost obscene in its magnitude, but things have now moved into a whole new ball game.

'First off I recommend you tell no one about this, and I do mean absolutely no one. Secondly, I'll have to check discreetly the rules of Powerball for you. But from my understanding what you have in your hand is the equivalent of a bearer bond. That means whoever has it in their hand upon presentation for payment gets the money.

'Turn it over, Robert. Is there a place on the back to fill in your name and address?'

'Yes,' replied Robert, looking at the back of the ticket.

'Well normally, now would be the moment for you to fill in that information and sign it, as a sort of extra security. But I think you ought to hold off doing that. If my memory is correct, I think the rules of the lottery state that the winner has to be at least a legal US resident, if not a citizen. I'll need to check out those things and how long you've got to come forward and claim the prize. It shouldn't take me too long, but I don't want to arouse any suspicions. I can probably get back to you later today or otherwise first thing tomorrow.'

'OK, but what good is that if you're right and I do have to be a resident or citizen?'

'That, my very excellent friend, is where I come in,' answered Andreas. 'I am both a citizen and a resident who, handily, happens also to be residing in New Hampshire. Of course, it means I would have to fill in and sign the back of the ticket and present it as the bearer, which in turns means you would have no choice but to trust me not to run off with all the money.'

Andreas was probably the only person in the world Robert would have no hesitation in trusting with such a huge temptation. Whoever collected the money would be its lawful owner and no verbal agreement on earth could alter that.

'Andreas, you know I would have no problem with that.'

'Flattery will get you nowhere when I am wrestling with the temptation of the devil sitting on my shoulder,' chuckled Andreas. 'OK then. Let me check out a few things and get back to you as soon as I can. Meanwhile can I be sure you will not either mislay, leave lying around, or throw away 260 million dollars again? We'll speak later. Until then stay calm, stay silent and whatever else you do keep that little piece of paper safe.' With that Andreas rang off.

Robert had always admired Andreas for being able to commit himself to a life of celibacy.

Although they had only first met at university, the bond of friendship that had grown between them was as strong as it would have been if they had known each other from childhood. Robert could not imagine having a closer friendship with anyone else he knew.

And yet, he had to admit, there was a small part of Andreas he did not know. A part that Andreas himself seemed determined to lock away and never acknowledge or talk about: his childhood. He always presented himself as if his life had started from when he was a young man in Italy.

When Robert had once pressed him about his family and earlier life,

Andreas had become silent and uncharacteristically morose. He would say only that his father's work caused them to live in different parts of the world and, after moving around quite a lot, they had settled in Italy. Andreas had explained that he had had an unhappy childhood and that he did not wish to talk about it. It was a closed book and he wanted to keep it that way.

Robert was saddened by this one exclusion from their otherwise close friendship, but he knew this was a position from which Andreas would not be moved. So, by mutual understanding and respect for each other, it was a subject that neither of them ever mentioned again.

The only vague hint towards Andreas's past occurred the night when both of them had been out celebrating the end of Finals. It was quite late and they had drunk a great deal more wine than was good for either of them. When they were finally thrown out of the bar the effect of the cool night air and alcohol had caused Andreas to collapse on the pavement. While he was trying to help his friend back to his feet, Robert had been surprised when he had detected a previously unnoticed, almost musical lilt to his friend's very slurred, but accented voice. However, he reasoned later that he had been so drunk himself he could not be sure what he may or may not have heard. Either way, he never raised the matter with Andreas.

Andreas did not call back until the following morning. Robert had slept only fitfully that night, his mind still trying to grasp the enormity of what might be about to happen to him. When at last the phone rang the morning was already quite well advanced in London and Robert had been up for some hours.

'Well, my most very excellent of friends,' Andreas had begun brightly, 'it seems we were right and what you have is a bearer bond that must be in the possession of at least a legal, taxable resident of these great United States. This means you will have to put your faith in me to collect all those fat winnings on your behalf and I will have to put my faith in you to see your old friend right for his trouble.'

Robert could hear the humour in his voice. He knew that if there was one person on this earth who would not have his head turned by so vast a sum of money, that person would be Andreas. Only he could have put the matter of trust that way round.

'So, what do you want me to do with the ticket Andreas? Shall I post it to you?'

Andreas did not reply before letting out a soft whistle, followed by a faint sigh. 'Oh you saphead. No wonder you joined the wrong church,' was his eventual response. 'You really don't get it, do you? What you have in your hand is actually 260 million dollars, cold cash. Try to think of it that way. Would you ever think of packing all that amount of money in a box, taking it to the Post Office and entrusting it to the efficiency, not to mention honesty, of the postal services on two different continents? Even if yours is loftily called the Royal Mail. You'd have to be mad.'

'Well, I would have sent it by registered post,' interjected Robert defensively, embarrassed at his own naivety.

'I have a better idea. You go today to your nearest travel agent and you book a first-class open return ticket to Boston with British Airways, TWA or PanAm. Book whichever is the most expensive, on the straightforward basis that you have no other way of telling which of them is more likely to make the most fuss of you, or coddle you in the greatest luxury. You need to start getting used to your vast wealth and what it can do for you.'

'Fine words, Andreas,' chuckled Robert. 'But I can hardly afford a bus ticket, let alone even the cheapest aeroplane ticket. And how am I supposed to get the time off? Do you expect me to just walk out of my parish and its duties? I'd be letting down all sorts of people.'

'Let me take your objections one at a time,' Andreas replied. 'You have a point about the need for ready cash and I can see the difficulty in trying either to pawn or raise a temporary mortgage against an overseas lottery ticket, especially for the purpose of buying an airplane ticket to America. Trying to borrow from someone would take too long and is likely to raise too many questions – even if you knew someone with the money, which I'm reasonably sure you don't. Am I right?'

'Yes,' chuckled Robert. 'So far so good. You're spot on.'

'I suppose it would be a little cheeky to try and tap your bishop for a loan?' suggested Andreas mischievously.

Robert laughed outright at the rather appealing nature of this thought.

'So here's what we need to do,' continued Andreas. 'It so happens that I am in possession of a modest little nest egg, which, contrary to what many people think happens when you join a religious order, I have been permitted to keep for my own personal use. So, when we're finished talking I'm going to go to the travel agent the college uses and pre-pay a ticket for you.

'You should then be able to collect this directly from the airline desk at the airport before you board the plane. However, unlike you, not being made of money, I'm afraid all I can afford to pay for will be the cheapest possible, one-way, economy class ticket that will, in all probability, have you sitting sandwiched tightly between two talkative, overweight ladies, somewhere down towards the back of the plane. You can console yourself with the thought that it will be the very last time you will have to fly in the discomfort with which most of us mortals have to cheerfully cope. Thereafter your life will be one in which you will be able to afford whatever you want. First-class luxury travel, where you will be completely cocooned from the rigours of the real world, will very quickly become the norm. Do you have a preference of airline you would like me to book for you, my liege?'

'Oh, Andreas, do stop talking your nonsense,' Robert retorted. 'I can't just walk out of here and fly off to America tomorrow, even if you were to buy me a ticket, which you know I could never let you do. Besides, I'm supposed to be having lunch with the bishop on Thursday. He wants to explain the whole St Mungo's situation to me.'

There was silence at the other end. The response, when it came, was softly spoken. 'Explain what exactly?'

Robert knew that Andreas was right. What was there to explain? It was quite obvious he had taken on St Mungo's under a false premise and that the exercise now would be one of damage control, smoothly undertaken over a good lunch, to persuade him to understand and accept the necessity for him to have been duped in this way.

'Why don't you just think about it for a little and call me back?' Andreas continued. 'But don't forget. Keep that little piece of valuable paper in a very safe place while you do your thinking. Remember it is a bearer bond for 260 million dollars,' he said again with emphasis.

'You might also want to think about how you could easily save St Mungo's yourself with that kind of money by buying the memorandum of agreement from the would-be purchaser. A property developer, I think you said. All they'll be interested in is a return on their investment. If you offered them that without their ever having to take the risk and hassle of actually demolishing the church and developing the site, they should leap at it, I would think. The sum of money required to do that would probably be equal to just a few days' interest generated from the fortune you now have, my oh so very excellent friend.'

Robert had always been impressed by Andreas's abilities in practical matters of business and finance, despite his vocation and apparent lack of worldly experience.

The two friends agreed to speak again the following day.

*

It was still only Tuesday. Robert tried to concentrate as he returned to the day-to-day work of the parish. The unopened post on his desk yielded a mixture of bills; a plea for funds to support a private well-digging project in Africa; a final demand from the London Electricity Board; and a letter from the headmistress of St Mungo's & St Barnabas' Church of England Primary School, reminding Robert of his promise to address the pupils and parents in introducing the school nativity play. Perhaps he would like to come to one of the earlier rehearsals by way of preparation for his speech?

This parochial school, affiliated with St Mungo's, was the principal bright spot in the parish. Thanks to its good teaching methods and adherence to the most sensible traditional standards in education and expectations of behaviour, it had long had a well-deserved reputation for excellence.

Robert set the post to one side on his already overcrowded desk. He was finding it hard to concentrate.

What should he do?

The phone rang. It was Logan from neighbouring LAMDA – the London Academy of Music and Dramatic Art: London's oldest drama school and considered by those in the know to be its finest. Logan was calling to confirm another year of LAMDA using the Church of St Mungo's for their academic year-end carol concert. The tradition of this and the very welcome income it brought in to St Mungo's had become a high point on the calendar of both institutions. Tickets for the LAMDA Christmas carol service – traditionally illuminated entirely by candlelight – were much sought after and the church was always packed for the jubilant and joyous occasion it unfailingly was.

Robert liked the idea of local community use for the church and was looking forward to seeing the church transformed when enthusiastically decorated and prepared by the LAMDA students for this annual celebration of Christmas. For that one night at least, he felt, the church could become a beacon of hope for what it might once again be.

Just then a robin flew in and alighted unhesitatingly on the top of his desk lamp. Small birds were not an uncommon sight in St Mungo's, particularly during the winter months for those species that did not migrate. Robins in particular seemed prone to making these visits. Perhaps it was because of their natural curiosity.

This particular robin seemed to be quite unafraid. Perhaps the light, or the relative warmth emanating from his office, had persuaded this little bird to fly down and perch on top of Robert's lamp. The small bird seemed to be staring at Robert as if appraising him, its little head cocked first on one side and then the other. Apparently satisfied, it flew over to the open bookcase against the wall, alighted briefly on the tallest of the books that protruded slightly above the others, turned once to look directly at Robert again, appeared to bow and then flew out of his office back into the body of the church.

Robert got up and followed him out. He was just in time to see the little bird fly straight to a hole in one of the upper stained-glass windows.

Returning to his office, Robert was about to sit back at his desk when his eye caught the book that the little bird had briefly alighted upon before flying off. He went across to the bookcase, took it down and was startled to see its title: *The Journey and Adventure of Faith in New England.*

The matter was settled. Returning the book to its place on the top shelf, Robert knew his mind was made up.

It did not take long to get directly through to the bishop. His request for immediate leave over the next two weeks was met with what Robert detected might be a mixture of surprise and relief on the bishop's part.

'That sounds like an excellent plan, Robert. A short break is just what you need and you certainly deserve it,' said the bishop. 'Are you going somewhere nice?'

'Just somewhere new in England,' Robert responded, hoping the bishop would not question him more closely, or start making recommendations. He knew this was being a little deceitful and a few weeks ago he would never have thought himself capable of acting like this with anyone, let alone with his bishop. But things were different now and he didn't feel as bad about it as he had expected to.

'Well, being winter it'll be cold wherever you go, but you're young, so I don't suppose you'll mind that. Give me a call when you get back and we'll reschedule our lunch. Enjoy yourself and, Robert, try and relax a bit,' concluded the bishop, trying to sound at his most solicitous.

Robert smiled to himself. The bishop didn't know how right he was about it being cold wherever he went in New England at this time of year: a lot colder than it was ever likely to get anywhere in old England, he thought.

When he had finished speaking to Robert, Bishop Rogers got up from his desk and went in search of his PA. The bishop was feeling quite pleased with himself. This fortuitous turn of events certainly took the pressure off.

'Ah, Christopher, we're going to need an immediate stand-in over at St Mungo's, Earls Court,' he said. 'Robert Melton just called me to ask for a fortnight's leave. I know it is very short notice, but under the circumstances I thought it judicious to agree. Obviously the lunch on Thursday is now postponed and it will give us more time to prepare a persuasive case for having kept poor young Melton in the dark. Do you have anyone in mind who could do an immediate stand-in? Doesn't have to be of the highest calibre or anything.'

Noticing the lack of reaction from Christopher Callow to this news, the bishop said, 'You don't seem too surprised.'

'No, your Grace, I'm not. I was worried something like this might happen. Robert Melton is, from what you've told me, an energetic, purposeful young priest who takes his responsibilities quite seriously and the unsettling discovery of the position in which he now finds himself must, I feel, be quite stressful to him.

'I suggest we, I mean you, might ask Horace Cruickshank to fill in for the two weeks. I know he's on a study sabbatical, but I don't think reduced and, I assume, rather minimal duties over at St Mungo's would be too arduous, or any obstacle to the continuation of his studies?'

'Excellent idea, Christopher. You're always one step ahead of me, aren't you? Cruickshank's just the fellow and he's easy-going enough not to mind being asked at the last minute like this. Will you get hold of him for me?'

'I've already left a message for him to call me back, your Grace ... on another matter of course, but it is quite convenient.'

Bishop Rogers felt again the familiar mixture of admiration and gratitude at the extraordinary prescient abilities of his assistant. Had he not known better, he might have had an uneasy feeling that something was not quite right.

'Well, Christopher, it would seem events might be moving in our favour over this little hiccup, don't you think?'

'Yes, on the face of it, it would, your Grace.'

That was a typical sort of equivocal response one might expect from a civil servant, thought the bishop returning to his office.

Christopher Callow was not so sure. He had, of course, listened in on the conversation when Robert Melton had called. With his Foreign Office training kicking in, there was something in the underlying tone of Robert's voice he had picked up on that had worried him. Sitting motionless at his desk, the heavy frown of concentration testified to the fact that it was still worrying him. Was it suppressed excitement he thought he had detected in Robert's voice? But what could possibly be the cause of that?

Christopher Callow had the unpleasant feeling that he and, by extension, of course, the bishop, might be about to be outmanoeuvred by this young priest, but he couldn't for the life of him work out how. It was a feeling he wasn't used to. He didn't like it one bit.

As soon as his watch showed him the time was eleven o'clock Robert telephoned Andreas.

'I've been given two weeks' leave by the bishop,' he explained, barely able to contain his excitement. 'I called to ask for some time off and he agreed without question.'

'You've probably helped ease his guilty conscience,' Andreas answered wryly. 'Anyway, don't ask me why, but I figured you'd work out just how important this was and find a way to get your sorry tail over here.'

'Just one small problem, Andreas, I can't afford the airline ticket.'

'Don't worry, I'd assumed as much and yesterday, after we'd finished speaking, I went to our travel people and bought you a one-way ticket for tomorrow with British Airways, flying to Boston.'

Reading his itinerary, as if from a script and without pause, Andreas continued, 'With your passport, you can pick the ticket up at the British Airways information desk in Terminal 4 at Heathrow Airport. You're on BA213 that will get you in to Logan Airport at one-thirty local time tomorrow afternoon. From there you can catch a bus up to Manchester, New Hampshire … I'm only joking, do you think I would let a man carrying 260 million dollars on him ride a bus? No, don't worry; I've arranged to have the day off. I've borrowed a car and I'll be there to meet you off the flight. Just make sure you keep that little piece of paper on your person at all times – not in a suitcase or even a briefcase.

'Should the Immigration and Customs people ask if you are carrying any financial instrument with a face value of more than ten thousand dollars, you'd better not say a lottery ticket. Although this would normally only make them laugh and wish you good luck, because of the frenzy of publicity this thing has attracted, it just might make them more interested in it than you would want them to be. As it isn't confirmed as the winning ticket yet, the truth is you are carrying no such instrument. But of course they'd never suspect a humble priest of having any money anyway.

'So, until tomorrow. You'd better get packing and be sure to be at the airport in good time, just in case there's any kind of hitch.'

'Thank you, Andreas. I will pay you back for the airline ticket, whatever happens.'

It was a sobering thought, of course, that the lottery ticket, although apparently having all the right numbers, had indeed not yet been confirmed as the actual winning ticket. Robert hated uncertainty.

18

ANYONE PASSING THROUGH King's Cross station during the busiest part of the morning rush hour might have seen the unusual sight of the dense crowd parting, pressing back in a continuous wave. The reason for this was the collective revulsion and the haste to move as far away as possible from a young woman making her way across the concourse.

She was horribly disfigured by neurofibromatosis, a disease causing wart-like, purple growths on her face, hands and neck, creating an almost reptilian effect all over her skin. Yet she held her head up high as she walked firmly through the parting crowd, staring straight ahead without looking to left or right. In the tube to Earls Court, despite the throng of people packed into the train, she had plenty of space to herself in the carriage.

Brenda didn't get many female clients. Unsurprisingly the majority of those who came to her were relatively young men, usually between the ages of twenty and forty she guessed. As a result, any female 'untouchables' tended to stand out.

This young woman was no exception to that rule. Anyone who could look past the hideously disfiguring growths would have been rewarded by the sight of the most beautiful, deep aquamarine eyes. But today there was something else besides: something more than the apprehensive, often furtive, fear that Brenda was used to seeing in clients coming to her for the first time.

'My name is Olivia,' the girl said, without extending her hand. A slight movement in the wicker basket hanging from her shoulder accompanied by a barely audible clicking sound caught Brenda's attention.

Olivia put the basket on the floor and opened it up to reveal a tiny baby, barely more than three weeks old. 'I had to bring my daughter with me,' she said. 'I hope you don't mind, but I've no one to leave her with. She won't be any trouble, I promise you.'

Brenda gestured what she hoped would be interpreted as this being no problem and her being quite happy about it. Olivia's understanding came as a wan smile of gratitude.

After a slight pause she continued. 'I expect you have already guessed there isn't much point in me having a massage. You wouldn't be able to find enough smooth skin on my body to work on, even with a finger tip,' she said with a weary, joyless little laugh.

'I've heard a lot about you from the disfigured people like me who live – if you can call it living – mostly unseen, either tucked away from the rest of the world in various institutions, or, for those of us who prefer to risk being seen, the dark corners of the streets, where we can at least see life carrying on around us.

'You've become quite famous in places most people don't even know exist. The kind of places they wouldn't be able to imagine in a million years. Cult status even. A sort of modern-day, female Robin Hood figure, only instead of feeding the poor the rumour is that you'll help with some very personal needs.

'Don't worry, I didn't come here for any of that,' she said flatly. 'But it's mostly about how you react to people like me and how you treat us with dignity and respect – even love, they say – that has made you so famous. But then, you're one of us aren't you? Maybe that's what makes the difference.

'Anyway, I'd like to spend the hour I've booked just talking to you, even though I know you can't speak. But I understand that makes you a very good listener. And I really, really would like someone to just listen to me for once, without being distracted by what I look like.'

Brenda tried signing her agreement, but seeing the blank look on Olivia's face, quickly wrote a note instead: 'Olivia, it would be a pleasure to listen to you.'

Olivia read it and gave Brenda another wan smile before starting to talk again. 'I could tell you about the viral infection that is the cause of my condition, or how I was once a beautiful baby and even a child until I was ten, when my body started to change into the hideous monster it's become.

'Gradually, I lost all my friends. Even my mother eventually became too embarrassed to be seen with me. She was unmarried and estranged from whatever family she once had somewhere in the southern part of America. Alabama, I think.

'When I was eighteen she got into some sort of trouble, drugs I believe, and she was deported back to the States as an illegal immigrant. I didn't even know she was here illegally. I was OK because I'd been born here and my father was British, a soldier, but he was killed by a bomb in Northern Ireland before I was born and before he and my mother could get married – if they were ever going to. And I'm not sure about that because my mother wouldn't ever talk about him.

'Anyhow, as I said, I was OK. By the time my mother was deported I had been getting regular treatment on the NHS for years, not that anyone can really do anything much for this condition.

'But look now, I've spent all this time talking about myself and I really didn't want to do that. Except, I suppose in some way it's important to me for you to know where I'm coming from. I really wanted to talk about my baby and the kind of future I'd like for her.

'I don't know who the father is. It was in a dark alleyway. I was drinking heavily back then and this man, a big young man, even more drunk than I was, came at me in the darkness. Technically it would have been rape if I'd offered any resistance but, truthfully, I didn't. Why would I? My only thought was to stay in the dark and pray he couldn't see me clearly until we'd finished,' she said with a bitter laugh. 'If this was going to be the first and only sexual encounter I was ever going to have, I wanted it to be good. So, instead of fighting him off, or yelling out, I gave it everything I had.

'Of course it was a big disappointment. Especially after all the hoopla you hear about it growing up. Satisfying in an animal kind of way I suppose, but I was too terrified of him being able to see me to relax enough to enjoy it I think.

'Anyway, after he was done he just stumbled away. But not before he'd seen what I looked like. I'll never forget his look of complete revulsion. He looked like he was watching a horror film and he put his hand up to cover his mouth. Stammered an apology of sorts as he zipped up his pants and kept repeating he hadn't realised. Would never have done it if he'd known and so on.

'Then he had this look of cold fear. He asked me if you could catch what I had. Suppose I should have said "Yes". Part of me wanted to, but I felt kind of grateful to him, so instead I just had a little fun and told him it would probably be OK. But, if he wanted to be absolutely sure, he should wash his bits that had touched me in camel's milk within twenty-four hours of contact. I said something about this being the only known source of the enzyme that was the natural antidote to what I had. I chuckled for quite a while after that, imagining him wildly searching London for camel's milk!

'Of course, it was a complete surprise to find out later that that one encounter had left me pregnant. At first I was in total shock, but once I found out the baby would be very unlikely to have inherited my condition, I relaxed and began to love the idea of becoming a mum. And look, now I have this completely beautiful baby that is a part of me, and a part of two mysterious families I never knew, one English, the other American. I have such dreams and hopes for her.'

Then she stooped down gently to widen the top of the basket and Brenda saw in her beautiful eyes a look of the purest, saddest, love she had ever seen as she gazed at the tiny unblemished figure of her daughter soundly sleeping.

'I guess our time is almost up,' she said, still looking at the baby. 'I can't afford to pay you for any more, I'm afraid. Before we go I wonder if you would be kind enough just to warm this bottle of baby feed for me? I know Rebecca's going to wake up any minute now and when she does she's going to want feeding, I can tell you!' she said with a smile that for a moment seemed to reflect genuine joy.

'I don't suppose you know how to do it, not having babies yourself. It's easy. Just warm a pan of water and stand the bottle in it for a couple of minutes,' she said, putting the bottle in Brenda's outstretched hands. 'Quickest if you warm the water in the electric kettle first and then just pour it into a pan. If you don't mind I'll just use your bathroom while you're doing that, then Rebecca and I will be all set for our journey home.'

Brenda nodded and, pointing at the bathroom door, took the bottle into the kitchen with her. She was struck by Olivia's use of American terminology: 'bathroom', 'all set' and 'pants'. There was more of her mother in her than Olivia realised.

With the noise of the kettle coming to the boil, Brenda never heard the soft click of the front door being quietly opened. When she returned with the warm bottle of milk she sat down to wait for her visitor to reappear.

While she was waiting she looked at the baby, now just beginning to stir in the bottom of the basket. Little Rebecca opened her tiny eyes briefly and looked directly up at Brenda with that uncluttered, inquisitive and uncomprehending innocence babies have.

It was then that Brenda noticed the envelope in the basket. It was addressed to her in large, bold writing. Immediately Brenda sensed that something was wrong. She knocked gently on the bathroom door. When there was no answer from inside, Brenda tried the handle. The door opened to confirm her mounting fear. The bathroom was empty.

Looking quickly around, she went to the front door and saw at once it had been opened and was now left standing ajar. She ran into the street but could not see any sign of her client in either direction. It was one of those moments when she was acutely aware of her own handicap. How she longed to be able to stop

139

a passer-by and quickly ask if they had seen a severely disfigured young woman heading towards them. At least she knew Olivia could never pass unnoticed, even on the busiest of streets.

Her head started to spin until the first faint, insistent cries of a waking baby demanding to be fed brought her back to her senses.

Now Brenda had a whole new set of worries and hurriedly dialled Nina's number, signalling the emergency code with her clicker.

After some initial hesitation Brenda heard Nina asking, 'Is that you Brenda? Is that a baby I can hear? Is this an emergency?'

Carefully, while trying to control the sense of panic that was rising in direct proportion with the baby's cries, Brenda clicked back 'Yes'.

'OK, I'll be right there,' she heard Nina say before the phone was hurriedly put down.

While waiting for Nina to arrive, Brenda picked up the basket with the baby in it and began swinging it gently backwards and forwards. She knew enough from remembering the times with her own brothers and sisters that babies like to be rocked. This had an immediate, if temporary, effect in quieting the cries of hunger.

It was only a matter of minutes before Nina joined her, wearing a look of enquiry poised on the edge of alarm. In order to explain and needing both hands to sign, Brenda put down the basket. Almost immediately the pitiful little cries began again, but this time with renewed intensity.

Nina knew exactly what to do. She picked up the basket and resumed the gentle swinging motion while Brenda explained the situation as best she could.

'So you're saying the mother was here as a client and now she's gone? Do you mean gone out to get something, leaving you to baby sit? Or do you mean gone as in you think she might have abandoned her baby with you deliberately?'

'I don't know,' Brenda responded with frantic motions of her hands. 'But I have this awful feeling she has left the baby here for good.'

'Well, I think it is way too soon to assume something like that,' Nina said, trying to sound both practical and reassuring. 'Maybe she had to put money in a parking meter, or she is diabetic and forgot some medicine she had to get, or something.

'Anyway, right now, it seems to me the important thing is to get this baby fed. Has that been warmed?' Nina asked, pointing to the feeding bottle standing on the table.

'Yes, but about ten minutes ago.'

'It should still be fine,' Nina said, gently lifting the baby out of the basket and expertly installing her in the crook of one arm. Taking the bottle with the other hand, she soon had Rebecca feeding hungrily and contentedly.

'It's a skill, a mother's instinct, you never really forget,' she said in answer to Brenda's look of grateful admiration.

It was only after she had been watching Nina for a while that Brenda remembered the envelope in the basket. She picked it up, tore it open and, with growing apprehension, sat down to read the letter she found inside.

Dear Brenda,

If you are reading this letter it is because I made a decision after meeting with you today.

Had my own instincts not confirmed the reputation you have amongst those of us who exist on the forgotten margins of society, I would not have left Rebecca with you. I had to come and meet you for myself to be sure I was doing the right thing for Rebecca in leaving her there.

Before continuing, I need to tell you not to bother trying to look for me. I realise how easy it would be for me to be found, were you to tell the authorities (I can't exactly hide in a crowd can I?). So, I want you to know I will have ended my life within less than half an hour of leaving you.

Brenda looked at her watch; it was now approximately thirty minutes since Olivia had slipped out.

She was about to resume reading when her doorbell rang. In a sudden moment of hope, Brenda sprang up and hurried to open the door. The anxious look of relief disappeared when she hurriedly pulled open the door and was confronted by her next appointment of the day. The dishevelled hunchback with the club foot and unkempt appearance was a fairly frequent client whom Brenda knew well. The massages she gave him genuinely relieved the constant pain he felt.

'Sorry I'm a bit later than I should be Brenda,' Dan said, stepping awkwardly into the room. 'They've closed off Earls Court station. Some woman threw herself under our train just as we were coming into the platform. They kept us cooped up before we were escorted off through a couple of doors at the front end.

'Of course I was more or less at the back of the train, still in the tunnel when we came to a screeching halt. Had to wait for everyone else to move up first before I could get off. They were just bringing the body up onto the platform when I got there, covered up of course. But I heard someone say whoever it was had horrible growths all over their skin. Decapitated they said.'

Then he saw Brenda's face. 'What's the matter? You look like you've seen a ghost or something. Are you all right?' his voice trailed off.

Brenda motioned to him to take a seat on the chair just inside the door, while she went back to where Nina was feeding the baby with a far-off contented expression on her face. She did not even look up when Brenda returned.

Brenda started quickly writing a note explaining that the woman who had jumped under the train was almost certainly known to her. Then, as a vaguely formed thought occurred to her, she crumpled it up and wrote instead, 'I'm so sorry Dan, but I'm not feeling too well. I have a fever, which I think may be flu. Please can we change your appointment to the same day, same time in two weeks? The massage will be free then.'

Hurrying back she handed it to Dan, while at the same time opening the door to let him out. Fortunately he needed no encouragement to leave. As the destitute all know, illness of any kind is the number one enemy and the golden rule is to stay well away from anyone who might be infectious.

'Thought you didn't look too good Brenda,' Dan said, shuffling as quickly as he could out of the door, taking care to neither shake Brenda's hand nor touch the door handle. 'Decent of you to make it a free one next time though. I won't say no as cash is a bit tight at the moment. See you in two weeks, then. Hope you're feeling better soon,' and, with a little wave of his hand, he headed for the ramp rather than the steep stone steps. Dan liked to talk to anyone who would listen. And Brenda didn't want him gossiping to all and sundry about the baby he'd seen in her flat.

Returning inside, Brenda gave Nina a grateful smile and sat down again to continue reading Olivia's letter.

> This is not something impulsive, I've thought about almost nothing else since Rebecca was born. But realistically, what kind of a mother could I be to my beautiful child?
>
> Please try to see and understand this from my point of view. I'm doing this for the good of my daughter and the great love I feel for her – a love which is even stronger because I feel no love for myself.
>
> If you are able to do this for me, I want you to know the enormous gratitude I feel as I write and (although it may seem perverse!) the honour I do you in entrusting my most precious little daughter to your love and care.
>
> I've made it as easy as I can for you. At the moment she is off any known 'radar'. As far as the authorities are concerned she doesn't yet exist.
>
> If you agree to this, I want you to be her mother and for her to grow up knowing and accepting only you as her mother. I'd like you to do this for as long as you can until you think the time is right to tell her about me.
>
> Please never tell her about this letter and destroy it once you

have made your decision. Also, please never tell her how I died. Just say it was my illness – which, in a way, it is.

At the bottom of Rebecca's basket you will find three envelopes. Two contain money. One is your standard fee (in case you decide you can't carry out my wish). Another contains all the money I have managed to save and scrape together before coming to see you. It's not much, but it is everything I have to give you towards what caring for Rebecca will cost you. I know it probably won't even cover the first six months of her life, but it is everything I could pull together (I even sold my blankets this morning).

If you decide you can't take Rebecca, please would you keep this money somewhere safe for her – maybe open a Post Office savings account?

The third envelope contains a letter for Rebecca. But, as it also contains a thousand kisses trapped in it, which must not be allowed to escape, it must remain unopened by anyone but her. It is for you to give her one day, when you judge the time is right.

I realise I'm asking a great deal of you and I'm putting you in an awful moral dilemma, but, as one of us, living on the outside of society, this will come as nothing new. I know enough about you from your reputation to know that, if you agree to be her mother, Rebecca will never want for love, care or protection. And what more could any parent want for their child?

It's getting late, and as I shall be bringing Rebecca to you in the morning I need to finish this so I can spend what remains of the night just looking at my precious little daughter as she sleeps so peace-fully and so unaware of the cruel burdens we carry in this world.

Oh, just one more thing you should know about me. Although I don't go to church, at least not when others are there (what church would want me?) and although I have a good deal of suspicion of religion – despite everything that has happened to me, I do believe in God and Jesus Christ. So, I would like Rebecca to know about God too.

In anticipation of your positive response to my outrageous request, I'm going to risk telling you of the enormous debt of gratitude I will always owe you. I could only wish we had had a chance to know each other before today.

With eternal thanks and love,
Olivia

PS. Whatever your decision – one further small request when you've made it. Please gently hug my little girl and give her tiny forehead one last kiss from me. Whisper to her that it comes from her mother with more love than she will ever know until, perhaps, she herself becomes a mother one day. After that, no more. All her maternal affection should come from, and be enjoyed by, her new mother – be that you (as I fervently hope) or an adoptive mother.

Thank you

Brenda put the letter carefully back in its envelope and sat deep in thought until her concentration was broken by the sound of Nina's voice as she spoke gently to the baby she was holding in her arms.

'There, I expect that feels much better now you're fed,' she said, putting the almost empty bottle to one side.

Resting Rebecca on her knee Nina looked over at Brenda. 'Are you going to tell me what all this is about?' she asked quietly.

After only a moment of hesitation Brenda gave the envelope to Nina who responded by handing Rebecca over to Brenda saying, 'You're going to have to hold her if you expect me to read this. If she starts to cry put her up front ways across one of your shoulders and gently pat her back. It just means she needs to burp.'

Brenda took the baby gingerly, but she was relieved that Rebecca seemed quite content to lie across her lap, looking up at her with a potent mixture of curiosity and (could it possibly be?) an expression of silent pleading.

Looking down at this tiny thing, Brenda was surprised at how she was unable to meet Rebecca's innocently enquiring gaze without soon looking away. It was as if she was afraid of being drawn into something by Rebecca that she wasn't ready even to contemplate, let alone decide upon.

Completely outlandish though it was, Brenda could see how Olivia's (was that even her real name she wondered?) wild plan for her daughter's future just might work – precisely because they were, all of them, outside the system.

But how could she possibly be Rebecca's 'mother'? She was sure Olivia couldn't have known her true gender and, if she had, would she still have wanted to entrust her precious daughter's future care and upbringing to her so passionately? Almost certainly not, Brenda thought, which now left little alternative but to hand Rebecca over to the correct authority. But that was something Olivia had made clear would be her least preferred option.

Brenda was torn between wanting to fulfil Olivia's last desperate wish for her daughter's welfare and the realisation that it might, in the end, be better for Rebecca to be taken for adoption into a normal family (whatever 'normal' might mean). It was, at that moment, an insurmountable dilemma that Brenda felt woefully inadequate to try and resolve.

Nina had finished reading Olivia's letter and now sat with it folded on her lap. She was studying Brenda and Rebecca together with a thoughtful look on her face. 'So the young woman who jumped on the line at Earls Court was Rebecca's mother?' she enquired in the sort of way that only required a hesitant nod from Brenda. 'I overheard your client telling you about it. Presumably, Olivia, Rebecca's mother, didn't know you were born male? Is that what's bothering you?'

Again Brenda nodded.

'Well stop it. Here's what I think. Just look at that baby. Happy, contented, interested and feeling totally safe with you. You're a natural mother in all but the biological sense Brenda. OK, so there may be some things down the line that only a real woman is equipped to help with. Not that you aren't a real woman in every way except biologically.

'But what is a grandmother for if not being able to step in when needed? And, Brenda, I want to be Rebecca's grandmother.'

Brenda looked over at her landlady in stunned amazement as she took in what she had said. For a while she just sat there in bewilderment before she finally got up and placed Rebecca into Nina's eagerly outstretched arms. In Sign she then asked Nina to explain exactly what she meant.

'It's easy really. Olivia was right. You will be a wonderful mother and I have the experience and the love to be a good mother to you and a good grandmother to Rebecca. Together we will be her family and give her the love, care and upbringing her mother wanted when she chose you to care for her.'

'It's just not that simple,' Brenda signed back furiously.

'Oh, and why not?' retorted Nina.

'Well, for a start it must be illegal. I could get us both into all sorts of trouble over this.'

'Brenda, what you do almost every day is illegal. Many of your clients are probably in this country illegally. Letting you do what you do in my building is breaking the law also. Why would either of us suddenly become concerned about the law? We know why we do these things. Isn't that good enough? One thing we can be sure of is that this little Rebecca will not want for love.'

And that was how the decision was made. Aided by Nina, Brenda would accept the challenge of being Rebecca's mother.

There was no time to lose and after the baby had been put to bed, Nina started straight away to teach Brenda the things she would need to know about the immediate practicalities of motherhood.

When she got into bed herself much later that night Nina painfully recalled the time when she had been so close to ending her own life in Dubrovnik. Now, just a few years later, here she was in a new country with a new life and a new family.

She drifted off to sleep bewildered that life could be turned upside down so suddenly, but still keep going in a wholly different and previously unimagined direction.

19

SITTING COMFORTABLY IN a window seat, following an airline lunch that was better than he'd expected, Robert sat back and started to ponder the whole extraordinary odyssey into which he seemed to have found himself suddenly plunged.

Things had been moving so rapidly over the last forty-eight hours that he had hardly had time to stop and think about them. Now, with five hours ahead of him before landing in Boston, he had, for the first time, the opportunity to go over in his mind all the events of the past three days.

Assuming that he had indeed got the winning ticket raised the moral dilemma of to just whom the staggering proceeds of this win might really belong?

Was it to the depositor of the ticket in the Sunday collection plate, who, were they to know its true worth, would now assuredly wish to claim it was put there in error?

Was it to the Church, which would make no claim on the personally abusive notes and other odd detritus periodically left in the collection plate, but who would surely mount an aggressive claim were they to know the value of this particular 'offering'? (Of this Robert felt certain, despite the fact that under the Powerball lottery rules, the Church of England could hardly claim the necessary qualifications of residency in the United States.)

Or was it indeed to him, the finder of the ticket in the collection plate, a proportion of the financial contents of which were normally used to boost the stipend of his living costs anyway?

Was he therefore free to give this ticket to his good friend Andreas Doria, a citizen of the United States, who could then, quite legitimately, claim the prize and, if he so chose, gift all his winnings over to his friend Robert Melton?

Robert knew too that had he taken this 'offering' seriously and called the bishop or Church Commissioners for permission to keep this peculiar American lottery ticket before the draw, they would almost certainly have agreed, but not before chastising him for wasting their time with such a frivolous request.

On balance, Robert felt the moral dilemma of ownership, although complicated, was at least tipped in his favour. He was, though, still worried by the uncomfortable knowledge that only he and Andreas knew how he had come into possession of the ticket and how much this might have a bearing on this self-justifying way of thinking.

At some point in his deliberations Robert realised he must have drifted off to sleep because he was now being awakened with instructions to prepare for landing at Boston's Logan Airport.

As he came through the doors leading out from the customs and baggage claim area, Robert immediately spotted Andreas waiting to greet him. It was very good to see his friend again.

Once they were in the car, he and Andreas began catching up on the four years since they had last seen each other. This was Robert's first visit to America and he was fascinated by everything he saw and by every new experience.

He marvelled at the tall buildings, and was even fascinated by the toll booths at the entrance to the Sumner Tunnel, through which, Andreas told him, they drove deep under Boston Harbor. He was intrigued by the concept of the 'State Line' as they crossed the border from Massachusetts into New Hampshire and was amazed at the quantity of snow, the trees, the frozen lakes and the increasing beauty of the countryside as they drove north up I-93 towards the state's largest city, Manchester, where St Jerome's Abbey and College were located.

'This is nothing, my friend. Wait until I take you further north, up towards the White Mountains,' Andreas told him. 'Then you will see real beauty and wide open spaces.'

Andreas had arranged for Robert to stay in one of the Abbey's plainly furnished but comfortable guest rooms. He had just finished settling in when there was a tap at his door from Andreas, who had come to collect him to go for a pre-dinner drink. 'Are you all cleaned up and ready to come and meet the Abbot?' his friend enquired.

'Before we do that,' Robert said, 'I want you to take a look at the lottery ticket. I can't stand the suspense of not knowing for sure that I haven't somehow got it all wrong and worrying that the little piece of paper I have will turn out to be worthless.

'If that happens I'll spend the rest of my life trying to repay you for the cost of my airline ticket over here and I'll have no way of ever being able to afford to get back. So, come in, close the door and let me give you the ticket to look at while I look out of the window and hold my breath!'

'I agree, it's a good beginning,' replied Andreas quietly, coming into the room and closing the door behind him. 'But, Robert, the only way we'll know for sure is when it is presented to the State Lottery Commission.'

'I'm beginning to think you love all this cloak and dagger stuff,' laughed Robert uneasily, while retrieving the ticket from the envelope in which he had placed it for safety in his pocket. Nervously, he now handed it over to Andreas.

'I don't think you have any idea just how big the media frenzy is about this huge, single-ticket, jackpot win,' Andreas responded.

He took the ticket over to the light, silently inspected it on both sides and then proceeded to do it again before looking up at his friend without speaking. The expression frozen on his face made Robert's heart stop.

'Come on Andreas. What is it? Say something – I can't stand the suspense. I've got it wrong haven't I? I can see it in your face.'

Andreas remained silently regarding his friend with what Robert had correctly recognised as a look of deep, compassionate concern. At last he spoke.

'On the contrary, my poor friend, I believe you have the sole winning ticket that will make you the inheritor of one of the largest gambling fortunes the world has ever seen.'

'So why the sad look on your face?' Robert asked, already knowing what the answer would be.

'Because, my poor very rich friend, you will now have to wrestle with Mammon in a titanic struggle between the forces of good and evil. I fear for you in this situation, where clearly the temptation to evil is surely going to have a long head start. In helping you with this, my moment of temptation will be just that – but a moment.

'After collecting the money, however that is done, I will immediately be handing all of it over to you, where that sort of staggering wealth and what it can offer you will begin working on your mind. Truly I don't envy you that and can only pray you are of a stronger character than I am. I know I would quickly weaken in any prior resolve and find myself insidiously and inexorably drawn towards the temptations and sweet attractions of self-indulgence, leading me inevitably deeper and deeper into sin.'

The serious tone of his friend's voice and the genuine look of compassion on his face touched Robert deeply. He put a hand on Andreas's arm and said as reassuringly as he could, 'Don't worry Andreas, I have already vowed to myself that, were this to happen, I would only undertake what I see as the administration of this mission in conjunction with the Holy Spirit, in whom I long ago learned to put my faith in times of any temptation greater than I felt I could withstand. He has never, ever let me down when I have wholeheartedly and genuinely asked Him for His help.'

'Therein lies the problem,' Andreas replied. 'When the sweet siren voice of temptation sings, all too often we deliberately *don't* ask the Holy Spirit for help, precisely because we know He will if we do! Nevertheless I'm reassured and comforted by what you say.

'One piece of advice before we get on with the task in hand. Try always to remember that if the "good" and "evil" that exists in each of us were to be likened to two dogs fighting, the question might be which one of them will win in the end? The answer is simple: it will be the one you feed!

'This is an old and wise saying of the native Americans, from long before the arrival of Christianity among them.'

And with that, Andreas handed the ticket back to Robert.

'Why don't you fill out your details and sign the back of it now for safety?' Robert suggested.

'No, my friend. The moment I do that it becomes mine and I am sufficiently weak of will as to not want to allow the forces of evil to have any more time to play havoc with my mind in tempting me than I have to. Tomorrow we will go together to the local offices of the State Lottery Commission, where I will sign and add my details to the back of the ticket, just prior to its presentation in registering my claim.

'It seems I will be required to fill in an official claim form and thereafter it will take up to five working days for the lottery authorities to authenticate the ticket and my claim to it. Meanwhile the decision has to be made as to whether I choose to receive the prize paid out as an annuity, or to select a reduced capital sum as a one-time cash payment.

'The choice is obvious. It must be the one-time cash payment, paid as a cheque, which I can then immediately endorse over to you in its entirety. There will of course be tax to be paid, but I think it's safe to say you will be left with somewhere very close to 200 million dollars to be rubbing along with. The Lottery Commission will, of course, want to put you in the hands of one of their recommended financial advisers to stop you, intoxicated by your stupendous new wealth, from going hog wild mad with the money and bringing the lottery unwelcome publicity.'

'You make it all sound very daunting,' Robert said apprehensively.

'Procedurally, I understand it is all quite straightforward, but the consequences and responsibilities attached to such great wealth will indeed be daunting, my friend,' Andreas replied.

'After supper I recommend you have an early night. The combination of jetlag and all this excitement will have made you quite tired I suspect, and tomorrow will be another day of high excitement and anticipation.'

Despite his nap on the plane Robert was indeed more tired than he realised and the prospect of an early night now seemed very welcome.

20

THE FOLLOWING DAY, after breakfast, Robert and Andreas set off on the thirty-minute drive north up to Concord, the state capital. This was where the regional office of the State Lottery Commission was located.

Father Jordan, the Abbot of St Jerome's, had agreed to give Andreas a week of leave from his teaching and spiritual duties to be able to spend time with his friend from England. They had all had an enjoyable evening together the night before when, after what had been intended as only an introduction, Father Jordan had invited them to join him for dinner. For Robert, it had been a welcome diversion.

The abbot had liked Robert. He had been impressed by his zeal and energy, especially when he had been talking about his passion for what he thought he could do in turning around the fortunes of St Mungo's, if only he could have a little support from his bishop in this task. However, the Abbot was shrewd and wise about both people and human nature, and there was something about Robert that worried him. He couldn't put his finger on it and he didn't think it had anything to do with the barely suppressed excitement that seemed about to bubble over in Robert once or twice during the evening. At first, he put this down to it being the start of his first visit to America – but no, it was something else. Something that made Robert seem vulnerable to him.

Not for the first time did the abbot find himself impressed by the calibre of priest attracted to the Episcopal or Protestant denominations. It was a pity, he thought, that such vigorous and charismatic young men were often lost to Catholicism over the issue of celibacy.

Now, sitting in the car outside the offices of the State Lottery Commission on State Street in Concord, Robert handed the Powerball lottery ticket to Andreas who, reluctantly, filled out the details requested and signed the back. That done, they went inside together to claim the jackpot win.

Andreas handed the ticket over to the bored-looking clerk behind the desk and then they watched to see what would happen next. They didn't have to wait long before they were rewarded by an audible gasp, widened eyes, a hand pressed over an open mouth and a softly spoken 'Oh my God, you have the winning ticket!'

All trace of boredom vanished as the now electrified clerk forced himself to become business-like in going through the process for handling a single win jackpot claim, something he had never had to do before. And what a jackpot!

As Andreas had correctly predicted, there were formal claim forms to be filled out and questions to be answered. One of these was whether or not Andreas would be happy for his identity to be divulged, or whether he would prefer to have anonymity.

The clerk couldn't hide his disappointment when Andreas emphatically chose the latter. Had he not, the humble lottery clerk in rural New Hampshire would have been catapulted from obscurity right into the centre of national attention. He could imagine the commentary he would be asked to give on television when he was asked about the winner's reaction when he first acknowledged the likelihood that Andreas had the winning ticket, subject only to verification.

He imagined himself vividly describing how the winner had almost fainted in front of him when given the news, along with similar little embellishments of the truth designed to feed the press stories that would keep him and his little office in the national news for as long as possible.

What a boost it would have given to the Powerball publicity machine too. They would be portrayed as wisely and responsibly throwing an avuncular arm around the winner in taking him into temporary protective hiding, to shield him from unscrupulous peddlers of everything from shady investment schemes to hard luck stories and phoney charities.

Sadly the truth was that, as the sole winner of the biggest lottery jackpot the world had ever known, Andreas was a disappointment. Showing no excitement, he remained frustratingly calm and unresponsive.

The clerk felt this muted reaction might be explained when he looked at the completed claim form handed back to him. Under 'Profession', Andreas had written 'Benedictine monk'. Having himself been raised as a Catholic, the clerk had some idea of what that meant and wondered at the irony of how a monk's vow of poverty could be reconciled to such sudden wealth.

Still, he was not prepared for Andreas's next comment.

'When this goes through, I want the prize to be paid in the one-off capital lump sum option. And I want to assign it all immediately to my friend here,' Andreas said, indicating with a nod towards Robert.

'What, all of it?' asked the incredulous clerk. 'Every penny?'

'Yes, every single penny,' Andreas answered emphatically. 'I'm assuming at that point it does not infringe lottery rules that he is neither an American nor even a resident of the United States?'

'Er ... no. Technically, at that point the money is all yours and you are free to give it to whomever you wish, I believe. But I'll check on that if you like?'

'Yes, please,' Andreas answered.

'Your friend's name and profession?' enquired the clerk.

Before Andreas could stop him, Robert had replied, 'A poor, lowly Church of England vicar, originally from Australia, by the name of ...'

'I don't see that his name matters,' interrupted Andreas. 'Especially as he also will want anonymity.'

The clerk nodded. But privately he could not look beyond the utter tragedy for the media who would be missing out on this extraordinary story that was becoming more bizarre by the minute. First of all for this vast jackpot to have been scooped by a Benedictine monk, who had taken a vow of poverty. And now to be told that he was immediately going to give the entire fortune to a friend, who just happened to be a vicar in the Church of England.

The clerk knew the press would go completely mad for this and would probably pay well for such a good story. The temptation of that thought had now entered his mind and would not easily be banished.

After they had finished the formalities of registering the claim, Andreas and Robert thanked the clerk and left. They now had five days to wait for the verification and actual payout to be made.

Back in the car, they commented on the change that had come over the clerk between the time when they had walked into the office and when they had left. On arrival, they had been met with bored indifference; but by the time they left, his whole attitude towards them had been transformed to one of great deference, almost obsequious sycophancy, as he rose from his desk to come around and hold the door open for them.

Andreas said, 'I'm afraid from now on you're going to have to start getting used to that sort of thing, Robert. It's the strange effect money seems to have on people. Unless you have achieved recognition as a living saint, the complete absence of money renders you invisible. Modest means brings you into circulation. Wealth brings you respect, and great wealth brings you awe and great respect. The sort of staggering wealth that will shortly be yours is likely to confer upon you almost the status of a deity. People will seek your opinion on every subject and will hang on your every word. That is what I worry about for you.

'Strange to think how, just a few days ago, I would doubt anyone, beyond your friends and maybe some of your parishioners, would either care about or want your opinion on anything. You would simply not be thought of as "interesting". Apprise these same people of your new net worth and suddenly your opinions on everything from geopolitics to matters of science or global economics will be eagerly sought. In effect, you will have quite suddenly become interesting.

'It is not you that has changed. It is they that have changed in the way they see and react to you. The frailty of human nature I suppose. Your challenge will be to remain unaffected by this wholesale change in attitude towards you. To remain grounded, to remember your vocational calling, your vows to serve God in his Church – even if in the wrong one – and to resist the siren call of Mammon with all his sweet temptations. No small task, my friend.'

Robert smiled at the friendly jibe at the Church of England. He knew Andreas did not mean it.

As it was still early in the day and the rest of it stretched before them, Andreas had suggested they might drive up to find the small town of New London, where the lottery ticket had been identified as having been originally purchased.

Leaving Concord, as they made their way over to Interstate 89, they drove past the world-famous St Paul's School, a co-ed boarding school, internationally renowned for its academic excellence.

'It's difficult to imagine, but some of the most likely future leaders of this great nation are right now probably to be found studying behind those walls,' Andreas remarked as they passed the relatively unassuming entrance.

'It is part of the enigma of New Hampshire, that one of the poorer, most easily overlooked states should be the home of so many schools and colleges offering such high standards of education – at least in the private school sector. You've got St Paul's at one end of Interstate 89 and Dartmouth College at the other, and numerous further excellent private schools scattered in between.'

They headed northwards on I-89 signed towards Lebanon and Hanover. Robert was again struck by the beauty of the state and its mixture of evocative

Anglo-Saxon, native American and biblical-sounding place names. Driving up a beautiful wooded river valley, they had passed towns called Penacook and Contoocook, another called Hopkinton, and were now approaching Warner.

From the highway Robert could see the white conical spire of a colonial-style, clapboard church nestling on the other side of the valley, surrounded by equally attractive, typically New England, clapboard colonial houses. Many of them had smoke rising straight up from substantial antique brick or stone chimneys into a vast, clear, deep blue winter sky.

From inside the warmth of the car, you could almost smell the still, crisp, coldness of the air outside. It was a very dry cold, devoid of humidity at this time of year. Robert, used to the less extreme, but much damper, grey, cold of London found it strange how much more bearable this dry, bright, cold seemed to be.

Once past Warner and now approaching the exit to Sutton, the highway signs had started to indicate the New London exit, twelve miles ahead.

'Almost there,' Andreas remarked. 'I wonder what sort of place it will turn out to be? I suppose it's quite likely that whoever put that lottery ticket in your Sunday collection plate, having bought it here in New Hampshire, might actually come from this area. Maybe they even live in New London and were on a visit to old London?'

'Perhaps visiting London, staying in a hotel near St Mungo's, they went to church on Sunday morning, discovered they didn't have much in the way of the Queen's currency and, worrying that it might be difficult to find somewhere to change money on a Sunday, found the lottery ticket in a pocket or purse and, on an impulse, decided to leave that instead?'

'OK, Sherlock Holmes,' joked Robert.

'Oh come now, I think it's more like a case for the dapper Hercule Poirot. My brilliant deduction is worthy of his little grey cells *n'est-ce pas*? But you've got to admit it's A, possible and B, quite logical,' chuckled Andreas.

Uncomfortably, Robert realised it was. Although the original purchaser of the ticket would be unlikely to know if it was the winning ticket, unless of course they had made a separate note of the numbers, or always played the same numerical sequence. He comforted himself with the thought that, anyway, if the claimant remained anonymous, it would be hard for anyone to prove. A story quite as fantastical as the journey of this lottery ticket would never be believed as grounds for a claim. How surprisingly often fact did indeed turn out to be stranger than fiction, thought Robert.

He was ashamed to admit to himself that he was already fighting off feelings of a furtive guilt about the true ownership of the lottery ticket and the windfall it was about to bestow on him. With an effort, he consciously pushed the matter from his mind.

They had reached Exit 11 marked to New London and Colby Sawyer College: New London was another college town it would seem. Coming off the exit ramp, they turned right on Route 11 East, continuing to follow the signs to New London. After about a mile they arrived at a crossroads at the crest of a hill. The view stretching in front of them was a breathtaking one of tree-covered rolling hills and distant mountains. On the right, taking full advantage of this view, sat a low, grey-painted building. The sign in front read simply 'Gray House Restaurant and Brew Pub'.

Turning left, the road took them higher up onto the spine of a long ridge, straddled by the town of New London. Robert and Andreas were immediately struck by its stunning location, its picturesque charm and its elegant, colonial architecture. There were one or two notable exceptions. On the left they passed a large, strangely futuristic building, fronted with what looked like opaque glass bricks. Robert delightedly drew Andreas's attention to the hanging sign proclaiming it to be 'Our Lady of Fatima Catholic Church'.

'Would you say that was a 1950s blight on this otherwise nearly perfect architectural landscape?' he mischievously ribbed his friend.

'A failed ecumenical experiment in which they must have employed an Episcopalian architect,' retorted Andreas.

Robert enjoyed his friend's quick comeback.

Over on the right, they passed the gracious, ivy-clad brick buildings that formed the crescent-shaped campus centre to Colby Sawyer College, immediately beyond which stood a handsome colonial-style church with tall symmetrical windows and a fine bell tower. Robert's hopes were raised that this lovely building might prove to be the Episcopal Church, only to be dashed when, on drawing level, they saw it was in fact the First Baptist Church.

'Well I guess the Baptists got here first,' sighed Robert with a wry smile.

They were now passing the Town Green with its traditional bandstand, already festively decorated for Christmas with garlands of evergreen foliage and big red ribbons. Next to this stood a very attractive, quite imposing white clapboard building that appeared, rather improbably, to house the town offices.

Behind this was a surprising building that looked like another 1950s architectural experiment. From the cross on its roof they could tell it was also a church. On an impulse Andreas pulled over beside a well wrapped-up man, head down, hunched against the cold, making his way carefully along the snow-covered sidewalk.

'Excuse me. What church would that be?' he asked pointing over at the building.

'St Andrew's Episcopal Church,' was the muffled response from behind a thick woollen scarf.

'I'm the priest there,' the voice offered as an afterthought, before continuing on its way.

Andreas was triumphant. 'So, unless we can find another building to outdo those two, it would be fair to say we are almost equal in our despoiling of the traditional architecture of this otherwise entirely picturesque town, wouldn't you say?'

'Well they clearly felt obliged to use a Catholic architect, who must have been hell bent on revenge,' retorted Robert.

Both men laughed.

Moving on past the historic New London Inn on one side of the street and the Tracy Memorial Library on the other, it was beginning to feel like New London was almost a prototype for a Norman Rockwell characterisation of a picture-perfect New England town. Even the bank and professional buildings were attractive.

Just past Morgan Hill Bookstore it was almost a relief to find the local telephone company occupying a large nondescript, utilitarian, red-brick building on one side of the street, with the Fire Station on the other. These served as a reminder that, however picturesque, this was still a working town and not a living museum.

Andreas spotted it first. Over on the right-hand side, just past the Fire Station and Funeral Home was a rambling old clapboard building painted a deep barn-red. It had a porch across the front supported by six oversized white columns. The sign on the street read 'Baynham's New England Mercantile'.

'Hey look – there it is,' Andreas pointed. 'The place where the newspapers said the ticket was bought.'

'Shall we go in?' Robert asked.

Andreas had already slowed the car and now swung into the parking lot.

Having taken a seat at one of the tables beside a cheerful wood-burning stove, both men were now enjoying steaming hot cups of coffee. It was surprisingly good. Robert felt unaccountably nervous, as if somehow in here he would be recognised as the holder of the much sought-after, winning lottery ticket. Looking around at the other patrons, he couldn't help wondering if any of them might be the original purchaser of the ticket.

There was a group of older men gathered around one of the tables, who looked as if they met here regularly, and a couple of young mothers holding their babies while chatting amiably to each other. A single man was reading a newspaper and periodically checking the watch on his wrist. Perhaps he was waiting for someone? And there were two professional-looking women with sheaves of documents lying on the table between them. Robert idly wondered if these two were faculty from the college, or perhaps executives from a local bank?

He could not see anyone who might fit his imagined description of the lottery ticket purchaser. They all looked either too sensible and practical to be the sort to waste money on such unlikely odds as those offered in the chance to win Powerball, or to have so recently travelled to London.

But then how could one ever tell? Some of the most unlikely people were avid subscribers to the football pools, lotteries, scratch-cards and other get-rich-quick opportunities of slim to no chance of success. And these days anyone might travel to and from London.

When they had finished their coffee, Robert and Andreas decided to wander about this intriguing establishment. As they discovered, it was an eclectic emporium of widely differing and very different merchandise, ranging from a beautiful, handmade wooden canoe to a magnificent dark maroon, solid cast iron cooking range from England, called an AGA. Robert recognised it at once. It was more or less identical to the one long ago installed in the vicarage at Pembroke Villas.

Delighted to air his recently acquired knowledge of this eye-catching cooking range, he explained its more unusual characteristics to Andreas, who was having some difficulty in grasping the concept of a cooking stove that was always 'on', twenty-four hours a day.

'You can't imagine what a friend the one at the vicarage has become,' Robert enthused. 'During the worst of this winter I've all but lived in the kitchen. I can't afford to heat the rest of the house on anything but the lowest setting, just warm enough to prevent the pipes from freezing, so coming down in the morning from a very chilly bedroom to a lovely warm kitchen is something to be so grateful for. Of course the one in the vicarage is a much older model, but they're essentially the same: indestructible, unchangingly straightforward in both design and function.'

'You sound like a salesman for these things,' Andreas grumbled good-naturedly. 'It looks like a monster to me.'

'Well, yes, you either love them or hate them, and people who love them do tend to get a bit evangelistic about all the other things they can be used for besides just cooking.'

They wandered on through the store until, passing the restrooms, their attention was caught. Instead of the usual two, there were three doors in a line. The left-hand door was clearly marked 'Gentlemen', the right-hand one 'Ladies'. The door in the middle was marked 'Politicians'.

They looked at each other in bafflement before Andreas stepped forward, tapped on the middle door and gently tried the handle. He stepped backwards in surprise as the door swung easily open in his hand. Staring out at him was a bald, middle-aged man sitting on the john reading the newspaper, the expression on his face one of mild surprise and annoyance.

Momentarily taken aback, Andreas had been about to stammer an apology before hastily closing the door, when he realised he was looking at a *trompe-l'oeil*. Closer inspection showed that the man was sitting on the john with his pants up, broad suspenders firmly in place over each shoulder. On the wall behind, the artist had painted a sign that read 'In New Hampshire you'll never catch a politician with his pants down'.

Both men roared with laughter. 'Someone here must have quite a quirky sense of humour,' exclaimed Andreas.

Robert drew his attention to the artist's signature in the lower right-hand corner: Clinton Sheerr. 'Well he does, at least!'

Just then they overheard someone at the soda fountain counter asking if anyone had been in about the Powerball lottery ticket.

Robert turned round quickly and saw the man he had noticed earlier sitting by himself reading the paper, periodically checking his watch.

'Nope,' was the taciturn response from the otherwise friendly, even chatty, soda jerk.

'You people up here just don't seem to get what a big story this could be – biggest my paper ever had – and what with prime-time TV and radio! Could put this sleepy little town on the map.

'All I want is a little help to sniff this one out. Can't be that many people buy lottery tickets here and you must know more than half the regulars. It's a statistical fact that most people who habitually buy lottery tickets, buy them from the same place every week. The chances of this ticket having been bought by a tourist passing through at this time of year are about as remote as winning the jackpot itself was. Someone around here's got to have some idea who it might be.' His voice changed from a tone of bullying frustration to one of desperate pleading as he spoke.

'As I've said before, folks round here like to mind their own business,' replied the young soda jerk, adding under his breath after the man had turned to go back to his table, 'And we don't care much for inquisitive journos either.'

Although barely audible, Robert had heard his parting shot as he approached the counter, ostensibly to get a refill for his coffee. He smiled, winking conspiratorially at the young man.

'The last one – staking out the place in the hope of a scoop,' offered the assistant, nodding towards the departing back. 'Unless of course you're one too? You're not from around here are you?' he enquired, now suddenly on his guard again.

'No,' admitted Robert, 'I am that unlikely thing he was referring to, a tourist. But, just to make it even more unlikely, from London by way of Australia. An Anglican priest staying with my good friend here, a Benedictine monk from St Jerome's Abbey in Manchester.' He indicated Andreas, who had now joined them.

'My friend is showing me some of the beauty of New Hampshire. I'm already quite impressed and this little town certainly is attractive,' he added, hoping to flatter.

It seemed to work. Although still wary, the young man relaxed a little.

'Big, big fuss over this lottery ticket,' he said. 'Had a pack of journos camped out here all last week. Convinced the purchaser must be someone local and, a bit like a criminal is supposed to, would somehow feel compelled to return to the scene of the crime, so to speak.'

Robert put what he hoped was a blank look on his face. It worked.

'Suppose you know about the big win?' the young man now enquired doubtfully, noting the look on Robert's face.

'I thought the whole world must know by now,' he continued, when Robert showed no sign of comprehension. 'Someone bought a Powerball lottery ticket here couple of weeks or so back,' he explained, nodding towards the state-owned lottery ticket machine protruding above the counter. 'Single ticket win of the biggest lottery ever: 260 million dollars. And whoever it was now seems in no hurry for the money. Driving the journos and the media mad. We've had nothing but TV and radio crews and packs of press hounds swarming all over the place ever since they worked out the ticket was purchased here.

'Most of them have only gone in the last day or two. This one's the last one holding out,' he said, gesturing over to where the man was again seated reading his paper. 'I almost feel sorry for him. Guess his editor won't let him leave.

'Of course they'll all be back big time if and when the winner does show up. It's my belief that whoever has the ticket either doesn't know it yet, might be away – a lot of people from around here go to Florida for large parts of the winter – or really wasn't from here. We get quite a few people passing through during the winter. People visiting the college; salesmen and people connected to the ski industry; as well as a few random visitors and tourists, such as yourselves. If anyone I can think of from around here had the ticket, and knew they had it, they wouldn't be able to hold out this long. Just calculating the amount of bank interest being lost on a daily basis would hurt too much,' he said with a laugh.

Just then Robert noticed that the man sitting alone with the paper was no longer reading it. He was studying Robert closely. Robert found the penetration of his stare, even from a distance, quite unnerving. Folding his paper, the man got up and came over to where Robert and Andreas were standing talking to the young soda jerk. Although uninvited, he joined the group.

'Don't suppose one of you two gentlemen would know anything about who the big winner from around here might be?' he said. Although addressing them both, he didn't take his eyes off Robert.

Andreas, sensing the rising panic in Robert, moved a step closer and replied. 'It's funny. That's just what we were hearing about from this young man. I gather it's a pretty big brouhaha in this town?'

'Of course, I knew about the win, being from Manchester, but my friend here, visiting from England, didn't know anything about it – he only arrived last night from London.'

'Is that so?' the man said, not moving his eyes from Robert's face. Being the seasoned gumshoe newshound he was, although still uncertain, he looked like a man who was fairly sure he had scented blood.

It was only when the soda jerk, now eager to contribute to the conversation, offered the information that Robert was an Anglican priest from London visiting his friend, a Benedictine monk from St Jerome's College in Manchester, that the man took his gaze off Robert and, with a rather crestfallen expression, turned towards Andreas. 'So I suppose that rules you two out anyway?' he said reluctantly.

Then, as if to be sure he was being told the truth, he turned back to Robert and asked in an outwardly conversational tone of voice, 'Is this your first visit to the States?'

'Yes,' replied Robert. 'I'm from Australia originally, but I live in England now. Apart from that I've not had much opportunity to travel, so I've really been looking forward to this trip, to see even just a little bit of America.'

'Well, Padre, if that is what I'm supposed to call you, sorry but I'm a lapsed Presbyterian myself, so I get a little confused with all the different denominational titles, I hope you'll have a great visit.' The disappointment in his voice couldn't be disguised. The moment of excitement gone, he returned to his table and glumly resumed studying the paper, but with one eye always alert for the door.

It had been a narrow escape. Robert gave Andreas a look of grateful thanks. Without either of them saying anything, both men felt it would be a good idea to leave as soon as they could but, to avoid arousing any further suspicion, not too hastily. They finished their cups of coffee, said goodbye to the young man who had served them and took their leave.

Back in the car heading south again on I-89 towards Manchester, Robert said, 'I just couldn't help feeling guilty and I know I was betraying it on my face. Even when I was a little boy I always hated having to keep a secret. It made me feel as if I was somehow being dishonest. If he'd asked me outright whether I had the winning ticket I don't know what I would have done, so thank you for coming to my rescue so swiftly.'

'Did you see the way he was looking so intently at me, as if he could read my mind? For a moment or two it looked like he knew he was on to something. I suppose investigative journalists are trained in reading people's minds and body language – just like Immigration and Customs Officers.'

'Yes, my friend, a close call,' Andreas agreed. 'But one easier to deal with before your win has been confirmed and you are the owner of an eye-watering fortune. Evasion may not always be so easy, so you'd better start thinking about how you are going to handle similar situations – and worse – in the future, when I won't be there to help you out.'

21

―――

SITTING IN HIS suite at the Ritz Carlton Hotel in Boston ten days later, a period that already seemed like a lifetime, Robert thought through the extraordinary events of the past fourteen days that had changed his life forever.

A few days after he and Andreas had returned from their visit to New London, the Lottery Commission had confirmed the win. As agreed between them, Andreas had collected the money, choosing the reduced amount in order to have it as a one-time capital lump sum. After taxes were also deducted he had received a cheque in the amount of 192 million dollars.

He had also carefully elected to have the full protection of absolute anonymity, as guaranteed under the rules of the lottery. This had been a source of great disappointment to the lottery officials who could only dream of the global publicity such a win by a Benedictine monk would have generated – only then to have been further amplified when, to their collectively stunned amazement, right there in front of them, Andreas endorsed the cheque and with it the entire amount it represented, over to his friend from England, explaining as he did so that, having taken a vow of poverty, he didn't want or need the money.

Later, in private, Andreas had admitted to Robert that when he had found himself briefly holding the cheque for that amount with his name on it, he had become aware of the enormous temptation such a thing could exert. He likened it to the ring in *The Lord of the Rings*. It was, he knew, a moment of decision in which he must act swiftly and decisively before the small 'voice on his shoulder', growing ever louder and more persistent, could persuade him with seductively tempting thoughts of all the perceived good he would be able to do with that amount of money at his disposal. 'The voice', cleverly trying to find a chink in his armour, had even tried to suggest it would surely be all right just to keep back some of it.

The services of the professional financial adviser on offer to all big lottery jackpot winners were swiftly directed to Robert, who had gratefully accepted.

The following couple of days had involved the opening of a number of bank accounts in Robert's name and seemingly endless meetings to hear his adviser's broadly outlined suggestions for a prudent investment strategy.

Robert had agreed with almost everything recommended to him, except the amount he might want in his easy access checking account. Bill Temple, his new financial adviser, had suggested he should initially have as much as twenty thousand dollars in this, readily available, but essentially non-interest-earning account. Robert had been adamant that he only wanted five thousand in this account. Only commenting on how Robert would probably soon want instant access to more than this, once he got used to his wealth, Bill had agreed without further questioning.

With the money safely, if temporarily, invested, Robert had begun to take the time to consider his own position. He already knew he didn't wish to return to St Mungo's at the end of his two-week leave. He felt he needed more time to think about his future from the perspective of the distance he was now at and also in the context of his complete and dramatic change of circumstances. However, he knew what he wanted to do in the immediate future and that was to save St Mungo's.

Taking the bull by the horns he had decided to call the bishop as soon as possible after checking into the Ritz Carlton Hotel, the choice of place to stay in Boston having been made on Bill's recommendation. He had been told that this was the sort of hotel that was now commensurate with his new financial status. Robert had initially demurred at the cost, until it was pointed out that the daily interest his money was now earning far exceeded the daily room rate of even this most luxurious of hostelries.

It was alarming to realise just how quickly he was beginning to get used to taking for granted the small things his new wealth could so easily provide. Three weeks ago he had agonised over the cost of making a transatlantic telephone call; now when he picked up the phone on the beautiful antique French writing table in his suite, he hardly gave the matter a thought as he dialled the bishop's number.

After being put through, as always, to Christopher Callow en route to the bishop, Robert became aware of a new and growing self-confidence as he felt a slight irritation at the way Christopher Callow patronisingly tried to persuade him that it might be best if he were to pass a message on to the bishop. The newly confident tone in Robert's voice as he insisted on speaking directly to the bishop himself was not lost on Christopher Callow either. Something was up. He'd guessed as much. He felt a frisson of excitement in anticipation of finding out just what when he listened in on their conversation.

When the bishop came on the line Robert hardly recognised the confidence in his own voice as he began, 'Your Grace, I've got the proverbial good news and bad news for you.'

Then, without waiting, he continued, 'Giving you the bad news first — I don't intend coming back to London for a while. However, the good news overwhelmingly outweighs the bad news, and that is that I want to give you the funds to save St Mungo's.

'You see, I've come into some money.' He hoped the implication here would be of a sudden inheritance from a distant rich relative. 'And, while I know you've already agreed a sale to Barrasford Holdings, I also know they will accept a sum of twenty-five per cent of the agreed purchase price, plus their deposit with interest, in return for withdrawing from the purchase.

'I know this because I spoke to Tim James, the Chief Executive of Barrasford Holdings, less than an hour ago. So, from memory, you had agreed with them a two million pound figure for the site in total. I propose to transfer an amount equal to three and a half million pounds into your custody, from which you can repay Barrasford their deposit, plus a sum of half a million pounds.

'The balance of the money will give the Church Commissioners the two million they were expecting from Barrasford, leaving something in excess of 900 thousand left over. You and the Church Commissioners then get to keep St Mungo's as a freely given gift from me. I make only one condition to this proposal. That is, with the excess funds, they undertake to repair and then maintain the fabric of the church.'

The long silence that followed made Robert think that maybe they had been cut off. 'Your Grace?' he asked. 'Are you still there? Did you hear everything I said?'

'Yes,' came the reply after the slight time delay that customarily occurred on a transatlantic connection. 'I'm just so surprised Robert. I'm afraid you've rather caught me off guard. Of course what you propose is very generous, very generous indeed. I don't think I had properly understood how deeply you must feel about St Mungo's to make you want to be quite so … so generous.

'I have to confess to feeling a little humbled by your extraordinarily magnanimous proposal in the face of what you might rightly see as my … perhaps less than candid approach to your work in the parish.

'Of course, I must put your proposal to the Church Commissioners, but I think I can confidently predict their response and the grateful thanks they will want me to extend to you. I'll speak to them first thing tomorrow morning. Where can I find you, to get back to you?'

'I'm staying in Boston at the moment,' Robert replied.

'Are you indeed?' said the bishop. 'When I was a young curate, my very first parish was in Lincolnshire. I used to cycle into Boston regularly. Such a delightful town, I always thought.'

Now it was Robert's turn to be thrown for a moment. 'I'm not in Lincolnshire,

Bishop,' he explained. 'I'm in Boston, Massachusetts, staying at the Ritz Carlton Hotel, telephone number 617-214-8484.' Then he couldn't resist adding, 'I'm in the Presidential Suite. You can call any time, the suite has a twenty-four-hour butler service, so you can always leave a message if I'm out.'

Robert thought for one moment he heard a muffled gasp somewhere on the line that hadn't come from the bishop.

'Are you indeed?' the bishop said again, in a far less self-assured and rather more impressed manner than a moment earlier. 'Very good. I will call you first thing your time tomorrow.'

Then he remembered to ask, 'Oh, and Robert, when do you think you'll be back?'

'I don't know, your Grace,' Robert heard himself reply. 'It may be some while, as I have a number of things to take care of first.'

Robert knew the bishop could order him to come back, but he'd calculated he wouldn't under the circumstances, and because of the proposal that had just been put to him.

He allowed himself a small smile of satisfaction as he pushed to the back of his mind the uncomfortable thought that his generous offer to rescue St Mungo's might be as much about assuaging his own guilt as any real desire to save the church.

How the tables had turned, he thought as he replaced the receiver and picked up the glass of champagne on the table beside the telephone. All in all he was feeling quite pleased with himself, although maybe a little worried at just how quickly he was getting used to enjoying this new lifestyle. That had been the only bone of contention between him and Andreas before he left the hospitality of St Jerome's Abbey.

Robert had wanted to give his friend five million dollars to do what he liked with, ostensibly as a 'thank you' for his help in making the jackpot collection possible, but also, if he was being truthful with himself, to strengthen the feeling that by having Andreas willingly share in the windfall, it would somehow make what he was doing less troublesome to his own conscience.

Andreas had been adamant in refusing to accept anything. Robert had tried every argument and persuasion he could think of, pointing out that Andreas could simply give the money away to any number of good causes if he so wished.

But Andreas would not be persuaded. Even when, in final desperation, Robert had tried to get him at least to accept just a token thousand dollars in cash for a few little personal luxuries, like the new stereo system he'd said he wanted, Andreas had remained steadfast in his refusal.

This had eventually become the source of an unspoken friction between them, with Robert being upset and increasingly irritated at his friend's adamant refusal to take any share of the money. To Robert, the position Andreas had taken made it somehow feel like an unspoken indictment of his action in accepting the money as his own.

For his part, Andreas was equally alarmed and upset at the sudden and rapidly growing change he saw being wrought in his friend. It had started almost from the moment he had taken possession of the cheque. More than ever he could not help making the comparison to the ring in Tolkien's book. It made him feel guilty that he had participated in what had seemed an innocent enough adventure to start with – outwitting the combined forces of the mighty media to collect the largest jackpot in history – only to watch it take control of his friend and ultimately, he now feared, possibly destroy him.

Robert had been intending to stay at St Jerome's College as Andreas's guest and, as such, also a guest of the Abbey, for the duration of his two-week visit. But with the growing friction between them ever since the collection of the money, Robert decided it would be best for them both if he left early.

Things had come to a head on the eighth day of his visit, three days after Andreas had endorsed the jackpot-winning cheque over to him. Robert, in his frustration at being unable to get Andreas to accept any part of the money, had finally accused him of being jealous of his good fortune.

Although the accusation hurt him deeply, Andreas's only response had been to regard Robert with a look of great sadness and pity. It was as if he saw the presence of pure evil now leading his hitherto innocent friend gently by the hand towards his inexorable destruction.

That look, with its penetrative insight, had been more than Robert could stand. He resolved to leave that day. Andreas did not try to dissuade him, beyond saying that, whatever happened, he could always be certain of a warm welcome at St Jerome's any time he might need it in the future.

The patronising smile of derision with which this was greeted seemed to form on Robert's face without his consent. He immediately tried to control it. It was not after all what he felt, or the response he had wanted to give. He hoped Andreas hadn't seen.

'It's not really likely I'm ever going to need to stay here again is it?' were the sarcastic words that had come into his head to go with that smile. Fortunately they remained unspoken. But where had they come from? He needed to get away. His friend was making him uncomfortable.

Andreas had, however, glimpsed the nascent formation of what would have been more of a sneer than a smile. He had also noted Robert's effort to control it and the look, almost of surprise, that had quickly replaced it. Andreas was now very worried for his friend. What had started out as something of a grand escapade over which they had both been able to laugh and joke in a harmlessly conspiratorial sort of way, had swiftly turned into something of a much more serious and sinister nature.

He knew he must pray ardently for his friend, in the same way he prayed daily for a situation from a long-ago childhood. The thought that he might now have been an unwitting party to the leading of another friend into trouble was, he knew, going to torture him.

Andreas had been surprised when, in coming to say goodbye, Robert had said, 'Andreas will you thank Father Jordan for the kind hospitality of St Jerome's for me, please?'

'I think he is in his study if you'd like to say goodbye and thank him yourself,' Andreas had answered.

Robert did not know why, but instinctively he wanted to avoid Father Jordan's wisely penetrating eyes reading into his mind. 'No, I ordered a taxi to take me to the airport. It's here already, so I don't want to keep it waiting with its meter running.'

'Robert, I was planning on driving you down to Boston,' Andreas had told him, trying not to sound hurt. 'There is really no need to fly. It's hardly worth it anyway. The flight may only be twenty minutes, but with the getting to and from the airport at both ends and the check-in process, it's much quicker by car. Only about one hour fifteen minutes from here, door to door. Much less expensive too. Not that I suppose that matters now,' he added.

Robert handed Andreas an envelope. 'The money I owe you for the cost of my flight over from London,' he said. 'I suppose you will accept that much from me?' he added with no attempt to disguise the sarcasm.

Andreas accompanied Robert to the front entrance where the taxi was waiting.

'Well, goodbye and thank you Andreas,' Robert said, holding out his hand. The uncustomary formality between them seemed alien to Andreas.

'Come, my friend, since when did we shake hands like strangers or acquaintances? Barely a week ago at Logan Airport we embraced with the hug of family and close friendship – we can surely do as much now?' And so saying he gave Robert a warm, brotherly hug.

Although it was imperceptible to anyone else, this spontaneous gesture of genuine affection from Andreas was, at first, not reciprocated by Robert, who seemed to freeze where he stood. Then, quite suddenly, he gave Andreas a hug so tight it seemed like he might never let go. Andreas likened it in his mind to the grip of a drowning man, out of his depth and clinging desperately to his only chance of rescue.

When he eventually relaxed his grip, Robert briefly held Andreas by the shoulders and looked him straight in the eye. What Andreas saw was a tortured combination of fear and pleading, mingled with a strange arrogance and pride that he had never seen before.

'Take good care of yourself, my friend,' Andreas said. 'Remember, you must learn to be the master of your money because, if you don't, it will become the master of you. That way you will lose your soul.'

It was over in a moment. Robert picked up his canvas holdall and turned towards the door.

'I will remember you in my prayers, as I ask that you remember me in yours,' Andreas said softly to his back. Robert stopped and looked back. He said nothing, but his blank expression was eloquent enough to leave no doubt about the mounting concern Andreas had for his friend.

An hour later Andreas knocked on the door of Father Jordan's study. 'I just wanted to let you know that Robert has gone. He asked me to thank you on his behalf for your friendship and hospitality, as do I Father Abbot,' Andreas said.

Father Jordan put down his pen, removed his glasses and sat back in his chair. 'Oh, I thought he was to be with us for two weeks,' he replied, adding, 'is everything all right?'

'He needed to take care of some urgent matters of business down in Boston, before returning to London it seems. I'm not sure, but I hope and pray everything's going to be all right in the end.'

'I assume by business you mean Church business? Albeit Church of England business,' he added with a wink and an encouraging smile.

Father Jordan was a seasoned enough priest to know from the worried look on Andreas's face that all might not be well. But he also knew when not to ask too many questions. Andreas was the sort who would tell him more if he ever felt the need to do so.

'Well, I'll keep him in my prayers,' he said, picking up his pen and glasses again.

'Yes, please do, and … thank you, Father,' Andreas said as he left.

As soon as he was in the taxi, Robert had instructed the driver not to go to the airport but to drive him instead directly to Boston. The driver was startled, and recognising him for a foreign visitor, felt compelled to point out that the taxi fare might be as much as 150 dollars on the meter, but he offered to do the trip for a fixed fare of 100 dollars, if Robert was really sure he didn't want to catch the Concord Trailways Bus, which would only cost him about fifteen.

Robert accepted his offer to do the trip for a hundred-dollar flat rate. The driver was delighted and happily engaged what he now saw as this important and generous foreign visitor in a running commentary on everything from the state of the roads to the difference between New Hampshire and Massachusetts politics. In the end Robert had to feign sleep to get some peace.

Back in London Bishop Rogers was sitting at his desk looking mildly bewildered; he had just finished talking to Robert Melton in America. There was a familiar tap on his door before Christopher Callow allowed himself in.

'Ah, Christopher, sit down will you. Quite a turn up for the books. Hard to believe really. Going to turn everything on its head – if it really happens.'

Christopher Callow knew he was going to need all his powers of acting and concentration to display just the right amount of surprise, so as not to betray any hint of his prior knowledge of the extraordinary turn of events the bishop was now about to unfold to him.

When the bishop finished telling him the details of his conversation and had outlined the proposal put to him by Robert Melton, he asked Christopher Callow for his opinion.

'Well, your Grace, it seems to me that, if this offer can be taken at face value, it is a gift horse into whose mouth we shouldn't look too deeply. It is an amazing piece of good fortune both for the Church and for St Mungo's, and of course very, very generous of Robert Melton.' It somehow no longer seemed appropriate to either think of him, or refer to him, as 'young' Robert Melton.

Christopher Callow's well-tuned antennae had detected something was up when Robert Melton had first called the bishop to ask for time off. He had not said he was going to America and neither he nor the bishop could have guessed at any such thing. Both of them had, without bothering to think about it, somehow just assumed he was planning a break in Cornwall, the Cotswolds, perhaps the Lake District, or somewhere similar. He simply didn't seem the type to go gallivanting off to America, nor did they ever think he could afford trips of that nature.

So it had been suppressed excitement he had detected in Robert's voice. He was also right about the feeling he had had that he, and the bishop, had been outmanoeuvred. But it was the money that puzzled him most. How had Robert Melton suddenly come into what must indeed be a very substantial fortune? Sufficient to be able to suddenly and immediately transfer the huge sum of three and a half million pounds to save St Mungo's.

If it was a surprise inheritance from some unknown, very rich relative, the inevitable delay for probate would normally make it impossible to access such a large sum so quickly. This left open a limited range of possibilities. Aware of his own weaknesses, Christopher Callow knew it was not unheard of for a rich widow to fall so madly in love with her parish priest as to willingly part with her fortune in return for love – even with minimal physical affection. Although usually more demanding of the physical, the same was equally true of some rich older men.

But he knew Robert Melton was not of the latter inclination and the likelihood of the former having happened in the parish of St Mungo's seemed so remote as not to be worthy of serious consideration. He was stumped and had to admit he had been completely outwitted. Robert Melton had played a very good game of poker in the end. But Christopher Callow knew Robert had only won because somehow he'd been dealt a killer hand in the last round. He, Christopher Callow, really did not like being beaten in the game of life, by what he considered a novice player.

On his way home that night, his attention was caught by a small piece lost in the centre pages of the *Evening Standard*. It stated that after a period of four weeks an anonymous winner had finally come forward to collect the huge American Powerball lottery win. Nothing was known about the winner except some wild speculation that whoever it was had immediately given all of it away to a friend.

Try as he might he couldn't make this fit either. It raised more questions than it answered. But he couldn't shake the feeling that somehow these two events weren't unrelated.

22

LUXURIATING IN THE soft vastness of his super king-sized bed, Robert noticed the clock on his bedside table read three o'clock in the morning, as it had, give or take five minutes, on the previous three nights. He seemed to be falling into a pattern where initially sleep came easily after a busy day – mostly taken up with meetings arranged by Bill Temple – before he woke in the watches of the night and his brain kicked in.

There had been endless meetings with tax attorneys and accountants specialising in Anglo-American tax affairs; with stockbrokers, and lawyers eager that he should write a will; insurance brokers, insistent that a man of his wealth needed immediate and hefty personal liability coverage; even a tailor, brought in to make him a range of the finest bespoke suits to reflect his important new status in life.

It had all been happening so fast that during the day he found he had little time to think. It was at night, alone in his magnificent suite, that in the early pre-dawn hours he would awaken to the gnawing doubt over the rightful ownership of the money that, try as he might, he could not shut out. Robert turned the details of the events leading up to it over and over in his mind. He knew that, had his acting church warden not had a bad cold, it would have been he who, as part of his duties, would have emptied and counted the contents of the collection, which would have made him the one to find the lottery ticket. It was only because Robert had suggested he go home early that he had not been the one to do so.

Following on from this line of thinking forced Robert to confront, uncomfortably, what the outcome might have been had his church warden also known about the lottery ticket. Would Robert have taken the path he was now on? Or would he already have returned to his London parish and handed the entire fortune over to the Church?

This raised the question again of whether, having been deposited in the Sunday collection plate, the lottery ticket had become the property of the Church? In which case, even in the extraordinarily unlikely event that anyone would ever have bothered to check an American lottery for the results, the Church would, technically and morally, have been ineligible to collect under the rules of that lottery, which required winners to be legal American residents. St Mungo's Anglican Church, firmly situated in London, would hardly seem to qualify.

Robert then asked himself the question whether, if somehow the ticket had been recognised and then identified as the winning ticket, the church authorities (and here he couldn't help thinking of Christopher Callow) would have simply sat back and said to themselves, 'Oh well, what a shame we don't qualify, but clearly those are the rules.' Or would they too, in recognising the instrument as a bearer bond, have done exactly what Robert had done and given it to a trusted American resident to collect on their behalf?

Although Robert was pretty sure he knew what the answer would have been to this moral dilemma, it didn't really justify his own actions sufficiently to give him the peace of mind required to sleep the undisturbed sleep of the innocent.

His decision, which at the moment he told himself was only an interim, temporary step, to take control of the matter himself in order to be quite sure St Mungo's was saved, was, he knew, influenced by the fact that there were only two people in the world who knew how the lottery ticket had come into his possession. Neither of these was his church warden. Only he himself and Andreas Doria knew the full story. Despite the recent unfortunate cooling of their friendship, Robert knew he could rely on Andreas's complete discretion, even with such a potentially explosive secret.

When he thought about Andreas this way it hurt him to realise that, unequivocally, he could still trust Andreas with his life, and that indeed his friend would rather die than betray him. If only Andreas had allowed Robert to give him some of the money. After all, his primary motivation, Robert told himself, had only been to share his good fortune with his good friend. Unfortunately however, Andreas had also recognised his secondary motivation: his desperate desire to share, in order to add a further degree of legitimacy to his actions.

Robert was of course aware of the possibility that there was a third, as yet unknown, person out there somewhere. Someone who, having deposited the ticket, might have the knowledge that it was his, or perhaps her, ticket left in London that had the winning numbers on it. Although unlikely at this stage, what if this person did know and eventually came forward? Just the knowledge of how they had put the ticket in the collection plate, with the inevitable publicity following such a claim, would immediately provide it with legitimacy, bordering on certainty in the light of his actions since that fateful Sunday. In short, Robert Melton would be unmasked.

These were the restless worries that, as with all worries, were greatly amplified in the still darkness of the early morning hours. Despite his luxuriously comfortable surroundings it was these thoughts that were preventing Robert from being able to enjoy undisturbed, restful sleep. He tried remembering his mother's admonition from childhood when he had been facing his first exams: 'Worrying is like riding a rocking horse: it may give you something to do, but it will get you nowhere.'

He was startled from his eventual return to a fitful sleep by the insistent ringing of his telephone.

'Hello? Hello, Robert, it's ... er ... Bishop Rogers here.' The momentary hesitation had been due to his uncertainty over whether to use just his Christian name, John, when addressing someone about to give three and a half million pounds to the Church. 'I've spoken to all the powers that be, from the Church Commissioners down and I've confirmed what you told me about the position with Barrasford Holdings. Everyone is in agreement with your generous proposal, so if you still want to, we can go ahead.'

'Fine – I'm delighted,' Robert answered, trying to overcome the early morning grogginess in his voice. Clearing his throat he continued, 'I'll have my financial adviser make arrangements to transfer the money to you today. Please will you have someone telex thorough the appropriate bank details for my attention here at the Ritz Carlton? Also, once you've concluded things with Barrasford Holdings, please would you send me a letter confirming the following points: one, that the Barrasford contract has been bought out; two, that you have received the equivalent of three and a half million pounds from me in return for not selling off St Mungo's; and three, that, within this overall sum, you have received ample additional funding from me for the renovation, continuing upkeep and repair of St Mungo's for the foreseeable future. You can send the letter to me in Boston, care of the Ritz Carlton Hotel. I'll be staying on here for a while yet.'

The Bishop of West London sounded slightly taken aback. 'That seems a little demeaning. Is it really necessary to have to confirm in writing that we are going to keep our side of the bargain, Robert?'

Christopher Callow, listening in from his desk, visibly winced. Even the bishop seemed to regret what he had said before the words were fully out of his mouth. There was a short, pregnant, silence.

'Yes, I'm afraid it is and I must insist upon it Bishop ... I mean your Grace,' came Robert's cold reply.

'Very well, I'll see to it as soon as the money gets here,' said the bishop. 'And thank you Robert, what you're doing is very generous. Perhaps I was wrong after all to overlook the importance of St Mungo's to the diocese.'

Robert wondered if this was as close as he was going to get to an apology from the bishop.

Instead of summoning his assistant as he usually did, on this occasion Bishop Rogers got up from his desk and walked over to Christopher Callow's office. He walked straight in to find his assistant leaning forward in his chair, elbows on the desk, his chin resting on the top of his clasped hands. He was deep in thought, lines of concentration furrowing his forehead.

'I've just been speaking to Robert Melton in Boston and, you know, I think he's really going to do it. At least he says he is so convincingly, either he both can and will, or he's become delusional and we'll have a different sort of problem on our hands.

'Christopher, you look like one of those chess champions trying to puzzle out his next move in a last desperate bid to avoid checkmate.'

'Do I, your Grace? I'm sorry, I was far away in deep thought.'

Christopher Callow thought just how close to the truth the bishop had been in characterising his pensiveness. This was a game in which he appeared to have badly underestimated his opponent. He hated the feeling that he had been outmanoeuvred, even checkmated, by Robert Melton.

With the urgent matter of saving St Mungo's now satisfactorily taken care of for the time being, Robert had had time to consider his next move. He had to admit to himself that he was enjoying being anonymous in America and rich beyond his, or most people's, wildest dreams. He felt in no hurry to return to England.

As a result of spending so much time together over the past few weeks his, initially business-like, relationship with Bill Temple had begun to show signs of developing into an early friendship, based largely on a mutual respect for each other.

Robert felt increasingly confident and comfortable with the advice and guidance he was being given. In William 'Bill' Temple he recognised he had found someone he could have complete faith in and rely on absolutely. Furthermore, he was beginning to find he had a natural understanding and aptitude for investing, or at least thus far in the underlying principles behind what made for a successful, diversified, investment portfolio.

For his part Bill Temple had been surprised and pleased by both the trust and genuine interest his new client had shown right from the start of his appointment. It was an unexpected pleasure to be acting for someone who, while freely admitting to his almost total ignorance of all matters financial, was now a keen student, eager to learn all he could.

Before going into the world of accountancy and finance, Bill Temple had been very tempted to go to teacher training college with a view to a career in the teaching profession. Conversely, before choosing the Church, Robert had been considering a career in accountancy and finance. From a business point of view, meeting as they had now, these two men were made for each other. One was a frustrated and gifted teacher of his art, the other an eager, naturally gifted student. They already knew they would get on famously.

23

FOR THE CLERK back in the State Lottery Commission's little office in Concord, New Hampshire, keeping secret the knowledge of the winner's identity was becoming unbearable. From the winner's profession as an ordained Benedictine monk at St Jerome's Abbey, to his extraordinary subsequent action, in immediately endorsing over the entire fortune to his friend, an Australian Church of England vicar from London, it was explosive. The clerk could no longer resist the temptation.

Even though he didn't know the name of the vicar, he knew it wouldn't take the media long to identify him. How many Australian vicars could there be in England? The clerk knew only too well that, if he played it right, he would get a good payoff for selling this story to the highest bidder: a payoff big enough to risk getting fired from his job at the Lottery Commission if he was ever identified as the source of the leak.

This thought had been gnawing away at him now for the better part of a month and he knew if he didn't act soon the story would go cold and lose most of its value. To minimise the chance of the leak ever being traced back to him, he planned 'accidentally' to leave the office copy of the originally completed claim form out on his desk while at lunch that Thursday. He would then call in from lunch to say he had been taken ill and not return to his office until the following Tuesday. He would leak the story to the press late on Monday.

Although, undoubtedly, his action would be viewed as careless, it would mean that the information would be visible, there for anyone to see on his desk, throughout the balance of office hours on Thursday, all day Friday and half of Saturday. Not to mention the contract cleaners who would be in to clean the offices on Sunday.

This would leave open the possibility for a large enough number of other eyes to have seen the information and perhaps been the ones to leak it. First thing on Monday morning he would phone his boss to tell her what he had stupidly done, so she would be the one to go and find the document lying openly on his desk. The only risk to this scheme was that, during this time, someone else might indeed see the completed claim form on his desk, recognise the value of the information and scoop him in selling it to the press.

The following Tuesday morning, after a mysterious tip-off, the press and media ran it. Although it was by now no longer as a top story in the national papers, identifying the winner of the Powerball lottery's biggest ever jackpot win was still considered to be of sufficient human interest to warrant an entry on page two and be worthy of a mention on most national radio and television news channels. Only the New Hampshire *Concord Monitor* and Manchester *Union Leader* ran with it as front-page news because of the strong local connections and interest.

Robert heard the bulletin on National Public Radio while shaving in the marble bathroom of the Presidential Suite at the Ritz Carlton, and froze. Andreas was mentioned by name as the big lottery winner who had, so selflessly, immediately made the entire fortune over to a friend.

The story was a compelling one because of all its extraordinary elements. Starting with the big win by a Roman Catholic Benedictine monk who, constrained from keeping the money by his vow of poverty, had given the entire fortune to an obscure, as yet unidentified, Australian friend who happened to be a Protestant, Church of England vicar from a poor parish somewhere in England.

The telephone in the suite began to ring insistently. Almost afraid to answer it, Robert eventually picked it up from the telephone hanging on the bathroom wall. His relief was palpable when he heard Bill Temple's voice.

'Have you heard the news this morning?'

Robert replied affirmatively.

Bill could hear the concern in his client's voice. 'It isn't what either of us would have wanted, but it's a situation that can be managed, as long as we remain in control of that process and stay one step ahead of the media,' Bill explained reassuringly. 'Right now I think we need to meet to plan a strategy. I've cancelled all today's appointments, so we can get together and do this. I don't think you should go down to breakfast in the hotel dining-room this morning. It won't be long before the press are on to you. Given the time difference with the UK, they may already have identified you and tracked you down as far as the Ritz Carlton. So I suggest you stay in your room until I can get over there.

'I'll check out the lobby for any likely press or media people on a stake-out and then come and get you. I'll bring my car and, if the coast is clear, we'll leave straight away. We can have breakfast in the Blue Diner at the end of South Street. I've not taken you there before, but it's a quintessential piece of working American history and probably the last place in Boston anyone would think of looking for you. They do a great breakfast too, by the way.

'I'll be over in about twenty minutes. Stay calm, it's going to be all right, maybe even fun.' And on that encouragingly cheerful note he rang off.

Forty minutes later they were seated in a private booth at the back of the Blue Diner. Bill Temple's office was just round the corner in South Street and he was clearly a well-known regular here. Despite his preoccupation, Robert was able to appreciate the authenticity of this original piece of Americana. The Blue Diner had indeed once been actual rolling stock from a transcontinental train. Its elegant, art deco chrome-clad exterior, long ago removed from its huge cast iron wheels, had been embedded at the far end of South Street at a time when this whole area had been nothing but red brick warehousing in a blue collar, working-class district on the edge of the city. Now surrounded by sleek glass and marble-clad high-rise office buildings, rubbing shoulders with those same red brick warehouses, renovated and converted into large, trendy, open-plan commercial spaces, favoured by high-end architects, art galleries and contemporary designers, the Blue Diner today catered to a very different, much more upscale, white collar crowd.

Inside it looked as if nothing much had changed from its glory days as a railroad dining car. Its soda fountain-style counter had red, leatherette topped, revolving mushroom-shaped stools on single chrome pillars. The booths, all with banquette seating, were similarly upholstered, while the counter surface and table tops were of grey-green marble-grained Formica, lightly trimmed around the edges with a band of chromed metal, decoratively pressed into parallel wrinkles. The centrepiece on the wall behind the counter was a large pink, neon lit, Art Deco electric clock. The waitresses, mostly mature women, wore 1950s-style uniforms consisting of a plain, fitted, maroon dress with a white apron and starched white headpieces. The men, working in the open kitchen and behind the counter, wore white uniforms with close fitting oval-shaped white caps, piped in maroon to match the colour of the waitresses' dresses.

With the early breakfast rush over, the place was quiet at this time of the day and Bill Temple was a well enough known and appreciated regular for him to request that the booth next to theirs be kept empty.

Looking around after ordering a full English breakfast, Robert tried to imagine all the places this diner must have been to in its heyday on the railroad; the famous people who must have eaten their breakfast, gently swaying to the rhythm of the track as they made their way across the Great Plains from Chicago, or over the Rocky Mountains towards Los Angeles. It seemed impossible to him not to get caught up in the romance of it all and yet, looking around, he saw only people oblivious to the provenance of its history, preoccupied as they were with the here and now, intent only on getting a bagel and coffee 'to go', with which to rush back to their desks in one of the nearby offices.

'Robert, you're not listening are you?' Robert finally heard Bill say with a laugh.

'I'm sorry, I was just imagining the past history of this place as a working railroad car.'

'OK, but you'd better listen now if we're going to make a plan for how to face the media, because within twelve hours, twenty-four if you're lucky, that is what you will be doing, whether you like it or not.

'But, first off, I think you need to tell me a bit more about yourself if I'm going to be able to help you. I know you're Australian, that much anyone could tell from your accent, although, surprisingly, there are those over here in the US who might not – you might be mistaken for South African, English or even Canadian.

'I didn't know until this morning that you are a Church of England vicar, "currently working in a parish somewhere in England". So maybe we could start from there?

'Are you married? How do you know Andreas Doria, the Benedictine monk who officially won the lottery? What is your relationship to, or with him, and what motivated him to immediately give his huge fortune entirely and solely to you? Though perhaps before you start it would be fair if I told you I am neither Episcopalian nor Roman Catholic. I was brought up, and still am, a sometimes practising member of the Baptist Church.'

Robert picked up the steaming mug of coffee that had been placed in front of him. He took a sip. It was delicious, strong and hot.

Starting from the beginning, he told Bill everything. About his childhood in Australia; his father's early death in a subterranean construction accident; how he had first met Andreas at Cambridge; to how he had taken on the appointment as vicar of the impoverished parish of St Mungo's. He was open and truthful about everything, except about how precisely the Powerball lottery ticket came

191

into his possession. This he simply explained as having been given to him by a visiting tourist to his church one Sunday morning and how, as a non-resident in America, he had needed to take into his confidence his friend Andreas Doria in freely 'giving' him the ticket, without any legal claim to it, in order for the money to be properly collected.

Robert was surprised at how easily he had been able to tell Bill that the lottery ticket had been given to him and how much less troubled his conscience already was over adopting this interpretation of what the intention of the mystery donor might otherwise have been.

Surely it stood to reason the ticket must have been meant for him? After all what good would it have been to the Church or anyone else? In any other scenario he could imagine the lottery ticket would already have been discarded, its extraordinary value almost certainly unrecognised or, even if recognised, frustratingly uncollectable.

No, he had been increasingly able to convince himself that whoever it was who had put it in the collection plate must have meant it for him. Besides, if the Church of England did have any moral claim to it, hadn't he satisfied that by his gesture of saving St Mungo's?

In finishing his story, Robert said, 'So there you have the whole background, Bill. Now you'll understand why I needed Andreas to collect the money and why he immediately handed it all back to me. By the way, your earlier implication that there might be more to my relationship with Andreas than friendship is very wide of the mark.'

'That's as may be,' replied Bill. 'But you'd better not be too sensitive about it, because for sure it is going to be the obvious conclusion drawn by many as the only possible way to explain why Andreas would turn round and give you all that money without keeping so much as a penny for himself. The problem is that that explanation, although fantastic enough, is going to be much more believable than the truth – even if you could tell it, which I'm guessing you won't want to?'

'No, you're wrong there Bill, I do want to tell the truth – firstly because I've done nothing wrong and secondly because it would be very unfair to Andreas not to head off any inaccurate implication of a relationship between us, other than that of a once close friendship.

'Remember, as a Catholic Benedictine monk, he has taken a vow of celibacy and that applies to physical relationships with either sex: primarily the reason I could never have considered the priesthood within Catholicism. Although I hasten to add, while I can understand same sex relationships, my own inclinations are very much towards women.'

'I don't doubt it,' interrupted Bill. 'I'm merely pointing out how the media are bound to insinuate things in an attempt to give some explanation to what otherwise looks like the most extraordinarily altruistic gesture on Andreas's part.'

'That's where the legality comes in,' Robert rejoined. 'I've checked with the lawyer you introduced me to the other day. When the lottery ticket legitimately came into my possession in England, as a gift to me, that little piece of paper became mine. I then gave it freely, as an unencumbered gift, to my friend Andreas. By writing his name and address on the back of the ticket he confirmed his absolute ownership of it. As the then owner of this bearer bond, he rightfully claimed the jackpot it had won. At that point, however briefly, the money legally became entirely his. He was then quite free to do whatever he liked with it. He could easily have chosen to keep it, given it all to a home for stray cats, or anything else. He chose to give it all to me. End of story.'

'Not quite,' Bill replied. 'Apart from the completely fantastic aspect of the true story you tell, which by itself is going to drive the media wild with joy at the prospect of where they can take this, you're forgetting one rather fundamentally important detail. That is, who gave you this ticket? How did it get into your possession over in England? Don't think for one minute the media are going to let you off without a satisfactory explanation for that. Just saying you were given it won't be nearly enough.'

'Again, the truth,' said Robert with conviction. 'It was given to me by a visitor to St Mungo's Church after a Sunday service; presumably an American visitor to London. I don't know for sure and I don't know their name, or any other aspect of their identity. You get given all sorts of random things from time to time as a parish priest. I wouldn't have paid it much attention at the time. In fact, I'd actually thrown it in the wastepaper bin after everyone had gone. What good was an American Powerball lottery ticket going to be to me? I only found out about its value when I happened to call my friend Andreas for a chat – something we only did occasionally because of the cost – and he told me about the unclaimed big win. That's when I retrieved the ticket from the wastepaper basket and discovered I had been given the sole winning ticket.'

'Oh boy, I want to be there when you tell this whole story to the media. They'll need more than one ambulance on standby to deal with the heart attacks brought on by over-excitement in even the most jaded hacks when the different dimensions of this story sink in. It's got just about everything: God and Mammon; straddling three continents; an American Roman Catholic monk and an Anglo-Australian Church of England vicar; extraordinary altruistic gestures that go way beyond even fantastic generosity; and an unidentified American mystery donor travelling to England to give the ticket away anonymously, almost certainly without realising they were giving away the largest lottery jackpot in history.

'The only thing that's missing is murder and sex. And most of the media, the press anyway, will bring that in by innuendo whatever you say: either hinting at a homosexual relationship between you and Andreas, or perhaps speculating that the original purchaser and donor of the ticket might be an American lady of a certain age, besotted by this rugged, handsome, young Australian Church of England vicar. She chose to remain anonymous because, of course, she is already married to a domineering husband who has promised to have her done away with if ever he caught her having an affair.'

Robert laughed. 'That's quite an imagination you've got there Bill,' he said.

'No, it's not my imagination. It's my experience of an uncontrolled, lusting media who are going to go hog wild over this story.

'My recommendation, Robert, is that we go back to your hotel, try to pick out some of the more responsible representatives from the press, TV and radio and invite them to an exclusive press conference with you. That way you can tell them your story and try to remain in control of events until it's all out there and eventually the whole thing becomes old news, or something bigger breaks to take the spotlight off you.

'We'd better plan to do that this afternoon because it's my bet that by this evening, if not sooner, the press will have found you. Also, that way the hotel is your contact address, so all the begging letters and calls, of which you are going to get thousands over the coming weeks, will come there. You'll need a secretary from tomorrow. I'll send someone from my office as a temporary measure until you have time to find your own.'

Just then the waitress came over. 'Mr Temple, I'm sorry but we can't keep the booth next to you empty any longer. We've got the early lunch crowd starting to come in and there's a line already.'

Both men had been so engrossed in their conversation that neither of them had noticed the time. Bill looked up at the neon clock and then, in disbelief, at his watch. It was almost noon. 'I'm sorry Stacy,' he said. 'No, of course, and you can have this booth too, we have to go. Thank you so much for the privacy and for letting us sit here so long. Thank Mitch for me too and tell him I owe him one, will you?'

They left, leaving a generous tip with payment for their breakfast.

Walking into the lobby of the Ritz Carlton Hotel Robert immediately recognised the face staring intently at him from behind a lowered newspaper. Knowing evasion would be useless this time, he hastily smiled in as friendly a way as he could. He just had time to let Bill know he had already been discovered before the journalist he had seen and spoken to three weeks before in Baynham's Mercantile up in New London was standing beside him.

'Hello. Good to see you again, Padre,' the journalist said pleasantly, holding out his hand. 'Where's your friend? The Benedictine monk if I'm not mistaken? By the way I'm Jason Keiffer, investigative journalist for the New Hampshire *Concord Monitor*. Don't often get big scoops and never big scoops with such an international dimension. I would be very much obliged if you would grant me an exclusive interview before the media at large find you.'

Against his better judgement, Robert couldn't help feeling a grudging admiration for this ageing, but still doggedly determined hack, patiently using his own instincts, shoe leather and old-fashioned ways to remain separate from, and sometimes ahead of, his generally younger, more impatient, techno-savvy competitors.

'OK, you win,' Robert said with a smile. 'Why don't you come up to my suite with us …'

Jason Keiffer cut him off. 'Don't look round,' he said under his breath 'But I've just seen the guys from the *Boston Globe* and *New York Times* walk in with someone else who I don't recognise. Give me your room number and I'll meet you there in ten minutes. Meantime I'll see if I can put these fellas off the scent, if it's you they're after – and I'm pretty sure it will be.'

Robert told him the floor and suite number in a low voice.

'Thanks. See you in ten,' he said walking over to where the other journalists were now standing by the reception desk.

'Trusting fellow, but why were you so open and honest with him?' Bill asked Robert as the elevator doors closed behind them. 'You could have given him any room number or we could get off at the next floor, catch the service elevator down to the basement and leave by the back entrance.'

Robert told him how they had first run into each other up in New Hampshire three weeks before. 'I suppose I feel a little sorry for him, operating as the odd man out, a bit of an anachronism in his profession. Also a realisation that there is probably a lot in common between an old-fashioned journalist, a detective and a priest. We all have well-developed instincts about people and whether or not they can be trusted to be telling the truth. He would have known if I'd tried to deceive him. Anyway, it's lucky those others arrived. It gives us ten minutes to prepare what and how much I'm going to tell him and he's being very useful in delaying the others. In return, the best I can hope to give him is a twenty-four-hour head start for a scoop if we can somehow hold the others at bay until tomorrow morning.'

Ten minutes later Jason Keiffer knocked at the door. Bill opened it. 'Well that's settled that, for a few hours I should think,' Jason said, coming into the room.

'What did you do to put them off?' asked Bill, introducing himself at the same time.

'The first thing is not to try and do that,' replied Jason, looking around the room for Robert and fixing his eye on the closed bathroom door. 'Before anything else you have to find out how much they know already. Not as much as you might think, as it turns out. Seems the Church of England authorities were not very forthcoming on the subject. They didn't, or I should say couldn't, give a name, but they did let slip that your client,' he said this with a nod towards the bathroom door, 'was last in contact from Boston. The *Globe* and the *New York Times* have got staffers in London working on finding his parish and when they do, which probably won't take them too much longer, they'll soon get everything they need to track him down over here. Because of the time difference he's probably got until tomorrow morning before that happens. When I found out how little they actually had on him, I knew they were only here at the hotel on a fishing exercise.

'It wasn't too hard then to tell them about the legitimate Australian businessman I had fortuitously found staying over at the Four Seasons. By the time they figure out he's not their man it will be tomorrow morning. Still, I feel sorry for that Aussie fella, he's going to have a very interrupted evening and his dinner spoiled by being pestered by my colleagues in the trade. I may be a humble, old-school reporter, past his prime, working for a small regional newspaper, but the advantage I do have is called experience. Only any use of course if you've managed to learn something from it. I've learned a few things, one of which is that the young, well-paid, bright boys working for the big, global brand, media names often have one glaring weakness, or perhaps I should say two, but they are really two sides of the same coin so to speak. It is that their propensity to overestimate their own skills and abilities is matched only by their propensity to underestimate the skill and ability of old regional hacks like me. I find sometimes I can exploit that to my advantage, and I've just done so downstairs.'

The muffled sound of an expensive lavatory being discreetly flushed rewarded his steadfast gaze towards the bathroom door. Moments later Robert entered the room and joined them.

'All right, I'm going to give you a head start on the story because I think you deserve it after all the effort you've put into tracking me down,' he said.

'Thank you. I only wish I'd trusted my gut feeling when I first set eyes on you up in New London three weeks ago. I was quite suddenly so sure it was you, but it was the monk-vicar thing that provided just enough unlikelihood to make me doubt myself instead of following my instinct. Another lesson learned. Whatever happens in future, I must always, always trust in my instinct and not be put off by any extraneous circumstances, however plausible. Trouble is you were telling the truth. I'd have known in an instant if you weren't.'

Robert smiled. 'Told you so,' he said to Bill knowingly.

For the next hour Robert unfolded the events of the past four weeks to Jason Keiffer, who listened without interruption, taking notes from time to time.

When he'd finished, Robert sat back, looking over at Bill, who gave a small approving nod. Together they studied the expression on Jason's face, while awaiting his reaction to what he'd just been told. Robert was fairly sure that what he saw was a struggle going on as Jason fought to suppress the excitement he now clearly felt for what promised to be the scoop of his life on a small regional newspaper – that would, for a moment, propel his name and the name of his newspaper around the world.

'Thank you. You've just given me the story of my career,' he said quietly. 'I know you're telling the truth. The only concern, or rather question, I have is over the identity of whoever it was who, while visiting your church in London, gave you the lottery ticket and why they would do such a random thing? Are you completely sure you have absolutely no idea who they were, or even perhaps what this person's name was?'

'I'm completely sure, Jason,' Robert replied, using his first name in the hope of further cementing the confidence he felt was being established between them.

'Well, whoever it was, the hunt is going to be on for them big time once this story breaks. The trouble is, in a situation like this we'll get hundreds, no thousands – literally – of chancers, gold diggers, attention seekers, calling in claiming to be the person who gave the ticket to you. Some will say they didn't mean to give it to you, it was a mistake or, because you are a man of the cloth, they gave it to you for safekeeping while on their visit to London. Others will just hope you will give them something, anything, and so on.

'You'll be amazed at all the different, imaginative ploys and reasons people will come up with. Yet, we – and by that I mean my fellow journalists and media editors – will have to trawl through every one of these spurious claims in the hope and belief that somewhere in there will be the person who really did give you that magic little piece of paper. Trouble is all the big media names will have armies of junior staffers to delegate this tedious trawling process to. I have no one to do the dirty work for me, so I guess my big moment in this incredible story ends here. The less scrupulous print publications will run with any claimant story that seems even faintly plausible, not caring whether it's true or not, because either way it will temporarily boost circulation figures. Get ready to see some truly fantastic propositions.'

'What do you mean by "propositions"?' asked Robert.

'I mean as to who, how or why you got given this huge fortune. Believe me you'll be reading about how it was divine intervention, sending your guardian angel, who, conveniently, just happened to be an American, to help you save St Peters and exact revenge on the wicked bishop.'

'St Mungo's ... and the bishop isn't wicked,' Robert interjected.

'Whatever,' Jason continued, 'he will be by the time some of my seedier colleagues have worked their magic with this story. That church might as well be called St Lucky if you ask me.

'Oh, and don't worry, you'll be getting plenty of the other sort of propositions too: from marriage to dubious business opportunities. Your life is about to change forever, my friend. I hope you are one strong, tough character,' finished Jason.

Robert was immediately reminded of Andreas by Jason's use of the term 'my friend'. How he wished he had his friend here with him now.

As if reading his mind, Jason asked, 'Oh, by the way, what's happened to your monk friend, Andrew wasn't it?'

'Andreas,' Robert again corrected him.

'I meant to ask you what you gave him for his trouble, considering the vital role he played in collecting the money for you?'

'Nothing,' replied Robert. 'He wouldn't take anything.'

Jason and Bill now both looked at him incredulously. It was a question Bill had forgotten to ask earlier on in the Blue Diner.

'Nothing? What do you mean, nothing? Nothing, or relatively speaking, nothing?' asked Jason.

'I mean absolutely nothing. Zero. He wouldn't even let me buy him the new stereo system he wanted. He's got a real bee in his bonnet about the corrupting effect of this money and he wanted none of it. It was strange how vehement and adamant he became on this point, as if he saw something almost satanic in its influence. It was like he had become afraid of it. Afraid to touch or be touched by any part of it, however small.'

Bill was slowly shaking his head in silent bewilderment. Jason was looking pensive. 'He's a wise man, that friend of yours,' was all he said.

The following morning the phone in Robert's suite started ringing at six o'clock. It was a journalist from the *New York Times* wanting a private interview before the hastily arranged press conference scheduled in the ballroom at the hotel for eleven.

Robert refused. By six-thirty, following a string of calls from other journalists and media people making similar requests, Robert asked the hotel to hold all his calls; the only exceptions being if the caller was either Bill Temple or Andreas Doria. He really hoped Andreas would call once he'd seen the front-page article in the *Concord Monitor* that morning, which he felt certain he would have.

At eight, Bill Temple rang from the lobby phone to say he was downstairs with Cynthia White, the best secretary and administrative assistant they had in their office. While they were coming up, Robert called down to room service and asked for breakfast for three to be sent up to his suite.

At the knock on the door, Robert first checked through the spy hole to see who was outside. Jason Keiffer had advised him to do this; he was having to learn fast how to adapt to his new circumstances. Opening the door to Bill Temple and Cynthia White he was surprised to discover that Cynthia White was black: ebony black, young, slim and very beautiful.

Bill introduced them. 'Robert, this is Cynthia White. Cynthia, this is Robert Melton. As I told you Robert, Cynthia is the best secretary and administrative assistant in our office – by far. You've got to be nice to her, because we can't afford to lose her. She's only on loan to you until you can find your own personal assistant. She'll even help you do that too.'

Cynthia smiled a shy, beautiful smile that made her whole face light up as she put her hand out to shake Robert's.

He noted the intelligence in her eyes. 'I guess I wasn't expecting the secretary you mentioned to be …' his voice trailed off in embarrassment.

'Black? Is that it?' suggested Bill after an awkwardly long pause, his voice now sounding a warning mixture of incredulity and protective outrage.

'No, no, not that at all,' Robert stammered in genuine confusion. 'I meant so beautiful,' he blurted out in his embarrassment.

'Oh,' Bill laughed, relaxing. 'Well, don't be fooled, Cynthia won't take any nonsense from you and she will expect the highest standards in the work you give her. She doesn't like things to be incorrect, sloppy or unprofessional.'

Now it was Cynthia's turn to laugh. 'Don't listen to Bill, he's worse than my father,' she said. 'I'm glad to meet you Mr Melton and happy to help out in any way I can while you get yourself established. Do you like people to call you Mister, Reverend or Father?'

'Oh please, just call me Robert,' said Robert, warmly shaking her hand. 'Thank you so much for coming to help me out.'

'You're welcome,' Cynthia replied in a way that made Robert feel she meant it.

'I suppose for the sake of others it would just be easier to go with "Mr" for the time being,' he suggested. 'I don't think "vicar" is a term much used or understood in America is it? And I don't feel very "Reverend" in the role I'm currently in. "Father" is mostly used by Catholic priests or High Church Anglicans and Episcopalians, and I'm neither of those.

'How do you like to be addressed: as Cynthia or Miss White?' he asked hesitantly.

'Oh, Cynthia, always,' she said.

'We call her the classic misnomer in the office,' interjected Bill playfully. 'And if she's looking grumpy I'll tell her to take that black look off her face.'

'Yes, and that's when I get to call you honky white trash,' Cynthia shot back defiantly with an equally playful look in her eye.

Robert could tell immediately that theirs was a genuinely friendly office, with happy, healthy working relationships, free of any of the stiff awkwardness sometimes masking hidden racism. He knew then that he and Cynthia would get along.

Over breakfast the three of them rehearsed exactly what Robert was going to say to the assembled media representatives gathering downstairs. Bill had brought along a copy of the New Hampshire *Concord Monitor*, which had the whole story emblazoned across its front page under a banner headline proclaiming 'Billionaire Monk becomes Billionaire Vicar' with an only slightly less prominent strap line underneath reading 'From Riches to Rags – Benedictine monk, winner of the world's biggest ever lottery jackpot, hamstrung by vow of poverty, gives it all away to Australian Church of England vicar'.

The headline allowed room for a small headshot of Jason Keiffer, with mention of his name as the scooping investigative journalist.

Having read it though twice, Robert felt, on balance, that it was a fair reflection of what he had told Keiffer the day before: a bit sensationalised in one or two places, but more by what was left unsaid than by what was said.

Maybe there was still some 'honour' among journalists, he thought. Robert made a mental note to call Jason Keiffer and thank him for his restraint in writing what was essentially an objective, factually correct, article, in which the sensationalism came mostly from its content, rather than from the way it was written.

After breakfast Cynthia suggested to Robert that they should plan the immediate things he would need her to do. First on this list was to set up a temporary office. Assuming the hotel would let them, she would arrange for them to install two extra telephone lines, a word-processing typewriter, a photocopier and a fax machine.

Cynthia herself would go out later and get all the office supplies they would need for the time being. It was agreed that she would start work at nine and finish at six, with an hour off for lunch.

This accomplished, it was time for the three of them to go down to the hotel ballroom for the press conference. They took their seats behind a long table covered with green baize cloth. Robert and Bill sat with Cynthia between them, looking out over a sea of eager faces, many with cameras already poised.

An hour later the extraordinary story of the biggest lottery jackpot ever won was being wired across the country and around the world. The interpretations were widely varied, ranging from factual to fantastical.

As predicted, the scoop by the New Hampshire *Concord Monitor* meant that none of the serious press would feature it as a front-page story. Only the smaller, regional or tabloid press would run it as their lead item, confident that it was still the right story to maximise their circulation.

For radio and television, Robert had agreed to one short collective interview, that was just long enough for a shared news clip.

The individual clamouring for an exclusive personal interview after the press conference was deafening. But all these requests were politely and firmly refused, as were the ones for Robert to appear on various well-known national television talk shows.

Back in his suite, Robert rang Andreas.

'How's it going, my friend?' came the immediate response. It was good to hear his familiar cheerful voice. 'You're a big celebrity now up here in New Hampshire.'

'You've seen the *Concord Monitor* then? Please let me reassure you, Andreas – it wasn't me who leaked the story.'

'I know that, and I'm not blaming you. Anyway, I've just said goodbye to Jason Keiffer. Poetic that he should turn out to be the fellow we met up in New London. On the basis that his article was both fair and relatively restrained, I allowed him a short interview with me for a follow-up piece in tomorrow's paper. It's the only interview I intend to give. All other requests will be declined.'

'That's really what I'm calling you about,' Robert told him. 'I'm afraid you're likely to be besieged by the media for a few days. I've just come from the only press conference I intend giving, but because of your role in this, and who you are, they all now want your story. Trouble is, when they realise you're not talking, some of the less scrupulous ones may write whatever stuff they feel like making up, if only in the hope of provoking a reaction from you. I'm really sorry Andreas, I never meant to get you involved in this in such a high-profile way.'

'Thank you, but don't worry, my friend. You know that nice friendly telephone receptionist we have here at the Abbey? The one you liked so much? Well, she's protecting us from unwelcome intrusion. Not even the President himself would get past her. I've already asked her to field any calls for me.

'Also, I don't read any papers or magazines of the sort to which you are referring, so I won't know what, if any, scurrilous stuff is being written about me. Actually, it provides a perfect time for me not to go about so much, but rather to get on with what I do best and that is quietly praying for all those who either feel too busy – perhaps like you at the moment – or don't know how to pray for themselves. There is so much real pain, hurt, hatred, violence and suffering in the world. And not nearly enough of us who take the time to put all these troubles into God's lap – absolutely the only one who can fix them.'

'You're a good man Andreas, and a true friend. Thank you.'

Robert felt awkward and humbled as he remembered with shame his arrogant departure the last time he had been with Andreas. Then, hesitantly, he added, 'Are you still adamant you won't let me give you anything at all, for enabling all this and for all the trouble I've now caused you?'

'I'm quite sure. More so than ever in fact. But thank you for offering,' was Andreas's uncompromising reply.

To his dismay, Robert again felt the strange, alien rush of anger surging inside him at what he saw as this surreptitious – even judgemental – rejection of his actions. He fought hard to control it. Why wouldn't Andreas just take something? Yes – if only to reinforce the still fragile self-justification of his friend's position.

Robert felt as if he was now finding that the steadfast goodness he had once always so admired in Andreas had become an irritant, silently accusing him in his own life choices. He realised he didn't want to be prayed for. He did not want any awkward feelings of guilt to get in the way of the enjoyment of his new wealth and position. The world was suddenly very different now. He had only just begun to appreciate this, but he was already intoxicated by the early realisation of the extraordinary power and pleasure great wealth can bestow. Drawing on both his direct personal experience and his theological training, there was a part of him that knew, categorically, that if you sincerely invoked the help and power of the Holy Spirit in times of great temptation, help would always be forthcoming.

For the time being, however, Robert very deliberately did not want to risk inviting divine intervention to spoil the fun he was beginning to have. Maybe there would be a time for that later, he told himself, if it became necessary.

But what harm was he doing now? The money had fallen into his lap, so to speak, and had he not already put some of it to good use in the generous way in which he had paid to save and secure the future of St Mungo's? He even began to allow himself to entertain the idea that perhaps it was the hand of divine providence that had entrusted him with this money, to do good with it. He told himself he would ensure he did do good with it and thus justify his 'stewardship' of it.

Forcing himself to do so, he again apologised to Andreas. 'Well, anyway, I'm sorry about all this unwelcome publicity – the intrusion and fuss I've caused you.'

'I suppose you'll be returning to London now, Robert, to your well-deserved triumph having saved St Mungo's. No doubt you'll get a hero's welcome home, not just from your grateful parishioners, but perhaps, ever so slightly more satisfyingly, from a shamefaced bishop too?'

But Andreas's mischievous attempt to lighten the atmosphere between them this time failed to spark a similar response.

'Actually I have no plans to return to London in the near future,' was all Robert would say. He was feeling uncomfortable and wanted to end the conversation.

'Well, my friend, please know you will be often in my thoughts and always in my prayers. I'll pray that you may learn to deal well and wisely with this big responsibility – perhaps even burden – you have taken on. Please stay in touch, Robert.'

'Sure,' was all Robert would say. But he knew then it would not be so. It would in fact be a number of years before he and Andreas would see or speak to each other again.

24

WHEN BISHOP ROGERS arrived at his office that morning, Christopher Callow was leaning over the receptionist's shoulder, reading an article she had spotted on page four of the *Daily Mail*.

'Good morning, Emily. Good morning, Christopher,' said the bishop. Then, removing his overcoat, he noted Callow's unusual expression: perhaps a mixture of envy and admiration, heavily tinged with curiosity? 'Something interesting happening in the tabloid world for once?' asked the bishop cheerily.

'Well, the source of Robert Melton's new-found wealth is, it seems, revealed. Although the extraordinary explanation ends up begging more questions than it answers,' replied Christopher Callow, lifting the paper off the desk and handing it to the bishop to read.

The report of the story began with Andreas Doria winning the lottery jackpot, and then giving the entire fortune to his friend, without mention of the ticket having been first acquired by Robert Melton.

'Hmm, I see what you mean,' said the bishop a few moments later, handing the paper back to Emily – the receptionist he and Christopher Callow shared. 'Given such a huge sum of money, it is indeed a very strange explanation. Even, I would venture to say, a most unlikely turn of events.

'Wouldn't you think that, having taken a vow of poverty, this monk would, in the first place, be the most unlikely purchaser of a lottery ticket? And, even if he had, having against all odds then won such a vast fortune, decided he couldn't keep any of it after all? Wouldn't he, more logically, have wished to divide it up in some way? Perhaps giving some to family members, favourite or deserving charitable causes, or even to the Benedictine Order?

'To give it all immediately – so vast an amount – entirely to Robert Melton seems very strange indeed and must inevitably raise the question of what their relationship is. A long-lost brother or half-brother perhaps? But even if their relationship is, as friends – what shall we call it – a deeply personal one, it still seems odd. Although it never struck me that Robert Melton would be the sort to have any inclination in that direction.'

'Nor I,' interjected Christopher Callow, noticing that Emily was blushing deeply.

'At the very least, wouldn't you normally expect to share it between you?' continued the bishop. 'Although almost equally far-fetched, a more plausible explanation might be that our Robert Melton has a secret gambling addiction and, unknown to any of us, had some way of buying American Powerball lottery tickets and in the very, very unlikely event of a win, might have needed someone to collect for him. Someone in whom he could place a great deal of trust and confidence? Hence the choice of a Benedictine monk?

'I don't know anything about this Powerball lottery, or what the rules say but, just from a taxation point of view, it might well be that winners have to be American citizens, or at least legal, tax-paying, residents? To the best of my knowledge Robert is an Australian citizen with the right to work and reside in the United Kingdom, so he wouldn't have qualified.'

Christopher Callow looked at Bishop Rogers as if for the first time, surprise and a new-found respect written openly all over his normally inscrutable face. 'I think, your Grace, you might have missed your true vocation: as a detective,' he said with a smile.

'You don't know how close to the truth you've come with that one, Christopher,' the bishop wryly thought to himself.

'Elementary, my dear Watson. Funnily enough, when I was a young man, had I not felt a stronger calling to the work of God, that is exactly what I wanted to be,' responded the bishop. 'I don't know how many times I read all the Sherlock Holmes stories growing up.

'If I'm right, the only part of my theory I can't find an explanation for is how our Robert got hold of the ticket in the first place. A puzzle, that one.'

Christopher Callow was struggling for an answer to that too as he returned to his office.

With both men gone from around her desk, Emily allowed herself to indulge in the fantasy she had only recently, since meeting him for the first time, begun to harbour for the tall, good-looking, young Australian priest. She had even been thinking of trying to find an excuse to go to St Mungo's on a Sunday morning, despite the distance from her flat in Finchley. Now it seemed he had suddenly joined the ranks of the super-rich. Sadly, she realised, any chance she might have had with him was probably gone. He wouldn't look twice at her now. In the way she was sure he very definitely had that first time he had come to see the bishop.

Although she knew she was pretty, even beautiful she had been told, how could an unsophisticated girl from Finchley hope to compete with the world's most glamorous, cultivated and sophisticated women? Women who would soon be discreetly, and not so discreetly, throwing themselves at the man she had hoped might ask her out? The man with whom she had dared to dream she might eventually get to spend the rest of her life?

Emily had met many suitable men, but none of them, even her current boyfriend, had so instantly captured her interest and imagination in the way Robert Melton had when he first walked into the office.

Back in his office, Christopher Callow was unable to concentrate on the work in front of him. He was convinced that the bishop's hypothesis was somehow close to the truth and he was now consumed with a potent mixture of naked envy, insatiable curiosity and a grudging admiration.

He badly wanted to know how Robert Melton had come to be in possession of this American Powerball lottery ticket. He could think of no plausible explanation. But, being the person he was, he was reasonably certain in his own mind that there was something suspicious about it. If only he could figure out what that was.

He smiled sardonically to himself at the memory of how he had once felt a degree of sympathy for this eager, trusting young priest, whom he had helped the bishop hoodwink – albeit with the intention for it to be only temporary. What a turn around in events. And he wondered what part, if any, St Mungo's itself had played in this. He couldn't help thinking it somehow had. But just how?

25

BACK IN BOSTON, with the story now fully out in the open, it took only a relatively short time for the media interest to die away. Andreas, true to his word, eschewed all further contact with the press, or any media representatives. The St Jerome's Abbey receptionist, normally renowned for her helpful welcoming manner, was as capable of being fierce as she was friendly when it was called for and, with her at the switchboard, Father Doria was left undisturbed.

Likewise Robert himself refused all further requests for interviews and declined numerous invitations to appear on radio or television talk shows. Although well protected from ambush on the telephone by the ever-vigilant Cynthia White, she could not protect him from physical ambush when coming and going from the hotel. For this and other reasons, after a few weeks, Robert decided to move to New York.

Bill Temple understood Robert's concern for preserving St Mungo's, recognising it as something rooted within him, something tangible and enduring from the previous life he had only recently abandoned. Bill could also see that Robert Melton, eager to learn the ropes of managing his own fortune, needed to be carefully introduced to the maelstrom of corporate investing. Real estate seemed a good place to start.

Thus, guided by Bill Temple, Robert bought a newly completed high-rise office block on the corner of Madison Avenue and 56th Street in Manhattan. At the same time he bought himself a spacious private apartment in the Carlyle

Tower above the Carlyle Hotel on 76th Street and Madison. This gave him a pleasant twenty-block walk along Madison Avenue when, on fine days, he might prefer to walk to and from his office rather than be driven. These were assets Robert could see and appreciate every day. Bill understood that they would always be there, reassuring and comforting when he and Robert ventured into the far more turbulent waters of Wall Street and the bond markets.

At one point, during the course of one of their first reviews of investment prospects, Bill had happened to mention a small company, Sundholm Oil, which had recently acquired a drilling licence for oil exploration in Alaska. The fact that the company was promising to put aside five per cent of its profits to benefit the impoverished local Inuit community had caught his attention as something he thought Robert might like.

He was right. Robert had shown a sudden heightened interest and had asked Bill to tell him more about this particular company.

'Well, actually not a lot is known about them, but their prospectus claims they are drilling with an expectation of finding a hitherto unexplored oil field, which they state their geologists have identified as having the potential to yield up to ten thousand barrels of oil a day. It's heavy crude, but nevertheless valuable if they've got this one right.

'On the downside, the company has no track record to speak of and not a whole lot of experience. The more established oil companies are sceptical and don't rate their chances. So, risky, but it might be worth a speculative investment.'

'And you say that they're going to spend five per cent of their profits helping the local Inuit community?'

'That's what the prospectus says,' Bill replied, not without a note of scepticism. 'But they've got to show a profit first and this sort of oil prospecting business isn't for the faint-hearted.'

'All the same, I like the sound of this company ... what's it called again?'

'Sundholm Oil,' Bill replied, passing Robert the glossy brochure he had been looking at.

'Sundholm Oil,' Robert repeated to himself. 'Sundholm Oil, eh?'

'So, do you want me to look into it?'

'Sure, why not?'

Later, after Bill had left him for the day, Robert took a call from his newly appointed stockbroker, Andy McDowd of Dawson, Heinkel and Goldberg, to enquire how big an investment he would like to make in Sundholm Oil.

Robert, whose earlier interest in the company stemmed primarily from the fact that Sundholm was his mother's family name and that the Inuit people living around the drill site stood to benefit if the company did strike oil, was caught off guard. Acutely conscious of the fact he was now out of his depth and not wanting to show his ignorance, he played for time by telling Andy he would speak to Bill Temple.

'That's fine, Mr Melton, but I suggest you don't leave it too long. Part of my reason for calling you now was to alert you to the fact that the price of the stock seems suddenly to be rising fast. We've heard no announcement from the company and at the moment I can't find anything out but, if past history is anything to go on, this type of situation is often indicative of some good results that haven't yet been released.

'It could always be a balloon of course, but it might mean they're about to prove out the oil reserves they've been drilling for. If so, they'll be off to the races and the price will have run away by tomorrow.'

'OK. Thanks. I'll speak to Bill now and get right back to you,' said Robert.

'Terrific, I'll stay right here by my phone awaiting your instructions. When something's hot like this you have to make a decision. I have no idea why, and professionally I probably shouldn't say anything, but I have a strange hunch about this one,' Andy said as he rang off.

After making increasingly frantic attempts to track down Bill Temple by phone, Robert finally found himself speaking to Bill's youngest daughter.

'Hello. This is Carrie Temple. I'm going to be seven years old tomorrow,' she informed him brightly, before letting him know that her parents had gone out to the opera and would not be back until much later that night, innocently volunteering the information that 'Daddy' hated opera and had been unhappily dragged off to it by 'Mommy'.

With Andy McDowd waiting by his phone for instructions, Robert realised he was now on his own with this decision. He had no idea what to do, or what size of investment he should be making. How much of the money – his money – although it didn't yet even feel like it was his – was he meant to put on something like this? Half of it? A quarter? Or just some of it? He had no idea and he found himself fervently wishing there was someone he could ask about it, guiltily recognising this did not seem like the sort of problem he could trouble God with.

What was it Andy had said? He had 'a hunch about this one …' and, portentously, the name of the company was his mother's family name. He'd grown up knowing that the Sundholm family motto was 'Fortune favours the bold and brave' and his mother had always advocated following this maxim.

As he sat pondering what to do, the phone rang again. It was Andy McDowd.

'Sorry to bother you again, Mr Melton, but we've got to decide about Sundholm Oil. The price has doubled in the last thirty minutes and we're almost at the end of trading for today. What do you want me to do?'

Robert made a concerted effort to make his voice sound calm and decisive, when he answered, 'Andy, I think we should invest twenty-five.'

There was a slight pause before Andy asked, 'Twenty-five thousand?'

Robert, mistaking the pause and a note of mild surprise in Andy's voice for derision at so small an amount for such a rich man, and now desperate not to be thought of as a timid, unsophisticated investor, panicked and replied in as steady a voice as he could manage, 'No, twenty-five million.'

This was followed by another, rather longer pause, during which Andy McDowd held his breath before emitting an involuntary low whistle, and saying 'Well Mr Melton, that's certainly a bold bet. Are you sure you want to put that much on "red" so to speak – although, more optimistically perhaps, I should say "black"? You'll own approximately seventy-five per cent of the company?'

Perhaps it was his panic, Andy's use of the word 'bold', or a strong desire not to seem indecisive, but whatever it was it made Robert determined not to acknowledge he had no idea what he was doing.

'Let's just say I have a feeling about Sundholm Oil,' was all Robert could think of saying. His mouth had gone very dry and he realised he was sweating profusely. How he wished Bill Temple was there; he could see now he had an awful lot to learn.

After Andy McDowd had made the trade – his last of the day – he sat back in his chair. He was trying to work out what had given his client the confidence to make such an enormous investment in a small, unproven oil exploration company he couldn't possibly know anything about. Was Robert Melton soon going to prove the old adage that 'a fool and his money are soon parted'? Or was he what they knew in the investment business as a 'lucky' investor? His quick decision to acquire seventy-five per cent of the company was either a very brave one, or a very foolish one. Either way it could have been based on nothing more than instinct. But how many other successful investments had been made on instinct too, Andy pondered?

On an impulse, looking at his watch, Andy McDowd picked up the phone again and hurriedly made one more investment in Sundholm Oil: twenty thousand dollars to his own account. He'd already had a bit of a hunch about it and now he thought that if Robert Melton was going to prove 'lucky' he would like to have a small part of it.

That night, neither Robert Melton nor Andy McDowd slept well.

Early the following morning, well before Wall Street trading had begun, Bill Temple was on the phone to Robert. 'Good morning Robert. Hope it's not too early for you? My daughter said you'd called looking for me last night. I gather she told you how much I like opera?' he said with a chuckle.

Robert's heart began to race. He hadn't felt like this since he was a small boy at school, up in front of the headmaster for some misdemeanour ... or foolishness.

He struggled to keep control of his voice as he tried to make light of what he'd done. 'Oh it was just that Andy McDowd called about one of the companies we'd talked about yesterday: Sundholm Oil. He wanted to know if I was still interested as the price was beginning to move.'

'OK, I'll call him later and we'll take another look. That all?'

Robert cleared his throat; his mouth suddenly felt full of sawdust. 'Well, no Bill it isn't. I'm not sure how to tell you this, but when I couldn't get hold of you, I made a decision to go ahead with an investment in the company anyway.'

'A bit of a long shot, Robert, speculative one as I said, but no problem. Actually that's great, shows you're already growing your wings. So how much did you and Andy decide to punt?'

Robert gulped silently, his heart pounding, 'Oh just twenty-five,' he answered, obfuscating in the desperate hope that Bill wouldn't ask for clarification, even though he knew this could only be a temporary postponement of having to admit to the enormity of what he now suspected he had done.

'Probably a bit more than I would have advised you for such a wild card, but that should be fine. It might prove to be an expensive lesson, but at least you can afford to lose twenty-five thousand. And, hey, you just might have picked a winner, Robert, in which case the danger is you could develop a taste for this kind of thing and that's when the trouble starts! I'll be over in an hour or so, we have a busy day ahead of us today, so get in a good breakfast.' With that Bill had rung off.

Robert had no appetite for any breakfast. His mouth remained stubbornly dry as he waited for the inevitable. He didn't have long to wait. Twenty minutes later his phone rang again.

Bill's voice sounded quite different. Firstly it was an octave higher in its pitch and secondly it oozed panic. 'Robert, you've invested twenty-five million, not thousand!' He was almost yelling down the phone. 'You've bought the whole fucking company!'

'Only seventy-five per cent of it,' Robert said lamely, largely because he could not think of anything else to say. He knew Bill was not someone given to gratuitous expletives, so it was a measure of his panic and disapproval that he had resorted to using such language.

The silence at the other end of the line was now so ominous, Robert thought he should say something else.

'Listen, Bill, I apologise. I didn't really know what I was doing and I guess I did get a bit carried away. I tried to get hold of you to ask your advice first.'

'Well, if you carry on like this you won't need my advice for long, because very soon you'll have no money left,' Bill retorted crossly.

'OK. It won't happen again – I promise. I'm very sorry, Bill. Is there anything I can do about it now?'

Then he remembered something else, 'Oh, by the way, please wish your daughter a happy birthday from me.'

Bill completely ignored Robert's attempt to distract and lighten the moment, telling his client pointedly, 'All you can do is pray they do find oil – and lots of it. But that is what you're supposed to be good at isn't it? Praying I mean. I hope you've got a hotline for this one Robert – you're going to need it. I'll see you shortly.'

Bill was still very disgruntled when he arrived at Robert's suite an hour later.

'I've just checked with Andy. The market just opened with no change on Sundholm Oil from the close last night, so at least that's something, not that you could unload what you've bought anyway. Seems you've really put the company in the spotlight though: everyone's scratching their heads in disbelief over who the mystery buyer of Sundholm Oil is and what it is he or she knows that they don't.'

He let that sink in before taking off his jacket, sitting down at the expensive antique writing table and opening his briefcase. 'OK, let's be down to work to get what remains of your rapidly diminishing fortune safely invested before you have any more wild ideas, Robert. We'll need to come up with something solid to replenish what you've just thrown away.'

Suitably chastised, Robert spent the rest of the morning evaluating and agreeing solid, blue chip, stock purchases with Bill that would give him a well-balanced cross section of sensible investments in a broad portfolio of commodities and companies.

It had been a long and frankly dispiriting morning for both of them and Bill had just suggested breaking for lunch when the phone rang. Neither man was eager to take the call, but in the end Bill picked up the receiver.

'Bill? Is that you?' Andy McDowd's voice sounded uncustomarily panicky.

'Yes, it's me, Andy,' Bill answered with weary resignation. 'You'd better give it to me straight. Robert is right here with me.'

'Rumour going around that Sundholm Oil is all puff and pastry – a purely speculative float. It seems the founders of the company couldn't believe their luck when along came this patsy out of nowhere offering to buy seventy-five per cent of their combined stakes at ten times valuation. Couldn't sell it fast enough. They've made their money now whether or not any oil is found. Price is already dropping back fast. As you can imagine, the market and big oil are laughing their heads off.'

'Why the hell d'you let him buy it, Andy?' Bill retorted irately.

'Look Bill, I'm not his keeper. I don't know anything about this guy except he's a big boy and a very rich one at that. I'm just a broker who does what he's told.'

'C'mon Andy. You've been around. This one had all the hallmarks of a potential scam in need of proper investigation before investing.'

'That's easy to say with hindsight, Bill. I guess I just missed the signs this time. I even put twenty thousand of my own money into it yesterday too. Proportionally that probably means more to me than your Mr Melton's stake does to him.' Andy was sounding particularly glum as he rang off.

Looking over at Robert, Bill asked, 'Did you get the gist of that?'

'Well, I'm guessing Sundholm Oil's turned out to be a bust and I've lost my investment?' Robert responded, looking as despondent as he felt chastened. 'But, Bill please don't blame Andy for this in any way. It was entirely my own decision and my own fault. He was just acting on my clear instruction to him.'

Bill was impressed by Robert's honesty and determination not to let anyone else share the blame. A lesser man would have been only too happy to let some of it slide off onto any others conveniently within range.

Their work on other investment strategies continued in the days that followed, with no further reference to Sundholm Oil. A week had passed since Robert's moment of madness, as he privately saw it, and he was in the bathroom one morning when Bill again answered the phone.

'Bill? Andy here.' Now completely unable to keep the excitement out of his voice, the stockbroker continued, 'You're not going to believe what's just happened. Hot diggedy dog, but Sundholm Oil has struck oil! And Bill, I mean big, big oil. Not the heavy crude either, but sweet, light oil. Twice as valuable. It seems they've tapped into one of the biggest reserves of the century. Forget ten thousand barrels a day. We're talking six times more than that at least – and that's a conservative early estimate!

'The price has gone through the roof and now everyone wants to know who last week's buyer of the company was and what they all missed. No one is laughing now.

'There's bound to be some sort of investigation, of course but, if it's kosher, your Mr Melton's stake has just quadrupled in value and will likely have doubled again before nightfall.

'He can't have known anything can he, Bill? It really must mean that Robert Melton is one lucky dude. I think I'll stop trying so hard and just buy a little of whatever he buys from now on.

'Hey, I've got to go, Sundholm Oil is like a runaway train and I have to keep up. Everyone wants a piece of the action now! I'll speak to you again later, when the markets close. Take good care of that oil baron. He's just put my three girls through college for me! Bye.'

Bill sat down on the sofa. He wasn't a very religious man, but he did now find himself wondering about this maverick priest with the Midas touch. Did he have a hotline to the big man up there after all?

He was still looking dazed when Robert came out of the bathroom, 'You all right, Bill?' he asked.

'That was Andy on the phone,' Bill explained. 'He was calling about Sundholm Oil.'

Now it was Robert's turn to lose the colour in his cheeks. 'Oh. What did he have to say?' he asked as calmly as he could.

'I've been in this business all my working life, Robert. You know that. But this beats everything. I have no idea how, but you did it. Sundholm Oil has hit pay dirt – big time.'

'I don't understand,' Robert answered. 'I thought you told me … Andy said … it was all a scam. That I'd as good as lost every cent I put into it.'

'It turns out that those were just rumours as well, Robert. Andy called to say that Sundholm struck oil yesterday – struck more oil than anyone could have imagined. Now the markets are going crazy as everyone tries to catch up. And all the big boys are scratching their heads because some greenhorn called Melton has just snatched the biggest piece of the pie from right under their noses.

'I've never known Andy to be like this. He even says all he wants to do is invest in whatever you put your money in from now on,' Bill said, allowing himself a smile.

Robert pulled the chair from the desk, sat down on it and ran his fingers through his hair. 'It's incredible,' he said with relief. 'Just incredible.'

'You can say that again,' Bill acknowledged wryly. 'I feel kind of dumb now, not taking a stake myself.'

Robert was trying to get his thoughts back on track and asked, 'This is going to sound dumb too, Bill. But what does it actually mean? How has what's happened changed things for me?'

'That isn't dumb at all. It's a new experience for us both.' Robert was looking worried and a tad bewildered; Bill gave him a smile of reassurance.

'Right now, you have masterfully bought yourself the hottest new property in the world oil market. And, according to Andy, who spends his life steeped in this kind of thing, you have turned your reckless twenty-five million-dollar gamble into something closer to 200 million. In round figures, then, I would say you've doubled what you got from that lottery ticket.

'That's not a bad day's work, Mr Melton. Not bad at all. There's got to be something in the power of prayer.'

'Yes. There is, Bill,' Robert told him quietly but emphatically.

Later, after Bill had gone, Robert realised that the overriding emotion he felt was one of relief. Huge relief. By a pure fluke he had not made a complete fool of himself after all.

He knew he had been very, very lucky this time but he would have to learn fast if he was going to retain any credibility in this fast-paced, although admittedly exciting, heady financial world.

26

THE POSTMARK ON the handwritten envelope showed that it had been posted in London five days before. Robert decided that it could not be the official confirmation he had asked the bishop to send. He knew his tone had left the Bishop of West London in no doubt that this was to be a formal correspondence in every sense; his letter, when it came, would be typed.

That thought dismissed from his mind, Robert was still surprised to read what lay folded inside.

Dear Reverend Melton

I have asked a friend to post this letter to you, because the priest now working at St Mungo's gave her an address. He said someone there would know where to send this on to you.

This is not an easy letter for me to write. When I first saw you I could see that you were approaching me in a friendly way and I was rude to you – very rude – and for that I would like to apologise. I really am very sorry. I think you are a good man. I hope you are, because now it is me who needs to approach you.

I had hoped that I could see you face to face to explain why I need your advice – and your help. People in the area where I live tell me they like you. They say that you seem to be the kind of priest who really cares about others. Whenever I saw you in St Mungo's I could see how sincere you are in your work. That is why I feel I can trust you with what I am going to tell you now.

I know that you know what I do for other people. This is something I hoped I might be able to explain to you when we met. But now you are gone for what may be some while and I am having to write to you instead.

Last week something amazing happened in my life – amazing, but deeply troubling at the same time. I think you know that I could never hope to 'create' a child of my own and I like to think that the little baby who came into my life last week was sent by God. Do you believe that is possible? I hope you do, because I am certain that God brought Rebecca to me.

I have a wonderful friend, who is older than me and who was a mother herself. She helps me care for Rebecca and already, in just a few days, I feel that we are becoming a family in the best sense – loving and caring. If you could see us, I think you would agree with what I am telling you.

But I am worried – terrified is probably a better word – that if someone in authority finds out that Rebecca is living with me and my friend they will come and take her away. Rebecca's mother entrusted me with her baby before she died. I have a letter from her to prove this. But the mother was like so many of us 'unseens'. She lived outside the system, with no social security reference, no doctor, no address. She had none of the things that 'normal' people have and that is why I worry, really, really worry that the authorities might take away my little Rebecca and I will never be able to bring her up as her mother wanted me to.

Will you help me? Please, will you tell me how I can keep Rebecca and keep her safe for ever? You can write to me at this address and I promise to do whatever you advise. I haven't told anyone else about Rebecca. Only you and my friend know about her. If you believe in miracles, as I think you must do as a priest, then you will understand the miracle that has happened to me. I pray now for that miracle to last for ever.

Yours very sincerely,
Brenda

Robert studied the letter carefully as though there was something he had missed. Then he slipped it back into its envelope, scribbled 'FAO Cynthia' on it and tossed it onto the growing pile of mail that awaited his PA.

Speaking into his dictaphone, Robert said, 'Cynthia, you'll find an envelope written by hand in this morning's post. There's an address in London to reply to. It's not exactly the kind of begging letter Bill has been telling me about, but I think you can use the standard reply he and I drafted. Just change it a little to make it sound more personal. And sign it on my behalf, will you?'

Cynthia headed the letter 'From the desk of Robert Melton'.

Dear Brenda

I was interested to read your letter and thank you for taking the trouble to write to me.

I hope you will understand that a lot of people write to me as you have done and, while I am sympathetic to everyone's individual situation, it is invariably quite beyond my ability to do what people ask of me.

Please believe me when I tell you that I give careful consideration to every request for help that I receive and I was deeply moved by what you told me about you and Rebecca. However, I have to tell you that I feel I am both unqualified and ill-equipped to give you the kind of support and advice you are asking for.

I am very sorry if my reply comes as a disappointment, but I believe it best to be honest with people. I hope you will respect that and take this as my final reply on the subject.

Yours sincerely,
Cynthia White

Pp: Robert Melton

27

Eight years later

'MASTERS OF THE UNIVERSE'.

Robert had been amused by the phrase when he had first encountered it in one of *Time* magazine's surveys of the world's wealthiest and most influential business leaders – amused and a little unsettled.

But gazing across the Manhattan skyline from the roof garden of his Madison Avenue penthouse he had found himself becoming more accepting as time passed, just as he had become accepting of other things that would have been wholly out of place in the life of the Reverend Robert Melton, minister to the souls of the few in the Parish of St Mungo's who found room in their lives for pastoral care, faith and the divine.

Some years earlier, *Forbes* magazine and the *Wall Street Journal* had started looking at him. Dismissive references to the 'new, accidental investor' had grudgingly given way year by year to the more measured and respectful tones in which they now referred to the man who had first burst into the business pages of the city's popular press under the gaudy headline 'MELTON'S MIDAS MIRACLE'.

At first he had been caught up by the intoxicating thrill of the interviews, profiles and public accolades. Bill Temple had urged him to be cautious, but Robert felt himself to be a phoenix, rising from the despairing ashes of St Mungo's and all the dismal drudgery that his work, trapped in that dead-end parish, had come to represent – not just in the eyes of the Bishop of West London, or of those few parishioners who paid barely disguised lip-service to his ministry – but most tellingly in his own eyes.

It had not taken him long to formalise his rapidly expanding financial activities into a properly incorporated investment vehicle, under the name Bicknor Wilmot Securities Inc. This company occupied the top three floors of what was now named the Bicknor Wilmot Building. It had two dedicated elevators to serve just the top three floors. The remaining bank of four elevators serviced the rest of the building that was leased out to a number of other professional businesses. These included a prestigious law firm, a leading public relations agency and a private client stockbroking firm.

The ground floor and basement were leased to a branch of Mellon Bank that specialised in discreetly catering to the retail needs of the well-heeled Park Avenue residents and Lower East Side New Yorkers. These were people Robert had passed in the lobby without a glance in his early days in the city. Now he found himself coolly appraising them, men and women, evaluating them dollar by dollar from shoe leather to facelift like an analyst running his finger through an investment portfolio.

Robert had, as Bill Temple noted, proved to be a very quick learner and was soon demonstrating a natural talent for shrewd investing, both for short-term and long-term gain.

After only its first year, Bicknor Wilmot Securities Inc had already taken the New York financial community by storm and was rapidly gaining a reputation for its big, bold investment strategies that had either already yielded, or were now promising to yield, huge returns on its positions held. As a consequence Bicknor Wilmot Securities and Robert Melton were names being increasingly referenced with respect in conversations over Manhattan power breakfasts and Martini lunches.

There were, of course, those who remained steadfastly sceptical, asking themselves how a man so recently devoted to the selfless service of God, could so quickly master the ways more often associated with Mammon, no matter how much available investment money he had started out with. They argued that Robert Melton's inexperience and lack of training were what was allowing him to take what they saw as dangerously large bets in his increasingly adventurous investment strategy.

Cynics joked that he had a hotline to heaven. The envious quipped that the Almighty was building up Melton for a spectacular fall from grace – a modern-day Lucifer to send them all scurrying back to church and synagogue.

Others, most often younger members of the investment community, were more inclined to feel the excitement of what they saw as the bold, visionary positions being taken by Bicknor Wilmot in its carefully chosen areas of investment, both nationally and internationally.

These were the ones who found themselves attracted to the fund and it was this that had facilitated the rapid building up of a team of young experts, all eager to get in on the action and get ahead of the game.

New technologies offered new horizons and not for the first time the old money back east, now being joined by billions of Middle-Eastern petro-dollars in search of a lucrative home, looked greedily westwards, following 'Melton The Messiah' (as an early bio-sketch in a Sunday edition of the *New York Times* had billed him) and his money to the promised land in California and the area of hi-tech industries known as Silicon Valley.

Despite the scepticism of the older, greyer heads, there was no lack of those wanting to invest in the fund. Demand was growing to such a degree that it became obvious that another fund would have to be started to take advantage of this deep well of capital. This necessitated the separate naming of the funds, although both were essentially operating under the same investment philosophy – if, nominally, in different sectors. Drawing on his ecclesiastical background,

Robert decided to name the top fund 'The Canterbury Fund' and, as a sort of tribute to Andreas, the second fund was called 'The Cardinal Fund'.

Robert himself had become completely absorbed in the action of his new life. In contrast to the way he had viewed himself when struggling to bring life back to St Mungo's, he now felt fully alive, engaged and in control, in a way he had never felt before. It was intoxicating. But the concentration required to stay abreast of events and circumstances was enormous. It left less and less room in his life for anything other than work.

It was as a result of this, rather than through any conscious decision, that he had stopped praying on any kind of regular basis. The refreshment and peace that prayer had previously brought him had simply evaporated, drifting away and disappearing out of his life. Initially, both in Boston and New York, he had regularly attended church and always at the very least on Sundays. Now it was many weeks since he was last at St James's Episcopal Church on Madison Avenue where he had become a regular Sunday worshipper when he first arrived in New York.

The truth was that Robert Melton was now being driven by a relentless determination to make money. After that first accidental and unbelievably lucky gamble with Sundholm Oil, his fortune had continued to grow inexorably. He had even tried convincing himself that, in some unfathomable way, this too was God's work: the Parable of the Talents being played out across the stock markets of the world.

Deep down, though, was the gnawing anxiety that what he was really building was a golden calf – a false god that would eventually ensnare him and bring about his downfall and damnation. Early on, charitable giving seemed to offer a kind of absolution. But no matter how much money Robert gave away to good causes – and he did give away a great deal – it was never quite enough to reassure him that the end justified the means.

The more he consolidated his position among the financial elite, the more seductive this brave new world became. Very quickly he had leapfrogged over

Business Class and started to fly only in First Class, where he revelled in the opulence, recognition and special attention this always brought him.

All too soon however, even this was not enough and he arranged for Bicknor Wilmot to buy a Gulfstream GIIB executive jet, fitted with extended-range fuel tanks, so he could travel whenever and wherever he wanted. Two full-time flight crews consisting of pilot, co-pilot and hostess joined the payroll, thereby ensuring that, with a refreshed and rested crew always at the ready, his plane could be called upon at a moment's notice, at any time of the day or night, to fly him anywhere in the world.

Not long after that he bought a 350-foot motor yacht, persuading himself it was a useful asset for 'power entertaining' and leveraging deals. Crewed and maintained at a permanent state of sea-readiness, the yacht was based in Fort Lauderdale, where Robert would fly down at weekends with business associates, or contacts he wanted to cultivate, impress and – increasingly – to intimidate.

In his darker moments he acknowledged a sickening empathy with the yacht's previous owner: the dictator of a left-leaning banana republic. Portrayed by state propaganda as a righteous champion of his downtrodden people, Felipe Cruz had acquired a taste for the better things in life. As a child he had seen the British royal yacht *Britannia* during a state cruise around Her Majesty's Caribbean colonies and, with his fingers thrust into his nation's pathetically small reserves, topped up by handouts from his paymasters in Moscow, he had placed an order for a vessel of similar style, if not quite the same proportions, celebrated by the propaganda ministry as the flagship of the nation's infant navy.

However, President Cruz had been deposed and then assassinated before he could take delivery. For reasons of political sensitivity his successor immediately cancelled the contract with the shipyard, which allowed Robert to buy her at a 'bargain' price.

He loved this boat. To him, she represented the pinnacle of his achievement thus far. As a private joke he had named her *Lucky Find* and, when he was on board, cruising across the southern Atlantic down into the Caribbean, or over in the Mediterranean, there were times when he could forget the gnawing guilt he felt he shared with *Lucky Find*'s previous owner.

Was his entitlement to her and all she represented any worthier than that of Felipe Cruz? If they were placed side by side on Judgement Day, was there really anything to set them apart? Hadn't they both appropriated fortunes that weren't theirs?

It was in the early hours of way too many similar mornings that Robert regularly awoke to the same recurring nightmare of being unmasked as a cheap, dishonest fraud. He remained haunted that someone, somewhere out there in the world, knew that they were the one who had put that lottery ticket in the collection plate at St Mungo's. And only they would know for whom or what purpose they had put it there.

This was a nightmare that had lost none of its clarity as the years passed. Even now, Robert pictured the worshipper to whom perhaps he had administered the Body and Blood of the risen Lord at Holy Communion, stepping out from the shadows of retribution, to proclaim to the world what had happened and how he, Robert Melton, had taken the money and put it to his own personal use when – and this was just before Robert was snatched from sleep every time – that winning ticket had been destined for a higher purpose in the hands of the appropriate authorities within the Church of England.

If only he had not become estranged from Andreas. Even thinking about him made Robert feel the now-familiar surge of anger and resentment. But, despite himself, this was always mixed with a grudging respect.

Anger – because Andreas had not and would not allow himself to benefit in any way from the decision he, Robert, had made.

Respect – because Andreas's position was unquestionably honourable, added to which was the bleak understanding that, however badly he treated his friend, Andreas would never, ever divulge the secret between them.

While these sentiments may have been sharply defined by a restless conscience churning inside the head of Robert Melton, formerly vicar of St Mungo's, for the bulk of the time Robert Melton, founder and brilliant CEO of Bicknor Wilmot Securities Inc, was growing increasingly out of touch with the world in which he had once lived.

Comprehensively absorbed by his success and the influence it afforded him, Robert was locked into a tailspin of ever more seductive luxury, and the attendant status, that was sucking him into a black hole of conceit and callous disregard for the feelings of others.

This was epitomised by the way he had tried one last time to persuade Andreas to accept a very substantial 'donation' for his original help in making the big win possible. Already so far removed from the world in which they had become friends, Robert had decided on the spur of the moment to visit Andreas to make his proposition, convinced as he was that Andreas would be unable to refuse this time.

He had been on his way to a lunch meeting in Chicago when he impetuously told his pilot to change course to route via Manchester, New Hampshire. Robert had seen nothing amiss in calling Andreas from his plane to imperiously announce his imminent arrival, without a thought for how Andreas would react to hearing from him for the first time in five years.

Forty minutes later, stepping out of the stretch limousine, hurriedly hired to meet his plane at Manchester airport, Robert had been pleased to find his friend waiting for him at the main entrance to St Jerome's College.

Andreas had a warm smile on his face as he delightedly extended his arms wide in welcome. 'Well I can see you have taken easily to the trappings of high office, my friend,' he joshed Robert gently, in the way they always used to.

Suspiciously, Robert's guilty conscience made him search for a hint of sarcastic criticism, but there was none.

'So come. It's a lovely sunny day. Let's take a walk before we have lunch. It's so long since we've seen each other and I have a lot to catch up on with all your doings over the past five years. You, perhaps less so with the unchanging life I lead,' Andreas added with a self-depreciating chuckle.

'Sorry Andreas,' Robert replied, placing his hand on his friend's shoulder and looking him straight in the eye, 'to build sincerity' as his style coach had instructed. 'I have to be in Chicago for an important lunch and then for dinner later in LA. I've got my plane waiting for me at the airport.'

Turning to the limousine driver without waiting for Andreas's response, he said, 'Meet me back here in half an hour. Also, would you call my pilot and tell him to be sure to be ready to leave just as soon as I get there?'

'I'm impressed,' said Andreas. 'But disappointed too. I had so hoped to see you for longer. But if you only have thirty minutes, I'd better leave all the talking to you.'

Robert had wanted to impress Andreas – intimidate him, even bully him – convinced this would make him bend to his will. He'd become used to how most people in Manhattan, from the doormen and maître d's at Lutece, to John Joseph Phelan, Jr, chairman and chief executive of the New York Stock Exchange, courted his favour and relished his good opinion.

'Andreas, it's good to see you again,' Robert began. 'I'm truly sorry not to be able to stay for longer,' he said, oblivious to the glib apology he did not mean.

'The fact is, my life has changed completely and my time has become very valuable.'

'It always was valuable, Robert,' interrupted Andreas quietly, but without reproach.

'I'm good at what I do now,' Robert continued. 'One of the best. There's purpose to my life and I feel fulfilled.'

There was a pause, long enough to make Robert uneasy while Andreas studied his friend.

'Do you?' Andreas asked gently. 'Or are you so busy running you don't have time to interrogate that properly?'

Robert again chose to ignore the question, but Andreas could see from his change of expression that he had touched a nerve.

'Look,' Robert continued. 'The fact is I'm good, Andreas. I'm seriously good, I've more than quadrupled the money given to me with that lottery ticket.'

Andreas noted the emphasis with which Robert had said 'given to me'.

'What I wanted to say to you is, if whoever put that lottery ticket in the collection plate at St Mungo's were to step forward now and want to claim back the money, all of it, I could easily afford to give it to them, with interest, and still be a very seriously rich man.'

'Even though you *could*, I wonder if now you would be able to?' Andreas asked, almost as a rhetorical question.

Suppressing his irritation, Robert once more chose to ignore him.

'Andreas, you deserve some of the money,' he continued. 'You know you do. Without your help I would never have been able to get hold of the money that gave me my start. I want you to accept at least something.

'Name any figure you like. I don't care if you give it all away to charity, or let the Benedictines have it. The point is, now you don't even have to think of whatever I give you as being part of that original fortune. This would be money I've earned since, from my investments – from my business successes. What do you say?

'I've even taken the liberty of writing a cheque, made out to you, for a very modest two million dollars,' he said, pulling the cheque from his pocket and holding it out towards Andreas.

Andreas kept his hands tightly clasped behind his back. He felt a strong, almost physical, urge to reach out and grab the cheque. A year ago St Jerome's had started a capital campaign to raise badly needed funds for a building and refurbishment programme of the campus facilities, including the Abbey church.

Fund-raising had been slow. A single donation of this magnitude, with a likelihood of more to be got from the same source, would transform the position and more or less assure the programme's complete success.

The temptation to take the money Robert was offering was compelling, but Andreas knew that the worst temptation was always sweet, reasonable and rational. It was indeed hard to see any harm in taking Robert's money now, especially as the depositor of the original lottery ticket had not stepped forward to lay any claim to it and, after all this time, would seem hardly likely to want to do so now.

Furthermore there was, after all, no reasonable way to try and find this un-known person who, perhaps, had no idea that the lottery ticket they had placed in that Sunday collection plate had turned out to be the sole jackpot-winning ticket.

But neither of these considerations addressed the unanswerable question of who the original depositor of that ticket would have intended to benefit from any winnings.

Andreas smiled and thanked Robert again for his kind and indeed very generous offer, but, ignoring the proffered cheque, he once more steadfastly refused to take one cent from him.

Despite having vowed to himself on the flight up that he wouldn't, Robert now became angry. Getting his own way was his stock in trade. These days no one said 'No' to Robert Melton – no one, that is, who valued their job or position.

He looked at his watch impatiently and ostentatiously.

'Well, it's almost time for my driver to get back. I have to be on my way. You're being very unreasonable, Andreas. You know there is no one else on earth I can talk to about this. Look at it from my point of view, for once. I make a special trip to come all the way up here to visit you. You stubbornly refuse to take any of the money by way of thanks. What am I supposed to read into this? That you're silently accusing me of wrongdoing?' he said crossly.

'Robert, I don't presume to accuse or stand in judgement of you over anything. You are my friend. However you're right on one point,' said Andreas quietly. 'There is no one else down here on earth you can talk to about it. But have you thought of talking to God instead of me?'

Back aboard his plane, Robert called for a scotch and brooded sullenly as the pilot headed westwards across the Hudson Valley and towards Niagara Falls, Lake Erie and on to Chicago.

Robert had singularly failed in his aim. Andreas had not budged. Worse still, he had left Robert feeling shallow and tarnished. Andreas's acceptance of just some of the lottery money was the only way Robert had of lending legitimacy to everything he had done since Andreas had passed the winning cheque to him in its entirety. Without his friend's support, Robert realised, there was no way to restore the peace of mind he craved.

He pondered the two comments Andreas had made that he had chosen to ignore.

Was he working so hard and keeping himself so busy precisely to avoid questioning the legitimacy of this new life he had so wholeheartedly embraced?

And, were a bona fide claimant to the lottery ticket to surface, would he really be able to hand over 200 million dollars?

Reluctantly he had to admit to himself that the truthful answer to the first question might be 'Yes' and to the second 'No'.

He had parted badly from Andreas, going so far as to suggest that his quiet life of prayer was a self-indulgent trifle: a waste of time, doing no good for anyone. Whereas he, Robert, was working hard to create wealth, with which he was investing many millions of dollars in charitable endowments, organisations, businesses and activities that would be saving lives and creating jobs, thereby helping huge numbers of people all over the world.

He had even angrily derided Andreas's relationship with God. Andreas claimed to be praying for all those too busy, too preoccupied or simply unaware of God's great love and mercy for them. But Robert had spitefully dismissed it as a soft option in contrast to the real and practical good he was able to provide from putting his money to use in what he now cynically referred to as 'love in action'.

Robert had wanted to hurt Andreas because he wouldn't cooperate with him. Although he knew he had at least succeeded in that, the look of pain and surprise it had brought to Andreas's face had brought no pleasure to Robert.

And pleasure was what he needed now. As his plane touched down in Chicago he decided to do what he had increasingly resorted to doing when he felt this way. Before alighting to the waiting limousine he asked his pilot to arrange for one of Chicago's most elegant and expensive 'escorts' to be aboard the plane waiting for him when he got back from lunch. She was to bring suitable clothing and be ready to join him for dinner in Los Angeles, following which they would be staying the night at the Bel Air Hotel in Beverly Hills.

By now both his pilots knew his taste in such women; his preference for dark eyes, dark hair and olive skin, making Brazilian, Columbian, Argentinean and other South American beauties always acceptable.

But Mr Melton also required these girls to be well educated and sophisticated. His pilots knew the success of the assignation, and therefore their ability to 'pick', would be determined by whether or not the lady in question flew with them back to Chicago – or even better to New York tomorrow – or whether she would be left in Los Angeles with a first-class ticket on one of the commercial carriers back to Chicago, while they flew non-stop to New York.

That disastrous trip had been three years ago. Countless numbers of women had drifted through Robert's life since then. But the one person he had really wanted to spend time with now seemed more unapproachable than ever. Although Andreas had made an attempt to contact Robert soon after their last meeting, it had been to reaffirm their friendship rather than to change his position over the money Robert had offered him. Robert was not interested in preserving their friendship

237

without Andreas's even modest participation in taking some of the windfall. Now, because of their last encounter, he had barred himself from contacting Andreas again. In the long watches of the night, after the same recurring nightmare had woken him once again, he felt more isolated than ever.

Tightening the cord of the bathrobe he had pulled on carelessly, he held the heavy cut-glass tumbler to his nose and breathed in the delicious aroma of the sixteen-year-old, cask aged, Lagavulin he had poured on his way past the eighteenth-century Boulle bureau, which he had bought on a whim in Zurich to serve as a drinks cabinet. Among other tastes he had acquired, these days Robert Melton drank only the finest malt whiskies.

Around him the city blazed, flashed and sparkled beneath the glowing canopy of the night sky. The sound of the traffic came to him as a softly murmured moan rising from the streets far below.

This was a view he had come to know too well. Marooned by sleep, despite the growing number of pills Dr Brubeck had prescribed, Robert had discovered whisky to help him forget. Whisky and those transient thrills between the sheets that no man of the cloth could ever countenance.

After Vanessa? A smooth, slightly smoky, Lagavulin. It was a natural segue.

That was something else that would have been wasted on the Reverend Robert Melton.

Things were different with Vanessa. Robert didn't pay her in either cash or kind. Drawn to the aura of sheer power she sensed in him, she had come to him at first willingly and then hungrily.

He wasn't proud of this conquest but the way in which he satisfied her craving for him was an aphrodisiac he had not experienced with any of the other women who had joined him in bed.

Outwardly Vanessa was the stunningly beautiful, slim, elegantly and expensively dressed trophy wife of Ivan Waverley, flamboyant founder of the racy Waverley Brokerage firm, one of Manhattan's new generation of titans in global finance and the most vociferous opponent of Robert Melton's rise to power and prominence in the domain to which Ivan Waverley believed he held an almost divine right.

Cool and aloof, Vanessa came across to most people as lofty and faintly disdainful – and as a result most people were in awe of her.

Robert was not. In fact, the first time they were in the same room, having observed the effect Vanessa was having on others, Robert had ignored her, preferring instead to 'joust' with her husband over the workings of the newly constructed, complex financial investments which were being disdainfully referred to as 'junk bonds'.

Vanessa had been struck by Robert the moment he walked into the room. It was as if some primitive instinct had been involuntarily awoken in her. An instinct that silently told her that this was the man to whose power she needed to submit herself.

After a while, she joined them at her husband's side. Conversation moved to the Independence Day holiday. The Waverleys would be at their estate home in the Hamptons; Robert taking some Caribbean sea air aboard *Lucky Find*.

But beneath the casual chatter and restrained point-scoring, Robert became aware of a suppressed tension emanating from Vanessa towards him, which she was struggling to conceal. Although a little uncertainly at first, this started to awaken an equally primitive response from somewhere deep within him.

Robert had not been surprised when Vanessa had contacted him a few days later. What had surprised him had been her dispensing with even a token vestige of romantic formality.

Although he himself had no particular penchant for it, from the moment of their first meeting in his penthouse, both she and Robert had abandoned themselves completely to the erotic thrill of sadomasochistic pleasure that Vanessa seemed to so urgently crave. They did so with a lust entirely devoid of any inhibition in a way he could never have imagined before.

At first Robert had been disturbed at his enjoyment of being cast in the role of master of this sophisticated, beautiful and willingly abject slave who had come to him. But as the sight of Vanessa kneeling submissively in front of him, trembling with arousal, became more familiar, he had grown more comfortable with it and now found he greatly enjoyed this controlling aspect in their relationship. He also found he had a particular talent for satisfying her in any way she wanted. It had as much to do with his intuitive understanding of the brain as well as the body.

For him the feeling was always heightened by the thrill of knowing the exquisite, if secret, superiority he had gained over his most critical and dangerous business rival.

Robert knew too what no one else had ever discovered – that Vanessa was powerless to resist. He had awoken a response in her that craved absolute domination, in the knowledge that with this man it would be safe completely to let go of her long-suppressed desire to, literally, physically belong to someone else, in the most basic animal way that a bitch-dog belongs willingly to her master.

What was it she had sensed in Robert that was so different to others?

Perhaps it was the priest in him, playing subconsciously to her strict Catholic upbringing, in which the sanctity and discretion of the confessional was absolute, bringing with it a feeling of relief, based on total trust and complete safety.

And perhaps it was a nod towards the priest in him that permitted Robert to indulge Vanessa in this way. Later, after she had left, he would console himself that what he was giving her was in itself a twisted form of 'ministry'. Physical and perverted as this ministry may have been, Robert believed he detected an underlying penance in Vanessa's passion.

Not content with just physical control of her when they were alone together, Robert had developed a system of signals so that when they met in public, sometimes at a restaurant, but more usually at the ubiquitous charity events, awards dinners or other black-tie occasions, he would still be able to exert his grip on her at a distance. In such situations, especially when she was with her husband, Robert delighted in being her puppet master.

Once, in the Four Seasons on East 52nd Street, Robert, lunching with business associates, spotted Vanessa and her husband arriving with some friends. Ivan nodded an obligatory curt acknowledgement in Robert's direction as he was shown to a table across the Bar Room. Vanessa gave Robert no sign of recognition.

Positioned as he was with his back to their table, Robert found an excuse to swap places with one of his guests. Now, with a direct line of view towards Vanessa, he had made eye contact with her before slowly and lazily pulling on the left lobe of his ear. This was the signal they had agreed upon that meant she was to present herself to him while he decided exactly what he was going to do with her.

Even at a distance, Robert had fancied he could see her silk-sheathed figure beginning to shift in her chair.

Whatever excuse she had had to come up with to satisfy Ivan, Robert had known his signal would compel her to come to him as soon as possible. His private elevator had ushered her up to him later that evening looking for satisfaction of her own.

His whisky tumbler was empty. Unhurriedly Robert went in search of the bottle before walking back to the bedroom, where he had left Vanessa deliberately lying face up, naked and exposed. He stretched and tightened the silk ropes he had used to bind her wrists and ankles to the four corners of his, extra large, king-size bed, poured more whisky into the tumbler and took a sip.

Obediently, Vanessa ran the tip of her tongue slowly and hungrily around her mouth. This was going to be an evening to remember.

28

WHAT ROBERT HAD no way of knowing was that that evening with Vanessa would be memorable for another reason: it was to be their last together.

She had been cold and dispassionate when she telephoned him two nights later to announce that she was not going to see him any more. Their affair had become an addiction – an obsession – she told him, and things were in danger of getting out of hand.

'That's rich,' Robert thought to himself. But he detected something in Vanessa's voice that betrayed another reason.

'I've finally got something out of my system,' she admitted. 'At last I feel free.'

'Free? Forgive me if I'm wrong, Vanessa, but I don't think it was me who was looking for domination and bondage.'

'That's what I'm telling you,' she persisted. 'I understand now that I can put all that in the past.'

'By "all that", I take it you include me?'

Vanessa bridled at this. 'Oh, come on Robert. Don't act the hurt little boy. You had your fun and don't pretend you didn't. There's something else,' she continued, as if she was dictating a grocery list. 'I don't want to lose Ivan.'

'Ivan?' Robert asked incredulously. 'Since when has Ivan been important to you?'

'Since I realised that I want us to stay together.'

'Since you realised losing Ivan meant losing the gravy train you're happy to luxuriate in, you mean?'

'Now you're being petty,' Vanessa snapped back. 'If Ivan and I lived separate lives, it was because of me – because of the way I was feeling about myself and … what I wanted. You know what I'm talking about.'

'And now I've given you that, you're ready to move on? Is that it?'

'Ivan and I can be happy, Robert. I see now that's what I want. I want my marriage to work with Ivan.'

'Good for Ivan,' Robert retorted sourly.

'I didn't think you'd behave this way,' Vanessa said. 'I had a higher opinion of you, Robert. I guess I was wrong.'

'Then that makes two of us, Vanessa.' He listened to the silence before she hung up and the line went dead.

Robert poured himself a generous measure of whisky and wandered out onto his balcony. He could not deny the powerful aphrodisiac Vanessa had been every time she had begged him to indulge those, previously undiscovered, sadistic tastes she had implored and encouraged him to explore fully with reckless abandon. Thinking now about his encounters with her in a detached sort of way, he realised that it was not the erotic thrills alone that he had enjoyed. Bizarrely, much of his pleasure had been in the giving; being trusted enough to give Vanessa discreetly all she craved. It was a strange feeling: disconcerting and at the same time enriching.

Their affair had lasted for almost two years. Robert had been rigorous in keeping it under wraps. But he had hoped its secrecy might allow him somewhere to escape from the perpetual torment of the combined demons of guilt and self-betrayal. Now Vanessa had deprived him of that small refuge and it was that, he realised, that made him bitter. She had stepped aside from his life to start afresh with Ivan, leaving Robert to reconcile himself to the deep-seated feeling that he was somehow a fraud, an impostor, in a world in which he didn't really belong.

*

Robert was not the only one to be having misgivings. Since moving to New York soon after the creation of Bicknor Wilmot Securities, Cynthia White had become indispensable in her role as his PA. She had relished the thrill of being a vital cog in the 'Melton Machine', as year on year Robert's stock had risen in Wall Street and the wider business community.

Working closely with him every day, she had grown fond of him and had found there were many qualities about him she greatly admired, not least of which were his focus and determination.

But as the years passed both Cynthia and Bill came to realise that Robert had grown into a man possessed by a relentless determination to make ever more money – and what worried them both even more was that there was no end in sight: no goal, nothing at the end of the rainbow that was luring him on. Despite all his success in multiplying, now many times over, his original fortune, and despite the numerous accolades, both public and private, being heaped upon him, Robert Melton was never fully content in his achievements.

Making money had become his narcotic, bringing ever-briefer moments of satisfaction at the cost of long spells of irritability and withdrawal. As a faithful Christian believer and regular churchgoer, Cynthia had become saddened and alarmed to see this former man of God so completely abandoning his background, his upbringing and his vocation.

She was also dismayed and discouraged by the way Robert's once courteous and solicitous concern and treatment of others had become impatient, intolerant and downright arrogant. Junior members of the Bicknor Wilmot team had once looked forward to a chance encounter with the boss. Robert had made no secret of the truth that he was on as much of a learning curve as they were and, no matter what deal he was engaged with himself, he had always made time to show interest and encouragement in the work others were doing on his behalf.

But these days younger employees who wanted to get on in Robert Melton's organisation were careful to keep out of his way. It wasn't so much that the man at the top lost his temper; they could live with bosses who behaved like that, knowing that the storm would pass and the sun would shine once again. What frightened them was the cold, almost cruel edge to Robert's voice when he found fault – and the young women who had been attracted to Bicknor Wilmot in part because of the dashing, daredevil man at the head of the firm felt this most keenly. Recently it had become commonplace for Cynthia to find some of them repairing tear-stained make-up in the ladies' restroom, crushed and humiliated by a scathing rebuke from the man they once had hopes of idolising. She wondered if Robert knew what hurt he could cause. Worse still, Cynthia wondered if he even cared any more.

Her loyalties were torn. She had loved the early success of Bicknor Wilmot, the attention it brought and her role in it. But increasingly she was questioning her attitude to Robert. Was she being hypocritical in continuing to work for a man now so different to the one who had once been eager to be mentored by Bill and her?

Bill was also questioning his position at Bicknor Wilmot, if for different reasons. Although he had been pleased and flattered, he could never understand why Robert had been so insistent that he retain an office and come down to New York almost every week. Bill was still being paid a very large consultancy retainer fee, which had started to make him feel uncomfortable. It was generous of Robert, very generous, Bill acknowledged, but it didn't make sense. The advice he gave Robert had long ago been completely overtaken by Robert's own shrewd, if largely intuitive, investment decisions that seemed so often to be unerringly correct.

From Bill's early introduction and tuition, Robert had rapidly gone on to prove himself the ultimate master amongst 'Masters of the Universe', displaying an uncanny knack of being able to anticipate and extrapolate the fortunes of a particular company's future, almost foretelling whatever unseen opportunity or disaster lay ahead.

Bill knew Robert didn't need him any more for any logical business reason. He suspected Robert's motives for wanting him to stick around were a complex mix of gratitude, the need for a security blanket and some equally deep-seated personal insecurity. Although they had become very close and their relationship was based on trust and friendship, Bill had always had the feeling that Robert was not telling him quite everything. He guessed it might be connected with his abrupt departure from the priesthood, but he couldn't be sure.

There was something else too that had convinced him it was time to leave and return full-time to his practice in Boston – and this was the concern he unknowingly shared with Cynthia.

Bill did not like to admit it, but Robert had changed. He was not the same man whom Bill had delighted in teaching, even protecting, when they first met. He knew it would be absurd and quite wrong not to expect Robert to have changed as he matured, grew in confidence and learned how to manage and live with his vast wealth. But, if Bill was being honest with himself, he did not like the changes he had watched unfolding.

From a man who had cared deeply about other people, Robert had turned into someone self-absorbed, selfish, impatient and arrogant. His intolerance of other people's failings and feelings, and his increasingly demanding, unreasonable expectations of those who worked for him, bordered on a depth of unkindness that Bill could no longer bear to witness.

The truth was he had sadly become disillusioned in witnessing his eager, innocent young protégé turn from a man of intelligent, passionate caring and considerable charm, into an arrogant, dismissive bully.

From what Bill could tell, Robert's sole aim in life seemed to have become the pursuit and accumulation of greater and greater wealth. Even more disturbingly, it was not as if this was solely for Robert's self-gratification. Bill had detected something darker. Robert was increasingly using his wealth to intimidate and command at least external respect and glorification from others; anyone who fell short of doing this to Robert Melton's satisfaction felt his displeasure keenly.

Andy McDowd had been one of the higher-profile casualties still licking their wounds in the wake of Robert's financial juggernaut. Andy had learned his trade in the cut and thrust of Wall Street dealing floors. He spoke his mind and respected those who did the same. Over the years he had worked with Robert Melton, Andy had made a practice of following Robert's personal investment strategies. It had paid off handsomely at the outset with Sundholm Oil and, with few exceptions, that success had been repeated time and again across a broad portfolio of investments. Alongside his clients, Andy would never have called himself wealthy, but by following Robert Melton's tips he had become comfortably well off – and this hadn't gone unnoticed.

Come Christmas a couple of years earlier, the in-house magazine of Dawson, Heinkel and Goldberg had printed an interview with him, in which Andy had been flattered to answer questions about his work and his consistent record of outperforming most other brokers – and not just his immediate colleagues.

Afterwards, Andy pleaded that he hadn't wanted to incriminate Mr Melton in any way by mentioning his name in the article. Maybe Andy had simply become so used to tailing Robert's success that he had lost sight of where his inspiration had come from. Perhaps he had enjoyed Thanksgiving just a little too much and was feeling very at ease with himself and the world at large when he was interviewed shortly afterwards. But that was the last Christmas when Andy McDowd was truly happy.

On his first day back at work after the holiday, the president had asked to see him and, when Andy was seated in his office, had handed him a short letter. There were times when Andy woke at night in a cold sweat still remembering what he had read.

Although the firm acknowledged his years of service they were, reluctantly, having to let him go. Apparently one of their most prestigious clients had telephoned the chairman of the board, at home on Christmas Eve, to complain in the strongest terms about Andy's professional misconduct. Robert Melton had read the interview with Andy McDowd and had taken grave exception to it.

'But what was I supposed to do?' Andy had asked the president. 'Sure, I followed the guy's trades. Who wouldn't? There's nothing illegal in that. It's not insider trading or anything. I've always been straight down the line. Ask anyone you like. They'll tell you the same about me. Every reader of the *Wall Street Journal* would follow Robert Melton, if they had the chance.'

'That is Mr Melton's point,' the president explained. 'You did have the chance and you took it. But you made no acknowledgement of the debt you owe to Mr Melton. None at all, as far as I can see and – most importantly from the point of view of this firm – as far as Mr Melton can see.'

As he cleared his desk, Andy McDowd breathed a silent prayer of thanks that at least his youngest daughter had finished college. Ahead lay an uncertain future; when Bill Temple caught up with him, Andy McDowd was selling life insurance in Elizabeth, New Jersey.

What stung Bill at the time was Andy's refusal to blame Robert for what had happened. 'I screwed up, Bill – big time,' Andy told him without rancour. 'I'd never have made the money I did if it hadn't been for Robert Melton. I guess I just got too big-headed. Lost sight of what he had done for me all this time.'

Business is business, Bill Temple had reflected. However, remembering Robert's defence of Andy at the time of the Sundholm Oil gamble, he had expected Robert Melton to be the kind of man who would still retain a modicum of compassion in his dealings, as Bill himself had done throughout his business life. That saddened him and the already tarnished gloss of Wall Street lost a little more of its gilt in Bill's eyes. He knew it would continue to lose its lustre as time went by.

The subject of Cynthia and Bill's concern and disappointment was more ill at ease than either of them realised, however. It was not just Vanessa, although her sudden departure from his life had contributed to Robert's malaise. It was that old, deep-down feeling of being haunted that wouldn't let him rest. Haunted by the fact that someone, somewhere out there in the world, knew that they were the one who had put that lottery ticket in the collection plate at St Mungo's. Far from abating, this feeling had amplified itself over the years, insidiously, corrosively taking over his life.

That had been eight years ago, but still he couldn't get over the fear of them coming forward, even now, to tell the world what had happened. His theological training helped Robert to know enough about psychoanalysis to understand that he was suffering from an irrational paranoia that, with professional assistance, he could almost certainly be helped to overcome. But he also knew it to be too big a secret to entrust to anyone, other than the one person to whom he had already entrusted it: Andreas.

And now, Robert wondered, would he find any redemption – even with Andreas?

29

BILL BROKE THE news to Robert when he got back from a business trip to Puerto Rico.

'What's on your mind, Bill?' Robert had asked casually, as he leafed through the papers Cynthia had left neatly piled on his desk. 'Have a seat. You look like you're on sentry duty or something.'

But Bill preferred to remain standing. 'Robert, I've decided it's time for me to go back to Boston,' he said.

'Sure thing,' Robert replied distractedly as he concentrated on the flickering screens on his desk. 'We can talk on the telephone if there's anything urgent before next week. I think my senior executive is entitled to take a little time off once in a while.'

'Robert please pay attention for once. You're deliberately not understanding me,' Bill continued. 'I'm twenty years older than you and I've been yo-yoing between Boston and here for almost eight years. It was OK at first, when I knew you needed me. But things are different now.' He just managed to stop himself adding 'And you're different now.'

'The point is, you know everything I can teach you. I want to go back home and run my own consultancy practice while I still can.'

Robert had looked up and abruptly stopped shuffling through the papers. He was now looking directly at Bill. 'But you can't,' he said incredulously. 'What about me? What am I going to do?

'If it's a raise you need, you know you've only got to ask, just tell me what you want. Come to think of it, I had been meaning to discuss increasing your holding in Bicknor Wilmot stock. Maybe we could realise an immediate cash sum to double your stake in the company – as a personal emolument from me?'

But he could see by Bill's expression that this wasn't the issue.

'It's not the money, Robert. It's never been about the money. Although, God knows, you've always been more than generous to me.'

'Then what is it, Bill?' Robert asked plaintively. 'Do you want more time away from the office. Is that it? How about we sit down and structure a programme that would let you work from home – coming down here maybe once every two or three weeks. That can't be bad, can it?'

But the shrug of Bill's shoulders and his weary sigh gave Robert his answer.

'I don't want this to sound ungrateful, Robert, because it isn't meant to. But this past couple of years Bicknor Wilmot has been all about you. When people mention Bicknor Wilmot, it's always your name that follows: Robert Melton. And that's how it should be. Don't get me wrong. You built this company. It's yours. Your success. Your triumph.'

And here Bill gave a sigh. 'But I can't honestly say it's got anything to do with me any more. Bill Temple? Who talks about him today?'

'You're being ridiculous,' Robert scoffed.

'Maybe I am,' Bill conceded. 'But, thanks to you, I've been able to build up sufficient capital to retire anytime I like. I want to return to my modest consultancy business and now I think is the right time to do that.'

'So, you're going to leave me high and dry?'

'You're hardly on your own,' Bill said, gesturing to the broad, open-plan office where the hundred or more Bicknor Wilmot staff were glued to their computer terminals, frequently talking animatedly down the telephone at the same time.

'You know what I mean,' Robert told him crossly. 'I always ranked you highly for your loyalty, Bill, and I thought you enjoyed our work here together.'

251

Bill Temple knew better than to react to this jibe, but Robert's words cut deep. 'I thought so too,' was all he said.

Bill was guarded when Cynthia started to prise from him this exchange with Robert. She had, and would always have, great respect for Bill Temple, who had been so much more than just an employer. He had believed in her, trusted her, empowered her and mentored her to get to where she was today. She knew how fortunate she had been in ever meeting a man like Bill and she had learned over more than a dozen years of working together how to read what was going on in his mind.

Right now, Bill was deeply unsettled; Cynthia had spotted that right away. Was he being disloyal to Robert, he worried? Was it selfishness, or pique on his part? Was he jealous of Robert's success? Bill didn't know. He really didn't know.

Cynthia did.

'That's baloney, Bill Temple,' she told him firmly. 'If Robert Melton doesn't know what a good man he could be losing, he doesn't deserve to have you working with him one minute longer.'

Bill smiled weakly, in acknowledgement of her support and encouragement.

But there was nothing weak about Cynthia White when she tackled Robert, after Bill had gone to lunch. Cynthia had marched into Robert's office, slammed the door shut and told him he was being a 'damned fool' for treating Bill the way he had.

Robert was so taken by surprise that he didn't know how to react, which left the way clear for Cynthia to offload the disillusionment and disappointment that had been building inside her for too long now. And she gave it to him straight, telling him it was entirely his own fault for having become so obsessed with money that he had forgotten how to treat people properly – 'good people, Robert, like Bill, who's the best'.

Robert still had enough of a grip on reality to know that if he attempted to remonstrate with his PA for daring to speak to him like this, she would resign on the spot and not mind one bit doing it. He knew it was almost a challenge, a test, and she was not going to take any shit from him.

He also knew she was very angry with him. He decided to sulk instead. This he did for several days until he had to leave for the Far East.

Cynthia, however, quickly regained her composure. More so than Bill, she felt she had an influence on Robert that could still be helpful in curbing some of his worst excesses and thoughtless acts of arrogance.

Deep down, she knew Robert was still a good person – Cynthia was convinced about this. He was acting wilfully, like a spoiled child in a candy store, and when he had finally overdosed on the candy, she desperately hoped his more balanced and reasoned sense of proportion and perspective would return. She still believed she could help save him from himself – though how long that would take was an entirely different matter.

Robert seemed to be in a more measured frame of mind when he returned from his whistle-stop tour of Australia, Indonesia, China and Japan. He had been at back-to-back meetings with government officials, including the Chinese premier, the Japanese prime minister and various Asian captains of industry: principally, but not exclusively, those involved in the mining sector, covering such diverse commodities as gold, platinum and coal.

It had been a very successful trip and Robert was feeling particularly good about the meetings he had had with Anglo American. He was impressed by this particular global giant's ethical approach to mining: their commitment to local employment; their regard for the safety and welfare of their local workforce; and their willingness to invest in the social infrastructure of the areas in which they mined. It reminded Robert of what had first attracted him to Sundholm Oil, all those years and billions of dollars ago.

On the flight home he had decided to increase his stake in the company significantly. He still squirmed when he remembered how Cynthia had ripped into him before his departure, holding up a mirror for Robert to see his own greed and disregard for other people. What she had said to him had struck home. That, and what he had learned from Anglo American, had inspired him to make a point in the future to seek out long-term ethical investments, rather than simply the ones that boosted the bottom line.

Amongst the correspondence that had been awaiting his return, Cynthia gave him a larger than usual, old-fashioned, blue envelope. It was handwritten in clear, bold copperplate, marked 'Personal, Private and Confidential'. It was addressed to 'The Revd Robert Melton'.

Straight away Robert spotted the postmark from Manchester, NH, but he knew from its neatness the writing was not Andreas's. Turning the envelope over, he looked at the return address. The envelope had been mailed by a Mrs Maude Kimball from New London, NH.

Robert held the letter in his hand for a long time, just looking at it. He sensed already what it was going to tell him and he couldn't decide whether his dominant emotion was one of fear, or relief.

Finally, he asked Cynthia to instruct Jill, his secretary, to hold all his calls. Then, having given orders that he be left undisturbed, he closed his office door and sat down at his desk.

Unlocking the secret drawer in which he kept his most private and personal documents, he took out the last envelope he had received addressed to the Revd Robert Melton. After eight years of reading and re-reading it, he could recite the letter inside word for word, but he still drew it from the envelope and smoothed it on the tooled leather surface of his desk.

Dear Revd Melton

I received your letter and I thank for you writing to me. Thank you too for being honest enough to make me understand that your life is following a new path.

I would not be honest if I did not tell you that I have read in the newspapers about what has happened to you and why you are now living in America. That is why I can see that the worries and problems of people like me and Rebecca are no longer your concern.

I hope your new life brings you happiness for as long as you want it to. But I also hope that one day you will come to value the work you used to do in London, at St Mungo's. In my prayers I ask God to bring you back to us when He wants you to return to His work once again.

Please know that I will always remember you every time I visit St Mungo's.

Yours, very sincerely,
Brenda

Leaving Brenda's letter on the desk, Robert turned over the envelope he now held in his hand and opened it. He was not prepared for what he read.

30

My dear Robert (for you are very dear to me),

Yes – I am the lady who put the Powerball lottery ticket in your collection plate at St Mungo's on that cold, wet Sunday morning in London eight years ago.

Do you believe in fate? At the time I had no idea this would turn out to be the winning ticket (what are the overwhelming odds against that?). It was the absurd gesture of an even more absurd old lady, giving a ridiculous spur-of-the-moment gift to a grandson, in which I was openly challenging fate to give me a sign. For, you see, you are my long-lost grandson.

Shortly before the outbreak of the Second World War, I was studying in England, where I fell madly in love with an English student, who was an undergraduate at Oxford. We had a brief affair. The result was an unanticipated and certainly unplanned pregnancy. As a Roman Catholic, brought up in a strictly Catholic family, there was only one thing worse than having a child out of wedlock: that was to have an abortion.

The scandal within my family, and for my family, in a small rural New Hampshire community was impossible to contemplate at the time. I also passionately wanted to complete my studies. So, against all my beliefs and upbringing, I resolved to have an abortion, secure in the knowledge that that way my parents need never know and would never be shamed by me in the eyes of their community.

However, with war looking increasingly likely, the talk amongst the undergraduates was all about how many men would once more have to fight and die, and how it was now the duty of women to have more babies. In the face of this, my already troubled conscience would no longer allow me to consider an abortion. That is when I made my bargain with God. If I gave up my studies (for which the potential onset of war gave me the perfect excuse) and had my baby, I would give it up for adoption at the very moment of birth and return immediately to the United States. (By now my parents, your great-grandparents, were begging me to come home anyway for my own safety.)

As part of this bargain, I promised God that I would never, ever, try to make contact with my child at any time in the future. I even instructed the nurse in the maternity wing of the hospital in Oxford not to tell me if I gave birth to a boy or a girl, but to take the child straight away. All I asked was for them to make sure it went to a good, deserving and above all loving home.

Not holding or seeing my baby, even once, was, it turned out, the hardest thing I've ever had to do in my life. Although I did in the end know he was a boy because the doctor unthinkingly let it slip by saying 'come on little man', while encouraging him at the moment of birth. I'm now so glad he did.

After that I returned to America, without completing my studies. I spent the war years back with my family in New Hampshire, where I worked down in Concord on the staff of Governor John Winant, until Franklin Roosevelt posted him to London as our ambassador, to replace the hugely unpopular Joe Kennedy, who was busy advocating cutting a peace deal with Adolf Hitler. When America joined the war, I worked as a volunteer in the munitions factory in Newport, which was closer to New London.

With what I had been through alone in Oxford, with the effect of the war on us all, and the eventual discovery that your biological grandfather had been killed in the Normandy landings, I never did get married. You see, it may be hard for you to understand, but I loved your grandfather. Neither of us was ready to get married at the time, let alone contemplate having children and raising a family. The hope I had secretly harboured throughout the war was that he

257

would come home safe and we would be able to get back together once again, to rediscover the love that had led us into our ill-fated affair.

He really did love me as much as I loved him. It was the timing that was terrible. We were both young, foolishly romantic students, and I think he panicked at the thought of being trapped into the responsibility of marriage. When I told him I was going to have the baby after all, that was when our relationship ended. But our feelings for each other hadn't changed.

When I found out Jack (Jack Talbot was your grandfather's name) had been killed on the D-Day beaches, I sank into a deep depression that lasted for weeks. The worst part was that there was no one I felt I could talk to, no one to share my feelings with. I was carrying a heavy burden all alone and in secret.

I never returned to England until, many years later, I came to find my son. All that time I'd kept my secret and my side of the bargain I'd made with God. But after the deaths of my parents and my older sister (who never had any children), I decided it was time to go back. Ever since giving birth to your father there had not been a single day when I had not thought about him and prayed for his wellbeing. Although I knew nothing about his adoptive parents, or what name they had given him, in my mind I had named him John, after John Radcliffe, the man who had founded the wonderful hospital in which he was born.

I spent a long time thinking about the solemn bargain I had entered into with God all those years ago, but I decided that, now I was older, God would permit me to try to find my son, as long as I made no attempt to contact him, or risk upsetting his life. (I had no idea even whether his adoptive parents would have told him he was adopted or not; you must remember that in those days it was not usual.)

All I really wanted to do was to see if I could find out from the hospital what they knew of my son's adoption. If I was able to get that information, all I hoped for, if I was very lucky, was perhaps the chance to be able to set eyes on him for what would have been the very first and only time in my life. I promised myself I would do no more than that. It was a long shot after so much time; I just felt I must try.

I wrote to the hospital and by an extraordinary piece of luck (or was it pre-destined?) in their reply I was told that, although the hospital records were incomplete, a researcher from the university had just finished a three-year study on tracing the orphans and children put up for adoption in the city of Oxford over a twenty-year period, spanning ten years either side of the outbreak of the Second World War. In this study, wherever possible, he had followed their lives right up to the present.

It was from this kind and intelligent man that I learned that the son I called 'John' had in fact been christened Stephen and that he had been adopted by a rather older than usual, childless, academic couple living in the small town of Burford, quite close to Oxford. They had not hidden from Stephen that he was adopted. I also learned that at some point, before he eventually emigrated to Australia, he had tried unsuccessfully to find out about and locate his biological parents.

I was delighted to discover that this researcher had been so thorough he had even followed up enquiries about Stephen in Australia and was able to tell me about your father's marriage followed by his tragic death some years afterwards. Finally he told me about your existence, my grandson, and how the last he knew was that you were studying to become a priest in the Anglican Church. He had never met you, your mother or your father's adoptive parents. Almost all his enquiries had been conducted by mail.

Armed with this information, and your name, it was not so hard to find out from the Church of England authorities where you were. Having done so, I travelled to London and got a room at a small hotel on Cromwell Road, just round the corner from St Mungo's Church. That was on a Thursday. For the next two days I spent a great deal of time, despite the inclement weather, walking up and down Earls Court Road in front of the church, not trusting myself to go in. I'd told myself that the commitment I'd made about my son should now equally apply to my grandson.

Finally, on Sunday morning I came to the 10.30 Communion Service, where I was able to look at you. I could hardly breathe with the emotion I was feeling. You reminded me so much of Jack – your grandfather. You have his same physical stature, his eyes, the same corn-coloured hair.

I had no way of being able to give you anything, so when the offertory was to be taken up, I'd planned to leave behind a postcard of New London. For some reason, at the last moment, I couldn't find it in my purse. It was then I decided, on the spur of the moment, to put the New Hampshire Powerball lottery ticket into the collection plate instead.

I'd only bought this ticket on a whim while having a cup of coffee at the soda fountain in Baynham's New England Mercantile in New London the day before I left for 'old' London. I would normally never buy a lottery ticket, but because of all the hype and excitement over this being the largest jackpot in the history of the lottery, I was persuaded to buy one. It was absurd of course, but I was in such a good mood at the thought of my trip back to England and maybe seeing you, I bought one for a bit of fun anyway.

I knew I shouldn't, but as I dropped it in the collection plate, I asked God for some sort of sign that seeking out this contact with you was OK with Him; I never dreamed for one second this would turn out to be the winning ticket.

I know, as a Roman Catholic, I'm not supposed to receive Communion in the Episcopal or Anglican Church, but I chose to follow my conscience rather than the dictates from Rome. So I came up with the other members of the congregation to be given Holy Communion by you. My only concern was that my hands were shaking so badly I was worried about spilling the wine!

Being that close to you, receiving the Body & Blood of Our Lord Jesus Christ from my own, long-lost, grandson's hand, was probably the most spiritually meaningful moment of my long and often lonely life. It was a feeling too intense to describe, but in that moment I knew I'd had my 'sign' and it was OK to be doing what I was doing.

Satisfied with that one precious moment, and not wanting to

risk upsetting, burdening or possibly even angering you, I left for Boston and my return to New Hampshire later that day. Though I fear they must have thought me a silly old lady, the cabin crew on the British Airways flight were so kind. I don't think I stopped crying tears of joy, mingled with those of a very profound sadness, all the way across the Atlantic.

It was a heavy burden keeping the secrecy of what I had done all those years ago from my own family (my parents died without ever knowing they were grandparents). Despite my determination to keep the bargain I had made with God, from even before the moment of his birth I never stopped loving your father, the son I never knew or even once set eyes on. I don't believe there has been a day in my whole life when I haven't thought of him, and always the constant wondering …

To stop myself from going completely mad with this, I developed my own phantom 'relationship' with him. This consisted of me writing a letter to my son every month. I did this without fail until I learned of his tragic death. Of course I had to ensure the letters were very well concealed from my parents and I kept them in a locked trunk under my bed. By the time I stopped writing to him I had over 500 unmailed letters to him. I still have them.

Ever since I found out about the winning lottery ticket being traced back to Baynham's here in New London, I did begin to wonder of course. As each day went by with no claimant coming forward, I started to hold my breath. But then I reasoned that even if the ticket I'd bought had turned out to be the one, you might not have known what it was, or what to do with it. How would you even know if it was the winning ticket? I was sure the likelihood was you would have just crumpled it up and thrown it away.

Since I couldn't do anything about it, I tried to be philosophical and let it go from my mind. I'd had my 'sign' after all and needed no further convincing that tracking you down was OK. I'd seen you and received Holy Communion from your hand. I needed and felt I deserved nothing more. I'd come home to live out my remaining years and to finally die happy, at peace with what I'd done and how the good Lord had planned it should all turn out.

I shouldn't have been either so complacent or presumptuous! It seems the good Lord had other plans indeed – plans I could never have imagined even in my wildest dreams!

You see, about six months ago I was diagnosed with cancer. Where it started doesn't really matter. The point is it seems to have spread to most parts of me and, despite my doctors' protestations and pleadings, at my age I have no interest in treatment other than palliative care. On that basis I'm told I have, at most, between three and four months left to live.

It is the knowledge of this that is my motivation for writing to you. If you would like to meet your grandmother, now would be a good time to do it. I cannot come to you, so you would have to come to me.

It will probably be hard for you to understand, but I really did love your father very much. In the hope you might be interested I am enclosing the very first and the very last letter I wrote to him.

With much affection and long imagined love,
Maude Kimball (your grandmother)

When he had finished reading Robert didn't move for a long while, deep in thought as he leant back in his oversized office chair, the letter still tightly held in his hand.

It was the insistent ringing of his private phone that dragged him back to the present. Robert tipped himself forward, grabbing the receiver.

'Jill, I thought I'd made it clear I was not to be disturbed under any circumstances?' he barked irritably down the line. Then, before Jill could even tell him who the caller was, he slammed the receiver down hard.

Robert picked up the large envelope and slowly pulled out the two other letters. Both were still sealed in their original, cream-coloured, handwritten envelopes. They were addressed only to 'John Radcliffe Kimball' and dated forty-seven years apart.

Robert turned the earliest one over in his hand. Although redundant, the return address was from a Miss Maude Kimball in Wilmot, New Hampshire. He now opened it hesitantly, smoothed out the neatly folded sheets and began to read.

September 1939

My darling infant son, not a day has gone by since your birth three months ago that you haven't been uppermost in my thoughts. You will never read this letter, or the others I intend to write you. I do so for my own sanity. The purpose is to stop me from going mad with the sense of guilt, grief and loss I feel at having given you up for adoption. This, and my future letters to you, will be a one-sided, very personal relationship in which I promise you complete truthfulness in the sharing of my innermost feelings, fears and thoughts.

To begin with, without any right to do so, I must beg for your forgiveness. When you were conceived, almost a year ago now, the stark choice I faced in an England preparing for war seemed to be only between abortion and adoption. Your father, a fine, handsome young man, and a student up at Oxford, was not any more ready or prepared for the responsibilities of fatherhood than I was for motherhood.

I loved and still do love your father very much. But perhaps the real truth (and I said I was going to be honest) is that in these uncertain times, neither of us loved the other with enough conviction and determination to overcome the obstacles and face the enormous difficulties we would have had in getting married.

As two impoverished students, the challenges to getting married and starting a family seemed insurmountable enough. Add to that the fact your father is from an urban, intellectual, traditionally Anglican English family of some social standing, while I am from a traditional, staunchly Roman Catholic, farming family here in rural America and you may, one day, begin to understand what we were facing.

The shame and disgrace that having you as a bastard child would have brought on my family was more than I could bear. So

I had decided to have a quiet abortion in England, well away from my family. However, my Catholic upbringing and the uncertainty of impending war, with what sadly will be its inevitable casualties, made me see the tragic waste of not having my child and then immediately giving you up for adoption.

The only way I could go through with this was to ask never to see you. I never have. The pain of this mistake will stay with me and haunt me all my life. If I could turn back the clock and have this chance again, I know now for certain I would face all the shame and scandal in the world. Nothing would persuade me to give you up.

Please don't blame your father. He is barely twenty years old. The war is now a certainty and he knows he is going to have to go off and fight. He has joined the army in the regiment of Royal Monmouthshire Royal Engineers and will be leaving for Europe any day now.

I pray daily that you are in a happy home with wonderful parents, surrounded by love. Already I am imagining the sort of family it might be and willing them to love you as much as I now know I love you. I am also assailed by doubts and fears.

Uppermost of these is that your new 'father' will almost certainly have to go to war too, with the real possibility he may never come home. To lose two fathers in your short life thus far would seem unthinkably hard. I will try to remain positive for you.

In future letters I will tell you, bit by bit, more about me and my life as it progresses here in New Hampshire: the 'forgotten' New England state. While I was over in England I found everyone seemed to know, or at least have heard of, Vermont and Maine, but few people had ever heard of my home state and had little or no concept of where within the United States it even was! It is the well-kept secret: the jewel in the crown of New England. Unspoiled, wild and achingly beautiful, it is already my dream that one day fate may bring you here. To the roots you don't even know are yours!

This is the beginning of my imagined relationship with you John Radcliffe. It may not be real to you – and sadly you will never see these letters – but my love for you is more real than you will ever know. I made a tragic mistake from which there is now no way back – one I will regret for the rest of my life.

With the warmth and love only a mother can give I am, and will always be,

Your loving mother,
Maude (Kimball)

After putting the letter carefully back in its envelope, Robert continued to sit motionless at his desk. Finally, before reaching for what was the last letter from his grandmother to his father, written forty-seven years after the first, he picked up the internal phone to his personal assistant.

'Cynthia, a change of plan,' he told her. 'Please cancel my trip to Houston and Dallas tomorrow. Also ask Jill to call Mike and have him find the closest airport to a place called New London in New Hampshire. Tell him to be ready to fly me there this afternoon. Oh, and please get Jill to find me a hotel as near as she can to New London. Have them arrange a pick-up from the airport. I'll be staying one night. Thanks.'

That done, he carefully opened the last letter from his grandmother to his father.

November 1986

Dear John,

Although I know now you were called Stephen (I like that name for you) you have always been John Radcliffe to me and as this must be my last letter to you I think I'll stick with the John I've known and loved so much for these past forty-seven years.

I finally met your adoptive father when I was over in England last week. (My first visit back since you were born!) The rules and regulations governing adoption have changed so much in the intervening years, and I was able to track him down through the records kept at the new John Radcliffe Hospital in Oxford. Although he is now a very elderly man (your adoptive mother died some years ago) living in a care home at Boars Hill, close to Oxford, his mind is still clear. He told me that you had got married at the age of twenty-one to a lovely Swedish wife, Pia Sundholm, and had emigrated to Australia.

He told me of your heroic death in an underground construction accident at a tragically young age and how the occasion of your funeral had been the one time he and your adoptive mother had journeyed out to Australia where they met your son, their grandson, then aged six, for the first time. He also mentioned that was the first and only time he and his wife ever went abroad.

Your adoptive father told me that although you never really 'fitted' as their son, you had nevertheless loved them as best you could and been a good son. (You were physically big, outgoing and gifted with a naturally easy way with people. They were both small, rather shy, retiring, academic types.) He said he knew you had had to get away and although his wife had found it hard to accept, he had understood and didn't ever hold it against you.

We talked for a long time. Noticing my height (I am still almost six feet tall even though now past sixty), he asked about your real father. I was able to tell him how your father had been a top oarsman at Oxford and how he had rowed for Oxford in the Oxford and Cambridge boat race in 1938 and again in 1939. How he stood 6ft 5in in his bare feet and was broad-shouldered with it. How he had always thought he was invincible and how he had been killed by a German machine gun while single-handedly giving covering fire for his men to make it safely ashore from the landing craft on 6th June 1944.

It was then your adoptive father told me how you too could have saved your own life had you run from the excavations. That your decision to warn the others, and use your size and considerable strength to try to support the twisting metal beam, had bought those invaluable, precious seconds that allowed your men to escape, but cost you your own life. Like father, like son, it would seem.

So you've been dead for nineteen years. But it doesn't really make any difference; the purpose of my writing you this lifetime of unsent letters was always for me. You were the only son I ever had and your father was the only man I've ever loved, or even 'known' – in the biblical sense. Had he not been killed, our dream, my dream, was he was going to come to America. We were going to get married and, in due course, take over my parents' farm in Wilmot. It was not to be.

Instead, after both my parents had died, I opened a bookshop in New London. I love books and have always loved reading. The bookshop provided me with a great source of solace and companionship for many years until I grew too old for it and sold it. It's still there, Morgan Hill Books, a wonderful place to browse and lose all sense of time. It's now the only bookshop in New London.

Of course, the life I have been imagining for you all these years bears scant resemblance to the real and tragically short life you led. I never imagined you emigrating to Australia, but I see now it made sense. You couldn't have known why, but that need for big open spaces and room to breathe must have been in you as part of your nature. It's in me and, although he was not born to it, was also in your father.

You were conceived during a week we spent together in a remote cottage we had rented on Dartmoor. It was out in the middle of the moor at the end of a long muddy track, crossed by a fast-flowing stream. The weather was wild and stormy. With no electricity we had only candles for light and an open fireplace for heat. We spent all day out on the moor with only ourselves, the wild moorland ponies and hardy moorland sheep for company. I don't think we were ever so carefree, so happy and so much in love. In the evenings we lay in front of a roaring log fire listening to the wind raging and howling at the sturdy stone roof tiles and the rain slamming in violent gusts against the small-paned windows. We felt so alive and so invincible.

I told your father of places in New Hampshire I wanted to show him. Of places like Rattlesnake and Ragged Mountain. Of inaccessible, uninhabited, magical ponds, hidden deep in the forest. Where the likelihood of seeing moose, bear, deer or beaver was considerably greater than that of seeing people.

That was when we first started talking about making a life together over here. Although he was brought up in London (his family came from Islington) he hated urban life and longed for the remote, wide-open spaces of places like Scotland and the Welsh mountains. I used to tell him if he didn't find New Hampshire wild enough we could always sell up and move out to Wyoming or Montana and live with grizzly bears!

So, your attraction to the rugged wide open spaces of places like Australia was always genetically programmed inside you.

Thank you for being a good son to your parents, despite what made you different. Not being able to have children of their own, they must have loved you all the more dearly and I don't doubt they always gave you of their best.

So, you have a son, Robert. And I have a grandson. He's grown to be a fine-looking young man, John. You would be very proud of him. I can't quite get over the irony that I, brought up a conscientious Roman Catholic, eventually resisted having an abortion, the result of which is that the Church of England has gained a handsome, energetic, dynamic young priest. I chuckle when I think that, perhaps, if that outcome had been foreseen, I might have been granted a special dispensation by Rome for an abortion!

Don't take that last remark seriously. I'm absolutely in favour of birth control, but against abortion, outside very exceptional cases. It's just that progressively, the older I get, the less and less time I have for all the other, often petty, hypocritical rules and regulations imposed on us by the hierarchy within all establishment religions. So many of these 'restrictions' have been designed as part of some sort of complex, burdensome control mechanism, often dreamt up without any historical or doctrinal basis. And in many cases only introduced in relatively recent times.

Robert is a big chap. Very like you I'm told. When I first set eyes on him as he strode out onto the altar from the sacristy at St Mungo's (have I forgotten to tell you he is now the vicar at St Mungo's Church on Earls Court Road in Kensington?) the years rolled back. I was a young woman again, seeing Jack Talbot, your father, for the first time. So his likeness has been dominant in passing down to the third generation.

I know, according to the rules from Rome, I was not supposed to, but nevertheless I went up to take Communion from him. It was a very, very special moment for me to be given Communion from my own grandson's hand.

Although there was a part of me longing to hang back after the service and introduce myself, I thought it unfair, even unnecessary, to do so – suddenly burdening Robert with something he might not want complicating his life. Also, his adoptive grandfather had seemed anxious I shouldn't. I think he didn't want anything weakening or disturbing his relationship with his grandson in the twilight of his own life. We had tacitly agreed to let things be. It seemed easier and kinder that way.

However, I wanted to challenge fate by making some small connection, however obscure. I'd decided that when the collection plate came round, I would drop in a postcard of picturesque New London I knew I had in my purse. Anyway, while I was rummaging for it, the collection plate had reached me and was being patiently, but discreetly, held in expectation. I couldn't find the postcard and I knew I couldn't delay further. The only thing that came to hand was the New Hampshire Powerball lottery ticket I'd bought in New London at the beginning of the week.

It was so unlike me to have a lottery ticket to begin with. I never buy them. On this occasion I'd been persuaded to by a friend. There was so much publicity surrounding the fact that it was to be the biggest jackpot payout in history. Anyway, on an impulse, I dropped it into the collection plate with a £5 note.

I know it's silly but coming back from Communion a little later I found myself wondering what if, by some extraordinarily unlikely quirk of fate, it did turn out to be a winning ticket?

Back at the hotel, I laughed out loud at my own foolishness. I hope you were smiling too, John.

Of course, tantalisingly, at the time of writing this and in closing what will be my last letter to you, I've read that the enormous jackpot has been won by a single ticket holder, who has not yet come forward to claim the win. In accordance with my strict and unbroken rule, once this envelope is sealed I will not and must not reopen any of my letters to you. The temptation to make revision or explanation with the passage of time would be too great.

Don't worry, the chance of your son having stumbled into a fortune of this size is so remote as to be unthinkable. And yet … and yet … my brazen challenge to fate to make some small connection, however obscure …?

I'm sitting writing this to you at a corner table by the stove in Baynham's Café. It's very quiet, almost deserted at this mid-morning hour so close to Christmas. Normally it would be busier, but I suppose everyone is off doing their Christmas shopping. Just as well, because I can hardly bear to say 'goodbye' after all this time. My darling, most precious John, when we finally meet in Heaven, as I believe we shall, my dearest wish will be for your understanding and forgiveness.

I will never forget you, but I'm afraid I must now end this very last letter I will ever write to you. I have no choice … I can no longer see through my tears.

Your mother – who has loved you <u>always</u>,
Maude Kimball

31

———

ROBERT SAT MOTIONLESS in his chair. This last letter from his grandmother to his father, folded and gently replaced in its envelope, lay on the desk in front of him, his left hand resting lightly on it.

Cynthia gave one soft knock on the door before going in without waiting for a response. She and Bill Temple were the only ones permitted such freedom of access to Robert at any time and under any circumstances. She was surprised to see Robert sitting back in his chair motionless rather than in his more customary position: earnestly leaning forward, hands on his keyboard, attention focused on the screen of his new computer.

As she approached, Robert hastily rubbed his eyes with the backs of his hands. Cynthia was too much of a woman not to notice at once that he had been shedding a tear and too surprised and too discreet an assistant to say anything, or give any indication of having noticed. She noted the two elegantly handwritten envelopes addressed to a John Radcliffe Kimball lying on the desk in front of him.

'Robert, Jill has made all the arrangements,' she told him gently. 'Mike will have the plane and crew ready and waiting for you at Teterboro in an hour from now. She's booked you the best room they had at a little place called the New London Inn. I gather it's a traditional New England Inn in the centre of what is a very small town. Although they do have a landing strip, the Eagle's Nest, the nearest regional airport capable of taking the Gulfstream is at a place called

Lebanon, about thirty minutes' drive away. All very biblical sounding I know, but that's New England for you. Every name is English, French, native American or biblical.'

Cynthia was gently trying to lighten the mood and Robert smiled at her gratefully. 'The hotel, or rather the inn, will send someone to Lebanon Airport to wait for you as soon as Jill calls to confirm you're in the air and on your way. Mike says the flight time is only about fifty minutes.

'I've been in touch with Houston and Dallas and postponed both meetings for forty-eight hours. They weren't happy about it, but what can they do? They need to see you more than you need to see them. I explained it was important and personal. They both suggested flying up to New Hampshire to see you there. I told them "no" and that anyway part of the purpose of you going to them was to see their operations.'

Robert cleared his throat. 'Thanks Cyn, you've thought of everything in your usual efficient way. It's going to be bad enough losing Bill, but I can't tell you how I'd miss you if you ever decided to return to Boston. How on earth would I manage?'

Cynthia smiled, 'Oh you'd manage. You always do. Within three weeks you'd have got used to someone else's efficiency and have forgotten all about me.'

Although said affectionately, from the way in which she had spoken, it was clear she meant it and was not fishing for compliments. As she had demonstrated before his most recent trip to Asia, Cynthia was one of the few people who viewed Robert Melton quite objectively and remained unimpressed by his wealth, while still respecting his undisputed talent for making money. Were she ever to leave him, he really would miss her, if for that reason alone. But he also knew she was right.

Ten minutes later Robert was in the back of his Bentley limousine heading towards the George Washington Bridge that would take him over to New Jersey and Teterboro Airport. He'd brought along the little suitcase he kept permanently at his office for quick, last-minute, overnight trips.

From time to time, Raphael, his driver, glanced in the rear view mirror. He knew something unusual was up. His boss was not reading papers, or dictating notes, and his briefcase lay unopened on the seat beside him. He'd never seen Mr Melton just sit and stare out of the window unseeingly like this before.

About thirty minutes into the flight Mike came back from the cockpit to speak to his boss. 'Just been on the horn to the ground. They wanted me to let you know that when we come in to Lebanon everything happens kinda suddenly. It seems the runway is carved into the side of a mountain, and with the wind direction as it is we'll be coming in from the valley end, so one minute we'll have several hundred feet below us and the next we'll be on the ground. Spooks some folks a bit when they don't know what's happening, so just thought I'd give you a heads-up on it.'

'Thanks Mike, I never worry when you're up front but I appreciate the warning.'

What Mike had not told his boss, because the pilot did not know at the time, was that the transport laid on by the New London Inn differed significantly from the sleek, highly polished limousines that Robert usually found drawn up beside the steps when he alighted from his plane.

Once down on the tarmac in this small rural airfield, neither Robert nor his crew could see the vehicle sent to collect him.

'Tell Mike to get on to the control tower, would you Louise?' Robert asked the pretty cabin attendant on duty that day – Robert preferred Fleur, who was more overtly sexy – 'And get him to find out where my car is.'

Louise returned a couple of minutes later with the answer. 'They say it's waiting out front for you, Mr Melton. Would you like me to fetch someone to carry your bag?'

Robert shrugged his shoulders. 'I guess the exercise will do me good. And don't worry about the bag.'

He made his way to the door, carrying his briefcase and overnight bag. 'I'll see you guys tomorrow,' he told the two pilots.

'Sure thing, Mr Melton. We'll be here,' Mike replied. 'You have a good day.'

The air was fresh and clean as Robert crossed to the small terminal building. After Manhattan, Beijing and Tokyo, he realised it had been a while since he had breathed air that pure.

He scanned the small parking lot. He could see no sign of his waiting limo. Robert checked the time on his watch and was about to turn back inside when he heard the toot of an automobile horn.

It took Robert a moment to realise it was meant for him. He looked at the few sedans parked randomly and then he saw the old, faded red Dodge Power Wagon pick-up, the original paintwork of which had long ago succumbed to years of being alternately bleached by the hot summer sun and 'sandblasted' by the harsh, stinging winter blizzards.

Standing next to the pick-up waving at him stood the driver – an attractive, dark-haired woman wearing a denim skirt, bandana and cowboy boots – Robert guessed her to be in her mid-thirties.

'You must be Robert Melton,' she said with a winning smile that made her eyes sparkle. 'I'm Mary Cotton.' She held out a hand, which Robert shook without thinking. She seemed open, friendly and genuinely welcoming. Robert had also noted that she took his arrival in a multi-million dollar private jet completely in her stride and showed no sign of being overly impressed.

'Sorry about the pick-up,' she said. 'It's what I normally come to work in. I'd have brought the sedan if I'd known I had a collection to make.'

'It's not a problem,' Robert said distractedly, as he peered into the dusty cab, wondering where to put his bags.

'Don't you want to throw those in the back?' Mary asked. 'I've cleared a space on those sacks – they're quite clean.'

'I think I'll just keep them on my lap,' Robert answered, after spotting the upturned wheelbarrow.

'Fine by me,' his driver answered, resuming her seat behind the steering wheel.

Privately Robert had to admit to himself he had been more than a little irritated when he had seen the informal mode of transport arranged for him by his office. He had quickly grown so used to being fawned on and always being surrounded by seemingly effortless luxury that, irrationally, he was annoyed by this presumptuous informality.

'Is this your first time in New Hampshire?' Mary asked as they drove away from the airfield.

'Not exactly,' Robert answered guardedly. 'I came here a couple of times several years ago, to visit a friend of mine.'

'OK,' said Mary. 'Only recently we've gotten quite a few business types from New York and Boston buying weekend and vacation retreats up here. It's really beautiful in the fall, of course. Cold as Siberia in winter, though.'

'I guess it must be,' Robert answered, noticing the dirt-encrusted flooring around his highly polished Oxfords.

Mary Cotton seemed quite happy to drive along in silence for a while, leaving Robert to gaze out of the window. He had forgotten just how beautiful the scenery was in New Hampshire.

They were heading south on Route I-89 towards New London and had just passed the exit to Route 4, marked to Enfield. Now feeling a little guilty over his earlier, petulant thoughts in the face of Mary's completely genuine apology and explanation, Robert wanted to make amends.

'So what is your job at the hotel?' he enquired, trying to make himself sound interested and feeling he had been quiet for long enough.

'Oh, just about a bit of everything and anything,' was her cheerful reply. 'It's not really a hotel in either the grand, luxury sense, or the budget, cookie-cutter sense. It's really an historic old New England inn. Quirky, charming and completely maddening all at the same time.'

Robert thought about the last hotels he had stayed in. He doubted if anywhere in New Hampshire would ever come close to the luxurious suites Jill habitually reserved for him – even in the less salubrious cities like Beijing.

However, intrigued by Mary's disarming honesty, Robert smiled a smile from within and started to relax in a way he had not for a long time. There was, he had to admit, something rather liberating about riding down this highway, through stunningly beautiful countryside, in a shabby old pick-up truck, being driven by this completely natural, friendly, attractive lady who did not give a damn that her passenger could probably afford to buy half the state, were it for sale.

Now keen to continue the conversation, Robert carried on, 'So, do you have a specific role at the inn, apart from doing a bit of everything?' he asked.

'Yes, I suppose I do if you put it like that,' she said. 'I own it. So for my sins I'm really responsible for the whole darn place. That also makes me responsible for my employees and the guests – in that order,' she added emphatically. 'Then there are responsibilities to the town, the surrounding community and to the bank – in that order,' she emphasised again. 'Let me tell you, owning and running an historic New England inn, at the centre of an involved and committed local community, is not for the faint-hearted. It's a true love-hate relationship and even after ten years I still haven't worked out which of those is my principal emotion.'

Robert laughed. Despite his initial reaction, he was beginning to enjoy the ride; Jill would be spared a reprimand for not coming up with something better.

'So, your turn,' Mary said. 'What brings you to our little town all of a sudden like this?'

Normally Robert would have given a very perfunctory and dismissive response to such an impertinent enquiry, however innocently intentioned it may have been. But coming now from Mary Cotton, after he had been questioning her, he knew it was meant only to be conversational. Nevertheless he thought he should be careful.

'I'm here to visit someone called Maude Kimball, an older lady who lives somewhere near New London, I believe.'

'Oh yes, Maude. Everybody's grandmother. Truly the sweetest, loveliest lady anyone could ever hope to meet. She lives alone in a cottage in Sutton. Next town down the valley from New London. There is more worldly wisdom in that lady than there is in all the self-help books that have ever been published.'

'Is that so?' asked Robert, hoping his enquiry sounded neutral.

'Yet, somewhere there's a deep sadness too,' Mary continued. 'It doesn't often show and she never lets you see it, but it's sometimes struck me that she's more serene and peaceful than she is ever really happy, if you know what I mean. A sort of carefully cultivated serenity and peacefulness developed over time, I would say too.

'She never married and didn't seem to have much time for would-be suitors. Too busy looking after her parents and helping them run the big old family farm they had over in Wilmot. But she was always there for anyone in any kind of trouble and would do anything to help a fellow human being – or animal for that matter. It's rumoured she'd had a boyfriend once. An Englishman she'd met while studying over in England many years ago. Maude doesn't talk about it, but people guess he might have been killed in the war. She received a black-bordered envelope from England at the Wilmot Post Office sometime before the end of the war, I think. After that I heard she wasn't seen for days and when she did start going about again her face and eyes were still swollen red from all the crying she'd been doing.

'So, how come you know Maude?'

'I gather she was a friend of my family when she was studying in England. As you say, many years ago, before the war. I've never met her, but she wrote to me in New York; I understand she's not well and can't travel herself.'

Mary glanced over at Robert now and seemed to be looking at him in an entirely new way, as if appraising him for the first time – comparing him to someone else she might know. Robert felt very uncomfortable. As she turned her eyes back to the road there was a ghost of a smile on her face.

'You old dark horse Maude, I'll bet there was more to your time as a student in England than your parents or anyone else ever knew about,' Mary thought to herself. The physical resemblance was uncanny.

'Everybody's grandmother' – the description was still ringing in Robert's head. And yet, if he was to believe what she had written to him, she really was his actual grandmother.

He knew he had to be careful. This could still turn out to be a very clever hoax, set up as an elaborate 'sting' to try and get at a share of his fortune. He wondered if he was getting paranoid when he even found himself briefly considering the possibility that Mary, and maybe others from the town, were all in on an elaborate plan to dupe him.

They had reached Exit 12 marked to New London and Colby Sawyer College. Robert began to take note of his surroundings as they now headed along Route 11 East. At the edge of town on one side of the road they passed Cricenti's Market, a big grocery store, and on the other side a fine-looking yellow building proclaiming itself to be the Ledyard National Bank. Opposite this were two other banks rejoicing in the more locally poetic names of The Sugar River Savings Bank and Lake Sunapee Bank. Robert remembered seeing the name Lake Sunapee Bank on that first brief visit he had made to New London with Andreas. That time they had approached the town coming up I-89 from the south and so had entered from the opposite end.

'How big is this town that it needs so many banks?' Robert asked Mary.

'That depends on the time of year,' she replied. 'In the winter the population can be as small as 1,500. In the summer it can grow to over three times that many. We have a lot of what we call "snow birds", people who summer here but fly south or west for the winter.

'The reason for so many banks is that although New Hampshire is generally a poor state, there are pockets of affluence. New London is about bang in the middle of a well-to-do corridor that runs along I-89 from Concord, the state capital, in the south to Hanover in the north, home to the world-famous Dartmouth College and the Dartmouth Mary Hitchcock Hospital and renowned Medical Center.

'Another big attraction for people with money is that New London is close to beautiful unspoiled lakes and mountains. Chief among these is Lake Sunapee itself. So we have long-established, elegant – if slightly frayed – family homes that have been passed down from generation to generation, alongside more opulent ones built in recent years that are the refuges and rewards for a lifetime of hard work and service in cities all over the country.'

Robert nodded his head. He got the message.

'People who have retired like the area too. They like the quality of life, the clean air, unspoiled countryside, skiing in winter, and the lakes in summer. Add to that the lack of any state income tax or sales tax and you can see why people might choose to come here to enjoy and protect their hard-earned savings.'

Robert understood that too.

Now they were passing Baynham's New England Mercantile and he noted how different it looked in summer. People were sitting at the tables out in front enjoying the late-afternoon sunshine and conversations over cups of coffee or ice cream. From here on along Main Street Robert started to recognise the landmarks he had seen before: Morgan Hill Books, The Art of Nature, the other branch of Lake Sunapee Bank and finally the historic old New London Inn itself.

Mary pulled into the driveway and stopped in front of the side door. 'If you want to jump out, Mr Melton, I'll just park up at the back and join you at the reception desk. Jennifer should be there to sign you in. But if not, I'll only be a moment. I never really know where Jennifer is and I'm not sure she does either,' she said with a smile.

The passenger door of the old truck dropped slightly as Robert stepped out. Placing his briefcase and overnight bag on the ground beside him, he brushed his trousers with his hands. Then, buttoning his jacket and straightening his tie, he picked up his bags and made for the entrance.

Mary was right. The reception desk was unattended. 'Jennifer' was nowhere to be seen. The inn itself was spotless and shining; the fragrant smell of beeswax polish mixed with the scent of fresh flowers.

Robert waited for Mary to re-emerge, wondering irritably when the last time had been that he had had to stand waiting in the lobby of a hotel to check in.

His thoughts were interrupted by a striking, slender young woman, hardly more than a girl, as she silently appeared out of nowhere, or so it seemed. She approached Robert with the warmest smile he thought he had ever seen. She was dressed in an almost translucent floral dress that extended to well below her knees. Her dark honey-coloured hair hung in curly profusion down to her shoulders, framing a face that was as open and innocent as her smile was wide and warm. Her eyes were cornflower blue and her skin softly tanned to a golden summer brown. At most she looked to be about twenty.

'Hello, I'm Jen. Welcome to the New London Inn,' she said holding out a slender hand. Robert, unused to the informality of shaking hands with hotel staff, was momentarily thrown. But he instinctively took her hand anyway. Today was turning out to be a day of surprises.

Having signed what was more akin to a guest book than a hotel register, Robert followed up the wide wooden staircase as Jennifer showed him to his room. She seemed to move soundlessly across the floor. It was then he noticed she favoured going barefoot. It was a touch that seemed to complete the rather ethereal, magical look so naturally worn by this elfin-like, unadorned beauty. He had to admit that New London seemed to have a freshness and informal originality to it that was different from anything he had come across in Australia, England, or thus far, America.

Ten minutes later Robert went back down to the reception desk. Mary was talking to Jennifer about the number of reservations for dinner that night. 'Looks like it'll be a quiet night Jen. If you're OK with it, I think I'll take the chance to have a rare evening at home. I've got so many chores to do there too. Who'd be an innkeeper and have a farm to look after too?' Mary was saying.

Then she caught sight of Robert, 'Oh, Mr Melton, I gather Jen took care of you. Sorry, I got distracted having a word with chef. Room all right?'

'Yes thank you,' Robert replied, looking around. He needed the concierge, but on current showing the nearest was likely to be a hundred miles down the road in Boston.

'Is there something you need?' Mary asked.

'I was wondering if there's some sort of taxi or car service available. I don't have a lot of time and I'd like to get out and meet with Miss Kimball. I was thinking about going over to her house now.'

So unused to rural life had he become, he realised neither he nor his office had considered how he was going to get around once he got to New London.

Mary gave a gentle laugh and Jen smiled. 'No taxis or limo services here in New London I'm afraid. Nearest place you'd find one of those would be Manchester or Concord I would think.'

Robert remembered the loquacious driver he'd had take him from St Jerome's down to Boston.

'Tell you what I can suggest,' Mary said, hand on hip looking at Robert thoughtfully. 'It's quiet tonight, so I'm about to go home for the evening and leave Jen to take care of things here. No problem for me to swing past Maude's house on the way. Show you where it is an' all. Then you ride along with me to my place. I'll jump out and leave you with my truck for the night. That way, you'll know how to head back to Maude's and later on back here too.'

Robert tried to remember the last time he had driven himself anywhere. The Riviera, maybe, the summer before last? There was no point in getting angry, although maybe he would have a word with Jill after all, when he got back to the office. Under the circumstances, it seemed hard to fault Mary Cotton's generous suggestion.

'You'd trust me to drive your truck?' was all Robert could think of to say.

'Why ever not? It's just an old truck. The workhorse of pretty much every small farm or homestead around here. Besides, I reckon you could afford to buy me a new one if you were to wreck it.'

Uncustomarily, Robert found himself fumbling for words. 'Well, maybe,' he muttered. 'It's very generous of you.'

'Who said anything about being generous? If you go and get lost and start driving about all over the place I'll have to charge you for the gas. It's only so you can go between Maude's place and here, understand?

'I'm doing it as much for Maude as for you. She'd probably try and drive over here if she knew you were stuck without a car. But she's in no shape to be doing that sort of thing unnecessarily now. Especially not at night.

'We can go whenever you're ready. Does Maude know you're coming, by the way?'

'I'm ready now,' Robert replied, conscious of both Mary and Jen eyeing his expensive suit with mild amusement. 'And ... no, she doesn't know I'm coming. I wanted it to be sort of a surprise,'

'Well, I'll bet it will be,' Mary said quietly under her breath, but not quietly enough that Robert hadn't heard. He shot her a look of alarm but said nothing.

*

Leaving the inn, they turned left onto Main Street heading south out of the town. Robert recognised the Episcopal and the Catholic churches as they drove by and remembered how he and Andreas had vied with each other over which of the buildings was the most jarring piece of architecture in this otherwise picture-perfect New England town. The memory should have been amusing, but it wasn't.

Although Andreas had tried to contact him several times during the first year he had moved to New York, Robert had not responded, and he had not seen or spoken to him since the complete failure of his own last clumsy attempt to buy Andreas's friendship back. The truth was he felt uncomfortable with Andreas now. His very presence made him feel guilty and he greatly resented that. He had desperately wanted to paint Andreas completely out of his life.

However, driving now along Main Street, New London, in an old Dodge pick-up, past the elegant, colonial-style town offices, the bandstand, the beautiful Baptist Church and the gracious buildings of Colby Sawyer College, Robert realised just how very much he missed his old and trusted friend. Did it have something to do with the antiquated vehicle he was being driven in, or being in close proximity to him in the little New England town Andreas had first brought him to?

Robert remained adamant that he would not be the first to break the long silence that lay between them, but in his mind he compromised by resolving to take his call next time, should Andreas ever try to contact him again. This way it was left to fate and it eased his conscience sufficiently for him to be able to forget about it again.

These thoughts were broken into by the sudden spectacular view of a beautiful lake on their right, with a magnificent-looking mountain rising majestically above and behind it as they drove down the hill. Mary had decided to fill the truck with gas before lending it to Robert, so she had taken the road down past the town lake to the little Park 'N' Go gas station. The lowering sun was sending long shafts of pale light between broken cloud that added drama to the scenery in front of them.

Mary saw him looking at the mountain. 'Beautiful sight isn't it? I see it almost every day and I never tire of it.

'That one,' she said, pointing at the mountain Robert was looking at, 'is called Mount Kearsarge. It was immortalised by one of America's great wartime sweethearts, Kate Smith, singing "When the Moon comes over the Mountain".

'It's one of the most romantic sights you can imagine in late summer, if you come this way on a clear night. Face towards the mountain and watch the enormous harvest moon rising slowly. It looks as if it's coming out of the very top of the mountain itself. Then it casts a broad, bright moonbeam of light across the whole lake.

'On a still summer night, it's just one of those extraordinary sights that make you shed all your doubt. Only God could have created such breathtaking beauty.'

Robert was looking at Mary thoughtfully. 'You'd really rather be living in downtown Detroit, wouldn't you?' he said, with mock seriousness.

'OK, OK. I do get carried away sometimes, but if you lived here and grew to know the beauty of the seasons you'd learn to love it too,' Mary said defensively.

They were approaching Sutton and she said, 'Pay attention now,' as she turned right to drive along the edge of Keyser Lake. After about a quarter of a mile they came to a short driveway leading to a small, well-kept, Cape-style cottage on the edge of the water.

'That's where Maude lives now,' said Mary, slowing down to turn around. 'She's been there ever since she gave up the old family farm in Wilmot. Hope she can stay there, but she has no family to care for her. At least none that any of us know of,' she added as a delayed afterthought. 'Trouble is, when she gets too sick she may have to be moved up to the hospice. Do you think you'll be able to find your way back OK?'

'It shouldn't be too hard. I've checked some landmarks to go by,' Robert answered. 'Including that lake,' he added wryly.

'I guess you're a big boy really. It's just that you're from the big city and we country folk tend to think of you city boys as being a bit hopeless, if left all alone out in the woods!'

Back on Kearsarge Valley Road, Robert noted they were now headed northwards running parallel to the base of Mount Kearsarge. They passed what Robert took to be the local golf club and shortly afterwards crossed the town line into Wilmot. A quarter of a mile later they turned onto a dirt track leading off into the woods. This brought them to a very pretty, small colonial-style farmhouse that looked badly in need of painting.

'This is home and where I get out,' Mary said. 'Don't have either the money or the time to look after it like I should,' she responded to Robert's silent observation. 'Everything I've got goes into keeping the inn going.

'Hope it goes well with Maude and you find your way back to the inn OK. There's no hurry. We never lock the place and Jen will leave your room key on the desk if she's gone to bed before you get back.

'Don't go tiring out poor old Maude with too much excitement now. We all love her deeply. Everybody's grandmother, as I said.'

Mary was looking directly at Robert as she said this. Then she got out of the truck, saying, 'See you in the morning', and with that parting shot swung the driver's door closed. It gave a surprisingly solid, reassuring sort of thud, normally associated with much more expensive vehicles. Robert suspected they weren't making pick-ups like that today.

Further thought was interrupted by the realisation that he had not driven a vehicle with manual transmission for many years. He put the clutch to the floor and tried to ease the gear stick into first. The resistance and grinding sound of crashing cogs in the gearbox made him wince.

In the rear view mirror he saw Mary stop, the front door of her house ajar in her hand. 'I forgot to mention the synchromesh is long gone,' she shouted to him over her shoulder. 'You have to double de-clutch to shift gears.' With that she walked into the house, closing the door behind her.

Twenty minutes later, having more or less got the hang of how to manage the gearbox, Robert found himself back at the little Cape cottage on Keyser Lake. He drew up outside and turned off the engine.

He got out slowly and walked over towards the front door with his pulse racing. A porch ran the length of the front of the house. Robert stepped on to this and reached for the old hand bell sitting on a rickety table next to the door, above which was a faded sign inviting visitors to ring loudly because the occupant of the house was often out in her garden down by the edge of the lake.

Before he could ring the bell though, the front door swung gently open and a striking-looking, elderly lady stepped out to greet him. She was still tall and the obvious beauty of her youth remained clearly visible beneath the tired mask of age and illness.

She gave Robert a lovely smile, but it was her eyes that caught and held his attention. He knew he needed no further proof. He was looking directly at his own and his father's eyes. This was no hoax or trick. He was standing face to face with his grandmother: a grandmother of whose very existence he had been unaware until yesterday.

He remembered now where he had once, briefly, seen those eyes before. It had been in the dim light of a cold, dark, dreary, wet Sunday at the Communion rail in St Mungo's.

32

FOR WHAT SEEMED like a long time neither of them spoke. They just stood looking at each other in a way that conveyed the acceptance of an obvious fact that negated any need for explanation, beyond what had already been resolved in writing.

Finally, in what seemed to be the most natural gesture, Maude held out her hand towards Robert – not in a way that invited him to shake it, so much as to hold it while she led him into the house. It was as if the years were rolled back to Robert's childhood and this was his grandmother in whose hand he could put his own with complete trust.

'Thank you for coming. We've both got a lot of talking and catching up to do,' she said.

'Yes,' was all Robert could say in reply. He was annoyed at the constriction in his throat and the rising feeling of an emotion he wanted desperately to control.

Maude led them to a couple of white Adirondack chairs out on the deck, overlooking the lake. There, they watched the sun go down and talked late into the night.

She told Robert all about his grandfather, Jack Talbot, and how much she had loved him. But how circumstances – the social strictures, religious intolerance and the war – had conspired in a perfect alignment to prevent the possibility of marriage at the time.

In turn, Robert told his grandmother all about his own Australian childhood memories of his father, the son Maude had never known, and what he knew of his father's earlier life growing up in England with his adoptive parents, the only grandparents Robert had been aware of until now.

Maude made no attempt to stem the flow of her own tears as she sat listening to Robert talk of his father. Nor did Robert make any attempt to console her, recognising instead the need she had to feel this moment.

Was it still the priest in him, he wondered, to know when to let tears flow and when to provide comfort?

It was after one in the morning before Robert finally took his leave for the night. Mindful of Mary's earlier admonishment not to over-tire Maude, he had suggested leaving much earlier, only to have the suggestion waved aside by Maude who, without any sentimentality or noticeable fear, had said, 'When you've been told you have no more than three months to live, you tend to resent spending any of it asleep.'

Before she kissed him goodnight, Maude made Robert promise to return the next day. Robert couldn't bring himself to tell her that he would be going back to New York in the morning.

Safely back in his room at the inn, Robert lay in his bed, his mind going over the tumultuous events of the past forty-eight hours. Sleep eluded him entirely until he fell into a brief fitful doze shortly after dawn. He awoke with a start to the insistent sound of the telephone ringing beside his bed. The clock next to his head told him it was already past eight o'clock.

It was Mike, needing to know what time he wanted the crew and the plane ready for his return to New York and the onward flight to Dallas and Houston.

As he tried to get his brain in gear, Robert knew it was not only the assurance he had given Maude to return that morning that made him hesitate – he realised he was not ready to leave either.

'Mike, I'd like you to take the plane back to New York for the time being. I need to stay here for a little longer than I'd expected. I'll let you know when I want you to come back and pick me up. Probably in a day or two.'

Robert lay back on the bed. He was tired and he had a lot to think about. Besides, he knew the phone would ring again within fifteen minutes. Mike would be calling Cynthia right now.

He had guessed correctly. The phone rang again after only ten minutes.

'Good morning, Cynthia.'

His response was greeted by a soft chuckle. 'You knew Mike was going to call me didn't you?' he heard Cynthia say.

'That's what I like about you, amongst many other things of course – you always get the whole picture quickly, without ever having to be told,' Robert said.

'So what do you want me to tell Dallas and Houston this time?' she asked.

Robert did not immediately reply. The pause was long enough for Cynthia to ask, 'Robert? Robert are you there? Can you hear me?'

His reply, when it came, sounded weary, even to Robert's own ears. 'Yes Cyn, I can hear you. I want you to tell them the truth. Tell them I've found a grandmother, my real grandmother, who I didn't know I had until yesterday. Tell them too that she's dying and only has weeks to live. Tell them that you'll reschedule with them in a few days.

'Oh, and Cynthia, tell them not to bother you. You'll call them when you've heard from me. Likewise go through my diary for the next five days and put on hold, or cancel, all my appointments will you?'

Cynthia could hear the tiredness in Robert's voice, but she could also hear something else: stirrings of hope, of optimism – a hint that Robert might be starting to rediscover something that Cynthia feared he might have lost for good: his humanity. And that thought rekindled feelings in her she had thought had been banished for ever as far as Robert Melton was concerned: pleasure and what had seemed like a kind of sisterly love.

'Robert,' she said softly. 'That's amazing. How on earth did you or your grandmother work this out? But I'm so very sorry she doesn't have long to live.

'Don't worry about a thing back here. Between Jill, me and Bill we'll take care of everything. You stay up in New Hampshire for as long as you need to. Just let me know what we can do for you. Would you like me to send Mike back up later with some clothes and anything else you might need?'

'No thanks. In the short time I've been here, I've already discovered I don't need half the things I thought I could no longer do without.'

'OK, but what about clothes? You only had one clean shirt and set of underwear in your office overnight bag.'

'Cynthia, stop worrying. You don't need to mother me. New Hampshire may be rural but they do wear clothes up here and I won't be needing New York suits and highly polished shoes. I'm sure I can buy a pair of jeans, a couple of shirts and some underwear for a tiny fraction of what it would cost Mike to fly back up with stuff for me.'

There was a silent pause before Cynthia said, 'You – in jeans? This I have to see. Get someone to take a photograph for me will you?'

That got them both laughing.

'OK,' Cynthia continued. 'But let me know at once if you need anything, or need me to take care of anything, won't you?'

They finished the call. In New York Cynthia sat back in her chair, the broad smile on her face reflecting the secret hope she suddenly felt. She said a silent prayer of thanks.

Sitting on the edge of his bed at the New London Inn, Robert was smiling too: a wry smile of surprise and bewilderment at what was happening to him. He felt a burgeoning sense of freedom and purposefulness he had not felt since leaving his parish in London eight years ago.

The clock beside his bed showed that it was now past eighty-thirty. He quickly shaved, dressed and went downstairs in search of breakfast. In the lobby he encountered Mary.

'Well, good morning sleepyhead' – a salutation that two days ago Robert would have found highly impertinent coming from an innkeeper to one of her guests, but which now simply seemed friendly in just exactly the way it was meant.

'I knew you were safely back when I saw my old truck out front. How did it go with Maude?'

'I'd like to talk to you about that,' Robert said. 'But first I need some breakfast. I'm starving. Will you join me? Oh, and is there some place in town I could get some clothes? Just basic stuff: jeans, shirts, underwear, maybe a sweater, that sort of thing.'

'First off, breakfast's done. Starts at six-thirty and finishes at nine, except weekends when it's nine-thirty. Most folk around here have breakfast between seven and eight; some of us even earlier. Latecomers and vacationers maybe around eight-thirty. But that's no problem. Jen'll fix you up something. What do you want? Eggs, beans, bacon, wheat toast and coffee?'

'Sounds perfect. Eggs over easy and lots of coffee. Thanks.'

'Secondly, I had my breakfast about three hours ago,' Mary continued, 'but I'll happily join you with a cup of coffee.

'Thirdly, there's a place called Huberts at the far end of town, where you'll be able to get everything you want. You don't look much like a jeans man though, but if you are going to wear jeans you might want to look for some shoes too. Polished shoes, like those,' she said with a nod towards his feet, 'worn with jeans might look a little too stylish around here. Besides, with the summer dust, they'll be impossible to keep shiny New York clean. Maybe a pair of chino pants would suit you better?'

Robert was a little stung by this second questioning from an attractive woman over the suitability of jeans for him. Surely he wasn't that much of an urban dandy? He determined more than ever he would get himself some traditional Levi jeans, the iconic sort he'd worn as a teenager and young man in Australia.

Mary joined him at his table just as he was finishing up one of the best breakfasts he'd had in a long while. It beat the hell out of the fruit and wheat germ, fat-free yogurt smoothies he always had at the Carlyle.

'You'll be needing transport today won't you?' she asked. 'Why don't you keep my old truck while you're here?'

'I was thinking about that and wondering if I could go and rent a car from somewhere?'

'No need, if you're OK with the truck. I can only drive one vehicle at a time and I'm happy to use my old Chevy sedan for now.'

'Well, if you're sure, that's really kind of you but you must let me pay you something for using it.'

'No. Just buy your own gas, and when you go, leave it with a full tank. What goes around comes around. I've always believed we reap what we sow. I've got this chance to do something nice for you, which, perhaps, will influence you when you have the chance to do something nice for someone else, and so it goes. And then maybe someday it'll be my turn.'

'That sounds very trusting,' Robert said, refilling their coffee cups, 'and very Buddhist.'

Mary cradled the cup in both hands to enjoy the aroma rising from the dark surface. 'Well, it's just the way I like to lead my life. It won't make me rich. But I sleep well, and with a smile on my face.'

'So, did you get your business done with Maude?'

'It feels like I've only just begun,' Robert answered, relieved to have someone to talk to about it. 'It turns out she's my grandmother. A grandmother I didn't know I had until I had a letter from her two days ago.'

'I hope you're not expecting me to look too surprised?' said Mary. 'When you told me what'd brought you up here and I got to taking a second look at you it was, literally, staring me in the face. The likeness between you is uncanny, and it goes way beyond the almost identical eyes.

'I'm so very pleased for Maude, but what a bittersweet thing – to unearth something like that in the last weeks of her life. Must be quite a story in there somewhere.'

'Yes, there is,' said Robert flatly. 'One that I don't think even Hollywood could have come up with. Treads hard on just about every pious toe. Fornication, sin, fear, judgement, religious intolerance, lack of compassion, enforced secrecy, tragically young deaths, aching loneliness. Even love,' he added with a bitter laugh.

'And, as if that wasn't enough, if I told you how I even came to be here, in America, you would simply be unable to believe any of it. One thing I learned as a priest though, and I do know to be true, is that so often it's fact that really is stranger than fiction. Maybe sometime soon I'll be able to tell you the whole story, but not now.'

'Oh don't worry,' Mary replied, 'You've given me more than enough to try and get my head around. Not that any of it's my business really. I wouldn't in a million years have had you as a priest. Can't be too many of those flying about in their own jets!'

Robert laughed. 'No, I guess not,' he said and then added wistfully, 'but then maybe I've lost my way somewhere along the line.'

Mary didn't respond. She just looked at him thoughtfully.

After breakfast, having equipped himself with two pairs of Levi 501 button-fly jeans, underwear, a couple of shirts, a sweater and some durable, oiled-leather shoes, Robert drove back to Maude's cottage. It was another beautiful day.

This time Maude came to greet him with outstretched arms. She had been waiting near the front door, pretending to do some gardening. She had hardly slept. The excitement and pleasure of finding her grandson had kept any hope of sleep at bay. Besides, with her own time at a premium, she already knew she had work to do to help her grandson rediscover his way in life, and maybe even his faith, but she wasn't yet sure about that.

Having been brought up a very strict Catholic, Maude had long since begun to question the rigidness, the rules and the rituals by which her parents had accepted, without challenge, every tenet of the Roman Catholic religion – especially those that seemed to be so patently contradictory, illogical, or founded on the most dubious historical basis.

Perversely, it seemed to her, looking back on her life, there was a direct relationship between what might be seen as the weakening of her unquestioning religious observances and practices, with the considerable strengthening of her own personal faith.

Yesterday Maude Kimball had been a stranger to Robert, but today, stepping into his grandmother's welcoming embrace already seemed the most natural thing in the world to him.

'I don't suppose either of us got very much sleep,' Maude said. 'I've got some coffee on. Let's go sit by the lake and continue where we left off last night.'

'Don't you have things to do I could help you with?' Robert asked.

'Nothing that can't wait,' came Maude's certain reply.

Sitting looking out over the lake, with the morning sun sparkling on the water, they had hardly resumed talking when their conversation was interrupted by the clear, haunting cry of a bird.

Robert had no idea what had made the noise and looked questioningly at his grandmother.

'It's a loon,' Maude explained. 'Probably a mother, calling either to her chicks or to her mate.'

'A loon?'

'Yes, it's an almost prehistoric water bird, closer to the size of a goose than a duck. It shares some of its evolutionary traits with the penguin, although, unlike penguins, loons fly quite well. They are native to the northern hemisphere and seem to like the New England states and Canada.'

Robert nodded in understanding. For a moment both of them felt the same connection, as if this were an eager young grandson being instructed by a wise grandmother. They smiled and chuckled comfortably together.

'So, where to begin?' Maude asked. 'I need to be practical about this as I may not have very much time.

'If you want to learn about my imagined relationship with my son, your father, the best thing would really be for you to open and read all the letters I wrote to him but never mailed. That way you'd also learn something of my life too. I know it's a lot, but they are all in date order stored in old shoeboxes in a big old trunk upstairs. If you wanted you could start off by reading just one in six and still get a pretty good idea. You can also take them all with you when you leave if you want to. I'd like you to have them anyway.

'First off though, talking of leaving, how long do you plan to stay?'

Robert wasn't really prepared for this question. 'I don't know,' he said. 'I had originally planned to return to New York today, but since getting here and finding you I know I want to stay for a while longer. I've already told my office I won't be back for a few days.'

'In that case would you like to come and stay here? Maybe move over tomorrow, or the next day? It wouldn't be fair to Mary to pull you out of the inn without notice.'

'Yes, I'd like that very much,' Robert said. 'It would be like staying for an extended sleepover with the grandmother I never knew I had,' he added with a broad grin. 'I'll talk to Mary about it tonight or tomorrow morning.'

Maude sat back in her chair and smiled. 'That would be nice.'

Then she let her gaze drift across the lake for a while, before turning her attention back to Robert. 'You know I had no idea that that lottery ticket I put in the Sunday collection at your church was the jackpot-winning ticket. How could I? The odds against it were almost incalculable – which, of course, is the idea of lotteries, isn't it?

'It was complete, spur-of-the-moment serendipity. I couldn't find the postcard of New London I'd wanted to drop in with my contribution and I desperately wanted to leave some sort of tangible connection for you with New Hampshire. I had this bizarre idea that if I did so, it might some day, somehow bring you over here.'

'Well, it certainly has, hasn't it?' Robert interjected with a gentle laugh.

'What's really strange about it though,' his grandmother continued, 'is that when I opened my purse back at the hotel later, right at the top, clearly visible, was the postcard I'd been so frantically searching for. Whereas I distinctly remember tucking the lottery ticket inside one of the tight little side pockets. How does one ever explain such things?'

'There are so many things in life that can't be satisfactorily explained,' Robert answered, sounding as if he could be a priest again. 'A behavioural scientist would probably say it had something to do with the urgency of your searching that made you overlook the postcard and, subliminally, search for the lottery ticket because your unconscious knew it was there.'

'Well, the behavioural scientist would be flat wrong,' Maude retorted tartly. 'Heaven preserve us from all the psycho-babblers in this world.'

'There is one thing I do want to ask you, Maude,' Robert said, leaning forward tensely. 'Did you always mean the lottery ticket to be for me personally – and consequently its proceeds?'

'I never gave it that much deliberate thought at the time, of course,' was Maude's matter-of-fact reply. 'It never occurred to me that it might even be a winning ticket, let alone *the* winning ticket. I was just trying to make some sort of symbolic connection between you, New Hampshire and, to be totally frank, me.

'But, yes, I've thought about that since and I realise my intention was for you to have that ticket and I can tell you that, had your ownership ever been contested, I would have broken my silence to come forward as the donor and declare it to be yours, as I had intended.'

The look on Robert's face told Maude that, not only had she given the right answer, but it was the answer her grandson desperately needed to hear.

For Robert the overwhelming relief felt almost physical. Maybe, he wondered, this is what absolution felt like for devout Catholics after going to receive the sacrament of Confession – a concept he and Andreas had often argued about.

'One other thing,' Robert asked. 'Why did you never come forward before this? I don't understand that.'

'I thought I'd explained that to you in the letter I sent,' Maude replied. 'Had you returned to London and your life there, I wouldn't have felt I had any right to intrude upon it, particularly at my stage of life and because I had freely chosen to give your father up for adoption. Remember I had signed papers at the time of the adoption promising not to try and contact your father for the rest of my life. It was only because I knew you had remained in America, and because I wouldn't be around for very much longer, that I wanted to give you the chance to meet me – at least if you had any wish to do so.

'I can't tell you how glad I am that you responded so quickly and so positively and now I can't think why I delayed so long. Still, one thing about having only limited time left is you try not to waste any of it on regrets for what is already in the past.

'Of course, as much as I could, I tried to read about you and follow your progress in New York. Much to the surprise of our local Park 'N' Go convenience store in Elkins, I even took out a subscription to the *Wall Street Journal*. For someone who'd never shown the slightest interest in business or financial matters, they must have thought it was the early onset of senility, I think.'

They both chuckled at that.

'Didn't you ever want any of the money from your winning lottery ticket?' Robert asked, feeling ashamed at his question even now.

Maude picked up on the apprehension in his voice. 'What for?' she asked.

'I already have everything I need and you're the only family I have. Yes, once in a while I thought about it, if only to be able to help some of the folk around here for whom I know life is a struggle. But I do what I can to help them anyway. When my parents died they left me comfortably enough provided for and knowing you won't be needing it, I've willed most of my estate to different charities I like to support.

'Anyway, would it have made me any happier or a better person?' It was a rhetorical question, which Maude answered by asking, 'Has it made you either happier or a better person, Robert?'

The pensive look on his face and the length of time it took Robert to answer told Maude all she needed to know.

'I see now I was meant to contact you,' she continued. 'Maybe you've lost your way in everything that has happened to you and you need someone – family – to help you find your way back?' she suggested gently.

Ignoring this, Robert replied. 'Well, it's opened many doors and shown me a whole world of which I previously knew very little. It's also allowed me to discover a talent I never knew I had. It's given me much greater confidence in myself and allowed me to meet people and do and experience things I would never even have dreamed of. So, yes, on balance, I see what's happened as mostly positive.'

'That's all well and good,' his grandmother told him, 'but your answer to my question is not really balanced. You've only given examples of what you see as the positive benefits. What would you say are some of the negative ones?'

'That's a lot harder to answer and I'm not sure I'm able to put what are still barely formed thoughts or feelings on that subject into words right now.'

Maude looked at him reassuringly. 'That's OK, but think about it and perhaps you'd like to talk more on that before you leave.'

Robert saw her grow tense momentarily, as she flinched at the pain that had been her unwelcome companion in recent months. 'Right now I think it's time we had a little lunch,' she said levering herself up from her chair. 'I'll go in and fix us both a sandwich. You happy with tuna salad?'

'I'll come and help you,' Robert told her, standing up and holding out his hand to her. 'Are you sure I'm not making you too tired? Should I leave you to have a rest?'

Maude smiled at her grandson. 'If you only knew the pleasure your presence and your company gives me, you'd understand why I don't want to waste a moment of every opportunity to be with you. Your being here is far more likely to keep me alive for a little longer than your not being here.

'But you're right, it is time I took some more of my pain control medication.'

Together in the kitchen, they fashioned two, generously filled, tuna salad sandwiches. After cutting them in half, Maude put three of the halves onto Robert's plate and kept a half for herself. They ate their lunch sitting on a bench Maude had installed at the bottom of her garden, right on the edge of the lake.

For the rest of the afternoon and well into the evening Maude made Robert tell her as much as he could remember of his father and his childhood growing up in Australia.

It was after ten o'clock when Robert got back to the inn. It had been another eventful day, one in which he had been given a lot more to ponder on and think about. Sleep, he knew, would not come easily.

Both Mary and Jen had left him separate messages to call his office urgently. It seemed that they had been trying all day to get hold of him.

33

ROBERT AWOKE VERY early after only a few hours' sleep. He lay on his back staring up at the ceiling. To his surprise he felt quite well rested and wondered if this was to do with the fresh country air, the freedom from a long-held, overbearing secret guilt, or that for once his thoughts were not of business, but what he now clearly saw were the far more consequential ones to do with his personal life. This new, fascinating, fragile and imminently finite thread, leading him back to a whole aspect of his family that, until days ago, he had known nothing of.

These thoughts convinced Robert of something else too: that he would not be returning to New York anytime soon.

At almost the same moment of making that decision, the telephone beside his bed began its insistent ringing.

Reluctantly he reached for the receiver. 'Hello Cynthia,' he said without waiting to hear who was on the line.

'Well, I don't know who Cynthia is,' came Mary's voice in response. 'I just wanted to tell you that it was me and not Jen who made the decision not to contact you down at Maude's house.

'Your office kept saying it was so urgent, but they made the mistake of telling me it was a matter of the greatest business urgency. Like a red rag to a bull to me of course. I just thought what on earth could be more important than the limited time you have with Maude? So I told them we didn't know where you were and couldn't reach you.

'First couple of times it was someone called Jill. She was really agitated and kept trying to impress me with the importance of it. Then it was someone called Cynthia … Oh, I guess the Cynthia you thought I was …? Anyway she was much calmer and I'm willing to bet, knew where you were and knew we knew where you were too. Without saying as much, she seemed to buy into the idea of protecting you. Sounded like a really nice lady.

'I hope I did the right thing, but if you're going to get mad at anyone get mad at me and not Jen. If I'd let them find you, I'm certain whatever it was, or is, that's so important would have started playing on your mind and broken the atmosphere for you and Maude.'

'Thanks Mary. You did absolutely the right thing. I'll call Cynthia in a moment and sort everything out with her.

'By the way, Maude's asked me to go and stay with her and it feels like the right thing for me to do. Would you mind if I checked out tomorrow and moved down to her place?'

'Yes I would,' Mary shot back. 'You should move to Maude's house today. She needs you and neither of you have got any time to waste. I appreciate you wanting to give me notice, but that's only because I've been nice to you. If I was just some Holiday Inn you wouldn't think twice about checking out today, would you? That's the difference between what I do and what cookie-cutter hotel chains do. It's probably also why they make good money and why I'll never be rich. But, hey, it's like I said with this place, it's a love-hate relationship and for some inexplicable reason today I love it.'

Robert laughed, 'OK, Mary,' he said. 'I'm not going to fight you.'

'Better not to,' Mary replied, unable to hide from Robert the smile in her voice.

'Oh, and you can keep the old truck for the time being. I'll let you know when I need it back. You be good to Maude. She so deserves a little family love right now, even at this late stage in her life.'

There was a brief pause before Mary continued. 'And, Mr Melton … oh darn, can I call you Robert?' she asked and then without waiting for his answer carried on. 'Please don't go back to New York if you don't have to. Not just yet. Maude wouldn't let you see her disappointment, but I'm very sure that having found you she won't want to lose you again, even for one precious second. There, I've said what I wanted to say and now I'll mind my own business.'

Robert hadn't expected this and he was glad he was alone to hear what Mary had said to him. He didn't mind her saying it at all. In fact he liked it. He liked her saying it.

'Don't worry, Mary,' he told her. 'I don't mind telling you it's mutual. Now that I've found the grandmother I didn't know I had, I don't want to waste one precious second with her and I don't want to lose her again either, until … I have to,' he said, his voice trailing off.

'There's something else,' he added before she rang off. 'Although you might think the need is all one-sided on Maude's part, the truth is I think I've already discovered I need her just as much as she needs me. Thank you, Mary for being so understanding and, yes, please do always call me Robert.'

After finishing the call Robert shaved and took a shower before calling his office in New York. Although it was still early, well before the official office opening time, he knew Cynthia would be there already. Whenever there was any kind of crisis, if he was away, Cynthia always covered for him, making sure she was in early and home late.

Cynthia picked up the phone on her desk after the first ring. 'Good morning Robert, I'm guessing it's you calling at this early hour,' she said with very little question in her voice. 'How's it going up in New Hampshire?'

'It's going very well thanks, Cyn. I gather you and Jill were trying to get hold of me yesterday. Message I got said it was very urgent. So here I am. What's up?'

'Well, it seems like the guys in Houston and Dallas have found an alternative investor and now think they can dictate terms to you. They've issued an ultimatum, the gist of which is either you get yourself down there today, or at latest tomorrow morning, or they'll go ahead and do the deal with the Bird Group, leaving you as an isolated minority stakeholder. They could be bluffing of course, but I don't think they are. Jill's sure they're not and she's very exercised about it.

'What do you want me to do? Would you like me to call Mike and send the plane up to get you?'

A few days earlier a situation like this would have had Robert on his way to Dallas already, to wrest back control of the deal. He had developed the reputation of being very competitive when it came to business, never allowing himself to lose a deal to a rival without a fight. In such situations he had become accustomed to winning. Having done so, he always made sure to exact a high price from all those who had either stood against him, or even just stood aside. They could expect no mercy. Only those loyal to him throughout the inevitable ups and downs of the process could expect to be rewarded.

This was how he had built his fearsome reputation for being a tough negotiator and a hard man. Sometimes in the dark loneliness of the wakeful night hours Robert would compare this man he had become to the naive, unsure, trusting young priest in Earls Court and smile to himself. If only they knew. So much of life was about other people's perceptions and so much of it was like a game. A game which, in the business world, he'd quickly learned how to play well – and how to play to win. Even so, he never let himself forget Brenda's last letter to him, safely locked away like a holy relic that Robert would take out and peruse at times of reflection.

Contrary to what Cynthia thought likely and Jill was sure of, all Robert's instincts and well-researched knowledge of the Bird Group led him to think that his targets in Dallas and Houston were bluffing. He knew the Bird Group didn't have that kind of firepower and, if they did, they would be so stretched in doing

303

it they would in turn become very exposed themselves. In which case Robert decided he would mount a direct attack on them and capture the whole enlarged group – something he knew he could easily afford to do and they would not be able to defend. He would have plenty of time to do that later.

'No, Cyn. Just call them and tell them I've got important things to do up here. Tell them I'm not coming. Oh, and be sure to tell them I wish them lots of luck with the Bird Group. OK?'

There was a short silence before Cynthia spoke. 'OK, Robert. As long as you're quite certain that's what you want me to do. Remember you were stalking this one for quite a while before we ever got the opportunity.'

'So when are you thinking of coming back to New York?'

'I don't know, Cyn. Something's happened up here that I really can't put into words yet. It's just, I know I have to stay here for the time being. I've never been so sure of anything in my life.'

The last sentence, although quietly spoken, was uttered with such emphatic certainty it alarmed Cynthia.

'Robert, you haven't been abducted into some kind of a cult have you? It's just your voice sounds strange, and this is all so unlike you. Do they put something in the water up in New Hampshire the rest of the country doesn't know about?'

Robert laughed, 'No, Cyn. Don't worry about me. It's just … oh, I really can't describe it yet. It's to do with my grandmother, and so many other things too.

'It's like, ever since I got here, this place and the people I've met so far are somehow, without realising it, holding up a mirror and letting me see myself in a way I never have before. I don't know, it's all so complicated. I'm just not ready to talk about it yet, but I promise you as soon as I am you'll be the first to know. Rest assured I'm fine and just look after things down in New York for me will you?'

'Don't worry about a thing down here, Robert. I'll take care of it with Bill. By the way Bill says "Hi" and he'll come down from Boston to spend more time here with me until you get back. As long as you're sure you're fine I'll relax, OK?'

'Thanks, Cyn. That's great. Just so you know it may be a while, but right now I've no idea how long. Will you ask Jill not to contact me unless it's life-threatening?'

'I will,' Cynthia chuckled. 'She gets pretty wound up in the competitiveness of it all, but batting on our team, that's no bad thing!'

'Give her my best and make sure I remember her birthday. It's coming up quite soon, I think. Take care, Cyn and ... thanks for everything.'

'You're welcome Robert. And you take care of yourself too.'

With that they both rang off.

34

WHEN ROBERT WENT downstairs for some breakfast, Jen met him in the lobby with a message. 'Maude called while you were on the phone. She says she needed to come to town to get groceries and asked if you'd like to join her for some breakfast over at Baynham's first.'

'Thanks, Jen, we passed it coming into town – back along Main Street just past the fire station I think?'

'Yes. That's it. Place in town where everyone likes to meet. Great stuff there and good coffee too.'

Robert remembered it from his first visit with Andreas.

Ten minutes later he was seated at a table next to the window. Maude was looking a little tired, but happy, he thought. It surprised him to discover how protective of her he already felt.

'I thought it would be a bit different for you to come here, and fun for us to get out a bit while I still can,' Maude began.

'Also, it seems fitting to round the circle with you in as much as this is the place I bought the lottery ticket that has changed both our lives so much and brought you to me.

'It's one of the older, more historic places in New London that has reinvented itself more than once. Started out being built as a farm, would you believe. Then, as the town grew up all around it, it was for many years the old New London Hardware Store.

'However, with the arrival of the big chain store models, it was too small to compete on price and, although it competed effectively for a long while on its reputation for knowledgeable, individual customer service, it couldn't survive without change. So it changed into what it is today. A sort of Aladdin's emporium, embracing the warm heart of the old American country store, but with enough useful stuff, sourced from all over the world, to be more a store of many countries than just a Country Store.

'The café does a great breakfast and the coffee's probably the best in town. Besides most days, if you sit here long enough, you'll get to see all of your friends. It's that sort of place and that's important to me.'

They ordered their breakfast, Robert opting for the full cooked breakfast and Maude for wheat toast with orange marmalade, and coffee. She had developed a taste for marmalade as a student in England.

'I've been here before,' Robert told Maude. 'Eight years ago when I came up with Andreas shortly after arriving in the States. We just wanted to see the place where the lottery ticket had been purchased.'

'I don't know if buying it here made it a lucky ticket for me,' said Maude, 'or if putting it in my grandmother's little blue jug on the kitchen table had anything to do with it. My grandmother gave me that jug when I was just a little girl. I used to think it was so pretty. It's an unusual shape and the white of the porcelain top contrasts vividly with the broad, cobalt blue, band in the middle. But as a child I was even more fascinated by the intricate shield and family crest embossed on each side: the crest of the Holroyd-Smyth family from Ballynatray in Ireland.'

'In Ireland?' Robert asked, sipping his coffee.

'My grandmother had some connection to the family, but how she came to be in possession of this pretty little jug I don't remember. Anyway, the story she always told me was that one day the family had been enjoying a very grand picnic, amid the romantic ruins of St Molana's Abbey, the remains of which still

307

stood in the parkland on the edge of the river Blackwater below the big house of Ballynatray itself. Somehow, when clearing up, the little jug was mislaid and when the butler reported the loss to the lady of the house later that evening she became very agitated and urgently requested another search be made at first light the following day.

'It had rained in the night and when, to her great surprise and joy, the housemaid who had been sent to look for it, stumbled across it, the little jug was full of water. As she stooped down to pick it up, she saw a badly injured young fawn from the deer park lying on its side hidden in the grass. It was nearly dead and appeared to be panting with thirst. So the housemaid put the little jug down next to its head, positioned in such a way that it could get the tip of its tongue into the water.

'The story goes that no sooner had the fawn drunk the rainwater from the little jug then it sprang up, its injuries no longer visible, and bounded off into the forest behind.

'If it's true, and if it is in any way "miraculous", was it the jug, the rainwater, or the hallowed grounds of St Molana's Abbey that might have been responsible? Anyway, ever since, people have believed that the little jug has magical powers. This was Ireland of course! But what I can tell you is true, is that when I got home from here, I put that lottery ticket in the little jug so as not to lose it.

'Why I later removed it to put in my purse before travelling to England I don't really remember. Except ... except against all likelihood, I suppose I must have thought somewhere, deep down in my subconscious, "What if it was a winning ticket? Would I want to leave it sticking out of a little jug on my kitchen table for anyone to see should they happen by while I was away?"

'Maybe lottery tickets are like that. It's all in the dream, just the possibility – however remote.'

Robert finished spreading marmalade on a piece of toast. 'That's a charming story, Maude,' he told her gently. 'And as such I love it. But I'm not much given to superstitions of that, or any other kind. Put it down to my rigorous theological training if you like,' he said with a smile.

The mention of his vocation caused Maude to change tack. 'Now that's something I've been wanting to ask you about,' she said cautiously. 'Presumably, it was an inner calling that made you choose to be trained for the priesthood? You are an ordained priest in the Church of England and, until I came along with my lottery ticket, you were a vicar with your own church and parish in London. What happened to make you turn your back on that? I hope it wasn't just the seductive lure of Mammon?'

There was a long, uncomfortable silence, which Maude seemed in no hurry to interrupt, content instead to wait patiently for her grandson's response. When it came, there was such a sad quietness to Robert's voice that Maude put her hand out to him. He took her frail old hand in his young, strong one and gently stroked it.

'I'd begun to have a crisis of faith quite some time before your trip to London and the appearance of the lottery ticket,' he began. 'I think it started with an increasing sense of hopelessness and pointlessness in my parish work after I started at St Mungo's. There I was, with my own parish in the very heart of one of the busiest parts of London, a major international city. Yet staring me in the face was the certainty that with the attrition of age, almost all my pitiful congregation of about two dozen regular worshippers would be gone within ten years.

'The church building itself was crumbling without any possible means of being able to pay for even basic repairs. The form of worship on offer to anyone under the age of about fifty seemed entirely irrelevant. To an energetic young man, full of ideas, zeal and optimism, it had felt like an exciting challenge at first and I had even begun to make some positive progress, but when I discovered the real purpose of my appointment, and the actual intention of the church authorities for St Mungo's, it felt like a betrayal, leading to a long, slow death sentence, as part of which I was to be condemned to squander at least two years of my life.

'On top of that I began to feel hypocritical, Maude. When I started at St Mungo's, I'd unkindly scorned my predecessors for their apathy, and then I found myself facing the same issue.

'I began to question a God who would let someone eager to devote their whole life to His service, find themselves so completely trapped in this hopeless position. For weeks I prayed earnestly for God to give me guidance over what to do. I knew I was supposed to seek His will in whatever situation I found myself, but try as I might I could make no sense of it.

'I felt abandoned and the ritual of the Holy Eucharist and other worship had begun to seem a hollow mockery, devoid of any meaning. I started to feel fraudulent in my role as a parish vicar and even began to dread the prospect of being called upon by any parishioners in need. Fortunately, with so few parishioners left, the likelihood of that was always going to be small.

'There was only one situation where I felt any continuing connection to my calling and even now the memory of it exerts a powerful effect on me.

'But this is a lot about me, Maude,' he continued, hoping to shift the conversation. 'Are you sure you want to me to go on? Shouldn't we be talking about you and your life?'

'We've already done a lot of that and there'll be time enough for more later. But right now I want you to continue. I have a feeling this is important and, whether it is or not, you and everything I can learn about you are absolutely the most important thing to me,' Maude replied.

'Well, as I was going to say, there was one parishioner, if she can be called that when she wasn't even on the parish electoral roll and never came to church services. She was completely different to all the rest. Indeed *was* different to anyone else I've ever known. She would just come into the church at random moments throughout the week, mostly in the mornings and never on Sundays. She always sat right at the back of the church, well hidden in the shadows, remaining quite still, and she'd usually stay between ten and twenty minutes. Sometimes I wouldn't even know she was there until I saw movement as she got up to leave. It took me a while to establish any kind of contact with her.'

Robert went on to describe Brenda and how eventually he had been able to establish what he characterised as a tentative relationship. One in which he knew there were boundaries that would not allow him to get too close to her. He did not, though, tell Maude about the two letters he had received from Brenda.

Maude seemed particularly interested when Robert told her about the last note Brenda had left for him to find in the pew at St Mungo's.

'You know where those words come from Robert, don't you?' Maude asked.

'No, should I?' Robert replied.

'Well, not the "stop worrying" bit, but the bit after that "All shall be well. All manner of things shall be well". It's a direct quote from Julian of Norwich, one of the great lady mystics of the medieval Church in England.'

'Ah yes, of course. I should have realised that.'

'It's strange, isn't it, that "he" was a "she". She was in fact a dame, so she might even have been known as Lady Julian of Norwich, just to make it even more confusing. She took her name from the Church of St Julian in Norwich, England, which belonged to the Benedictine community at Carrow, where it's thought she might have been a nun.'

'You seem to be very well informed on matters of English clerical history, Maude. I'm impressed,' Robert said with a broad grin.

His grandmother chuckled. 'No, it just happens I read a short history of her life about a year ago. And it was short, because despite her own prolific writings, not a great deal is known about her.'

'I wonder why Brenda chose her to quote from?' Robert asked himself, as much as Maude.

'Oh come on, Robert. For a clever man, you're being slow in seeing that obvious connection, aren't you?' Maude interjected almost impatiently. 'Didn't you say she'd changed gender?'

'Oh, of course! You're right. That was stupid of me. Typically clever of Brenda too, to echo her own situation in her choice of spiritual writers to quote from.'

'She sounds quite mysterious and, being unable to speak, is perhaps inclined to write in ways that have more than one meaning: to maximise the impact of every one of her written words, if you see what I mean,' offered Maude.

'Yes. You're probably right. I'll have to think about that. But what I was going to tell you about Brenda is that, despite not really practising the rituals of her religion in any conventional way, I always had the strongest impression that whenever she was near I was somehow in the presence of … I don't really know how to describe it … but I suppose "goodness" is the word I'm looking for. It was as if she had a closer connection to God than any of us who practise our religion in the conventional way.'

'Robert you're talking with the naivety and innocence of a churchman who's never known anything else. Which is, perhaps, what you were when you first arrived in this country. But don't pretend the intervening years haven't exposed you to a lot, and taught you a great deal about life in all its complexities, its messiness and even – sometimes – its beauty.

'You're forgetting that I've been following what you've been doing over here ever since you arrived, not just in the pages of the financial press, but also in the tabloids and society gossip magazines. *Town & Country* did a very glamorous piece covering the exotic birthday party you threw last year: the one that started in New York and finished four days later on board the *Lucky Find* in Fort Lauderdale, with all those bikini-clad beauties surrounding you.

'By the way, I was disappointed in the name you chose for your yacht. *Lucky Find* is boringly unimaginative. It reeks of guilt from the confessional and, frankly, is rather vulgar. After what you've told me about Brenda, *Silent Beauty* or *Black Beauty*, or something along those lines would have been so much more intriguing and elegant.

'So don't pretend to an innocence you've only recently lost – and don't expect me to either – just to play to your idea of social sensibilities. I lost my own innocence years ago and I've been living with the consequences ever since.'

Robert was looking uncomfortably startled, but Maude didn't back away from what she wanted to tell him. 'What you've experienced and learned about life and yourself over the last eight years will either be the making or breaking of you. Should you decide to return to your true calling, it will be the making of you. Should you decide to devote the rest of your life to the pursuit of hedonistic pleasure and ever-increasing wealth, it will ultimately prove to be the breaking of you and you will forever remain the man with the unsatisfied mind.

'Don't get me wrong. I'm not against the making of money. Whoever it was who famously said, "There is no doubt whatever that, under the capitalist system, man exploits man. Whereas, under the socialist system, it is completely the other way around" knew a thing or two about human nature. Perhaps cynical, but true. I'm realistic enough to know that no system is perfect.'

It was clear that Robert didn't know how to respond. Maude patted his hand and said soothingly, 'Now I've said more than enough and anyway, I think it's high time I did the grocery shopping I came into town for and then went home.'

Robert was sitting back in his chair. He didn't move. He was looking at his grandmother with amazement and admiration. When he had come up to New Hampshire he hadn't known what to expect. A scheming fraud, exploiting emotion to try and get at some of his money? A simple, little old lady at the sad end of her life, wanting only to be patronised with forgiveness and platitudes? He hadn't reckoned on this independent-minded, highly intelligent, dignified old lady, able to hold her own with any trained philosopher or thinker.

'Come on Robert,' said Maude, getting up. 'It's time we went home. We've got a lot more talking to do. But first some groceries. We'll stop at Springledge Farm too and get ourselves something delicious to have for lunch down by the lake.'

*

Two hours later, seated where they had been the night before, they were enjoying a light lunch of locally made Buffalo mozzarella with thick slices of home-grown tomatoes that tasted of warm sunshine, accompanied by a crusty, round loaf of freshly baked sourdough bread and a glass of chilled Simi, Californian Sauvignon Blanc.

'We're so lucky with our local producers. Springledge Farm is a gem,' said Maude, nibbling her slice of cheese. 'After lunch, Robert, I'm afraid I'm going to need to take a rest. Jen Rupa, my doctor, would already be very cross with me if she knew what I was up to,' she chuckled.

'That sounds like a good plan, Maude. You need to do your best to keep your strength up. While you're resting I'll pop back to the inn, pay my bill and get my things. Then, if it's OK with you, I'd like to make a start reading through all those other unmailed letters you wrote to my father?'

'They'll be waiting for you on the kitchen table when you get back.'

'I'm looking forward to reading them,' he told her, raising his glass to her.

35

BACK AT THE inn, Robert was pleased to find Jen on duty rather than Mary; he knew Jen didn't know about Mary's refusal to accept any payment in lieu of his early departure.

After collecting his things, Robert paid his bill, insisting on paying for that night as well. Jen tried to object, saying she didn't think Mary would want to charge him for the extra night he wasn't going to be there, but Robert brushed her objection aside, saying it could be considered as a small contribution towards car rental if nothing else.

It was a lovely afternoon. Driving back to Maude's house Robert was in no hurry, so he decided to take a detour and drive around the town lake again on his way back to Sutton. At the south end of the lake, he pulled into the small parking area by the Town Beach, opposite Marshalls Garage.

The view up the lake towards the old Pleasant Lake Inn in the far distance was as beautiful as it was tranquil on this still summer day. The mirror-smooth surface of the water was only slightly disturbed by a pair of ducks swimming idly about and a lone Indian canoe being paddled quietly and expertly across the middle of the lake.

It was a tranquil scene, just as Robert had hoped. He stilled the throaty engine of the old Dodge pick-up and sat back in the driving seat. He wanted time to reflect. So much seemed to have happened to him over the last three days; his mind felt divided.

If he allowed himself to think about his New York life, the business deals and responsibilities he knew he should get back to, he was in turmoil and could feel the competitive excitement and stress levels rising together within him. It was very alluring and seductive. Yet, when he thought about this current life he had been leading over the last few days, one into which he had almost literally parachuted, the inner sense of purpose and meaning was so profound and brought with it such a feeling of deep calm, familiarity and happiness, he knew he couldn't risk losing it – at least not yet. Besides which, in remembering Mary's words imploring him not to leave Maude now they had found each other, he realised he couldn't do anything to hurt this extraordinary woman who just happened to be his grandmother. He also sensed he had much to learn from her in whatever precious time she had left.

But all of these thoughts were very much immediate ones at the forefront of his mind. He realised that there was something much more profound taking place deep inside. Something momentous that he didn't want to face up to, but equally something he knew he would not be able to deny forever.

Had Maude in her wisdom already sensed his dilemma? What had she really been thinking when she presented him with the two stark choices she had outlined? How could she know, despite all his outward success, of the deep dissatisfaction he felt with himself, or of the deeply buried, but nagging, pull of the priesthood that tugged at his mind?

Looking out across the limpid water on that somnolent afternoon, Robert sensed he was at a critical fork in the road of his life. What extraordinary circumstances had brought him to this point and this place? What did they mean in the decision he must now make?

Down one road lay the guarantee of continued success, power, fame and fortune, with the comfort of certainty and the certainty of comfort. Down the other lay the possibility of obscurity, service, modesty and the discomfort of uncertainty.

Between two such choices it should not, he knew, be hard to decide. And yet it was. He tried in his mind for a compromise that would allow him to travel both roads, but his training and his intelligence told him that was impossible. He could not serve two masters.

Having resisted doing so for a long time, but now, desperate for peace of mind and facing a situation where he knew he must make a decision, yet was completely unable to, Robert did what he hadn't done since leaving St Mungo's. Sitting there in the cab of the old Dodge truck, looking out over the lake, Robert blurted out loud, 'Over to you Lord. I can't handle this one. Please, please help me.'

Robert had no idea what to expect any more than he had done that last time, kneeling down in St Mungo's, when he had handed over to God the whole dilemma of his betrayal by the Bishop of West London. He remembered also the note Brenda had left that time, telling him to stop worrying and that all would be well. Against all possible rationality, it had indeed turned out that way – at least as far as the saving of St Mungo's was concerned.

But there was no Brenda now to leave him another signpost or reassuring message. Instead Robert's uneasy conscience was a reminder of what she had written to him eight uncomfortable years ago – and what he had got Cynthia to write to her in reply.

He dragged his thoughts back to Brenda's note, back to her reference to Julian of Norwich. Had that been more than a message? Had it in fact been a portent, a sign from God that He had heard Robert's cry for help and had indeed taken over the problem?

Then there was Maude's letter that had arrived on his desk out of left field. He remembered the churning in his stomach at the sight of her New Hampshire address. But he remembered too that this was swiftly followed by the sense of inexplicable relief he had felt descending on him. It had brought the same enormous peace of mind that had come to him on that bleak day in London: something he hadn't experienced in years. And now, parked by the lake in New

317

Hampshire, he was enveloped by that feeling once again. Was this the 'jubilation in Heaven' of one sinner taking a first faltering step towards returning to the fold, he wondered? He would have liked a 'Brenda' to be there to give him some reassurance.

Coming out of his reverie, Robert was surprised at the amount of time that had slipped by. He started the engine, carefully double de-clutched before coaxing the gear stick into reverse and was about to look over his shoulder to back up when something caught his eye out on the water, not far from the shoreline where he was parked. Peering hard, he made out the upturned hull of the Indian canoe he'd seen earlier being paddled across the lake.

He had no undue concern for its two occupants. Any moment now, he expected to see them in the water next to the boat. The water was warm and calm, they were near the shore and Robert knew they should be in no danger. From his own experience growing up in Australia, Robert knew Indian canoes. Although they were by far the most graceful of all canoes, they were inherently unstable in the hands of those who didn't understand the dynamics of the design. But Robert acknowledged that this didn't fit with the professional, splash-free expertise with which he had seen the boat being effortlessly guided across the lake.

Just then he noticed an outstretched forearm and hand reaching up from behind the half-submerged hull. Whoever it belonged to seemed to be waving frantically.

Robert opened the door of the cab in time to hear, above the laughter and happy squeals of children at the beach, what seemed to be a woman's voice screaming for help, before it was muffled into silence again beneath the water.

With all time for further thought instantly banished, Robert was simultaneously running the short distance to the water's edge while ripping off his shirt and kicking off his shoes. Having worked vacations as a teenage lifeguard in Australia he knew the importance of speed and bringing help to the distressed couple as quickly as possible.

He found himself bizarrely thankful that he was not wearing a belt with his Levis. As he took a long, shallow, running dive into the water he had just had time to rip open the button fly. The drag of the water on the fabric of the loosened jeans was sufficient to allow him to swim right out of them within the first thirty feet. Clad now only in his underwear he was able to swim as efficiently and quickly as possible out to the upturned canoe.

It took Robert less than three minutes to reach it. There he found a young woman struggling desperately to keep the head of a man above water. She was in a state of shock, bordering on hysteria. The young man with her was quite still, scarcely conscious, floating awkwardly in a semi-upright position; without the aid of the woman he would clearly have drowned.

Robert swam up beside them, expertly took hold of the man and guided him into the orthodox life saving position for the swim back to the shore. The man was unconscious, which made Robert's task easier, though he was solidly built and it took all Robert's strength to manoeuvre him back.

With the arrival of help and the situation having been taken out of her hands, the young woman regained some of her composure as she swam alongside. Confident that Robert knew what he was doing, she was able to relax enough to tell him that the young man was her husband and he suffered very occasional bouts of epilepsy.

'Medication normally keeps it under control,' she said between breaths. 'He hasn't had a seizure for three years. Something must have brought this one on quite suddenly. There weren't any of the usual warnings. Maybe it had something to do with the brightly reflecting sun spots each time we lifted our paddles.'

'You did very well,' Robert gasped back. 'He's a solid guy, your husband.'

'During the seizure it was all I could do to stop him from drowning while he was thrashing around unconscious in the water. Kept me so occupied I couldn't even shout or wave,' she said beginning to get her breath back. 'God, I don't know what I would have done without you.'

As they neared the shore other people who had hurried over from the beach area and Marshalls Garage waded into the water and helped Robert carry the man over to an area of flat grass, where a young mother had laid out a large towel in readiness.

The postmistress came out to say the doctor and ambulance had been called and were on their way. The couple seemed to be known and amongst friends. The young man was beginning to regain a groggy half-consciousness, unaware of the alarm and excitement he had caused.

As the excitement died down, Robert became aware that he was the stranger, standing there in nothing but wet white Jockey trunks. Covered with sudden embarrassment, he was about to start a frantic search for his clothes, when a woman he recognised stepped forward with a broad grin to hand him a towel she had borrowed from one of the beachgoers.

'I was driving past and saw my old truck parked up,' Mary Cotton said. 'Knew you must be about somewhere. Saw the group gathered at the water's edge and when I heard the engine still running figured you'd got yourself into the middle of something, or were up to no good.

'Nice bod by the way!' she said playfully as she handed him the towel.

After gratefully wrapping the towel around his waist and with his modesty somewhat restored, Robert went over to where he had kicked off his shoes and dropped his shirt.

'Don't worry, I collected those up for you, along with your jeans, which I fished out of the water. Thought you could use a towel first, though. Besides, you haven't noticed, but all the women on the beach are enjoying getting an eyeful of your rugged Australian physique! Kinda surprising for a New York moneyman really.

'Can't blame them, though. A tall, handsome stranger suddenly appears from nowhere in their midst. Without a second thought for his own safety, risks life and limb to rescue one of their own from drowning. Emerges from the water, wearing only wet, form-flattering underwear, with water running off a well-developed, manly chest and walks modestly away ... move over James Bond!'

Robert smiled sheepishly. 'You've got an overdeveloped sense of the dramatic Mary,' he laughed. 'But thanks for the compliments.'

Just then the young lady from the lake came running over. 'How can I ever thank you properly for saving my husband's life?' she said. 'I don't even know your name. I'm Annie Foster and my husband's Jake.'

Still with only the towel wrapped around his waist, Robert self-consciously took her outstretched hand. 'Robert Melton,' he murmured. 'No thanks needed. It was instinctive. I would have done it for anyone in that situation,' he said, not meaning to sound either dismissive or conceited.

Just then two of the men from Marshalls Garage, who had swum out to retrieve the half-submerged canoe, came up and put it on the ground. 'Want us to put this up on the car for you Annie, or keep it in the garage overnight?' one of them asked.

'Hey, thanks guys. I'd forgotten all about the canoe. That's so kind of you. I guess the roof of the car would be great.'

Looking now at the canoe, Robert noted what a beautiful boat she was. From the traditional woven cane seats, richly varnished wooden interior, beautifully scalloped bow and stern curves, to the glossy dark green paint of her hull, she was a very elegant craft.

As the men hoisted the canoe up again Robert noticed a name painted in a flowing script on either side of the bow. It was unusual for a canoe to have any name other than that of its manufacturer. In near disbelief at the coincidence only he would understand, Robert now read the name: *Brenda*.

'*Brenda*?' he asked, trying not to sound too surprised.

'Yes. It was Jake's grandfather's boat. His pride and joy. He named her after a girl he'd met somewhere before he was married. Very mysterious. He wouldn't ever talk about her. Just said she wasn't as others saw her and that she was his

321

muse. He had to tell me what a muse was. Some sort of inspirational goddess apparently.'

Robert was stunned. Wrapped in the borrowed towel, he stood rooted to the spot with a far-away look of concentration on his face.

Eventually, somewhere far off, he heard a voice asking, 'Is he all right?' It was someone talking to Mary.

Then the reply, 'Yes, I think so. Looks like something just jumped into his mind.

'Robert? Robert, the lady whose towel you've got wants it back.'

The threat of finding himself again exposed in his wet underwear was sufficient to snap Robert back to the present with a jolt. Instinctively he tightened his grip on the towel at his waist.

Mary laughed. 'I thought that might wake you up. Where'd you go? You had us worried for a moment.'

'Sorry, I was miles away,' Robert replied.

'Best get into some clothes,' Mary said, walking towards the truck.

The people on the beach had by now turned their attention to Annie and Jake as Robert followed her, holding the towel tightly around his waist.

Mary held open the passenger door round the far side of the truck, so Robert would be sufficiently screened to change. 'I'll give Louise the towel when you're finished with it,' she said. 'And don't worry. Your modesty is safe with me.'

'Thanks, Mary,' Robert mumbled awkwardly. But as he let go of the wet towel to reach into the cab, it slipped to the ground.

'Not the best moment to show off,' she laughed, bending to pick the towel up from the sandy grass. As she did so her hand brushed lightly against Robert's when he too simultaneously reached down in his haste to grab the towel. With their heads close, their eyes briefly met and a volume of unspoken words passed between them in the way only the eyes can communicate the thoughts of the soul.

Instinctively both of them knew something had changed. To Robert it felt like a moment of absolution. It could have lasted an afternoon, or a nanosecond. Time did not matter. Although as yet unacknowledged, when they parted, he had found an eternity in Mary's smile and she had found the answer to a deep yearning in his.

'See you back at the inn sometime,' she said softly as Robert began to struggle into his wet jeans. Then, waving the towel, she called across the hood of the truck, 'OK, Louise. The gentleman is decent now!' before leaving Robert to pull on his shirt, socks and shoes.

Climbing back into the old pick-up, Robert started the engine, waved goodbye to Annie and Jake and, pausing only to let a construction truck go past, pulled out onto the road. Setting off back towards Maude's house, he heard himself condense his thoughts into two words, formed as a question. He muttered them out loud: 'God or Mammon?'

That was when the bells diagonally across the road from the post office began to ring out. Robert knew he could not fight or doubt it any longer. He had his answer.

The bells were being rung in the Chapel of the Epiphany.

36

BACK AT MAUDE'S house all was silent. Robert let himself in very quietly, anxious not to disturb his grandmother's rest and grateful to have time alone to settle his mind by concentrating on something quite separate to that afternoon's events by the lake.

As promised, Maude had left the boxes of unmailed letters on the kitchen table. Robert went to the beginning of the row in the box labelled 1939–1941. He picked out the first envelope, slit it open with the kitchen knife and began to read.

For the next few days, between time spent with Maude, Robert became fully immersed and increasingly absorbed in reading through this one-sided correspondence from a mother to a son she had never known – from his grandmother to his father – whom he himself could now only dimly remember.

The letters were mostly quite short and were written in a style that recognised and reflected the changing age of her son as he grew up. Mostly they were a summarised diary of events and feelings that gradually built a picture for him of Maude's earlier life, predominantly spent in helping her parents on the Wilmot farm, where she was born and had grown up.

The birthday and Christmas letters were always more poignant and revealed the tragic sense of loss and sadness Maude felt, which stayed keen and sharp as the years passed. They were written without a shred of self-pity and instead concentrated on providing the sort of advice and encouragement any good mother would wish to give her son as he progressed through early childhood, followed by the more difficult teenage years and so on into adulthood. Overwhelmingly, Robert was struck by the gentle, worldly wisdom and love expressed in every letter.

During one of Maude's afternoon rests, Robert had become so absorbed, he completely lost track of time. It was only when a movement outside the window distracted him that he looked up to see his grandmother walking down to the lake in the last rays of evening sunlight. He marked the place he had got to, closed the boxes of letters, stretched himself, and went out to join her.

'I'm sorry, I had no idea how late it was, Maude. How long have you been up?' Robert asked.

'Oh, at least a couple of hours,' she replied. 'I looked in on you but you were so engrossed I didn't want to disturb you.'

'Are you surprised?' Robert asked. 'The letters you wrote my father are completely captivating. They're a wonderful mix of family history and parental advice. And they're so beautifully and eloquently written, the care and love they express is almost … I guess, "poetic" is the right word.'

'Oh, hush now,' Maude told him, waving a dismissive hand.

But Robert wasn't finished. 'Above all, they're love letters, Maude. Not of the romantic sort of course, but still full of the purest form of love.

'I just keep thinking how tragic it is my father never got to see them.'

'Maybe they weren't ultimately meant for him. Maybe it was always you who was meant to read them?' Maude responded enigmatically.

Now it was Robert's turn to ask a probing question. 'Did you ever resent having to spend most of your life as a young woman hidden away with your parents on their farm, after the glamour and excitement of Europe?' he ventured.

'No. I wasn't in any way a captive,' Maude assured him. 'After the war, my parents really wanted me to leave, to go and experience the world again. It was me who wanted to stay. It was in my soul. After the trauma of two such enormous personal losses, neither of which I could talk about, I felt at some sort of peace at last. I had always been so happy here as a child.

'I'd have kept the farm on after my parents died, but as I got older I knew it was right to let it go before it became too difficult for me. Also, I felt it needed a family again. We never really own these special places. They own us for a while and we are privileged to take care of them for future generations. Not necessarily from within our own families either.

'Funnily enough, the family who bought it were from England: three children, mostly grown up now too. All of them seem to have fallen under its spell and love the place as I did – and still do.'

Robert felt his grandmother reaching for his hand. 'This would seem a good moment to tell you I want to be buried there,' she told him softly. 'The family who live there now know about my wish and have agreed to it. There's a special place up on the hill behind the house, an acre of dappled trees and open grass known as Top Wood.

'At more or less the highest point the land levels out. There's a huge rock just in front of the rough farmer's wall that marks the upper boundary of Top Wood from the endless miles of forest that lie beyond to the north. The view southwards looks out over the farm, its fields and its ponds, and over the southern stretches of forest, towards Mount Sunapee in one direction and Mount Kearsarge in the other.

'I used to love going up there in the evening to watch the sun setting over on the western edge of the forests. The shafts of pastel, pale pink light silhouetting the tall scotch pines in long shadows. Beautiful in all seasons, but somehow especially so in early winter, after the first fresh fall of snow, before it becomes too deep to get there without snowshoes.

'Have you ever seen truly pink snow? The still quietness and perfect softness of the forest floor, all its blemishes and regenerating debris concealed under six inches of still pristine snow. The branches and twigs of every tree sugar-coated in white? You should go there sometime.'

Robert gently squeezed her hand and nodded.

'Oh, and that's another thing,' Maude remembered. 'Only now I'm not telling you, I'm asking you. It would really make me happy, Robert – very happy – if you would consent to conduct my funeral service. Despite the path you've taken since coming to America, you're still a priest aren't you? I know that of course you are an Anglican priest and I'm a Roman Catholic, but we're quite fortunate here in that we are a long way from the controlling eyes of either Rome or Canterbury.

'By and large, over here in America, the Episcopalians and Catholics get along famously. In fact the Reverend Ron Striker and Father Bob Goodlow have the utmost respect for each other and are good friends – as they are also both good friends of mine. More broadly than that even, all the Christian, non-Christian and Judaic denominations, at least those stemming from the same Abrahamic root, seem to be in a more enlightened place around here.

'Every year on Thanksgiving morning we have an inter-denominational service in New London, and again on Ash Wednesday, at Easter and at Christmas, taking it in turn in each of the others' churches. This year Thanksgiving will be at the Baptist Church.

'These special services are all well supported by what I call the more independently minded members of the different denominations who, of course, are friends and neighbours, always happy to share in almost everything else anyway. It is a wonderful experience of collective worship, in recognising our common humanity and, with gratitude, the gifts we all receive from God, regardless of how we may choose to format that worship at other times throughout the year.'

Robert remained silent for so long after Maude had finished she felt compelled to give him a verbal nudge. 'Well? Say something, Robert. Even if it is to say you disapprove of my homespun theology!'

'No, Maude. I don't disapprove. Far from it in fact. If more people were less strait-jacketed by ritual and, as it were, less tribal – more what you call independently thoughtful in their approach to religion – the world and humanity would almost certainly be in a much better place. However, I don't think the hierarchy in control of most of the world's establishment religions would welcome that. And they would be able to advance many theoretically sound theological arguments for not doing so. None of which would address, or admit to, the advantage they see in having and maintaining control of their own flocks … or should I say tribes?

'Sadly, as we know only too well, there is, and always has been, more fighting, killing, torture and injustice in the world perversely conducted in the name of some sort of God than for any other cause. Religion, whipped up into a toxic cocktail of fear and imagined loathing by any of the many zealots and fanatical extremists, of any denomination, be they Christian, Islamic, Jewish or any other you care to think of, including all the sub-sets and different sects thereof, can be as potent as a nuclear explosion. That is a heady power to wield over others and those who do, be they priests, pastors, imams, rabbis or whatever, if corrupted – and history has shown us that some always are – can be very dangerous indeed.

'I'm often reminded of the wisdom in the words of an eighteenth-century French philosopher, whose name I can't now remember, but who I understand was himself a man of deep faith. Famously, he once said, "There is nothing that obscures the face of God quite so effectively as religion".

'I don't want to give the impression I'm against religion. That would be rather illogical of me wouldn't it? But I'm vehemently against the manipulation and exploitation of, or by, religion. Religion as instruction to an informed faith is essential, but there should always be room for the freedom of the individual to think and sincerely follow their own conscience. Religion should never be used as a ritualised substitute for personal faith.

'Fortunately, however, religion tends to exert a generally more positive influence than it does negative. And, as with all large institutions, there will always be a mixture of good, bad or indifferent leaders at every level. The important thing to remember is that your belief and your faith should always be firmly rooted in the song and not the singer.'

Maude had stopped walking. She turned to give her grandson her full attention. 'Do I take that as a "Yes" or a "No" to my straightforward request?' she asked, a teasing expression on her face.

'Sorry, Maude. I got carried away. The answer is "Yes", of course, although it will be a bittersweet honour for me. But, related to that, there's something I need to tell you.

'Can we go and sit on the bench? It may take a while to explain.'

Now that he was confident that his grandmother would understand him and with her seated on the bench beside him, looking out over the flat evening calm on Keyser Lake, Robert told Maude about the ruthless repression of his true inner calling all the time he had been so successfully making money in New York. He told her how he had never spoken of this to anyone before, not even really to himself. This was the first time he'd been able to put it into words. He told her how, in the short time since arriving in New Hampshire, the pressure on him to admit to himself the dilemma he was facing had rapidly grown, to the point where it could no longer be contained.

He then recounted the events that had occurred when he'd stopped at Pleasant Lake that afternoon and had handed the whole unbearable dilemma over to God. He finished by putting into actual words for the first time the decision he had made.

'I'm finished with New York – for good,' he told her. 'I'm going to give it all up: the business, the apartment, the corporate jet, the Bentley – even the *Lucky Find*. I'm done with that life, Maude. It's taught me a lot about myself and others, but it also became my master. I don't want to spend the rest of my life enslaved to a way of life that offers no lasting satisfaction.'

'Are you completely sure this is what you want?' Maude asked hesitantly.

'I've never been more certain of anything in my life,' Robert answered.

'But what about all your money, Robert? I always read you're worth billions now.'

'It won't have been wasted, Maude. I'll either donate the entire proceeds to an existing charitable foundation: one that's up and running – and running well – like the one set up by that savvy investor, Warren Buffet, the Sage of Omaha. Or, maybe, I'll establish my own foundation. I haven't decided which yet. But either way I intend to see that something good will have come from this last eight years.'

Maude scarcely dared to ask her next question, but she knew she had to. 'And what about you? What do you plan to do with your life afterwards?'

'That's easy,' Robert replied. 'I'm going to go back to London, submit myself to the Bishop of West London and ask his forgiveness for having absconded for eight years. There's only one thing I want now and he's the only person who can give it to me. I want to be reinstalled as the vicar of St Mungo's, if there's any way that can be arranged, and finish the work I started there. I don't know how much things have changed in my absence, of course, but it's still important to me to prove that St Mungo's can be saved and recast to be relevant in the London of today. Most of all, Maude, I want to prove that to myself.'

If he'd learned anything in business, he told her – and he'd learned a great deal – it was that no business could stand still and survive. Almost by definition, standing still meant falling backwards. Only businesses that were constantly adapting and reinventing themselves could continue to prosper long into the future. The Church and its role in a constantly changing society was no different. There were those, of course, who would advance this as the very argument for the Church to remain constant in a world changing all around them – a view firmly held by traditionalists, who seemed unable, or unwilling, to grasp the inevitability of the inexorable decline this approach meant.

But Robert had also learned enough now to know that change should not be imposed for the sake of itself and nor should it necessarily be allowed to replace what went before. Rather, change should be introduced and allowed to develop organically, alongside what was true, tried and tested. He also knew that change, in the context of the Church, must out of caution and necessity move at a slower pace than would be required in the more rapidly moving world of business.

'Only when I've done this for St Mungo's, and proved its success, will I feel ready to move on to other challenges in my life,' he explained. 'But whatever and wherever these are, I know now I will be facing them as a priest.'

His voice took on a passion Maude had not heard before. 'Something very tangible happened this afternoon at the lake, when I went to help that young couple. I felt useful, Maude. But it was more than that. As I was swimming out to them I felt this enormous empathy – almost like love – for other people in their moment of crisis. And that's something I haven't felt since I first encountered Brenda in St Mungo's eight years ago.' Mentioning Brenda's name now made Robert wonder at her recurring connection to all these signposts in his life.

There was another feeling too, but for the moment Robert decided he should keep that to himself.

When he had finished telling Maude his plans, Robert sat back to await his grandmother's reaction and response. He was surprised when it came.

'Annie Stearns, or Foster as she is now, and Jake are a nice young couple. Good people. I've known Annie since she was born. Jake's parents had a summer home here and he went to Colby Sawyer College. But I'm curious as to their significance in the jigsaw puzzle of your life?'

Robert couldn't help showing his surprise and a little bewilderment. 'Well Maude, that's certainly not the response I was expecting,' he said with a small laugh of nervous relief. 'Why should there be any particular significance to the random coincidence of my being by the lake when they got into trouble?'

'If you're expecting me to be surprised by your decision to resume your vocational calling to the priesthood, the answer is I'm not in the least surprised. I've been expecting it from after the first five minutes I spent in your company a few days ago.

'What I am surprised at is your stubborn unwillingness, or inability, to understand the coincidence that was so clearly the catalyst that led you to be able to make the decision. You said, because you felt completely unable to make the decision without help from God, you had just handed your dilemma over to Him, when the incident with the Foster couple occurred in front of you? You were in effect seeking divine guidance.

'What did you expect Robert? Did you think a thunderbolt would come down from Heaven? Or a shaft of intense celestial light envelop you? That's all so Old Testament and may have served a less cynical, less sophisticated society well. But I think the way God works today is usually more subtle, don't you?'

'Of course I had considered that connection being a possible explanation but, I'll admit, I'm not sure my faith is strong enough to accept that kind of direct intervention yet,' replied Robert.

'That's all part of why our so-called civilised society today has become so sceptical about accepting, or even allowing for, the existence of a higher power. Unless we are able to clearly identify, with proof – and maybe therefore to control – we can't believe. Our cynical minds have lost their sense of wonder and amazement at all that is out there in our daily lives that defies rational explanation and so gets explained away as merely "coincidental". Without faith in a higher purpose than we can see or control, the only alternative is to dismiss everything inexplicable as coincidence or serendipity, be that good fortune or bad.

'The problem that atheists have is that they can no more disprove the existence of God than believers can prove His existence. I may be paraphrasing, but, after forty years as an avowed and vociferous atheist, one eminent member of the global scientific establishment admitted that the possibility of life having been created by accident was about as likely as the preposterous idea of a small boy walking into a scrap metal yard, waving his arm and thereby assembling one of the new, fully working, Boeing Jumbo Jets. Therefore, on an overwhelming balance of probabilities, he had decided it was factually more likely that the complexities of life were attributable to a higher force of some intelligent design than that they can be explained by an unlikely random cosmic accident,' concluded Maude.

'You make a persuasive argument,' Robert told her. 'But why is there such a trend towards doubt, disbelief and deepening cynicism? To declare any kind of faith in God is becoming deeply unfashionable and even faintly embarrassing for those who have still got the moral courage to do so. Especially amongst younger people.'

'Have you considered it might have something to do with what you were saying earlier about the failure of most of the establishment religions to progress and adapt to changes in society in any meaningful way?

'Take just one example. The antagonism and ridicule of prominent atheists means the very idea of any kind of faith has been successfully equated with ignorance, even low intellect. Which of course encourages fear and doubt amongst those who might otherwise be inclined to believe and have the confidence to say so. This doubt then creates concealed feelings of guilt. And in the end it becomes a vicious circle which it is simply easier to ignore than to face.

'Perhaps if religion was to focus as much on the core essence of a simple, straightforward faith, as it does on the repetitive rituals of worship, it might have more relevance to young people and those struggling with what, if anything, to believe in.

'Let me tell you about something memorable that happened to me in this connection,' Maude suggested, knowing that she had Robert's complete attention.

'Please do.'

'Shortly after the death of my parents, I wanted to go away for a break and chose to take a trip to the wine country of California,' Maude continued. 'I was in San Francisco on a Sunday and decided to take myself off to Grace Cathedral, the beautiful High Church, Episcopal Cathedral on the top of Nob Hill, to which I could walk from my hotel, rather than go to the very modern, less aesthetically pleasing, Catholic Cathedral way off on Gough Street.

'In his sermon, the priest posed the question, "If hot is the opposite of cold, what would you say is the opposite of faith?"

'After giving us a few moments to think about it he proposed that many of us in the congregation would have decided that the opposite of "faith" was "doubt". A showing of hands, including my own, proved him overwhelmingly right in this assumption. He then tested our thinking by proposing that in fact the opposite of faith was not doubt at all, but rather "certainty" – as he said, a grim certainty, but nevertheless certainty.

'Therefore, almost by definition, faith must encompass doubt. In fact, arguably, you cannot have faith without doubt.

'For me, as I suspect it was for many in the congregation that day, this was a seminal moment in which we realised we need feel no guilt or fear over our recurring doubts, now or ever again. This simple analogy was of more help to me in my journey towards faith than years of going through the motions of repetitive, ritualistic prayer.'

'Maude, I'm not sure the rules of your church permit such thinking,' Robert said with a chuckle.

'That question should really be, does it permit any kind of challenge to its thinking? Or would it rather do its thinking for us?' Maude replied with a resigned sigh. 'The Roman Church has always been good at thinking. Too much so if you ask me. It's what all those Curial cardinals in the Vatican do best. But it's the way in which it often seems to direct and adapt that thinking to suit its own purposes that might sometimes raise an eyebrow. Even create a whiff of self-serving hypocrisy. That's when the line between scheming, or what is sometimes referred to as "Jesuit thinking", and honest, open-to-question thinking, becomes blurred.'

By now Robert and Maude could no longer ignore the long shadows of a late sunset over the lake. It would be dark soon. They went in to make supper together. After the meal Maude declared her need for an early night and went to bed leaving Robert to his own thoughts and the chance to resume reading his grandmother's unmailed letters to his father. Before that, though, he had an important call to make.

Although it was almost nine o'clock, he knew it would not be too late to call Cynthia at home. She answered on the second ring. Robert could hear the sound of the television in the background before it was switched off.

'I hope I'm not interrupting a favourite programme?' he asked jokingly.

'No, and funnily enough I was expecting it to be you,' Cynthia replied.

'Why so?'

'C'mon Robert. You've been silent now for almost a week. When have you ever managed that before? Normally you call twelve times a day, at least, and often half the night too. We've almost been worried about you,' said Cynthia, sounding strict to anyone who didn't know she was really laughing.

'Cynthia, I've got something important to tell you and Bill,' Robert began. 'I've been doing a lot of thinking since I got up here and I've made a big, important decision about what I want to do with the rest of my life.'

'Yes?' Cynthia's voice was a mixture of anxiety, curiosity and caution.

'Well, first off, Cyn, I'm not coming back to New York. My place is definitely here with my grandmother ...'

He wasn't able to complete what he was going to say before Cynthia interrupted. 'What do you mean, you're not coming back to New York?' Cynthia was sounding bossy and demanding in the way that only a very trusted PA-cum-friend can do. 'Not coming back as in ... not yet? Not anytime soon? Or never?'

'Well I guess if you put it like that I really mean never,' Robert replied after a short pause. 'At least not until after ... after I've buried my grandmother.' He found it hard to say the words. 'And then it will only be for as long as it takes to collect a few personal things and return to London.'

The silence at the other end of the phone was deafening.

'Cyn? Hello, Cyn? … Are you still there?'

'Yes, I'm still here Robert. But I'm waiting for you to explain,' Cynthia replied warily.

Robert spent the next forty minutes telling Cynthia everything that had happened to him since his arrival in New Hampshire, culminating in his decision to renounce all his wealth and return to the priesthood – hopefully to the impoverished parish in London where he'd first started.

'That's if the Bishop of West London will have me back,' he concluded.

'Of course he will,' retorted Cynthia. 'If the allure of the lost sheep returning to the fold isn't enough, you can always point to your solid gold fleece and offer him a little wool by way of inducement.'

Robert laughed outright. 'Now, now Cyn – that puts him and me in a worse light than either of us deserve,' said Robert.

'I'm not so sure about that,' replied Cynthia, laughing too. 'I think you've lost your mind. What do they put in the water up in New Hampshire? Whatever it is, it's scary and I must remember never to go there.'

Her voice then took on a serious tone as she asked, 'Do you intend to have someone else handle your business empire over here? What do you plan for that?'

'No, Cyn. I know Bill wanted to leave soon anyway and I've always thought you would like to return to Boston one day. But I want to ask you both to stay long enough to handle the dismantling and sale of everything for me. In return I want to give you both a bonus of one million dollars each, on top of all remuneration and any redundancy payments due to you.'

The silence that followed was finally broken by the sound of a stifled sob from Cynthia.

'You're really serious about this aren't you, Robert?' she asked in a small, quiet voice, expressed more as a statement than a question.

'Yes, Cyn, I am. I'm really deadly serious about it. I've also been inexplicably happy about it ever since I made the decision. I know it's right and I know it's what I want to do with the rest of my life. I'm impatient now to get on with it, although not, of course, for my grandmother's death. She really is the most remarkable, well-read, perceptive and intelligent woman, Cyn. She's teaching me so much, and I want to be with her for as long as possible without any distractions.

'That's why I want you and Bill to take over right now in dismantling and selling everything. And I really do mean everything: the business; the office block; the *Lucky Find*; the plane; my apartment; the Bentley; the Rolls-Royce – absolutely everything. I want it all liquidated for cash.

'I've decided that the cash should then all be channelled into a charitable foundation to be administered by a carefully selected group of trustees, headed by you and Bill, if you will do it? I neither want, nor can I have, any part of it, beyond being able to make suggestions as to worthwhile beneficiaries and charitable causes for you to consider from time to time. My only request would be that the foundation be called The St Mungo's Trust.

'When everything has been liquidated, Cyn, the foundation will be starting off very well endowed, so the administration and responsibility for overseeing it will be an important job. It's a job that must be properly remunerated. It will provide you and Bill with a career for the rest of your working lives. Incidentally, it goes without saying that the foundation and its administration will be headquartered in Boston.

'To get this under way, you and Bill will need a comprehensive power of attorney from me, enabling you to act on my behalf in all matters. It should cover both personal and business matters. As soon as you've got this drawn up, I'd like it if you and Bill would come up with it so we can get it signed off. One of the local lawyers here in New London can witness everything and ensure its legality.

'I know Harcourt & Boodle will want to insist on sending one, or even two, of their highest-priced lawyers up with you to do this, but at 500 dollars an hour it isn't necessary. If we do need to make any changes, which I don't envisage needing to do, we can talk on the telephone with Joshua and get the changes made locally here.

'By the way, this can provide one last run for Mike and the crew before you sell the plane. And, before you say anything Cynthia, I assure you it is of course my intention to see to it that Jill, Mike and all the staff everywhere are well rewarded for past service and more than generously compensated for any period of unemployment.'

'I wasn't going to say anything,' protested Cynthia. 'Other than to ask you if I have to come up there?'

Robert was taken aback. 'I thought you'd want to come?' he said sounding almost hurt.

'Sure, there's part of me that can't wait to see this strange magic land that seems to have had such an effect on you, but there's another part of me that's scared as hell. Still, I can always bring my own bottled water I suppose ...'

When she started to laugh, Robert knew the bridge had been crossed. Cynthia was sounding more like her old self again. Robert felt the tension easing from his shoulders and he started laughing too.

37

SLEEP ELUDED ROBERT that night and he stayed up into the early hours of the morning reading his grandmother's letters to his father. He could only begin to imagine the pain, guilt and crushing sadness she had gone through – not to mention the unalterable regret – in deciding to give her baby son up for adoption. It infused all of her letters to him.

Yet, to anyone of a judgemental frame of mind, it would be easy to have scant sympathy for a woman, not handicapped by lack of family or grinding poverty, who was capable of doing such a thing. Robert knew, however, that taking a strictly moral stance like that ignored the circumstances of the time.

And those circumstances had been heavily stacked against the young Maude Kimball. England was on the brink of war. There was a deep gulf of hostility, sheer ignorance and enmity between Protestants and Catholics. The father of her child, scarcely himself a man, was likely to have to fight for his country, possibly thousands of miles from home. Maude was a single girl – barely a woman – a student in a foreign land, while back home, family shame, disgrace and opprobrium awaited her return, pregnant, to a small rural New Hampshire community. These would all have conspired into a maelstrom of moral, spiritual and emotional confusion. Even someone as wise and strong as his grandmother could be forgiven for having given in and given up her baby amid the fears and uncertainty that reigned back then.

In its own way, by turning her back on the easier option abortion presented, her decision to choose life via adoption was commendable enough and, in the context of that time, a brave act in itself.

When he had put the last letter carefully back in its envelope it was almost four in the morning. The sky was already beginning to lighten in the east. Robert sat back rubbing his eyes, sore from the concentration of the past seven hours. Although he yawned and felt tired, he knew sleep would elude him for a while longer.

His mind was still in overdrive processing and analysing much of what he had read and learned from his grandmother's letters; at some point in the future he knew he would like to edit them into a book. The events of the time, combined with the commentary on daily family life over a period of nearly fifty years, beautifully chronicled and infused throughout with the poignancy of love and loss, provided a unique insight into a period in American social history that was both parochial and yet sometimes global in its perspective.

He had been particularly struck at his grandmother's knowledge and intuition in the earlier letters through the war years, in which she had displayed her utter contempt for old Joe Kennedy. She shared the opinion, expressed by many in subsequent years, that Kennedy, who had been the US ambassador to London at the time, had secretly, and later openly, advised President Roosevelt to seek an accommodation with Hitler on the grounds that Great Britain was finished. Her pithy observations on Kennedy were as much about him as a person as they were about his appeasement and self-serving policies.

It was clearly a matter of great pride to her that in contrasting him to his successor, John Gilbert Winant, a three-term Governor of New Hampshire, who took over from Kennedy in 1941, she was able to show the stark difference in moral fibre between the two men. The former ambassador displayed all the characteristics of a bully and a coward, exemplified in his refusal to sleep at the ambassadorial residence in London for fear of being bombed, insisting instead on having himself driven out of London every night, whereas Gil Winant eschewed even the relative safety of the official residence in favour of a small flat as close

340

as possible to the heart of things at the US Embassy, in Grosvenor Square. This he did in order to work tirelessly in helping to convince President Roosevelt of Churchill's determination and resolve to bring the British people through.

In this task Winant was ably supported by two other prominent Americans sent to London at the time: Averell Harriman, the fast-living, hard-driving millionaire, who ran FDR's Lend Lease programme in Europe, and Edward Murrow, the prominent radio journalist and head of CBS News in Europe.

Robert marvelled at his grandmother's interest and depth of knowledge in such worldly affairs. He also found himself becoming as intrigued as she was clearly fascinated by the truly remarkable contribution and achievement of this extraordinary, self-effacing New Hampshire man. From reading his grandmother's letters, Robert understood that it would be no exaggeration to say that Winant had played a significant role in helping protect the free world against the onslaught of Nazism. Without steadfast men like Gil Winant, and with the all too ready capitulation of weaker men like Joe Kennedy, the evil ambitions of the Third Reich might have prevailed. Yet it seemed to Robert that Winant was a forgotten hero, largely unrecognised in history and even, according to his grandmother, in his home state. Robert decided that this remarkable man merited more research after his return to London.

When she came downstairs at half-past six, Maude found her grandson fast asleep, stretched out on the sofa. She left him at rest and went through to the kitchen to make herself an early morning cup of tea. This was a habit she had quickly taken to all those years ago during her time in England and she couldn't imagine now doing without this ritual that always began her day.

She must have slept well as she was late this morning. Most mornings she was normally up by five-thirty, although this would sometimes slip towards six during the long, cold New Hampshire winters. Now, of course, with time having suddenly become her most precious commodity, sleep frustrated her. She was always grateful for any rest she could get, while at the same time resenting her continuing need for it. How useful it would be, she thought, if nature had devised things so that anyone under sentence of death could happily function without need of sleep for the last three months of life.

Maude wasn't afraid of death. In fact she was secretly quite looking forward to the experience. It held the promise of much adventure. Her original enthusiasm to travel and see the world had been suppressed after her premature return from England. This was compounded by the practical difficulty of foreign travel in the years during and for some time after the war. Besides, somewhere in the back of her mind lurked the notion that it was a mother's place to be at home. And, although she may be the only one to know it, she was nevertheless a mother.

In the end these maternal instincts had been redirected into looking after her parents as they lived out their years on the old family farm in Wilmot. However, Maude had always envisaged seeing the world one day, if not with someone special, at least with a good friend with whom to share the experiences, the laughter, the sunsets and the local wines.

Now the thought of the ultimate travel experience: that mysterious journey to be undertaken without need of passport, papers, visas, injections, or luggage of any kind, presented the rather appealing concept of the sort of complete freedom she had never known. She likened it in her mind to the thrill and sheer exuberant joy of a skinny dip dive into the calm waters of a clear, pristine lake, before surfacing into the bright sunlight of an exciting, adventurous new dawn.

No, Maude Kimball was not afraid of death, but she had to admit to herself that she was a little afraid of the process of dying. Whoever it was who had flippantly said that they weren't afraid of death, they just didn't want to be there when it happened, had made a good point! Dying, she concluded, would likely require an act of conscious bravery in being able to let go with complete confidence when the actual moment came.

She was reminded of a sermon she had once heard at the little Catholic

Church in Potter Place, just across the Andover town line from New London. The priest had likened the fear of dying to the fear of birth, using the analogy of twins in the womb in which he imagined them talking to each other. Happily ensconced in secure, familiar, comfortable surroundings, warm and well fed without a care in the world, suddenly, as the moment of birth approaches, one twin says to the other, 'I don't want to be born. Who knows what happens out there in that big daunting, unknown! No thanks. Not for me. I'd rather stay in here and stick with what I know.'

This twin resists the birth process with all his or her might. The other, more adventurous twin, embraces the idea of change with a level of trust and confidence in whatever the future holds. And it is this twin that is always born first.

Maude liked the simple idea that the surprise of dying might indeed be as wonderful as the miracle of birth.

Robert stirred. Opening his eyes he glanced at the grandfather clock, just then rudely and loudly proclaiming the hour to be seven o'clock. He stretched, yawned and stood up, rubbing his eyes.

'How long have you been up?' he said to Maude.

'Only half an hour. I overslept a little this morning I'm afraid,' Maude replied. 'It's going to be another beautiful day. This summer is on track to be one of the best we've had in New Hampshire since I was a child.'

'Yes? I'm so pleased about that for you Maude,' Robert said, coming over to give his grandmother a gentle kiss on the forehead. She sat with her now empty teacup by the window looking out over the lake.

'Have you had breakfast?' Robert asked.

'No, I was waiting for you to wake up. Besides, if it's OK with you, I'd like to go up to Baynham's for breakfast. It's a chance for me to get out and see people while I still can, and pick up some groceries in town. They say in New London that you can either go and visit your friends or go to Baynham's and let your friends come to you. Right now it's more efficient for me to do the latter,' and the prospect made her smile.

'Fine with me. Just give me fifteen minutes to shave and I'll drive us up there,' he replied, heading towards the bathroom. Turning his head at the door, he asked casually over his shoulder 'Does Mary ever come to Baynham's for breakfast?'

'Not usually. She's too busy at the inn doing breakfast for her own guests. She sometimes comes in for coffee a little later, when her breakfasts are done. Mostly that would be after about ten-thirty. Do you need her for something? We could stop by the inn on our way there, or on our way home.'

'No, not really. It's only that she's been so kind lending me her truck and everything. I thought it would just be nice to see her.' Heading on towards the bathroom, he didn't see the slow smile of surprised, wistful satisfaction spreading across Maude's face.

Second only to her grandson now, Mary was the person of whom Maude was most fond in all the world. That hint, giving rise to even the possibility that Robert and Mary might begin to form a relationship, filled her with an inexpressible delight, even excitement – tinged only with the sadness of the knowledge that she wouldn't be there to see it.

Thirty minutes later Robert and Maude pulled into the parking area in front of Baynham's. Despite the relatively early hour, the place was already busy and the front lot was full. Robert dropped Maude off at the door before finding a place to park at the back. He rejoined her at a table on the outside terrace, located at the front of the building, with its narrow porch and oversized white columns.

'This time I've ordered us both the full "Baynham's breakfast", with eggs, bacon, sausage, wheat toast, orange juice and coffee. I hope that's all right,' said Maude. 'We won't need much lunch after that, which should allow us more time to talk. I've still got a lot of things I want to say to you and much I'd still like to hear more of from you too.'

'Sounds great. Just remembering it from last time makes me feel hungry.' Robert was glad she was also going to have such a hearty breakfast, although he knew she probably wouldn't be able to finish it. She needed to eat. The cancer was destroying her from the inside and she had already become alarmingly thin, although, he was pleased to note, not yet frail. Eating well was the only way for her to keep up her remaining strength for as long as possible and, to do this, breakfast was the most important meal of the day.

Coffee came first and while they were enjoying their first cup, Maude asked bluntly without preamble, 'Robert, do you believe in God?'

Sitting back, sipping from the steaming hot mug in his hand, Robert did not immediately reply. He knew it was not such a strange question to ask an ordained clergyman as it might seem. Sadly there were a number of vicars, and probably priests too, who had, somewhere along the way, lost their faith and no longer believed in God. Either unable, or too old, to face life outside the protection of the Church, they opted for the safety of remaining as practising priests, concealing their lack of conviction from their fellow vicars, priests, peers and bishops, while continuing to go through the ritual motions for those for whom they had been charged with pastoral care.

The sad hypocrisy of this situation sometimes led to an impatient, patronising disdain for what would increasingly seem like the weak-minded needs and beliefs of their flock. At other times it led to them taking solace in alcohol. Ultimately, for the bravest ones, the only honest course of action was to leave the Church.

'That's a question I've been asking myself a lot over the last year or so,' Robert replied when he finally spoke. 'When I first arrived in America and collected the lottery win, I think I was too intoxicated by the excitement, the power, the attention and even the adulation that great wealth brings with it.

'At the beginning I had some perspective, some control, because I knew my good fortune, as I saw it then, was down to luck, to pure chance and I couldn't give myself any credit for it. But, as I found and tested a talent I never knew I had for making money, bit by bit I got so drawn into the excitement of being what business pundits call a Master of the Universe, that I found less and less room for God in my life.

'The power, the influence, the ability to have and do whatever I wanted, however I wanted, whenever I wanted, all seemed to push God so far into the background that eventually I simply had no time for Him and lost all sense of any need for Him.

'At some point I think I simply stopped believing in God, choosing to rely instead on my own strength and invincibility. For a long while, several years, this didn't worry me. I even looked back on my years in the Church of England as a quaint and faintly embarrassing period of my younger life: one on which I preferred not to dwell and never acknowledged unless I was forced to.

'During that time, with the power and control over others my status had brought, I developed ways of making it clear to people that this period of my life was a no-go area. Very few, and eventually no one, were brave enough to risk incurring my displeasure about this – or anything else in fact.

'It was like I was always running in some sort of race, Maude. I knew I had to win, but I could never quite see, let alone reach, the finishing line. If I slowed down, even for a moment, I felt vulnerable and self-doubt would start to creep in. But as long as I kept running, doing what others saw as brilliant deals, the proof of my worth was always going to be validated by my fortune, which just kept on growing.

'To eliminate self-doubt, and with that any thoughts of the role God might want to play in my life, I kept running harder and harder until I had lost all perspective of the difference between material success and personal happiness: every possession you could imagine balanced against inner contentment I guess. Nevertheless, somewhere buried inside I was becoming increasingly restless and dissatisfied.

'Although I couldn't, or perhaps I should say wouldn't, admit it to myself at the time, deep down, I wanted to turn back to God. I had become so lonely and isolated. Superficially of course, I was surrounded by friends and people hanging on my every word. If I wanted someone to join me for dinner I had only to ask. I had become so arrogant, that I knew they would change their plans for the chance to bask, and be seen to be basking, in the aura of my wealth and wisdom. I was spoiled, but miserable at the same time – with no one to whom I felt I could turn, except perhaps my PA, Cynthia, who probably knows me better than I know myself. But I didn't. It was a line I think that neither of us wanted to cross.

'By the time your letter arrived I was in turmoil. I could see no way out. I had no family to speak of. I'd turned my back on Andreas, the Benedictine monk from St Jerome's I told you about: my one true friend. I'd walked away from my priesthood, my church, even my faith. Worst of all, I didn't even understand that I wasn't happy. I just didn't question it. I had it all. I had everything everybody wants and strives so hard for. How could I not be happy?'

He drained his cup, offered Maude a refill, which she declined with a wave of her hand without speaking, and poured coffee into his own cup. His grandmother didn't want to interrupt him. She wanted him to say it all.

'Although I resisted it,' Robert sighed, 'looking back I see now that I had all my priorities wrong – that my life was a mess. That realisation began with the arrival of your letter. It gave me something meaningful to search for at last. Something I now clearly see as far more important to me than another clever business deal.'

Robert saw the warm smile of pleasure this last statement had brought to Maude's face. He saw something else too that he couldn't quite identify. Was it gratitude?

He could not know that, for Maude, this was more than she could ever have hoped for, even dreamed of, in her long-awaited answer to years of patient prayer.

She now offered a silent prayer of thanks to the God in whom she had, despite all, persistently held to in her own faith.

'Although I wouldn't characterise it as an Epiphany or Damascene moment,' Robert added, 'looking back on it, things started to come rapidly into focus for me more or less from the moment of my arrival in New Hampshire. Perhaps it was the sudden contrast to my pampered life in Manhattan, which caught me off-guard. To be greeted off my private jet by someone so grounded as Mary, in a shabby old Dodge pick-up she had made no attempt to smarten up on my account, was just the check I needed.

'Fortunately, as things turned out, there was no other way for me to get to the inn. I had to decide right there whether this particular Master of the Universe was going to swallow his pride and climb into that dirty old truck, or whether he was going to turn right around and fly straight back to New York. I'm ashamed to admit it now, but the only thing that prevented me getting back on my plane was the urge to meet you and confirm that you really were my grandmother.'

He took a gulp of coffee, to let Maude say something if she was going to. But Maude, sipping her coffee, encouraged Robert to continue.

'That was another thing,' he said. 'The easy and natural way Mary chatted to me on the drive back to the inn was another testing moment. She seemed to take me completely in her stride. She couldn't have failed to note I'd arrived in my own jet. I'm quite sure Jill, my secretary, would have emphasised this in a way Cynthia never would. It's important for Jill to make sure everyone knows just what a big shot she works for.

'Anyway, I could tell Mary was clearly unfazed or unimpressed. She was easy and friendly and from the start she treated me the same way I guess she treats everyone. At first I was suspicious that it was all part of an act. I hate to admit it now, but I thought you might even have been part of some elaborate sting – you know, to blackmail me or somehow engineer a way to get at my money.'

Maude smiled broadly at the idea of this. She was enjoying Robert's catharsis.

'Mary was treating me the same way she treats everyone she meets, regardless of who they are or what they might look like. What surprised me was finding how quickly I responded to this direct, down-to-earth, even humorous approach to life. I found myself relaxing in a way I hadn't done for years. It just felt so good, Maude – really, so good. Sort of like coming home.'

His grandmother had finished as much of her breakfast as she could manage. Most of it was still on her plate, but she'd eaten more than Robert had expected. He'd been slower to finish as he'd been talking so much between mouthfuls. Now, pushing his plate away, he sat back.

'Meeting you, Mary and everyone I've come into contact with since arriving in New Hampshire has really opened my eyes to what's important in my life; what was missing from it and what I must now do to rediscover the vocation I thought I'd lost. I owe so much to you – and a lot to Mary.'

At that moment, as if on cue, Mary walked across the porch towards them. Her face lit up when she saw Maude and she came straight over. Maude noticed at once the immediate change that came over Robert. He looked bashful, even nervous, like an awkward little boy.

'Hello Maude. I'm so glad to see you out and about enjoying yourself up in the town,' Mary said. 'I was going to pop by later to see how you were doing.' A brief look of genuine concern crossed her face as she took in the pushed aside plate of unfinished food. She noted how thin Maude had become.

'Hello Robert. I see you prefer the Baynham's breakfast to mine at the inn,' she said teasingly.

'No, no it's not that at all. Maude wanted to come here,' he stammered. Then, seeing the mischievous twinkle in her eye, he recovered himself sufficiently to add, 'But now you mention it, the breakfast here is pretty good. Must keep you on your toes!'

Maude interrupted. 'Mary, will you join us? There's something I'd like to tell you. Robert, will you be a dear and get Mary her coffee? Thank you.'

'Just a small splash of milk, no sugar,' she added.

Mary sat down beside Maude while Robert went to get her coffee.

Without preamble Maude, looking straight at Mary, said, 'Robert is my grandson.'

Mary put her hand on Maude's arm and said. 'I know Maude. I worked that out for myself on the drive back from Lebanon Airport, the day I picked him up. He looks just exactly like you. I'm so very, very happy for you and could only wish you'd found each other sooner. You don't have to explain anything of your past to me, or anyone else. No one has the right to judge you. I love you like the mother I hardly knew. I hope you know that?'

'Yes, yes, I do,' said Maude, feeling a lump rising in her throat. 'And I'm so grateful for your love ... and now for your understanding.

'I may not need to explain, but I would like to tell you about it. All about it. Because I would so like you and Robert to be friends after I'm dead.'

Mary looked away, but she couldn't hide from Maude the shadow of sadness that momentarily passed over her at this stark reminder of what lay just ahead.

Robert returned with Mary's coffee.

'Robert, I've told Mary you are my grandson,' Maude announced. 'Now I'm going to tell her all about my past and how it comes to be you are here. Why don't you go and get the things we wanted and come back to meet us in an hour?'

Robert hesitated for a moment, undecided whether to stay and hear the whole amazing story for himself again. Then he sensed that this was time Maude and Mary needed to spend alone together. He looked at his watch, and told them, 'I'll be back around eleven-thirty to take us both home.'

Mary threw him a grateful smile. He could see the moistness already in her eyes.

'Is there anything in particular you'd like me to get from the supermarket?' he asked Maude as he prepared to leave.

'No, thanks. Just get what you like the look of for yourself. You can put it on my account if you like.' Robert smiled, and with a nod to Mary took his leave.

Spellbound by the whole unbelievable story Maude unfolded for her, Mary managed to keep her emotions in check almost until the end. Several times while Maude was speaking she had, quite unconsciously, reached out to put her hand on Maude's arm in a gesture of comfort.

It was only when Maude told her about the extraordinary bond that had formed so quickly between her and Robert, how the loneliness and sense of loss that had filled most of her life had finally disappeared with his arrival, and how her one regret was she wouldn't have more time with him, that Mary lost control and was unable to stop the tears flowing freely down her sunburned cheeks.

She no longer cared what other customers might think. She leant over in her seat and held Maude in a tight hug, punctuated only by the occasional violent and uncontrollable sob. Maude silently stroked her hair, saying nothing. A faraway look on her face had room to include the maternal love she felt, had always felt, for Mary.

This was how Robert found them when he returned a little after the agreed hour.

38

ON THE SHORT drive back to Sutton, Robert asked Maude, 'Was Mary OK with it?'

'Oh, yes. Her tears were just ones of compassion and joy.' Then she added, almost as an afterthought, 'Mary has such a generous, giving nature.'

'Yes, I think I can see that,' was all Robert said by way of response.

Later that afternoon, after Maude had had a short rest and they were again sitting beside the lake, Robert said, 'I don't think I finished giving you my answer to your earlier question as to whether or not I believe in God.

'I suppose the short answer is an unequivocal "Yes I do", perhaps more so than ever in the light of my recent experience. But it's more complicated than that and there are still things I'm trying to understand better and come to terms with. Mainly to do with the simplicity, the purity of faith – as in belief – and the practice of religion as expected, even demanded, of me as a priest.

'On the one hand religion seems so often to complicate, even as I've said, to obscure the face of God, while on the other it should, and can, be the pathway to knowledge of God. I think perhaps faith and religion should be more clearly seen as separate – if only because in many cases it must be possible to have faith without religion, and in other cases, equally possible to ardently espouse the practice of religion without a shred of faith.

'I suppose that's really what I'm wrestling with in my desire to return to the priesthood. It's like having unfinished business. I was just beginning to feel I could make a difference in the small community of St Mungo's and I was excited about the plans I had to rescue and transform the parish. I was keen to reach out to the young and disenfranchised living and working in the area, many of whom may well have grown up with scant or even no knowledge of God in their lives.

'Without some basic knowledge it's hard to have faith. Yet, if you start by preaching the importance of the sacraments with all the emphasis on the traditions, rituals, ceremonies and obligations of religion, that always seemed to me to be completely counterproductive. The more I thought about it, that kind of orthodox approach just seemed to make religion exclusive, even divisive, if you know what I mean?'

His grandmother nodded her agreement; she knew exactly what he meant.

'Although I can't pretend they were fully formed, I had plans to do things differently. I wanted to reach out in a way that would focus on God's love in action. I wanted people to see God's love as open-minded, tolerant and above all extending a loving welcome to all, regardless of background, race, religion, sexuality or circumstance.

'To my way of thinking, the cornerstone of that kind of religion is admitting we have a common bond, in the certain knowledge that, from whatever background, we are all broken vessels just trying to make sense of our disordered and disorderly lives. Whether prince or pauper, most people's lives are messy at some level or another. The really important, the really joyful, thing about this is that God doesn't care. He loves us all equally – just the same.

'I've always loved that old Celtic saying, "Bidden or not bidden, God is present". So you see it's really up to us.

'Talking of broken vessels, look at me. I deserted my parish. I walked away from my vocation. Defied the authority of the Church I had solemnly sworn to serve and, worst of all, abandoned all those who had put their trust in me – not least of all my parishioners.'

'And in the end you'll be a much better priest for it,' Maude said quietly but emphatically.

'I don't know about that,' Robert replied. 'But I've definitely been on a journey in which I've learned a lot about other people and a great deal more about myself. I just hope the bishop and my former parishioners will have me back for a second chance.'

'They will Robert. I'm sure they will.' Maude's conviction was reassuring.

Later that afternoon Robert had a call from Cynthia to let him know the power of attorney documents were ready and that she and Bill, together with Joshua from Harcourt & Boodle, who had insisted on coming in person, would be coming up the next day to get them signed as he had asked.

Robert thanked her for her usual efficiency, teasingly telling her before he rang off how much he was looking forward to welcoming her to New Hampshire.

'Yeah, I know, magicland,' she responded. 'Don't worry, I'm coming prepared. I'll have a rabbit's foot in one hand and a four-leaf clover in the other.'

At eight-thirty the next morning Mike rang from Lebanon Airport to say they'd landed and Cynthia and Bill were already on their way down to New London, in a rental car sent up from Concord.

Robert had told Cynthia to come straight to Baynham's where he would meet them all for a cup of coffee and even breakfast if they wanted it. He had asked Maude if she wanted to come, but she had declined, saying she had things to do that she'd been putting off since his arrival. He told her he'd have everything done by early afternoon, so they agreed she would meet them up at Baynham's at three. Robert wanted Cynthia and Maude to meet before Cynthia returned to New York.

He hadn't long arrived at Baynham's himself before he saw them pulling into the parking lot. Bill was driving with Cynthia beside him and Joshua sitting in the back. Robert went out to meet them.

'Welcome to beautiful rural New Hampshire,' he said, smiling broadly as he opened the front passenger door for Cynthia. He was genuinely pleased to see her, as she was to see him.

'Is it safe to breathe the air?' she whispered. 'Or will it make me want to put on a hair shirt and give away everything I own? Not that there's much to give,' she added.

They gave each other an affectionate hug.

'Don't knock it, Cyn,' Robert told her. 'When this is finished you'll have a lot to give away, should you ever want to.'

'Don't worry. I'll make a point of never coming back to New Hampshire, then. Just in case it affects me as it seems to have you!'

'Hello Bill,' Robert said, shaking him warmly by the hand. 'Good to see you. Hi Joshua. Thank you for getting the paperwork done and for coming up today.'

He gestured to the entrance. 'Shall we go in? Have you had breakfast, or would you like some? Breakfast is great here,' he assured them as he held open the door.

Although Cynthia had tried to prepare him for a change, Bill was still taken aback by the man standing beside him looking relaxed and comfortable in jeans and a polo shirt in a way he never quite had in his expensively tailored suits.

The diffident insecurity, even sense of inferiority, Bill had noted when he was first introduced to Robert at the time of the big win had long since gone, but gone too now was any sign of the excessive confidence, bordering on arrogance, that had taken its place.

Now, as far as Bill could judge, he was looking at a man at ease with himself, completely comfortable in his own skin. The ceaseless questing and nervous energy appeared to have morphed into an almost Zen-like confidence that needed no external trappings of power and wealth to prove its worth. Bill was impressed, but not quite ready yet to believe the change could be a lasting one.

Joshua too had been completely thrown off stride. He was never normally at a loss for words and it was very unusual for him to be intimidated by any of the firm's clients. Although he didn't know Robert nearly as well as Bill and Cynthia, he nevertheless had had regular dealings with him over the past seven years or so, during which time Robert had become by far the firm's most important client. Joshua's partnership in the firm had without doubt been hugely boosted by his efficient handling of the affairs of Bicknor Wilmot Inc, and indeed those that were concerned with the personal side of Robert Melton's life.

He now found it very difficult to reconcile the clear image he had of Robert, his principal client, as the immaculately groomed and attired figure, radiating an energy and personal power that seemed to dominate everyone in the room, with the relaxed, calm, casually dressed man now holding open the door, courteously inviting him to breakfast. For the first time in his life that he could remember, Joshua was spooked. He was also alarmed.

When Cynthia had first called him to tell him what was wanted and broadly what Robert's intentions were, he'd assumed this was some sort of passing phase brought about by the emotion of his circumstances and that, given a little time and the cold light of day, preferably a New York day, Robert would come to his senses, or at least could be talked round to a less extreme position. Joshua was certain that a sensible compromise could be found. He didn't really believe it was feasible for anyone who had such vast wealth and power to give it all up willingly and voluntarily. It just hadn't seemed possible to him. Now, seeing Robert as he was here in New Hampshire, he wasn't so sure.

This would mean big changes in the firm. While fees would no doubt remain substantial during what would be a period of complicated reconciliation and reorganisation, after that there would be an inevitable decline as the daily business activity of Bicknor Wilmot Inc effectively ceased. Of course, he would aim to secure the firm's role as legal advisers and counsel to the proposed charitable trust, but nevertheless the decline in fee-earning potential for Harcourt & Boodle would be substantial. His bonus for this year would be safe, but thereafter he could no longer be certain. In fact everything was suddenly being plunged into a turmoil of uncertainty. If there was one thing Joshua Roundel hated it was uncertainty.

Keeping his thoughts to himself, Joshua tried his best to project his normal image of affable dignity. It was an image that had been carefully cultivated and encouraged amongst the partners of the firm who felt it created just the right air of friendly approachability, while at the same time reassuring clients of the gravitas of the firm.

'Robert, you look younger, more relaxed and happier than I've ever seen you. This good clean mountain air must suit you!' Joshua said, unconsciously putting a hand on Robert's back. Even as he did so, he realised this gesture was the kind of presumptuous informality he would not have dreamt of making before. He quickly removed his hand but, to his surprise, saw Robert had either not noticed or not minded.

That was it! Cynthia had been studying Robert. There was something new radiating from him that wasn't power. She couldn't put her finger on it until, quite unconsciously, Joshua had said it. It was happiness. Robert was glowing with a relaxed contentment and happiness she'd never seen before. It was as if he had finally found his place in the world.

During breakfast, over which they talked mostly about New Hampshire, Robert quietly observed the three of them. Cynthia, who of the three knew him by far the best, clearly had now taken him at his word. She was able to accept the radical change in her boss's choice of lifestyle and his decision to return to his vocational calling. This acceptance was, he thought, no doubt helped by her own position as a firm believer and person of faith.

Bill, although fully briefed by Cynthia, still seemed doubtful, although this doubt did not necessarily stem from Robert's sudden desire for such a radical change. Bill had for some while been worrying that Robert was fast losing touch with reality, buoyed up by the false sense of his own invincibility. Bill was old enough, wise enough and human enough to know that a correction in this arrogance was needed. He had no problem with that. Indeed he would have welcomed it for his friend. It was the sheer scale of the proposed change that he couldn't yet fully grasp with any degree of acceptance.

Robert knew it would be more difficult for Bill to understand. A very good, kind and moral person, Bill was, of his own admission, a bit of an agnostic when it came to his relationship with Christianity. Although, if pressed, he was inclined to lean more towards believing than not, he had often been known to describe himself as a ceremonial Baptist. He enjoyed weddings, baptisms, even funerals in the full ceremony of the church rituals and he wouldn't think Christmas was Christmas without first going to church to sing wonderful, reassuringly traditional carols. Easter also, he felt, should be properly marked by attendance at church. It was the concept of faith, and what was required to have faith, that Bill struggled with.

Joshua was far more difficult for Robert to read; not least because he did not have the advantage of knowing him as well as the others. At Robert's request Cynthia had told both Bill and Joshua there was no need to wear suits for this day trip to New Hampshire. Cynthia herself had come more casually dressed than she would have been in New York, although she still managed to look strikingly attractive – but then she would in whatever she wore. Robert had not failed to notice heads turn to look at her as she walked into Baynham's and it was not because she was black. The appreciation of her striking, natural beauty was transparent on the men's faces and almost as much so on the women's faces too.

Bill had managed to swap his near trademark grey suit for a pair of khaki chinos, dark chestnut loafers, pale blue Oxford cloth shirt and navy blazer. He was wearing no tie. Robert knew this was about as dressed-down as Bill liked to get and was his concession to what he perceived to be 'New England preppy' casual.

Joshua, on the other hand, had ignored any concession towards casual. He was dressed as he always was in his Manhattan finery: expensively tailored dark blue suit, well starched crisp white shirt, Hermes tie, and highly polished black tasselled loafers that he had shined every day by the Puerto Rican shoeshine boy who had the concession in the lobby of the building in which Harcourt & Boodle had its headquarters. Although his well-heeled appearance would have gone unremarked on or even unnoticed in New York, the same would not be true in New London. His sartorial elegance shone like a beacon of big-money capitalism in this relaxed, laid-back community. Here many people's idea of dressing up would be to swap practical footwear for dress shoes; in winter, jeans for chinos and in summer, shorts. Jackets and ties were largely reserved for weddings, funerals or perhaps court appearances.

For different reasons, then, Joshua attracted almost as much surreptitious attention walking into Baynham's as Cynthia.

Robert wondered if Joshua really knew who Joshua was any more. He had been projecting the image of himself he wanted others to see for so long now, that the boy who'd grown up in a devoutly Jewish family on Long Island, loving nothing more than to go fishing or sailing in the small dinghy his parents had given him at the time of his bar mitzvah, had been almost completely suppressed; Joshua Roundel, the much-acclaimed corporate lawyer, with a fearsome reputation for ruthlessness and efficiency, would have been a complete stranger to him. It was true that Joshua loved the competitiveness of doing battle against other corporate lawyers, but only if he didn't lose. He very rarely did – which was why his clients liked, admired and trusted him.

Seeing him now across the breakfast table Robert felt a little sorry for him. Was he too so caught up in a way of life and a carefully constructed image of himself that he no longer even knew if this was what made him happy or not? It frightened Robert to realise that, just a short while ago, across the table he would have been looking at a mirror image of himself.

'Thank you all for coming up here today,' Robert began as they finished eating and were able to sit back with coffee mugs in hand. 'What I aim to achieve should be quite straightforward really. I intend to give full and complete power of attorney over all my business and personal affairs to Bill and Cynthia together. My instructions to them are to liquidate everything I own, either directly, or through any of my companies. All the cash raised is to be aggregated into a charitable trust that I would like you, Joshua, to set up for me. Bill and Cynthia are to be trustees together with two others I've yet to ask. I'll let you know their details when and if they agree. And that's it really. Frighteningly simple.'

Robert sat back and studied the expressions on their faces, judging the effect his words had had on each of them.

With Cynthia it was a mixture of sorrow, acceptance and admiration. With Bill it was incredulity, trying to come to terms with an acceptance, struggling to give way to admiration. With Joshua it was outright disbelief and fear.

The silence that followed his statement of intentions was eventually broken by Joshua, as Robert knew it would be.

'Robert, I'm not sure I fully understand. What do you mean by "everything you own"? Surely you'll keep something for yourself? Where are you going to go and what will you do?'

Unknown to them, Robert had painfully come to understand now just how right Andreas had been to accept absolutely nothing, not even one penny of the big win. To have done so would have opened up the floodgates of temptation.

'Joshua, I know this will be difficult for you to understand but, yes, I really do mean everything. The last flight of my Gulfstream, before it gets put up for sale, will be later this afternoon when Mike flies you all back to New York. My businesses, my investments, my apartment, my yacht, my cars, my art collection – absolutely everything is to be sold for cash to fund my charitable trust, for which, by the way, I want you to secure the name: The St Mungo's Trust. I'll explain that in a moment.

'I want my apartment to be sold with all its contents, including artwork and antiques. When I come back to New York it will be for just long enough to pack a suitcase with the few clothes I'll need and one or two small personal items. The remainder of my clothes and shoes can be given away. But Cynthia will see to organising that with Jill.'

'After a quick stop in New York,' Robert continued, 'I intend to fly on to London where my hope is that I will be able to resume the post I deserted eight years ago as the vicar of St Mungo's Church on Earls Court Road. For that I won't need more than I can carry in one suitcase. I intend to return the way I arrived.'

The colour had drained from Joshua's face. He was aghast and stunned into a disbelieving silence. The truth was he had no idea where to begin. This was just something so far beyond his very considerable powers of comprehension or previous experience, he was unable either to grasp completely all its implications, or to fully believe it. It would have been far easier for him to understand if Robert had died.

'I hope I've given you all a sense of the urgency with which I would like these wishes to be carried out? I want it to be very much a priority. Now that I have made my decision, I want it all done as soon as possible. Before I change my mind,' he added, smiling at them.

At these last words, Robert saw the gleam of hope ignite at once in Joshua's eyes. So that was it. This was a temporary madness from which perhaps, given time, Robert would be, even could be, dissuaded?

But Robert could not allow his attorney to indulge false hopes. 'Sorry Joshua, I didn't mean to create any doubt about my resolve over this. There is none. I was just trying to lighten the mood,' he said with uncustomary gentleness, putting a hand on Joshua's arm for a moment.

This was a gesture that was not lost on either of them. Joshua knew it was meant to make him feel OK for his earlier welcoming hand on Robert's back.

'When do you intend to come back to New York?' Joshua was finally able to ask. 'Can I at least take you to lunch or dinner while you're there?'

Although Robert knew at that moment it was a spontaneous and well-intended gesture of friendship on Joshua's part, he also knew that by the time it took place it would have become just another expense account client entertainment. Over the past eight years he had had enough of those to last a lifetime.

'When I come to New York it will be for no more than one night at the most, so I hope you'll understand and allow me to decline this time. As to exactly when I will be passing through New York is uncertain.'

He paused before continuing, 'I intend to stay here to be with my grandmother until she dies. Although she herself is a Roman Catholic, she has asked me to officiate at her funeral service. She has cancer and isn't expected to live for more than a few more weeks at most. After that I intend to return to London as soon as possible with, as I said, only an overnight stop in New York on the way.'

Although he had done his best to hide any emotion, Robert was surprised at just how difficult he had found it to talk so frankly and so openly about his grandmother's limit on time.

Cynthia said nothing, but put a hand on his arm, where she let it rest for a good few moments. Bill and Joshua both looked uncomfortable, not sure what, if anything, there was to be said.

Finally, trying to be kind, Bill said, 'Why don't you let Mike fly up with the plane to get you? Just one last time. It's very unlikely to be sold so soon.'

'No thanks, Bill. Having made the decision, I want to be very focused and very pragmatic about achieving my aims. I don't intend to let the disposal of material possessions get in the way. Which means everything I own must be fairly priced for a quick sale. I want you to ensure Mike is well paid off, with a generous severance package, as soon as the plane is sold. No period of notice will be required of him and I'd like him to have a good bonus on top of his severance.

'When I'm ready to leave here I may well drive down to New York, just to have some time to think and give myself a chance to ease myself from my old life into my new. Or, perhaps I should say, from my new life back to my old! If not, I'll fly down commercial from Manchester.

'Cynthia, that reminds me, would you ask Jill to get me an open, one-way, ticket to London on British Airways? Not first class, just in regular economy.'

Bill sat back and looked at Robert in amazement and admiration. Joshua had his head down and was studying his hands on the table in front of him.

'OK, I think it's time we headed over to the lawyer's office,' Robert said looking at his watch. 'It's just up the street, opposite the magnificent Baptist Church, which you have to see. As it's such a lovely day, we can walk from here if you like?'

Then, seeing the look of apprehension on Joshua's face and noticing again his pristine city shoes, Robert quickly added, 'No, maybe we should drive. I'll ride with you in the car.'

Five minutes later they were ushered into the offices of Dufrère & Dufrère. The co-principal, Gary Dufrère, had come out to greet them. He and Robert had never met, but he handled all Maude's affairs and also Mary's over at the inn. He was a well-known, well-liked, and highly respected pillar of the New London community.

Two hours later the two principal documents and related paperwork had been pored over and read in detail. Both lawyers had offered their opinions and advice as to their legality and the responsibility that would be vested in Bill and Cynthia. To Joshua's evident relief, Gary pointed out that the broad-reaching mandate given under such a power of attorney placed an enormous amount of personal trust in both Bill and Cynthia. Robert confirmed he wanted it that way and had deliberately intended for them to have something of a free hand in making the decisions over the liquidation and disposal of his assets.

With everything agreed, all that was left was the formal signing of the documents. Joshua's throat was quite dry as he held out his elegant, expensive and highly prized Mont Blanc fountain pen to Robert. It was a courteous gesture he had never before made to any of his clients.

Taking the pen with an appreciative glance, Robert signed both documents and the triplicate copies of each. He did so unhesitatingly and with a confident flourish. He wanted no one to see the dilemma of uncertainty he was wrestling with in his mind. Was he mad to be taking such drastic action? Was there, as Joshua had tried to suggest, perhaps a more moderate middle course of action that would have allowed him to retain some of his wealth, or at least control over it?

When the two lawyers had added their signatures as witnesses to the documents everything was done. Gary looked at his watch and asked the assembled group if they would like lunch.

Joshua immediately took the opportunity to insist that lunch should be on Harcourt & Boodle, saying it was the least he could do if he wasn't going to be able to take Robert out in New York.

Turning to Gary he asked tentatively, 'Is there somewhere we can get a good lunch around here?'

Gary didn't betray the amusement he felt at Joshua's uncertainty. 'Yes, as a matter of fact there is. We'll be able to get a pretty good lunch over at the inn.'

Robert was secretly delighted at this unprompted endorsement of Mary's establishment.

Ten minutes later they were seated at one of the round tables on the window side of the restaurant, facing the Town Green on which stood the impossibly attractive building that housed the Town Offices. A little further up they could see the picturesque bandstand, behind which was the giant flagpole and the elegant bell tower of the Baptist Church.

Looking out over this idyllic scene, Cynthia leant over to Robert on her left and confided to him she could perhaps now see why he had fallen under the spell of the place.

'Sure beats the view of Madison Avenue from my office window,' she said to the table at large.

Gary smiled. 'Yes, maybe. But you have to be careful the tranquillity of it doesn't lull you to sleep sometimes.'

Joshua was studying the wine list. He wanted to order something special and was agreeably impressed by the selection in front of him. He already knew Robert preferred to drink Californian wine, having previously heard him say on more than one occasion that he'd tasted enough Australian and European wine to last him for a while. From the extensive choice of fine Californian vintages, Robert could tell the New London Inn must have a discerning clientele that belied the bucolic atmosphere of the place. Judging from the prices at the high end, a well-heeled clientele too.

Jen came to take their orders for lunch. She greeted Gary with an easy familiarity and Robert with a friendly nod of 'hello'.

'Welcome to the New London Inn,' she proffered to the other three with a warm smile.

After she had gone Robert was amused to see their reaction. Bill had seemed to lose his concentration, completely forgetting whatever it was he had been saying to Joshua, while, for his part, Joshua had been rendered temporarily speechless for the second time that day.

'This place really is magicland. Don't tell me,' Cynthia said putting up her hand, 'she's called Tinkerbell, isn't she?'

Above the laughs coming from Bill and Joshua, Gary said, 'No, she's called Jennifer, but everyone calls her Jen. She helps Mary run this place, which they pretty much do between them, aside from a chef to do dinner in the evening, some part-time helpers in the kitchen and help with the cleaning. They're both of them hard workers.'

'Does she always go about barefoot?' Bill asked.

'Yes, pretty much, for most of the year anyway, but not outside in the winter

365

of course. Then she'll wear clogs, or boots if the snow's deep. I'll admit there is an ethereal, fairy-like quality to her. But she's completely unconscious of her own beauty, which is as fresh and natural as a fine spring morning. Never wears make-up. Doesn't need to. But it's the very lack of her self-awareness, her complete innocence, that makes her so attractive.'

Robert was impressed by Gary's romantic eloquence. 'Not bad for a lawyer.' he thought.

'I think I'm in love,' Bill croaked hoarsely. 'I think she must have put a spell on me.'

Now it was Gary who chuckled, 'You and every man in New London.'

'Uh oh. Here we go again in magicland,' Cynthia chipped in. 'I suppose you're going to tell us she was found abandoned in the snow and brought here by the gypsies one cold winter night?'

Cynthia made as if to reach for her purse, saying loudly, 'Where are my rabbit's foot and four-leaf clover?'

That got them all laughing.

'No, but she is an orphan,' Gary confirmed. 'Jen's parents were killed in an automobile accident when she was about six. She lives with her aunt and uncle who never had any children of their own. Mary, the owner of this inn, is like a cross between a mother and a big sister to her too. She kind of adopted her some years ago.'

'She must be a nice lady,' Bill said.

The lascivious, vulpine gleam that had started to form in Joshua's eyes when he had first taken in the lithe shape of Jen's firm young body, the outline of which he fancied to be almost visible through the translucence of her loose summer dress, was suddenly extinguished. He too had experienced the loss of his own parents, shortly after his bar mitzvah. They were also killed in an automobile accident: on the Long Island Expressway. Lloyd and Bessie Roundel had been returning from a night out at the theatre with friends in Manhattan, when they were hit head-on by a drunk driver. Due to some botched legal technicality and a clever lawyer, the driver, who unquestionably had caused the accident and had survived unscathed, was able to get off without charge.

Meanwhile Joshua's beloved parents were dead and at the age of thirteen he was left an orphan. He too had been taken in by a childless aunt and uncle. But in Joshua's case their compassion had come reluctantly. As he remembered it, the carefree enjoyment of his childhood ended there. His aunt and uncle were dutiful and did their best, but it was a household without the warmth, love and laughter he was used to. It was the bleak injustice of his situation that had first inspired Joshua to consider becoming a lawyer.

Casting his eye across at Jen as she took the order from another table, he felt ashamed of himself. When she had first appeared, Joshua's mind had filled with the fantasy of her succumbing to his charms as a seducer. As he watched her disappear into the kitchen, all he could think of now was casting himself as her protector and guardian.

Enjoying a cup of coffee after what had indeed turned out to be a surprisingly good lunch, Robert was the first to spot Mary entering the room. He had been talking to Cynthia who, without making the connection, became aware of a sudden, subtle change in Robert's attention and body language – even his voice.

Cynthia glanced up to see a very attractive woman, not yet middle-aged, but just too old to be called young, with a luxuriant head of raven hair, wearing a faded denim skirt, bandana and cowboy boots. She had a good figure, emphasised by the wide leather belt around a trim waist. Cynthia was instantly reminded of the female country singers she'd once seen on a trip to Nashville with her grandfather.

But it was not so much her admittedly striking appearance as her face that caught Cynthia's attention. Cynthia prided herself on being a good reader of people and she was instantly captivated by the mixture of warmth, compassion and kindness she saw in Mary's large dark brown eyes. Set in a face of such good-natured, open candour, it would be impossible for anyone not to be drawn to her, she thought. But Cynthia detected something else. A sadness, perhaps born of some long-ago regret? She couldn't be sure what, but she was sure there was something.

Mary came over to the table and greeted Gary with the warmest of smiles. Cynthia noted she had that rare gift of smiling with her eyes as well as her lips; the effect was hypnotic in making you feel happy and special, if only for that moment.

'Hello stranger,' she said to Gary in a voice both mellifluous and soothing in its tone, an octave or so lower than one might have expected. 'It's been a while since you've been in.'

'I know, Mary. I've been busy for weeks now down in the Concord Courthouse. Besides, it's not every day I have such distinguished guests from New York I need to surprise with the quality of our restaurants here in little New London,' Gary responded with a wink towards Bill and Joshua.

'Let me introduce you to Joshua Roundel, a senior partner with the prestigious New York law firm of Harcourt & Boodle; Bill Temple, who works for Bicknor Wilmot Securities Inc and Cynthia White who is Robert's PA. Robert of course you know already. This is Mary Cotton, owner of the inn and, I'll hazard a guess, owner of the hands that cooked our lunch today,' he said turning towards the others.

They all complimented Mary on the delicious food they had just enjoyed. After exchanging pleasantries Mary excused herself to go back to work.

'A remarkable woman,' Gary said after she'd gone. 'The mystery is why none of our young men from around here ever snapped her up.'

Cynthia noted how Robert had remained silent and appeared to be tongue-tied throughout the encounter. This was so out of character. Robert would normally have been out front and centre in taking charge; she knew something must be up.

For a fleeting moment Cynthia felt a pang of jealousy, but dismissed it immediately. Her relationship with Robert was both professional and one of close personal friendship, but it was not more. Both of them had always known that that would never work. They were eminently unsuited and would drive each other mad in their need to be the one in control.

Cynthia had never felt any jealousy towards the girlfriends who had passed briefly in and out of Robert's life since she'd known him – although it made her cross with him when, on more than one occasion, she had reluctantly helped him fend off unwanted further attention from disappointed young women in whom he had shown enough interest and on whom he had lavished enough money and attention, to give them hope that they might be the one in his future. Cynthia knew that none of these girlfriends had ever meant anything to Robert beyond the voluntary exchange of their beauty and their bodies for the high living and elevated status he temporarily bestowed upon them in return.

What she saw now was different. His interest in Mary was almost equally matched by her disinterest in him – or at least in his money and position. It was a refreshing turnaround.

Noticing it was now after two-thirty, Robert declared it was time for him to meet up with Maude back at Baynham's as they'd agreed earlier. He explained to Bill and Joshua that it would be too confusing and too tiring for his grandmother to meet them all and, as it was Cynthia he particularly wanted her to meet, he suggested they might like to remain behind at the inn lingering over another cup of coffee. He and Cynthia would only be an hour at most.

Gary suggested at once that he take Bill and Joshua for a tour of the town and bring them over to Baynham's at four.

'Do you mean to tell me that we need as long as an hour to see the whole town?' Joshua asked mischievously.

However, Gary did not miss a beat when he replied. 'Of course we do, Joshua – when you factor in the slower pace of life in the country!'

Maude was already waiting for them when Robert walked into Baynham's with Cynthia at ten minutes to three. Maude had a moment or two to study Cynthia as Robert guided her between the tables over to where she was sitting by the far window. She was struck by Cynthia's natural beauty and elegant dress sense, but even more so by the intelligence that showed in her eyes and the easy, comfortable way in which she moved. Maude liked what she saw.

'I hope we haven't kept you waiting, Maude,' Robert said with a genuine concern and gentle courtesy that took Cynthia by complete surprise. This was a side of Robert Melton she was not familiar with.

'No Robert, I was early and, for that matter, so are you,' Maude said tapping her watch.

Cynthia was impressed. This was just the sort of no-nonsense, no-humbug, sort of woman she liked.

'Well, as Robert isn't going to introduce us, it seems, I am going to assume you must be the Cynthia I've been hearing so much about?' Maude continued, holding out her hand and smiling warmly. 'I'm Maude Kimball, Robert's grandmother, but I'm sure you already know that too. I gather you are my grandson's brain and without you he couldn't tie his shoelaces, let alone run his life! Welcome to New Hampshire and especially to New London.'

Cynthia smiled, taking Maude's frail thin hand in both of hers and holding it gently but firmly. 'He's perfectly capable of running his own life and would do so if I wasn't there to do it for him. Just like he's well able to tie his own shoelaces, but he's just too lazy to buy shoes with laces.'

That had both women laughing: one with a robust, merry laugh, the other with more of a soft, higher pitched laugh that seemed to be something of a struggle. Cynthia saw the look of concern again on Robert's face.

'So Robert was lucky enough to find you in Boston and then rudely moved you to New York, I gather?' said Maude. 'Is Boston where you're originally from?'

'No, I was born in North Carolina where my parents came from, but I spent most of my childhood with my grandparents in Savannah, so really I've always thought of Savannah as my true home.'

'Savannah? I've always wanted to go there. It sounds so romantic somehow. A few years ago now, quite by chance, right here in Baynham's as a matter of fact, I met a really lovely woman from Savannah. She turned out to be a nun: Sister Lucy. She was recovering from a serious illness and had come up here to see the beautiful fall foliage. She'd not come as part of one of the usual tour groups, choosing instead to come alone. She was staying in a local motel. Anyhow, we got talking over our cups of coffee and after a bit I decided I liked her enough to invite her to come and stay with me. She did. Stayed for almost a month and we've been friends ever since. Sadly we don't get to see much of each other, but we write regularly and call on the phone at least a couple of times a year.

'She's an exceptional person. Not what you might perhaps expect from a nun. Not piously religious, at least not overtly so, but a perfect example of Christ's love in action I would say. She told me a lot about Savannah and how wonderful it had been growing up there. Soon after leaving seminary college she'd been sent by her order – she's a Dominican nun – down to Trinidad where she worked as a nursing sister. She'd been trained as a nurse before ever becoming a nun. She said she'd loved Trinidad but had always missed Savannah, particularly in the spring.

'She remained in Trinidad for almost ten years before returning home to Savannah, where she's been at the Dominican convent ever since. Just the way she describes Savannah makes it come alive. It sounds so historic, elegant and so atmospheric. Even a little mysterious. I'd really love to have seen it for myself,' Maude finished wistfully.

Cynthia had been on the point of saying she must still go, when she remembered that wasn't going to be possible. Unable to recover herself smoothly enough, she stammered some incoherently awkward response. Maude smiled with an understanding tenderness as she put out a hand to pat Cynthia on the knee.

'Don't worry. Everyone does that all the time. As human beings we're conditioned to always think there will be a future without end. We can't help it. And it's probably right that we should. Even now I catch myself doing it sometimes.

'What you should know is that I'm not afraid of death, it's just the actual dying bit I'm a little apprehensive about,' she said with a wry chuckle. 'Robert knows how I feel about it. Get him to tell you sometime. While you're about it, arrange to take him and show him Savannah for me sometime will you? That way at least I'll have fulfilled my ambition by proxy.'

Robert was annoyed at the tightness he suddenly felt in his throat. He coughed loudly as if to clear it. Cynthia too found herself having to look up at the rafters as she reached out to take Maude's hand.

Still looking up, she said quietly but emphatically to Maude, 'That's a promise.'

Robert and Maude both knew she meant it. Robert was pleased. This was something he could now plan to do for Maude in the future.

'When we go, which we will at some point, we'll raise a glass of champagne to you, Maude. And that's a promise too,' Robert confirmed.

'Excellent. I love a glass of champagne to mark special and memorable moments. When you do – and if I can – I'll try to send you some special feeling, some sort of sign, that I'm enjoying the moment with you.'

'So,' she said, turning back to Cynthia, 'what do you think of my grandson's life-changing decision?'

For several moments Cynthia made no reply. When she finally responded it was in a quiet, serious voice. 'I think it's truly amazing and truly wonderful. It's also very, very brave.

'Many people, particularly from the professional and financial world, will be very unsettled by what Robert is doing. They'll see it as very extreme. They'll seek to hide their own discomfort in trying to explain it away by saying things like

372

"he's had some kind of breakdown"; "he's become a victim of his own success"; or, more mockingly, "he's found God".

'Robert will probably lose most of his new-found friends and – once they figure out he really is nothing more than a poor parish priest – all of his business peers and acquaintances. Not that that will matter to them, but, curiously, I do think it will matter to Robert. Maybe even hurt him a little to see just how insecure, shallow and self-interested so many of those in his present firmament of so-called friendship really are.

'That said, not all of them will be like that. Some, one or two at least, will be filled with genuine admiration and will write sincere letters of congratulation. They will also probably want to, and make the effort to, stay in touch. Not everyone in the world of finance and banking is bad. I know that, or I wouldn't have been able to work for Robert for so long.'

Maude was studying Cynthia with a look of profound respect.

'No wonder Robert always speaks so highly of you,' she said. 'You're a very perceptive person and clearly have a good understanding of human nature in all its frailty – and good intentions. I'm truly glad you're friends, and happy to think you will always be so. I'm also very glad to have been able to meet you.

'But it's been a long day for me and I feel my reserves of energy are beginning to fade. Time for me to be going home for some rest. I've got to try to keep my strength up to be able to enjoy to the fullest as much time as I've got left with my grandson. It's hard not to look back over one's life and not have regrets, but for me to do so now would only be adding to the tragic waste of what might have been.

'There's a humility that comes with age as we accept the inevitability of our increasing infirmity and eventually our own death. But lest I, or anyone, be tempted to pass too harsh a judgement on these mistakes and missed opportunities in life, it is important to remember to view them through the prism of the time in which they were made.

'Now, would you be kind enough to help me up?' Maude said to Cynthia extending her hand towards her.

With linked arms, the two women walked slowly towards the door while Robert paid the bill. He noticed how much Maude was leaning on Cynthia and how tired she had become. Her deterioration seemed to be accelerating with alarming speed. He felt an unfamiliar sense of panic rising within his normally calm and well-controlled mind. This was something he felt powerless to influence.

Robert followed them out to the parking lot, where he fretted about his grandmother driving herself home and suggested he could do that before he took Cynthia up to Lebanon Airport. Taking Cynthia to the airport was something he wanted to do, so he could talk to her without Bill and Joshua.

'What nonsense, Robert,' Maude retorted. 'I'm quite capable of driving myself home. Besides which, Sutton is all downhill from here and even if I was to succumb to fatigue or confusion, by now my little car, like a good horse, knows its own way home from here!' and she gave Robert an affectionate but firm pat on his arm. Cynthia was amused to see who was in charge.

'I've so enjoyed being able to meet you,' she said to Cynthia as they spontaneously embraced each other in as tight a hug as Maude could manage and as Cynthia dared, noting how desperately thin and frail Maude's frame was in her arms. 'I should have liked to have known you better. We would have been close friends I feel. But I want to thank you again for all you've done for my grandson. I really think it might have been your conscientious and steadying influence that stopped him going off the rails completely.'

Cynthia, looking steadily into Maude's still bright but sunken eyes, said nothing. Tears welling in her own eyes, she just looked at this remarkable woman; there was nothing to be said and anyway she couldn't speak. And yet she couldn't bring herself to let go.

'Now don't go upsetting yourself on my account, my dear,' Maude told her, her own voice betraying the emotion she too was feeling at saying goodbye to Cynthia for what she knew would be the last time. Both women had instantly recognised in each other a kindred spirit and it seemed almost cruel of fate to have shown them a closeness and friendship that might have been and yet was not to be.

'I'll be just fine,' Maude continued. 'I really do have faith in the purposes of the good Lord for each of us. I've nearly done my time in this world and, although I have to confess to a little apprehension that I can't deny, I'm actually quite excited to experience what comes next.'

With tears now rolling unchecked down her face and unable to stifle entirely the sob that shook her, Cynthia whispered hoarsely, 'I wish I had your strength. Your faith. I wish you could send me some small sign, just so I would know you are all right. I don't know why I care so much, but I really do – for you and for Robert.'

Maude smiled tenderly at her. Old enough to be her mother, she felt a mother's instinct now in her wish to reassure. 'It's not for us to challenge God in asking for signs. But doubt is OK. Without doubt, there would be no requirement for faith.

'I'll tell you what, I promise you this Cynthia,' she said, using her name for the first time. 'If it's given to me to be able to send you a sign, I will. What shall we agree upon?' she asked as a distraction.

At that moment a little chipmunk scampered in front of Maude's car and stopped. It sat up on its back legs and looked confidently over in their direction, before flicking its little tail and darting on across the parking lot. Both women were momentarily distracted by its boldness in coming so close to where they were standing beside the car.

Looking back at each other they agreed in unison that, if it were possible to send a sign, a chipmunk would be that sign. 'If I can, I might send a loon too,' Maude continued with a smile. 'Only because I'm so very fond of them and they always remind me so much of New Hampshire.'

She saw Cynthia's questioning frown and added, 'Get Robert to tell you about them. Loons are the most handsome and mysterious of water birds, with a distinctive and hauntingly beautiful, warbling cry. Once you've heard it you will never forget it.'

Just then Joshua and Bill pulled in, fresh from their tour of New London, a little after the appointed meeting time as it happened. Gary had dropped them off back at the inn to pick up their rental car. Robert walked over to meet them.

'Sorry we're a little later than we said,' Bill began. 'This town really has got some beautiful places to see, but it's quite spaced out …'

'No problem, Bill,' Robert interrupted. 'We've only just finished up ourselves. But I wanted to ask you if you'd mind going on ahead to the airport. I'm going to bring Cynthia up myself. We'll be about fifteen minutes behind you. Tell Mike we're on our way and to get everything ready for departure. By the time you've turned in your car, we should have just about caught up with you.'

Bill had been half expecting something like this. He'd known from early on in their relationship, in fact not long after he'd introduced Cynthia to Robert, that it had become more than just professional but without ever being carnal. He'd watched a deep friendship develop between Robert and Cynthia. He wasn't in any way jealous of it, because he himself had always felt like a father keeping an eye out for Cynthia from the time when she'd first come to his company a shy, young, insecure person looking to better herself in life. He'd soon recognised her deep intelligence and integrity: both qualities that made her shine in his profession. But she was too creative a person, with too active a mind, to have been satisfied forever within the confines of a financial advisory service. She had positively blossomed from the start of working with Robert Melton in the building up of his business empire.

'No, that's fine,' Bill said. 'We'll get on our way, but not before Joshua's had a chance to say goodbye.'

Joshua was already out of the car. Taking Robert's hands in both of his he thanked him for everything, for his business, for his confidence in him, for his friendship. And he wished him well in his return to his past as the Anglican vicar of St Mungo's in London. Robert was touched by the absolute sincerity in his voice.

'When I get over to London sometime, I'd like to come to your church one Sunday. That's if you'll allow a Jewish boy like me to cross your threshold?' Joshua said, smiling broadly, but at the same time surprised at his own disparaging use of the diminutive 'boy'. Had that been to do with the earlier reminder of his childhood, he wondered vaguely?

'You can have no idea how much I would welcome that,' Robert responded with equal sincerity. 'And I wouldn't have the slightest intention, or even wish, to try and proselytise you from your Jewish faith, for which all informed Christians and Muslims should have a profound respect, if only because of our shared historical root in being one of the three great Abrahamic religions.'

Joshua looked momentarily confused, unsure whether his memory of early religious education had covered that particular topic or not. Nevertheless he was pleased to hear the genuine welcome in Robert's voice.

With that Bill and Joshua got under way, leaving Cynthia with Robert and Maude.

'I hate long emotional goodbyes,' Maude said in a voice that betrayed the emotion she was trying to hide. 'Cynthia, you have a good moral compass. You'll be fine. But sometimes it's best not to think too much. Periodic tribulations are a part of life. Be positive. Be happy. Be kind and above all never be afraid to take the risk of loving. Now, I wish you a long and happy life.

'Robert, I'll see you later. Be quiet when you come in, I may be sleeping. I'm a little tired today.' With that Maude got in her car and drove off in the direction of Sutton.

Gary was hurrying out of his office, already late for another appointment, when he saw Maude's car driving slowly past. The angle of the sun was such that he had a clear view of her face. He couldn't help but see the stream of tears glistening on her hollow, sunken cheeks and the infinitely sad expression on her face.

He felt the same wave of compassion he always felt when encountering any form of suffering in his fellow man. As a lawyer he had always fought his hardest when representing someone wronged, particularly if they were poor or disadvantaged, regardless of whether they could pay his fees or not. Now he felt powerless to help. He remembered he'd be seeing Maude the following Monday. She'd asked to come and see him to review and make some small changes to her will. Gary had suggested he go to her, but Maude had been insistent on coming to his office.

Turning back into his office, he asked his secretary to make sure they would have chocolate cookies and Earl Grey tea on hand, two things he knew Maude had retained a liking for from her time spent as a student in England long ago.

'Oh, and Grace, don't forget to use Maude's tea set on Monday.' He knew Maude liked it served that way. Brought in on a tray, teapot, proper china teacup and saucer. Milk, not cream, from a small china jug, with a plate of chocolate covered wholemeal cookies. He had bought the plain white china teapot with matching cup and saucer years ago after observing how Maude liked to do things when he went to her home. It was universally known in the office as 'Maude's tea set' and was only ever used when Miss Kimball came to the office.

It was little personal touches like this that had helped to establish Gary Dufrère as one of the most popular lawyers in town. To him it seemed a small thing, but he was aware enough of his individual client's circumstances to know that Maude's life had now shrunk to the point where it was the little things from which she was still able to derive the most pleasure.

To take the trouble with a bit of ceremony and punctuate their meeting on Monday with a pleasant tea and, in his case, a coffee moment, would, he knew, give Maude great pleasure and underscore their long friendship. He realised now it had also become very important to him. He wanted to see the pleasure this small gesture would bring to her face.

For what seemed the longest time, Cynthia did not move. She stood looking in the direction of Maude's car slowly receding until it disappeared behind the Lake Sunapee Bank building on Main Street. When she turned back, Robert was holding open the passenger door of the old Dodge truck for her. She got in, softly crying the tears of real pain.

Getting in on the other side Robert said nothing. There was the familiar and unavoidable roar from the powerful old engine as he turned out in the opposite direction from Maude, taking them towards I-89 up to Lebanon Airport.

It wasn't until they reached the interstate and headed north that Cynthia broke the silence and spoke. 'Your grandmother is one hell of a lady, Robert. No wonder you don't want to miss a moment of her remaining time.'

'I know, and I'm so glad you understand. She really wanted to meet you and I know doing so will have made her very happy, in a bittersweet sort of way, if you see what I mean.'

For the next couple of miles they sat in companionable silence, absorbed in their own thoughts as they looked out over the spectacular scenery on both sides of the highway.

'Robert, you know I promised your grandmother I'd go with you to Savannah sometime? It's a promise I want to keep,' Cynthia said quietly, breaking the silence. 'I don't mind if magic Mary comes too, but I do want us to go and raise that glass of champagne you promised.

'I'll be happy to buy the champagne because, as a humble vicar, you'll struggle to afford the cost of the flight from London!' Cynthia said, recovering her sense of humour a little.

'Who said anything about Mary coming?' Robert asked with a note of alarm.

'Oh, come on, Robert. It was staring me in the face the moment Mary walked into the restaurant. You're head over heels in love with her in a way I've never seen you with any other woman. What's more I think you'd be ideally suited. She's perfect for you in what's now going to be your future, in a way she never would have been if you'd remained Mr Big Captain of Industry, the toast of corporate Manhattan.'

'OK, Cyn, I guess I can't hide it from you, even if I am doing a pretty good job of trying to hide it from myself,' Robert said with a sheepish smile.

'But it's hopeless really, isn't it? If the bishop will have me back it won't be long before I'll be leaving for London to pick up where I left off as the impoverished vicar of St Mungo's. That's what I'll be doing from then on. Mary won't want to leave everything and everyone she knows and loves to come with me to London. Her life is here – and it's a good life.'

'That depends on only one thing, doesn't it?' Cynthia replied. And when Robert didn't answer, she did. 'It's whether she loves you or not, and whether she is sure of your love for her.

'If she does – and if she is – it wouldn't matter if it was Moscow you were going to take her to. One look at a woman like Mary and you can see she has love and loyalty stamped right through her. Now, I grant you, she wouldn't have looked twice at the big-shot Robert Melton wanting to take her to New York to turn her into some sort of socialite trophy wife. But the real Robert Melton, who nobody over here knows, except perhaps me and, to a lesser extent Bill, is someone Mary could fall in love with – and would travel to the ends of the earth to be with.

'So, my advice to you, is practise all you've learned from your willingness to take ever-bigger risks in your business life, and take the biggest risk of all. Risk rejection and follow your heart. If you win, you'll have found a depth of happiness that will enable you to be the best you can be in whatever you do. In your case I suppose that means being the best vicar in the Church of England and, who knows, maybe in time becoming the Archbishop of Canterbury.'

That idea made them both smile, before Cynthia continued, 'If you fail, it doesn't matter, because you'll have given it your all, your best shot. Remember the old adage "If you have tried to do something and failed, you are still vastly better off than if you had tried to do nothing and succeeded".

'And what's all this about the bishop maybe accepting you back? I should think he would after the way he treated you and after the donation you made to save St Mungo's! Also, Robert – and this is relevant to Mary – I know you well enough to know how you can't ever leave anything unfinished. I've long thought the reason St Mungo's in particular rankles with you is because of two things: your feelings of guilt at having walked out on your priestly vows, and the abandonment of your mission and your parishioners. Meaning for you St Mungo's is unfinished business.

'Because of this it's probably the right place for you to start. But that is all it will be, a start in your second calling as a priest. You won't stay at St Mungo's for any longer than it takes you to achieve what you had set out to do before – and nor should you.

'Everything you've learned and the enormous confidence you've gained in your business life over here would be wasted for you to stay on in one small church for any longer than it takes to fulfil your commitment to yourself and your parishioners. And that is to save the church by breathing life back into it. Not forgetting the likelihood that some of the more elderly parishioners you've described to me may well no longer be with us. But I know you'll still feel you owe it to their memory to finish what you promised to do.

'Now, I said this was relevant to Mary. If you told Mary your time in London might be regarded as a finite, kind of overseas posting, after which, if you and she both wanted, you might think about returning to America and perhaps even New Hampshire, that would demonstrate your consideration for her, which would, I'm sure, help her to view your proposition more favourably.

'You clearly like America and seem to have fallen under some sort of spell here in New Hampshire. It's not as if the work of God isn't as necessary in America as it is in England. Think about it.'

For a few moments Robert didn't reply, but when he did it was to suggest, 'I don't think the English would stand for having the Archbishop of Canterbury living in New Hampshire, do you?'

When they had finished laughing about that, Robert said, 'Well Cyn, that was quite a lecture! But you could be right. I'd not thought of it, but meeting and spending this time with my grandmother up here has opened my eyes to so many things and changed everything for me.

'As you well know, my private life hasn't all been about high-class prostitutes. I've met and entertained some of the most beautiful, intelligent and sophisticated women in the world over the past eight years, but none of them have even got close to doing for me what Mary does. I know I don't deserve it but I feel like I really need Mary in my life and, after Maude dies, it's entirely possible this place will feel more like the home where my roots are than anywhere else.'

'Whoa, be careful now. Just be sure you don't love Mary because you think you need her. You must be certain you need her because you love her,' Cynthia told him sternly.

'OK, you're right to make that distinction and, yes, it is that way round.'

They were now just pulling in to the airport entrance; their time talking together had run out.

'Cyn, thanks for coming up here today. It's meant a lot to me and, I can tell, to my grandmother too. I'll keep in touch to let you know how things are going. As soon as I know the date I'll be passing through New York, I'll let you know, so you can give any interested members of staff a time when I'll come by the office to say "goodbye and thank you" to them all. I know you'll treat them well and generously, as I've requested. Have a good trip back to the city.'

'Don't worry about a thing in New York. Bill and I know your wishes and we'll take care of everything. You just concentrate on your grandmother. Please tell her how very much I admire her. We'll speak soon. Bye for now.'

Cynthia leant over and gave him a kiss on the cheek before jumping out of the cab. They both knew the informality of this was a first between them. But it now felt the most natural thing in the world. All the rules seemed to be changing.

'By the way, you look surprisingly at home in blue jeans, behind the wheel of this old pick-up. Ruggedly handsome even. You might want to consider making your proposition to Mary from in here. I think she'd say yes,' Cynthia said as she pushed the door shut.

Robert caught the wink and smile as she turned and walked into the little terminal without looking back. He waited just long enough to see her reunited with Bill and Joshua before easing the old Dodge into gear and heading back down to Sutton. He'd finally got the hang of the double-declutching and took some pride in the fact that he could now change gears with almost the same silent, butter-smooth softness of a Rolls-Royce.

Twenty minutes earlier Bill and Joshua had been driving up the same highway. Bill would have been happy to talk, but was surprised to find the normally loquacious Joshua in a silent and reflective mood. Thinking about it, he wondered if lawyers were encouraged, even trained, to be talkative in law school. It would make sense in a profession where hefty charges were levied by the hour, or fractions thereof.

For his part Joshua was going over in his mind the tumultuous events of the day. He'd found it all very unsettling and deeply discomforting. He didn't like one bit being forced to recognise the grudging esteem and admiration in which he now held Robert for having the extraordinary courage to turn his back so totally on material gain. The founder of Bicknor Wilmot Inc was giving up luxury, comfort and status for the rest of his life, to follow the star of his calling, with all the hardship, depravation and risk it was inevitably going to entail.

This was the cause of a terrible conflict going on in Joshua's mind, and he was torn. On the one hand he felt resentful, even betrayed, by what he saw as a fellow member of the capitalist class defecting to a sort of utopian socialism —

but not a socialism with which he could argue or one he could rail against. On the other was flat-out envy that Robert had enough moral courage and insight to readjust his life totally to what was really important in making him fulfilled and happy.

Ever since becoming a qualified lawyer, Joshua had become adept at suppressing any feeling that he might not actually enjoy his work. He had been so successful at this most of the time that he no longer truly knew if he did or he didn't. But sometimes in the quiet dark hours of night he would lie awake remembering wistfully the little boy he had once been.

The dream Joshua Roundel had harboured in secret all his life was to be a boat builder. He had wanted to design and build beautiful sailing boats that would be renowned worldwide for their speed, their gracefulness and their seaworthiness. It had been a passion so strong he dared not speak of it to a family that he knew had very different expectations of him.

It was a dream that, remaining unmentioned to anyone, had died with his parents on the Long Island Expressway on that night long ago, eclipsed by the rage and over-riding passion to fight the injustice of laws that could allow the drunken killer of his beloved parents to go unpunished.

After graduating from college and law school, Joshua had begun his legal career flushed with altruism and motivated by an ambition to right the wrongs he perceived within the criminal justice system. But the passage of time and an early marriage to Caitlin, a beautiful but demanding girl he'd met at college, had weakened his drive to fight his way up among the handful of elite criminal lawyers who dominated the criminal justice system. He had opted instead for the more seductively lucrative area of corporate law, which was both less demanding and offered many more opportunities to a greater number of practitioners. It was a milieu in which he was able to excel and thus had quickly risen to the top.

Now, very well paid, with a spacious apartment on Park Avenue's Upper East Side and an elegant weekend and summer home in the Hamptons, he led a life of sybaritic luxury. A member of both the Country Club and Yacht Club in Southampton, he dined regularly at Manhattan's finest restaurants and enjoyed all the perks of partnership in the prestigious legal firm that Harcourt & Boodle was.

But right at this moment, if he was being truthful with himself, he felt angry with, and certainly resentful of, Robert Melton for inadvertently challenging the comfort zone of his self-satisfied complacency, for cocking a snook at the outward success of his life and all the trappings that served to confirm it.

Yes, sadly, Joshua recognised, he was stuck. Trapped.

When he pondered Robert's break for freedom, Joshua was envious. Hearing what Robert planned to do and seeing the ease and peace of mind it was giving him, made Joshua realise just how much regret he had over his own personal life.

However, he was too much of a realist not to know it was too late for him to have the courage to give it all up. Yet the temptation, the dream, even now, to sell everything and buy a small firm of boat builders was strong. But with two children in private schools, yet to go to college, and a high-maintenance wife who, on the only occasion he had ever dared mention his boyhood dream, had responded sharply that she had 'married a lawyer and not a boat builder', he knew he would never go through with it.

Now he felt an urgent need to push these troubling thoughts far from his mind. He had never been so keen to get back to New York. Although he knew she had only been joking, perhaps after all Cynthia was right. Maybe there was something about the self-reliance of New Englanders that made people take stock of their lives.

He couldn't wait to board the private jet that would fly him to the waiting limousine, that would whisk him in insulated comfort to the safety of his luxurious home. He and his wife would be dining at the Carlyle that night with one of the other partners in the firm. The prospect of this made him start to feel better, more like his old self again. He didn't think he'd be coming back to New Hampshire any time soon.

But why did he feel such deep-down insecurity? Perhaps this was why his best-loved holiday in the Jewish calendar had always been Sukkot: the Feast of the Tabernacles – a festival of joy. Joshua had been struck long ago when this had been described to him by a rabbi as being 'like a tutorial in how to live with insecurity, while still being able to celebrate and enjoy life'.

Enjoying life had never been a problem for him. It was the fear of insecurity awakened by Robert Melton that he was struggling with as Mr Melton's private jet sped him southwards back to where Joshua reluctantly accepted he belonged.

39

MAUDE HAD LOOKED tired and drawn when Robert had last seen her and he didn't want to disturb her afternoon rest by going back to her house too soon. This also gave him the opportunity to stop at the inn on his way back. This time in the afternoon was often a good time to catch Mary when she wasn't too busy. That was if she hadn't already gone home to do her chores there before returning to the inn for dinner.

Mary was standing at the reception desk with Jen, reviewing the dinner reservations they had for that evening, when Robert walked in. 'Looks like we've got a full house tonight, Jen. We'll be busy right through. You'd better call Maggie and see if she's able to come in and help. We probably could manage without her, but best not to take the chance if she's available,' Mary was saying.

She smiled when she saw Robert coming over to them and then she turned her attention back to the reservations register before Jen had had a chance to notice.

'Hello Mary, I was passing by on my way back from the airport to Maude's place and thought I'd drop in to see if I could buy you a cup of coffee or tea?' Robert began, trying to sound both natural and casual.

'Sure, I've got about an hour before I need to start getting ready for what promises to be a busy night, so it's not really worth going home anyway. But you can't buy me tea or coffee. That much we can run to here.'

Then a sudden thought took hold of her. 'Is there something particular you wanted to talk to me about? Is Maude OK?'

'No, don't worry. Maude's at home resting and I didn't want to go back and disturb her just yet. She's had quite a tiring day one way and another. So, as I had time to spare, I thought it would just be nice to visit with you.'

The faintest blush of heightened colour passed across Mary's cheeks as her expression of concern turned to what he hoped he correctly identified as one of pleasure.

Emboldened by this, he added, 'But as it happens though, there is something I want to talk to you about.'

They went through to the lounge, which was deserted at this time of day. Jen brought them a pot of coffee on a tray. Although Robert would normally have preferred tea at this time of the afternoon, the Australian and English habit dying hard, he said nothing. He had more important things on his mind.

He did not know where to begin, and admitted as much to Mary. 'The thing is, a lot has happened to me in a remarkably short space of time since I first arrived in New Hampshire. It will probably sound crazy to you, but I came here as the person I thought I was and have since rediscovered who I really am. A lot of that is of course down to the surprise discovery of an extraordinary grandmother and a whole family history I didn't know I had. But some of it is down to other things that have happened while I've been here and to the people I've met. Not least among whom I would include you.

'So, if it's OK, there are some things I'd really like to tell you.'

And Robert did. For almost an hour he told Mary everything about himself, from his appointment by the Bishop of West London to his first parish, to how he had arrived in America. About the Powerball lottery ticket Maude had bought. How he had discovered his natural talent for business and had quadrupled his fortune. Finally how ultimately empty and unsatisfying he'd found his new life and how he was now intending to give it all up, to return to his work as a humble Church of England vicar.

Mary said nothing throughout. She sat back and listened quietly, the expression on her face only changing slightly to register surprise at the revelation that, although he was the one who had become the beneficiary of that famous Powerball lottery win, which had caused so much excitement in the town eight years earlier, it was in fact Maude who had bought the ticket at Baynham's, and not the Benedictine monk from St Jerome's, as had been widely reported at the time.

After Robert had finished, and when she did finally speak, it was to say, 'I've often heard it said that fact is stranger than fiction and if ever there was a story to prove that, this must be it.

'That old dark horse Maude. How did she ever manage to keep that secret to herself all this time?' Then adding after a pause, 'Although I do think she's good at keeping secrets.

'Robert, thank you, I'm really very honoured you've entrusted me with this. Does Maude know you were going to tell me?'

'No, not yet, but I plan to tell her I have later today. I know she won't mind. She trusts you completely.'

Mary started fidgeting. Robert thought she looked suddenly uncertain in a way he had not seen her look before. 'I should tell you,' she continued quietly, 'that I'm also humbled by what you've decided to do. It is extraordinary and ... I don't know how to express it properly. The magnitude of it ... it's truly ... awe-inspiring. I guess that's what I mean.

'I don't have any interest in big business. Why should I, trying to make ends meet with this place? But even I had come across the name of the great Robert Melton – and that was before you showed up here. I knew that this Robert Melton was fabulously rich and, to be honest with you, I had him down as the kind of brash tycoon who sometimes swings through here with a briefcase full of cash they want to throw at some super-expensive holiday mansion hideaway. A lot of them don't make it into their third winter before they sell up and hurry back to the city.'

She put down the linen napkin she had been fiddling with absent-mindedly and exhaled deeply. 'But I see now I was wrong about that Robert Melton – wrong about a lot of things.

'To give away all your enormous wealth and return to being a priest … I don't think we normally call them vicars in the Episcopal Church over here,' she added as an aside. 'I can't tell you how much I admire you for really being able to do that. I've always had a soft spot for a man who treats those who can do nothing for him with the same respect as those who can. It's a good judge of a man's character.'

It was Robert's turn to blush.

'Well I suppose I should be getting back to Maude,' he said, making no effort to leave. 'She'll have finished her rest by now, I should think.'

Finally standing up, Robert said almost as an afterthought to their conversation, 'Mary, I wondered if you'd care to join me on a hike up Mount Kearsarge sometime? I've not yet been up and I've been meaning to ever since you first showed me the mountain and told me how much it meant to you. I thought perhaps we could go one afternoon while Maude was having her rest.'

'Oh Robert, I'd love to!' Mary replied, giving his hand a squeeze. 'I can't think of anything nicer. It's years since I last hiked up there, so long in fact I can't remember the last time. Funny how when something is on your doorstep you just take it for granted and never get around to visiting it. I'll bet it's the same for you with the Statue of Liberty or the Empire State Building.'

Keeping his pleasure at Mary's response in check. Robert replied, 'Yes, I visited both in my first week in New York eight years ago and haven't been back to either since. Anyway, if the weather cooperates, let's see if we can find an afternoon soon.'

'Sounds perfect,' Mary told him, smiling with a pleasure she felt no need to conceal.

'That's great. I'll be in touch. Oh, and thanks again for being a good listener and giving up your precious time for me.'

'Say "Hi" to Maude from me, would you?' she called after Robert as he walked towards the door.

40

ROBERT FOUND MAUDE sitting at the kitchen table when he got back. She hadn't been up long from her afternoon rest, for most of which, to her surprise, she had slept soundly. She must have been even more tired than she had realised. Now, she felt much refreshed and, as the kettle had just boiled, she got up to busy herself making tea for them both.

'I can't tell you how much I liked Cynthia,' Maude began after she greeted Robert. 'I took to her instantly. There's just something about her that is so lovely, so genuine, so free of guile. Unusual in many young people today – their lives seem so complicated.'

'Well I know she took an instant liking to you too, Maude, probably recognising pretty much the same qualities in you as you have in her.' Robert was aware how pleased Cynthia would be to be categorised as a 'young' person, despite this being only relative from his grandmother's perspective.

He was also deeply impressed and pleased that his grandmother had made no reference whatever to Cynthia being black. Taking it completely in her stride, it was as if she hadn't even noticed that obvious physical characteristic. It was wonderful for him to realise that, in spite of her age and the differences in attitude between their generations, this was something that was of no consequence to his grandmother.

Just as if she was reading his thoughts, Maude suddenly added, 'So beautiful too. What a pity she hasn't found the right man to marry yet. Perhaps she will when you're no longer around needing to be mothered and demanding all her attention.'

For the second time that day Robert found himself blushing. How worldly wise and perceptive his grandmother was. Her reading and understanding of human nature was quite remarkable for someone who had lived such a sheltered life.

Changing the subject, Robert told his grandmother of his stop-off to see Mary on the way home and how he had told her all about himself. About his past and what he now planned to do with his future.

His grandmother seemed genuinely pleased. 'I'm glad you did that Robert. Mary needs to know who you really are if there is to be any chance of her being a part of your future.'

Robert no longer felt capable of being surprised by this extraordinary woman. Was he so transparent in showing his feelings? He did not think so. But where then did her perception come from? Perhaps, indeed, Cynthia was not so wrong about this place being 'magicland'. Everything that had happened to him since he first arrived in New Hampshire seemed, upon reflection, to have a magic quality to it. But there was also an inexorable, if indiscernible, pattern.

'Forgive me for being so blunt,' his grandmother continued. 'But with time running out for me, I no longer have the luxury of employing subtlety to make the things I say more palatable, or even less startling. Your reaction has confirmed that my instinct – my hope, really – was not wrong, at least on your part.' Maude smiled. 'There is nothing I would like more than to go happily to my grave in the belief that you and Mary might make a future together as man and wife.'

At that moment it seemed to Robert there was somehow more than a 'kindred spirit' connecting Cynthia and his grandmother. With so little to go on, how had these two, admittedly remarkable, women, quite separately identified his own secret wish that Mary might agree to marry him – a wish that was growing stronger as the prospect grew clearer in his mind?

Cynthia had been absolutely right, and Mary had as good as confirmed it.

Unlike all the other women he'd associated with in recent years, Mary would never have been attracted to the man he had become in New York. His anxiety now was in knowing if she would be sufficiently attracted to the real person he had been before and was now determined to be again. He longed to feel more confident she would be able to believe in his transformation and have sufficient faith in him to consider moving with him to London.

Maude sensed enough had been said on this matter for the time being and changed the subject. 'I know it's very unlikely, but I'd like you to try to do something for me once you're settled back in London. My friend, Sister Lucy, the Dominican nun from Savannah I was telling Cynthia about, has a great wish she shared with me a while ago.

'It seems that shortly after she first arrived at the hospital in Trinidad, a young man of mixed race, well I suppose only a boy really – I think she said he was only about sixteen – was brought to the hospital in a terrible state. He'd been dreadfully mutilated in a vicious physical attack that his attackers had never meant him to survive. But somehow, against overwhelming odds, he did – thanks in large part, it seems, to whoever it was who found him by the roadside and took him to the hospital. After which it was down to the expert care he received there.

'Well, it was Sister Lucy who mostly took care of him after the doctors had done what they could. Apparently, amongst other unspeakably terrible things, his cowardly attackers had cut out his tongue, so he could no longer talk. Anyway, Sister Lucy believes there was something very special about this young man and she says there is nothing in her life that she would like better than to find him again. All she knows is that, after leaving hospital and being banished from his family, he'd been forced to leave Trinidad forever. She's pretty certain he went to London.

'A bit like looking for a needle in a haystack I know, but I was wondering if you might be able to trace him through some organisation or institution with which he might be registered. There must be some organisation to help mute people over there. Sister Lucy said she had given him a book on how to teach yourself Sign Language.'

'Of course, I'll do what I can, Maude,' Robert answered. 'But it's a bit of a long shot. Did this Sister Lucy tell you anything else about him that might help me track him down?'

'She did say he had exceptionally striking hands,' Maude remembered. 'She described them as being beautiful and sensitive. She had urged him to use this gift and perhaps consider a career as a musician, artist, sculptor or something, none of which occupations need or require great verbal skills.

'I know it's not much to go on, but to hear Sister Lucy talk about him, I'm more than half convinced her instinct that he was somehow special may be right. Anyway, although I won't be around, I'd really love you to see if you could help her for me in this search. She will understand if it's a dead end, but she'd be very grateful to you for even trying. As I would too on her behalf, Robert. It would just mean so much to her. Will you do it?'

'Of course I will, Maude. I'll start investigating as soon as I get back. Funnily enough, Brenda, the young lady — who's also a mute — the one I told you about from St Mungo's, might be able to help me find him. If she's still there that is. I think she's the person who would best know how to go about finding him. Did Sister Lucy ever mention his name?'

'Sorry, yes of course. She didn't remember his family name but, from memory, I think she said his Christian name was something like Bernard.'

Robert sat bolt upright. For a moment he didn't speak. But when he recovered himself he asked Maude, 'You did say he was of mixed race didn't you?' And, of course, the beautiful, sensitive hands!

'Maude, I'm just about certain the woman I know is in fact the young man Sister Lucy is looking for. I don't know why I didn't put two and two together sooner. But it came to me immediately, once you suggested his name. You see the woman I know, Brenda, was born a boy. I told you all about her.'

Now it was Maude's turn to feel a moment of revelation. 'I believe you may be right, because, come to think of it, the name Sister Lucy mentioned was actually Brendan, not Bernard. I remember now thinking it must be a Celtic name. Quite unusual – probably Irish.

'Also it makes complete sense now. Sister Lucy did tell me that part of his mutilation had included a brutal, crude castration. Robert, do you think the young woman you know could really be him? Sister Lucy would be so very happy to have found him again.' Maude had become quite animated.

'The more I think about it, the more certain I am it must be one and the same person,' Robert said. 'The similarities are uncanny. "Brendan" to "Brenda" is such an obvious transition. Both are of mixed race and probably a similar age. Both have remarkable hands. But the clincher for me is your saying Sister Lucy recognised a special but indefinable quality in Brendan. Brenda has exactly that quality too. As I told you, I would describe it as being almost spiritual in its magnetism.'

'Is Sister Lucy right about her working with her hands? Is she an artist or something?' Maude asked.

Robert smiled as he hesitated in his reply. 'In a manner of speaking, yes, in answer to both questions,' he said. 'But not in any way that either you or Sister Lucy could ever possibly imagine. I think you might both be shocked.'

'Oh Robert, do stop tantalising. What on earth do you mean?' Maude asked tartly. 'I'm not as prudish as you might think, you know. I thought you knew that by now after what I've been through in my life.'

'OK,' Robert continued, 'I think Brenda gives … massages … to people with disabilities.' He hesitated before going on. 'She specialises in giving massages to the severely deformed, disfigured and disabled.' Still concerned for her sensibilities, Robert looked carefully at his grandmother, but as she showed no sign of minding, he continued. 'I believe these can sometimes include the provision of what is euphemistically referred to as giving relief – a practice more normally associated with the arts of a prostitute. In massage terminology it goes under the heading of a "special", apparently.'

Robert was now conscious of his own embarrassment. 'I'm sure she is very good at what she does and therefore could be considered a sort of artist in this unlikely field,' he ended lamely.

There was a long pause, during which Maude regarded her grandson with a look of affectionate amusement before replying. 'Don't be so coy about it, Robert. Can't you say the word masturbate? What a pompous long-winded way to describe a perfectly natural activity. Usually conducted alone and in strict privacy I grant you, but nevertheless normal. In Brenda's case, perhaps even rather wonderful if, as I suspect, she is offering this as a service, sensitively provided to those who have a real, if unspoken, need for it.

'I think she should be congratulated, not condemned, for showing compassion to those poor unfortunate souls for whom sadly such a need exists.

'Did you expect me to be shocked? I may live in the backwoods of New Hampshire, but I grew up on a farm where earthy things happen as a daily occurrence. I also read a great deal and, as you know, travelled abroad as a young person. I never married and never had a physical relationship with any man after your grandfather. Do you think I became a saint and gave up all my basic physical urges for ever more? To have a really good physical relationship with a man a woman needs to feel love first and, as I understand it, most men find this preferable too.

'What an extraordinary coincidence, but I really think Sister Lucy might be right about her Brendan and your Brenda. She sounds rather intriguing and remarkable. Although it will clearly be a big dilemma for her, once Sister Lucy understands what and why Brenda does it, she might not inwardly disapprove as much as she might outwardly have to, if you see what I mean. In the end only the good Lord will be able to stand in judgement of such matters. It is my belief that, in knowing the intentions of men's hearts, He will be a great deal more wise and compassionate than we are in our judgements.'

'Maude, it would be best if I definitely confirm Brenda's identity as formerly being Brendan before saying anything to Sister Lucy,' Robert advised. 'After all, I have no idea if Brenda is even still around. It's been quite a while and she may have moved, or gone away.'

'Yes, well, I'll leave that up to you, Robert as I definitely will have gone away,' Maude quipped. 'I've made a short list of just a few people I'd like you to contact after I'm dead. People not from around here. Sister Lucy is top of that list with her address and telephone number. I agree it's sensible to be sure of Brendan's or Brenda's identity as the right person before telling her. No point in raising her hopes only to disappoint. But I do believe she will be delighted if he is the young man she remembers so well. Even if he is, as you say, now a mature young woman.'

Robert's stomach tightened again. He knew his grandmother's days were numbered, but the knowledge didn't make accepting the reality of her imminent death any easier. He marvelled again at her calm, almost matter-of-fact acceptance of it.

Later that night, just before going to bed, Maude said, 'Robert, I think I'd like to go to Mass on Sunday. Would you be happy to accompany me to the Catholic Church?'

'Of course, Maude. After my long absence from the clergy it's very important for me to brush up on what the competition is doing now,' he said with a broad wink and a smile.

The following day being Saturday, Maude and Robert elected to stay away from the town and remain quietly at home, filling in more of the gaps in their respective lives.

On Sunday, Maude requested they go to the earlier, eight-thirty Mass at the little Church of the Immaculate Conception hidden in the woods at Potter Place, rather than the ten-thirty Mass at the bigger, main parish church in New London. As she always awoke early, it seemed sensible to allow themselves the rest of the day uninterrupted. Besides which, at the earlier service there would be fewer people to see afterwards and, anyway, she just liked the basic simplicity of the smaller church.

Maude had not been to Mass for a while and Father Goodlow, a tall, spare man with a profusion of thick, close-cropped grey hair and merry blue eyes, greeted them warmly at the door. 'Maude, I've been meaning to call on you for some time now and I'm sorry I haven't got around to it. How are you managing?'

He had wanted to say how well she was looking, if only to be encouraging, but he was shocked to see the dramatic change in her and honesty stifled any thoughts of insincerity. He also knew full well that Maude would see through any platitudes he trotted out.

'Father Bob, good to see you,' she replied. 'I'd like to introduce you to my grandson, Robert Melton, an about to be reformed, runaway, renegade Church of England vicar, from a parish in London. He's here on an ecclesiastical espionage mission to see what he can learn from we Catholics to take back to his parish when he returns there shortly,' she said, giving him an impish grin.

'Maude you've always had the ability to surprise, even sometimes startle people, but that's quite a lot of different information for me to process all in one go. I think you lost me when you said your grandson ... unless I misunderstood?'

'No, you didn't, Father Bob. But that's a long story that neither of us has time for right now. Perhaps you would come over to the house sometime next week, as I'd like to tell you all about it. I'd rather you heard it directly from me than Robert and, as you know, I may not have much time left.'

'I'll call you later today. That's a promise,' the priest said.

'Now then,' he continued, extending his hand and turning to Robert with a broad smile. 'Anyone of good intention is always welcome. But whoever you are and whatever you're here for, any friend or, better yet, relative of Maude's is always especially welcome.'

With that it was time for them to go in and take their places.

As was normal on most Sundays, the little church was filling up fast. By the time the Mass began the church was full with people of all ages. Some came with young families, others as couples, some alone. It looked to Robert like a good healthy cross-section of the local parish community. He knew many a priest in England and Australia who would be envious of this tangible evidence of success in God's ministry in this small, out of the way parish.

When the time came for the distribution of Holy Communion, Robert had intended to stay quietly in his place out of respect for the teachings of the Catholic Church. However, Maude whispered, 'Robert, I know what the rules are, but just this once I would so love it if my grandson were to take Communion alongside his old grandmother.' It was unnecessary to add that there might not be another occasion to do so.

'Will Father Goodlow mind? I don't want to compromise or embarrass him,' Robert whispered back urgently.

'Not in the least, I assure you. He knows the difference between the real core of Christian belief and doctrinal hair splitting,' was Maude's pragmatic response.

When it was Robert's turn to receive Communion at the altar rail, Father Goodlow's expression of concentration didn't waver as he gave the Communion host to Robert. It was only the slightest hint of a wink that told Robert they were completely at one in a conspiracy to recognise this sharing in the love of Christ amongst all sincerely practising Christian believers.

Robert knew enough about the discipline of the Catholic Church to realise that Father Bob Goodlow had gone out on a limb in giving him Communion. Were the diocesan bishop to become aware that he had knowingly given Communion to a non-Catholic, and especially to an Anglican vicar, it would almost certainly have resulted in an official reprimand.

What Robert did not know was that Father Bob had already assessed the situation with Maude, and guessed how much it would mean to her. He felt certain the bishop, whom he knew well, would have agreed to let this one go on compassionate grounds. The danger for both of them always lay in a pedantic parishioner making an official complaint to the bishop in writing.

Over the years both Father Bob and the bishop had come wearily to recognise that in every parish, every congregation of any denomination, there was always someone who took it upon themselves to be vociferous and fastidious in their strict adherence to the rules, regardless of any extenuating circumstances – the modern-day Pharisee who loved to draw attention to any doctrinal misdemeanour, to which they could triumphantly point in hypocritical outrage.

Later that afternoon, Father Bob Goodlow kept his word and telephoned Maude to arrange to go and see her. They settled on Tuesday afternoon at three o'clock. This gave Robert the perfect opportunity to arrange the hike with Mary to the top of Mount Kearsarge.

Robert had wanted to stay with his grandmother until Father Goodlow arrived, but Maude would have none of it. 'You're wasting the best part of the day,' she protested. 'Stop fussing about me so much. Go and get Mary. I'll be fine. It's almost two o'clock already and if I know anything about Father Bob it's that he'll be punctual and, more than likely, even a few minutes early.'

So, just after two Robert was at the inn to collect Mary. He was surprised and pleased to find her ready and waiting for him. He guessed Maude might have called to let her know he was on his way.

When Father Goodlow arrived at Maude's house at just before three he found the front door standing open. He knew it was the customary local invitation for him to let himself in.

Calling her name to let her know he had arrived, he walked through the house. She was nowhere to be seen, so he ventured out into the garden on the lake side. There he saw her sitting back in one of the two white Adirondack chairs down at the water's edge. At first he thought she might be asleep so he approached quietly until he inadvertently stepped on a small stick, snapping it loudly.

'There you are Father Bob,' Maude said, half turning towards him. 'I'm sorry. I've been deep in thought and I didn't hear you arrive. But don't give up your day job as a priest, you'd make a terrible Indian tracker!

'Forgive me for not hoisting myself out of the chair to welcome you, but take a seat yourself,' she said, indicating the other chair next to hers. The truth was she knew she was losing her strength rapidly now and the effort of getting herself up from the comfortable semi-reclining position in which the Adirondack chair was holding her would have taken too much out of her.

'Thank you for coming. It's time for you and me to have a chat,' she said. 'I don't really go in for formal confession, so I hope just sitting here together, with me telling you what I need to tell you will count, if I promise to be completely open with you and keep nothing back?'

Father Bob smiled and gently patted the back of Maude's frail hand, resting palm down on the broad arm of her chair. 'Don't worry, Maude. That's a fine way to make a confession as far as I'm concerned. And when have you ever been anything but truthful? You must be the most truthful, trusted and honest person around here.'

'But I've hardly been a model of regular church-going propriety have I? Besides, as you well know, I'll as happily attend the Episcopal Church as the Catholic Church on any given Sunday. There's a reason behind that of course. Which I'm about to tell you.'

It was well over an hour later by the time Maude had finished telling Father Bob all about her early life. Her time in England. The fellow student with whom she had been madly in love and who had been killed in the war. The son she bore and gave up for adoption. How she had discovered the existence of her grandson.

The fate of the lottery ticket. How it had brought her grandson to her. And how, as a result, she felt she had been instrumental in saving her grandson from himself and the seductive clutches of Mammon.

'I said earlier I would explain to you my interest in the Episcopal Church, which I must tell you I hold in equal respect to the Catholic Church.

'Well, Jack Talbot, the man – I suppose boy would be more accurate – I was so madly in love with, came from a staunchly Anglican family just as I come from a staunchly Catholic one. We would have long, often spirited, discussions together about the virtues and vices of both faiths, me always defending Catholicism and he Anglicanism. With the certainty of youth, neither of us would give any ground. He loved me as much as I loved him, I'm sure of it, and had the war not interrupted I'm certain we would have got married after finishing university.

'However, it was not to be. I think he felt trapped once I had decided against an abortion and expressed my determination to have the baby and put it up for adoption. As I said, he was really only a boy at the time. Had he come back from the war, I'm certain our love for each other would have overcome all these problems and eventually we would have been married. Until the arrival of the baby, he'd always said that's what he wanted more than anything else. I often think his willingness, even eagerness, to enlist at the outset of the war had a lot to do with my pregnancy and determination to give birth to our child.

'Anyway, after getting the news of his death I was inconsolable, the worst of it being I had no one to turn to in my grief. After a couple of weeks, during which time I had seriously considered the possibility of suicide, just to escape the completely intolerable pain and despair I was feeling …

'I told you I was going to be ruthlessly honest with you in this confession Father Bob, didn't I?' Maude interrupted herself.

'… I happened to be driving past the Episcopal Church here in New London one day, and on the spur of the moment I pulled into the parking lot. For a while I just sat there in the car feeling uncomfortable and out of place. Then the door of the church opened and I saw the priest at that time coming out to look up at the sky, as if he was checking the weather. As he turned to go back in he caught sight of me and smiled such a warm smile of welcome I decided to go in.

'The church was empty and at that point there was no sign of the priest I'd just seen either. So I sat quietly at the back and allowed myself to think about Jack. After a bit it was as if I heard him laughing, not at me, but with me, at the whole silly argument about the differences between the denominations to which we had both given our implacable allegiances, more out of cultural upbringing than from any independent thought. Suddenly it just all seemed so pointlessly divisive. The longer I sat there, the closer I felt to Jack and I discovered my despair and suicidal thoughts giving way, not to happiness exactly, but to a sort of calm acceptance.

'Eventually, after what must have been almost an hour, as I was leaving the church I ran into the priest I'd seen earlier. He showed no surprise at finding me there and all he said was he hoped I'd found what I'd come looking for. After that I never looked back and became as comfortable with the Episcopal Church as I have remained with the Catholic Church.'

As a priest of a certain age Father Bob Goodlow had heard many confessions and many life stories, but what he had now heard from Maude still had the power to move him in a way that no longer seemed to happen very often. Sitting next to this good, kind, wise woman, now frail and elderly, ravaged by cancer and probably in the last days of her life, he was deeply moved by all that she had just told him. But for the circumstances and social conventions of the time, everything in her life would, in all probability, have turned out so very differently for Maude Kimball.

In his mind he railed against the outdated, judgemental mores that could be so ruinous to people's lives, especially to women's lives. He knew only too well how widely respected and loved Maude Kimball was in the New London and wider community, yet he knew that, even today, there would be some who would censure her if they knew Robert was her illegitimate grandson – and especially so if they also knew she was the original winner of the largest Powerball jackpot ever. Envy was a very strong corrosive force. Not for the first time Bob Goodlow was glad of the absolute secrecy of the Confessional he had solemnly sworn to uphold.

'Well Maude, as confessions go, I would have to say yours was one of the most dramatic and soul-baring I've ever heard. It was also the longest.' Maude smiled and gave a small chuckle.

'I can't give you any penance as you've already endured a lifetime of that. All I can do in my capacity as a priest is absolve you, in the name of Christ Jesus, of any of your perceived wrongdoings. Even though I do so with little conviction that what you did even qualifies as wrongdoing in the eyes of the good Lord.

'So, if you will bow your head and ask God for His understanding and forgiveness of these and any other sins of your life, I will grant you His absolution.'

That done, they both took a moment to sit back with their thoughts as they looked out over the lake, in the direction of the sun which was already beginning to tilt towards the west this late on in the summer.

'Father Bob, thank you for giving me and my grandson Communion together on Sunday,' Maude told him. 'It meant a lot to me and was something I really appreciated.'

'I know that Maude, which is why I didn't hesitate. After what you've just told me, I'm so very glad I did.'

'There's something else I wanted to ask you today,' Maude continued. 'Robert has agreed to officiate at my funeral but, maybe it's because my Catholicism is so deeply rooted in my subconscious, I wanted to ask you if you could and would conduct the service with him?'

'I'd be honoured to Maude, although for me too it will be with very mixed emotions – as I am sure you understand. You know we priests are not exempted or protected from our own emotions. I'm sure, if someone wanted to, they could make mischief for me for agreeing to officiate with Robert acting as an equal, but that's a risk I'm more than prepared to take. I know the bishop would only pay lip service to any reprimand if forced into a position where he had no choice but to give me one.

'Will you give us any guidelines over your wishes for the service, or are you happy for me and Robert to work out the details between us?'

'I've left an envelope on my desk setting out the few wishes I have. But I'm happy to leave the planning of the service and choice of hymns to both of you. Lots of good hymns though, please. I've always loved hymns. Oh, and try to make it cheerful too will you? Happy memories, with lots of love and laughter is how I'd like it to be.'

Father Bob grinned, before saying, 'Typical of you Maude, to leave a tantalising hint of mystery behind in an envelope!'

41

AT ITS START the fairly well-worn trail up the north side of Mount Kearsarge had seemed unremarkable as a challenge. Robert felt a little self-conscious in his brand new walking boots, when deck shoes or even, at a pinch, flip-flops would, he felt, have been equal to the task. Especially as the trail they had chosen was marked as 'more difficult' and, at almost three miles, was the longest.

This feeling did not last long, though. Soon the trail became much steeper, rougher and narrower. Quietly Robert conceded to himself that his Anglo-Australian prejudice against what he thought of as American softness and love of specialist, protective kit for even the simplest of physical challenges was wrong again.

Up to that point, Mary had been content to walk behind, letting him lead the way and, out of a sense of chivalry, Robert had set off at a modest pace, confident Mary would have no difficulty in keeping up. She didn't. Climbing steadily, she chatted all the while about the times she had come up here as a child, and later as a teenager to smoke cigarettes with her friends.

But with the trail getting steeper and rougher, Robert began to find the effort of talking and maintaining even the modest pace he had set harder and harder. Soon he was breathing heavily. Mary seemed to be having no such trouble and Robert was relieved to be able to take advantage of an excuse to stop for a short rest at a point where the trail levelled out, briefly offering a panoramic view back over the treetops back towards New London and Wilmot. It was a magnificent vista that aptly demonstrated the extraordinary extent to which the state was forested. Until you saw a view like this, it was hard to comprehend that ninety per cent of New Hampshire was covered with trees.

When they set off again, without giving him the option, Mary took the lead, telling Robert, 'As the local girl I'll go ahead and point out all the landmarks we come across.'

Whether deliberately or not Robert wasn't sure, but Mary set a pace that was considerably faster than the one he had set for her. Determined to keep up, he soon found that, without sounding completely out of breath, he was less and less able to continue chatting in the same way they had done before. Mary continued to demonstrate no such difficulty.

From his position, with Mary up in front of him, Robert could not help but notice and appreciate her small, shapely butt, emphasised by the snug-fitting jeans she was now wearing, as opposed to her more usual denim skirt.

As they were close enough to the same age, Robert realised that this was an active demonstration of something he'd read about and long suspected might be true. It was the difference between someone who is trained 'gym fit', as he was, and someone who is 'active fit' as a result of their daily lives.

Mary's stamina, flat belly and firm, shapely body, were due to years of a continuously active lifestyle and well-balanced, home-cooked meals. His was down to the restorative effect of rigorous one-hour training sessions, four times a week, with a personal trainer in the corporate gym on the penultimate floor of the Bicknor Wilmot Building, designed to compensate for the excesses of too much rich food and fine wine in some of the world's best restaurants – plus, of course, a hectic schedule of travel with its attendant disruption to sleep.

By the time they reached the summit, coming out above the tree line onto vast, bare, windswept slabs of granite, Robert was breathing hard and found himself unable to talk in anything but the most halting manner.

He was also uncomfortably conscious of the fact he was drenched in sweat.

By contrast, Mary appeared completely untested by the ascent and showed no sign of this having been any kind of undue exertion for her.

'I guess I'm not as fit as I thought I was,' Robert conceded with a sheepish grin after he had recovered his breath.

'Well, I'm sure it's just different when you're more used to walking the streets of Manhattan. I've been doing this sort of thing all my life,' Mary said kindly.

'Mary, you're never despondent or negative about anything are you? Do you ever get depressed?'

'Of course I am. And, yes I do.'

'What do you do when you're down … to snap yourself out of it … to cheer yourself up?'

'Oh, that's easy. I go out and find someone to help. It's surprising but true. Helping someone else, even in quite small ways, always makes you – the helper – feel better. Fortunately there is never any shortage of people in need of help!'

Both of them smiled.

They were sitting down now at the foot of the fire tower lookout post that was securely anchored with long steel cables to the very highest point of the granite outcrop. The tower was unmanned today, signifying that the risk of forest fire was not considered extreme, probably due to the lack of any wind rather than the conditions, which remained dry. Forest fires were a constant danger during the summer months. Every mountain above a certain height had a fire lookout tower that could be manned at short notice by a member of the Forest Service.

As he got his breath back, Robert had time to look around. The 360-degree view was breathtaking. The ocean of trees, stretching to the horizon in every direction, was awe-inspiring, broken only by bodies of water, glinting with the reflection of the weakening rays of the afternoon sun. These marked the different lakes and ponds nestled in this mountainous part of the state.

'It must be incredible to come up here in the fall,' he said.

'Yes, it is. Although I've not been up here in a long while, I try never to miss going up some local mountain in the fall. It's part of why I can't ever imagine being able to live anywhere else.'

Robert's heart sank a little, but her comment also spurred him on. 'Mary, there's something I want to talk to you about on that point.' He had decided he had now to face the question that, in a different time and place, he would so much rather have delayed, to give himself and Mary more time to become better acquainted.

'Very sadly, I don't think Maude has much time left to her,' he began, noting as he said so the look of intense sadness immediately begin to cloud Mary's normally sunny features. This was one subject she desperately did not want to face up to. 'She's asked me to officiate at her funeral. Ideally she wants me to do so with Father Goodlow, if he's willing and able to agree to that. She's going to ask him this afternoon.'

'Of course he will,' Mary cut in. 'He's that sort of man. He doesn't need the Vatican to lay down the law when it comes to knowing God – and what He wants.'

'Good. Anyway, coming straight to the point; after the funeral I intend to return to London just as soon as possible, hopefully to resume my post as the vicar of St Mungo's Church. Because of this shortage of time and the fact that, although we're still youthful, neither of us is exactly young any more, I wanted to ask you if you would consider becoming my wife?'

To his surprise Mary's face betrayed no shock and no indication of her emotions as she sat staring past him way out into the far distance.

'Please don't say anything yet until I've finished what I wanted to say,' he continued. 'I know that by any conventional standards we hardly know each other, but I know my own feelings and I've never, ever, felt this way about anyone else on earth before. In trusting my own instincts and the whole serendipity of how we've come to meet, it's a risk I'm willing ... no, wanting, to take, if you feel the same way and are willing to take it with me?

'When I arrived in New Hampshire I had everything in the world to offer you materially and would, I suppose, have been what is crudely called a "good catch" by most people's standards. Now I've got very little to offer you by way of material security or comfort, beyond the humble living of a Church of England vicar. But in terms of security in my love for you, I think I have everything to offer.'

For what seemed to Robert like a very long time, Mary did not move or say anything, but continued to stare silently off into the distance. When she did finally speak, she did so looking directly at him.

'When you first arrived in New Hampshire, you interested me only in an academic sort of way. I was curious to see what a seriously rich person was actually like. If I'm being honest, I suppose I was, subconsciously at least, predisposed not to like you, but I was determined to keep an open mind and to treat you no differently from the way I would anyone else.'

'I think that may have been the moment I started to like you,' Robert interrupted with a shy smile.

'Anyway, to my surprise you weren't at all as I'd expected. Yes, you were a little petulant and spoiled at the very beginning, but you soon seemed to change – and after meeting Maude you changed completely. It's hard to describe, but it's as if you changed from the person you were pretending to be into the person you really are.

'That's so rare, you know. Most people never do. They spend so long making themselves into someone they are not, but think the world will be impressed by or approve of, that in the end they forget entirely who they once really were. And, deep down, still are, if they could only find their way back. Mostly they never can. I think your grandmother saved you. You owe her a lot.'

'I know I do. More than anyone could ever imagine.'

'Somewhere along the way during your short time here, I suppose I started to have the same feelings towards you, Robert, that you say you have towards me. I think it may have begun as soon as the time you mangled the gears on my old truck. When you drove off that afternoon with my poor old Dodge, lurching along in giant kangaroo hops, I smiled to myself as I imagined you being so much more used to being whisked silently and smoothly along in the back of luxurious limousines, or at the wheel of a Rolls-Royce.

'I actually felt sorry for you, but at the same time I found qualities in you that I'd never expected to find. I knew I liked what I saw. Not many people in your position, with your sort of money, would ever have dreamed of borrowing my untidy, dirty old work truck, when you could so easily have afforded to have a car and driver sent up from Boston.'

Then Mary hesitated, before saying, 'I suppose you're telling me that if I was to agree to marry you, I'd have to be prepared to move to London?'

'Well, yes ... sort of anyway. Perhaps not immediately. That wouldn't really be fair or practical for you. And it wouldn't be forever. Once I've fulfilled what I originally set out to do in revitalising and re-establishing a relevance and new direction for St Mungo's – if that need is still there – to the point where it can be handed on to someone else, I have a feeling I'd like to come back to the States. But this time to serve the interests of God rather than Mammon. Perhaps adapting some of the skills and lessons I've learned from serving the latter over the past eight years to better serving the former in future. Finally, when it comes to retiring, I can think of nowhere in the world I'd rather settle down than right here, with you, in New Hampshire.'

Mary was again silent for a while. She seemed to be considering what Robert had just said. Eventually all she said was, 'I never thought I'd be tested like this.'

'What do you mean? Tested like what?' Robert sounded alarmed.

'My life was comfortable, settled, content, even mostly happy. I'd got past the point of needing a man, or so I thought. I love my neighbours and this community, who are anyway mostly all my friends. I even love my old inn most of the time. I like the people.

'It's the sense of place and purpose I have here. I was born and raised here. I love the seasons, the smells, the winter snow, swimming naked in the cool, crystal clear lakes in summer. Emerging, dripping wet, to lie on the hot, sun-baked granite. And perhaps, most of all, the magnificence of the autumn colours in fall. It's become my family. It's my home. I have very, very deep roots here.

'I didn't believe anything or anyone could tempt me away from here and all this. And now you've come along.'

'I know. But I'm not sorry,' Robert said gently before falling silent. There was nothing more he could say, but inside he was daring to hope.

'If I say yes, I'll be following the instincts of my heart and I would do so in the belief that, in the short time you've been here, this place has worked its magic on you too and we will one day return, together ... for ever.'

'That's a promise, Mary,' Robert said solemnly, looking her straight in the eye. 'Anyway, I have to come back over to the States sometime soon. I've given Maude my word that Cynthia and I will visit Savannah for her and raise a glass of champagne to her memory. You'll have to come with us.'

At this Mary smiled for the first time since they had sat down. 'How typical of Maude,' she said. 'Yes, I know she'd developed this interest in Savannah ever since befriending that nun, Sister Lucy, when she was up here on a visit. She'd really wanted to go herself but it's too late now, isn't it?' Her voice trailed off on the back of this rhetorical question, expressed without any hope.

Seeing the sadness return to Mary's eyes, Robert tried to distract her thoughts. 'Did you meet Sister Lucy? What's she like?'

Mary, unconsciously putting her head on one side, looked thoughtful for a moment before she said simply, 'She is like love ought to be.'

After that they sat for a few minutes in silence together, each lost in their own thoughts, staring out towards the late afternoon sun, low in the sky. The few stunted trees, bravely determined to grow at the highest point possible on the upside of the tree line, were casting boastfully long shadows. Knowing how quickly the light would soon begin to fade, it was Mary who said it was time to go, getting to her feet and holding out her hand.

Robert took it as he stood up. Briefly Mary's fingers closed tightly round his, before she let go to lead them back down the trail.

Not long into the descent, Robert noticed a lone, silver birch tree, out of place at this height, barely managing to cling to survival in the thin soil. Its bark was peeling in small tight curls, probably as a result of the dry conditions.

Robert put out an arm to stop Mary. Without saying a word, he carefully pulled a narrow strip of the tightly curled silver bark from its trunk. It formed a small perfect circle in his hand. Then, turning towards Mary and dropping on one knee he took her left hand in both of his. Now gently coaxing the silver circle around her ring finger, he formally asked her if she would marry him.

Mary stroked the top of his head with her right hand and, with tears filling her eyes, she slowly nodded her assent before saying 'Yes' in a scarcely audible whisper.

42

THE SLEEK, SHINY black Cadillac stretch limousine with darkened windows looked incongruous parked next to Mary's old, dented, muddy brown Chevrolet sedan in the parking lot of the New London Inn. All its windows were closed, giving the impression that the chauffeur was anxious not to breathe the New Hampshire air and had no intention of leaving his hermetically sealed environment. He looked bored and disdainful of the humble inn outside which he was being required to linger.

Robert pulled up alongside in Mary's old pick-up. Curious, he smiled at the chauffer but was unfazed when this friendly gesture was ignored. At this moment he was, he thought, the happiest man in the world as he opened the front door to the inn.

He could sense something was wrong the moment he walked in.

Mary was standing next to Jen behind the reception desk and looked up when Robert entered. But there was no smile of welcome – just a nod to acknowledge his arrival, before Mary abruptly turned away and headed into the kitchen. The door swung firmly shut behind her.

'There's a lady here, asking to see you, Mr Melton,' Jen told Robert, who was looking bewildered and worried. 'She's very beautiful and sophisticated,' Jen added involuntarily. This was the type of film-star woman Jen had only ever encountered in the pages of glossy, high-society magazines: the type of woman she secretly held in awe.

Robert's confusion drained away with the colour in his face.

'She's waiting for you in the lounge,' Jen said.

Opening the door, Robert took in the sight of Vanessa stretched languidly on the sofa over by the big French windows. She was alone in the room, idly flicking through a thin copy of *New Hampshire Life*, looking mildly amused at its contents. The sun shining onto where she was sitting caused the large diamond ring she was wearing to sparkle brilliantly as she looked up to see Robert entering the room.

Vanessa nonchalantly tossed the magazine onto the sofa beside her, sat back and stretched out her long, gym-toned legs. Robert could not help noticing that the top button of her Gloria Vanderbilt jeans was undone.

Anger and panic rose inside him. Panic, he could accept; but he knew he had no right to feel anger. Vanessa's cool reminder from the last time they had spoken – that he could not pretend he had not had his fun – was suddenly pounding in his head like a migraine. Now the consequence of his stupid, reckless self-indulgence was staring him in the face, threatening to obliterate the prospect of happiness and peace of mind that had been eluding him for so long.

'Hello, Robert. You don't seem very pleased to see me when I've come all this way specially to see you. Are you cross with me? Are you thinking you need to punish me?' she said expectantly, throwing her head back to expose her long, evenly tanned neck, while letting her legs slide open just a little in a gesture of submission.

'What on earth are you doing here, Vanessa?' he asked, ignoring her last remark. Deliberately choosing not to sit down and trying to keep his voice steady, he continued, 'Surely you're not thinking we can start again? Because we can't. That's over. Finished – period. You were the one who said you wanted to end it and move on. Well, surprise, surprise, so do I. And the very last thing I want to do now is to go back to satisfying your secret fantasies.'

'Oh, don't worry, Robert. I'm not really that serious about it,' Vanessa said, sitting up and straightening herself out. 'Actually I've come up to this outlandish, hillbilly backwater to tell you something – and to thank you.

'Ivan and I are in Boston for a couple of nights at the Four Seasons. He's in meetings all day and then we're the guests of honour at a gala dinner tonight at the Ritz Carlton; Ivan's being recognised for his generous philanthropy to the Museum of Modern Art.

'It was just on the long, tedious drive, I had too much time to start thinking about the way we used to enjoy each other's company. I suppose I thought it might be fun to have one last fling.'

Robert tried to close his mind to what she was saying. 'Listen Vanessa, I'm not going to waste time explaining it all to you, but my whole life has changed completely. I'm a different person and I realise now that's the person I've been wanting to be for years.'

'Well, I can see your style of dress has taken a new direction,' Vanessa said, studying Robert coolly.

He ignored the jibe and carried on. 'I'm giving up being a financier. In fact I'm in the process of liquidating all my assets, so that all the proceeds can be put into a charitable trust. I'm shortly going back to London, where I intend to resume being a priest – hopefully, back in the parish I deserted eight years ago.'

On hearing this Vanessa dropped her guard. While she sat taking in what Robert was telling her, he found the composure to add, 'I'm also newly engaged to Mary, whom I gather you may have met: the remarkable lady who owns and runs this inn.'

Vanessa was now looking at him thoughtfully. 'Well, that is quite a change, isn't it? And do we have your friend … no, I'm sorry … I mean your fiancée, Mary, to thank for the jeans and open-necked check shirt look? I must say they do show off your rugged physique more appealingly than your Manhattan suits ever did.'

'Stop it, Vanessa,' Robert interrupted. 'You said you'd come to tell me something. Well, please tell me and then leave, before you do more damage than you may already have done by coming up here.'

Vanessa smiled enigmatically. Robert knew she was playing with him and he also knew there was nothing he could do to stop her.

'So, what is it?' he snapped.

'OK, Robert. I'll come right out with it. I'm pregnant and you're the father. I'm not quite such a hussy that I left open the top button of my jeans just to get you excited!'

Robert was speechless, his throat dry as the awful implications of this news sank in. 'Are you sure?' was all he could say.

Vanessa smiled wryly. 'By that I assume you don't mean to patronise me by asking if I'm sure about being pregnant. But rather whether you are the father? Well, yes. I am sure.

'As I said at the beginning, I came up here to tell you something and to thank you. You see, the great sadness in Ivan's life was my inability to bear him children – he'd always wanted a son and a daughter. But when nothing happened after a few years, it was tacitly assumed that I was infertile. Ivan's ego couldn't have borne the problem being his, but I always had my suspicions. Anyway, it was better for my marriage not to question that assumption.

'Then you came along. There was never anyone else. So, you can see I'm now going to give Ivan the child he so desperately wanted. What he doesn't yet know is that he's going to have twins – a boy and a girl if we're lucky.'

Robert sat down, trying to process everything he had just been told. His immediate thought was that these children would be bastards.

But Vanessa interrupted his thoughts, as though she was reading his mind. 'That's why I also came to thank you, Robert. Ivan thinks they're his, of course. He's deliriously happy that at last there's proof of his masculine prowess. And I don't ever intend to let him know otherwise.

'It's curious, you know. We'd finally gotten around to talking about adoption.

But now, thanks to your parting gift, you've made an otherwise childless couple happy and fulfilled.'

She leant towards him, resting her elbows on her knees and her chin on her slim-fingered hands. 'Just as I was certain I could trust you with my special secret – but it would be wrong to say we didn't indulge it together – I want you to know that you can trust me completely with what I now know will always be this secret shame of yours.

'I don't need, or want, anything from you. Which from what you've told me is probably just as well,' she added sardonically. 'A dirt-poor, Church of England vicar is hardly a good bet for child support payments.'

Then Robert detected an edge to her voice when she told him, 'Don't think I couldn't have considered a quiet abortion. If Ivan knew you were the father, he would have insisted on it, before almost certainly filing for divorce. If Ivan were ever to find out what I have done, these children – our children – will be put up for adoption. I'm not equipped to manage them on my own in penury.'

She gave him a cold, hard smile. 'So you see, Robert, what you have done, if for all the wrong reasons, is bring life and happiness to what will soon be a complete family unit. It's that – and your silence – that I want to thank you for.'

In his turmoil, Robert thought he could hear Maude's practical advice telling him not to be so concerned with clearing his own conscience that, in doing so, he might wreak something catastrophic that would result in the babies being given up for adoption, perhaps even being parted from each other in the process.

His wise and wonderful grandmother had lived long enough and through enough to know that life was often messy, but that through it all what mattered most was love. With Vanessa and Ivan, whatever their faults, Robert knew that these twins would be loved and want for nothing. No matter what price he might have to pay, he could not deprive them of that.

Robert's silence eventually prompted Vanessa to speak again.

'Thanks to you, Ivan and I will now have the one element that was missing in our arrangement … our marriage, I mean: the perfect nuclear family unit he always wanted,' she said cynically.

Had he been in any mood to do so Robert might even have smiled at this Freudian slip.

'I will continue to be the expensively dressed, glamorous trophy wife, dutifully at Ivan's side. The consummate society hostess and all-round asset in his business dealings. In return for which I will retain free access to limitless wealth, an assured social position and the thoroughly pampered, luxury lifestyle I've grown accustomed to enjoying.

'I know you will never divulge the affair that we had and, more especially, my particular preferences, that you so expertly catered – perhaps I should say ministered – to, if I can put it in a way I know you will understand.' She raised a perfectly sculpted eyebrow to reinforce her point.

'I suppose a psychiatrist would say it was a throwback from the sense of utter worthlessness I had in my own insecure, poverty-stricken childhood down in Georgia. Who cares? You gave me something Ivan never can – and I don't just mean the twins.

'But, I now want your assurance that you will never, ever, lay claim to, or at any time try to make contact with the children I'm carrying. Also you must never divulge your role, your connection to them, to anyone. The children will be Waverleys and nothing else. I insist on this – for their good of course. When I leave here shortly we will never see or acknowledge each other again. Do I have your agreement and your word on this?'

Robert was looking closely at Vanessa. She gave every impression of being the one in control, able to dictate terms; but he could see she was worried. He admired her chutzpah. On the face of it, she had more to lose than he did. It was her threat to put the children up for adoption if he didn't comply that gave her the upper hand. This was a trump card and she knew it.

And now fate had just given her another ally. Without his money or position, and in his desire to return to the priesthood, the revelation of bastard twins, born as a result of a frenzied, sadomasochistic affair with a woman married to his biggest rival, would not play well in any religious denomination. Vanessa knew she was safe. He had no choice but to agree.

When he spoke Robert was very clear. 'All right, Vanessa, as I don't seem to have much choice, I will agree to your terms, with one exception. There are three other people who must know. Mary, whom I can't deceive. Now that I know, it would be unthinkable to still expect her to marry me without my telling her I am to be the father of twins with you.'

'Oh Robert, how sickeningly pious and noble you've suddenly become … it's so bourgeois of you … quite unlike my pragmatic and robust approach towards Ivan. It must be the effect of this intolerable rural wholesomeness,' Vanessa interjected scornfully, waving a slender, bejewelled hand towards the window.

Ignoring her, Robert continued, 'My grandmother – who will probably be the only one to understand – and will anyway very shortly take the secret with her to the grave. And Cynthia, my long-time PA, friend and confidante, who knows and accepts me with all my many faults; her loyalty to me and her discretion are absolute.'

Vanessa smiled, trying to hide the amusement she felt at all this. No fight back from the great, fearsome Robert Melton, Master of the Universe, determined and ruthless in getting his own way, always the one in control?

She had not expected this easy capitulation on his part. The transformation from the Robert Melton she had known – and worshipped – in New York was remarkable. It was almost disappointing.

However, Vanessa could not help now experiencing what felt very like jealousy towards the woman whom she was sure must be behind this extraordinary change in him. The feeling was exacerbated by her patronising view that Mary, unfashionable, bucolic innkeeper that she was, was no worthy opponent.

'Well Robert. What a surprise. You know, as I left the barely sophisticated environment of Boston to come all the way up here, I nearly turned round. I kept asking myself, why bother? Had I known it was your intention to relinquish your wealth and forsake your current way of life to return to being a poor pastor in London, I wouldn't have come. I could have saved myself the journey. You'd never have found out, so there would have been no need to tell you.'

The word 'pastor' had been carefully selected from her arsenal of terms to be used derogatorily, now delivered with such derision its intention was unmistakable.

'I was concerned back in New York that you might well have begun to suspect something at some point. Why I was able to terminate our exciting affair so abruptly, for example? And, in the future – what if either of the children were to look like you? I couldn't take that chance without first having your agreement to silence and, if ever necessary, unequivocal denial.

'Thank you, by the way, for not insulting me by asking if it was an accident. Naturally I wanted Ivan and myself to have the best possible genes for our children, physically and intellectually. It was Cambridge University where you graduated, wasn't it? We wouldn't want there to be any doubts about that, in the light of – how shall I put it? – recently surprising and frankly, to me, incomprehensible revelations. It's a shame really that you will never know your children.'

'I suppose I should be flattered,' Robert answered, 'But you make it sound as if you've cleverly managed to cheat me out of my stud fees. And all the time I thought I was the one in control,' he ended bitterly.

Vanessa smiled without any warmth and continued, 'So, was it a wasted trip up into this awful, uninhabitable place where – I paraphrase some English wit – even the birds brazenly fly about uncooked? No, it's been worth it just to see with my own eyes the unbelievable transformation of the esteemed Robert Melton. To see you standing there in jeans and an open-necked check shirt looking … well … almost like a cowboy.

'So, if you must tell that bandana-wearing hayseed you're engaged to, fine. We don't, and never will, move in the same circles. I hope you'll be ...'

She had been about to wish Robert happiness but he cut her off. 'Vanessa, I'd like you to leave now. You've said what you came to say and you've got what you came to get.' Robert could barely contain his anger as he stood up and moved to open the door.

Vanessa uncoiled herself from the sofa and, without hurrying, made her way out to the reception area, where Jen now pretended to be very busy with the reservations book.

At that moment the door from the kitchen swung open and Mary walked through, flushed from the heat of the stoves, sleeves rolled up.

Vanessa appraised her knowingly and gave Mary a cold smile of self-satisfaction. 'I've just been congratulating Robert on his engagement,' she said disdainfully.

At the entrance door she turned. 'Well, goodbye Robert,' and then looking again at Mary, added, 'I hope you'll both be very, very happy.' With that she was gone.

Seeing her emerge from the inn, the limousine driver jumped out to hold open the rear door. He was eager to leave this place and head back to Boston.

The last sight Robert had of Vanessa was from behind. Her tall, slender figure accentuated by the skin-tight jeans. With the limousine door shut, Vanessa was hidden from view behind its darkened windows. The absurdly long car pulled out onto Main Street, its grateful driver relieved to be pointing it back towards Boston.

Robert turned to face Mary. He hardly knew how or where to begin, but he knew he must tell her everything right away. 'Can we go into the lounge Mary? There's something I need to tell you,' he added unnecessarily. 'Jen, please will you see to it we're left undisturbed? Thanks.'

Jen nodded solemnly, overcome with a premonition of concern for them both as she watched Mary walk uncomfortably into the lounge, Robert holding the door open for her.

In the back of the limousine, Vanessa was struggling with her emotions in a way she had not since she was a teenager.

In the end, her meeting with Robert had been brief and perfunctory. She had been chastened, however, that her allure had diminished so rapidly in his eyes. Diminished, or been substituted? In the privacy of the blacked-out limo, that stung her more than she might have expected.

Robert's passion for this latter-day Annie Oakley was just about understandable, but what Vanessa found almost impossible to reconcile was his extraordinary decision about his business future. She didn't know whether to laud this or laugh out loud. She could not help but admire Robert's self control, his altruism – even eagerness – to give up his entire fortune and with it his power, position, lifestyle and influence, to return to being a humble priest in some backwater of London.

It was the pure conviction, determination and sheer strength of character she had glimpsed in him that was so unnervingly attractive.

For a moment she could almost imagine throwing away everything in her own superficial, sybaritic world just to follow him, to be with him wherever he went – content to have nothing except the security of the certain, steadfast love of this strong, self-assured man. Vanessa had never come close to experiencing the concept of goodness as so powerfully alluring before.

The feeling had frightened her badly. Even now, irrationally, she was still unsettled. Why else was she so jealous of that cowgirl Robert was engaged to?

Vanessa retrieved a pair of oversized dark glasses from her handbag. Putting them on, she forced herself to thoughts of Ivan. How happy he was going to be with her at the news of the twins – now due in just over six months. And then there was the enormous, elegant De Beers diamond ring, with matching necklace, she'd seen at Tiffany's that she knew he would buy her in celebration. She made a mental note to go in as soon as they returned to Manhattan tomorrow and ask them to discreetly put it on hold for her.

She thought about the fabulous Park Avenue triplex apartment, like a baronial castle in the sky, sitting atop one of the most exclusive buildings in the city. The private jet, the spectacular home in Beverly Hills, the enormous mansion in Palm Beach they had just bought and the inaugural party she was planning to throw there to impress all their friends. Perhaps she'd ask Ivan to let her buy the home in Cap Ferrat she had always had a hankering for. She liked the idea of mingling with sophisticated European aristocrats and minor royalty, in the process gaining a little European glamour and chic with which to further impress her friends back home in the States.

Just then the music channel on the limousine radio, which she had set low to suit her mood, began playing Peter Sarstedt. Vanessa caught her breath at the familiar words of the song, 'Where do you go to my lovely?' and stifled an involuntary sob.

Despite hurriedly brushing her cheek as she thrust herself miserably back into the soft leather seat, one hot tear escaped from behind her theatrical dark glasses to roll unchecked down to the left corner of her trembling top lip.

She switched off the radio hurriedly and, in a determined attempt to pull herself together, clicked on the intercom. 'Can't you go a little faster?' she asked the driver imperiously. 'I'm going to be late for a dinner and I have to have time to dress.' She suddenly wanted to put as much distance as possible, as soon as possible, between her and the 'what might have been' in her life.

The driver of the Four Seasons limousine was only too happy to oblige. The quicker he left the boondocks behind and returned to the familiarity of Boston the better. Even Boston did not satisfy his aspirations. He was hoping soon for a promotion to become one of the fleet of drivers at the Four Seasons hotel in Manhattan.

43

MARY WALKED ACROSS to the sofa where Vanessa had been sitting, plumped up the cushions and picked up the copy of *New Hampshire Life*, which lay casually discarded in one corner.

'Don't you want to sit down?' Robert asked tentatively.

Ignoring him, Mary studied the cover of *New Hampshire Life* and then went to return it to its place on the sofa table where it belonged. 'Are you sure things have really ended between you and that woman?' she asked. 'Only, if a woman as attractive as that hires a chauffeur-driven limo and drives all the way up here to see you again, she has to have a reason, doesn't she?'

Robert was not expecting this and answered without thinking. 'Vanessa and her husband are staying in Boston for a couple of days. I guess the limo comes with the suite.'

'Her husband?' Mary asked. 'So this … this ice maiden, is actually married, is she? How many other surprises are you going to spring on me in one day, Robert?'

'She and Ivan don't have a proper marriage. They stay together because it's convenient – it suits them both,' he responded distractedly.

Then, before she could say anything, and not knowing what else to do or say, Robert decided now was the time to make a full confession.

Without excuses, he told Mary everything about Vanessa and how he had had no idea she was carrying his children until today. By way of explanation he said, 'I was always looking for escape from my own demons, my guilty conscience and, at first, with Vanessa I found I could forget.'

'And you say it wasn't love?' Mary asked, desperately wanting to believe him.

'No it wasn't, Mary. Please hear me out, I beg you, because now, with you, I'm fortunate enough to know what real love is.'

Admitting to the enjoyment he got out of forcing Vanessa into complete submission, he tried to explain. 'Vanessa needed me to do these things for her … no, that's not right. Do these things *to* her, I mean. She had these darkly hidden cravings, urges, fantasies, whatever you want to call them. She wanted someone – a man she could trust absolutely – to take power over her. To bend her forcefully to his will.'

'Are you trying to tell me that the woman who was here just now is a masochist?' Mary asked incredulously. 'Seemed more likely to be the sadist type from what little I saw of her,' she added.

'That's exactly what I'm saying. The trouble was I got to enjoy it. I got to like the power thrill it gave me. However, after a while, as with any drug, in order to get the same thrill, things started to escalate dangerously. It was like a narcotic. I knew it had to stop, but by then I was so addicted I was powerless to end it.'

For all her confusion, disappointment and the private turmoil raging in the back of her mind, Mary had to admit Robert had been admirably, if brutally, honest. He could have skipped this, she thought. He could have passed over it, leaving her none the wiser. But he had wanted her to know everything, regardless of the possible consequences. She had to give him credit for that. Also, was there, perhaps, something in the fact that even Vanessa recognised in Robert a man she could trust with her innermost secrets?

'I see now why you said it wouldn't be easy telling me this,' she acknowledged.

Robert sighed. 'I had no idea I was capable of being like that,' he told her. 'It shocked me and, in the end, sickened me as much as it turned me on. It was a low point for me and I felt deeply ashamed of myself. So you see it's not just my fame and fortune I now want to – and must – put behind me in returning to my vocation as a priest. I hope you can understand and believe that.'

'I'm not sure what I understand or believe any more,' Mary replied. 'But I do think I need to sit down. Maybe you should too. You look terrible.'

So much of her wanted to stand by her man, to appreciate his honesty and be able to reassure him that nothing had changed. But another part of her was, at that moment, very afraid. It was not yet too late to pull back to a safety she knew well, a comfortable, reliable safety she was familiar with and liked. Could she now really take the risk of giving up everything she trusted here in New Hampshire to go with this man she knew so little about to another country on a different continent?

Robert watched her pull the birch bark ring from her pocket, drawing it open and letting it spring back into a curl. 'As you know Robert, even before this bombshell exploded, the idea of giving up everything I've ever known and loved all my life, to marry a man I've known for barely a few weeks, was always a really difficult decision for me. To now take the risk that you are the man I believed – and still want desperately to believe – you to be, and give up everything to move with you to London, is an even bigger one.'

'I know it is Mary. Don't think I don't appreciate that. It's the reason why – the moment I knew myself – I wanted to tell you about Vanessa and the fact that she is now going to have my children. There aren't any more skeletons in my cupboard, I promise,' he finished with a wan smile.

After a long silence that Robert judged best not to interrupt, Mary said, 'Robert, I can't pretend that I'm not hurt – even a little angry – at your deviant, loveless dalliance with this unfortunate woman. I just find it so hard to understand and reconcile with the man I thought I was getting to know well enough to want to marry.

'But, if I'm being as honest with myself – and with you – as you have been with me, my overriding emotion is one of intense jealousy.'

At this point Mary paused, as if unsure of whether to go on or not. Looking at him now she seemed to be re-evaluating Robert. 'You see I also have a skeleton, or rather a confession to make ...' Mary's voice trailed off in misery.

'Go on,' Robert said, trying to sound encouraging. 'There's nothing you can have to tell me that I don't deserve, or that would change my love for you in any way. I can't imagine how you can be jealous of Vanessa when, compared to you, she is as nothing in my life.'

'I wish I could be certain of that,' Mary said wistfully. 'I knew I had to tell you this before we got married anyway, but I just wanted to enjoy being engaged to you, at least for a few days, before I faced up to it. I see now that was wrong of me. You see, the reason I'm so jealous of Vanessa is that she is going to have your babies and not me. Robert, I'm afraid that is the one thing I can't give you – I'm unable to have children.'

Mary's misery and shame in telling Robert this was matched only by a cold, irrational fear of how he would take this devastating revelation.

'When you said yesterday you wanted to marry me, I was so happy. But I was also terrified. I was so scared you wouldn't want me when you found out that I'm flawed. Imperfect. Unable to do the one natural thing that God put women on earth to do ...' Mary's voice trailed off into a fearful silence again as she scrutinised Robert's crestfallen face for his honest reaction to what she knew would be a devastating blow.

Only because he was frantically processing what Mary had just told him, Robert hesitated fractionally too long before holding out his arms to embrace her.

Mary registered his delay and mistakenly read it as a sign of his disappointment, his doubt maybe. She had dreaded this moment for so long that now she had confessed her secret her thoughts became focused on survival, on protecting herself from the inevitable, unbearable hurt she knew must follow.

She pushed away his arms and quickly said, 'It's no use, Robert. I think it's best for you to go back to London without me. My heart breaks telling you this, but I know in the end it will be for the best – for both of us. I've made up my mind and I'm adamant about it, so please don't make matters worse by prolonging this discussion.

'From a practical point of view, right now the biggest difficulty will be in deciding when and how to tell Maude. She'll be devastated.'

Robert clenched his fists in silent despair. In the space of less than twenty-four hours his world had been turned upside down. The joy he had felt yesterday on the summit of Mount Kearsarge seemed like a lost horizon that he was seeking forlornly from a pit of deeper despondency than he had ever known.

But he knew he did not deserve any better. He had only himself to blame. It would have been naive not to anticipate, even expect, his past reckless, decadent lifestyle not to catch up with him at some point.

'I'll tell Maude,' he said hoarsely. 'She deserves to hear it from me.'

At the door he lingered and then asked, 'Is there anything – anything – I can do, Mary, to change your mind?'

Not able to turn and face him from the window she was fixedly staring out of, Mary's only response to this was a slow, sorrowful shake of her dark hair.

Robert left the room quietly. Passing through the reception area, he deliberately did not look over at Jen as he left the inn for what he realised wretchedly would likely be the last time.

Mary did not move. She let the tears fall freely as she watched Robert drive away in her old red truck, in the direction of Maude's house. It was only when Jen put her skinny, sun-kissed, arms tightly around her from behind, and silently laid her corn-coloured head on Mary's back, that she felt strong enough to move again.

Only Jen, nature's child, could be so sweet, so in tune with her feelings and so understanding to know that words were useless.

44

ROBERT FOUND HIS grandmother out in the garden. Maude could tell right away from his expression that something was wrong, but it was the aura of deep melancholy surrounding his whole being that worried her most.

She watched him approaching across the lawn before calmly saying, 'I'm just going in to make us both what would be a welcome cup of tea to enjoy out here in the sun. Sit down while I do that. I won't be long.'

With that she went inside. Robert sat down, happy to do as he was told for once. His mind was all over the place and he was glad to have a few minutes to collect his thoughts before his grandmother returned.

It wasn't long before Maude was back with a pot of Lapsang Souchong, the delicately fragrant aroma of which did indeed hint at how welcome it was going to be. Sitting herself next to him she quietly waited for her grandson to speak.

When he did, it was with a heavy heart that Robert told his grandmother everything that had happened over the last three hours to change him from being the happiest person alive to the most despondent he'd ever felt in his life.

Maude listened attentively to everything Robert told her. He had originally thought to tell her only about his affair with Vanessa and that she was pregnant with his children as a result, but now he was in the reassuring presence of this wise, tolerant woman who, as his grandmother, was also all he could count in the world as his family, he knew he wanted to tell her everything. The whole unalloyed truth, however damaging it might be to her image of him.

By the time Robert had finished the sun was low on the western horizon.

Maude now glanced obviously at her watch and said, 'Heavens, look at the time. I'm famished and you must be starving. Let's go and get something to eat.' With that she got up and went briskly towards the house.

Robert was surprised. Having just opened up his heart to his grandmother and confessed what he regarded as his gravest sins, he was uncertain what to make of this reaction. He sat alone for a few moments, and then rose to follow in a bit of a daze.

In the kitchen, he found Maude busying herself cutting slices of freshly baked, whole wheat bread. Thin cuts for herself, thicker for her grandson. Then looking in the cupboard above the old Glenwood range, she said without turning around, 'I'm afraid it's going to have to be a tuna melt and salad again, unless you'd rather have the remains of the egg mayonnaise left over from yesterday?'

'Honestly, I'm not very hungry, so I'd be happy just to finish up the egg mayonnaise.'

'Good, while I'm fixing that I'd like you to open a bottle of wine. I think you could use a drink – I know I could and any damage it does to my health at this point is irrelevant,' Maude said, handing Robert a bottle of Sterling Vineyards Chardonnay from the fridge with a kindly smile.

It was only when they were seated at the kitchen table that Maude finally addressed her grandson's confession to her.

'It seems to me, Robert, that for a very bright man you can be excessively stupid at times – and I'm not talking about what you got up to in bed when I say this. Clearly you and Mary both still love each other very much. Equally clearly Mary has, quite understandably, had a big shock at the unexpected arrival of what sounds like a bit of an apparition from New York, announcing that she is shortly going to be giving birth to your twins. Hardly the same as the announcement of the virgin birth is it?' Maude said, looking wryly at her grandson.

'At the moment Mary can't see beyond the fear and uncertainty this change to the situation puts her in. But it is the fear and uncertainty, combined with her own feelings of inadequacy and insecurity, that are the problems, not whether or not she still loves you, or you her. That is her greatest fear – whether your feelings for her will change after what she has had to tell you.'

Maude's hand trembled slightly as she lifted her glass to her lips and sipped the pale yellow wine.

'Poor Mary. My poor, poor Mary. What a cruel, lonely secret to have to carry all these years.'

'You didn't know, then? About her not being able to have children?'

'Not a clue,' Maude answered, carefully placing her glass back on the scrubbed, weathered surface of the table. 'And I know about keeping this kind of secret. It's funny, isn't it? There was me, unable to share with anyone – except God, of course – that I had a child. And here is Mary, in precisely the same situation, but for the completely opposite reason.

'I don't blame her one bit for sending you packing and deciding to hang on to the security she knows and loves here in New Hampshire, rather than cast herself adrift with a man she hasn't yet had time enough to get to know properly. A man who she now finds, contrary to everything she has thus far imagined him to be, has been fathering children with a married woman, while at the same time indulging her penchant for masochistic sex. Set against this record, the fact that you have decided to return willingly to the servitude of the good Lord, would now do little to dispel those fears and anxieties.'

Robert drained his wine glass in a single swig. 'You don't mince your words, do you, Maude?'

'I never have – and I certainly won't when I don't know how many I have left.'

She refilled her grandson's glass. Robert tried to take the bottle from her wobbling fingers, but she shooed away his hand.

'My view is that you and Mary need some time. Time to decide what is really important to both of you and time for her to get a sense of perspective in looking back over your dubious past and forward to your, hopefully, more promising future.

'You need time too, Robert. You shouldn't easily dismiss Mary's condition. I know modern medicine can do marvels for infertile couples and I know that adopting children is so very different to … well, let's say it's better these days. But if you are lucky enough for Mary to still want to marry you after all this, you will both be entering into a marriage when you know that making a family together will present particular problems.'

Maude took a long sip from her glass, which made her cough. She dabbed her lips with her napkin. 'But you mustn't let these problems stand in the way of being happy together. You know about me and your grandfather, Jack Talbot, and you've read my letters to John Radcliffe, so you understand that aching pain when you are parted from the people you love.

'This isn't going to be easy Robert and, frankly, you don't deserve it to be. I'm not sure, but sadly I fear it is possible you may really have lost Mary over this. I know that when she makes up her mind about something it is nearly impossible to get her to change it. But that doesn't mean you shouldn't try.

'Now, if you're expecting me to comment one way or another about your dubious sexual exploits down in New York, I'm sorry to disappoint you but I'm not very interested. I'm reminded of Sally, a wonderful old, gravel-voiced, Bourbon-drinking, cigar-smoking character, sadly now long dead, who, when approached one day by the town gossip with the exciting news that someone's wife had been caught in bed with someone else's wife, famously responded in her laconic drawl, "Brad, the closer and closer I get to the tomb, the less and less I care about who is sleeping with whom."

'At this moment, I think the best thing you can do is get right away for a day or two. There's no point in you moping about here and, besides, it'll clear your head and help you to think straight again. I shan't be telling Mary where you are, because she needs the space to see her life in perspective once again.'

'So, where do you suggest I go?' Robert asked, emotionally drained and content to be guided by anyone with a grip on the situation.

'I'm not going say anything, because I don't want to tell even the whitest lie to Mary when she asks where you have gone – which I know she will. All I will tell her is that you will be telephoning me at noon the day after tomorrow. We have to pray that gives enough time for everyone to sort themselves out and get a grip on the future instead of being transfixed by the rather depressing past and present.

'What I will say, Robert, is stay well clear of Boston and Manhattan. Beyond that take care and God speed. I think you are going to be needing Him to watch over you and guide you more in the next few days than you have at any time in your life.

'And if you should find yourself short of immediate cash, you'll find five hundred-dollar bills rolled up in the little jug where I kept the lottery ticket. Take them, they were going to be yours soon anyway.'

Robert protested, 'I can't take your money, Maude.'

'Don't be silly,' she answered. 'It's our money and I wouldn't have mentioned it if I didn't expect you make use of it. I think I understand enough about the law to know that once you've given away all your money, as you have done, you can't get it back again.

'On the other hand, I think it might be tactful if you took my car on this occasion and left Mary's truck here.'

She could see Robert was about to object and cut him off before he could speak. 'I won't be needing the car now,' she told him, reaching for the keys hanging on the old iron nail driven into a beam. 'I don't want to be the cause of an accident and shorten even further my appointed time, do I? Besides, in extremis, I can probably drive Mary's old pick-up better than you – I was brought up driving farm trucks.'

'Maybe you're right,' Robert conceded, smiling at this.

'On this occasion, I think I am,' Maude replied. 'You get right away. Get out of the state altogether, I suggest. Explore somewhere new. You'll find distance gives you perspective.'

Robert smiled at this. 'Distance gives perspective. Very eloquent, Maude.'

'It may have been half a century ago, but I did graduate in English,' she reminded him with gentle self-mockery.

'Now, you go and pack a bag and get on the road until it's time for that telephone call.'

'What will you be doing in the meantime?' Robert asked.

'Leave that to me. I can't decide whether I really helped my grandson or not when I left him that lottery ticket eight years ago. This time I'm going to do my utmost to do what I can.'

Robert knew he shouldn't push it, but he felt compelled to ask, 'Are you going to speak to Mary?'

Maude heard the anxiety in his voice and saw the fear in his eyes. 'If she will talk to me, of course I am,' she told him gently.

'Off you go now, get your things from upstairs and leave your old grandmother to get on with what needs to be done.'

Robert gave her a hug and kissed her on the cheek. A few minutes later as he was on his way out of the door, Maude called out, 'Remember the message your phantom parishioner, Brenda, left you in London.'

Robert looked back questioningly.

'From Julian of Norwich: "All shall be well and all manner of things shall be well."'

Robert gave a wan smile of recollection.

'It worked the last time,' Maude told him. 'God moves in a mysterious way, Robert. You of all people should understand that.'

45

ROBERT HAD FOLLOWED Maude's advice. He had driven away in her car heading vaguely northwards and in time had been swallowed by the night as the car headlights picked out place names and road signs against the dark forest backcloth shrouding him on either side.

Some time around one in the morning he had pulled off the road and had sunk into an exhausted sleep, squeezed on the back seat. It was not comfortable and Robert didn't want it to be. If his mind was in torment, his body might as well be too, he reasoned. But all he achieved was waking up from a fitful doze, cold and stiff at a little before five o'clock. The world was just beginning to stir with the arrival of the morning sun.

He found his night-time meandering had delivered him to the northern edge of New Hampshire's White Mountains. Memories of his hike up Mount Kearsarge with Mary made this the last place he wanted to be. He needed to be somewhere totally different, somewhere as far from associations with New London as he could get. He caught echoes of his childhood and teenage years in Australia, echoes of his time aboard *Lucky Find*, and Robert knew he needed the sea.

After a few false turns, and a stop to fill the tank and grab a coffee and a bagel in Gilead, Robert had found his way to the interstate that led him towards Bangor, beyond which lay the rugged coastline of Maine that he had admired in one of Maude's books.

Having reached the sea, he was drawn to surround himself with as much of it as he could and he had driven south to Deer Isle until he arrived at the small fishing harbour of Stonington where the road ended and he could go no further.

It was mid-afternoon when Robert had switched off the engine and clambered stiff-legged from the driver's seat. The sunshine was warm and the air soft on his skin. But it was the reassuring smell of the ocean that had confirmed he had made the right decision as he stretched, breathed in deeply and leant against the harbour rail watching lobster-fishing boats swinging lazily on their moorings.

Stonington carried the same carefree atmosphere as Robert had gone in search of somewhere to stay. He had settled for a small bed and breakfast overlooking the water.

And that was where he had remained, holed up for that day and the next, not once getting back into Maude's car, preferring instead to walk the trails that led around the wooded promontories or sit on the shoreline gazing out across the water to the wooded islands dotted around. This was one of the loveliest seascapes that Robert had seen in a long time – fresh and unspoilt, he thought. But those two words whipped his mind back to Mary: fresh and unspoilt. What a fool he had been. What a weak-minded, weak-willed fool.

He had been tempted to ask for God's guidance and help out loud, but Robert had felt too ashamed. 'Over to you, Lord,' he had whispered uncertainly, hoping now, rather than trusting in His mercy.

46

IT WAS MID-MORNING the day after Robert had left when Maude called the offices of Bicknor Wilmot Securities Inc in New York. A pleasant voice, infused with a suitably professional expression of competence, answered the phone after only two rings.

'This is Maude Kimball, may I speak to Cynthia White please?'

'Just a moment,' came the efficient response.

After a short pause and a click on the line Maude heard Cynthia's voice, a note of concern in it.

'Hello Maude. What a nice surprise to hear from you. Is everything all right up there in magicland?' Cynthia enquired.

With the compression of her remaining time, Maude had learned to eliminate conventional social pleasantries by way of introduction.

'No Cynthia it's not,' she answered bluntly. 'Frankly only a death, and I don't mean mine, could be worse.'

With that Maude gave Cynthia a summary of everything that had transpired between Robert and Mary. She concluded by saying, 'Cynthia, I don't normally waste time worrying, but now I'm very worried that the man you and I both love in different ways and the young woman I have long loved as a daughter, may be about to throw away their chance of future happiness together. Something that, from my own bitter experience, I can say they will both regret for the rest of their lives if this situation isn't salvaged.'

It was Cynthia's turn to be practical. Before Maude had even finished speaking she had been automatically checking her diary.

'Listen Maude,' Cynthia said. 'What you've told me is potentially bad enough, but above all of that is my concern for you right now. You said you're worried – worried enough to call me down here in New York. This is no time for you to be worrying and certainly not alone. I'll be with you in New Hampshire late this afternoon. I'll stay at the inn. Please don't tell Robert I'm coming.'

'I won't, and … thank you, Cynthia.'

Cynthia could hear the relief and gratitude in Maude's voice, already weakening from the emotional worry and the effort of talking for so long.

'I'll be at the inn tonight, and I'll try and talk to Mary. I'll leave it to you to try and knock some sense into that clever financial brain sitting between your grandson's ears. So I probably won't see you before the morning. In the meantime please try not to worry. If anyone can sort this situation out it will be two wise women with some worldly experience of life's messiness.' With that Cynthia had rung off.

Reassured, Maude went to make herself a cup of tea, grateful to Cynthia for being so responsive and so willing to get immediately involved. There was no point in going for a rest. She knew she would never be able to sleep. She would take her tea down to the lakeside instead and just try to let the surroundings relax her, as they so often had in the past.

In New York Cynthia had no sooner finished talking to Maude than she picked up the phone again – this time to Mike. Even before finishing her conversation with Maude she had made an executive decision to commandeer the Bicknor Wilmot Gulfstream for one last flight. There would be no other way of getting up to New London tonight in time to talk to Mary – and time was of the essence if she was going to ease Maude's anxieties.

Mike had been delighted. He had shown and flown the plane earlier in the day to an executive from General Electric who was considering it for the expanding fleet of GE executive aircraft. The guy from GE had been very impressed and had left agreeing to buy it – but technically it was not sold yet.

Cynthia arrived unannounced at the inn at just past six o'clock. Jen, recognising her at once, seemed very pleased to see her and was delighted to be able to offer her a room for the night.

After checking in, Cynthia asked Jen if Mary was around. Guessing the connection between Cynthia's sudden and unexpected reappearance in New London and what had transpired between Robert and Mary, Jen replied conspiratorially that Mary was in the kitchen where, distracted as she was by her thoughts, she'd only been getting in everyone's way as they were trying to prepare dinner that evening.

Cynthia had an idea. 'Jen, would you fix a table for two in whichever is the quietest corner of the dining room and, if possible, ensure the immediately surrounding tables remain empty? Then let Mary know I've come up from New York to have dinner with her? I'll be down in thirty minutes.'

At seven, when Cynthia came downstairs for what to her would be an early dinner, she found Mary already seated at a table laid for two over in the corner at the back of the dining room.

Fortunately the dining room was not crowded that night. There was a first night performance of *My Fair Lady* at the New London Barn Playhouse and many of those who might otherwise have been dining had gone to see it.

Although profoundly distracted, Mary seemed genuinely pleased to see Cynthia as she approached the table.

'I suppose Robert must have already told you what's happened and that our very short engagement is off?' Mary began miserably as she stood up to shake Cynthia's hand warmly.

'No. I've not spoken to Robert for some days now. Not in fact since he called me so happily to let me know you were engaged. He sounded ecstatic.'

Mary frowned, looking puzzled. 'Then what brings you here now at this late hour of the day?' she asked curiously.

'Maude,' was Cynthia's succinct reply.

'Maude? Is she all right?' Mary asked, the sadness in her face momentarily turning to a look of apprehension.

'I don't know is the answer to that. If you mean is she still dying, well yes, of course, she is. Sadly, as far as I know, nothing's changed there. No, she called me because she's so concerned at the terrible mistake she's convinced you and Robert are both making. She thinks you're jeopardising your whole future happiness together because of what happened yesterday.'

After they had both decided on their food order and were alone again, Cynthia continued. 'Mary, I've known Robert for eight years now, and I've got to understand him pretty well. Beyond wiping his butt, there isn't much I haven't done for him in that time, including covering for some of his more egregious indiscretions when necessary.

'There is no question, he's not always been a saint or even a good boy and, when he hasn't been, I've always let him know it. But do you think I'd have stayed in his employment if I didn't know for a certainty that, deep down, he was a good man?

'Shortly before Maude's letter arrived for him at the office, Robert's personal conduct and behaviour had really gotten out of hand. Bill Temple and I had, reluctantly, come to the conclusion that the Robert we'd known, admired, respected and felt privileged to work for, was perhaps lost to us forever. Bill so much so that he'd already resigned. I wasn't quite ready to give up on him yet, but with great sadness I was preparing myself to do the same, if something didn't make him pull back. I think that must have been the time when he was coming to the end of his relationship with the woman who I gather came here yesterday to tell him she was going to give birth to twins.

'Robert did a pretty good job of keeping that particular assignation a secret from all of us and, even now, I'm not quite sure who it was. Maude was either being discreet or she genuinely couldn't remember the name; all she knew was that Robert had said she was married to one of his rivals in business. Well, there were plenty of those but, if I had to guess, I'd say it was Vanessa Waverley – known to all behind her back as the Ice Queen.'

At this Mary nodded her head. 'Yes, that's what her name was.'

'Well, why am I not surprised? I could tell she had a thing about Robert, almost more a sort of smouldering obsession if you ask me. Anyway, they both did a very good job of keeping it a closely guarded secret, which should have given me a clue, because Robert normally couldn't care less about people knowing who he'd bedded – and not always single women I'm afraid to say.'

Mary smiled wanly at this tartly shared confidence.

'I know it doesn't put Robert in a very good light to tell you this,' Cynthia continued, 'but in all the time I've known him I've never seen any of his conquests or assignations mean anything to him. He was never in love with any of them. At least half of them were paid in cash and the other half in kind – often with expensive jewellery and the taste of an otherwise unattainable lifestyle, which usually involved being feted on board the *Lucky Find*.

'The first and only woman I've seen Robert properly in love with is you. When I met you and saw the effect you had on Robert – before even you knew it – I could tell right away you were made for each other. I was even a little jealous of you Mary, not because Robert and I were, or could ever have been, more than the closest of friends, but because, up until you, Robert needed me.

'It's a nice feeling to be needed, even quite seductive. Anyway, now I'm over my jealousy and I just want you and Robert to be happy together, which is why I came up here to see you tonight, before it's too late – for both of you.'

There was a silence before Mary responded.

'People don't really ever change though, do they? We'd like to think they're going to, or at least be capable of it; perhaps they even mean to, but after a while they always seem to revert to type,' Mary said despondently.

Appetising though it looked, both women were playing with the food on the plates in front of them. Cynthia was not very hungry; dinner for her in Manhattan was usually never before eight-thirty and frequently not until well after nine. Mary was simply too wretched to care about food or eating.

'You're absolutely right about that,' Cynthia responded, 'And that's my point. Robert *has* reverted to type. To the caring priest he was before he got seduced and intoxicated by a way of life that was essentially alien to him and completely out of character.'

For the first time since they'd started talking, Mary looked as if Cynthia might have a point worth considering. A way of looking at the situation she'd not herself thought of before. With it came the faintest look of someone daring to have a glimmer of hope that maybe all was not lost after all.

Noticing this, Cynthia felt a private surge of relief that just maybe her trip up to New London was not going to turn out to be a failure and a waste of effort.

Just then the door opened and Maude walked in. She was moving slowly and looked strained. Cynthia was dismayed to see the rapid deterioration in Maude's health, even in only the short while since they'd said what they'd both thought would be a final goodbye this side of heaven. Mary was surprised to see Maude out at this late hour at all.

'Cynthia, thank you so much for coming so quickly,' Maude said, as Mary hastened to pull up another chair for her to join them. 'I called and Jen told me you'd arrived and where I'd find you both. And, as I don't know how much, or how little, time I might have left, I've none to waste, so I decided to come up at once.' Maude said this unsentimentally as a statement of practical fact.

Turning now to face Mary, Maude began. 'Mary, before you give up on Robert, I want to tell you that in giving up on Robert's father – my only child whose real name I didn't even know – I made the worst mistake of my life. A mistake that was to rob me forever of any chance of real happiness. Now, from the perspective of an older and perhaps wiser woman, in the very last glimmer of her life, I look back and see what an awful misjudgement I made and what a tragic waste it all was. I now want desperately to try to stop history repeating itself.

'The two people I love most in all this troubled old world are you and Robert. Please, please, for both your sakes, don't now give up on Robert, as I did on his father. What he's done and the life he's been leading over the past eight years may be reprehensible and indefensible, but for that too I am responsible.

'Yet, without that winning lottery ticket, Robert would never have come into your life or mine, so I make no apology for it. The little peace of mind and lasting happiness I've been lucky enough to enjoy in the very last furlong of my journey here on earth has been in the finding of my grandson – the real person – and in seeing the blossoming of the purest love he has for you, the daughter I never had – and, I believe, the deepening love you have for him, Mary. Don't now throw it all away because of mindless errors in his past – because that is what I am sure they were – or in the mistaken belief you can't trust Robert. You can – this I know.'

With that Maude sat back, worn out. She had spoken, almost pleaded, with such concern and passion that the effort had exhausted her, despite the deliberate economy of words. However, she had said as much in the detail of what had to be left unsaid as what was said.

Mary and Cynthia sat in silence, neither woman trusting themselves to speak.

Putting a protective hand on Maude's frail arm, Mary could feel the trembling. When she did speak it was through her tears.

'Oh Maude, I don't know what to say. I no longer know how I'm feeling, or what I think. My mind is in turmoil. I need time to think things through for myself.'

'All right, but speaking selfishly, I don't have much time, so let me ask you just one question. Do you still love Robert?'

Mary's answer to this when it came was in a whisper, 'Yes, yes Maude I do – more than I can say. But I had to tell Robert something yesterday that I think may have made him change his feelings about me.'

'It hasn't,' Maude replied gently. 'I told Robert that you and he would be starting life together knowing that creating your family – however that turns out to be – would now require patience and understanding on both sides. But without you, Robert could never have the family I know will make him happy for the rest of his life. Please don't deny yourselves that chance. You will have children to raise; I know you will. And I also know you and Robert will love them all the more because of whatever special way God brings them to you. I had that chance a long time ago and not a day has gone by when I haven't regretted not taking it. Don't do that to each other. That's all I'm saying to you.'

Mary gave Maude's arm a squeeze of thanks.

'Robert's gone away somewhere to be by himself, but I asked him to telephone me at mid-day tomorrow,' Maude said.

Mary cleared her throat, 'Please will you ask Robert to come to the old covered bridge at Kimpton Brook, at three o'clock the day after tomorrow?'

'I'll make certain he's there,' was all Maude said.

With that Maude got up to go home, refusing all attempts by Mary, Cynthia and Jen to drive her back. Even in Mary's old pick-up she could manage this short journey and she needed to be alone with her thoughts before she spoke to her grandson again.

Cynthia, left with no other option, retired to bed earlier than she had in years, wondering if this was why people from the country always looked so much healthier than city types.

Mary half-heartedly offered to stay and help Jen shut the inn down for the night, but Jen insisted she went home. Giving Jen a grateful smile, Mary acquiesced without argument for once. She too wanted time and space alone to think things through at the end of what had been a long and emotionally tumultuous two days.

Robert telephoned his grandmother from Stonington the next day, as they had arranged. Maude gave him Mary's message and directions to find the rendezvous the following afternoon.

'I'll make a start this afternoon,' Robert replied in answer to the news.

But Maude cautioned him not to be over-eager. 'You've put that poor girl through an emotional wringer. If you take my advice, you'll treat this delicately now, not like one of your business deals, Robert.'

'Trust me, Maude, I wouldn't risk doing anything else,' Robert reassured her.

A little before three the next afternoon he pulled up at the old covered bridge that straddled Kimpton Brook at Potter Place. There was no other car and no sign of Mary. The day was hot and his mouth felt dry from the anxiety of not wanting to get this wrong.

Growing increasingly anxious and despondent when there was still no sign of Mary at ten minutes after three, Robert got out of the car and walked over to the bridge.

It was a fine example of one of the old covered bridges still to be found throughout New Hampshire, Vermont and Maine. This particular bridge was no longer in use for vehicular traffic of any kind, but the worn grooves in the thick boards were a reminder of the old steel-banded wagon and buggy wheels that would once have regularly traversed it.

Robert's eyes gradually adjusted from the strong sunlight to the cool shade enclosed within its solid wooden sides and allowed him to focus as he looked down the full length of the bridge. His heart leapt. There, clearly silhouetted against the bright sunlight at the far end, stood a figure quietly watching him.

'Mary?' he called out, but any reply was carried away by the noise of the rushing water underneath.

Resisting a sudden childish urge to run to her, he strode towards the light where he knew it was Mary waiting for him. His footsteps echoed loudly in his ears as he urgently paced the heavy, uneven boards.

On reaching Mary he stopped. Standing still, his eyes searching hers, he waited for her to speak. For a while they remained like this, neither of them saying anything, letting their eyes communicate far more eloquently than words.

It was Mary who spoke first. 'Robert, if I come with you to London you must promise me that if ever the twins … need you in the future, for any unforeseen reason whatsoever, we … you … will be there for them and, should the need ever arise, we will welcome them into our home so that it becomes their home too.'

Feeling relief and happiness flooding over him at this reference to 'our' home, Robert knew he had the answer he had been so desperately hoping for.

It was an hour or so later, with the tension of their separation not yet fully dispelled, while sitting together on a large flat rock in the middle of the brook, their legs stretched out in front of them, dangling their feet side by side in the cool, clear mountain water, that Robert asked Mary what had made her change her mind.

'Maude and Cynthia,' was Mary's direct, succinct and surprising response.

'Cynthia?' Robert asked incredulously. 'How did she know? I hadn't told her.'

'Yes, well Maude called her and she flew up to New London right away, there and then. She stayed at the inn two nights ago. She and Maude made me see things differently and I'm so glad now they did.

'You're not to be angry with Cynthia, but she used your plane – although, technically, I suppose it's not yours anymore. Anyway, there was no other way she could have gotten here so easily.

'She said to tell you that if you're going to be cross with her for doing that, fine, but you're not to blame Mike and you can deduct it from the bonus you owe her for the years of cleaning up after your more badly conducted affairs.'

Mary said this with an uncertain, fragile smile. It was her first smile in two days. 'No more affairs, Robert. Badly conducted or otherwise,' Mary now added in mock severity.

'No. None. Never again,' Robert hastened to reassure her, before continuing. 'I owe Cynthia and Maude a debt of gratitude I don't think I can ever repay. It's so typical and understanding of Cynthia to have done that and then disappear as quickly and quietly as she came. I must call to thank her when I get back to Maude's house.

'But Maude? I don't quite understand. After I told her everything that had happened, she advised me to give it … give you … time before trying to say or do anything. Only now I find she's gone straight to see you … and with Cynthia.'

Mary looked at Robert as if he was a dolt. 'Men,' she said rolling her eyes heavenwards. 'You don't and never will understand a woman's mind. Maude knew that because I'd said I didn't want to see you, you were likely to be more of a liability than any help in finding a resolution, if one was to be found.

'Under normal circumstances her advice to you would have been quite right. I felt I did need time but because Maude wanted to help, she couldn't take the risk of giving me that time. It's the one thing she doesn't have much of any longer.

'Robert, she really did change the way I see things. She made me look at them differently. That's how I know now I must always be there for you.

'You certainly do owe a lot to those two wise women who, in their different ways, love and understand you in all your faults. And now I owe them my gratitude too, for not losing my chance of happiness with you.'

Later, as Robert and Mary arrived back together, Maude felt immense relief as she said a silent prayer of thanks to God.

In spite of her fatigue, she had not slept well the previous two nights and now felt suddenly tired, more tired than she'd ever felt before. The emotional strain and responsibility of the past few days had taken its toll on her already much diminished reserves of energy. She'd go to bed early that night, she thought.

For the moment though, she was able to relax in the contented knowledge that what she had wished for was finally going to come to fulfilment.

'All shall be well, and all manner of things shall be well,' she repeated quietly.

'Indeed they shall be,' agreed Father Goodlow, whom Maude had invited for tea and moral support.

47

MARY FELT STRANGELY uncomfortable, even awkward, at the prospect of their engagement being made public. It would be a while before she could reconcile the thought of leaving the place she loved to go and live in London with a man whom, after all, she really knew very little about as yet. All she did know at present was the urge to follow the instincts of her heart, wherever that may lead.

The truth was that no man before had ever caught her attention or disturbed her contentment in the way Robert Melton's arrival in New London had. He had also, she now realised, reawakened the spirit of adventure she used to have growing up. Living in London, with Robert, as the wife of an Anglican vicar, would certainly be different. Initially at least it would take her way, way, outside her comfort zone and probably challenge her at every turn. But it might also be very exciting and rewarding. What was troubling her most was how to explain it all to Jen, and what to do about her and the inn.

She had been distracted from these thoughts by the look of pure, ecstatic happiness radiating across Maude's face when she and Father Goodlow were the first to be given the happy news. Maude was transformed. For a moment she no longer looked old or ill. It was almost as if she was a young girl again, clapping her hands in a gesture of unselfconscious, spontaneous, childish delight. Mary was aware, however, that there was no surprise in her delight. It was as if she had been hoping for it, even perhaps planning for it to work out like this.

'You canny old thing Maude,' Mary thought, smiling to herself.

Father Goodlow had noted the lack of surprise in Maude's delight too. But he had also seen something else. Something so imperceptible as to go unnoticed by anyone not finely in tune with such matters.

Before Robert had even finished breaking his news to them, Father Bob had seen Maude lift her face quickly and openly for the briefest of moments towards the sky. Her eyes were closed but the barest, silent movement of her lips betrayed the thanks she was giving to God for this answer to her prayer. It was a gesture Father Bob had seen many times before and one he always admired as a simple, sincere, act of gratitude and faith. How very typical of Maude, though, to be so accepting of the limited time left to her and to fill it with thoughts and prayers for others, he thought.

'Well, many, many congratulations Robert,' said Father Bob, shaking him warmly by the hand. 'Were I ten years younger and if the Church I serve allowed we priests to get married, Mary is exactly the woman I would have set my sights on.' This was said in such a way that all three of them knew he meant it only as the highest of compliments to Mary.

Disentangling herself from Maude's embrace, Mary turned, and simultaneously giving Father Bob a big hug, said, 'Had things been different for you and had Robert not come along, I think I would have been responsive to your approach, regardless of your age, Father Bob. But I'm honoured to think of you as one of my closest and most special of friends, despite the fact I'm not a Roman Catholic.'

'No, but I might have persuaded you to see things differently and correct the error of your ways. You know how we priests love to save lost souls!' he said with a broad wink and a warm smile that made everyone laugh.

Looking fondly at Father Bob, not for the first time Maude thought what a pity it was that such men were prevented from the happiness, companionship and assistance that marriage might afford them in their often difficult and tedious parish work. Although it was admittedly imposed some 600 years ago, the still relatively recent historical basis for the imposition of celibacy in the Catholic Church seemed dubious at best. Why, Maude wondered again, couldn't the Catholic Church make such a matter more vocational by differentiating between those priests pursuing a monastic life and those whose calling was to parish or pastoral work?

'So, when and where do you plan to get married?' asked Father Bob.

Mary and Robert looked at each other questioningly. Neither of them had yet thought that far ahead.

The seed of an idea sprang into Mary's head. 'It will either have to be fairly soon, before Robert returns to London, or it will have to be later on, over in London. As I believe it is customarily the bride's prerogative to choose in such matters, I would like it to be here, sooner rather than later. I know, Father Bob, we cannot ask or expect you to officiate, but as I have no one to give me away, would you be willing to walk me down the aisle of the church and give me to Robert?'

'It would be an honour and I would be delighted,' Father Bob replied. Then, addressing himself to Robert, he said, 'You know Robert, I really ought not to like you. You come flying in here, one of the richest men in America, maybe even in the world, able to have almost anything or anybody you want. Yet you give away all your wealth in order to attract and, worse, carry off the one girl we all want and your money could never have bought you.

'Furthermore, while you're here you monopolise the remaining time of the one woman we all love the most, just by turning out to be her hitherto unknown grandson and, just to really put the boot in, you turn out to be an active member of the competition to me. Yet, despite myself, I can't help liking you. Maybe even admiring you – just a little!'

That got everyone laughing and, not for the first time with Father Bob, Robert was reminded of Andreas.

The unspoken thought going through both Mary's and Robert's minds was would they be able to organise their wedding in time for Maude to be there? Knowing the enormous pleasure it would give her, this now seemed very important.

Maude caught the look they exchanged and said, 'Don't you worry, I'll be there whatever happens. Miss my only grandson's wedding to my surrogate adopted daughter? Not likely. But I suppose you'd better hurry up with it.' Again, she said this as a statement of fact without a shred of self-pity.

After Father Goodlow and Mary had left, Maude and Robert sat down to talk and spend the evening quietly together. The excitement over, Maude was looking grey and hollow-cheeked again.

'Robert I'm tired but I'm thrilled and so happy that my dream and, yes, my prayer, has been answered before I die. Your arriving in New Hampshire has been so completely life changing for many of us and none more so than you. And to think it all started with a lottery ticket bought right here in New London! You couldn't script it in a movie really, could you?

'In a sense it's true what they say about when you throw a pebble into the ocean – that you don't see the effect of the ripples thousands of miles away. Well, the ripples from that lottery ticket have been the catalyst for enormous waves of change. The world really is a mysterious and wonderful place and in some respects I shall be sorry to leave it.

'On that note, I've spoken to Father Bob, who is happy to officiate with you at my funeral. I'd thought to be buried from the church in Wilmot Center, close to where my parents' farm was, but as it's a Congregational church, as opposed to a Catholic church, I think it would be kind not to make things too awkward for him – he is already taking a risk on my behalf. So I'd like to have my funeral service at the Catholic Church in Potter Place where we took Communion together on Sunday. But I want to be buried at the spot I told you about, under the big rock on the hill up above the old farmstead.'

Robert saw a wave of pain momentarily distort his grandmother's wise and gentle face.

'I'm afraid it's getting worse. I don't think the self-administered pain relief will work much longer,' Maude said matter-of-factly when the acuteness of the pain had subsided a little. 'In the morning I'd like you to call the Kearsarge Valley Visiting Nurses for me. It's time, I think, to have regular nursing care. You know we're very lucky, morphine really is a blessing in the management of aggressive pain. And now I think I'll go to bed. I've had quite enough excitement for one day!'

Robert slept soundly all night, awakening later than usual. He went at once to his grandmother's room, but found she was up and gone already. He smiled as he noted how tidy her room was, with even the bed made. He knew his grandmother was determined to cope and maintain her standards for as long as she possibly could. He dressed quickly and went downstairs in search of her.

It was another beautiful late summer morning and already the early morning chill had been dispelled. His grandmother was nowhere to be found in the house so he made tea, then went out into the garden. Maude was sitting in her favourite spot down by the edge of the lake. The air was very still and the surface of the water mirror flat, the early sunlight sparkling as it reflected off the concentric ripples flowing out behind a loon swimming past in search of its breakfast.

'Good morning, grandmother. I've brought you a cup of tea,' he said, placing the steaming cup down on the broad arm of her chair. 'What a beautiful morning. How did you sleep? How are you feeling today?' Robert asked solicitously as he let himself slide back in the Adirondack chair beside her.

Maude turned to greet him, with a look of surprised delight at hearing him address her as 'grandmother' for the first time. 'Oh, Robert, I'm so pleased to see you. Isn't it utterly beautiful,' she said, nodding to indicate the lake and the day itself. 'How sweet of you to bring me a cup of tea.'

She put out a frail hand for him to take gently and hold in his. 'Why do we only finally learn to live in the moment towards the end of our lives? I don't think I've ever felt happier than I do now, at this very moment, sitting here in this beautiful place with you. Knowing you and Mary are to be married is the icing on my very rich cake.

'You know I'm hardly feeling any pain today. I don't think you need bother calling the Kearsarge Valley Visiting Nurses just yet after all. They are such wonderful, wonderful, dedicated people, but they work so hard and have so many other more important cases to be dealing with. Time enough to call upon them only when I really can't manage the pain any more. I even slept very well last night and I'm feeling much restored.'

'Good. Don't worry, I'm here to look after you too and I'll only call the Visiting Nurses when you want me to.'

After that they sat silently side by side, each appreciating the beauty of the day and each lost in their own thoughts.

Robert was thinking about Mary. He could hardly wait to see her again and guiltily couldn't stop himself from wondering when his grandmother might be planning a rest that would free him to go up to New London.

His thoughts were interrupted by Maude saying. 'Would you be a dear and make me another cup of tea? I'm afraid I've let this one get cold.'

'Of course, Maude, I'll be back in a moment,' Robert said, picking up the cup and saucer and hoisting himself from his chair. Maude caught hold of his hand with a grip that surprised Robert by its strength.

'You know, when you came down just now you called me "grandmother". That's the first time you've done that,' she said. 'I've been longing for you to do so, but I didn't want to ask. It makes me feel so much more connected to you, it makes us – you and me – family. The only family I have. Robert, I hope you know how very much I've come to love you and how very, very happy I am that you and Mary are to be married. I'm so proud of you both.'

'Thank you, grandmother,' Robert said deliberately, smiling as he patted the back of Maude's hand, gently lifting it back onto the arm of her chair. 'I'll be back with your tea in a moment.'

Carrying the teacup and saucer in one hand, Robert walked briskly across the lawn and into the house. He put the kettle on and, while waiting for the water to boil, reached for a fresh teabag. Opening the packet he laid it down beside the saucer. As he picked up the teacup to throw away the cold tea he was surprised to discover how hot it was.

He took a sip from the cup. Strange he thought, the tea was not cold at all and normally his grandmother never liked it too hot anyway. Distracted as he had been, he had lost all track of time so he had no real idea of just how long it had been since he had taken the cup of tea out to her. But he realised now that it could not have been very long.

Suddenly Robert had what he could only describe later as a keen sense he was not alone in the kitchen. He looked around but could see no one. Puzzled, he turned back to reach for the kettle when what he took to be a cobweb brushed lightly against his cheek. But there were no cobwebs free floating in the middle of the room. It was then that all his thought processes seemed to accelerate and focus in one clear flash of understanding.

He wanted to run down to the lakeside to where he had left Maude – no, his grandmother – sitting in the early morning sun, but something told him this was not the moment to run. Not to turn a moment of private peace into a panic of pointless activity. Instead he walked quietly over to where Maude was sitting, her head slightly to one side, resting against the high back of the chair. He found himself hoping against hope she had fallen asleep.

As he came up to her, he saw at once she was dead.

Mechanically he tested her vital signs and could detect no trace of life. Part of his training as a priest had been how to determine as accurately as possible if someone was dead or not. Leaning over he kissed her fondly on her forehead then, telling her he would be back in a moment, he walked up to the house. He knew there was one call he must make before all others.

Luckily Father Goodlow was in when Robert called. 'Father Bob, I'm afraid my grandmother … Maude, has just died. Probably no more than five or six minutes ago. I know she wanted you to be told at once so you …'

'I'll be right over to give her the sacrament of the last rites,' Father Goodlow interrupted him, 'And Robert, don't be afraid. Be sad for yourself by all means, but be happy for her. She'll have been spared a lot of pain and I for one am pretty confident Maude will already be with God in heaven. I'll be with you in less than ten minutes.'

Replacing the receiver, Robert was genuinely humbled by Father Bob's straightforward expression of faith and his gentle chiding of one priest to another. He was, he realised, a little rusty in the depth of his priestly relationship with God.

Ten minutes. Robert knew there were other calls he should make. The hospital, Maude's doctor, Chadwick's the undertakers. But there would be time enough for that after Father Bob arrived. He had just ten minutes left to spend with his grandmother alone.

As he approached her, Robert noticed that the loon, which he had seen swimming by earlier, had returned and was now close to the water's edge, barely ten feet from his grandmother's chair. The bird seemed quite happy and showed no fear at being close to a human. Did it somehow know his grandmother could no longer be any kind of threat to it? Did birds and animals know instinctively when humans were dead, he wondered?

Robert sat on a rock on the other side of his grandmother's chair, so as not to disturb the bird. He took her lifeless left hand gently in his and talked softly to her, thanking her and telling her how grateful he was for everything she'd taught him, shown him and done for him. He told her what an inspiration and influence she had been to him in just the short time he had been privileged to know her.

How proud he was of her and how bravely and selflessly she had handled all the difficulties in her own life.

Most of all he thanked her for opening his eyes and helping him to turn his life around from the path of self-indulgent destruction he had been on, to one in which, he now knew, he would work tirelessly to recapture the value and excitement of his original vocation to serve God, by serving his people – in whatever form, shape, creed or colour they came.

His thoughts were disturbed when he heard the door from the kitchen open and close. Looking up he saw Father Bob hurrying across the lawn towards him. He was carrying a small briefcase.

Before letting go of his grandmother's hand to get up and greet Father Bob, Robert silently reaffirmed to his grandmother the esteem in which he held her and how she would, for the rest of his life, be an example and role model for him to try and live up to going forward.

The action of standing frightened the loon, which now slid silently away, swimming out to what it considered a safe distance some thirty feet off-shore, where it remained, as if on self-appointed guard, watching them.

'I let myself into the house, Robert, and when I couldn't find you, I guessed you must be out here on such a beautiful morning. Oh, this is so perfect for Maude,' he continued. 'It's just how she would have wanted to die. Quietly, peacefully, sitting outside in a place she loved deeply, after one of the happiest days of her life yesterday.'

While he was talking Father Bob opened his small briefcase to take out his stole, a broad band of silk cloth nine feet long, which he put around his neck. Next he removed a small silver vial of Holy Chrism, an exotic oil of balsam and olives that had been specially blessed by the diocesan bishop.

When he was ready, he knelt down beside Maude's body and with a nod of his head, invited Robert to do likewise. Although familiar with the procedure from his own theological training, Robert had not been practising in the priesthood for long enough to have had more than a couple of occasions in the past when he himself would have been conducting an anointing of the very sick or recently deceased.

After marking the sign of the cross on Maude's still warm forehead with the holy oil, Father Bob proceeded to say a number of short prayers commending Maude's soul to the care and mercy of an all-loving God. He concluded with the reassuringly familiar words of the Lord's Prayer, in which Robert joined him.

Father Goodlow was removing the stole from around his neck after finishing the brief ceremony when the silence of this perfectly still summer morning was broken by the cry of a lone loon coming loudly from close by. Glancing towards the lake both men clearly saw the bird looking straight at them, at a distance of no more than the same thirty feet from the shore that Robert had earlier observed.

With its mournful cry still echoing across the water, the beautiful bird now unhurriedly dived out of sight while they watched intently to see where the great bird might surface again. When they heard the call again it came from far off and the distant V-shaped ripples breaking the glassy surface of the water seemed to emanate directly from the path of the morning sun, shining brightly across the water. They could no longer see the bird. It was far too bright a light for either man to look directly into.

'Robert, were you with her at the actual moment of death?' asked Father Bob.

'No, well almost I suppose, but not quite.' Robert then told him about Maude sending him in to make her a fresh cup of hot tea and how, when he found that the tea already in the cup was still hot, the realisation and premonition of her presence in the kitchen had hit him.

'How typical of Maude to manage her own precise moment of death so as to be of the least trouble to anyone else,' said Father Bob. 'You know it's not uncommon for some people to do that? They are surrounded by family and loved ones and still they contrive to find a private moment to let go of life at a time and in a way so as to cause the minimum distress to those they love. Others seem to need reassurance and even the permission of loved ones, or those around them, before they can let go. Maude was a woman of great faith and would have needed no such reassurance, let alone permission.

'Funny isn't it, even after almost forty years as a busy priest, every time I see a death, and I've seen many, I still marvel at the almost immediate separation of the spirit, what we would call the immortal soul, from the body. If ever there was compelling visual evidence, if not quite proof, of life after death, it is that moment, when the spirit seems to literally leave the body. Look at Maude's body now. Although in form it still resembles her, she clearly and simply is no longer there in her essence of being as we knew her. It isn't even the peace of sleep to which many like to refer. It is more like a much loved, but now empty, inanimate suitcase. Maude herself has gone, having no further need of her mortal body: her suitcase for the soul.

'The eternal question, over which there is so much disagreement, can only be, gone where? The depressing view of the atheist is there was nothing before and nothing afterwards. In my opinion this view is simplistic and unimaginative in its determination to overlook the clear evidence of life both before birth and after death. After all, life itself, as we know it, is full of mystery all the time if we only look around with open eyes and minds. Oh well, lucky old Maude, with what she now knows, she wouldn't swap places with any one of us left down here on earth!

'Have you called the various agencies and services that will need to be notified?' Father Bob asked, returning to matters of a practical nature.

Once again Robert felt humbled by the sincerity and certainty of Father Bob's faith and had to remind himself that it was OK for even a priest to have doubt sometimes. He remembered Maude's wise words learned from that sermon she'd heard in Grace Cathedral years before – 'Without doubt there could be no faith'.

'No, I wanted to have a few moments with Maude before starting the formal

461

processes. I also wanted you to be able to minister to her in peace and quiet before anyone else got involved. Maude would have wanted that. I'll make the calls now but I was wondering, Father Bob, if you would be able to stay with Maude while I go and fetch Mary? I want to be the one to tell her.'

'Absolutely, I'd like that, in fact, to have a few minutes alone with Maude's mortal remains myself. But while I'm here, why don't I make the calls so you can get off at once to Mary? I know exactly who to call and they will accept my assurance as to the certainty of Maude's death, so we won't get the full, high-speed, siren-wailing, blue and red flashing light treatment that would shatter the peace to no purpose, while advertising the worst to all and sundry.'

'That's a good idea – and a very kind, thoughtful offer. Thank you Father Bob. I'll be back with Mary as soon as possible, hopefully even before any of the appropriate authorities have arrived.'

Father Bob Goodlow sat down in the chair next to Maude's. He too was in no hurry to call the authorities. Like Robert he hoped this short delay would allow Mary time to see and be with Maude for her own private moment of goodbye, before the intrusion of the necessary actions that would soon have to follow.

Also, the truth was, he wanted his own private moment with Maude. Now taking her hand in his just as Robert had, he talked gently to her, telling her things he had long held in his own heart, but would never have been able to tell her in life. He told her how, when they were both younger, despite her being ten years older than him, he had realised he loved her and how, had he been free to, she was the only woman in the world he would ever have wanted to marry. But it was more than that. He had had to pray constantly for the strength to contain his feelings for her, even sometimes going so far as to deliberately avoid her, or any situation in which they might end up being alone. He would not have been able to trust the strength of his own feelings, or his own willpower to overcome the temptation that assailed him to hold her in his arms, if he had allowed her into his private thoughts.

Looking at her now, he so clearly saw that the beautiful person, with whom for years he had been secretly in love, had gone. It was as if the light of her life, and thus his, had gone out.

He found he could regard Maude's lifeless mortal remains with a deep affection and an acute sadness, but not with the love of old. That person simply was no longer there.

'Oh Maude, Maude where are you?' he said aloud to himself as he finally arose to start the business of telephoning. No sooner had he turned towards the house than, as if in reply, he again heard the distinctive cry of the loon.

Looking back he could see nothing except the flat, unbroken calm of the water. The call had come from out of the light mist still lingering over the surface, but now suffused with rays of bright morning sunshine. Somewhere, deep inside, he knew with certainty the call had been for him.

48

ROBERT WAS BREAKING the speed limit by some considerable margin; he wanted to get to Mary as quickly as possible.

Five minutes later Mary's attention was caught by the unmistakable sound of her old pick-up racing into the parking lot and rattling to a screeching halt beside the inn. From her position behind the front desk, where she was going through the week's bookings with Jen, she glanced out of the window that overlooked the entry driveway, a frown of concern forming on her face as Robert came hurrying through the front door.

'Mary, you need to come with me at once. I'll explain to you on the way.'

'You can hold the fort for an hour or two can't you?' he asked Jen, who nodded.

Mary's expression was now clouded with fear: the fear of her own unwillingness to accept the likelihood of the inevitable bad news she knew she would have to hear at some point quite soon.

'Please God not yet,' was her frantic thought as she tried irrationally to stave off the inevitable by saying, 'Just give me a moment to have a quick word with the kitchen about tonight's arrangements.' As if this strict adherence to normality would somehow make any unwelcome news go away.

Robert stepped towards her and taking her arm gently but firmly said, 'No, Mary, you have to come with me now – at once. Jen will look after everything here for you.'

She did not resist as he led her out to the pick-up, its engine still running, ready to go.

Left behind, Jen's unrestrained tears for Maude, for Mary and for her own sense of loss, needed no formal confirmation. She knew exactly what Mary was being taken to face. Although not religious in any formal sense, Jen understood that in the natural world, the most beautiful of plants had to die in order to regenerate and flower again. The thought had always brought her comfort when having to come to terms with a death of any kind.

Although the day was already quite warm, Mary found herself shivering in the passenger seat of the cab sitting next to Robert as he sped along Main Street in the direction of Sutton.

Passing the town hall and police department headquarters the noise and speed of the old pick-up immediately attracted the attention of the officer on duty just as he was stepping out of his patrol cruiser. Chief Gray, or Buckie, as he was affectionately known to most of the local residents, was sure it was Mary's old pick-up he had seen racing past. Although he'd not been able to get a good look at the driver, he was reasonably sure it wasn't Mary herself. He was also quite sure she would not have been driving with such a reckless disregard for the law, or the safety of other road users and pedestrians in New London.

Chief Gray jumped back into the cruiser and, switching on his siren and flashing lights, gave chase. Even so, he didn't catch up with the old pick-up until the far edge of town, after it had crossed the junction with Route 11 by the Four Corners Bar & Grill. Hearing the siren and seeing the flashing lights in his rear-view mirror Robert hadn't wanted to stop, but knew he must. However, before Buckie could get out of his patrol car, Mary had jumped out of the pick-up and run back towards him. 'Buckie … it's Maude,' was all she said.

It was all she had needed to say.

'Follow me,' the policeman yelled to her through the open window, already pulling the cruiser out in front of the pick-up.

Robert grated the gears badly in his haste to get going again. On any other occasion this would have resulted in a suitably sarcastic comment from Mary, springing to the defence of her old, much-loved Power Wagon. Today she remained silent.

Buckie led them down the twisting road towards Sutton at a speed Robert was hard pressed to keep up with. At Maude's house he turned without stopping, only taking the time to yell over to Mary, 'Call if you need me or any other assistance.'

'I'd like to see the NYPD doing that,' Robert said, waving after the retreating patrol car.

'That's just one more thing that makes New Hampshire so special,' Mary answered. 'Commonsense, old-fashioned policing. Maude was very fond of Buckie Gray.'

'You can see that was mutual,' Robert told her, giving her hand a gentle squeeze. 'Come on. I know she's waiting for you.'

On the way Robert had had time to break it to Mary that Maude had died, that Father Bob was with her and the need for speed had been only to try and buy Mary some short time alone with Maude before the relevant agencies arrived to remove her body, as they must. He had also had time to tell Mary how peacefully and painlessly Maude had slipped away, choosing exactly her own place and time to do so. Mary had smiled at this through her own silent tears and had been grateful to Robert for being able to give her that comfort at least.

Hurrying through the house with Robert they found Father Bob sitting with Maude, in much the same place as Robert had left him.

'I've telephoned all the agencies who have to be informed. Dr Rupa said she'd be here right away to certify death. The ambulance is on its way to collect Maude's body and deliver it to Chadwick's Funeral Home, whom I've also spoken to and they will be expecting it. My guess is Dr Rupa will be here in about ten minutes from now and the ambulance in about twenty. So, Mary, you'll have about ten minutes alone with Maude if Robert and I go up into the house,' Father Bob said, holding Mary affectionately by the shoulders and looking directly at her.

'Thank you,' she said as she sat down in the empty Adirondack chair next to Maude's.

'Robert, you know it's a strange thing but the moment someone has died, even someone as well known and deeply loved as Maude, it suddenly seems entirely natural to refer to that person's corpse as an inanimate object. No longer "him" or "her" but rather "it". You'd think it would be difficult to make that adjustment so quickly, but one look and you just know the person themself has gone. The body that's left behind is just that, an empty outer casing, no longer needed,' Father Bob said, leading the way into the house.

An hour later, after the ambulance had gone and both Father Bob and Dr Rupa had taken their leave, Robert made two mugs of coffee and carried them out to where Mary was still sitting, lost in thought as she looked out over the lake, the occasional sob escaping as waves of emotion engulfed her with the memories of Maude flooding in.

'You know, Mary, it was about as perfect as it could be for her,' Robert said gently. 'There is never a good time, but the rest of us would be fortunate indeed to have a death like Maude's. It was, as the Irish like to say, a good death. She'd been so happy with our news and the lovely day spent with Father Bob. I really think she'd had a premonition or something and the good Lord was looking after her, because she'd told me she was feeling better. At least the pain had eased enough for her to ask me not to bother calling the Visiting Nurses.

'Sitting here, in her favourite spot looking out over the lake she loved, in the still peace and tranquillity of a perfect early morning in late summer, it would be hard to imagine a better way to say goodbye to this often troublesome world that had not always been so kind to her. She was never any trouble to anyone in life and now she has managed to be of no trouble to anyone in death. She would have liked that, I think. No fuss, just something else to be faced up to.'

'Yes, but she won't be at our wedding, will she? She'd said she would be and wouldn't miss it for the world,' Mary managed to get out in a small, grief-stricken voice between the sobs convulsing her again.

Getting her up from the chair Robert enfolded her in his arms. 'I wouldn't be quite so sure about that, Mary. Maude was always resourceful and determined. She may not be there in any sense we would recognise, but I'm willing to bet she'll be there in some form or another.'

'There's an envelope Maude asked me to open as soon as she died. She left it on her desk. I'm just going in to get it, I'll only be a moment.'

Two minutes later he was back. He sat down in the chair which had so recently been Maude's. Turning the envelope over in his hand, he inspected it before opening the flap. The envelope was disappointingly flat. He guessed there could be no more than two sheets of paper inside at most. Opening it he found just one. He reflected on how Maude had always been succinct in her approach and this was going to be no different.

His grandmother's bold, clear handwriting covered both sides. He read it aloud. The short preamble was an expression of love and appreciation for Robert and Mary together with the secret expression of hope she held that they might fall in love and make a life together. She ended this by stating that nothing could make her happier in life or death.

Mary smiled at Robert through her tears as he read that out. Reaching across from her chair, she took his hand and squeezed it hard. The letter continued with a reference to Maude's official last will and testament that she had only very recently updated following Robert's arrival. This was lodged with her lawyer, Gary Dufrère. She explained she had changed things after Robert had told her of his decision to give away all his great wealth and revert to being a poorly paid clergyman. To this end she wanted Robert to have her little house on Keyser Lake, unless he and Mary were to get married. Should that be the case, knowing they would have Mary's farm, she wanted her house to go to Jen.

Momentarily forgetting her sorrow, Mary's eyes widened. This was perfect. A perfect solution for Jen, who would be able to manage the inn for however long it might be that Mary was going to be over in London. The house was so perfect for her too. Small and compact, in the most beautiful secluded, lakeside setting. It would also give Jen the security and independence she deserved if she was going to manage the inn alone while Mary was away. Furthermore it would give her security for life.

Robert continued reading. The remainder of the letter was a reconfirmation of exactly where she wanted to be buried, but with a specific request to be buried not in a traditional coffin, but in a coffin-shaped basket woven of willow, and that her grave be dug, not by Chadwick's as the neat rectangular straight-sided, deep coffin-accommodating hole, such as they would normally do, but rather by a man from Andover called Caleb Stearns. A man who, when younger, Maude had had do much of the land clearing and reclamation work on the farm after the death of her parents. Describing him as a man of independent thought and a bit of a law unto himself, it was clear Maude had had a great deal of respect, even fondness, for the man, impressed as she was by his intimate knowledge of, and connection to, the land, the surrounding forests and the numerous watercourses that were so abundant on the property.

The letter finished with a heartfelt plea that at her funeral service all denominational differences between the Catholic and Protestant religions be put to one side. She wanted it to be a true, ecumenical celebration of a 'rather less than perfect life', conducted joyfully and without judgement.

Keeping the biggest surprise to the end, the letter concluded with the frank admission that she had, for some years, been in love with Father Bob Goodlow. She described this as tacitly understood between both of them, although it never strayed beyond the recognition of an extraordinarily close friendship.

Robert quietly folded the piece of paper and put it back into its envelope. 'Did you know about Maude's undeclared love for Father Bob?' he asked Mary.

'Not as a certainty, but I think I guessed at it – even felt it – whenever they were together,' she replied. 'But I don't think anyone else ever did. Best leave it that way too, don't you think?'

'I was going to suggest the same thing,' Robert replied.

The next few days kept Robert and Mary busy organising and planning Maude's funeral arrangements, and coordinating with Father Bob and Chadwick's. Mary had put the inn's kitchen in production to handle refreshments after the funeral service, which the owners of the old Kimball-Moss Farm had kindly consented could take place down in the big field fronting the house.

The weather was continuing set fair so they decided to gamble on only having a small tent, sufficient to act as shade from the sun and a place for the more elderly to be able to sit. Being outside in a newly mowed field would be so much more Maude's style than closing people in if it was not necessary.

The day before the funeral, on the long dirt driveway leading up to the old farmhouse, had anyone been there to see, they would have witnessed an old mechanical digger being driven slowly along towards the open woodland up at the back of the house. Sitting up on the driving seat was a large, bear-like figure of a man, apparently absorbed in the complicated art of guiding this unruly machine that ran on tracks rather than wheels. Caleb Stearns had known Maude and her parents for many years and the respect in which they had always held him he reciprocated in kind. Going now to dig the hole for her grave, at her specific request, was an honour and duty he was proud to undertake.

49

SO MANY PEOPLE turned out for Maude Kimball's funeral service that there were as many standing bare-headed, and respectfully silent, outside the large double doors left standing wide open at the back of the church, as there were those who had managed to pack themselves into every available space inside. The little Church of the Immaculate Conception, nestled amongst the trees in Potter Place, had never been so full. A hastily rigged-up loudspeaker extension meant that those unable to get in would still be able to hear the words of the funeral Mass.

Surveying this enormous turnout minutes before beginning the service and, realising he knew almost every face in this congregation, Father Bob Goodlow allowed himself a moment to wonder who, if anyone, could possibly be left in the small town of New London. A chance visitor, he thought, might be forgiven for thinking the worst at finding a whole town suddenly and literally abandoned. He knew that many of the local businesses and shops had closed as a mark of respect, but also to allow their owners and staff to attend the funeral.

At the beginning of the service Robert, now once again attired in the robes of an officiating priest, stood at the lectern and introduced himself as Maude's grandson. The audible intake of breath at this revelation from those amongst the congregation who had somehow not yet either heard the rumours or worked it out for themselves, was smaller than some might have expected. That there were any who did not yet know was perhaps less surprising given the still relatively short time Robert had been amongst them and the low profile he had been keeping while spending most of his time with his grandmother.

Those more familiar with the dynamics of a small rural town, not really much bigger than a large village, would not have been surprised. Everyone knew secrets were impossible to keep in a place like this. It was perhaps one of the few downsides of living in a small community where everyone knew everyone. Rumour and gossip were rife.

But it was also part of the basis for the many ways in which neighbour could look out for neighbour. If a recognised pattern of behaviour suddenly changed there would always be someone to question it. Thus no one in trouble could fall through the net unnoticed, and the generosity of this tight-knit community knew no bounds. Besides, in most people's hands, this type of 'gossip' tended to be more of the well-intentioned passing on of information of local interest than in any way malicious – although this was not always the case.

Robert finally finished telling everyone the background of Maude's earlier life. How he came to be her grandson – the very existence of whom she had only discovered some eight years ago. How events had brought him to New London, drawn by the extraordinary thread of consequences stemming from Maude's random, out-of-character, purchase of the lottery ticket at Baynham's. And finally how, over the past few weeks, his grandmother had rescued him in changing the course of his life, directing him back to his true vocation.

The silence in the congregation following this was palpable, broken only by the stifled sobs of many of the older women, able to identify with the awful and agonising dilemma Maude had had to face over her baby, the son she never knew, and the loved and loving 'husband' who was never to be.

Wide-eyed with outright astonishment, the panoply of reaction amongst the congregation to Robert's explanation of events ranged from an inability to fully comprehend – amongst some even a cynical disbelief – to a further posthumous deepening of affection for an already enormously well-loved and respected member of the community. Added to this was the regret that they would now never be able to tell Maude just how much they admired her for her wisdom and strength in handling the enormous pressures of what she went through so admirably when so alone and so young.

All of them already knew about the lottery ticket. It had of course been more or less the sole topic of conversation in the town at the time of the big win. But what they had not known was that it was in fact one of their own, Maude Kimball, who had originally bought the ticket. Its subsequent odyssey to London and into the Sunday collection plate at St Mungo's Church in Earls Court was to become the stuff of legend. It was a story so beguiling, so intricately woven with unforeseeable consequences, as to be beyond even the most fertile imaginings of Hollywood.

There were those in the congregation, mostly men, who, now understanding just who Robert was, or had been when he first arrived in town, could not quite believe that he – or anyone for that matter – could completely turn his back on such fame and breathtaking fortune voluntarily to resume the mantle of an obscure parish priest. They were cynically speculating as to how long this new-leaf-turning would last and just how 'irrevocable' the giving away of his entire vast fortune had been. At the very least they assumed he must have salted away a parachute of several million dollars, if only against the failure of his ability to readapt to poverty after having grown so accustomed to the influence and seductive luxury of great wealth.

After the funeral Mass, those who wished to attend the burial followed the funeral cortege up into the Wilmot hills. As requested, the hearse carrying Maude's coffin stopped in front of the Congregational Church in Wilmot Center. The double doors stood open and a single candle could be seen burning in front of the altar. Robert, Father Bob, Mary and Jennifer went in alone to kneel for a few minutes in silent prayer. Having been previously warned, the many cars following behind the cortege waited patiently, pulled over to the side with engines

473

stopped. The long line stretched all the way back to the bottom of Teal Hill – a distance of more than a mile.

Later, as near to the graveside as cars could get, Maude's willow basket coffin was carried easily up the grassy slope, through the well-spaced trees, to the spot she had chosen. With everyone gathered round, Robert and Father Bob conducted her burial in a relatively short interment ceremony.

Had anyone looked beyond the large circle of those gathered round the irregular-shaped hole, they might have noticed a lone figure, standing some distance off, up against the farmer's wall of loosely aligned rocks that he himself had built for Maude years earlier. Caleb Stearns, freshly washed and cleanly attired, was holding his hat tightly scrunched up in his big hands. Tears were rolling unchecked down his rugged, weather-beaten face.

Quite suddenly, in the moment of absolute silence at the end of the ceremony, when no one was quite sure what to do next, the clear, distinct and unmistakable call of a loon echoed up the hillside from the larger of the two ponds down below the farmhouse. Normally a mournful, haunting cry, somehow this call sounded different, almost joyful. Several people turned in surprise to look. The pond was nowhere near big enough to attract loons and could never before have been visited by one. Those looking were in time to see this majestic bird take off across the water, flying out over the open field to gain height, circling round once to come directly overhead and then flying south in a straight line, out over the vast forests stretching past the mountains to the far horizon.

Robert watched until the bird had shrunk to a tiny spec in the sky before disappearing from his sight altogether. With Mary now holding on to his arm, he bent his head towards her ear to say quietly, 'That was Maude telling us she is free and happy now.'

The weather that afternoon continued to cooperate as Maude's many friends and well-wishers made their way on foot down from the hilltop graveside to the big field where all the cars had had to park and where refreshments were now being served.

Robert, Mary, Father Bob and Jennifer did their best to follow Maude's wishes that this should be essentially a happy occasion in the celebration of her life, rather than a gloomy and regretful goodbye. They circulated amongst the throng, encouraging people to remember the best and funniest incidents and anecdotes of Maude's life among them. Soon the sound of general merriment and laughter overtook the sombre mood that had prevailed at the graveside. There were those, however, who were still too much in shock at the revelation of Maude's hidden past to allow themselves to participate fully in this way, preferring instead to question all they had learned of this one-time pillar of their community, whom they thought they had known so well.

Later, as the last of the mourners were leaving, Mary found Robert to tell him, 'I've been thinking. With the way things have turned out, I know you'll be wanting to leave for London as soon as you can. Realistically there's not enough time for us to get married here now. And anyway, I've come to realise just what the Church of St Mungo's must really mean to you. So, if it's all right with you, I'd like us to be married there, over in London.

'I've got some things I need to sort out here before I can follow you over, but when I do, maybe in six weeks or so, let's plan on getting married in the church where Maude's impulse started this whole fantastic odyssey that led to our meeting.'

For a moment Robert said nothing. He just looked at Mary, squeezing her shoulder affectionately. She could tell how pleased he was at her suggestion.

'If you're sure you're OK with that Mary, I think it's a lovely idea. As you say, it not only rounds the circle, but it gives Maude a role in it too. I think we'd both like that. But it is the prerogative of the bride, so, if you do change your mind, I'll completely understand and go along with whatever you decide.'

50

WITH THE HOUSE and its contents having been given to Jen and arrangements made for Maude's letters to be stored at Mary's house, the task of distributing his grandmother's few personal possessions to those she had stipulated was done. Chief among these requests was that her well-worn, much-loved old Bible be given to Father Bob. This accomplished, Robert was ready to leave.

He was impatient too. Not wanting even to take the time to drive down to New York, it was only three days later that Robert found himself tightly strapped into the small, well-worn seat of an old Fokker Friendship aircraft, en route from Lebanon Airport to New York's La Guardia. Sitting next to him on the aisle was a large, overweight man whose bulk rebelled against every valiant attempt he made to confine himself to his own assigned seat.

It was another warm day and the air was stiflingly hot inside the plane. Mopping the sweat from his brow with a sodden grey handkerchief, the man muttered something between a complaint and an apology to Robert over the cramped conditions. The plane had eighteen seats. All were filled.

Shortly after take-off the pilot advised them not to take off their seat belts. It was going to be a bumpy ride. Looking at the chunky, scratched chrome of his seat belt buckle Robert noticed the engraved outline image of a kangaroo. As he was reasonably sure there were no kangaroos in New England, or indeed anywhere in the North or South American continents, he deduced that this plane must have first seen service in Australia, before being sold to Pilgrim Airlines for its regional routes linking Maine, New Hampshire and Vermont to Boston and New York.

The plane was unpressurised and thus could not fly high enough to avoid lower level air turbulence – and the pilot had not been wrong. Soon they were bucking and diving like an unbroken wild horse. As the body of the small plane twisted and flexed in the violent air, it was possible to see periodic glimpses of daylight appear around the cabin door through which they had boarded at the back. Robert hoped it would manage to remain shut. He found himself wondering if, in its former life, the plane had been used for passenger service somewhere in the Australian outback, or for crop dusting, maybe even fire-fighting.

However, he thought better of exploring these possibilities with the man overflowing the seat next to his. From the tight, white-knuckle, grip on the arms of his seat and the ceasing of any attempt to staunch the sweat now left to pour freely down his brow, Robert knew his fellow passenger was a nervous flyer. Trying to reassure him, he ventured his own knowledge of smaller aircraft and the advantage they often had in being able, if needs be, to make a survivable, safe landing in an open field, or even on a straight stretch of highway if necessary, an option not open to larger aircraft.

Turning white, tinged with green, the man looked at Robert as if he were mad. Then he hastily pulled at the sagging elastic of the seat pocket in front of him in a desperate search for the little blue paper bag provided for the 'comfort' of passengers suddenly overcome by travel sickness. He only managed to open the bag just in time.

With the unavoidable smell so close to him, Robert tried to breathe more through his open mouth than his nose. He put his head back and closed his eyes, remembering how Cynthia – or had it been Bill? – had wanted to send Mike up with his plane one last time to bring him back to New York and how he had resisted the temptation, refusing to allow it. He smiled inwardly to himself at the

477

irony of this stark contrast between the insulated luxury of flying privately and taking a commercial flight.

Was his resolve being 'tested' so soon? Was it God's idea of a good practical joke? Or was it just an ironic coincidence? he wondered. Whatever it was, it was a baptism by fire in his return to his old way of life.

An hour later the plane landed safely, on schedule, at La Guardia Airport and taxied noisily over to an undistinguished, shabby-looking shed, set apart from the main terminal building, for small aircraft.

Once inside this structure that passed for a terminal, Robert debated whether to call Cynthia from the solitary payphone on the wall. She knew he was coming sometime soon because he had called her to let her know of Maude's death. She had wanted to come up for the funeral, but her own mother was ill in hospital and Robert had told her not to.

He decided he would call. Lifting the receiver to his ear, he at once noted there was no dial tone. The phone was quite dead. It was then he saw that the coiled metal cable from the handset to the phone had been ripped free from the wall. Another reality check for his return to his old life, he thought.

Only because he wanted his time in New York to be as short as possible, he decided he would allow himself the luxury of a taxi from the airport to what he must now learn to think of as his former office.

Soon, sitting back in the spacious old Checker cab that had long ago lost the efficacy of its suspension system, he was rattling his way towards Manhattan. The jarring and knocks from every pothole sent a cacophony of loud bangs up into the cab.

Robert gave the driver the address of his destination, but not long into the journey he became aware that the man was scrutinising him in his rear-view mirror, with a frown of concentration on his face.

Suddenly the driver relaxed and smiled. 'You're that big financier with the Midas touch aren't you?' he said triumphantly. 'I dabble in the stock market and

I like to follow the financial news. I've seen your picture in the *Wall Street Journal* more than once, and on television too. I pride myself on almost never forgetting a face, especially when it's connected to the world of big money. You and that Mr Buffett are the stars of the financial world, I'd say. Wait till I tell everyone I've had you in my cab.

'It was the address that got me thinking. That's the Bicknor Wilmot Building I said to myself, headquarters of the Bicknor Wilmot Securities Fund. I've seen that name in the papers a fair few times too. I'm almost as good with names as I am with faces. I think what threw me off the scent to start with is that I'd never expect someone in your position to take a cab. I'm sure a limo would be more your style, more fitting too really. Don't get me wrong though, it's not that I'm not delighted to have you in my cab, it's just I would never have expected it. Not in a million years. About as much chance as getting the President in my cab I'd say.'

By now they were just crossing the Triboro Bridge into upper Manhattan. Robert had not said a word. He would not have been able to, even if he had wanted to.

'Sorry, I do talk a lot, I know. My friends all tell me I talk too much, but it's the result of having an enquiring mind. I ask questions and I learn things. They all sit in their cabs with the radio on, listening to music or to lying politicians. Either way, they learn nothing. So, what's it like being one of the richest, most powerful men in the world then?'

The question Robert had always most dreaded had been asked. He was at a loss as to how to respond succinctly and yet truthfully. Unable to imagine the effect his words might have, he finally just said, 'That was my life until I gave it all up a few weeks ago. Tomorrow I'm going to return to London, to my former life, to my original vocational calling as a priest in the Church of England.'

The cab driver again looked intently at him via the rear-view mirror, unsure whether to laugh at what he assumed must be some kind of a joke, or whether he had simply misheard.

'You're kidding me, aren't you?' The response was left hanging with a question mark; one way or another, what he thought he had heard could not be right. He had always hated dry, deadpan humour: it got him every time.

'No, I'm not joking. It's perfectly true,' Robert explained. 'For the past eight years I've served Mammon pretty well and now I'm going back to my original training to see if I can make as good a job of serving God.'

At a complete loss for words for only the second time in his life (the first having been the moment of birth of his first child), the cab driver tried his hardest to rationalise what he had just been told. The thought then occurred to him that perhaps the great Robert Melton was having a mental breakdown. He had read of such things happening to very clever, very bright people.

'So what are you going to do with all the money you've made? You're not going to give it to the Church are you?' The tone of his voice was now rising, with a ring of alarm to it.

'No. Don't worry about that,' Robert said, smiling, even allowing himself a little chuckle. 'I now know enough about money and priests to know that the two don't often mix very well. I've established a charitable foundation to look after and administer the funds. It will be well managed.'

'Tell me you've kept enough at least for yourself?' came the driver's voice, almost pleading, dry-throated and sounding a little hoarse.

'Well, no to that too. I just couldn't have done it in some half-hearted way. Any priest really committing to serving God has to trust Him completely for everything and in everything. If I'd allowed myself a safety net, an escape route if you like, it would only mean I wasn't truly following the vows I made when I became a priest. Does that make sense?'

'Are you saying you now think it's wrong to become rich like you?'

'No. Not at all. The honest making of money is not wrong. Money itself is morally neutral. It's in the attachment to money, and what one may or may not do with it, that the problems usually lie. Getting money, and the power it bestows, can be a strongly seductive force. Money can corrupt even the strongest, most upright of men.

'However, if you're asking whether I now think it was wrong for me to have pursued the acquisition of great wealth, the answer is more complicated. I would say it was both a "yes" and a "no". "Yes" because clearly what I did in just walking away from my position as a parish priest and ignoring my vows was wrong. And yet, perhaps "no" – although this still remains to be proved, because with what I've learned, both about myself, the world and others, I now feel so much better equipped to return. Now I can be a far more effective priest than I would ever have had any hope of becoming beforehand. Then there's the good that can now be done through the charitable foundation I've established to make the best use of the money I've made.'

By now the cab had come to a halt outside the Bicknor Wilmot Building, but neither Robert nor the driver seemed in any particular hurry to end their conversation.

'You really are serious about this aren't you?' the driver said, collecting the fare from the little tray that protruded through the toughened glass screen.

'You know, I'm from Gallipoli. A Turkish Muslim myself, and also a bit of a history enthusiast. I know you're from Australia originally. Did you know that we Turkish Muslims gave you Aussie Christians a gift after the disaster of the fighting for the Dardanelles in the First World War? It's a memorial that stands at Gallipoli to all the Australian and New Zealand soldiers who lost their lives there. But today, to properly understand what the inscription on it says, you need to first know that a hundred years ago the most common boys' name among the Anzacs was Johnny and in Turkey it was Mehmet. My father made me, my brothers and sisters learn it by heart. I've never forgotten it. It's more beautiful than any poem to me. It reads: "Those heroes that shed their blood and lost their lives ... you are now lying in the soil of a friendly country. Therefore rest in peace. There is no difference between the Johnnies and the Mehmets to us where they lie side by side here in this country of ours ... you, the mothers, who sent sons from far away countries, wipe away your tears ... after having lost their lives on this land they have become our sons as well."

'Muslims, Christians, Jews – all sons of Abraham – why do we have to fight each other before we realise that a stranger is only a friend we haven't yet met?'

'Mr Melton, I really respect you for what you're doing. Did you say you're flying to London tomorrow? That'll be from JFK, right? Call me later and tell me what time and where to pick you up. It'd be an honour to take you,' Mustafa Kaleed said, passing Robert a slightly grubby business card.

The receptionist and security staff were very surprised to see Mr Melton suddenly back. Having failed to recognise him immediately, dressed as he was in jeans and polo shirt instead of his more customary formal business attire, they now snapped to attention.

Riding the elevator up to the twenty-fourth floor Robert knew that by the time he got to his office his staff would have been notified of his return. He had seen the lobby receptionist reach for her internal phone almost before he had passed the desk.

In the elevator, smiling to himself, Robert could not help thinking about how strange it was that in a small way he had begun his return to ministry in the back of a New York cab. It had felt surprisingly good.

Jill had only just reached the elevator doors when they opened. She was unconsciously adjusting her skirt and checking her hair as Robert walked out. He knew she must have almost run down the long corridor from her desk outside his big corner office to get there in time. Momentarily taken aback by his informal appearance, she smoothly recovered and, proffering her hand with a warm smile said, 'Welcome home Mr Melton, it's good to have you back.'

'Thank you Jill, but I think you know it will be a very short visit. I'll be leaving for London tomorrow night. On that point, would you confirm my flight with British Airways? I think I'm on the one that leaves about six pm and gets into London nice and early the following morning.'

'Absolutely, Mr Melton.'

Then, almost apologetically, she added, 'I'm afraid the Rolls and the Bentley have already both been sold, but if you'll give me a time and where you want to be picked up from, I'll arrange for one of Rafael's new limos to take you out to JFK.'

'No need for that,' Robert said glancing at the dog-eared business card he still had in his hand. 'Mustafa Kaleed is going to take me in his cab.' With that he handed the oil-stained card to Jill saying, 'Ask him to pick me up from here at around two-thirty tomorrow afternoon will you? Oh, also Jill, a window seat would be nice on the flight home if they have one left.' The use of the word 'home' was not lost on Jill.

At another time Robert might have enjoyed watching the rollercoaster of emotions passing swiftly across Jill's pretty but earnest face as she struggled to take in these instructions from her boss, a man she had had on a very tall pedestal ever since she began working at Bicknor Wilmot Securities more than five years ago.

Gingerly taking Mustafa Kaleed's cheaply printed card from Robert's outstretched hand, she held it as if it might in some way contaminate her. She was barely able to disguise the astonishment and horror she felt on Robert's own behalf at the outlandish requests for his travel arrangements.

Robert had been on the point of walking on to his office, but he stopped, put a hand on his secretary's arm and said, 'Jill, I'm sorry this is all a bit of a shock for you. Although I know Cynthia has told you about my future plans, I suppose it was hard for you to accept them fully without seeing me. But it really is true and I want you to try to be happy for me. Your position will be safe for you for as long as you want it, the only difference being you will be the Executive Secretary to the newly formed charitable foundation, continuing as before to work with Cynthia and Bill.

'If at any point you decide you don't want to do that, I've made generous provision to cover you while you go out and find a comparable position with another financial services firm or a bank. You will have the best professional and personal references from me and, given the high profile of this firm, and your position in it, I don't believe it would take you very long to find a similar – or better – position.'

So it really was true. Jill had been told by both Cynthia and Bill. She had also seen the cars sold, the yacht and the plane put up for sale and Robert's luxury apartment go on the market. She had even participated in preparing the particulars for the sale of the office building. Yet, despite everything, she had not quite been able to accept it.

Now, seeing Robert, how different he was and hearing direct confirmation from him, she could no longer deceive herself into thinking that somehow there had been a mistake. She was devastated. Her whole self-image and the one she projected had been, by extension, one of reflected importance in her role as Executive Secretary to the great and famous Mr Robert Melton.

Irrationally, she felt betrayed, let down, even embarrassed to be asked to book a grubby taxi and economy-class ticket on the flight to London. It was somehow beneath her and certainly beneath the way she felt her boss should be behaving. Against all the evidence, Jill had allowed herself secretly to harbour the belief that Cynthia and Bill had somehow got it wrong, or, if not, that Mr Melton himself would surely change his mind once he got back to New York – to his real life.

No one, Jill thought, could ever willingly allow themselves to give up wholeheartedly everything they had. Surely that would change once he had come back and seen for himself just how much that really was.

Robert gave her arm a sympathetic squeeze and with a reassuring smile turned towards his office. Jill remained rooted to the spot. Too stunned to move, the look with which she followed his progress down the hallway was one of disbelief, mixed with betrayal.

As soon as he entered his office the interconnecting door between his and the adjoining office opened. Cynthia entered, smiling warmly as she came over to greet him.

'Welcome back. I guess Jill took it hard, huh?' she said. 'We – Bill and I that is – tried our best to prepare her, but we could tell she wasn't ever really going to totally believe us. Sorry Robert.'

'Don't apologise. It's not your fault. It'll be good for her. She needs to be free of my identity to become herself again. Looking back, I realise now just how many high-level, young, and particularly not so young, executive secretaries there are out there who, to a degree anyway, assume their boss's identity. It gives them a reflected glory, a status, a vicarious sense of power and purpose they wouldn't otherwise have. The bad part is that their bosses sooner or later become aware of it and, far from discouraging it, surreptitiously encourage it, to take full advantage of the self-inflicted dependence they've created for themselves.'

'Well, it never worked like that for me,' Cynthia retorted.

'No, Cyn, it didn't, which is probably why you're my PA – and good personal friend – rather than my executive secretary.

'But I really must try to start putting all this in the past tense. No one here works for me any more. They either work for the firm, Bicknor Wilmot Securities, which is being sold, or they will work for the St Mungo's Trust. We all need to remember I have no further responsibility or authority over either.'

'So, not only did someone scatter fairy dust all over you in New Hampshire, but now you've come back full of atonement for all your past sins?' Cynthia said bluntly before allowing herself to smile. 'Cup of coffee?'

'Yes please, I'd love one.'

Cynthia was about to reach for the phone when she changed her mind. 'I suppose, in keeping with the new hair shirt policies you've adopted for yourself, I should go and make us both coffee.' She said this with a smile of mock servitude. 'I'll be back in five minutes with the best cup of coffee you'll have had since you left New York.'

Ten minutes later they were seated comfortably in the oversized leather armchairs that, with a pair of matching sofas, formed the sitting-out area of Robert's office with its spectacular views over Central Park. It was with a pang that the realisation, not so much of regret as shock, came to him that this was now on a courtesy loan and would only be so for a few more hours. Very shortly he would be turning his back on even this luxurious remnant of his former lifestyle.

Asking Jill for a cup of coffee on his way in, Bill now came to join them. He and Cynthia updated Robert on exactly where they were in the process of liquidating all his assets, the sale of the firm and the progress on the formation of the foundation. Jill came in with Bill's coffee and a file full of papers for Robert to sign, mostly pertaining to his resignation from various organisations and directorships.

Later Cynthia and Robert went out for lunch. Bill declined to join them, claiming a prior meeting. In fact, by earlier arrangement with Cynthia and Jill he stayed back to assist with and oversee the organisation of a small farewell party planned for Robert that evening. Not knowing when, or for exactly how long, Robert would be back in New York, of necessity this had had to be left somewhat to the last minute.

Robert and Cynthia walked down to Demarchelier, a low-key, semi-subterranean French restaurant on Lexington Avenue, with good food, good wine and a quiet, unhurried atmosphere. It had been a long-time favourite of Robert's.

Cynthia had been discreetly assessing the 'new' Robert ever since he had come in that morning. The difference between the Robert she had known and the Robert sitting in front of her was so marked, it was hard to comprehend them as the same person. Yet she recognised now the resemblance to the younger, more humble, man she had been introduced to in Boston and for whom she had first been drawn to come and work.

Gone was the arrogance, the increasingly offensive sense of entitlement, the swashbuckling 'Master of the Universe' aura. Replacing it was a very different, quiet sense of self-confidence of the sort exuded by a man who knew what he was doing, what he wanted and where he was going. It was very compelling and, Cynthia had to admit, very attractive. No wonder Mary had fallen in love with him, she thought.

'By the way Robert. Do you remember when I was with you up in New Hampshire, standing in the parking lot of that coffee shop place saying goodbye to your grandmother? How she and I agreed that, if she was able to, she would send me a sign to let me know she was OK – and rather improbably we'd agreed upon that sign being a chipmunk?

'Anyway, I'm sorry to say I'd forgotten all about it. Then right after you called to tell me she'd died, I felt the need to be by myself outside for a bit. Although it was still early it was a beautiful day, so I decided to go and take a walk over in Central Park. Well, I don't know if it was a coincidence or not, but as I came out onto the street, I saw this small group of people hurrying to work who had stopped right outside our main entrance. They seemed to be looking at something. As I stepped towards them the group parted and I saw what they'd been looking at. It was a little chipmunk perched happily and confidently on top of a fire hydrant, showing no fear of the people standing close by. As soon as I appeared it jumped down and raced off back towards Central Park. I can only hope it made it safely across Fifth Avenue.

'It's very unusual, but not unheard of, for chipmunks to be seen in Central Park. Usually those that are there have been released by city families who've caught one in the country and found out too late that chipmunks don't make good pets, especially in a Manhattan apartment.

'Strange or what? But what I can tell you is that from that moment I no longer felt sad for your grandmother.'

Robert looked at Cynthia and smiled, but said nothing. He'd tell her about the strange appearances of the loon over lunch, he thought.

Once they were seated and had ordered their food Cynthia asked, 'So, how are you feeling now the die is cast and you really are about to turn your back on your luxurious jet-set lifestyle to return to the gruelling work of a parish priest? It must hurt some to be back here seeing everything you've given up – doesn't it?'

'I was very afraid it might Cyn, but the strange thing is, now that I'm here amongst the trappings of what I now think of as my middle-life period, it's not nearly as difficult as I thought it was going to be. In a way it all just seems like so much stuff – and noise. Perhaps I was imprisoned by golden bars, but I think it will be ... you know ... liberating to leave it all behind for good when I return to London tomorrow.'

'Have you spoken to your bishop yet? Does he even know you're on your way back?' Cyn asked in an impatient, no-nonsense sort of way.

Robert looked sheepish. Cynthia always had a way of getting to the heart of the matter. 'Well, no. The truth is I've been putting off calling him. I suppose it's the guilt I feel,' he said smiling.

'Robert, in the corporate world you'd never have been afraid to call anyone and here you are now avoiding calling a fellow priest – even if he is a bishop,' Cynthia said scathingly.

'As I said, I think it's the guilt I feel. But you're right. I'll call him as soon as we get back to the office – I promise,' Robert replied.

'By the way, I'll take you out to the airport tomorrow if you like,' Cynthia said, changing the subject.

'Thank you Cyn, but I've arranged for Mustafa Kaleed to take me in his taxi.'

Cynthia gave him a questioning look of surprise.

'He brought me in this morning from La Guardia. We got talking, but we didn't really get to finish the conversation. Besides, you know how I hate goodbyes, especially long lingering ones at airports.'

'OK then, we'll just make it a quick goodbye when you leave the office.'

'Thanks, Cyn.'

After lunch, back at the office Robert sat down at his old desk. He said a quick silent prayer before picking up the telephone to dial the Bishop of West London's number. It was already seven-thirty in London, but he knew Bishop Rogers was likely to be working late.

The phone was quickly answered. The voice of a polite but efficient secretary came on the line. 'Bishop Rogers' office. How can I help you?'

Robert hadn't been expecting any receptionist or secretary to still be on duty. This threw him at first, and he paused for a moment, at a loss as to how to begin.

'Could I speak to Bishop Rogers please, it's Robert Melton here?' Happily, Robert could tell from the tone of her response that his name meant nothing to her.

'Will he know who you are?' she asked politely.

Robert smiled broadly to himself as he said, 'Yes, yes he will know. Tell him I'm calling from New York.'

There was a click, followed by a short silence before the bishop's familiar voice came on the line. 'Hello Robert. How nice to hear from you. I've been hoping for a call from you for a very long while now. Are you all right?'

Robert was surprised at how good it was to hear his voice. 'Yes, Bishop, I'm fine. But you'll recall that I've never been any good at preamble or diplomacy, so I'll just plunge in and tell you the reason for my call.'

Robert was unable to see the affectionate smile spread across the bishop's face as he remembered, not without a sense of guilt, the trusting and straightforward young priest who had taken on St Mungo's with such enthusiasm – and all that had happened since then.

'I hope you're sitting down. What I've got to ask you may come as a bit of a surprise.'

After a short pause Robert continued. 'I'm coming back to London tomorrow to ask you if you will let me go back to St Mungo's to pick up where I left off eight years ago.'

The bishop was thunderstruck. It was not so much the unexpected nature of Robert's request that had rendered him temporarily speechless, as this stunning demonstration of the power of prayer. Ever since Robert had left, Bishop Rogers, partially driven by his own feelings of culpability, had been praying fervently that Robert Melton would somehow return to his calling as a priest. However, his temporal understanding of the world and its ways logically told him that no one would ever be easily persuaded to walk away from such vast wealth, fame and power as Robert had attained.

'Bishop? ... Bishop, are you still there?'

'Yes Robert, I'm still here. It's just your request, out of the blue like this, is a lot for me to take in all at once. What has brought this about, if I may ask?'

This time it was Robert's turn to pause. The bishop said nothing, giving him time to reply.

'That's too long an answer for me to explain properly now, but the short answer would be the realisation of how brief life is for all of us and that it is not a dress rehearsal. In order to have a satisfied mind you cannot deny who you are or what your calling, your vocation, might be, if you happen to have one. All the time I've been making money and living a life of extraordinary privilege, I haven't ever been truly satisfied with either what I've been doing, or with myself.

'Time recently spent with a wonderful, wise, dignified old lady up in New Hampshire, who turned out to be my grandmother, made me see that to be satisfied, to be fulfilled and, yes, happy, I needed to stop pretending to be someone I wasn't. Stop denying who I really was. And stop refusing to acknowledge my calling to serve God in His Church.

'The problem was how to go back and where to begin. Then I realised, more than anything else, I wanted to start by going back to where I so abruptly left off. Quoting a friend, "to attend to unfinished business", if you like.

'I'm not worried about what happens after that. It's such a relief to leave the future, mine and everyone else's, in God's infinitely more capable hands. There is so much more to tell you. I've really hardly begun, but can I do that back in London? I've got a lot to do if I'm going to be on that plane tomorrow night.'

'Robert, I shall be delighted to see you. What you've said and even what you haven't said intrigues me greatly. It also humbles me and reminds me always to have hope – and faith. Shall we talk about your future when you get here?'

'My future after St Mungo's, yes. But could you give me your answer now to my request to first return, at once, to St Mungo's to finish what I left unfinished eight years ago? I really hope that it will be possible. You can have no idea how important this is to me.'

The bishop, never fond of making quick decisions, would, by instinct, have preferred to be non-committal. To give himself time to think about Robert's surprising request and of its possible consequences. He had not always been like this – so guarded, so careful. As a young priest he had been impetuous, energetic and instinctive in his approach, always more often getting things right than wrong. It was only as he rose through the hierarchy of the Church that he had learned the need for caution, especially in the politically charged atmosphere now surrounding him. He envied Robert his ability to remain straightforward and uncomplicated in his goals. He also knew he owed Robert this chance he was requesting.

'All right Robert. I recognise I owe you that. But will you come to my house when you get off the plane? You can spend your first night with us. My wife will be delighted to see you again. She'll probably want me to kill the fatted calf.' Although intended only as a figure of speech the analogy to the return of the prodigal son was not lost on either of them and it made both men laugh.

'Robert, I can't tell you what pleasure the thought of your return gives me. I'll really be looking forward to seeing you tomorrow. Travel well.'

'Thank you, Bishop. Tomorrow then.' He rang off.

*

Bishop Rogers sat back at his desk, the tips of his fingers pressed together. He was looking at an envelope on his desk. Already stamped and ready to go, it was addressed in his own hand to the incumbent vicar of St Mungo's rejecting his request for an immediate transfer. It was only by accident that the letter had missed the evening post; it had been underneath some other papers and been forgotten until discovered too late for the last post that day.

Was it serendipity, providence, or some other higher guiding power that made these things happen, he wondered? Was he simply a small cog in some vast unfathomable plan of which he was maybe now and then privileged to catch but a tiny glimpse? As a younger man he wouldn't have doubted it, but life had made him less trusting and more cynical.

He picked up the envelope and methodically tore it in half, dropping both halves in the wastepaper basket beside his desk. Then, reaching for his pen, he wrote another letter accepting the vicar's request for a transfer with immediate effect. He would deliver it by hand on his way home.

The bishop knew Father Ridley would be both surprised and delighted. Surprised because he'd only been in post for nine months and the usual minimum period was three years. Delighted at the swift granting of his request and what he would see as the importance of a special hand delivery.

What was it about St Mungo's that made it such a graveyard for most vicars, and yet Robert Melton couldn't wait to get back there?

Had he been wrong in his dealings with Melton from the beginning? Wrong to have misled him over the true nature of his task when he was first appointed? Wrong again not to have changed his mind and supported him when Robert had produced a viable plan, that might well have succeeded in turning around this failed parish for a minimal cost?

For a long time Bishop Rogers continued to sit at his desk allowing himself to reflect again about the whole question of serendipity. Who could ever have foreseen that his shabby treatment of young Robert Melton would in the end result in the saving and guaranteed future financial security of St Mungo's? Also, he suspected, there was its effect on this once naive young priest who was now returning, older and wiser, full of self-confidence, with a demonstrable talent for the world of high finance and a determination to complete the work he had started at St Mungo's. How strange it was that not one of the three vicars since Robert's departure had been able to understand or get to grips with the parish. All three had given up at some point and requested transfers – and this despite the long-term financial security Robert had ensured.

It was as if St Mungo's itself was rejecting them – was it waiting for Robert's return?

Shaking himself out of these thoughts, Bishop Rogers told himself to 'get a grip'. The Church of St Mungo's was an inanimate structure, incapable of exerting any influence, or being anything other than what it was, just a building. He was allowing himself to dwell at the entrance to a dangerous fantasy world, normally the domain of conspiracy theorists and the mentally unhinged. And yet, and yet, the unfolding of events as they had was more than a little curious and seemed to be leading inexorably to a conclusion he was absolutely powerless to influence one way or another. Life was strange indeed.

Back in New York, putting down the telephone in his old office, Robert Melton was surprised by two things. Firstly, the genuine warmth and sincerity he had clearly detected in the bishop's voice. Sincerity was not something he had come to associate with his memory of the Bishop of West London. Secondly, the unexpected pleasure he had felt at being back in contact with his former 'boss' and spiritual leader.

He was more anxious than ever now to get back to London.

51

THE FAREWELL PARTY with the staff had mostly been an awkward affair. Apart from Cynthia and, to a lesser extent, Bill, everyone seemed not to know how to react to their former boss. They were embarrassed by him and the position he had put them in. It was like watching people handle bereavement. They did not seem to know whether to congratulate him or commiserate with him. Most simply wished him good luck, but were unable to disguise the fact that they thought he had taken leave of his senses to give up all his material success to go and serve God – a God with whom many of them had only a shaky acquaintance at best and one or two no acquaintance or belief at all.

There was one exception: a new junior secretary who had only very recently joined the firm. Having never met him, her only knowledge of Robert was from his reputation and from reading about him. At the party she was the last to speak to him and had first to be introduced by Jill. Her name was Michaela.

This young lady, hardly more than a girl Robert thought, looked him straight in the eye (something Robert had noted almost none of the others had been able to do), warmly shook his hand and told him with complete sincerity how much she admired him for doing what he was doing. Then, without a trace of irony and with complete conviction, she told him his decision would make him a very happy man.

It was Robert's turn to be discomfited by this direct and certain declaration. He thanked her warmly, making a mental note to suggest to Cynthia that such a person should be recruited to the foundation side of the split, before the business side was sold off.

Robert knew it was incumbent upon him to bring this uncomfortable gathering to a close. Although well-intentioned, he could see everyone was looking for a sign it was OK to leave. Oddly he felt the same way himself. It was as if it stood in testimony to the fact that he had already given up his old life. He was no longer part of it and it was no longer part of him.

Robert spent his last night in New York sleeping on the pullout bed in the small apartment Bill maintained for those nights of the week he spent in New York. Jill had wanted to book him into the Carlyle Hotel. He had almost weakened, not for the luxury it would provide, so much as just not to disappoint Jill again.

The following day he spent most of the morning with Cynthia and Bill reviewing the aims, principles and mandate of the St Mungo's charitable foundation.

At eleven Joshua from Harcourt & Boodle came by to have a cup of coffee with them. Up in New Hampshire he had made Cynthia promise to let him know when Robert was going to be back in New York. Good as his word, he had immediately rearranged his appointments for that morning to be able to come over to the Bicknor Wilmot Building to say goodbye to Robert.

Robert was very touched. He had not expected Joshua to react as he did. He had assumed, wrongly, that once he'd made his decision to return to the priesthood as a penniless vicar, Joshua, calculating Robert to be of no further value to him, would very quickly wish to distance himself, eagerly moving forward in his search for the next Master of the Universe with which to replace him.

There was something else though. The staff in his own office seemed to be avoiding him. With the exception of Michaela they were all deliberately staying out of his way, clumsily averting their eyes whenever he walked through the office. The atmosphere was one of awkward embarrassment.

By contrast, Joshua could not have been more open in demonstrating his genuine sadness and regret in coming to say his goodbye. This he expressed with warm sincerity and good wishes for Robert's future, underlying which was his sense of admiration for what Robert was doing.

The irony in this was not lost on Robert, that his relationship with someone whom he had always taken to be just a business acquaintance, in a strictly self-serving commercial arrangement, should turn out to be so much deeper when it came down to it.

The irony was only added to by the fact that here, a man of the Jewish faith had come to wish him well in his future as a Christian priest and was doing so with undisguised admiration. Meanwhile, although he didn't know for sure, the probability was that most of his own erstwhile office staff were, at least nominally, Christian, and yet they were unable to get beyond their own self-conscious embarrassment at having the very idea of serving God, as an alternative to making money, thrust upon them. It was as if they felt betrayed by Robert for swapping sides.

It was a good lesson to him never to pre-judge anyone, nor necessarily to accept circumstances at face value.

After Joshua left, Robert, Bill, Cynthia and Jill had a sandwich lunch together in his office. The sandwiches were brought in by Michaela and before she left the room, in front of everyone, Robert asked her if she would like to transfer from Bicknor Wilmot Securities to work for the St Mungo's Trust after the two entities became separated. The expression of delight that spread across her extraordinarily pretty face gave him her answer.

'Good, then Cynthia will see to it with you,' Robert said.

'Just who do you think you are,' retorted Cynthia, 'giving instructions around here, acting as if you owned the place?!'

The happy expression on Michaela's face turned to one of horror. Jill looked nervously uneasy and even Bill was momentarily surprised, until they all saw Cynthia giving Robert a broad wink. Robert burst out laughing and, seeing the joke, everyone joined in.

Not for the first time Jill secretly envied Cynthia's ability to have this close, special relationship with her boss. It was a talent she had never had with Robert and she knew she would never be able to have with whomever she was to work for next either.

At two-thirty she came to tell Robert that Mustafa Kaleed, the taxi driver, was outside.

'Thank you Jill, please would you go down and ask him if he would mind waiting for me for twenty minutes?'

If they felt ill at ease about coming to him, Robert knew he must go to them. He walked out into the open office area and going to each desk he shook hands with every employee, one by one. He thanked each of them for everything they had done for the firm and wished them all the very best in their futures. He also told them that if ever any of them were to find themselves over in London for either business or pleasure they were to look him up. He would be delighted to see any member of Bicknor Wilmot Securities, the firm he had founded, at any time.

Finally, he went to say goodbye to Bill in his office. It was a heartfelt, if gruff, goodbye between two men determined to keep their emotions under control.

At the elevator door Robert gave Jill a big hug and thanked her for everything. She was by now openly crying. Cynthia came with him into the elevator. Just before the elevator doors closed, as he turned to face outwards he had a chance to see across the open floor of the main office area. Every member of the staff had stood up from their desks and were facing towards him as a mark of their respect. In that moment he could also see it wasn't only the women who were fighting back their tears.

As the elevator descended he thought perhaps, yet again, his judgements had been wrong.

In the lobby Cynthia looked him in the eye. 'Robert, I'll say goodbye here,' she said firmly. 'I don't want to disgrace myself in the street. Will you call me when you can after you get to London? Just so I know you're safely there? I hope it won't be too long before we see each other again, but I fear it might be a while. Also, will you write or call me once you are properly settled back at St Mungo's? If you can't afford the call, reverse the charge – call me collect. I figure I owe you that much and a lot more – maybe even more than you'll ever know,' she said wistfully, her eyes beginning to well with tears.

Robert went to take her in his arms, but she pushed him away. 'Now go,' she said. 'You told me you didn't like long goodbyes, well neither do I.'

Then she turned abruptly and walked briskly back towards the bank of elevators. Cynthia didn't look round. Robert watched her for a moment, wanting to go after her. Then he turned to leave himself, stopping only to shake hands and say goodbye and thank you to the clerk and security guard at the lobby desk. After that he walked out of the Bicknor Wilmot Building for the very last time.

Back in the elevator Cynthia pressed the button for the mezzanine floor. She could have walked up the one flight of stairs from the lobby but she didn't want Robert, or anyone, to see where she was going.

Stepping out of the elevator, she walked over to the plate-glass windows overlooking the entrance to the building. Cynthia knew that the solar-reflective glass would screen her from the street. She stood there and watched as Robert got into his taxi and drove off into the Manhattan traffic.

Had anyone been able to see her, they would have seen this beautiful, smartly dressed, black lady with tears streaming unchecked down her cheeks. Slowly she lifted one hand, kissed the palm and softly blew the kiss in the direction of the disappearing taxi.

She took a few moments to compose herself before returning to the elevators. When the doors opened she was ready with a smile for whoever might be inside. She knew she had to lead by example on the twenty-fourth floor now that their leader really was finally gone.

As good as his word, Mustafa Kaleed was waiting for Robert. Getting out of his cab to hold open the passenger door and take the small suitcase from him, he noticed the set look of determination on Robert's face. This time the determination was with himself, but in that instant Mustafa Kaleed could see how that same determination set against others would have been a deciding factor in the success of so many of his business dealings. In business he could see it as a good quality to have but, as a priest, he wasn't so sure how useful it would be.

Neither man said anything until they reached the Triboro Bridge. Instinct, born of being a cab driver for many years, told Mustafa Kaleed that Robert needed this time to sit in silence, uninterrupted and alone with his thoughts. Somehow the act of leaving Manhattan Island was the punctuation mark needed to differentiate the leaving behind of his 'middle life' and the heading back towards his old, 'new' life.

Unable to keep silent any longer, Mustafa Kaleed ventured, 'So, you really are going through with this then? Is that little suitcase your only luggage, or have you sent the rest on separately?'

Robert smiled. 'Yes, I am and, yes, that little suitcase is my only luggage. I've got nothing else to send on separately.'

'Was it very difficult for you leaving everything behind, saying goodbye to it all for ever?' Mustafa asked, unable to keep the disbelief he felt out of his voice.

'Surprisingly no. It was hard saying goodbye to friends and employees, but it wasn't hard to say goodbye to all the things I used to think of as important. Worse still, things I used to think identified me and who I was. Letting go of that bit has been cathartic.'

'Do you think those who make lots of money are now bad people in some way?' Mustafa asked. It was almost the same question he'd asked the day before and Robert knew he must be looking for reassurance.

'No. The world needs those who can make money with which to do good, as much as those who prefer, or are more suited, to give of their time in doing good. Being generous with your money, or generous with your time, are of essential and equal importance when it comes to actively doing good. But those who choose to make money would do well to reflect on Thornton Wilder's wise, pithy words from *The Matchmaker*, "Money is like manure. It is only any good if you spread it around."'

'Well, Mr Melton, if I was wearing my hat I'd take it off to you. I really admire what you're doing and if I wasn't quite happy with my Muslim faith I'd certainly want to look into this Christian God you're so determined to serve.'

Robert laughed. 'No need for that Mustafa. Good Muslims, good Jews, good Christians and countless others will all meet in heaven one day. And by good I only mean those who try.'

'I'm glad you said that, because I'm not sure how good I am, but I do try to be!'

They both laughed.

There was little traffic and they were at the airport in less than forty-five minutes. Pulling up at the British Airways departure point, Mustafa jumped out to open the door for his famous passenger. Getting out, Robert tried to hand him the thirty-dollar fare but it was waved away.

'No, I always intended this ride to be on me. If I may just shake your hand and tell you it has been an honour and a privilege to meet you. I'm awed and humbled by what you're doing. I know I couldn't do it, even from the precarious financial position I occupy – which in comparison to what you are giving up counts as nothing.'

Then, almost as an afterthought, he added, 'Although, if you had a stock tip to give me before you go, that might be nice!'

He asked this with such an innocent, mischievous twinkle in his eye that Robert couldn't help smiling.

Having thanked him for the ride and after picking up his small bag, Robert said, 'You could do worse than buy stock in Bicknor Wilmot Securities. I can say no more. Thank you again. Goodbye Mustafa.' And with that he headed towards the departure desks in the terminal.

As he walked into the terminal, Robert vowed to himself that that would be the last stock tip he would ever give anyone. He was determined now to leave that part of his life behind him forever.

Driving back to Manhattan, Mustafa Kaleed was trying to make sense of the stock tip he thought he had just been given by the great Robert Melton. It didn't add up. Ever since it became known that Robert Melton, the man with the Midas touch, was leaving, the stock price in Bicknor Wilmot Securities had crashed and had kept on tumbling as it became daily more apparent that Robert Melton really meant to leave and would not be changing his mind. How could that now be a good stock to buy with so much uncertainty attached to it, Mustafa wondered?

Perhaps the secret lay in what Robert Melton did not say, rather than what he did say? Suddenly Mustafa smiled to himself. Of course, that was it. With the stock now severely undervalued, if the company was about to be sold into good, capable hands, its underlying value would soon be recognised and start to rise, if not soar again. Robert Melton would surely know what the future held for the company he had founded, would he not?

Glancing at his watch, Mustafa Kaleed accelerated hard back towards Manhattan. He wanted to get back in time to buy some Bicknor Wilmot stock for his modest portfolio.

He really did try to be a good Muslim, he told himself.

At the British Airways check-in desk Robert handed over his ticket and passport to the smiling young lady waiting to undertake the check-in process. Seeing the name in his passport and on his ticket, her demeanour remained friendly but he immediately detected the adoption of a more formal approach. He'd seen this happen many times before when people had worked out who he was.

Then, looking more carefully at his ticket, she frowned before saying, 'I'm sorry Mr Melton, I think a mistake may have been made. This ticket is for an economy-class seat. I'm sure you're meant to be up in our first-class cabin.' This last part was said in the form of a statement rather than as a question.

'No, there's no mistake. I booked to fly in economy,' Robert responded gently.

The young lady looked more puzzled than ever. 'But you are the Mr Robert Melton of Bicknor Wilmot Securities?' she said enquiringly, after quickly glancing at her list of VIP names for the flight.

'Yes, I suppose so,' said Robert. 'But not really any longer – I was that person yesterday, but today and in future I'm just ordinary Robert Melton, metaphorically speaking.'

Now thoroughly confused, the young lady resorted to calling over a supervisor. After a quick consultation between them, the supervisor, eager to get the credit and to be of service to the great Robert Melton, smilingly came over to tell Robert he had been upgraded to first class on the flight.

To his total amazement, Robert thanked him politely and kindly, but declined, explaining he wanted to fly on the original ticket he had booked in economy.

The young desk clerk and her supervisor looked at each other. The supervisor shrugged imperceptibly and said, 'Absolutely no problem, Mr Melton. Whatever you wish. Stephanie here will get you checked in at once.'

The window seat Jill had managed to book for her boss had moments ago been released and was now gone. It was a busy flight and the back of the aircraft was full. After take-off, with people on either side, Robert, sitting in the rather narrow, upright position provided in economy-class seats that were not really designed for men of his height and build, resigned himself to a sleepless night.

Mercifully the pilot announced that due to the favourably strong trade winds, the flight would be a quick one. They would be in London in less than six hours.

Although physically strong, Robert had underestimated just how tired he had become after everything he had been through since his grandmother had died. Closing his eyes and putting his head back for a moment, he fell fast asleep. The next thing he knew he was being shaken quite firmly by a stewardess announcing they were coming in to land at London's Heathrow Airport.

52

AFTER TAKING THE tube from Heathrow to Kensington High Street, Robert walked up Kensington Church Street towards the bishop's house. Although it was still early, the streets were already busy with people hurrying to work in every direction. He felt uncustomarily nervous as he arrived outside the bishop's residence.

Although not a palace, the house was a substantial, classically proportioned building dating back about 160 years. Constructed of aged red brick over four floors, it had matching tall Georgian-style windows, four on each floor, divided in the middle by an elegant front door with a cantilevered neo-classical portico above. It was set back within a courtyard of similar buildings that were prominently attractive, without being overly grand or pretentious – suitable to the dignity of the Bishop of West London at the time of its building.

Robert was surprised at his sudden apprehension; he was more nervous now than he had been when he first crossed the bishop's threshold some eight years earlier. It was not something he had felt since getting himself established in America. As a highly successful and very rich financier, he had become more used to observing the nervousness in others meeting him than the other way around.

After pressing the white ceramic button in the centre of the well-polished brass doorbell surround, he stood back. He did not have long to wait until he heard footsteps from within, crossing the bare wooden floor.

The door opened. Camilla Rogers stood there with the same broad welcoming smile she had had when she had brought him coffee with homemade biscuits and a bright welcome to the diocese. Hand extended, she said, 'Robert. What can I say, other than welcome back to London and in particular to our home. I've got a room ready for you and we want you to stay with us for as long as you like. Come in,' she said with a wave of her hand, as she stood aside to let Robert enter.

At the same time Bishop Rogers came hurrying across the well-polished floor of the generously proportioned hallway.

'My dear fellow. Camilla's beaten me to it, but welcome back. It's so very good to see you again. Did you have a good flight?' He spoke with genuine warmth and sincerity.

'Yes Bishop, but largely because I slept the whole way, I think,' Robert said, smiling as he shook the bishop's hand.

'Please call me John from now on, Robert. I can't tell you how happy I am you have returned. But here I am talking when I expect you'd like to go up to your room for a wash before we all have breakfast? Camilla insisted upon preparing a hearty breakfast for you as she thought you might be hungry after your travels. I told her you'd get pretty well fed in first class but she still insisted,' the bishop said, glancing over at his wife with a good-humoured chuckle.

'Bishop ... sorry, I mean John, I didn't fly in first class. In fact, at my own insistence I had an ordinary, economy seat at the back of the plane. I'll explain everything to you later but, in making my decision to come back and pick up where I – wrongly – left off, I need to return to the starting point, to where I was then. I'm no longer a rich man. In fact I have nothing but the clothes I'm wearing and the few things I have in my bag,' Robert said, indicating the small suitcase he had brought with him.

'Mrs Rogers is right. I'm starving. I don't even know if dinner, or any food, was served on the flight. I fell asleep right after take-off and I didn't wake up until I was woken by an air hostess informing me we were coming in to land. So, a hearty breakfast sounds wonderful.'

Camilla Rogers gave her husband a triumphant smile that told him he should be more ready to trust feminine intuition and, in particular, that of his wife. Robert had the impression this may have happened once or twice before.

Overcoming his surprise at what he had just been told, Bishop Rogers regarded Robert with a new respect. He had so many questions to ask and so much to find out from Robert about what experiences he had had over the past eight years. He could already tell that this was a different person entirely from the thrusting, idealistic young man he had appointed as the vicar of St Mungo's.

In his place now stood a mature, worldly wise man who, although still young in relative terms, was definitely no longer wet behind the ears. In the prime of his life, he had a presence now that clearly marked him as someone who was used to being a decision-maker and a leader of men. He could immediately see that this Robert Melton was destined to go far.

Having shown Robert up to his room the bishop went down to help his wife put the final touches to the breakfast he had been so wrong about.

Twenty minutes later, freshly washed and shaved, Robert joined them in the dining room. Camilla Rogers had excelled herself in the kitchen. Robert was soon tucking in to a full, cooked English breakfast that even included his favourite grilled tomatoes and mushrooms, along with the requisite scrambled eggs, proper pork sausages, bacon and beans.

Afterwards, sitting back over steaming hot, freshly brewed coffee, served in large, white, bone china cups, Robert recounted all the main events that had taken place in his life since his abrupt departure from St Mungo's.

Although time at this moment would not allow for a full recounting, even abbreviated to its essential points it was, he knew, an absolutely breathtaking story. But already instinct told him that the bishop and his wife were destined to become friends, so there would be other opportunities to fill in all the details at another time.

Over two hours later, when Robert had finished his outline of events, and questions had been asked and answered, the bishop brought the subject round to the present. He did so by again apologising to Robert for what he now clearly saw was an act of deceit and betrayal over the way in which he had persuaded him to take that first appointment at St Mungo's.

'It was wrong of me, Robert. I know that now. The only explanation I can offer you by way of excuse is that, with everything else going on around me in the diocese at the time, I was getting pretty desperate about St Mungo's and I genuinely thought the experience would be a good grounding for you. I salved my conscience by telling myself that if, by some miracle, you were able to come up with the funds – I didn't know how, perhaps by bringing in a rich benefactor – I would be prepared to try and get the Church Commissioners to reverse their decision to close your church.

'The irony is of course that you did come up with a miracle. A far more unlikely and far bigger one than I could ever possibly have imagined and, as a result, you did save St Mungo's – despite me and not because of me. Who says God doesn't have a sense of humour?

'The whole episode has taught me a lot about faith, miracles and the powerful and mysterious manner in which the good Lord chooses his own way of doing things. But the other part of the miracle for me is that, against all the odds, you've given up your life of wealth and luxury to return to the priesthood. I've prayed diligently for that ever since you left, but what was the likely reality of that ever happening? I'm still stunned by the whole turn of events. It simply defies all logic, and yet, from what you've now told me, it would seem that, for you, it was all meant as part of your destiny. I wish I could have met your grandmother.'

'Yes, she was a wise and amazing woman. I think you and she would have liked each other a lot. But I'll let Mary tell you about her when she gets over to England. By the way, on that note, would you consent to officiating at our marriage at St Mungo's? We'd both like to get married as soon as we can after she gets here in six weeks or so.'

'I'd be honoured and absolutely delighted, but I'm very surprised you'd even consider me after the shabby way I treated you,' responded the bishop.

'Well, I think I need to apologise to *you*, for the shabby and disobedient way I treated you and the Church of England by just walking out. But the way I see it now, St Mungo's brought me and my grandmother together, and I'm delighted to be able to come full circle and get back to serving my church and my parish.'

'All right, can we call it quits?' the bishop asked, smiling and offering his hand. Both men stood and shook hands warmly. Camilla excused herself to go to the kitchen and make some fresh coffee. There, as she wiped a tear from her eye, she said a silent prayer of thanks to the God she had all her married life tried to believe in as fervently as her husband did.

'Now,' said the bishop sitting down again. 'Do you really want to go back to St Mungo's as soon as possible? Would you at least consider going back as the area dean, with responsibility for more than just that church?'

'If it's all right with you, Bishop ... sorry, John ... I'd like to go back to exactly where I so abruptly left off, just as the vicar. At least for now ... and the immediately foreseeable future. I feel I owe it to the parishioners and to myself to do that. Call it unfinished business if you like.'

'Well, in that case, I'm pleased to tell you you're in luck. Call it providence or coincidence, but just before I got your call from New York, I'd had a letter from Father Ridley, the incumbent at St Mungo's, requesting an early transfer. He's only been there nine months and I wasn't going to agree until you telephoned out of the blue. Anyhow, I contacted him right away. He's ecstatic. Didn't expect me to say yes and now he can't wait to leave and hand over to you. We've found him a parish down in Cornwall, quite sleepy most of the year, but it wakes up a bit during the summer holiday period. Should suit him fine. He wanted to know how long you'd like him to stay and overlap with you.'

'Not long at all really. Of course I'd like to meet him and get an update on the current regular parishioners, but he doesn't need to show me the ropes.'

'I thought you'd say that, so I've suggested he stays just through this weekend and leaves on Monday. However, if you like and can manage all right, I know the Cornish parish could use him right away, starting this Sunday, which would mean him leaving to travel down there on Saturday at the latest.'

'That's fine with me. After we finish here I thought I'd walk over there anyway. I can't tell you how much I'm looking forward to seeing St Mungo's again – excited really. I'll introduce myself to Father Ridley. After we've had a chat and he's updated me, he can give me the keys and feel free to leave any time. Tomorrow even, if he likes.'

'Good. His name is James. Not Jim. He likes to be called James. Oh, and by the way, there is something that is different. The old vicarage in Pembroke Villas has been sold. Sold shortly after you left in fact – far too big for a parish like St Mungo's to justify these days. The present place is a much smaller house the diocese already owned up on the back of Campden Hill. Callcott Street, near Notting Hill Gate. Not as convenient. A bit more of a walk I'm afraid, but you can always catch a number 27 bus. That'll take you down to the top of Earls Court Road if you like.'

'The longer walk should suit me fine. I'll enjoy it, especially in good weather.'

'Excellent. Well I suppose I should be getting on,' the bishop said, glancing at his watch. 'I told the office not to expect me before noon today, so I still just have time to take you down to St Mungo's and introduce you to James Ridley if you'd like?'

'Thank you, but there's no need, John. In fact I'd really like to walk over there on my own if that's OK with you?'

'That's fine. I completely understand,' replied the bishop, standing up.

'Just one more question. A matter of curiosity really,' said Robert, also getting to his feet. 'Your mention of your office reminded me. How is your assistant, Christopher Callow?'

The bishop stopped in his walk towards the front door and turned to face

Robert. 'I'm afraid he's in prison,' he said. 'He had a weakness for prostitutes of the streetwalker variety and was caught in a sting operation when he picked up what he thought was a hooker, but who in fact turned out to be a policewoman. It seems in his haste he was already indecently exposed when she produced her badge and arrested him. He wouldn't have gone down if this had been a first offence. Unfortunately he had a long history of it.

'Poor Christopher. He was a little too clever for his own good. His mistake was not so much in overestimating his own, not inconsiderable, intelligence, but in always underestimating the intelligence of others around him. He didn't think I knew of his past when I first took him on. Nor did he think I knew about his habit of listening in to my telephone conversations.

'He was only given six months and that was four months ago so he'll be ready for parole soon. I've been to see him in Ford Open Prison and I've promised to help him try and find another job. Unfortunately, because of the nature of his conviction, it is no longer possible to keep him on as my assistant.'

'I'm sorry to hear that,' Robert replied sincerely 'But I can't say I'm entirely surprised. There was always an air about him that was a little too smooth – as if he was hiding something that didn't quite add up.'

Bishop Rogers held open the front door and, while Robert thanked his wife for the welcome breakfast, he noted that the morning, which had started out so bright, was beginning to cloud over. The rain that had been forecast would not be far behind.

'Robert, welcome back. It's so good to have you home. I'm sorry we're out for dinner this evening, but I expect you'll be tired and pleased to get an early night. Remind me and I'll give you a key later.' This was spoken with such genuine warmth and sincerity, a formal handshake didn't seem quite enough. Both men spontaneously gave each other a hug.

'Thank you, John. It's good to be back,' said Robert, stepping outside. 'I'll see you this evening. So kind of you to give me a bed for the night.' He gave a final cheery wave before turning and setting off back down Kensington Church Street. From there he decided to walk along Holland Street, running parallel to the High Street, but much quieter.

Closing the door gently the bishop turned to his wife with a thoughtful look on his face.

'You know, all the time Robert was here my experience and training was telling me to be on the lookout for some other motive, some other reason behind what, on the face of it, looks like the most extraordinary altruistic course of action he has taken. It's almost unbelievable really that someone could willingly give up so much to resume life as the vicar in what is still essentially a dead-end parish like St Mungo's. I can't figure it out – and yet I'm having the hardest time in accepting his explanation at face value. Maybe I'm just too cynical in my old age, but if it's true, I really envy him.'

'No you don't,' said his wife. 'You envy his faith. And that's all right because what he's doing can act as an inspiration to reawaken and invigorate the faith of many an old priest like you.'

Her husband pulled a face of mock outrage.

'You know, I'm a pretty shrewd judge of character and I believe him. He's not some pious hypocrite and, God knows, we've got enough of those in any and all religions.'

'You're defending him because you like him. He's still as charming as he was when you first met him.'

Giving her husband an affectionate push with her hand, his wife responded teasingly. 'Now, now, no need to be jealous, you're the man for me and, anyway, I'm practically old enough to be his mother. In fact, I'll bet I *am* old enough to be his mother.'

Heading towards the dining room to clear away the breakfast things, Camilla Rogers added over her shoulder, 'I'm serious about his faith being inspirational, though. And not just to old priests in need of a little renewal.'

Bishop Rogers smiled to himself as he picked his umbrella out of the stand by the door and prepared to let himself out. He knew exactly what his wife meant and he was pleased. He made a mental note to be sure to invite Robert over for a family supper from time to time. He wondered what Robert's fiancée, Mary, would turn out to be like. He very much hoped they would all get along and become friends.

53

AT THE BOTTOM of Phillimore Gardens where it joins Kensington High Street, Robert paused, waiting for a break in the busy morning traffic.

Now on reassuringly familiar territory, he found himself directly outside the courtyard entrance to Our Lady of Victories Roman Catholic Church. On an impulse he diverted into the church to say a quick prayer for Andreas. Robert often found since he had broken off contact that he was reminded of his old friend whenever he saw or passed a Catholic church and this was one he knew well.

Morning Mass was being celebrated as he walked quietly in at the back of the church. The first reading had just begun. Not really listening or intending to stay for more than a moment or two, Robert's attention was caught when he realised the reading was from Matthew, Chapter 5, in which Jesus admonishes those to whom He is talking '... to leave these thy gifts before the altar, and go thy way; first be reconciled to thy brother, and then come and offer thy gift'.

Robert left the church as quietly as he had entered and the thought came to him that of course Andreas would know nothing of his time spent up in New Hampshire, nor of his decision to give up his wealth and return to the priesthood. Unless, of course, Andreas were to have come across it in some of the low-key press stories that had been run, or perhaps might yet be run before Robert's news value had evaporated.

Surprisingly, most of the business press and magazines had so far chosen to give the story only the most muted coverage, as though they felt betrayed by one of their own and were almost too embarrassed to mention it. Many in the business world would have liked to explain away Robert's actions as something to be pitied sagely and only mentioned in the same hushed tones as one might in referring to a nervous breakdown. Robert resolved to write to Andreas; he felt suddenly full of remorse and sadness at the wasted years of a friendship he had lost.

Walking the last familiar few hundred yards down Earls Court Road towards St Mungo's, what, he wondered to himself, had led him to enter that Catholic church at that precise moment?

At Our Lady of Victories, the priest, considerably younger than his head of white hair would imply, had noticed Robert's silent arrival and departure at the back of the church. There was nothing unusual in this. People were always coming and going from the church and most of the time it attracted no notice. On this occasion though it had, for some reason, caught his attention. It wasn't just that Robert was a large man. Monsignor Seamus Corrie could not quite put his finger on it, but this particular stranger had an aura about him that was made of more than just a self-confident bearing and height of stature. It was as if a sort of joyful energy seemed to emanate from him.

Passing the main Kensington Police Station, Robert smiled to himself as he recognised the familiar overhead, blue glass 'Police' lantern that had always reminded him of the affable Sergeant Dixon, that fictional police sergeant from the popular television series *Dixon of Dock Green*. He had always thought there was more than a little of the priest in that wise and gentle 'copper'.

At the Earls Court Road end of Pembroke Square, Richard, the proprietor of Kensington's much-loved garden centre, Rassells, was stepping out to get his obligatory morning coffee from everyone's favourite café, Le Monde. He did a double-take as he almost bumped into Robert.

Richard apologised profusely before having one of those moments of delayed recognition, triggered by the broad grin on Robert's face. 'Robert?' he asked uncertainly.

'Good to see you again, Richard,' Robert said warmly, holding out his hand.

'You're back?' Richard said, unconsciously stating the obvious as everyone does in such situations.

'Yes, and to stay this time,' responded Robert. 'At least for the foreseeable future.'

These two had formerly been neighbourhood acquaintances rather than friends, but had always been on first-name terms in acknowledging they were both there to serve the same community, if in rather different ways. Rassells had supplied the church with flowers and plants from time to time and Richard made it his business to know all his local customers.

'Well, it's good to see you and good to have you back,' Richard said with a parting wave as he turned towards Le Monde and the cup of morning coffee he could never do without.

From Rassells, Robert could easily see St Mungo's as he strode towards his final destination. Yes, it felt really good to be back.

With the money he had provided, the building had been outwardly restored in accordance with his instructions. Nevertheless he could tell at once from its forlorn aura that it was still suffering – not so much from physical neglect as a lack of direction. Robert saw right away that St Mungo's radiated no purpose – no mission.

Perversely this gave Robert a feeling of guilty excitement. He felt as if St Mungo's was stubbornly waiting for him. His money had saved it from the inevitable, but the church still needed Robert himself to bring it back to life. And they would do this together through serving the community that teemed around them on every side.

As he headed over to the side door, he noticed that the church clock, hanging on its bracket out over the pavement on Earls Court Road, had been repaired and was no longer permanently proclaiming the time to be eight-thirty. Striking the hour, it was now loudly announcing that it was eleven o'clock.

Robert paused with his hand on the door handle to listen to its chimes and remembered the day that he had stepped out through that same door and headed for America. What had happened in between then and now seemed like some sort of fantastic dream, and yet one in which he could not help feeling there had been – and still was – a purpose all along. Whatever it was, that purpose had now brought him back.

Stopping at the first row of pews, Robert knelt down to say a prayer. It was a prayer of heartfelt feeling to the God he knew loved him and whom in return he was determined to serve and love back. He felt an extraordinary sense of gratitude at being given this second chance, but it was also something more than that. The realisation dawned on him that he was, at this very moment, feeling more excited, more challenged and far happier than he had ever felt deal-making as an acknowledged 'Master of the Universe'. 'May today there be peace within; May you trust God that you are exactly where you are meant to be' – St Theresa had got it right in Robert's favourite prayer.

By the time he stood up his eyes had adjusted to the darkened interior and Robert looked around. He was surprised at how little had changed. The stone font and the flagstone floors had been cleaned of the years of blackening London grime. The broken windows had been repaired. But, beyond that, he could not immediately see anything very different from when he had left.

He was on his way to the vestry when he heard behind him the sound of the big front door of the church being quietly opened. Robert stood motionless, hardly daring to breathe, the clear and vivid memory of that same sound bridging the years for him. He knew exactly what it meant. Seconds ticked by as he strained his ears to hear if Brenda was just arriving or just leaving. The complete silence told him it was the latter. Turning to look, he could see the back of the church was empty. Nevertheless he decided to walk back just in case.

Brenda must have already been in the church and seen him arrive. He marvelled again at her chameleon-like ability to render herself more or less invisible. Robert saw at once the small piece of white paper, taken from the pad he remembered Brenda always carried with her. It was folded over. The side facing upwards on the pew where it had been left clearly bore his name. In eager anticipation he reached down and unfolded it.

'Welcome home Robert,' it read. 'I knew you'd come back. Unfinished business. I've been praying for you. Brenda.'

Folding the piece of paper back over, Robert put it carefully in his pocket. He smiled as he remembered Brenda's ability to convey much with the greatest economy of written words. It was a skill she had had to learn and had learned very well. But it was her choice of the exact same two words – 'Unfinished business' – that first Andreas and later Robert himself had used that intrigued him most.

The door to the vestry on the right of the altar stood ajar. Robert made his way towards the front of the church where he noticed the figure of the vicar moving around inside. Pushing open the door and holding out his hand, Robert asked mischievously, 'Father Jim Ridley?'

With what Robert thought sounded like a rather irritated and petulant correction, Father Ridley replied, 'James Ridley. My parishioners call me Father James,' he added to emphasise further that there was no form of address in which he would accept the diminution of the full 'James'.

'You must be Robert Melton, I imagine?' he said, taking Robert's outstretched hand. 'I've been looking forward to your arrival.' Then, scarcely able to conceal his eagerness, he added, 'I believe you know all the ropes of this place already, so I can't imagine there is much I need to show you or tell you?

'Do you know when I might be free to leave for my next parish? It's rather a long way down in the south of Cornwall and I know they'd like me to get there as soon as possible.'

For a moment Robert was tempted to suggest he might like to stay for the normal ten-day handover period, just to see the reaction this might provoke. But the truth was he too was eager to get on and did not really want anyone around who wasn't as fully committed to St Mungo's as he knew he was. In his business life he'd always hated the toxic, debilitating effect of having negative people around him.

Just as Robert Melton was a notably tall man, blessed with an athletic build, James Ridley was notably small of stature. He had a sunken chest and a rather sallow complexion that implied he did not spend more time outside than he had to. His unprepossessing appearance was not helped by the thin, wispy grey-blond hair flattened across his balding head. He was still only fifty-four but looked older. He had the aura of a man easily defeated by the problems of life, complicated by a blustering attitude that tried to demand respect, without the willingness or ability to earn it. It was not the first time he had run away from a failed posting.

Looking at him, Robert better understood his desperate need for the insistence on the full 'James'. It was not so much that he liked the name better than the more informal 'Jim', it was that in its full form it was, or seemed, more respectful of him.

Over his years in America Robert had seen such people many times, usually full of a latent resentment at being abused in the employment of powerful men to whom they were almost always fatally attracted by the idea that they could somehow, at least vicariously, share in their power. Looking now at James Ridley he suddenly felt a wave of compassion and sympathy for him.

'Well James, how about we spend the rest of today going over things and you leave at your leisure tomorrow morning? Would that suit you?'

Somewhat to his surprise, Robert thought he saw a look of disappointment pass over James's face. He realised that in his desperation to leave, James's wishful thinking had allowed him to believe he might even be relieved of his post before the end of that very day. Just as James Ridley was on the point of reluctantly acquiescing to that idea, Robert had another thought.

'Tell you what, if we go over everything today, this evening I'll take us both out to dinner somewhere halfway decent to celebrate my return and your new appointment to the staff of the Bishop of Truro. Besides, I'll need you to show me how the house works too. If it's anything like the last place I'll need to know the idiosyncrasies of the plumbing if I'm to have any hope of a hot shower in the morning!'

Visibly brightening, James Ridley smiled. In fact that idea filled him with pleasure. The fame of Robert Melton's extraordinarily successful achievements in the world of international business had not escaped him. James Ridley was also more than a little intrigued at how Robert Melton could possibly have voluntarily relinquished such enormous temporal power and fabulous wealth to return to St Mungo's of all places.

The fact that this man was willing, even wanted, to take him out for a celebratory dinner flattered his pride. For the first time in a long time he felt needed – even appreciated. The Bishop of Truro could wait one more day.

Over dinner at Julie's Restaurant that night, James Ridley was able to fill in some of the gaps in parish life since Robert's abrupt departure and his almost equally sudden return. A number of the older parishioners had died, or left the area to be cared for in nursing homes, or by relatives. It seemed there were few replacements and a respectable Sunday congregation had now dwindled to a mere ten to fifteen people.

Robert asked about Brenda.

'Oh, she's one of the deadbeats from the back streets off Earls Court Road, on the wrong side of Cromwell Road. Rude, arrogant woman. I tried talking to her once. She just looked at me in a totally expressionless sort of way and walked off without saying a word. If I didn't know better, I'd say she might have been assessing, almost reading me, but it's more likely the blank expressionless look she portrayed is induced by a lifetime of street life and drug abuse. I think she comes into the church for somewhere to go. It's warm in the winter and dry when it's wet. She never comes on a Sunday, or to any of the services. Not interested.'

Robert debated whether to tell James just how wrong he was in his judgement but decided against it on the basis that he was leaving. Instead, wanting to please, he said, 'I understand you're badly needed down in Cornwall and they're very anxious for you to get there?'

'When it was known I was leaving here, the Bishop of Truro telephoned at once asking for me specially to join his staff.'

This may not have been precisely how Bishop Rogers would have phrased it, and it made Robert feel sorry for the man sitting across the table from him.

Robert felt some sympathy for James Ridley. But for that lottery ticket he might easily have found himself looking back on a life where, somewhere along the way, all the promise, hope and energy of youth had been extinguished in disappointment and disillusionment.

He wondered what James's dreams had been when he was a young man first joining the priesthood, with hope in his heart and wings on his heels, burning with a determination to do the work of God. He resolved to pray for James that even at his age, his 'lottery ticket' moment might find him down in Cornwall and lead him on a journey that would ultimately fill his life with purpose and a genuine sense of self-worth.

As it was a pleasantly warm evening the two men decided to walk back to the vicarage house in Callcott Street. An understanding had grown between them – not a friendship so much as a mutual acceptance and respect between two men, each pursuing very different paths, but nevertheless committed to the same cause.

The Callcott Street vicarage was a small, double-fronted, terraced Georgian house located in the picturesque area between Notting Hill Gate and Campden Hill, rather prosaically known locally as 'Hillgate Village'. Built in 1850, it had all the characteristics and quirkiness of a house this age that had been adapted and updated over the years to suit the lifestyles and requirements of countless different occupants. After the spaciousness of Pembroke Villas, Robert knew it was going to feel very small.

The following morning, after warmly thanking Bishop Rogers and his wife for their generous hospitality, Robert took his things up from the bishop's house to Callcott Street and said goodbye to James Ridley.

Setting off for St Mungo's, Robert decided it was the first day of the rest of his life, doing now what he knew he was meant to be doing. He felt elated walking down from the top of Campden Hill, through Holland Park towards Earls Court Road.

54

THE NEXT THREE weeks sped by.

Robert was engrossed in reacquainting himself with his parish, although he was also mindful of the need to take time for himself. He still needed time to grieve for his grandmother, and time to think and pray, to ask God to help him as he found his way again. He was also keen to reconnect with those of his former parishioners who were still there. Far from being delighted, initially one or two of them seemed to regard his return with grave suspicion, even resentment. To begin with, Robert had to work hard to overcome this, but he began to feel that he had succeeded to a large degree by demonstrating his daily commitment to St Mungo's and its parish outreach.

It was a cause of frustration to him that he had seen nothing of Brenda since that first day of his return. He needed to confirm if Brenda could also be the 'Brendan' Sister Lucy was looking for, as he had promised his grandmother he would. But he also wanted to see if he could enlist Brenda's help in trying to create a link with the people in the parish who lived on the south side of Cromwell Road. She had asked for his help once – long ago. A request he now regretted having brushed aside. Was he hoping for too much now? He found himself thinking how sad it was that she never came to any of the regular church services.

Although Robert had immediately written to Andreas in America, as he had promised himself he would on that first day back in London, he had had no reply. This was perhaps the only sadness he felt in his now otherwise focused and purposeful life. He knew he would not stay for ever at St Mungo's, but he would stay for as long as it took to set its course and direction before accepting a bigger challenge, as he knew he must in his continuing service to God.

In less than a month Mary would be joining him, and they would then have a wedding to plan. It was a delightful prospect. He could not wait to show her something of London and in particular St Mungo's. He knew she would be of great assistance in his parish work. He also thought she might be very helpful to him in reaching out to Brenda and others like her.

It was in this positive and happy frame of mind that the following Sunday he celebrated the ten-thirty Holy Communion service. It was surprisingly well attended. Word of his return, coupled with knowledge of his extraordinary achievements in the world of high finance before his sudden return to the priest-hood, had made him, if not a celebrity, certainly a man of interest. People were intrigued enough to use the excuse for a one-off attendance at Sunday church.

Robert, of course, knew and understood this, but he also felt it was part of the opportunity he had been given to reach out to as many people as possible. He regarded it as the equivalent of the first 120 seconds he had been given when pitching his first early business proposals; a habit he had in turn learned to employ when the proposals were all being pitched to him.

Understanding the importance of these first two minutes, he worked very hard on his sermons and the personal manner in which he engaged with all those who came to St Mungo's. He knew he would not win them all, but he was motivated and excited to win as many as he possibly could, whatever their initial reason for coming to the church may have been.

After the service on this particular Sunday and after everyone had finally gone, Robert was in the vestry removing his vestments when his church warden, who had been counting the money in the collection plate, said with a chuckle, 'Well, Robert, some wag seems to have put an American Powerball lottery ticket in the plate. It's from the State of New Hampshire,' he said, handing it to him.

As far as Robert was aware, apart from the bishop, no one in England knew of the original Powerball lottery ticket having been deposited in the Sunday collection plate all those years ago. Immediately he understood there was only one person in the world who had the knowledge – and the sense of humour – to use this as his calling card.

Going at once back into the church, with the lottery ticket still in his hand, Robert thought at first that the solitary figure kneeling, head bowed, at the back might be Brenda. But of course Brenda never came to the church on Sunday. Whoever it was had chosen the exact same spot in the shadows where Brenda always sat.

With a rising sense of excitement, and not a little guilty apprehension, Robert made his way towards the kneeling figure.

'Andreas?' he enquired, speaking quietly.

The happy expression on Andreas's face when he looked up with a broad smile told Robert at once that he had been forgiven.

The two old friends embraced. They needed no words to convey forgiveness, or confirm the immediate re-establishment of their friendship.

'I was so happy to get your letter a couple of weeks ago,' Andreas began. 'When I showed it to the abbot he was delighted too and immediately agreed to give me leave to travel here and see you. I wanted to come straight away but there were things I had to do. I came just as soon as I could.'

For the rest of that day, the two friends talked. First over a cup of coffee at Le Monde where, unconscious of time or those around them, it eventually fell to the good-natured Belgian patron to ask them to vacate the table they were hogging, it being a small establishment with only room for five tables in total. Then over a good lunch, sitting outside at the Hillgate Pub, around the corner from Callcott Street. Both men had the signature homemade fish cakes, with a poached egg on top, following which they went for a long walk through Kensington Gardens and

Hyde Park. Their route took them past the famous Round Pond, and along the edge of the Serpentine, where on an impulse they rented one of the small tourist rowing boats.

Sitting out on the water just gently adrift on this fine autumn day provided an ideal environment for Robert to extend the unequivocal apology he had long felt he owed Andreas. As he did so, he acknowledged how right Andreas had been in his honest, if uncompromising, advice – and how wrong he had been in not only ignoring it, but in allowing himself angrily to dismiss it to the point of cutting off their friendship.

However, Andreas refused to accept that any apology was either owed or necessary. In his typically generous way, he said that he was as much to blame as Robert for having encouraged him in the first place. 'If anyone was to blame, it is a blame we must both share,' he had concluded as a compromise.

'Andreas, you are a very good, kind man and a wonderfully loyal friend,' Robert said, thanking him for what he knew he must now accept as the forgiveness he sought.

His friend's response was not what Robert might have expected. The expression on Andreas's face changed from one of warm, even affectionate, camaraderie, to a faraway look of infinite sadness. Turning away from Robert, he stared silently across the water, seeing and saying nothing.

For a while, neither of them spoke. Robert sensed this was a moment when words would be of little help. But he was shocked by the sudden change that had overcome his friend. Andreas's face had turned into a picture of pain and melancholy and as Robert looked at him he thought he caught Andreas wiping away a tear.

When Andreas finally broke their silence he spoke in a quiet voice, full of a deep sadness. 'No Robert, I'm not good or kind – and I'm most certainly not a loyal friend. At least I haven't always been.

'I've spent a lifetime trying hard to be all those things, but it can never make up for the past. The feeble best we can all do is to try and learn from our mistakes in seeking redemption and perhaps, one day, gaining forgiveness. There is not a day that goes by when my past doesn't haunt me, without any prospect of deserving or gaining either. I cope and console myself with the thought that, just perhaps, it is the actions of my past that have driven and instructed me all these years to be the best possible priest I can be. In a similar way, that is how I know you too will be a very good priest from here on.'

Robert didn't understand this reaction in Andreas. Or whatever it was he had unwittingly said that must have struck such a raw nerve. He wanted to ask his friend about it, but sensed this was not the time.

It was agreed that Andreas would be Robert's guest at the rectory and later that evening, Andreas had recovered his spirits sufficiently for them to pass a very pleasant couple of hours over a leisurely dinner at Thai Break, just around the corner. Andreas was a tennis enthusiast which made him wonder if the play on words in the name meant the owner was, or had been, a famous tennis player. The food was excellent.

The following morning, Robert said he needed to be down at St Mungo's by eight o'clock. He suggested Andreas get over his jet lag by taking an extra hour in bed and joining him at the church later.

Thus it was just before nine when Andreas opened the big front door to St Mungo's. He stepped quietly inside and, wanting to say a quick morning prayer before going to find Robert, went over towards the pew in which he had chosen to kneel the day before.

At first glance the church appeared to be empty, so it was a complete surprise to find someone kneeling in that exact spot. Because his eyes had not yet fully adjusted from the brightness outside, and because of the dark shadow cast by the big pillar, it took him a moment to distinguish this person as a very attractive, mixed-race woman.

At the moment their eyes briefly met in the gloomy light, Andreas was overcome with an inexplicable conviction that they had not only met somewhere before, but that they might even know each other. But where? How?

Reason and logic told him this could not be possible. And yet ... Andreas thought he had also seen the fleeting light of recognition pass over her face in that same instant. For a split second what appeared to be a glimpse of pure joy had illuminated her face, before her features were again composed into a cultivated inscrutability.

In the muted tone people instinctively adopt when speaking in church, Andreas murmured an apology for disturbing her before going to find another place to kneel. Oddly, she gave no recognition of his apology, nor made any pleasantry in return, choosing instead to ignore him and remain quite silent. Unknown to him, however, the woman had noted and memorised the name on the tag attached to the briefcase Andreas always carried.

He knelt down and tried to say the prayers he had intended to but, unable to get the image of the face he had just seen out of his mind, found he could not concentrate. Giving up, he made his way towards the vestry in search of Robert, but not before turning back to glance again towards the stranger he had just disturbed.

The pew was empty. There was no one there. Andreas had not heard the woman leave and he began to wonder if what he had seen was a ghost. There was something about the face of this strangely beautiful lady – something that bothered him.

Finding Robert in the vestry, Andreas mentioned his encounter with the silent, shadowy figure at the back of the church.

'Oh, that'll be Brenda,' Robert said. 'She often comes in like that during the week. She always comes alone, mostly about this time of the morning. She never comes to any of the formal services, though.'

'Strange that she didn't reply when I apologised for disturbing her,' Andreas mused aloud.

'No, not when you know about her,' Robert replied. 'She's dumb. Not as in stupid – far from it – but as in mute. Brenda's completely unable to speak.'

'Oh,' Andreas said rather lamely, after the uncharitable thoughts that had been building in his mind. 'That's quite unusual, I suppose.'

'Is she still there?' Robert asked. 'Actually, I want to talk to her. Ask for her help with something.'

'No, that's another odd thing. She's gone, but I never heard her leave.'

'Typical Brenda. She's very private – slightly mysterious, in fact. She's been coming to St Mungo's, very much on her terms, since I first arrived. She's definitely one of the more interesting members of the parish.

'As a matter of fact, Brenda is the one parishioner who seems never to have judged me for leaving as I did.' He hesitated for a moment and then continued, 'Nor has she looked for any explanation of my behaviour after my return – though she more than anyone deserves it.'

Robert could see Andreas's questioning look and switched the conversation.

'You see, technically she's really a prostitute, but not in the way you might think. She provides a sort of service – a basic need I would describe it as – to the disfigured and disabled outcasts we all ignore or pass by. The sort of people whose appearance makes us wish we'd never seen them, because they make us feel guilty when we reject them all the same. You know the kind I mean, I'm sure.'

Andreas nodded.

'In their desperation, when they ask for it, she gives those poor people the closest they'll ever get to a sex life with any sort of empathy or affection. But, once you understand what Brenda does, how sensitively she does it, and most importantly, why she does it, I would question anyone's right to stand in judgement of her.

'I admit I struggled with this one for a long time. I know what the teaching of the church – mine and yours – would be. But after I found out what Brenda herself has been through and understanding how this helps her connect with her particular clients, I find it hard, even impossible, to condemn her.'

'Robert, I'm not sure what exactly you're talking about,' Andreas interjected. He didn't know why, but he was starting to feel very uneasy at these half-explained revelations about the woman he had just seen.

'I'm sorry,' Robert said. 'I should have told you more of Brenda's background first for it to make any sense. None of it is as it seems.

'To begin with, Brenda has not always been Brenda. She was once Brendan and she came to this country from Trinidad. It seems something happened to her out there that resulted in her being horribly mutilated. A crude and total castration. She – or he, of course – wasn't meant to survive this and was left for dead. But, as a sort of macabre warning to anyone else, whoever did this to her – a drugs gang I heard – also cut out her tongue. That's the reason she can't speak.

'Luckily some Good Samaritan found her. Got her to the hospital just in time to save her life. However, it wasn't safe for her to remain in Trinidad. Whoever it was who wanted her dead would almost certainly have found her and come back to finish the job. It seems that whatever it was she had done, or got herself mixed up in, had also caused her family to reject her completely. So, having barely recovered from that ghastly ordeal, she came all alone to England.

'I gather it was her mutilation, which left her physically neither a man nor woman, that led to her new life as Brenda. And even though she can't speak, she communicates eloquently enough in Sign Language, or by writing things down. She supports herself, working with her hands, giving massages. But not the kind of orthodox massage you or I might have when the muscles ache a bit. She only offers her service to the physically disabled or severely disfigured.

'As far as I understand it, she aims to communicate an acceptance, a love, an understanding and friendship between herself and her clients. She devotes herself exclusively to this marginalised, forgotten group of people. I'm quite certain that if an able bodied multi-millionaire turned up, willing to pay a hundred times more than her normal rate for a dodgy massage, she would be no more likely to do this for the money than you or I would. I'm quite sure she'd send them packing.

'So, you see, even though I suspect Brenda feels she's unworthy to come and receive the sacraments at our church services, who are we to judge her life, or what she does? Only God can do that and I suspect we might be surprised at how He sees and judges these things. I also have this feeling that when she comes in here to pray, it is as much for her clients, her 'untouchables' as she calls them, as it might be for herself.'

In the poor light of the vestry Robert had not noticed all the colour draining from Andreas's face while he had been talking. His friend was now sitting opposite Robert looking as though he was in a trance.

'Andreas? Andreas, are you all right? You look as if you've seen a ghost or something,' Robert said.

After what felt like the longest silence, Andreas replied hoarsely, 'Robert, I think perhaps I have. The ghost of my past. The ghost I've been unable to escape all my life.' Then he leant forward, burying his face in his hands.

Eventually, lifting his head and now addressing Robert as a priest, Andreas asked wearily, 'If we went into the church would you hear my confession, Father?'

Robert hesitated briefly, then slowly standing up, nodded his assent. He was taken aback by this complete change in his friend and was now feeling very uncomfortable and very apprehensive.

Both men made their way to the same spot in the pew where Brenda always sat and where Andreas had chosen to sit the first time he had come to St Mungo's. The church was empty.

Sitting down, Robert turned to his friend, 'Andreas, this doesn't have to be a formal confession in the way I know you do them in the Catholic Church. Just talk to me as your good friend. When you're done, I'll grant you absolution within the limitations of my own feeble ordained powers, but most importantly in the name of Christ our Lord who sees and forgives all who ask.'

'Thank you, Robert.'

After a short silence, during which Andreas struggled to choose his words, he continued. 'You see, nothing here is as it seems. Just as Brenda is not really Brenda, but Brendan, I'm not Andreas. At least not the Andreas Doria you think you know.

'No, my real name is, or once was, David Thornton. My parents moved to Trinidad when I was twelve – my father was posted there in the Diplomatic Service.

'Neither he nor my mother ever really wanted children. I was a mistake and they always made that clear to me. I just got in the way of their selfish, self-centred lives. My mother was an aspirational socialite, who lived only for parties, and my father was ambitious – very ambitious. I don't think they ever made much of an attempt to find me after I left. They'd probably got used to me doing my own thing a lot of the time, Then, anyway, they both died in a plane crash shortly afterwards – on their way back from a big costume party in Bermuda I heard later – they didn't think my absence was a significant enough reason for them to cancel an important invitation like that.'

Over the next forty minutes Andreas told Robert the whole story of his childhood in Trinidad; his close, teenage friendship with his schoolmate Brendan and his cowardly betrayal of that friendship; the terrible guilt and shame of that betrayal that had led him to leave Trinidad and come to Europe where, eventually, he had found a sort of peace within himself when he had recognised a vocational calling to the priesthood.

When he had finished, Robert asked him where the name Andreas Doria had come from.

His friend smiled and said sheepishly, 'It was the name of the ship I took to Rome. She was a cruise ship called the *Andrea Doria* and, although they weren't supposed to take on any crew, I managed to get work as a junior steward. Just for the transatlantic voyage back to Italy. They'd had some illness on board and were temporarily short-handed so they didn't ask too many questions. I felt so guilty and so miserable I just wanted to break with my past completely – to make a new life, to try to forget what had happened. To forget Brendan and what I'd seen done to him without even trying to help him. So I began with a new name. It seemed like a good name to adopt. A good omen I reasoned. I even took the necessary steps to have the name legalised.

'After a while there were, eventually, times when I thought I'd succeeded in burying my past. I no longer even felt like David Thornton and I began to feel comfortable – even to believe – in my new persona. I had already started learning Italian from the crew onboard ship and when we got to Rome I stopped speaking English altogether.

'During my years there I learned to speak Italian fluently. I began to dream in Italian and without even realising it, I was soon expressing myself with my hands as much as with my voice.

'But then something would happen. I'd see something, or someone would say something, and my past would come flooding right back. I'd see so clearly the look of awful hurt, then the compassion, and finally the complete forgiveness on Brendan's face. It was worse, much worse, when I had been drinking.

'The only thing from which I can take some small grain of comfort, was the fact that I was the "Good Samaritan" you mentioned. I came back after the attack and found Brendan. At first I thought he was dead, but when I saw he was still alive, although mercifully unconscious, I carried him to the main entrance of the hospital. Even then I was too scared of getting involved, so I just left him lying across the threshold. I waited in the shadows for someone to come and find him. Then I left. So you see I wasn't even a very good or brave Samaritan.'

Robert now remembered the occasion he and Andreas had celebrated too hard after completing their studies, when a look of awful melancholy had overcome his friend and he had heard a lapse into what he had thought at the time resembled the musical lilt of a random West Indian or Caribbean accent.

Robert had not thought too much about it then. A lot of people who drank too much became maudlin. Thinking back now though, he realised how few those times had been; how fiercely restrained Andreas would become in his drinking after just two or three glasses of wine.

Andreas interrupted his thoughts. 'Are you going to give me absolution, Robert?'

'You know your Church doesn't accept absolution from an Anglican priest as a beneficial sacrament in the way that you do?'

'I know that, Robert,' was all Andreas said by way of reply.

'All right. But before I do, I have two questions. The first is to ask you if you became a priest out of guilt, or because you were running away from your past? Did this play any part in your decision?'

'I asked myself that many times in the beginning and, no, truthfully, it did not. My finding of God, in more than the standard ritual of going to church in childhood, may well have had to do with the loneliness and low point I'd reached in my life. But isn't that often when God reaches out to touch us? When we need Him most and don't even realise it? It was after I recognised God's great love for me – for all of us – that I decided I wanted to give my life to serving Him. Before we ever seek God, He is always seeking us. And so, no, I didn't find God. He found me.'

After a pause for Robert to say something, Andreas continued, 'You said you had two questions?'

'Yes,' Robert replied. 'Don't you think it's Brenda's, or Brendan's, forgiveness and absolution you should really be asking for now that you've found him again?'

'Of course, and I intend to waste no time in doing so. But I needed to tell you – my most trusted friend – this truth about my past that I've kept buried for so long. Having presumed to stand in judgement over your actions with the money from the lottery ticket and having tried to counsel you over the moral predicaments you faced, I let you perhaps believe that I was in some way better than you – both as a man and as a priest.

'Now you know the truth and the hypocrisy of any thoughts like that. Through all our years of friendship I was never quite the person you believed I was. And I was never honest or brave enough to tell you of this deceit before now. That is why I needed to tell you first, to ask for your forgiveness and your priestly absolution. The truth is, you're a better man and a better priest than I have ever been.'

'No, Andreas. The truth is we are all deeply flawed. But if we believe, as you and I do, that we are made in the likeness of God, with His help – which is there for the asking, if we only ask – we can each find our own redemption. We're all on our own, often lonely, journeys towards this goal. That's the purpose of life. It is also, I think, what any truly meaningful friendship is about. Helping each other through all the ups and downs, sometimes simply just by being there.

'That's why I admire Brenda so much. She understands and she never passes judgement.'

Andreas smiled ruefully. 'Have no worry on that score, Robert. If you thought I was going to try and seize the evangelical high ground by muttering piously about hating the sin and loving the sinner you need have no concern on that issue.

'"Before you presume to judge any man, first walk a mile in his moccasins", that's what native Americans say. No, it's now the priest who should go on his knees to the prostitute. To beg forgiveness for what I did – or perhaps didn't do – all those years ago that played the pivotal role in bringing my friend to where he … she is today. I just want to go and talk to … Brenda and ask for this forgiveness.

'How do I find her, Robert?'

'There will be time for that tomorrow. I'll take you to her. But now let me give you that absolution. I don't suppose I'll ever hear such a sincere and heartfelt confession again and, as I have no doubt the good Lord has forgiven you long ago anyway, I don't intend to pass up on this opportunity.'

55

THE FOLLOWING DAY, having taken the precaution of making a telephone appointment for Andreas to see Brenda, Robert walked with his friend to the corner of Trebovir Road. From there he pointed out the building and told him to use the basement door.

He was on the point of leaving when he noticed the two uniformed policemen standing outside. Watching for a few minutes to see if they would move on, both men became aware of the arrival and departure of official-looking men dressed in suits. These were clearly not people who would be numbered among Brenda's clients.

'My God, what's going on? It looks like Brenda must have been raided,' said Robert. 'Probably not the best moment for a priest to get mixed up in something you can't explain and that's nothing to do with you. Let's go back and wait for the air to clear.'

Turning earnestly towards him, Andreas put a hand on his friend's shoulder, 'Robert, it is to do with me. I turned my back on my best friend once before. I'm not going to do it again.' With that Andreas started walking firmly towards the two policemen.

Seeing the look of determination on his friend's face, Robert did not try to stop him. Instead he called after him, 'Good luck. I'll wait for you in the Café Rouge I pointed out to you.'

Robert could tell that something was wrong the moment he pushed open the door. The normally welcoming, if sometimes professionally cheerful, atmosphere in this Café Rouge had gone, replaced by an air of shocked, even angry silence. There was a sense of sadness too. Robert made his way to the bar and noticed that the waitress passing him had been crying.

Late now for the breakfast crowd and early for the lunchtime customers, the place was not too busy. Robert took a seat on one of the bar stools; when Andreas joined him later they would move to a table in whatever was the quietest area.

He recognised the barman, although he had not yet had a chance to get to know him. Robert ordered his coffee and ventured an exploratory, 'Place seems a bit subdued today?'

The barman looked intently at him before taking in his dog collar. He seemed to make up his mind that Robert could be trusted.

'Yup,' he said, 'One of our best customers,' he began before appearing to pause for thought, '… only so much more than that really. Sort of neighbourhood angel. Mascot of this place too if you like. Would do anything to help anyone in trouble no matter who they were … Anyway, she was murdered last night. Strangled by one of her … particular massage clients … the disfigured and disabled. Someone else she was trying to help.

'Brenda had a special quality about her. She really saw these unfortunate people as people … as equal, fellow human travellers. She understood them in a way the rest of us never would. She was one of them. Wounded herself in some horrific brutal gang attack when she was just a teenager, I heard. Left for dead. Tongue cut out. She couldn't talk. Before the attack she'd been a boy, so you can guess what the bastards did to her down there,' he said, nodding towards Robert's crotch.

At any other time Robert would have been taken aback at this innocently irreverent, but he thought healthy, approach to treating a priest as just a regular guy in need of no special deference. But he was too shocked to take in any of that now. All he could think about was Brenda and Andreas. Should he go at once to find his friend, he wondered?

Putting his coffee down on the bar in front of him, the barman seemed to notice for the first time the look of complete shock on Robert's face. He wondered if perhaps he had said too much, or whether this was how priests always reacted to such terrible events.

'The massage thing,' he said hastily, 'it wasn't like what you might think. Brenda never did anything for herself. There was nothing dodgy about her, She wasn't a prostitute in any conventional sense. It's just there isn't a word for what she is … what she was. Except perhaps … an angel of sorts. But I suppose she wasn't one of those in any conventional sense either. It's just she was … so … so … such a good person. Never a thought for herself, nor a shred of self-pity. Always thinking of others and their needs, how they were feeling, in ways no one else ever would.

'Although she couldn't speak, she had this aura about her whenever she came in here … which was most days. It made everyone feel better about themselves and be kinder to each other. Even the customers noticed the difference in atmosphere between when she was in here and when she wasn't. Didn't know why of course, or that it had anything to do with her presence. Uncanny really. But Brenda was special like that. To communicate she would write notes or speak in Sign Language. It made me want to learn it. So I did. We'd often talk together when I wasn't too busy. Won't be any use now though will it?' he said wistfully, reaching mechanically into the washer for a glass to polish as he talked. 'I can't think what Nina and Rebecca must be going through. Nina was her landlady originally, but they'd really become a family, the three of them …'

Robert felt as if he was in a daze. Taking a pound out of his pocket, he put it down beside his untouched cup of coffee as he rose to leave.

'Don't you want your coffee?' the barman asked, pulling himself back into the present with an effort. But Robert was already halfway to the door.

Just then it swung open and Andreas walked slowly in, ashen-faced, with a look of such inconsolable grief Robert felt compelled to hug him tightly – never mind what anyone else may have thought.

He turned back towards the bar and pointed questioningly to a table over in a quiet corner of the restaurant area. The barman nodded, pouring another cup of coffee before picking up Robert's untouched cup and following them over to it.

'Andreas, I've just heard about it and I'm so terribly, terribly sorry,' Robert said quietly to his friend, putting a comforting hand on his arm.

'The awful timing of this just seems so cruel,' Andreas responded. 'Although I've prayed every day for years to see Brendan again one day – to be able to tell him how truly sorry I am for deserting him and to beg for his forgiveness, I'd long ago begun to give up hope of it ever happening. Now, against all the odds, just when my prayer seemed finally to have been answered, suddenly everything is snatched away. And once again so brutally – so violently. Sometimes it's so hard to understand the ways of the Lord and easy to see why people, even very good people, get angry with Him.'

Robert didn't know what to say. Trained as he was to bring comfort and hope to people in such situations, this didn't include fellow priests. All he could muster up was, 'Andreas, maybe you haven't seen the full picture yet. Wait a little bit. Perhaps there are other pieces of this jigsaw puzzle still to be put in place?'

'What? You mean the old platitude of God's time and man's time being on a different scale?' Andreas replied abruptly.

'No, I didn't mean that.' Robert said. 'I mean that this terrible thing has only just happened – a matter of hours ago. Wait until you have all the facts. Maybe even have had a chance to speak with Brenda's landlady, Nina. From what the barman's just said it sounds as if she was really more of a mother to Brenda than a landlady. There's also the child, Rebecca. Brenda's daughter, so I suppose in effect Nina's granddaughter.'

He pushed the cup of coffee towards Andreas, but he didn't touch his own. Something from Robert Melton's past had suddenly struck him – something he hoped he had confined to a far distant memory: 'I can see that the worries and problems of people like me and Rebecca are no longer your concern.'

Behind Brenda's courteous acknowledgement, Robert still felt her disillusionment and disappointment. Her words had left his unwillingness to bother himself with her still as raw as the first time he had read that last letter to him in America.

Robert stumbled on, hoping Andreas was too absorbed by his own shattered emotions to pick up the change in his demeanour. 'Brenda and Rebecca were probably living below the radar. People like you and me did nothing for her. No wonder she felt abandoned – right to the end.'

'Do you think we should go and see if we can find her landlady and see if there's anything we can do to help her and her granddaughter?' Andreas suggested quietly.

As if on cue, at that moment the door swung open again and an attractive older woman accompanied by a pretty little girl of around eight or nine came in. Her swollen red eyes showed that the little girl had been crying. The expression on the woman's face was more resigned. Looking at her, an observer would get the feeling that, whatever the cause of her sadness, she had seen it all before and wearily, if reluctantly, accepted it as the random cruelty of fate.

'Nina with Rebecca, I would guess,' Robert said quietly to Andreas.

Somewhat to both men's surprise, grandmother and granddaughter made their way over to a table next to theirs. The barman gave a brave smile and set about preparing a coffee and a cup of hot chocolate.

Robert waited until he was about to bring their tray over, before he caught his attention and indicated that he wanted to pay for them. But the barman shook his head.

Putting down the tray in front of Nina and Rebecca, the barman nodded towards Robert and Andreas before saying in a voice loud enough for them to hear, 'The two … priests there wanted to pay for these, Nina, but these ones are on me.

'We are all so sorry about what's happened. You know how Brenda was very special to us all in here. Probably the loveliest person I'm ever likely to meet in my life.'

This simple gesture and the kind words about her mother were too much for Rebecca. She could no longer hold back her next wave of tears and put her head face down on her folded arms where she sobbed uncontrollably.

Nina rested an outstretched hand on Rebecca's back, while indicating to the young barman that it was all right and he had not upset her. There was, she said to him quietly, simply 'good sorrow' and 'bad sorrow' and it was 'bad sorrow' that Rebecca was suffering at the moment.

Relieved, the barman returned to his work.

Nina sipped her coffee and then looked across at the table next to them. 'You're the prodigal vicar of St Mungo's from up the road aren't you?' she asked Robert bluntly.

'Yes,' he said awkwardly. 'I'm … I mean we,' here he indicated towards Andreas, 'are so very sorry about Brenda. Your … daughter, I understand, and of course, your mummy,' he added gently to Rebecca.

'Brenda was a regular visitor to St Mungo's. Not to the services, but she was there more often than most people in the parish. I always welcomed that and I had been hoping to work with her one day. I felt she could connect me and St Mungo's to the side of the parish I really want to reach out to.'

'Yes,' Nina replied. 'I think her visits to your church helped Brenda. Her spirits were troubled and going there comforted her. But you were the only vicar who seemed to understand. She said you were the only one who made her feel welcome.

'She was so pleased and grateful that you had the compassion to sign to her in the church once. I think she wanted to work with you too, but then you suddenly left St Mungo's. At first, Brenda was very disappointed in you for doing that. But after some time, I think she understood. She told me it was just something you had to do and that one day you would come back and be a better priest for it.

'Brenda had a kind of sixth sense about people and things, and she wasn't usually far wrong. She would sometimes say that when she went to St Mungo's, she just sat and talked with God and it was His wisdom, not hers. But I was never as convinced as she was about that. I tried, but I just didn't have the strength of faith Brenda had.'

At that Rebecca, lifting her head up off the table, asked, 'Why didn't God help my mummy? Why did He let her die?'

The three adults said nothing.

After an awkward silence it was Andreas who spoke. 'Perhaps Brendan … Brenda, I mean … your mommy, believed in God so much, that He knew she would understand what would have to happen to her. Although my friend and I are priests, your mommy was possibly closer to God than we are. And now she will be with Him for ever, to help Him look after you and your grandmother.'

At his trip over Brenda's name Nina had shot a look at Andreas as if to say, 'Who are you and how much do you know of Brenda anyway?' The little girl was also studying Andreas's face, but said nothing.

Robert stepped in and introduced Andreas, explaining their long friendship.

Andreas sighed heavily before saying, 'I knew Brenda in what now seems like another life, years ago when we were teenagers in Trinidad. We were best friends, only …' He stopped, unsure how to continue in front of Rebecca.

Rebecca was confused, and looked questioningly towards her grandmother. Nina put an arm around her granddaughter's shoulders and slowly nodded. She knew Rebecca well enough to know that it would be very confusing at first. But Nina also knew that provided she handled it the right way and gave Rebecca plenty of time to ask questions and gradually take in what she was being told, her love for the only mother she had ever known would remain strong and unflinching. Brenda had wanted to tell her daughter all about her past, but Nina had counselled against it saying, 'Wait until she is a old enough to be independent, if she feels the need to be,' she had advised.

'This is something private for you and me to talk about at home, but not at the moment,' she told Rebecca. 'You think about your mummy and the happy times we had together. Those are what made her love you so much.'

Andreas continued, careful in what he said now. 'To my eternal shame, in my own fear I abandoned my friend, who protected me when we were both in great danger. I have never forgotten that. Nor what it means to be a truly brave person — not the coward I was.

'It wasn't only Brenda's whole life that was shaped by the awful events of that one night, it was mine too. From that moment to this I've prayed daily that I might one day find my childhood friend and be able to beg — yes, beg — forgiveness.

'Yesterday at St Mungo's, I did find my friend — only I didn't recognise who it was. Then, after Robert explained everything, I booked an appointment to see Brenda this morning. I was on my way to her studio to be reconciled with her, to ask for that forgiveness. Now, after this lifetime of waiting and praying, even that last chance has been snatched away.'

No one spoke after Andreas had finished what he had to say. Robert, still struggling to come to terms with this part of his friend's life, of which he had known nothing, never mind his own self-centred dismissal of Brenda and her daughter, seemed lost in thought. Rebecca was looking at Nina for explanation and guidance. Nina was steadfastly studying Andreas's face, looking as though she was trying to decide on something.

When, at last, she appeared to have made up her mind, it was she who broke the silence. 'If, as I suspect, you are not quite who you appear to be either, then I would only say don't be so sure. From everything Brenda has told me and I've now heard from you, I would say that she was always one step ahead of you.

'Last night Brenda gave me two letters for safekeeping. She said it was in case she was ever raided and the police took away her things. The first was a letter for Rebecca. The second was a letter addressed to David Thornton from Trinidad. Only she had put a tentative line through this name and written underneath 'Andreas (Priest)' with a question mark. I could tell from the writing and the envelope that the letter had been written a long time ago, but the change she'd made to the name on the envelope was new. Very new, as it's turned out.

'I was going to ask her if this meant she'd found out something about you, your whereabouts or perhaps just how to reach you through this Andreas, only she seemed excited and impatient. She had one more client to see, it was getting late and so we agreed to talk in the morning. She said she'd tell me all about it then. Rebecca was spending the night in my flat, as she quite often does, so I went to bed early.'

Now looking directly at him, Nina said, 'Andreas, knowing Brenda as I do … I suppose I must say as I did … my guess would be that Brenda's letter to you contains the forgiveness you need.'

With that Nina opened her bag and took out an envelope, which she handed to Andreas.

'If you don't mind, I think I should read this when I'm by myself,' he said.

'I would want to do the same,' Nina told him.

'Can you come and find me in St Mungo's?' Andreas asked them. 'Give me half an hour.'

'We'll be along in a bit, you'll find us in the vestry,' Robert said. 'And remember, whatever you're feeling now, this too shall pass.'

Andreas seated himself in the same shortened pew in the shadows at the back of the church that Brenda had always chosen. Although it only took him a few minutes to read the letter, almost twenty minutes elapsed before he could fold up the pages in his hand and carefully replace them in their envelope.

Nina had been right. Brenda's letter to him, addressing him as David, was an exhortation not to blame himself in any way for what had happened, or for how he had reacted to that terrible event in Trinidad so many years ago. In the letter Brendan urged David only to remember their close friendship, the shared angst of being teenagers and all the many wonderful and happy times they had had together.

As the older of the two, if only by three months, Brendan took upon himself the full responsibility for what had taken place in the warm surf on that beautiful moonlit beach. Brendan knew right away that David had been very confused and had not felt the same sense of love, of happiness and connection, that Brendan had enjoyed.

The one thing Brendan knew they had both agreed on, however, was the absolute determination to have a lifetime bond of friendship that would never be broken.

Andreas read that part of the letter several times. That was the bond which only a few hours later he, David, had betrayed in so cowardly a way.

In the letter, Brendan explained that his devout wish and daily prayer was one day to find and be reunited with his childhood friend. But in the event of that not happening, he wanted to leave this letter for David, in the continuing hope that David might also be searching for him.

Andreas felt a surge of anger – directed primarily at God, he had to admit – at the cruel fate of the timing. He felt deep sorrow too at the thought of the apology he could no longer give in person. And there was a loss, which at that moment seemed fathomless, over what might have been, if he and Brendan could have learned about each other's lives since that awful night.

'I'm sure God can take it – and much worse,' was Robert's only response, after Andreas admitted his lapse of faith when he joined the others later.

Standing next to them, Nina finished reading Brenda's letter to Andreas –

only, of course, confusingly, it was Brendan's letter to David. Folding the pages she now handed it back.

'You shouldn't be angry with God,' she said quietly. 'You either believe it was coincidence, a big, big coincidence, or God wanted you to have that brief meeting in St Mungo's yesterday, so you could see in Brenda's eyes that she recognised you and forgave you. If you believe that, didn't God answer your prayer?

'And you've got the understanding and forgiveness you have been seeking all this time – in Brenda's own handwriting. To be angry at God when what you wanted has happened, on His terms not yours, would be a little ungrateful, don't you think?'

'Yes, putting it that way, I suppose I must admit you're right,' Andreas said. 'But it just seems so harsh, after all this time.'

Then, as though it were time to change the subject, Nina turned to her granddaughter. 'Rebecca, I think your mummy would like everyone to say good-bye to her here, at her funeral in St Mungo's, don't you?'

The little girl gripped her grandmother's hand and nodded bravely.

'Yes, of course,' Robert answered encouragingly. 'It seems most appropriate. The coroner usually releases the body for burial after three days. Is there a particular day next week that you'd like to have the funeral service? I don't suppose you've had time to think about where you'd like Brenda to be buried either?'

'Well, as a matter of fact, yes, I have,' Nina replied. She looked at her granddaughter again, to say, 'I don't believe your mother left any written wishes about where she wanted to be buried, so what I know only comes from a conversation we had a few years ago. It is all connected to the Dominican nun who nursed her back to health in Trinidad – Sister Lucy. I think that was her name.

'I think we should cremate Brenda here, then at some point, when we can, Rebecca and I will take her ashes to Savannah, where Sister Lucy came from. Brenda used to talk about her, and the way she described Savannah, I know she would have loved to go there herself.'

'I know of this Sister Lucy,' Robert interrupted quietly. 'She is the same Sister Lucy my grandmother befriended when she visited New Hampshire some years ago.'

It was Nina's turn to look surprised.

'Before she died, I promised Maude, my grandmother, I would make a trip to see Sister Lucy and enjoy the beauty of Savannah as a tribute to her – my grandmother I mean. She had wanted to go there too ever since Sister Lucy had first told her about the city, but sadly she left it too late. In the end she wasn't well enough to make the trip.'

'Well, perhaps when we go we should all go together,' Nina said. 'Do you think Mummy would like that?' she asked Rebecca.

The little girl looked solemnly at the two priests and then at her grandmother, before smiling shyly. 'Yes, she would,' Rebecca answered.

'That will be something to look forward to,' Robert said, before gently returning to the matter in hand.

'Shall we plan the funeral for next Thursday? That allows just over a week for arrangements to be made. I don't suppose you'll expect it to be a big funeral, will you?'

'No, Brenda didn't have many friends outside her small family,' Nina replied. 'Of course we'll need to contact Amanda and Mike later today – I don't know how I'm going to tell them.'

As far as Rebecca was concerned, Amanda was her godmother. A wonderful godmother who always had little treats and lots of time for her goddaughter. On hearing Amanda's name and knowing how upset she would be, Rebecca covered her face with her hands, her eyes running with tears once again.

'Oh, and also Naomi, if we can find her,' Nina added, hugging the little girl at the same time. 'But they were about the only friends Brenda ever had. There are a number of acquaintances and neighbourhood friends from the area who may want to come, but there will only be a few of us. No more than twenty at the most.'

Robert asked Nina if she would like him to find a suitable funeral director, to which she readily agreed.

After this, Nina and Rebecca returned to Trebovir Road. Rebecca went straight to her mother's room where, lying face down on the bed, she gave way to all the unbearable sorrow and sadness she was feeling. Nina sat on the bed beside her granddaughter silently and gently stroking her hair, while she pondered all that had happened.

There was of course another connection with Brenda: her own. One that no one else knew anything about, not even her granddaughter. The fact that, at one of the lowest points in her own life, Brenda had unexpectedly come into it, filling the huge void left by the tragic deaths of her husband and son. Brenda had stepped in as both the son Nina had lost and the daughter she had always wanted. But this was her own secret and she wanted to keep it that way.

What was she to make of all these connections to Brenda, though? The fact that they were drawing together the people whose lives she had profoundly touched in this extraordinary fashion, at the very time of her unexpected and untimely death, must in some way, Nina felt, be the answer to a series of puzzles she didn't understand.

Did these constitute a 'force' beyond all of their control or comprehension? Something that held the answers to understanding the significance behind this pattern of intertwined coincidences and events that none of them could fathom?

Nina knew she was groping in the dark, perhaps allowing herself to get dangerously close to superstition. Nevertheless she thought that after Brenda's funeral, she would like to go and talk to Robert about it all. She had liked Robert today and now better understood why Brenda had liked him too. She was right; he would be a good priest.

After a while, when Rebecca's sobbing had calmed itself a little, Nina got up to go and call Amanda. She knew it would be a very difficult call.

56

ON SUNDAY ROBERT had decided he wanted to shake his congregation out of what he saw as their comfortable and, no doubt comforting, complacency. Standing at the lectern facing his mainly middle-aged, mostly middle-class, parishioners, he began.

'I've put aside the sermon I had prepared for today. Instead I plan to tell you all about a parishioner; a regular visitor to this church for many, many years, whom I would be surprised if any of you have ever set eyes on, or even knew existed, let alone actually knew in person.'

One or two of the faces in front of him registered a surprised curiosity at what he was about to say. Most remained passive and expressionless, their thoughts already having drifted away towards their Sunday lunch.

Robert continued, 'The parishioner to whom I refer was what many people might choose to call a prostitute.'

It was as if he had exploded a bomb. The changes in the expressions were as electrifying as they were unanimous. Yanked from their own thoughts at the mere suggestion of some salacious tittle-tattle within their midst, he now had everyone's rapt attention. In one or two cases he saw hearing-aids being adjusted.

'Although this description could be considered technically and probably legally correct, what this parishioner does, or I should say, did, for a living, I for one would strongly argue was not the practice of prostitution as you or I would understand it. If you knew her background and understood it from her situation, you would see that her activity, her actions, were rather more motivated by a selfless, generous compassion than by the sleazy avarice of commercial prostitution. The reason I corrected myself to say 'did' rather than 'does' is because, tragically, this person, a beautiful, still young, black woman called Brenda, was murdered earlier this week, right here in Earls Court.

'Brenda came to this country from Trinidad as a teenage boy. Yes, boy — but from here on I'm going to refer to her in the gender she adopted. She came all alone, knowing no one. The reason she came was because after witnessing a crime, a big international drugs deal in which even her father was involved, she was brutally attacked. Before being left for dead, her tongue was cut out, no doubt to serve as a warning to others. Only she didn't die. She survived, and for her own safety had to flee. So, not only did she know no one, but she couldn't speak and had to rely on writing notes to communicate.

'It was not only her tongue that was cut out. I will spare you the gruesome details of what her attackers did to her. Some of you may be able to use your imagination, if you so choose. What I will say is that it was a comprehensive mutilation. From that point, for the rest of her life, Brenda was without a definable gender. So when fate determined that she should become a woman, it was an understandable transition.

'However, it was this truly ghastly experience and her own less than whole body that enabled Brenda to empathise so closely with all those others who are severely disfigured or mutilated in some way or other.'

This heady mixture of mystery, mutilation, sex, race and now murder in their midst, was more, much more, than any of his parishioners had bargained for when they had come to church that morning. One of the elderly ladies in the pews closest to and immediately facing Robert, now let out an audible gasp of horror. But it was a horror mixed with a certain lurid fascination. She didn't want him to stop.

Looking out over his congregation Robert saw he now held their complete attention in a way that almost never happened during the course of a normal sermon. Without even being aware they were doing so, most were leaning forward in their pews in their astonishment and eagerness to hear more.

Robert went on to tell them all he knew about Brenda: how he had come to meet her and how he regretted that he had never had a chance to get to know her better. Explaining what she did, and why she did it was more difficult. As a churchman and theologian he knew that whatever the mitigating circumstances, a sin was a sin and he could not appear to be condoning it, whatever he himself might think.

It was when he told them why they had never seen Brenda at a church service – how she herself, driven by a compassionate conscience, but also recognising herself as a sinner, felt unworthy to receive the sacraments, or to claim any kind of acceptance as part of their church community – that Robert noticed one or two of his parishioners dabbing at moist eyes.

He paused.

Silence filled St Mungo's.

Concluding his sermon, Robert said, 'As a congregation and as a church community we have one last opportunity to meet – almost all of you for the first time – and show our acceptance of, Brenda as a part of this parish and what I now know must be its work. Brenda had few friends and it would be a lovely tribute if as many of you as possible might consider coming to her funeral. It will be held here at eleven o'clock on Thursday. If, after what I've told you about Brenda and her lifestyle, any of you feel you can't come to show respect, maybe you would consider coming anyway if only to show support for her little daughter and her grandmother? Thank you.'

From the surprised, but generally positive response as he said goodbye to everyone, Robert was encouraged to believe that many of them would now make the effort to come to Brenda's funeral. He was pleased about this. It was always much sadder when only a handful of people showed up. Early on, as a very new priest, he had officiated at one lonely funeral where he and the undertakers were the only people present.

There had only been a single objection: one of his younger parishioners, who had only started coming to St Mungo's a year or so before Robert's return and somehow had not yet made the connection between his local priest and the titanic financier from Wall Street. This self-important parishioner now made it quite clear he would not be coming, telling Robert he would be at his desk in the City, which of course was a valid excuse. But he also wanted it known he would not come even if he had not been working. He felt strongly that Robert had trivialised, even excused, sin. The way Brenda made a living was, he thought, undoubtedly sinful in God's eyes and therefore was in his own, he told Robert in no uncertain terms.

This was the first time since his return that Robert acutely felt the contrast between what he was doing now and what he had given up in America. Robert knew how this same young man would have listened obsequiously to everything he said, had he been aware that the Reverend Robert Melton he was now arrogantly addressing was the same Robert Melton so admired by his contemporaries in the financial powerhouses of Wall Street – and by extension, the City of London.

Robert felt tempted to retaliate, to put him in his place, but he bit his lip and accepted that this was a good lesson in humility, something he knew he must get used to.

57

THE FOLLOWING THURSDAY, the day of Brenda's funeral, Robert, accompanied by Andreas, arrived at St Mungo's early. It was still only just a few minutes past eight and the funeral was not due to begin for another three hours. Nina and Rebecca were already there, standing outside the side door on Stratford Road.

'Good morning Nina. Good morning Rebecca,' Robert apologised. 'I hope you haven't been waiting long. If I'd known you wanted to be here so soon I'd have willingly come earlier to open up. The undertakers aren't due to arrive until some time between nine-thirty and ten.' As he said this he and Andreas gave them both reassuring and comforting hugs.

'No, it's fine,' Nina replied. 'We only got here about two minutes ago ourselves. It was just because I thought I heard you say you'd open up at eight o'clock today instead of the usual eight-thirty. Neither of us could sleep much last night anyway, so as we were up early we decided we'd like to spend some quiet time alone together, just sitting in Brenda's pew to say our own private goodbyes before the funeral.'

Robert was suddenly reminded of Mary. It was just the sort of thing she might have said and wanted to do in similar circumstances, as she had before Maude's funeral. It was now only ten days before she was to finally join him in London, as the slow progression of his calendar constantly reminded him, but he was brought back to the present by the realisation that Mary would never now meet Brenda. The thought made him sad. He had told Mary so much about

Brenda and he had always felt that Mary and she might have become friends. He was sure that Brenda would have quickly come to understand Mary well enough to allow her closer than she would let anyone else – Nina excepted of course, and perhaps Amanda and Mike.

That reminded him to ask Nina, 'Did you manage to contact Amanda and Mike? Are they coming?'

'Yes. Poor Amanda is completely devastated. Mike wasn't going to come, but only because he's supposed to be leaving for a business trip to America. He didn't think his company would understand since Brenda wasn't family. But Amanda said she'd divorce him if he didn't delay by a day and if that meant him losing his job, so be it and she wouldn't be one bit upset or angry with him. So, anyway, he's going to fly out tomorrow and join his colleagues a day late.'

'Amanda sounds quite a character,' Robert said, smiling gently.

'Oh, that she is,' Nina said with emphasis.

Nina and Rebecca went to sit quietly together in Brenda's pew. From time to time Nina took Rebecca's hand and held it for a while, but otherwise they both seemed to be absorbed in their own thoughts, memories and prayers.

Just before ten the hearse bearing Brenda's coffin pulled up outside the main entrance to the church. Robert went to out meet it. The sight of the coffin being carried in by four strange men formally dressed in black was more than Rebecca could bear. Reduced once more to sobs, she turned and buried herself in her grandmother's lap.

Amanda and Mike had arrived at the same time as the hearse and, waiting respectfully until the coffin had been carried into the church, followed in behind.

Amanda was wearing big dark glasses and holding Mike's hand tightly in hers as tears ran down her cheeks. For someone who was so relentlessly positive, it came as a shock to Nina to see her deep anguish. Although Amanda was capable of a dramatic display on occasions, Nina saw at once that this was not one of those occasions. Perhaps, Nina thought, she had never fully understood just how protective Amanda had always felt towards Brenda.

Stepping out of the pew, Nina took Amanda in her arms. Neither of them spoke. Mike hugged Rebecca tightly in an effort to comfort her and calm her sobbing. It was a difficult moment for him too. The truth was he was close to losing control of his own emotions.

Shortly after this people started arriving. It began as a trickle but soon became a steadily growing tide.

By a quarter to eleven, to everyone's complete amazement, the church was already full. Looking around, Robert realised he knew almost no one. When it became evident what was happening, he had instructed that the choir stalls up on the altar be kept free for those parishioners he had asked to attend. One or two were already there in place looking around in bewilderment at their church that no one in living memory had ever seen so crowded. St Mungo's was not just full, it was packed. Every conceivable space, standing or sitting, was now occupied, including up in the organ gallery.

Surveying the crowd, Robert realised these must be the kind of people Brenda had catered for – or would it be more correct to say ministered to, he wondered. It was a very motley collection of humanity, embracing all colours, ages and religions – or none. The one thing most of them had in common was injury, physical deformity or disfigurement. There were some in wheelchairs, some on crutches and many others whose terrible disfigurements did not affect mobility, but ensured they were none the less made to feel outsiders: the invisible 'untouchables' in our midst whom we either cannot, or will not, see.

Still more were coming. No longer able to get into the church, they were gathering outside the main double doors, both of which had now been flung wide open. This relentless tide of forgotten humanity had now grown so large that it had spilled out onto this busy part of Earls Court Road and was causing considerable problems with pedestrians and even the flow of traffic – which was emphasised by the angry honking of horns.

A uniformed policeman had somehow managed to elbow his way into the church to see what was causing this growing problem. As it was almost time to begin the funeral service, and Robert would anyway have had difficulty making his way through this crowd to the back of the church, he looked over at the pew where Nina was sitting. Catching Mike's eye he indicated the policeman now not far behind him, who was trying to make his way through the throng with a look of bewilderment on his face. The policeman was in fact wondering if he should call for back-up to help him handle this highly unusual situation.

Mike understood right away what Robert was getting at and, with some difficulty, made his way back the short distance to where the policeman was marooned.

Seeing in Mike someone who might have some handle on the situation, the policeman told him, 'You can't conduct a church service that is going to draw such a large crowd without advance warning and permission from the police and traffic enforcement. Do you realise that the crowd outside is now blocking all but one lane of Earls Court Road? I can see the numbers here in the church are way beyond safety capacity. I'm afraid you're going to have to get people to leave, or cancel and reschedule this service – even if it is a funeral.'

Then, glancing in amazement at the tightly packed pews and throng of mourners standing four deep all around the walls, curiosity getting the better of him, he asked 'Whose funeral is it anyway?'

'Brenda's,' was all Mike was able to say. Brenda so seldom, if ever, used a family name that he had forgotten what it was, if he'd ever even known it.

'You mean Brenda, as in the Brenda from Earls Court? Trebovir Road Brenda?' asked the policeman.

'Yes.'

'Well, I suppose I should have guessed from the make-up of this crowd,' the policeman admitted, scanning the mourners again. 'Of course we knew about her murder. Such a loss. Woe betide the bastard who did it when we catch him – and you can be sure we will. If only you'd let us know her funeral was here today we could have told you what to expect.

'Of course you can go ahead as it's Brenda's funeral. I'll radio traffic control to come and help outside. We'll just have to run Earls Court Road on one lane for the duration of the service. Or even close it if we have to. Motorists won't like it, but they'll just have to be patient and put up with it.

'Will you do just one thing for me? Help me get to the coffin. I'd like to pay my own respects before the service starts.'

With help from Mike, but still with difficulty, they cleared a temporary path for the policeman to reach the coffin.

Not sure what was happening and checking his watch to see it was now only four minutes to eleven, Robert watched the policeman as he reached the coffin. Taking off his helmet, he genuflected with one hand on the coffin, made the sign of the cross and turned to go. The congregation burst into a spontaneous round of applause.

Robert was stunned. How did this policeman know Brenda, he wondered? There were just so many mysteries surrounding her, he was not sure he'd ever fully understand who and what she really was.

The funeral itself went off flawlessly. The singing was as robust as it was heartfelt. Andreas did the readings and Robert gave the eulogy.

In this Robert told the congregation everything that had happened to Brenda as a teenager in Trinidad and how the appalling events there had led her to being here in their midst, mostly unnoticed, unseen, and certainly unheard, for the rest of her life. He spoke of all that she had had to overcome: the loneliness, the hardship, the rejections and judgements. Yet, despite all, she was not bitter or angry and had devoted the rest of her life to the service of others – people like herself who existed on, or even beyond, the margins of normal society.

Looking at the shocked faces in front of him, he could see that almost none of those who might have encountered Brenda had had any real idea of what she herself had suffered. Many of them were now weeping openly.

Out of respect for Brenda, Nina and Rebecca – and perhaps for many of those in the congregation – Robert found himself trying to focus on Brenda's attributes. He decided it was best not to make too close a reference to what Brenda actually had to do with those hands that Sister Lucy had so admired and urged her to use.

It was at this point, when he was about to conclude, that Robert noticed Amanda had stood up, her arm raised high in the air to attract his attention. Mike was frantically pulling on her other arm, trying to get her to sit down.

'Yes. Amanda, isn't it?' Robert said, easily side-stepping convention in this less than conventional funeral.

'Vicar, you've said some lovely things about Brenda today. But you've avoided the issue of what Brenda did. I know it's difficult to talk about, especially for someone like you … I mean a vicar like you. I expect there are a lot of people in this church today who are only here because of experiencing what that was – what Brenda did for them and therefore who Brenda really was. I just wanted to say to anyone who might feel embarrassed or, worse, ashamed: don't.

'Brenda wasn't afraid to take on the gritty reality in people's personal lives. What Brenda did she did for one thing, and one thing only: love. Brenda's whole life was about love, understanding, tolerance and – amazingly – forgiveness. It's proof of the purity of those qualities in her that so many of us are here to honour her memory today.

'Brenda was my best friend and I couldn't be more proud of her than if she'd been the Queen of England herself.'

After that Amanda sat down – shaking.

For the second time that remarkable morning the congregation burst into spontaneous, heartfelt, applause. Robert noticed that even those older members of his regular congregation, up in the choir stalls, who had avoided joining in the first time, were now standing up and openly clapping their hands too.

The look on Mike's face as he put an arm around his wife's shoulders had turned from one of panic to pride.

Nina nodded her gratitude to Amanda and Rebecca smiled happily at her godmother.

Andreas had managed to retain control of his feelings until the moment when Amanda had stressed Brenda's quality of forgiveness. At that he had had to leave the altar for the vestry where he had sunk to his knees and humbly thanked Brenda, and, more importantly, God, for his personal forgiveness. Although it took less than two minutes, it was one of those rare moments of intensely connected prayer from which he arose feeling fully refreshed and at peace. Once more in control of his emotions, he returned to the altar.

After the funeral, it took some time for the huge crowd to disperse. When the last of them had finally gone and before it was time to escort Nina, Rebecca, Amanda and Mike to the crematorium with Brenda's body, Robert noticed the door open again. It was the same policeman who had been there earlier. Removing his helmet, he knelt down in one of the back pews. Robert went down to the back of the church. After a few minutes the policeman made the sign of the cross and rose to leave.

Robert approached him to say, 'Thank you for allowing us to continue with the funeral, and for helping with the traffic. No one expected such a large crowd.'

'No problem this time,' the policeman replied with a friendly, but cautionary smile. 'If anything had happened as a result of that crowd, particularly with it spilling out all over Earls Court Road like that, I could have been disciplined, lost any chance of a promotion and looked forward to a reduced pension. But once I knew it was Brenda's funeral and the effort some of those people must have made to be here for it today, I couldn't stop it. Only wish you'd told us up at the station. We could have told you to get ready for a big crowd.'

'I'm curious.' Robert said. 'It's none of my business, but I hope you don't mind me asking how you know Brenda?'

'No, I don't mind. Fact is, I don't know Brenda, at least not in any way you would recognise. I only ever spoke to her once. In the street outside this church, as it happens. And that was only to say "Good morning". She didn't reply of course. Couldn't, could she? But she smiled. It was a beautiful smile.

'No. So you see it's not so much that I ... we that is ... the police, at the Kensington Station, knew Brenda, as that we knew all *about* Brenda.

'Unfortunately the public rarely get to see the human side of policing. We knew what Brenda did. More importantly, we knew why she did it. That's why we always left her alone. In fact – and even she didn't know this – we used to keep an eye out for her. Unfortunately, we missed out badly on that particular night last week and I can't tell you how sorry some of us at the station feel about that.

'We know all the pimps, prostitutes and most of the regular Johns here on our patch. It's part of our job to know. We regularly raid and generally harass them. But we knew what Brenda did was different. We never thought of her work as prostitution. In fact we admired her. To the best of my knowledge she never once betrayed her mission. Any regular, able-bodied John hoping for a massage and sex session with Brenda was always turned away. It didn't get tried often, but when it did I'm told it's the only thing that would make her angry. The more money they offered, the angrier she got. No, Brenda was never on the game.

'As a priest I'm sure you must know that the law is blind. Well, sometimes we use that blindness to our advantage. The letter of the law can be a blunt instrument. Technically what Brenda did was against the law. Technically she was a prostitute. But, because more often than not her massages were just that, and because if some of her special clients couldn't afford to pay anything she made no charge, it allowed us the loophole to make an exception.

'Of course, over the years we got to know a number of those special clients of hers and to hear them talk about Brenda with such reverence and gratitude you'd think they'd been to see a saint, not a sinner.

'We police get to see a lot of the really messy side of life most of the general public don't know about. I know it can't be spoken about, at least not in so-called polite society, but we think what Brenda was doing was wonderful. She was a brave, exceptional person. Brenda will be greatly missed – and that's a fact. But that's the price we all pay for love, isn't it? Grief.

'Anyway, that's why I popped back in here. Just to say a prayer for Brenda and to ask God to try and see her life in the way we did up at the station. To see only the good in what she did and turn a blind eye to the rest – know what I mean?'

Robert knew all right. He liked this policeman. 'Please stop in any time you're passing in future,' he said, extending his hand. 'I'm Robert Melton. I'm the vicar here at St Mungo's.'

'Constable Sean O'Conner. Thank you father, but I'm afraid you won't want me. I belong to the competition up the road. Our Lady of Victories is where I tend to pop in from time to time.'

Just then Andreas, who had been tidying up in the vestry, came over to join them. 'Oh, don't worry about that officer,' he said, holding out his hand. 'Andreas Doria, Benedictine monk from St Jerome's Priory in Manchester, New Hampshire in the United States. The vicar here may have joined the wrong church. I tell him that all the time. But he's as good a priest as any I know in either the Roman or Anglican tradition. If his church, St Mungo's here, is good enough for me, a Roman Catholic priest, I'm sure it won't do you any harm. God really does reside here too – that is if you want him to. Anyway, as my friend says, I know you'll be made warmly welcome here anytime you want to stop by. I'm off back to my abbey in the States tomorrow, but wouldn't it be nice to encourage a little more interaction and understanding between two neighbourhood churches as these are?'

'Well, thank you both. Maybe I will do just that. Have a safe trip home, Father,' he said, addressing Andreas.

Then, turning to Robert, he said, 'Maybe we could have a cup of coffee together at Le Monde just next to the station up the road, sometime, Father? Perhaps I could even persuade the parish priest in charge of Our Lady of Victories to join us. Monsignor Seamus – he's a really good sort. I think you'd like each other.'

'That would be great. I'd like to do that. Thank you,' Robert replied warmly.

'Good. I'll be in touch, then,' said Constable O'Conner, replacing his helmet and making his exit.

It was time for Robert and Andreas to rejoin the others at the crematorium.

58

THE NEXT DAY Robert left the house first. Andreas stayed behind to pack his few things before going down to join him at St Mungo's. It was a sunny morning, his little bag was not heavy and he was in good time, so he decided to enjoy his walk from Callcott Street to Earls Court Road by taking the slightly longer route down through Holland Park.

It was almost as soon as he entered the park from the pedestrian alleyway in front of Holland Park School that he encountered the robin. It was hopping and chirping about almost as if it had been waiting for him and was pleased to see him. Its antics made Andreas smile as he stopped to watch.

Then, before continuing on down the hill, he said aloud, 'Goodbye little bird and thank you for making me smile.' But the little bird had other ideas. It flew alternately alongside and ahead of Andreas, alighting occasionally on fence posts or branches of neighbouring trees to rest and chirp happily, while seeming to wait for Andreas to catch up. Once, towards the bottom of the hill, it even briefly alighted on the suitcase Andreas was carrying. Andreas laughed. 'Well, little friend, do you want to come with me?' he said, addressing the bird. 'You certainly aren't too heavy for me to carry.'

At this point he had reached the gate at the bottom of the park where it joins the junction of Kensington High Street and Earls Court Road. The little bird suddenly flew in front of his face where it hovered for the briefest of moments before it flew back into the park. Andreas turned to watch, but the bird was flying back up the park to where it had first encountered him. Robins, he knew, were very territorial, and it would not leave its special patch unguarded for too long. 'Goodbye little friend,' he said to himself as he continued across Kensington High Street and down Earls Court Road.

It had been Andreas's intention to spend half an hour or so with Robert at St Mungo's, say his goodbyes and then walk on the short distance to Earls Court Road Underground Station and take the tube out to Heathrow Airport.

When he arrived Robert greeted him. 'Good news. No need to take the tube to the airport. The bishop called to say goodbye and when I told him what you were doing he said he'd like to drive you out to Heathrow himself. Said it was the least he could do for someone who he feels played a part in bringing me back to the priesthood and in particular to his diocese!'

'Well I'm honoured that the Anglican Bishop of West London, no less, should want to take pity on me, a poor Roman Catholic monk, but there is no need for him to do that. Let me call him and tell him not to bother. I don't mind going on the tube one bit.'

'Too late I'm afraid. He's on his way; should be here shortly.'

'Oh well. Perhaps it'll be good for ecumenical relations. Maybe I'll try and convert him on the journey. That'd be quite a coup wouldn't it?' Andreas said with a broad smile. 'Oh, by the way, I must tell you about the little bird I saw in Holland Park on my way down here just now.'

After Andreas had finished, he noticed the curious look on Robert's face. 'What is it?' he asked.

'Nothing really. Only … you're sure it was a robin?'

'Well yes, as sure as I can be without being an expert ornithologist. It was quite small, perhaps smaller than usual, but it had a red breast and brown feathers.'

Robert continued, 'It's probably just coincidence, but twice before birds have featured in my own life in ways that I have never forgotten. On both occasions, rightly or wrongly, I took them as signs.

'Once was after talking to you on the phone – I was trying to decide whether to really leave here and come over to the States. The other time was when Maude, my grandmother, died. She and Mary had agreed ahead of time that, if Maude could, she'd send a loon to let people know she was OK.

'Silly really, I know, but it is odd how on each occasion a robin and a loon appeared. The robin flew right in here, into this vestry. On the second occasion a loon made an appearance both at the time of Maude's death and again at her burial.'

Andreas was regarding his old friend with a quizzical look. 'And I thought it was the Catholic Church that had all the superstitions,' he said smiling. 'So you think maybe this robin I saw was some sort of message? A sign from Brendan? I'm afraid, Robert, I'd take more persuading than that.'

'Well, think what you like, my friend, but I don't share the same certainty as you about the black and white nature of these things. A mystery is not something we can't know anything about, it's just something we can't know everything about. Brenda was a mystery to me – and to you as well.'

'OK. I'll tell you what,' Andreas said. 'In a sense Brenda was "broken" so to speak. If, in the extraordinarily unlikely event of an injured, "broken", robin happening into your life anytime soon, maybe, just maybe, I'll be prepared to think you might be on to something.'

It was then that Andreas noticed the lottery ticket. The one he had bought specially and brought to use as his calling card in the collection plate at St Mungo's. It was still lying on Robert's desk where he had left it, protruding from under his pen holder. 'What shall we do with this?' he asked, picking it up and holding it out to Robert.

'I know exactly what we'll do with it,' Robert said, taking the lottery ticket from Andreas's hand. Stopping only to pick up a candle-snuffer – he remembered he had not yet extinguished the altar candles from the morning service – Robert led the way into the church.

Except for the two of them, St Mungo's was completely empty and silent. Taking the longer route, via the back of the church, the two priests walked together the full length of the nave up to the main altar.

Robert paused to pick up one of the big polished brass collection plates and removed the green baize cloth from where it lay inside. Then, standing in front of one of the altar candles, he indicated his intention to Andreas. 'Shall we do this together?' he said.

With each of them taking a corner of the lottery ticket, they held it up to the candle flame. In a moment it was ablaze. When they could not hold it any longer, they let it drop into the collection plate where, in a matter of seconds, what had once been the possible instrument to a fortune was reduced to ashes.

Both men looked at each other and smiled. It was the smile of satisfaction that close friends give each other when they have come successfully to the end of a long and perhaps difficult journey together. From dust to dust and ashes to ashes, the symbolism of God's victory over Mammon was not lost on either of them.

Just then they heard the side door to the church being hastily opened. It was the bishop hurrying in to say he was double-parked and that anyway he thought they had better be going as the traffic was a lot heavier than usual.

Robert went out to see them off. Neither he nor Andreas went in for prolonged goodbyes. On the way to the car Robert said he did not think it would be more than about six months or so before he would be back over in the States with Mary, Nina and Rebecca to make the visit to Savannah that they all seemed to have different reasons for making. Promises to keep.

Robert waited until the bishop's car had made the turn into Earls Court Road and been swallowed up in the heavy traffic before going back to busy himself in his office. He had plenty to do if he was going to try and harness the impact of Brenda's extraordinary life and astonishing funeral into widening the welcome of St Mungo's to a much broader spectrum of the community to whom he was supposed to minister. He felt too that he would at least now have the understanding and support of most of his regular congregation.

He was glad to be busy. It is always worse being the one left behind, although he had the assurance that his friendship with Andreas would now be as solid as it had been before the rift that had set them apart. A close and strong friendship that would last the rest of their lives.

Passing Brenda's pew as he walked back to the vestry, Robert paused, put a hand on the pew and said softly to no one but himself, 'Well, Brenda, look what you've started. But I wish I knew you were all right.'

Robert stayed later than usual in his office that day. When he did leave, the sun was going down and twilight had already arrived. He walked up on the north side of Earls Court Road, as was his custom. That way led him to the pedestrian crossing over Kensington High Street, which was directly in front of the entrance to Holland Park. He was smiling to himself. In less than a week Mary would be here. He had missed her more than he could ever have imagined since leaving New Hampshire. Now he would have so much to show her and share with her. Besides, they had a wedding to plan. It was a happy thought – one of many that evening.

As he was approaching the top of Earls Court Road, something in one of the shops on the other side caught his eye. It was in the window of the Geranium Sunshine Shop selling donated, used clothing and knick-knacks to benefit the blind. He could not quite make it out from this distance so, as he was in no particular hurry and he had become curious, he crossed over the road to take a closer look.

There in the window was a porcelain figurine of a small robin. Robert was slow to consider the significance of what he was looking at when, suddenly and unmistakably he noticed the otherwise perfect figurine had a broken right wing, which, having been rather badly reattached with glue, was left with a wide discoloured line, that only served to emphasise the break. The card beside it read, 'Porcelain. Robin Figurine – damaged. Reduced price 30p'.

For a long time Robert stood motionless in front of the window. The shop was closed. Tomorrow he would come first thing to buy that 'broken' robin. He knew just where to give it a good home.

Continuing on up to Kensington High Street he had to wait at the crossing. A red double-decker bus passed in front of him. Emblazoned on its side was an advertisement, placed by the tourist board of the US State of Georgia. It was promoting the charm and beauty of historic Savannah.

ABOUT THE AUTHOR

With a small loan received in 1966 from their local bank in Herefordshire, England, teenage brothers Tom and Oliver Vaughan co-founded Juliana's Discotheques Ltd. Over the next twenty years they steered this embryonic business from its origins in the back of an old van into the largest entertainment group of its kind in the world.

Juliana's Holdings Plc, as it became, would go on to employ some 500 people, operating in over forty countries on four continents. After being taken public, by blue-chip merchant bank Morgan Grenfell, the then global company was two and a half times oversubscribed at its very successful launch on the main London Stock Exchange in 1983.

Tom's experiences were chronicled in his 1986 book *No Ordinary Experience – the Juliana's Story*; thereafter Tom and his brother were involved in the setting up of a number of other businesses, some of which became very successful (others less so).

Although often described as a serial entrepreneur, Tom prefers to describe himself as a 'vigorous muddler', an occupation he defines as 'someone who goes to his office every day and muddles vigorously'. It is the vigour with which the muddling is undertaken that he considers to be the important part!

Tom now divides his time between business interests in London and New Hampshire.

The Other Side of Loss is his first novel.